AS FIERCE AS STEEL

A GOLD & STEEL BOOK

Anita!
Thank you so
much for everything
you do for Kyra.
I hope you like the
book!

CHRISTOPHER WALSH

COVER DESIGN AND
ILLUSTRATION BY:
CHRISTINA HAMLYN

This is for my mother,
Thank you for your love, support and patience and for nurturing my
young mind with reading.

And to my dear friend, Stacey Smith,
Thank you for rekindling my love of writing and for all your guidance
and encouragement along the way.

1

ELLARIE

Ellarie had dreamt she was lying on the shores of Great Valley Lake, a warm summer breeze flowing over her slender, naked body. Beneath her lay the ripped frame of Lazlo Arbor, his tight chest her pillow as they snoozed in the shade of an elm tree beneath the sun of summer.

The pair of free spirited lovers had taken the day to enjoy a long swim together, away from the prying eyes of the inland island they called home. Alone, in a private, sandy beached alcove on the western shore of the body of water they embraced and loved from noon to dusk. It was a favourite memory of Ellarie's, a dream she often came back to when she slept soundly enough to dream at all.

The frenzied cry of "Fire!" roused her roughly from the dream, cries that were emanating from the lungs of Joyce Keena, the lover of Ellarie's sister, Merion. The three were all lieutenants in the rebel faction known as The Thieves. Until now, they had been lodging in a farmhouse in the town of Argesse, south of the nation's centrally located capital of Atrebell.

Joyce yanked her from the straw-stuffed bed she had sunken so comfortably into and forced her to embrace the madness around them. "Get out! Go! The house is on fire!" Joyce came again, slapping the sleep from Ellarie with an open hand.

Clad only in a tunic, Ellarie took off from the room, grabbing the long, narrow dagger hanging on her belt on the bedpost and forgetting her boots and trousers. She found herself standing in the hallway of the house, half naked and unable to see for the smoke. Bare feet halted at the threshold of the main entrance as her mind went to her sister. Turning toward the stairway, Ellarie shouted for Merion who had been on the second floor in a private room with Joyce, but got no answer.

Seventeen members of the Thieves had been squatting in that farm house, a half of a day's ride outside the capital city. They were to make for Atrebell to intercept their leader, Lady Orangecloak, and return her to the relative safety of their hidden, underground cavern home known as Rillis Vale. Failure meant that Orangecloak and her bodyguards would walk into a trap within the city walls - one that was to be sprung by an ambitious lord of Grenjin Howland, himself the Lord Master of the nation of Illiastra to which they were in open rebellion of.

The smoke was overpowering Ellarie, but she would not leave until she was sure the others had escaped.

A bronze blur with a flowing golden mane of curls was in front of her from nowhere, shoving her into the night air with strong arms. Lazlo, she knew at once, having descended from the second floor of the burning home. The sinewy framed man drove her out of the house before she could resist, urging her not to remain in the burning husk and to run far away. She wanted to protest - she was Ellarie Dollen after all, the head lieutenant on this task force, there was no option for her to evacuate and leave everyone behind.

He was gone just as quickly, but before Ellarie could step back inside, she was violently tackled to the ground. The shock of the blow jarred her senses and sent her belt with her sheathed blade flying from her hand and out of her sight.

No sooner had she hit the ground than she realized there was a man in a uniform atop her. The soldier grasping for her arms wore a black jacket with gold and white epaulets, an outfit that marked him as a man of the prison city of Biddenhurst.

Soon, another had piled on to Ellarie, and they forced her over onto her stomach in a struggle the numbers made futile. Ellarie yelled, for Lazlo, for Joyce, for Merion, for anyone. Her bare feet kicked at the dirt, looking for purchase while gloved hands wrenched on her arms to try and bring them behind her back.

The next thing Ellarie heard was the roar Joyce let out as she burst forth from the front door of the farm house. The fearsome woman bore her axe in hand, swinging the flat of the blade into the face of one of the Biddenhurst men trying to subdue Ellarie and sending him reeling out of sight. The other abandoned Ellarie and turned his focus to Joyce, brandishing a sword to face off with her.

Ellarie scrambled to her feet and caught sight of her belt a few meters away. She yanked the dagger from its sheath and went to the door of the burning home, sticking her head in long enough to yell, "It's an ambush! If anyone can hear me, get out and run for the forest!"

For her, running was no option, no more than it was for Joyce, Lazlo or Merion. They were lieutenants, chosen by Lady Orangecloak, Field Commander of the Thieves, to lead their fellow members. Tonight, the duty fell to her to ensure that the others escaped. Nothing else mattered.

The front yard of the house was occupied by several Biddenhurst soldiers. All were armed with either bayonetted rifles or cutlass swords that glowed orange and yellow in the light of the enflamed building behind her. There were other Thieves outside as well, some fighting, some trying to get away, but none properly armed or armoured. "Run!" she called as loud as her lungs would allow. "Run for the forest and don't stop!"

Nearest to her was Joyce, batting at the brandished sword of a soldier who was ordering her to drop her weapon and lie in the dirt. The one who had taken the flat steel of the axe to the face was kneeling over a growing pool of blood.

As he inspected the state of his nose, he received a running kick to the teeth from Ellarie as she charged past to aid Joyce. "Give them no quarter, Joyce! Tonight we fight!" She declared with a roar.

"I won't have to be told twice!" Joyce roared back. In one fell blow from the axe, the guard on his knees had his head cut clear from his shoulders.

His cohort cursed loudly and lunged for Joyce, and he might have stabbed her but for Ellarie's slashing at his sword arm. He gasped, looked to his bleeding arm and was cut down when Joyce's axe was driven between neck and shoulder.

"I'll guard the front door and keep it clear for anyone trying to get out," Ellarie commanded as Joyce took her axe back in two hands. "You cover the back door and drive the Biddenhursters away from it."

"Leave it to me," Joyce said with a nod. She darted off towards the side of the home, charging headlong towards a throng of guards harrying one of their own.

More soldiers were coming forth to engage Ellarie, their orders to surrender falling on deaf ears. A rifleman stepped up, levelling his rifle on her and roaring commands as he held the tip of the bayonet mere centimetres from her face. She stepped to the right, closed in and drove the dagger deep into his chest. He gasped, groaned and sputtered as his lungs filled with blood. As he hit the ground, Ellarie lost her grip on her dagger and let it go before his weight could drag them both down.

Unable to pull it from whatever bone it had lodged in, she gave up on the dagger and grabbed the fallen man's rifle instead. Ellarie had never fired one before and had never desired to do so. There was no turning back now, she knew, for the ambush would force a great many hands this night.

To her left a guard had begun a blind rush at Ellarie and with no time to dodge she faced him with the rifle held to her side. The roar of the gun rang loudly and it kicked in her hands quite powerfully when she pulled the trigger. Through the ruckus the shot had found the soldier's abdomen and he stumbled and fell to the dirt with a heave and a moan.

A swordsman stepped in from the right and ate the butt of the rifle and a thrust to the left sent another flinching backward to avoid the bayonet aimed at his face. There seemed to be more coming toward her now, summoned by the blast from the gun in her hands. They were closing in on all sides, armed with a mixture of sabres, pistols and rifles.

"Drop it and lie down on the ground, thief!" one among them demanded of her.

Ellarie swung at him wordlessly and tried to move away from the semicircle they were attempting to form around her.

Three moved as one and converged on Ellarie faster than she anticipated. The rifle was plucked from her grasp by two of them and the third tried to move in close with his sword and grab her with his free hand. In a single swift motion Ellarie grabbed the sword-carrying arm in both of hers, spun around so it was over her shoulder and snapped it downward. She heard a loud snap and wrenched the sabre free from the now limp limb and spun once more, flashing the blade into the face of the guard. He shrieked and grabbed at the gash she had made in his cheeks, stumbling into his fellow guardsmen.

Armed once more Ellarie began to retreat hastily from the encroaching group, feeling the heat of the fire upon her back as she neared the house.

A sword emerged from the stomachs of one of her attackers and he cried out in horror at the sight of it before it was withdrawn back. When the man fell forward it was Lazlo standing there, clutching the bloody sword that had maimed the soldier. Across his nose and mouth he had tied a bandanna, but Ellarie knew the piercing blue eyes and mop of blond curls and whom they belonged to.

The posse seemed divided for a moment until one among them ordered the group to split in two in order to advance on Ellarie and Lazlo alike. *They're not trying to kill anyone,* she realised as they slowly kept advancing on her.

"Put the weapon on the ground and lie down with your hands behind your head!" one soldier called out.

To Ellarie's right, she spotted the cornfield that stretched for half a kilometre. Running crossed Ellarie's mind, but she knew she could not. It was her duty to stay.

"Where are *you* going?" a rough voice called out from behind her and Ellarie spun to meet its owner, regretting the decision as fast as she made it.

A single man managed to grab her sword arm from behind and the rest of the group pounced on her as one. The ground rose up to meet her while several bodies held her firmly to it. The sword was pulled from her grasp and despite her struggle, the men above her soon had her arms pinned behind her back. Thick iron bands were clamped over her wrists tightly and Ellarie found out painfully that they were pure, ridged iron, with no chain linking them.

She kicked and screamed for help as they lifted her up and her protestation was rewarded with a swift punch to the face. The blow shook her whole head. Her vision spiralled, the ears rang deafeningly and her legs were suddenly limp and clumsy beneath her.

The soldiers began dragging Ellarie away from the burning farmhouse to a waiting wagon with little resistance.

Things came back to her slowly as she was roughly bundled inside the wrought iron cage on wheels. The intensity of the fire emanating from the house continued to wash over her and the bars themselves seemed to radiate with heat. Ellarie's vision cleared itself enough for her to make out the figures battling one another in front of the mass of flames that once was their hideout.

Joyce Keena was the first she spotted, having returned to the front of the house and turning about in every direction with her reddened axe at the ready. The woman was calling Ellarie's name frantically and fending off soldiers with long, wide swings. The odds were against Joyce, she was tall and strong, but the outnumbering Biddenhursters were too many.

A man leaped onto the blonde's back, but she kept her balance. Joyce slashed at the men ahead of her with the axe, connecting with one soldier who cried out as the sharp steel tore through clothing and flesh alike. The blade sliced through the forearm holding the barrel of his musket like tallow and his mouth opened wide for a scream even Ellarie's ringing ears could hear. Joyce's swings became more unwieldy as the soldier on her back tightened the grip he had upon her throat. Other soldiers began to pile on her from behind and soon she disappeared from Ellarie's sight in a sea of Biddenhurst uniforms.

The ringing in Ellarie's ears slowly began to subside and the sound of the wooden home being reduced to ashes and embers dominated the sound spectrum. Competing with it was the shouting and screaming of the Thieves and Biddenhurst soldiers alike. A man to her right with a tall captain's hat and a breast full of glinting medals was barking orders beside the wagon. Between repeated calls to bring the captured Thieves to the wagon, he bellowed a loud command to spare the women at all costs but kill any man that resisted.

It dawned on Ellarie that she should try to get her hands free of their restraints. These were not the standard shackle and chain restraints she had encountered before, rather, there was no chain at all. Her hands were back to back in solid, unforgiving iron, forged cuff to cuff directly. They offered no movement whatsoever and kept her wrists so tight that she could find no way to slip the arms beneath the legs to get her hands in front. Never had Ellarie felt so utterly helpless to do anything, discovering it be a difficult task to even get into an upright position that wasn't uncomfortable.

From directly beside the cornfield on the left of her she spotted Lazlo almost immediately, unarmed, breathing heavy and spattered with blood that seemed to not be his. Upon tripping in the first Biddenhurst guard Ellarie had slain, she saw him reach down and yank her dagger free. Without a second of hesitation, Lazlo brought it down in an arcing swing on the back of one of the soldiers that had collectively mounted Joyce for an arrest. The man screamed in agony as the life burst from the gaping wound Lazlo had created with the dagger Ellarie had lost. The soldiers broke off from Joyce, now bound at the wrists like Ellarie though still struggling fitfully as a single man dragged her by the legs across the rough ground.

Now the lone member of the Thieves on the front of the burning house, Lazlo was left to fend for himself. Ellarie was certain that the remaining riflemen were going to open fire on him and make an end of it. He was a resisting male fighter after all, and there was no reason for him to be spared. Yet, the soldiers circled him and barked orders to surrender as they had to Ellarie and Joyce and made no attempt to attack.

It became apparent to Ellarie at that moment that the men likely thought Lazlo was a woman. With his face masked, that lithe body and his hair flowing in luscious, natural, golden blonde ringlets, he certainly looked the part.

Almost directly above Lazlo, a second floor window burst outward, with a spearhead thrusting through glass and knocking off the shards that remained. The slender figure of a female member of the Thieves that Ellarie knew to be Ami Rosia climbed out through the frame and leapt into the night air. Her landing target was one of the men accosting Lazlo and she hit her target with precision and grace. The two went down in a brief struggle, but as the thief had only escape on her mind, she broke free and darted for the tall corn stocks. The soldier took off after her, though Ellarie had no worries. Ami Rosia was the fastest runner in her unit, there was little odds of her being caught now. With a longing glance, Ellarie looked to the window again and was dismayed to not see any sign of her sister and her spear.

Ellarie scanned her trappings for any weaknesses and it was then she became aware she was not alone in the wagon. A skinny figure with reddish hair fell in to her sight, lying on her side with iron bonds matching Ellarie's on her wrists. At first Ellarie had to wonder who this red haired woman was, but it was then she realized the hair was wrong. It was not red at all, but blonde and soaked with blood. "Nia?" Ellarie all but shouted, thudding along on her now sore knees to the incapacitated girl. "Nia, can you hear me? Nia, please answer me," she frantically pleaded while fighting to keep her voice down.

The skinny woman from Holliford was given the first watch of the house and Ellarie hadn't even thought of what became of her in all the chaos. She was the first taken down by the look of it, and barely alive from her ordeal.

Blood caked lips slowly opened, the slightest hint of a whisper emanating between spits of crimson. Nia's eyes stared at the floorboards of the cart, lids scarcely apart. Ellarie had to put her ear to the girl's mouth to hear her whisper, "They're coming, they're coming." Nia was vainly trying to warn her.

"Stay with me, Nia." Ellarie surmised she had been ambushed to avoid alerting the other thieves of the soldiers' approach. A quick look at the back of the girl's head showed that blood had matted her braided hair, indicating they'd caught her from behind. *Nia had run,* Ellarie deduced, *and the soldiers couldn't finish the job with one blow, so they had gone to work on Nia's bloodied and swollen face to silence her.* "Stay awake, Nia, stay with me, keep talking."

Ellarie shifted into a sitting position, her back half turned to her ally. The girl had taken a hard blow to the head and likely was suffering a concussion. As a lieutenant, Ellarie had received basic medical training by the elderly doctor living in the ruins of Phaleayna, an abandoned city inhabited by the Thieves. She had learned that with a serious head wound, a concussion was highly likely and Nia showed every sign that Ellarie had been taught to look for. As best as her restraints would allow, Ellarie started shaking Nia to keep her awake, talking to her constantly in a soft voice.

A shape moving in the broken front window on the second floor caught Ellarie's eye and in a blink, a wild little thing with hair as red as the fire behind it flew through the flames and dove out. Ellarie's heart jumped in her chest. She almost screamed her sister's name as her younger sibling, clad only in trousers and a laced brassiere replicated Rosia's overhead attack onto a soldier.

Merion had come to fight, as was expected of her as a lieutenant. The spear in her hands plunged deep into a soldier's chest as Merion descended upon him from above. With a forward roll through the momentum the wild haired woman came to her feet close to the next intended target. The blood covered and masked Lazlo was almost impaled until Merion stopped at the last second, the tip of her spear mere inches from his stomach. The two realized who each were as the soldiers circled around them demanding obedience that they were not likely to get from Lazlo and Merion of all people. The pair went back to back and held their ground, much to the chagrin of the soldiers encircling them.

A roar emanating from Joyce caught the attention of Ellarie in the wagon and Merion in the midst of battle alike. The lone soldier dragging her had made the mistake of trying to stand Joyce up and she had knocked him down with a kick to the midsection. The soldier called to his unengaged comrades and a pair dropped their muskets to throw themselves atop the embattled lieutenant of the Thieves. When it dawned on Merion that her partner was the one being dog piled, she charged through the circle of would-be-arresters. With a mighty thrust, Merion plunged the wooden shafted spear into the first body she saw wrestling her love. Noiselessly, Lazlo went down behind Merion after she broke through, the circle of humanity closing in on him. The last Ellarie saw of her dagger was Lazlo having it wrenched from his hand by a guard who outsized him by about twenty kilos.

The soldier bearing Merion's spear in his back yelled enough for all to hear as he jolted backward, the point of the spear searing through his flesh and sprouting through his chest on the right side. *A lung has been ripped apart for certain,* Ellarie deduced. *Only death would follow that scream.*

A shot rang out behind the house and it gave Ellarie a sickly feeling in the pit of her stomach. The sound of a gun always had for as long as she could remember. Immediately she began to wonder if one of her own had taken the burden of lead. There were none among her ranks who carried firearms. A loud, single shot weapon was of little use among the stealth based tactics of the Thieves, but Ellarie supposed one of them could have stolen one, just as she had done moments before.

Attention of the captors turned away from Joyce, now writhing on the ground to escape her bonds, to Merion, clutching the spear still lodged in the unfortunate soldier's back. With a thrusting kick, she broke her weapon free and readied another charge. The leader of the ambush shouted out and Ellarie's eyes locked onto his tall, plumed hat as its feather bobbed along to where the two women were embattled.

Ellarie noted the pistol that was in the white gloved hand of the leader, its hammer pulled back and a bead drawn on Merion's lover on the ground. "Drop the spear missy and reach your hands for the stars," the man called in a gravelly voice. His uniform was well decorated and immaculate. This captain had expended no effort nor collected any dirt this night, Ellarie knew. A slick, black moustache that curled into two fine tips rested above a square jaw that hoisted his mouth into a stupid grin. Ellarie wanted nothing more in that moment than to rip it from his face. Her hands began to clench with anger, until she heard a whimper at her side. *Nia*, Ellarie realized at once. She had dug her fingers into the injured woman's leg.

The petite blonde's breathing picked up then, as if she had just come above the surface of the water and taken that first deep breath of air. "Ellarie, Ellarie you need to flee, they're coming," she spoke as loud as she could.

"Shh, Nia. I'm here, sweetie, don't yell," Ellarie cooed softly.

Hearing her leader's voice seemed to calm Nia enough to rest her head, though Ellarie resumed shaking the woman's leg to keep her conscious. Hearing her name said aloud made Ellarie wonder if anyone knew who she was at this point. If she could prevent it, it would be in the best interest of all the women to keep her identity from becoming known. Unlike her fellow lieutenants, Ellarie had the distinction of having no distinction and could blend in with a crowd quite well. The bisexual Lazlo was nicknamed 'Pretty Lazlo' on account of his effeminate good looks. Merion had that head of red curls and Joyce was the tall blonde with shoulders nearly as broad as a man's. Ellarie, by contrast, was an average woman of dark hair, standard height and a slightly muscled frame, but no defining features like the others. If the Biddenhurst men wanted the Sisters, it begged to reason that they might only be sparing the other women on account of not knowing which of them was Ellarie. It was on that premise that she would keep her name unspoken.

Ellarie's attention was drawn back to the fight at hand when she heard her sister. "You have but one shot, you piece of scum," Merion spat through gritted teeth at this captain. "You put a shot in her and I put my spear through your throat."

"What, you plan to jab me with your pointy stick?" he mockingly retorted.

"This stick is no stranger to blood," Merion gave back, lowering herself into a stance to ready a charge. "And I know you won't kill me, you know who I am."

The man laughed deeply at that. "That's where you're wrong. I have orders, aye, but if 'The Red Bitch' of the Sisters attacks me, I have the right to defend. Or at least that's what I'll say should anyone ask."

"Then let's see what that little pistol can do against my spear." Merion taunted, trying to divert the man's aim away from Joyce.

"So it comes down to the simple question of which would win: a bullet or a spear?" the Captain asked condescendingly while raising his pistol to Merion. "Here's your answer, queer."

Time seemed to slow for Ellarie in that instant and she heard herself and Joyce both shouting a blood curdling 'No!' in unison. Merion however, was the very face of focus, sidestepping away as the hammer fell forward. A soldier took the shot to the abdomen behind Ellarie's sister as spear and woman became a blur. A red haired, half naked flash of a woman darted towards the captain as he stood there with nothing but an empty pistol in hand. Too late he realised what was happening and by then Merion was airborne, her spear tearing throat and neck to ruin in a single thrust. Gurgling on his blood, the leader took Merion down with him as he tumbled backwards. The wide brimmed hat flew off his head as the grin he had so proudly worn minutes ago turned into a wide mouthed look of horror. With a masterful leaping twirl she and spear alike danced clear of the soldiers, landing gracefully at the ready to strike once more.

A wave of shock rippled through the soldiers as the red life of the captain pooled onto the dirt before them and their eyes fell solely to Merion. "Which of you is next?"

"She is, if you don't drop your fucking spear." All eyes turned to see the thickly built guard pressing Ellarie's missing dagger to Joyce's exposed throat.

Merion gasped. "Let her go!"

"I say fuck that," said the Soldier, letting loose a ball of phlegm on the ground beside him. "Put the spear down and drop to your knees or I open her throat."

"Do that and you'll die as your captain did, I promise you," Merion countered.

The broad fellow looked about quite confidently. "Do you want to risk that? All I have to do is draw the blade across her tender flesh. Meanwhile, you have to fight through all of them to get to me to keep your promise. Best case, you keep your word and I die, either way though, the Big Bitch will bleed out in front of you and the rest of the lads here jump your skinny bones. Weigh your options carefully, but do so quickly, I have no patience anymore."

"Run, Merion," Joyce spoke up, offering a third option. "Don't let them take you."

"That's no good. If you run, I'll still slit her throat," the big lug answered before Merion could even think about it. "The only way this one lives through the night is if you drop your spear and go to your knees. I'm counting from five."

"Don't listen to him, Merion. Run!" Joyce commanded.

"Four."

"Hurry up and run, Merion!"

"Three."

"Please, Merion, listen to me!"

"Two."

The spear clattered to the dirt and Merion followed after it, the very face of defeat. "I'm sorry, Joyce. I can't watch you die."

A pair of soldiers approached cautiously and took control of Merion's arms and forced her to the ground. More joined in needlessly on her limp frame, closing shut those horribly rigid cuffs on her slender wrists in seconds.

Ellarie slumped back against Nia, sighing sombrely as she watched the embers rising into the starry night sky from all corners of the peaceful little farmhouse. In no time at all, the four lieutenants on the mission had been captured. *It was such a simple mission,* Ellarie thought to herself. *Intercept Lady Orangecloak before she reached Atrebell, inform her that her own plans were compromised and return to Rillis Vale to regroup.* The Sisters had completed similar tasks before. As had Lazlo, on his own in one instance. In one night, somehow, despite all their combined experience, all their work had gone up in flames like the house before her. Now their fate was out of their hands, and the band of Thieves that had gathered to do this job were now prisoners and wards of Biddenhurst. *Was it all in vain?* Ellarie wondered. *And what of Lady Orangecloak, now in greater danger than ever and walking unknown into a trap.*

An interruption in her train of thought came when a man's voice broke through the chaos. "Father, I caught one! Look, Father, her hair is dark as coal. She must be the oldest Sister!" Ellarie's stomach fluttered as she lowered her eyes to the procession emerging from around the side of the house. The approaching guards dragged and pushed along more Thieves with their hands bound behind their backs. The men were Lazlo's cousin Donnis and close childhood friend

Etcher, his most trusted companions who had followed him as closely as Merion and Joyce followed Ellarie. They were beaten and bloody, but so were the soldiers holding them.

Orangecloak would be quite upset with all of us for fighting and killing, but they tried to burn us alive, what were we to do? Would she be so different were it her in place of me?

There were women too: Jorgia of Prive, Allia and Coramae of Aquas Bay, and lastly Bernadine of Layn, the woman falsely believed to be Ellarie. "Here she is, Father. Look, she has dark hair, pale skin and a short haircut, it's the Queen Bitch for sure!" the voice called again, though no one moved forward to answer the call for his father.

With one hand on her arm and another on the back of her neck, Bernadine was marched forward ahead of all the others. The southlander woman had kept her coal black hair cut short, with a long blade to fall over her left eye. Ellarie's own locks were of the same colour, though her own was normally kept just off the shoulder where it hung with a natural curl. The two also had a similar build and were only a few centimetres different in height. Indeed, to anyone who didn't know their faces, it would be very easy to confuse the two.

The Thieves captured on the rear of the house were all dressed in various stages of undress. It was doubtless that the heat of the fire was the only thing keeping them warm.

The young man who held Bernadine's bound arms was a scrawny fellow with a curly mop of hair atop a tall, clumsy looking frame in a loosely hanging uniform. The faces of his comrades were silent and sullen and none dared to speak as he unknowingly approached the bloody mess before them. "What is it? Why are you all so quiet? Where's my father?" he asked nervously just before his eyes fell on the Captain's body, soaked in blood and lying mere steps from his boots.

"Father, no!" the man cried out, throwing Bernadine haphazardly out of his way. She tripped and tumbled onto her stomach, groaning in pain as the air was driven from lungs. A soldier stepped forth and yanked Bernadine back up to her feet, holding her tight before she could get any ideas.

Tears ran freely down the lanky man's red cheeks as trembling hands touched the face of the slain captain. His uncontrollable sobbing and shaking quickly turned to seething rage. "Who?!" the Captain's son shouted atop his lungs. "Who took my father?!"

All went deathly silent, soldiers and Thieves alike who had been battling in front of the house just seconds before. Reluctantly, one of the men who held Ellarie's sister finally spoke up. "Sergeant Hoyt, it was this one." The soldier stepped forward, pushing Merion ahead as he went.

She stumbled and caught herself short of falling in front of the enraged son, now standing tall. There was no less than a third of a meter in the height difference between the two. Merion was totally vulnerable in her restrained position and stepped back in a crouch, her head cocked up at her foe, making the offsetting height seem even greater. The fear was plain to read across her face and Sergeant Hoyt stared with pure malice at the slender woman with the red hair.

"You touch her, I swear I will tear you asunder the minute my hands are free of these shackles," Joyce growled, entirely out of nowhere. Two Biddenhurst men tried their best to hold her by either arm, but the fierce woman was nearly too much to contain in her fury.

"Then you'll die in them, you dyke," the big man fumed as he unleashed a massive backhanded blow to the side of Merion's head. She dropped in a heap and Joyce let out a guttural roar that would strike fear in the bravest heart.

The two men holding her stumbled back, losing their grip as she burst forward. Charging with incredible speed, she took Hoyt unawares with a shoulder to the stomach, sending him to the ground where he lay breathless and gasping beside Merion. The soldiers rushed in to drag Joyce away and began barking orders at the fellow manning the jail cart Ellarie and Nia occupied.

It took five men to carry Joyce, writhing and twisting in their grasp, to the barred wagon. Once she was stuffed inside, she immediately began kicking at the door, even as the key was still turning in the lock.

Ellarie left Nia for a moment, sliding on her bottom to Joyce and nudging the shouting woman with her foot to get her attention. Joyce turned to see her and Ellarie leaned in close. "Don't say my name, they don't know who I am and if they know they have all three of us they may kill the others."

A look of total defeat crossed Joyce's face as she realised who Ellarie was. "Not *you*, how could they get *you*? When I didn't see you again I had thought that at least *you* had gotten away," she despairingly whispered back.

"That filthy dyke, bring her back out," the sergeant exclaimed hotly between gasps of air before Ellarie could say anything more. "I'll kill her right here and now!"

A line of guards appeared from behind the wagons and formed up in front of the burning farm house before any action towards Hoyt's command could be taken. A thinly bearded fellow with soft, dark ringlets of hair cut just above his ears stood at the front of the pack. His cold eyes surveyed the mess that had become of their operation.

"What do you want, you worthless steward? Father's dead now, no thanks to you." Young Hoyt hissed. He did not seem to appreciate the other man's presence, but the other hardly seemed to notice or even care, for that matter.

The man, who looked no more than twenty five or so by Ellarie's estimate, calmly removed a pair of leather gloves, taking in the flame engulfed house as he did. Strangely, his uniform and those of his followers were in immaculate condition and he seemed to be disturbingly unfazed by, and perhaps, even enjoying, the carnage that lay before him.

Finally, after letting the silence grow unbearably uncomfortable, he spoke: "My orders were to keep the neighbours at bay, to which I followed to the letter. Just as we were instructed by forces higher than Captain Hoyt to bring all the women to Biddenhurst alive. I intend to see that order through as well." The man spoke with a detached, apathetic demeanour, which seemed to only infuriate sergeant more.

"Silence, Lance. I'm in charge here now, I'm highest rank," Captain Hoyt's son shouted.

The man he called Lance seemed entirely unmoved by Hoyt's outbursts, as if he was entirely accustomed to it. "Furthermore, your grief has rendered your capabilities for making sound decisions nil." He added, "Therefore, as per section fifteen of military code, I am relieving you of your duties until such a time that you may be assessed by our superiors."

"No!" screamed Sergeant Hoyt, like a child in the midst of a temper tantrum, angrily stomping the ground as he pointed a finger at the man who dared challenge his authority. "You have no right! I call you a traitor to the realm! Men, seize him at once!"

The soldiers looked to one another uncertainly, none among

them daring to move toward one side or another.

All the while, the steward caressed his beard as a derisive smirk came over him. "Well, it would seem that they have disobeyed you, Anders. Now be a good boy and stand down. I have a job for you to do in the meantime while you're coming to terms with your grief: I'm going to prepare you a letter for you to take to Lord Taves in Atrebell. That's a big job. I should say that it is one fit for a sergeant. You can even say you wrote it. Lord Taves doesn't know you can't read or write. Come now, we will get your horse and some companions and you will be off. I do not want to see you hurt anyone else and I know your father would not either."

Hoyt was heaving hard, trying vainly to not show weakness. Slowly, the steward stepped forward, offering a bare hand to Anders.

The sergeant seemed like a boy on stilts to Ellarie. It made no wonder that the steward treated him as such and even less surprising that it worked for him. A quick nod over Lance's shoulder to the others was all it took and command was his. Without needing further command, the soldiers went to work collecting the captured and cleaning up the dead.

The first order of business for the men of Biddenhurst was to place the remaining women alongside Ellarie, Nia and Joyce in the prisoner wagon. It filled quickly once they were all piled in beside one another, leaving no place for Lazlo, Donnis and Etcher.

A party of soldiers convened to decide what to make of their predicament before the wagon. Beyond them, Ellarie could see others carrying the soldiers that had fallen in the fight out of sight, while the body of Captain Hoyt was tightly bound in a white, canvas tarp.

Though the fire raged on, the cold, dry autumn air nipped harshly at the huddled women. There was sobbing going on among them and moaning as their arms and wrists became sore and cramped in their restraints.

Beyond the mobile cage, the soldiers were convening and exchanging details of what they had experienced from their various posts. Ellarie was able to overhear some of it, confirming that the assault on the rear of the house resulted in two deaths among the Thieves. It also emerged through several witnesses that a single male was to have fled through the rear of the house and had managed to avoid capture entirely.

After what felt like hours, Ellarie heard horses galloping off in the distance just as the steward returned from whence he came.

"Corporal Cornwall!" bellowed a short, squat, bearded soldier who had been seen earlier accompanying the steward. "We've no place for the men, the wagon be full."

"We have spare horses now, seeing as how we lost a few men," the corporal surmised. "Lash their men over them like potato sacks. Also, while the fire still burns toss their dead in to it. We will bury all of ours except the Captain here. Wrap him up tight in that tarp and we will take him back with us for a proper funeral." He lifted his head to look at the scarcely clothed women before him then. "Get them some blankets or something as well, it will do us no good if they freeze. My orders were to deliver them to Biddenhurst alive. Letting them succumb to death is not an option."

It was no kindness he offered Ellarie and her companions. His tone said that they were only cargo that had to be kept fresh, like produce on its way to market.

A tarp was thrown to the women and with nothing but their teeth and feet they had to pull it over themselves. It smelled of horses and another indecipherable odour and really did little to aid warmth. Nia, gone unconscious once again, was left to lie in between them all in the motley circle they had formed.

Ellarie heard a moan as one of the Thieves men went over a horse's back. Just able to see over her shoulder enough, Ellarie espied the corporal approaching the man with the luscious head of hair she knew was Lazlo.

"You, you're familiar. What's your name?" Cornwall asked.

"Lazlo Arbor," he answered with venom, meeting the corporal's glare with his own as best as his position allowed.

Without a hint of intimidation at the mention of the name, the corporal let out a snort. "Oh, what a treat, it is the famous outlaw: Lazlo Arbor. My word, this raid netted us not only the prized lesbians that are the Sisters of Seduction, but also the girly-man Lazlo." He paused only long enough to spit on Lazlo. "What a merry band of freaks you all are. I would say the gods will thank us for taking care of such unfortunate mutations." The derisiveness with which the corporal spoke was contemptible.

Ellarie did not think she could bear more hate for any one person than she did for Cornwall in that moment, but he was not done. "Also, I will lay down one ground rule of utmost importance: If it comes to my attention that these men hear any of you cretins talking I will stop this sorry excuse for a convoy and have the lot of you beaten mercilessly." Lance turned his gaze on the wagon and the women within. "Try my patience further and I may even turn a blind eye should one of the soldiers wish to have his way with you. After all, no one stipulated what condition you were to be in upon delivery, just so long as you were alive."

No one dared bat him an answer and that seemed to satisfy the shrewd corporal. Without another word he disappeared from sight towards the front of the convoy with a smirk of self-satisfaction.

The corporal might even be thankful for Merion having killed the Captain. Ellarie considered. *Lance Cornwall went from lowly steward to commanding the whole convoy in the span of minutes and only the Captain's simple son had opposed his rule.*

The wagon was brought to the center of the convoy, with soldiers on horseback going in front and behind. The horses bearing the three lashed men of the Thieves and the deceased Captain Hoyt were lined up and flanked with mounted soldiers to either side.

As the Biddenhurst men formed up they talked amongst one another and Ellarie heard one alleging that they had two bodies from the Thieves that were discarded into the burning remnants of the house. From what she picked up from the descriptions of the dead, it seemed likely that one of them was Harris, the short, portly, openly gay man who looked after the house. A full-fledged member of the Thieves, but no fighter, at any rate and certainly not one that would provide anything near what could be called resisting arrest. It broke Ellarie's heart to think that the kind, soft spoken fellow was likely killed just for sport.

The other deceased man was one of Lazlo's crew and his description of having short brown hair and a shaggy beard meant it was either Errol or Bernarian. The Biddenhursters only spoke of having one dead man that matched those descriptors, which meant the other was the escapee they spoke of earlier.

Ami Rosia and either Errol or Bernarian, that's all that managed to get away. Ellarie realised as the convoy started moving and began pulling away from the collapsing inferno.

Fourteen Thieves had arrived on Harris' doorstep that evening. That sweet and gentle man had wined and dined them all at his table and given them his roof for the night. Now his home was gone, his life had ended and all but two of his guests were either dead or captured.

    The whole reason we were here was to counter a leak within the Thieves. Ellarie realised. *No one within the Elite Merchant Party should have known of the operation to rescue Orangecloak.* A sickening thought crept in as she watched the second floor of the farmhouse cave in on the main level below it. *Someone is still leaking information to the enemy.*

2
TRYST

A toast then, to another successful session of Parliament," one man said to another. Their crystal tumblers of rum clinked together audibly as they stood before the roaring hearth against the south wall of the expansive banquet hall.

The man offering the toast was Robick Mahash, Minister of Galren region and the newly made Lord of Agriculture. For the better part of half an hour he had been boasting of his new position to Minister Ike Slake of Galdourn. However, it seemed that the Lord of Agriculture was more concerned with mining a newly found cache of cobalt in his region than he was with potatoes and turnips.

It was a dull conversation for the man sitting in a nearby darkened corner, yet he listened all the same. For listening was exactly what he had been paid to do.

Lord Mahash and Minister Slake were lesser ministers of the Elite Merchant Party, - or EMP, as they were more commonly known - the controlling body of the government of the largest nation on the largest continent of the known world: Illiastra. Situated on the eastern edge of the Casparian Sea, it lay bordered by mountains to the east and south and a frozen desert of inhospitable cold to the north.

It was a country of lush green forests, fields and rolling hills and rivers that cut and flowed where they may to the lakes and ponds they fed. Amidst it all were the cities of man: made of brick, stone, iron and wood, many were walled to the outside and all pumped to the beat of industry. Those ruling over it were a wealthy group of sixty administrators of the sixty regions. Most were titled minister and a dozen again called Lord with one Lord Master to rule over them all.

Upon the dais, behind a small string quartet and seated in a chair of polished wood decorated with gems and gold, Grenjin Howland did just that.

The man watching the ministers on Lord Master Howland's behalf was a swordsman of considerable skill from the Midlands Republic of Gildriad. Itself a country on the continent of the same name found on the far western side of the known world.

Men like Mahash and Slake did not have much of a care for the swordsman in the shadows strumming on his guitar. They tolerated him within their walls and borders, yet this man had never felt welcome by most of the leaders of Illiastra. Regardless, Tryst Reine was hired to protect the Lord Master and this was the task his employer had asked of him.

To Tryst's credit, he at least dressed for the part, albeit only in black. Tonight he had chosen a tight vest over a shirt of silk with its sleeves rolled to the elbows, his finest leather boots polished to a bright shine and a pair of light, cotton trousers.

Even in matching finery, however, there was still a level of contempt rained upon him by those who felt themselves to be his superiors. Tryst Reine was born in a foreign land to modestly wealthy parents and in the eyes of these aristocrats, that made him lesser than they. Yet, for all their snobbery they still feared him. These men all knew that their wealth made poor armour against a man who bore the title of Master of Blades.

From the corner of his eye Tryst caught sight of Minister Slake excusing himself and wandering back into the herd of suits between the hearth and the dais. Lord Mahash lingered, took a sip of his brandy and glanced about. For the briefest of moments his eyes fell on Tryst and he saw Mahash's unease. Their stare was broken just as quickly as it had begun and Mahash departed for the centre of the room hastily.

I suppose I should go among them as well and see what the sheep are bleating about this evening. Tryst thought to himself while laying his guitar back in its wooden case.

It was part of Tryst's duties to report any conversations of interest he overheard to the Lord Master and he would hear no more by the hearth.

To the credit of the old man's paranoia, the Lords and Ministers were certainly the liars Lord Master Howland suspected them to be. Every last one of them held an unmatched conviction to their part that could rival the actors of the stage. To one's face, the government leaders could pay the sweetest of compliments with a feigned sincerity to fool all but the most observers. However, when the back was turned, they could plunge it with the daggers of their true intent.

That deception made the EMP appear to be a unified body on the surface. Yet, there was no doubt in the mind of the Lord Master's sworn shield that every man of the party was holding that unity for the betterment of themselves alone.

Then there was the woman, and once more Tryst felt her eyes upon him. She was Marigold, the daughter of the Minister of Daol Bay, Lord of Fisheries and Seas and Warden of the West, Marscal Tullivan.

Tryst's eyes had befallen her several times that evening upon the dais where the Lord Master and his two warden lords had supped. Now, however, she was weaving her way through the maze of Ministers and heirs who were all taking their turns to remark upon her appearance. With her slender yet curvaceous body, her long, dark hair and a face of green eyes and flawless features, there was no denying she was a rare beauty.

Tonight she wore a gown of crimson lace and samite that fell to the floor, the sleeves of which flowed down her delicate arms, flared around her hands and hung ostentatiously long. Its neckline was open and plunged low, revealing just a small taste of the supple skin beneath. There was no denying that she was truly a vision of loveliness walking amid an ugly game.

It was doubtless that she would proposition Tryst yet again, as she had been doing since the Parliamentary session in the spring of the year.

Marigold's time grows short and as time becomes lighter on the scale her desperation works to tip the scale away, Tryst said to himself.

Currently she was in the throes of what he knew must be a thrilling banter with the Captain of the Manor Guards, Egland Barrid. The rotund Captain's self-appointed duty consisted of waddling around the floor and inflating his own sense of importance by engaging with the ministers. However, that didn't save the affluent leaders from regarding him only slightly better than they did the serving staff.

Unfortunately for Barrid, despite his finely pressed cream coloured military jacket with its golden epaulets and collection of medals, he was afflicted by being born into only modest wealth. In the world of the EMP, a man's worth was less in his abilities and more in the loins he originated from.

As Tryst made his way into the sea of suits milling about, he noticed Captain Barrid's lone contribution alternating guard posts. They were the Honourable Guardsmen, Barrid's handpicked group of the most handsome and skilled men-at-arms the Illiastran military could provide. Tryst watched them move, clad in their violet and gold jackets and black trousers with a vertical stripe of gold upon either leg. The unit was one of special purpose and were convened to guard over the seasonal Parliamentary Sessions and any other major functions the Lord Master was expected to attend.

There was but one that Tryst knew as more than a name: Freyard Archer, First Class Rifleman, and Expert Marksman. When not summoned to duty, he was the Master-at-Arms and Captain of the Rangers for Fort Dornett, one of several military forts dotting the south side of the Varras River. However, at present Tryst saw no sign of his friend and thought it likely that he had been given a break for the next fifteen minutes.

As it was, there were only a few of the ministers on the floor that glanced in Tryst's direction as he passed. Though he had no doubt that his presence was noted amongst the noblemen. Many of them would be talking as he sauntered through, hoping that he would overhear their conversations and bring the choicest bits of information back to the Lord Master. Of course, nothing any of them spoke of could be deemed valuable. The duty fell to Tryst to extract any minor worth from the thickly spun webs of lies and general kowtowing and tonight there was little and less to note.

Truth be told, this had been a rather dry session. The two main items were a new tax that had been levied on produce farmers and the passing of a law that permitted landlords to issue arrest warrants to delinquent tenants.

There were several other pieces of legislation, though they served no other purpose than to funnel funds from the underpaid many to the wealthy few.

For all intentions, the autumn sessions and the talk around

them were just an effort to maintain the current status of affairs going in to the winter season. Everything would go into a holding pattern before the frost fell in a few weeks and the Winter Parliamentary Sessions would go sparsely attended due to inevitably poor weather.

No, Tryst knew that the next time there would be anything worth hearing it would be in the spring.

The loud voice of one Minister Braggen came close to Tryst's hearing. Craiginald Braggen was the Minister of Farmourd, a city located in the southeast. In a tone of grand overacting, the minister began to boast of how the mountain air had yielded his outlying farms the best harvest in all of Illiastra. The statement behind it was plain enough: Braggen had been among the ministers that had been vying for the Agriculture lordship that been granted to Robick Mahash. There was truth to the matter of the crops, however. But Braggen had little and nothing to do with that. It was no secret that Craiginald was a largely incompetent oaf propped up by his five city councillors.

There was nothing else to hear on the floor at this time outside of empty praise and idle banter. The ministers parted away from Tryst wherever he walked, giving him a clear path through the throng.

The dais fell into his vision as he turned in its direction, particularly the Lord Master sitting atop it in his gilded chair of finely polished elm. At present, the old man was speaking to his Warden Lords of the East and West that were seated to either side of him.

Lord Marscal Tullivan of Daol Bay sat on Grenjin's right. Aside from being the father of Marigold, he was also the Lord of Fisheries and Seas and the Warden Lord of the West. His face was pale and gaunt, a dark brown suit drooped from a sickly frame and he constantly had a handkerchief to hand to mop his perpetually moist brow. It was said in whispers that the consumption disease had taken hold of him, though no one would dare say as much to his face.

In addition to Lord Tullivan's woes, the eldest of his two daughters, Serephanie, had been kidnapped by a common fisherman, or so the story was presented. The truth as Tryst knew it was that she had run off of her own free will, abandoning her family, inheritance and legacy to avoid an arranged marriage.

Seated to the left of the Lord Master was the soon-to-be-father-in-law of both of the Tullivan women: Lord Eamon Palomb, Warden of the East, Minister of Hercalest and Lord of Fuel and Mineral Resources. His mile deep mines dotted the lands east of Atrebell, marring innocent and otherwise picturesque landscapes for their precious coal, metals and jewels buried within.

Twin sons of his sat in smaller, but no less lavish chairs. Closest at hand was the elder by two minutes, named Eldridge. With his short, wavy dark hair atop a tall, strong frame and a handsome face of striking, sharp features, he was the apple of his father's eye. Barring the unforeseen, Eldridge was also the destined Lord Master of Illiastra. Aside from his betrothed that abandoned him, he was loved amongst the women of the upper crust and adored from afar by those beneath. With his easy smiles and gentlemanly façade, Eldridge Palomb made for a fine heir that would make any father proud.

Beside Eldridge sat his twin, who looked more like a distant cousin than a twin brother, truth be told. Pyore was shorter by several centimetres, with a mop of dirty blond hair atop a wide head and a stocky body. Though none would ever say it in his hearing, he was a homely lad. Had he been born to anyone else he would have been not looked at twice. It was being Eamon Palomb's seed that made him somebody and this somebody lacked the outward courtesies of his elder sibling and father. Nonetheless, the lad was destined to take the Wardenship of the West, the ministerial seat of Daol Bay and Marigold Tullivan's hand in marriage, much to her continual chagrin.

That marriage had been sealed long ago, starting when Grenjin Howland's wife perished and left him without an heir. Rumours persisted that he was impotent at any rate, though regardless, the powerful Howland family's patriarch was a childless widower.

Despite the nepotistic ways of the Elite Merchant Party, Lord Master Howland had already annulled any claim to the Lord Mastership from his four junior siblings and their lines.

There had also been offerings from highborn ladies to remarry and ministers offering their sons to be taken to ward so that they might become the Lord Master's heir. Grenjin Howland had rebuffed them all, effectively extinguishing his family name for what he deemed 'the good of the party'.

Instead, Grenjin had concocted a plan with the two men seated beside him to unite the West and East by joining the Warden Lord houses together in marriage. Of course, with only daughters, Marscal Tullivan's name was also due to be inevitably extinguished. That being a product of chauvinistic, theistic law enacted by the Elite Merchant Party and the Triarchy religion a century ago that prevented women from ruling in any capacity.

Marigold Tullivan, however, had no intention of being so obliging of the laws of men or gods, even if she did stay when her older sister had run away.

The absurdity of it all was that if Serephanie were found, the marriage would still proceed. Even a cuckolded Palomb would not be so foolish as to cast away the eldest daughter of the Warden Lord of the West. Her name bore power, even if the law prohibited her from wielding it directly. Marigold, on the other hand, had decided on a different means of fighting her fate and was conspiring to annul the marriage contract in order to rid herself of it entirely.

"Mister Reine, a pleasant dinner party, is it not?" she asked by way of greeting as she approached his left side, sliding a hand into the crook of his elbow. Tryst had hoped to avoid conversing with her, but the woman was admirably persistent.

"It most certainly is, my lady." Tryst gave by way of reply, doing his best to keep the conversation to a cordial level. "I trust the food and hospitality has been to your liking?"

"It was quite delicious and I do intend to pay my compliments to Chef Ruggard before the evening ends," she said with a warm smile while the ministers on the floor pretended not to notice the two.

Tryst decided it would be prudent to end the banter then and there. "Would it be bold of me to assume that your being here means the Lord Master is ready for his report?" he asked in a tone that still carried friendlily, allowing the words to cut to the heart of the matter without harming feelings.

"Why yes, as it is, the Lord Master was going to send his steward, Mister Hossle, to get you, but I offered in his stead. In truth I felt the need to stretch my legs, I had been sitting for quite some time and I had feared my bottom had gone to sleep." The woman offered up a soft laugh, taking a quick glance up at Tryst. Soft painted lips pulled into a pretty little smile, though mischief lurked in those glimmering green eyes of hers.

"Then I shall not keep him waiting any longer," Tryst replied back, detangling his arm from her hand and excusing himself from her company. It was a little curt, though it would be improper for him to be seen as being overly friendly with the eventual wife of one of the Palomb twins. Twins, Tryst noted, who had also left the dais and seemingly the room itself.

"As you wish, Mister Reine, I hope you enjoy the rest of your evening. If you'll excuse me, I think I may refresh my wine glass and pay the staff my respects on another fabulous meal." Marigold said, ensuring the last word was all hers before walking away. Her high heeled shoes gave her backside a lift with each step that she fully intended to be noticed, by Tryst himself above all.

Tryst shook his head and headed towards the steps of the dais. Before which stood the small, grey haired, middle aged form of the Atrebell Manor's steward, Breyer Hossle, tasked for the evening with managing the audiences with the Lord Master. Despite asking for such not being a step Tryst needed to abide by, he did for the sake of appearances anyhow. Tryst waited while the assistant to the Lord Master strode up the steps and across the dais to the three older men in the high-backed chairs.

Howland looked to be nearly asleep as droopy eyelids fluttered open at the sound of Hossle's footfalls. The old man gave Tryst a glimpse before beckoning him forward with a quick flick of his index and middle fingers. Tryst joined the Lord Master and his colleagues, all of whom seemed to share in Grenjin Howland's exhaustion with the evening.

"Mister Reine," the Lord Master addressed Tryst as he approached the lordly trio. "Come to make your report, I trust?"

"Aye, ser," Tryst replied as he took a knee. He always took care to never refer to Grenjin Howland as 'my lord'. The reason for that being that Howland was Lord Master of Illiastra and Tryst Reine a mercenary born on the continent of Gildriad. A mercenary from a foreign land was not a soldier or a subject of Illiastra, merely a man who sold his sword and the arm swinging it. The Lord Master and Tryst were simply an employer and an employee, respectively. For that, Tryst begrudged the man who paid him the title of 'ser', but he would never call Grenjin Howland by the name Lord Master.

This titling arrangement was one Howland had been made aware of early in the time of Tryst's employment in bluntly honest and straightforward terms. The Lord Master had formed a respect for Tryst based on that and he had granted Tryst's request with no further argument.

"So what is it tonight?" the elderly man asked.

Tryst made sure to look at each of the three lords in turn as he spoke, lest they feel disrespected. "In truth, there is little to tell." He explained. "However, it would seem that Minister Braggen is not pleased that Minister Mahash is the new Lord of Agriculture."

"Not pleased, is he?" Howland replied in a bored tone, his gaze darting to Eamon Palomb, who sat silently with his hands intertwined and resting atop his belly. "I am sure he had more to say than that and I'll hear it, but not before you get up off the floor. It won't do me any good to have a highly paid protector with a poor knee."

"As you wish, ser," Tryst said, standing once again before continuing on. "Minister Braggen also stated that he would have been the more suitable choice, basing this on his perception that Farmourd had a more bountiful harvest than Galren."

Eamon Palomb gave a snort at that. "Braggen is the greatest fool in the entire caucus if he thinks I'll ever make him lord of anything, let alone agriculture. If we depended on him to oversee the farming industry, we would be spending our winters with only melted snow and wild game to eat. Even that fishing captain from Tusker's Cove is a more apt minister. At least he has the sense to keep his mouth closed and do as he is told, and that one is merely an upjumped commoner."

"Braggen is indeed an oaf in fine clothing, Lord Eamon." Grenjin turned in his seat in saying, coming to face the Warden Lord of the East and Minister of Hercalest, the most populous city in the realm. "Considering he is one of *your* Easterly ministers, I am sure you have a suggestion as to how to proceed in dealing with him?"

"I should say so." Eamon sat forward and addressed his fellow lords as he spoke, ignoring Tryst entirely. "He is a fool and a weak link in the chain that is this government. We should cut him out and find a more suitable minister."

Grenjin stroked his chin in contemplation, staring blankly into the crowd of ministers below the dais. "Would you make me ask whom you have in mind or will you tell me without a prompt?"

"Why of course, my Lord." Eamon answered quickly. "I would nominate my good cousin, Patton Palomb."

"He would certainly be an improvement from Minister Braggen." Howland put back. "Though Craiginald's brother may disapprove and certainly so may yours."

"Mine own brother is an invaluable asset in my council and in his role as the executive of finance within the department of Fuel and Mineral Resources." Eamon said, seeming to be entirely put off by the idea. "I could not spare him to leave for Farmourd. Patton would serve, and faithfully at that.

"As for Councillor Arneld Braggen, I should think he would be relieved to no longer have to worry about keeping his inept older sibling from ruining their family."

"You raise fine points and they'll all be considered another time." The old Lord Master commentated as he slid himself to the edge of his chair. "Bring this to my attention again when we near the election in the spring and we will discuss it further. In the meantime, I think I am thoroughly exhausted and ready to retire for the evening. Mister Reine, if there is nothing further would you be so kind as to escort me to my chambers?"

"Certainly, ser." Tryst said with a nod as he offered the Lord Master his arm to help the arthritic seventy four year old to stand. The man walked with a slow gait and usually a cane when the Parliamentary sessions were out. Though for that single week per season when the Ministers gathered at the Atrebell Manor the old fellow hid his weakness behind a call for an escort between chairs. Whether or not he actually believed he fooled anyone with the charade, Tryst couldn't be certain.

"I suppose I should address the good fellows before I leave." Howland said as he reached a papery thin hand for the sculpted post at the top of the dais and stepped away from Tryst.

With a single wave of his hand, the Lord Master brought silence over the hall, with even the musicians coming to a halt mid-song. "My good fellow Lords and distinguished Ministers, the evening grows late and I fear in my age I can no longer endure being awake in the wee hours. I shall take leave of you all for the night to get my rest, though feel at liberty to stay in my absence. Tomorrow we adjourn this latest parliamentary session, to be followed by another exquisite meal with you all and your families that will join us then. Until such time, I bid you all a fond goodnight."

Hossle joined Tryst to assist the Lord Master down the steps as the gathered men gave a polite applause for their vaunted leader. After crossing the floor and exiting through the oaken double doors to the expansive lobby, the Lord Master dismissed Hossle to move on ahead of them. This left Tryst alone to help Howland across the floor and over the tall stairs while the steward saw to having the elderly man's bed readied for him.

After a journey that seemed to take forever, with each step up the marble staircase that led to the second floor a battle in itself, they stopped to rest. A chair sat beside the balustrade that overlooked the lobby and it was there that Tryst helped seat the geriatric. Grenjin looked about nervously to ensure that only his own guards were about before addressing Tryst.

"Mister Reine," the old man began. His watery eyes flicked up and down Tryst's form critically, before meeting Tryst's own. "I couldn't help but notice you haven't worn a sword all week at the evening dinners. How is it a man can have a title like 'Master of Blades' and not visibly be wielding one? Is the sword I gave you to hang from your hip not acceptable?"

The comment caught Tryst a little off guard. When the old man spoke of noticing something in Tryst, the lack of an apparent weapon was not what he had envisioned. "My apologies, ser," Tryst began. "To be frank, the epee I was gifted from you is a beautiful piece and nothing more." He worded his criticism of the blade carefully to avoid causing his employer offence, yet he had never been one to mince words. "It is improperly balanced and the blade is made of cheap steel. The gold plated hilt, though a marvellous piece of craftsmanship, is clumsy and uncomfortable to the grip. It is aesthetically pleasing, no doubt, but as an honest weapon it is not adequate. I did not want to insult you by equipping my standard sword, so I thought it wise to wear none at all."

"Oh Tryst, the only thing blunt about you is your honesty. Believe me it is much appreciated to hear it from time to time." Grenjin showed no signs of being put off by the disparaging remarks Tryst made towards the sword in question. "Do not worry about that sword I gave you then, I would rather that you equip yourself with what suits you best. Just don't arrive unarmed, for it makes me nervous. If someone was to make an attempt on my life, they would be most inclined to do so when they thought you were empty handed."

The weapon under Tryst's scrutiny had likely cost an exorbitant amount of coin, but it would hardly be noticed in Howland's expansive bankroll.

Tryst's words were not entirely as honest as Grenjin would like to believe. Certainly the sword was useless, but he was not without a weapon. Hidden in either boot was a narrow pocket above either ankle in which he could conceal a throwing knife. The slender blades were adequate enough to serve in their intended form or to be pressed into service as a dagger. The knives, combined with his expertise in Kav-Do-Roe, an Elven style of hand-to-hand combat, made him a dangerous foe, regardless of whether or not he had a sword on his hip.

They lapsed into silence for the rest of the walk once Grenjin had resumed his slow, plodding trek. The last flight of stairs led to the third floor, the entirety of which was Lord Howland's living quarters. The door to the expansive apartments was opened by the steward when he heard Tryst and Grenjin approaching. Tryst made a customary sweep of the suites for intruders to the old man's satisfaction and left him with Hossle to prepare for sleep.

Going back the way he came to the Great Hall, Tryst went in search of Freyard. The hope was that his friend would join him in breaking the seal on a bottle of rum of good vintage that he had acquired while recently in Aquas Bay. His eyes scanned the remaining occupants of the room, finding that the Warden Lords of East and West had also retired for the evening and their stewards with them.

At first glance Tryst missed sight of Freyard and was about to leave when he caught him subtly waving Tryst over.

The sandy haired rifleman had built a reputation as ranger and had all but eradicated one of the three raiding gangs plaguing the Southlands. It was a feat that in its own right earned him a great measure of respect with Tryst, despite his usage of firearms, which Tryst wholly detested. As they came to know one another, that respect had turned out to be mutual and Freyard had eventually become one of the few people that Tryst called friend.

"Another dull affair, wouldn't you say, Reine?" Archer commented in a bored tone, referring to Tryst by his surname.

"Entirely, though dull is not without its benefits," Tryst answered with a smile as he closed the gap between them. "What's the word, my friend?"

"The word is that the Lady Marigold went into the kitchens some time ago and hasn't returned," Freyard noted.

"Hasn't returned?" Tryst was a little perplexed. He had seen her heading in that direction after their conversation earlier that evening, though that had been some time ago. "You've been monitoring the exits the entire time?"

"Aye Tryst, there's only three: the west door near to me, the south door from the servant's hall and the north one behind the dais. She hasn't emerged through either one, though she could have gone outside. Given that she went without a cloak or coat and it is more than a little chilly outside, I have my doubts about that," Freyard answered with a little concern in his voice. "Seeing as how you're not on duty like I am, I was hoping you would investigate on my behalf?"

Tryst nodded, himself wanting to figure this puzzle out. "Aye, leave it in my hands. I'll see what's going on."

After a quick thank-you from Freyard, Tryst left him and headed for the kitchen.

Inside the air was always warm, even after meals were finished being cooked and served. At this hour, no one was working. The cooks, bakers, dishwashers and servants had all gone across the west yard to the servant's quarters to take their own meals.

Only Ruggard remained within. The man was a giant of a master chef who stood a head and then some over Tryst. The big fellow was frequently called 'Lord of the Kitchen', a title lovingly bestowed on him by his workers and one he wore proudly. Tryst thought he was a good man of honest nature who was kind and fair to those who answered to him. Even now, the Lord of the Kitchen was working alone to clean up while his staff ate and rested.

Upon entering, Tryst found the tall man drying and sorting away the pots, pans and other cooking tools of the night. Ruggard turned his face to look over those wide shoulders as Tryst came through the door and turned back without a word, no doubt hoping Tryst would leave quickly.

Despite Tryst's best efforts to be friendly and pleasant with the staff of the manor, they all fostered a great deal of fear and hatred for him. Of course, Tryst knew that to be the doing of the Lord Master, who had taken great pains to spread false tales of Tryst to inspire such reactions.

In the towering cook there was no such fear, though the detestation was plain enough. "Can I help you, ser?" he asked with that deep bass he called a voice.

"Good evening, Ruggard, I was wondering if you had seen Lady Marigold lately? I had heard she came through here some time ago." Tryst posed the question quite amiably. He bore the man no ill will, regardless of how that was reciprocated.

"She did." Ruggard Helmsworth answered brusquely as he

turned his head away, putting his full back to Tryst as he worked a towel over a large boiler.

"I see, how long was she here might I ask?" Tryst put back, keeping the tone friendly.

"I don't know, not my job to keep track of the rich folk," he replied again, laying the boiler off to the side and reaching for a heavy looking iron pot.

From the corner of his eye, Tryst watched as Ruggard lifted it easily with one hand, like it was no heavier than a bowl.

"What was she doing, could you at least tell me that?" Tryst gingerly asked.

"Thanked me for dinner," he shot back as he put the pot down with a loud bang.

"That was all?" Tryst prodded, maintaining his poise in the face of the cook's rudeness.

The man finally looked at him, his brown eyes gazing out under thick, bushy eyebrows of near black that matched the short cropped hair on his head. "Talked to her butler and then took two stemmed glasses, a flagon of wine and left, like I wish you would do."

"I apologise for troubling you, Ruggard and will take my leave of you shortly." Tryst assured. An eyebrow arched curiously as he caught on something the chef had said. "You said 'her butler', are you referring to her steward, Oire?"

"That's him, yes. He went out the north door and she went out the south one, to my workers hallways. Pick one and follow it yourself if you're done here." Ruggard put the pot in the boiler, lifted them in his arms like they weighed nothing at all and walked out of sight to the storage pantry around the corner.

Tryst took the cue and turned towards the south exit to the servant's hallway.

Opening the door on the darkened passage, Tryst found it illuminated only by the electric lamps shining through the windows. The big, pole mounted bulbs served to light the outside walkways during the night. His eyes adjusted to fall on the figure of Marigold Tullivan, standing before one of the windows. A pair of wine glasses rested on the sill, one full and the other only half. She had taken notice of him as soon as the door had opened.

The pale lights from outside fell across her face and upon which Tryst could see a slim smile as she turned to meet him. "Mister

Reine, I see that Captain Archer passed along my message."

Freyard played me coy, he thought before following her game. "That he did. I understand that you wished to speak with me?"

"I do," she admitted. "I took the liberty of procuring us some wine, a fine red from the vineyards in the Bay of Fog. It's got a blueberry taste to it and a tender sweetness that just clings to the palette. It is quite nice if I do say so. Care to try some...Tryst?"

He couldn't recall if she had ever called him by his first name before. It had always been 'Mister Reine', just as all the lords and ministers had always done.

Nervously he stepped into the narrow hallway, closing the kitchen door behind him. "I...um...What is it you wish to speak to me about, Miss Tullivan?" Tryst heard the words stumbling out of his mouth as soft footfalls brought him closer to the brunette beauty.

She had a slight waver in her stance when she had been speaking, one that became more pronounced as she turned her body towards him. As she pivoted, her foot struck against the flagon on the floor and it rang hollow and empty.

She's been here since I last saw her, drinking up the courage to ply me again to help her break her marital bonds.

"The same thing I have been trying to speak to you of for some time," Marigold said, confirming Tryst's suspicions in a low voice that still found a way to bounce off the walls.

"Miss Tullivan I-"

She cut him off with a pointed look. "Marigold"

"Pardon?" Tryst nearly stammered.

"Please, call me Marigold. There is no need of formalities between us." She had picked up her wine glass in two hands as she said it, taking a gentle sip of the red.

"Fine then, Marigold. I don't know who you think I am, but I am not in any position to help you with what you seek." Tryst inched closer, so that they might talk in whispers.

The second wine glass that had been resting on the sill was offered to him and he had taken it to hand while speaking.

Marigold lifted her own glass and softly tapped it against his. "To calm your nerves, Tryst. You are quite worked up. Be at ease, for I will not hurt you." She said as she took another sip, to which Tryst responded to the toast by taking a similar portion to tongue.

It was indeed as sweet as she claimed, but not in a sickly way.

It had notable texture and a good body that he swished in his mouth before swallowing.

"You give me cause to be nervous Miss Tul-er...Marigold." Tryst caught himself from saying her family name.

"So you think you have cause to be nervous, Tryst?" she asked rhetorically with a humorous scoff. "After tomorrow I am to return to Daol Bay with my father, who as you know, is in very poor health. Either by his death or on the birthday of the Palomb Twins on the sixtieth of winter, the Tullivan's will lose Daol Bay. My family name, all of its holdings, titles and lands will all be assimilated into the greater wealth of the Palombs and rendered extinct. This arrangement also relegates me to the useless role of being a voiceless trophy wife of Pyore." Tryst noticed a fire in her eyes as she spoke the names of the twins before pausing to drink. She truly loathed them as much as she claimed. "My sister... My dear older sister Serephanie... Ran off into the night with a fisherman to escape it all, but I lack her free spirit it seems. I cannot ignore my people as she can, I cannot put my needs above theirs. I stay to fight as best I can to keep that marriage from happening, for their sake. So tell me again, Tryst, who is the one that should be nervous here?"

"I'm not saying you have no cause to be nervous," Tryst began. "What *I am* saying is that I am of no use to your cause and if we are caught together cavorting like this they will take my head." Tryst finished his wine, placing the glass on the sill.

"You are of much use to my cause, Tryst. You do not realise the power you wield and the power I could grant you if you were to join me." Marigold put to him for consideration.

Tryst pursed his lips in a firm line and gave a little sigh of annoyance. "I am a mercenary under contract to the Lord Master of Illiastra, a different sort of mercenary than usual, but a mercenary nonetheless. I am not the answer to your woes and you would be wise to forget about me." Tryst gave her his back as he attempted to leave.

"As you would forget about me?" she queried as he walked back the way he came, "You would leave Daol Bay and I to the mercy of the Palombs?"

To himself, Tryst rolled his eyes. He knew that she was making an attempt at shaming him into accepting her offer and Tryst was having none of it. "What would be my alternative?" he asked, by way of reply. "While your sister remained, you wanted me to marry you and whisk you off to Gildriad, now what? You would have me marry you and assume power in Daol Bay?" Tryst's tone was more than a little sarcastic, even a little stinging.

"No one would question you, Tryst. No one would dare challenge your rule." Marigold shot back, her tone just as biting as his.

"Eamon Palomb would challenge my rule. He and the entire might of the eastern half of Illiastra. Goodnight, Miss Tullivan." Tryst left her with that, returning to the dining hall.

Even Ruggard had retired for the evening, it seemed and the lights in the kitchen had been turned out, save for one over the exterior door. The hall had grown nearly empty, with only a few ministers lingering. Mattersly of Tippard, Slake of Hawk's Cove and Feyman of Holliford, all Western ministers, were seated together at one of the tables in the back corner. A raucous bout of laughter from Mattersly and Feyman at some jape of Slake's managed a snort from Craiginald Braggen, snoring softly from a nearby table. The old fop nodded off once more despite the noise, his empty wine cup pointing to a spreading stain of red across the white embroidered tablecloths.

"You found my lady, I trust?" Tryst heard over his shoulder, turning to see his smiling friend leaning against the same wall he had left him at.

"Why yes, Freyard, I did, thank you ever so much for delivering her message." Tryst replied sarcastically.

"Anytime, old friend, I shall see you on the morrow." Freyard chortled, evidently quite amused at himself.

"Aye, do me a favour before then, though. Keep our meeting between us and the tall cook and see Marigold safe to her quarters. She's had a lot to drink." Tryst said with a handshake before leaving his friend.

Alone once more, Tryst returned to the bench by the fireplace to collect his guitar and put the dining hall and its occupants behind him for the night.

3

ELLARIE

awn. After the night of horrors they had endured it would have been a welcome sight to most. In this realm of misery that Ellarie, Merion, Joyce, Lazlo and their unit had found themselves in though, it was just a reminder that they still lived, nothing more.

There had been no sleep, as if anyone could with their hands clasped roughly behind their back in unforgiving iron. Ellarie's shoulders screamed for respite and the elbows bent what little they could in protest of the bonds. The wrists had long ago been chafed raw and if she had to spend much longer bound up it wouldn't be long before they began to bleed. Her allies that shared the caged wagon being pulled to the Atrebell train station had shivered and sobbed the whole night. None among them dared to speak, however, not after Lazlo, Donnis and Coramae had all opened their mouths a few hours into the slow trek.

It had started with Donnis, who had made the mistake of asking to be allowed off his horse to urinate. Like Lazlo and Etcher in the same predicament, Donnis was having trouble breathing, but he had summoned the strength to speak up loudly enough to be heard. The guards had commanded him to be silent, but Donnis persisted and Ellarie thought they were going to beat him to death right there.

They were kicking and whipping Donnis with sticks by the time Corporal Cornwall had sauntered to the rear of the convoy to see what the commotion was. Lazlo called the soldiers cowards and slung a few other choice words at Cornwall and soon found himself beside his cousin and beneath a hail of boots and rifle butts.

Poor Coramae was Donnis' lover going on two years and Ellarie felt terribly for her as she shuddered, trying to keep herself to a quiet sob. When Coramae finally broke and begged the guards to stop they responded by unlocking the wagon and dragging the slender blonde out by her legs, beating her as well. Ellarie had thought about making a break for it herself, but she couldn't have gotten to the door without tripping over the others.

Even if I could, what could I have done with my hands back to back in solid iron? she reminded herself. *Besides fall on my face and take a lashing with the three already enduring one, that is.* So her tongue stayed still.

The same could not have been said for Lazlo, though Ellarie and every other member of the Thieves present knew there was a small chance of that happening. To Lazlo's credit he had been quiet until they laid the first blow on Donnis, which had been minutes longer than Ellarie had expected him to be silent.

After being thrown to the ground, Donnis' back had been to the wagons and he had been unable able to notice that Coramae was in peril. When Corporal Cornwall called an end to the beatings, the shaggy haired man was dragged to his knees and only then did he see his wife. The yell that came from him in that instant would stick with Ellarie forever. Almost instantly Laz and Donnis began calling their captors unsavoury names again, causing Cornwall to lose his temper once more and resulting in a backhanded blow for each man.

The two lay in the dirt, shirtless and shoeless, spitting blood and shivering as Cornwall stood seething above them.

It was then that the corporal gave what he had threatened when the sad procession had gotten underway hours ago. Both men were pinned down on their stomachs, faces turned towards the wagon as Coramae lay between them and it. Four guards piled onto Donnis and five onto Lazlo while the corporal grabbed the bound woman on the ground by the arms and drew her back to her feet.

"This is what you make me do," Cornwall uttered in a sickeningly amorous tone as he yanked down Coramae's smallclothes. "Private Hobelan, please come forward and remove your belt," the corporal ordered. "I have a job for you."

The same large fellow that had put Ellarie's dagger to Joyce's throat hours before stepped up and grabbed Coramae roughly by the tunic, tearing it as he yanked her away. "How badly do you want her beaten, Corporal?"

"I want her skinny little arse cheeks to look like two, big plump plums by the time you're done," Cornwall decided in an obnoxious tone. "Oh, and do make sure their men see everything. I want them to remember this for the rest of their miserable days."

Etcher, the lone male spared a beating, raised his head as high as he could and spat on Lance, calling him scum and cursing the name of Cornwall. The corporal gave him a kick straight to the face for his troubles and the blood from his shattered nose began to trickle almost instantly to the dirt road below.

Merion looked about to join the roars of anger from Donnis and Lazlo as two guards bent Coramae over and exposed her naked bottom towards Private Hobelan.

"Look at me, Merion," Ellarie had whispered, locking eyes with her sister. "Just keep looking at me. I need you to be strong." They held the gaze of one another and tried to focus on nothing else. The others cried quietly and either tried not to look at their friends outside the bars or shut their eyes and put their heads between their legs. Joyce was the exception, committing to watching every second of it, seething so hard that her face quivered with rage.

Coramae continued to wail as the leather belt loudly cracked against her soft flesh over and over again. Donnis and Lazlo both kicked and screamed in protest and tried to shake off their captors to no avail.

The big lug who had taken Donnis' wife stood a swarthy two meters tall with arms like tree trunks and a bulbous red nose above a stubbly jaw. It was a face Ellarie had committed to memory in the dim light of the oil lamps that the sentry guards carried.

If there is anything left for me to do in this life, it will be to make him suffer for this, she decided.

When the guard let the horrified woman go she tumbled to her knees then to her side and wept into the cold dirt. Donnis was hollering a hollow promise of vengeance at his captors that continued to press him to the ground. "I'll kill you all, do you hear me?! Every last one of you cowards deserves nothing less than death!"

Ellarie wished in that moment she could find some source of

superhuman strength to shatter the irons and the bars and rip every guard around her asunder. Some part of her hoped the Hero of Old Phaleayna would come crashing through the trees in his shining, teal coloured, plate armour atop his big destrier like the stories told. With his sword swinging above his head, he could make the guards run and scream around him, raining down blood and death wherever his blade touched flesh.

But Ellarie had no strength to break her bonds and she had seen herself what the Hero was now: dusty bones in rusted chainmail and steel plates, lying in an old tomb behind Great Valley Lake.

"Kill us? Why, you'll do no such thing, thief. You're going to Biddenhurst where you will be summarily executed for all your heinous crimes against the Illiastran Government." The corporal laughed, taking some sick pleasure in it all. "I told you all to stay silent, but you had to open your Ios forsaken traps, didn't you? I'll give you one chance, here and now: close your damn mouth or I start a line of guards who will fuck the sore little arsehole clear off that guttersnipe."

A silence fell over them, penetrated only by Coramae's sobs and Etcher's coughs as he cleared the blood from his throat. When it stretched on long enough Cornwall finally relented and ordered the soldiers to mount the men back on their horses and throw Coramae in the wagon once more.

Before the door had even slammed shut, Coramae crawled her way to Allia, the pear shaped girl with a long, dark braid, embracing one another as much as their restrained wrists allowed.

They were childhood friends from Aquas Bay who came as a pair to the Thieves two years ago. As it was told to Ellarie, the Elite Merchant Party had forced Allia's father's tailoring shop out of business and drafted her lone brother into the army. The loss of both their income and a breadwinner had sent her whole family spiralling into poverty. Not long after, her family had become destitute.

Lady Orangecloak had made a stop in Aquas Bay and held another of her demonstrations, convincing Allia then and there to join the cause and fight back. Coramae had refused to let her closest friend go alone and together they pledged themselves to Orangecloak and travelled with her to Rillis Vale as members of the Thieves.

While Ellarie had mused about the girls, the soldiers had mounted their horses once more and soon enough the procession was moving once more. There were no further complaints or requests from the prisoners and even the guards themselves fell into silence.

Hours later, for the first time since setting her head on a pillow in Harris Snelrowe's house in Argesse, Ellarie felt her eyelids flutter. Her exhaustion had inevitably caught up with her, though she fought the urge to sleep, feeling that she, as the commanding lieutenant of the failed operation, did not deserve rest.

There was still no movement from Nia, now curled in a ball, covered completely by the tarp and encircled by everyone else. Nia, due to being on guard duty when ambushed, was also the only one fully dressed. The others were all in their small clothes, with tunics and nightshirts here and there. Among them all, it was only Merion and Joyce who had managed to don trousers and even then, Merion was bare above that save for a laced brassiere.

The smell of the dampness in the dark fir trees drifted in, trying to wade its way through a cloying stench that had permeated the rolling, iron cage.

The guards were as hushed as their captives, and the wind had died to a whisper, falling so still that Ellarie could hear for miles.

A squirrel chirped noisily at them and the song birds came alive with their happy tunes, and for a time nature continued this melancholy elegy for the macabre parade.

After a time more noises reached Ellarie's ears: rushing rivers and human life, much of it, and bustling with activity. *We're outside Atrebell*, she realized suddenly, glancing at the forward end of the convoy to see the brick and mortar walls now in view. The walls still bore their pale blue hue, stretching for kilometres as far as the eye could see. Before them lay wide, iron bound, spruce lumber gates, sealed shut at this hour to all. Above the gate ran a covered bailey and a face soon emerged through one of the many windows to ask the party awaiting without of their business.

"We're from Biddenhurst!" shouted Corporal Cornwall, annoyed at having to wait even this long. "Open the fucking gate."

"I can see where you're from," answered the man above, apathetic despite the volume of his voice. "What are you doing all the way out here in Atrebell?"

The corporal groaned quite audibly before responding to the query. "We were deployed to Argesse to intercept and capture a band of Thieves operating in the area."

"That's interesting," the Atrebell guard commented casually, lifting a leg onto the windowsill and looking about languidly. He produced a big, green apple and began munching on it loudly. "The last time I checked a map, it seemed to me that Argesse was Atrebell's jurisdiction, not Biddenhurst's."

"I dare say, what sort of insubordination is this, guardsman?!" Cornwall sounded fit to be tied at that moment and Ellarie could only imagine he was growing more irate by the second. "We are soldiers of the government of Illiastra, same as you. If you continue to refuse to open that gate, I will have to demand to see your commanding officer."

The guard in the window was amused by that and was quick to counter. "You are in no such position to demand any such thing. By the look of the patches on your sleeves, you're a steward with the rank of corporal. I would like to see *your* commanding officer before I open any gates here."

"My commanding officer was killed in the skirmish, would you like to see his corpse?" the corporal replied, now on the verge of outright rage.

"Killed in a skirmish with the Thieves?" the guard above the gates said in a tone of mocked disbelief. "By Ios' name, you fellows certainly must have bungled that mission. You were able to goad the Thieves into not only attacking you, but you addled them so much that they killed your commanding officer. That's impressive, Corporal."

If Ellarie was not in her current predicament, she might have found that to be humorous. As it was, her own pain and misery ruined any chance that she might take any delight from the antagonising of a deserving target.

"Enough of this insolence, guardsman, you will open this gate at once!" Cornwall roared, now having reached his limit and becoming fully consumed by his fury. "My prisoners need to be boarded on the fucking train this morning. If you inhibit my ability to do that I will be bringing this directly to the attention of Lord Mackhol Taves himself! Open the fucking gate!"

"Alright, keep your knickers on," the guard relented, leaning his head inside. "Darbus, open the doors for Lord Mackhol's goons."

"Goons?! Goons?!" Cornwall shouted incredulously. "I will have you charged with obstructing the lawful policing duties of a soldier of Illiastra. Let's see you call us goons when you're in one of our cells!"

The corporal continued to rant, even as they got underway once more and proceeded toward the opening double doors ahead.

It was the guard in the bailey that got the last word from upon his lofty perch while discarding his apple core to the ground below. "I don't see anything lawful about the state of those prisoners."

The cobblestone streets of the city were teeming with people at this hour, just as Ellarie remembered from days gone by. Most of the people out and about in the streets were men on their way to their place of work. Rarely was there a woman to be seen and when Ellarie did spot them, it was almost always in the company of a male.

One of the few women she did spot was a poor, scrawny thing struggling in the middle of the road with a large basket. Unable to scurry out of the way of the Biddenhurst convoy, she scrambled, but not fast enough and her wicker basket went airborne. Turnips and carrots rolled out into the street and under the hooves of the soldier's horses, where they were crushed and mashed against the stones.

The blonde, lean woman scrambled to pick up the few vegetables that remained to her while able bodied men in all directions ignored her plight. As she crawled on her knees to grab a rolling turnip Ellarie saw the reason why the girl couldn't avoid the convoy and no one was helping her. *Her ankles are fettered, the girl's a slave.* It was an unsurprising revelation to Ellarie as an inordinate number of women wound up that way.

Most slaves were given jobs that kept them out of sight and, more importantly, away from a position that might make it easy to escape or be liberated by the Thieves. When slaves were allowed in public unsupervised, it was expected to see them fettered to prevent them from running or getting far without making noise. It also ensured that everyone who heard their rattling chains knew what they were.

Ellarie felt eyes on her from all directions. *Everyone loves a show*, she thought to herself. *Even one as grim as this.*

A brother of the Triarchy thought the wagon full of half-naked women was a good example to preach the ills of promiscuity, mistaking them all for prostitutes. When he was corrected by a Biddenhurst soldier, the holy man segued from prostitution to the sins of homosexuality smoothly, going from one memorised script to the next without wasting a breath.

The robed and hooded brothers and patriarchs of the Triarchy bleated the same spiels in every community across Illiastra, oftentimes verbatim. For Ellarie, however, worship was something she had never had any use for. Prior to becoming an outlaw though, she and Merion were forced to attend the daily mass by their overly religious father and she was familiar with the Triarchy's teachings.

Ellarie imagined that by now her father had applied to the City council office for the right of abandonment of his two eldest and unmarried daughters. Though they were both adults, being unwed women meant they technically belonged to their father until husbands could be found. If their father's request for abandonment was granted, Ellarie and Merion could be declared wards of the city and taken from their homes. In absentia of course - it was an empty gesture and simply a way for their father to absolve himself of any legal responsibility towards the runaways.

For abandoned woman that didn't run to Phaleayna or seek out the Thieves, there were two paths in life they could choose: they could become Sisters of the Triarchy and devote their life to worshipping the gods or be housed in an Espousal Dormitory. Either one seemed like a fate worse than death to Ellarie, though the espousal dormitories were especially insulting manifestations in her eyes. In the dormitories, unwed women were forced to wed any working man who might come through the door and pick them. Ellarie had always reasoned that at least women had been joining the temple priory to be Daughters of Ios as a career choice for eons. The dormitories were nothing more than a prison for women whose only crime was being unwed.

It was only in the last century that they saw their rights evaporate in a religiously motivated puff of smoke. In ancient days gone by women were warriors, serving the former monarchy as soldiers and even knights. They were free to live as they pleased and marry whom they wanted. With the rise of the EMP came the evaporation of anything resembling equality. What now remained made the stories of centuries past seem like they were no more than a fable concocted by wild dreamers.

There is no freedom for women anymore. Not in Illiastra and certainly not here in Atrebell, Ellarie thought while watching the slave girl trying to hobble away with the remnants of her vegetables.

It felt strange to Ellarie to be back in Atrebell again. This was her birthplace and she had lived here for the first half of her life, but it had not been a home to either her or Merion in six years.

The city seemed familiar enough, with the two southern

districts still looking as run down as they ever had, perhaps slipping even further into decay than she had remembered. The further north one went in Atrebell, the better things appeared. Beyond the Perrion River but before the Yanxes were the residences of the middle class folks. Their charming little homes were painted in a variety of colours and were nearly uniform in construction. These sort of citizens were generally management within the various companies that operated out of Illiastra, and like their jobs entailed, their homes stood as a barrier between wealthy and poor.

Beyond what was generally known in the south district as Rainbowtown stood tall hotels and sprawling mansions surrounded by the very vision of opulence. In all her years in Atrebell, she had never set foot on that side of the Yanxes River. It was seen as practically a crime for a peasant of the south districts to be seen uninvited amongst that lot.

The convoy had come to a stop, bringing Ellarie back to reality. There was chattering up ahead, and from what she could make of it Corporal Cornwall was trying to discover when the next train bound for Biddenhurst was set to depart.

The train station lay in the Southeast district, something the people north of the Yanxes were only too eager to complain about. This was despite the fact that the people of Atrebell were the only walled community to have such a luxury due to two massive steel gates. The engineering marvels sat in the city walls in both the west and east districts of the southern half of Atrebell. Unlike any other walled city in Illiastra, those gates allowed the trains to pass through Atrebell rather than outside it. This measure of safety and the geographical and political centralisation of Atrebell had made the station the main hub for all train-bound travellers in the country.

The entire party veered west, much to Ellarie's surprise. It was no mystery to either Dollen sister that they were not heading towards a train any longer. No, what lay ahead for them was the Gadlan Street Law Enforcement Station.

A glance to Merion illustrated that her sister fielded the same concern as Ellarie in being back in this neighbourhood after so long.

After they turned west, a squad of mounted men in immaculate Atrebell guard uniforms rode out to meet the Biddenhurst men. One among the Atrebellians rode in front and bid the Biddenhurst party to follow them the rest of the way to the guard station. It struck Ellarie just how uncourteous and cold the voice of the Atrebell guard was.

To him, this is duty and nothing more. This man wants as little to do with this as we do.

Of course it was no secret that the soldiers of Biddenhurst were held with little regard by other soldiers and guardsmen elsewhere in Illiastra. In all her years as an outlaw dealing with uniformed lawmen, Ellarie had never experienced such a level of contempt towards Biddenhursters as the Atrebell men had thus far displayed.

The procession finally stopped once more, when it was before the light blue building that camouflaged into the wall beside it like a great stone chameleon. It lay so close to the City walls that stepped catwalks had been built to bridge the nine meter high roof of the station to the top of the walls that stood a full six meters taller. The roof of the building, like the wall beside it, was topped with crenellations and sported an imposing black cannon head poking its way between every second merlon.

Ellarie spotted at least half a dozen guards walking the roof, knowing more were likely standing on the other side of the gunner slits along the front of the building. Beneath that were heavy steel doors flanked by barred windows, all set into a deep porch atop a tall set of cement steps.

Once it had been a formidable fortress and the base of Illiastra's military might. In its current state, it was a relic used to instil fear and intimidation amongst the populace. Ellarie's father had used it to just that effect on Merion when he first tried to "scare the queer" out of her. That incident six years ago had been the catalyst that started the sisters on the road that had ultimately led them home.

Ellarie recalled what Yeoll Dollen, the man the two girls had once called father, had put Merion through. Where the wagon now rolled, Ellarie had stood and pleaded with him, having been the lone member of her family that stood for her sister in her time of need. Much to the disgust of Ellarie, their mother had been stoic and silent, like she always was.

That was Linny Dollen's way as a godly woman of Ios, passively deferring all authority to her husband. All their mother's passivity had accomplished was to make things decidedly more difficult for Ellarie. Who, as the eldest, felt the need to protect and defend her six other siblings, even from their father.

Yeoll had threatened to abandon Merion and hand her over to the guards to be a ward of the city - a fate all children wanted to avoid at all costs, especially those like Merion.

To stave off Yeoll's rash decision, she promised to hide her feelings. For years afterward she pretended to be interested in men and told anyone who would listen that her goal in life was the pursuit of a husband. It was a lie, of course, and Ellarie suspected that everyone knew it, though it was only her that Merion freely admitted as much to.

For all his bluster, their father's behaviour had served only to permanently sever any trust Ellarie and Merion could possibly have for him. All the love and respect they once held for him had evaporated into thin air, replaced by contempt and mistrust. It was the law alone that kept the two sisters beneath Yeoll Dollen's roof and they both agreed to flee the city together for Phaleayna when the time was right.

All of Merion's false promises were upheld for four arduous years afterwards, right up until Ellarie's younger sister met the maiden named Joyce Keena.

A tall, strong and earnest young woman, she had disguised herself as a man named Joel Zangen and found work on a dairy farm south of Atrebell.

Upon seeing Joyce on one of their regular walks through the marketplace, Merion had pointed her out to Ellarie, noting both her disguise and her beauty radiantly shining through it. Ellarie had prodded her sister to introduce herself and say hello, though fear and shyness kept her from following through.

After a third of a season of watching Joyce riding into market leading her ox-drawn wagon of milk cans, Merion finally worked up the courage to talk to her. It turned out Joyce had taken a shining to Merion as well, making note of the redhead that came to market every week to eyeball her from afar. Joyce had been afraid it was the disguise Merion had fallen in love with, but was overjoyed when Merion expressed that she was interested in Joyce, not Joel.

Ellarie's dear sister and Joyce quickly fell for one another, with Merion running off to market every week to meet up with the woman in disguise as a farmhand. Their love was one of the sweetest things Ellarie had ever seen and she worked diligently to help them keep it a secret from everyone.

It was mere days after Merion's eighteenth birthday when it had all fallen apart, during a particularly snowy winter that had extended itself well into the spring. Merion was eager to celebrate a one year anniversary with Joyce and had managed to scrounge together enough coppers to buy her love a red woollen scarf. The beaming smile on Merion's face as she showed Ellarie the gift she had lovingly chosen was the last warm memory Ellarie had within Atrebell's walls.

On the day that Joyce arrived at the city to deliver the milk it was all Marion could do to contain her excitement. Though somehow, she managed to keep herself in check long enough to not give Yeoll any reason to think her behaviour suspicious. The sisters went off together, parting at the market as Merion all but skipped away to find Joyce and Ellarie went off to visit their older, baseborn brother Dolph.

Besides Merion, Dolph Farhart was easily Ellarie's favourite sibling. They shared a mother and had shared a roof until Dolph had turned fifteen. At that point, Yeoll had turned him out onto the street, much to Ellarie's chagrin. Their mother, Linny, had said nothing then either. Dolph was five years Ellarie's senior and fathered by Linny's first husband who had died tragically young before Dolph was even old enough to walk.

When Yeoll had forced Dolph out, he decided to follow in the footsteps of the father he never knew and joined the military. Since then he had married and bought himself a home in the Southeast district just beyond the train station in one of the better neighbourhoods in the south.

Despite her inaction, Dolph still loved his mother and his half-siblings, welcoming them all into his humble home whenever they called. Most took the time to visit him regularly, except for Roy, the eldest son of Yeoll's who was still Ellarie's junior by four years. As Dolph had followed after his father, so too did Roy, embracing the teachings of the Triarchy as Yeoll had to a nauseating degree. His goal in life was to become a Patriarch of the Triarchy, who long labelled both bastards and queers as vile beings worthy of scorn and death respectively.

Once he had settled on this career choice and begun reading *The God's Gift* and the *Proclamation of Ios* he took on an unnatural hatred towards their brother Dolph. That same, disquieting rancour was projected on Merion as well, once it became known in the family that she was gay.

Ever the dutiful son, determined to be obedient to both his father and the laws of the Triarchy, Roy had eavesdropped when Merion had shown Ellarie the red scarf. Upon hearing his sister talk of a lover named Joyce, he took it upon himself to follow her to market and catch her in the act.

Merion had ridden with Joyce through the south districts and Rainbowtown in the wagon while the latter was doing her deliveries and Roy later claimed to have followed them the whole day. After the last of the milk had been dropped off, the two found a quiet hayloft to retreat to, unknowingly leading Roy along with them.

Once he had seen the two women get undressed and embrace, Roy ran home and told their father and the pair waited for Ellarie and Merion to return that evening.

Father and son had grabbed Merion by the arms and dragged her kicking and screaming into the root cellar and locked her there. Yeoll promised that come morning he was giving her two choices: he could bring her to the guard station where she could admit to her crime and be sent to Biddenhurst or be presented at the Temple of Ios to join the Daughterhood. Either way, he would disown her.

Ellarie had protested until her face was red and her eyes puffy from crying. It was only when her father threatened to disown her as well that she relented at last. It had not been fear that had made Ellarie acquiesce - it was loathing. When her father had shown Ellarie how quick he was to shed himself of daughters, she realised there was nothing for her to hold on to either. She knew then what must be done, for Merion and herself alike, and she retreated to their room that night to prepare.

While her family slept, Ellarie stole Yeoll's keys and his hunting rucksack and packed clothing, food and water enough for herself and Merion. At the midnight hour she left her childhood house for the last time, set Merion free from the cellar and together they left home and family alike behind.

That one act made them fugitives, women on the lam from their male guardian after curfew and running through the maze that was the South district of Atrebell. They had little provisions and could think of no way out of the city, so they sought the one person they knew would aid them: Dolph.

Dawn had nearly arrived before Merion spotted their brother

on his patrol duty. After a time, they were finally able to get his attention and tell him of what had happened between them and Yeoll.

When he had heard it all, Dolph pressed his military-issued dagger into Ellarie's hand and a handful of coppers into Merion's. "You two need to get out of the city immediately," he had said in agreement with their plan. "Go to Phaleayna, they'll surely take you in with open arms there."

With their farewells said, the sisters left their last ally in Atrebell behind and snuck out through the west train gate when it opened to admit the morning cargo train. That seemed like an eternity ago now, even though it had only been six years in truth.

The party was before the wide doors of that same station. Soldiers atop the nearby wall and the roof of the stone building were calling orders to one another and soon it seemed like there were eyes on the convoy from every vantage point. All hands stood at the ready, bearing long, bayonetted rifles. As she looked up at the line of bluecoats, Ellarie had to wonder if Dolph was among them.

What would he say if he saw that his little sisters had come home to Atrebell as prisoners, shivering and half naked?

A line of guards had already emerged from within the maw of the station and had flanked the Biddenhurst men and their captives alike. Ellarie noted that without counting the riflemen above, the men in the midnight blue coats outnumbered the men in the black and gold two to one. The tension was practically tangible between the two groups of guardsmen and for once, Ellarie saw fear on the faces of the men from Biddenhurst. *You're outnumbered as we were. Now you know how it feels.*

Ellarie couldn't see Corporal Cornwall at the front of the line, but she had hoped he was as nervous as the others were.

She took the time to scan the faces in the blue coats for anyone familiar and saw only strangers looking back.

Beyond the uniforms a crowd of spectators had begun to multiply from a dozen to hundreds as word spread quickly of the unfolding scene.

A pair of heavy boots on concrete brought the muttering masses to silence. Prisoner, guard and onlooker alike all let their attention fall upon the immaculately pressed and medalled uniform of the man who was no doubt the Major of Atrebell. "Who among you leads this outfit?" a booming, gravelly voice called out.

Ellarie tried to jog her memory for the name of the Major and came up empty. It stood to reason that he was the same one who had been serving while Ellarie and Merion had still lived in Atrebell. There had been no news of a new Major being appointed since she left and such a lofty placement in the capital city would have been news worth hearing.

"I do," Cornwall called back, still beaming with arrogance.

"'I do' what?" the first voice replied, evidently annoyed.

"I do, Major Burnson, ser," Cornwall said in correcting himself, having forgotten that he was still just a corporal in the presence of a high-ranking officer.

The two conversed near the front of convoy, their voices so low that Ellarie could no longer hear what they were saying. From the tone of voice the Major took it was clear that he was openly reprimanding the younger soldier before everyone.

Burnson, yes, he is indeed the same man who had been the Major of the Guards when Merion and I lived here. He's decorated, tenured, and a meticulous stickler for the rules. Ellarie remembered as he approached.

The Major paused as he came upon the prisoner wagon holding the women and the three men of the Thieves and the body of Captain Hoyt slung over horses behind them.

Ellarie was sitting on the side of the wagon that faced Burnson, but dared to give him no more than a glimpse, as did Jorgia beside her, and Bernadine against the front of the wagon, opposite the door. Merion, Joyce, Allia and Coramae, with her head on Allia's lap, could only look at the other three women, and the latter two did so fearfully.

Burnson's finely pressed, dark blue coat bore a variety of coin shaped gold and silver medallions suspended from a spectrum of coloured ribbons. Atop the man's head was a black tri-cornered hat, gold trimmed along the top, with a tall, magnificent white feather sprouting out of it. The man's face was worn and his hair was a grey horseshoe that ran the perimeter of his skull. The hairiest part of the Major was a pair of thick, muttonchops that ran below the temples and almost to the mouth. A square jaw outlined his defined face and his eyes were a dull green with noticeable bags beneath them that gave his face a sorrowful appearance.

It was those sullen, green eyes that took in the sorry sight of the prisoners and their guards before them. The Atrebell guards had pushed back the growing audience, themselves orderly and silent in the presence of the most visible authority figure of their district.

Burnson took a step forward, poking a hand between the bars to grip the wrist of Allia and look closely at her bonds. "Corporal, do you care to explain what you have used to restrain this woman's hands?" he asked in a tone knew full well what they were.

Lance stepped up beside his superior and seemed short for words until the older man turned to meet his glance. "Well?" the major asked again.

"Iron pinions, ser," the corporal meekly replied.

"Cornwall, do you know how long I have been in uniform?" he asked flatly.

Cornwall hesitated long enough to clear his throat. "No, ser. I do not, ser."

"I have been serving Atrebell and Illiastra as a soldier and a guardsman for four decades now, seems like a lifetime to someone as young as you, I should say. I was wearing a uniform the day you came squalling into this dreadful world. Most likely I was atop the walls of Fort Layn, before they built that monstrosity of a cannon. If not, then I was right up there." The Major looked toward the high wall nearly touching the station. "Since then I've served in most of the holds north of the Varras River, aside from Biddenhurst, of course. In all that time I've seen iron pinions used to restrain a total of five people, Corporal. All five of them died at the end of a rope that was fastened to their neck. That's what iron pinions are made for, the forsaken on their way to the gallows. I thought that was something I should not have to tell a Biddenhurster. So tell me honestly, Corporal Cornwall, are you intending to execute these people right now, in my yard?"

"No, ser. I am not, ser," Cornwall answered with an angry curling of his lips.

The major held out his hands, palms up towards the captives. "Then by all means, explain to me why you have seven women and three men restrained in such a manner?"

Lance Cornwall glanced at the tarp wrapped body of Captain Hoyt at the end of the line, glowering at it, to which the Major noticed and commented on. "Your dead captain's orders, is that the way of it?"

"Ser, yes, ser." Cornwall responded while staring at his boots. "Captain Hoyt decided that regular shackles would not suffice, ser. Given that the Thieves have escaped them before, ser. The chain allows too much movement and they're able to get their hands in front of themselves, ser. So the Captain ordered us to gather pinions, ser."

He's gone from a roaring hill cat to a house kitten since passing through the gates, Ellarie noted.

"I'm guessing that Captain Hoyt is the fellow under the tarp?" Burnson asked rhetorically. "So tell me, as his steward, was there any chain-linked restraints of any kind counted as inventory when you left Biddenhurst?"

Cornwall practically flinched before he answered. "No, ser, just the iron pinions, ser."

"Just the iron pinions, I see." The Major sighed, quite finished with the conversation. "Corporal, have your men open the wagon. Vickers, Cadwell, take those male prisoners off their horses."

"Ser, with all due respect, what are you doing?" the corporal finally met the other's stare and anger flared in both men's eyes as they locked.

"What am I doing? You've marched ten people that you've mistreated and inhumanly restrained into my domain, Corporal. You would not dare ask me to house them for the night and turn them back over to you in time to catch a train in the morning I hope? No, Corporal, that will not do. I am taking command of these people at once, as per Section Eighteen of military code, Chapter Seven: Wardenship of prisoners. You brought them here, aye. Though as a superior officer, by six ranks no less, I reserve the right to seize them from you if I suspect undue hardship, of which I have plain evidence. Until such time that either Lord Taves or your superior officers come to claim them, they are my wards and will be housed here."

A pair of guards who were presumably the two named Vickers and Cadwell stepped out, slinging their rifles across their backs as they did. Their bayonets pointed towards the sky over their shoulders as they approached the three men lashed to the steeds. The three were soon panting and gasping for air as they slid to the ground and were forced to their knees. The major looked them over disapprovingly, inspecting the wreckage of their faces and the purple welts and bruises on their exposed skin.

Cornwall was visibly seething, with his fists balled at his sides, though he made no move to unlock the door of the wagon. Had Ellarie not been in so much agony herself she might have even laughed at the emancipation of the corporal by Major Burnson.

The brash, young steward was not yet done. "But ser, I have orders from Lord Taves to deliver these prisoners to Biddenhurst," he whined like a spoiled child. "If you will not allow me to do that by train on the morrow, I ask that I be allowed to leave the city again. My men and I will march them there overland ourselves."

Burnson had bent low to look at the men of the Thieves before him, glancing over their battered faces and scarcely paying any heed to the Corporal's whining. "What are your names?" the major asked the prisoners before him.

There was suspicion in Lazlo's eyes and for a moment he hesitated in answering. When a tense few seconds passed, Lazlo allowed his lips, swollen and crusted in dried blood, to slowly part. "Lazlo Arbor, this is my cousin, Donnis Arbor and my friend, Etcher Stables," the lieutenant of the Thieves answered for the three of them, keeping his eyes on the Major the entire time.

"*Lieutenant* Arbor, is it not?" Burnson sucked his teeth in saying. "You answer to the one they call Orangecloak, yes? By all accounts I have heard you were a highly skilled and capable soldier. Believe me when I say that I am sad to see such a worthy foe brought down by the likes of this." The major turned back to the Biddenhurst corporal. "Cornwall, you and your men are dismissed from my sight. I suggest you find lodgings north of the Yanxes as I don't want to ruin my day further by coming across you and your kin again. It shall be a shorter trek to the manor for you from there and you'll need to make a point to do so. Your Lord is still housed up there on the hill until the morrow. Send him my regards and inform him that I will only turn these prisoners over to him and him alone. If he chooses to give them back to you afterwards, that's his own doing, but I will do no such thing myself. Am I clear, *Corporal*?" Burnson placed heavy emphasis on the last word, to remind Cornwall of his standing.

For an instant it seemed like the younger man might disobey his superior's orders. Lance glanced to his men still atop their horses, outnumbered, exhausted and wounded, rubbed his jaw and finally relented, reaching to his belt for a thick ring filled with keys.

Major Burnson's own steward, a short, sinewy man with a long blond ponytail running down his back turned and held his hand out to Cornwall wordlessly for the exchange.

After the Biddenhurst man turned his keys over, he curtly walked off to his own horse. Once mounted, Corporal Cornwall silently and quickly led his men away through the parting throng of people without so much as a farewell to the Atrebell guards.

Silence fell across the people gathered before the station again, and some of the gathered civilians started to disperse.

Ellarie had to wonder if her parents or younger siblings were in the crowd, seeing what had become of her and Merion.

When the Biddenhurst soldiers had departed, the Atrebell guards holding the perimeter closed in tightly and faced outward, to form a human shield to block the view of crowd. The Major regarded the tarp covered body of the Captain that Cornwall had left behind for a moment before turning to his steward beside him. "Get a pine box for him after we're done with the living. Deliver him to the train station and mark him for a cargo car. His family will want to bury him in the town outside Biddenhurst's walls."

His eyes then fell to the three men on their knees, aching and bedraggled from their ordeal throughout the night. "Start with these three," the major bellowed for all the guards to hear as the steward went about fitting keys in the door of the wagon Ellarie and her friends were seated in. "Bring the men to the second floor single cells. Give them a hot meal, clean shifts, wraps for their feet and dressings for their wounds. Above all grant them five minutes each at the basin to wash. Then start on the women. We'll put them up in the drunk's cell with the same provisions."

The iron door creaked open on the fourth key the steward tried and he gave a sympathetic nod to the passengers inside.

Lazlo threw back threw his head, sending the matted blond locks of hair tumbling back out of his eyes to look up at the major. "Ser, on behalf of all my allies, I thank you for kindness. It's a mercy in light of our treatment thus far."

"You're welcome," Major Burnson replied as his eyes fell on the members of the Thieves staring up at him from on their knees. "I encourage you to enjoy the little comfort I can give you while it lasts. Mackhol Taves will be here at sunrise, I suspect. Where he's taking you all, you're not like to see any kindness again."

Soldiers began to step forward then. Lazlo, Donnis and Etcher were helped to their feet and led away with two guards for each man. Further down, four men were undoing the hempen ropes that had been used to lash the dead captain to his horse. The Major had begun to walk away when a guard reached into the wagon and dragged out the dirty tarp that had been covering Ellarie and the others out onto the ground.

The steward, still holding the door looked in at the uncovered women out of the corner of his eye and gasped when he caught sight of something that shocked him. "Major Burnson, ser, you should come see this, ser!" the young man called out, prompting the Major to turn back and walk to the door of the wagon.

"Richard, when you go to get that pine box, order two. We shall bury her in the graveyard outside town," the Major said before looking at the seated women and speaking to none of them in particular. "What was her name?"

Merion glanced from the body at her feet to the Major, a glint of fire still in her eyes. "Nia," she said. "Her name was Nia."

4

TRYST

In a flickering dream, Tryst heard his classmates cheering wildly for him and his opponent. The two boys were circling one another in a raised, roped, pentagonal fighting ring, their newly acquired bow staffs in hand.

Tryst was watching every move made by his close friend and sparring partner, Myolas Himmato, waiting him out. The bigger lad always went first, Tryst knew, and it was just a matter of time before his patience fled him.

That confident smirk Tryst knew so well ran across Myolas' face from ear to ear. It was a young face, barren of the thick, dark beard he would become known for.

They were but sixteen, yearlings at the University of the Combative Arts nestled amidst Fuwachita Mountain in the southwest prefecture of Drake. At sixteen, both had reached the rank of Weapons apprentice and as was tradition, their title had earned them each a finely crafted, yew bow staff. From the day they were handed the weapons, the pair had taken to wearing them proudly across their backs wherever they went.

A tournament had been held over the past month, pitting all the armed apprentices in a blunt weapon, round robin contest. Before this tournament, they were but two young eager faces among many. By the time they had reached this match, everyone in the school had taken notice of them.

Tryst and Myolas had run through the lists in their respective divisions, winning soundly at every turn to the surprise of the other students and the instructors alike. Myolas had even accomplished a single blow victory when he had knocked a young man out the instant the referee had clapped his hands to start the match. Even in that though, the two were competitive and Tryst resolved to earn an equally impressive victory. That moment came when Tryst was able to win by driving his opponent between the second and top rope of the three roped ring to the wooden floor outside.

After fighting their way through seven other matches apiece over eight days and with neither having suffered a loss, the time had come to determine a tournament champion.

Residents from Fuwachita City at the base of the mountain had made the trek all the way to Ritoh Arena within the University to spectate. The townsfolk sat shoulder to shoulder with a great many students from both the Combat and Academic institutes and the building had been filled to the rafters.

The combatants had dressed in their proper combat uniforms: a vest and trousers of silk belted with a sash, coloured black with gold trim for Myolas and red and silver for Tryst.

For some time, neither one was willing to give an inch. Both knew the first blow could be an opening for the other to capitalize on, a critical mistake, and both sought to be the defender in such an instance. Even Myolas showed a level of restraint Tryst had no idea his larger foe possessed. As Tryst knew though, Myolas' patience had an expiration point. His sash swayed behind him as he made a quick thrust at Tryst. It was a ploy, the thrust was only half length and Myolas pulled back at the last second. It was too late for Tryst to pull his own parry, and with no recourse, the two began exchanging blows.

The spectators erupted into a raucous roar of approval as the two yew staffs clacked loudly against one another in rapid fashion. Myolas laughed as Tryst backed him toward the ropes and Tryst was well aware that he was being toyed with. The Drakian born lad had always been the stronger of them and was a full quarter of a meter taller and a dozen kilos heavier. It was no secret that of the two, Myolas hit harder, lifted more and threw further than his rival. Tryst's counterbalance to that were his speed, agility and endurance. There was no doubting that as the match wore on, the odds would tilt further in Tryst's favour.

Tryst swung his bow quickly and rained blow after blow for his friend to check until Myolas finally pushed back and powered through him, going on the offensive himself. The battle went back and forth, and neither one could seem to land a blow on the body of the other. They parried, blocked, dodged and weaved around the ring, focused and sure, for what seemed to Tryst like a dozen minutes.

Tryst watched Myolas' breathing deepen, checked the heavy blows and felt their increasing sluggishness as Myolas spent his energy. The larger lad parried a slash to the leg when Tryst took the offensive. The parry was thrown quickly, Myolas stumbled and his staff lowered, giving Tryst the opening he sought. Tryst swung upward at Myolas' exposed head but hit only air. As he ducked the headshot, Myolas tried to sweep the legs from under Tryst while he crouched low. This was a gambit Tryst countered by leaving his feet and twisting into a sideways roll over Myolas' back, coming to a firm landing on the canvas mat.

Myolas had been baiting Tryst into making such a flashy move all along and as Tryst's feet touched down, Myolas was leaving his. The thick bodied Drakian went spinning in the air with his staff whirling overhead. The blow he landed sent a shock of pain across Tryst's shoulder blades and the weight drove him to the mat with his face roughly absorbing the impact. A knee shot into Tryst's back and the staff went across his neck.

As the realization came to Tryst that he was pinned, he released the staff in an effort to gain purchase, but try as Tryst might, the bigger teenager was immovable.

The referee overseeing the match slapped the mat, seeking a five count to end the contest. Despite Tryst's physical protest on the matter, it was an inevitable result. The hand came down for the fifth and final count and the audience erupted.

After releasing his opponent, Myolas celebrated with his staff above his head, soaking in the adulation from his peers. Instructor Himmato, who was Myolas' father, stood from his seat in the front row, and father and son bowed to one another as the younger regained his composure. Repeating the bow to the other instructors, including the referee, Myolas turned to Tryst, who had moved into a sitting position on the mat, his staff still beside him. An outstretched hand pulled Tryst back to his feet and the rivals gave a final bow to each other.

A sudden clangour rattled Tryst from his sleep.

Someone is in my armoury making a racket.

The night's shade still clotted the sky, but the autumn meant later sunrises. His head was still full of the dream and Tryst tried to shake it while quickly climbing into his green silk trousers and vest. A sash of golden silk was hastily tied to hold the trousers in place as he shoved his feet into sandals and stepped onto the landing of the stairs outside his room.

While not the most luxurious of accommodations, Tryst enjoyed his living arrangements at the manor. What he called home was a cylindrical brick and mortar tower that in the past had been the armoury of the Atrebell Manor. A blaze had burned all but the armoury to nothing and a new manor had been built around it. After the blaze, a separate building was constructed for the guardsmen to use as both a barracks and an armoury. What would become Tryst's quarters, which had once belonged to the Captain of the Manor Guards, and the armoury below it had proceeded to fall into disuse until Tryst's arrival. Despite having his choice of one of the many suites within the building, Tryst saw the rustic tower and decided almost immediately on making it his home. The apartment offered unmatched privacy and the empty armoury made for an ideal space for him to train. Where there had once been rows of weapon racks there stood now a fully equipped gym for his personal use.

After Tryst descended the steps noiselessly, he stopped before the entrance to the gym and craned his head in to take in the large room. A rack of wooden weapons encircled a quarter of the wall, with everything from daggers to heavy weighted spears at his disposal. Beneath the lone window, there was a raised platform lined with cushions and encircled in candles where he meditated before training to clear his mind.

In the centre of it all were a trio of down filled, leather encased, wooden target dummies, one of which had toppled over and taken the other two down with it. Standing over them in a fine suit of black with a white, button down shirt complete with a bow tie was the diminutive slayer of the dummy. Tryst watched as the boy laid a short, steel sword aside and tried to right the heavy, inanimate fellow, failing miserably at the task. The dummies were anthropomorphic, with adjustable limbs so that they could be set in various fighting positions, and they were quite heavy, especially for a child.

Through it all, the boy had not noticed Tryst enter and the elder stood for a moment without saying a word to observe the futility. It was a fruitless effort, for as soon as the boy tried to upright the torso it clunked to the ground in a heap again. As the dummy tumbled to the floor and took the boy down with it, Tryst let out a chuckle that sent the boy jumping.

"By the gods!" the boy exclaimed in the drawling accent of the highborn Hercalest folk.

"To what do I owe the pleasure, young mister Palomb?" Tryst queried lightly.

"Mister Reine, you startled me. My breakfast was finished and I wanted to try the sword father gave me, so I came here to battle the dummies," the boy answered, having finally caught his breath again.

"I see. Might I see the sword then?" Tryst followed his question up as he leisurely stepped into the room.

"Very well," he replied again, picking up the sword from the floor beside him. The boy held it by the grip, blade pointed at Tryst.

"First lesson: that is not how you offer your blade," Tryst explained while reaching to the rack on the wall and drawing a wooden short sword from it. Imitating the act of having a sword in a sheath, he drew it up from his right side with his left hand. Slowly, so the boy could follow, Tryst laid the flat of blade across the back of his right wrist while keeping the left on the hilt.

"Take this one and try what I showed you so that you don't cut yourself," Tryst instructed, opening his left hand palm upward so that the boy could claim the practice blade.

The young fellow looked thoughtfully at the wooden practice sword and replaced his own to attempt to replicate the act. The lad was right handed and pretended to draw the blade from his left. Twice he dropped it, but on the third time he managed to get it right. After three more correct attempts, Tryst allowed the Palomb boy to draw his real steel. He was more careful this time, nervous of cutting himself or dropping his new sword. When the lad had offered it correctly, Tryst accepted the blade.

"It is done that way so you offer the hilt." Tryst explained. "No one wants to take a sword blade first. You present it as such so that the receiver might take it to hand properly."

Tryst held the small sabre to the light of the tiny window. Its blade was just over a foot long with a large, rounded guard over the decorative hilt, making its weight slightly disproportionate as a result.

The guard made for a good safety measure, but hindered a sword of otherwise good quality and excellent steel. However, as Tryst cut the air with the blade, he noticed the young man following his every move with a look of awe and decided against stymieing the boy's enthusiasm.

"Not bad, young Palomb, this is a fine sword for you. You're a little young, but your father must think you're ready to be taught," Tryst commented, offering the sword back in the same manner he had just instructed the boy in.

"Father won't teach me anything. He didn't even give it to me himself. Instead he had one of the servants deliver it to me before he left for sessions." The boy disappointedly sighed, taking the sword back in his hand. "And I'm eleven, that's plenty old enough."

"That's unfortunate," Tryst said sympathetically. "Surely one of the men-at-arms in your home will be assigned to teaching you?"

"No, not them either. They all said I'm too young and they were afraid I'd cut myself." He stared at the floor as he spoke, looking up at Tryst only once he had finished.

Tryst knew the right of it: no man in Eamon's service wanted to face the old man's wrath should the boy slice himself open. The Palombs had a reputation of never taking responsibility for their own actions and that went double in matters pertaining to their offspring.

"Will you teach me?" The boy jumped, the idea suddenly coming to him. "I always wanted to go to the 'Academy in the Clouds' like you did, but Father forbids it. Perhaps I can at least learn from the Master of Blades?"

"I'm afraid not, young ser. I'm no instructor, nor do I think your Father would approve in the least." Tryst moved to the door, laying the wooden sword back in the rack in doing so. "Your breakfast may be finished, but mine's yet to begin and I must ask that you not linger here in my armoury."

"Wait!" Dorian jumped again. "May I at least join you?" The boy looked at Tryst with hope in his eyes.

"If the young ser wishes, he may." Tryst bowed his head, holding open the heavy oak door. There was a pang of pity in Tryst for Dorian Palomb. It was said that in his home of Hercalest he was entirely friendless, for having inherited his family's ill reputation meant other children weren't inclined to play with him. In his frustration, he had come to bully them, which did little to improve his standing.

Soon the pair had taken seats in the corner of the large hall Tryst had guarded over the night before. The tables were back in their usual placements and adorned with beige tablecloths for the morning meal. No one else of the upper crust had yet rose from slumber and only the kitchen staff were about, toiling at their duties.

Tryst had helped himself to coffee, hard boiled eggs, a rasher of bacon, a breakfast bread roll and a bowl of oatmeal layered with a fine gob of honey. It was the last day of his workout routine and he allowed himself a larger meal than usual, one that stood against his rigorous diet. The boy had grabbed an apple as he had followed Tryst through the kitchen, eyes agog as they fell on the behemoth Ruggard who was overseeing his cooking staff.

While working on his morning meal, Tryst was plied with questions by the loquacious lad munching loudly on his apple. Dorian claimed that as of late he had been reading a book called *The Fantastical Creatures from the Unseen World* and he proceeded to tell Tryst of all the beasts found within. minotaur, griffins, sea serpents and dragons, Dorian insisted they all were real and lived in droves somewhere over the Endless Ocean, beyond the mountain ranges of either continent. "You must have travelled around the world quite a bit," Dorian said. "I bet you've seen all sorts of monsters like that."

"Can't say that I've seen anything quite like that," replied Tryst with a gentle chuckle. "I suppose I'm glad for that, I don't know that I would want to."

Dorian answered quite assuredly, "You're the Master of Blades. If any of those things found their way here, you could slay them easy."

"Perhaps you're right," Tryst answered in amusement. "Maybe it will be you who will get to go beyond the Endless Ocean to discover all those great beasties."

"You think so?" the boy said, his eyes going wide at the suggestion. "Nareen says I could grow up to be a warrior too, and sister knows a lot, she's very smart," Dorian explained, before going on to tell Tryst of the further adventures he and his older sister had in Hercalest.

The more the boy spoke, the more it became apparent that Dorian had little to no interest in his older brothers or father. Rather, his free time seemed to be spent in the company of his one sister and mother, and every story revolved around the two. Nareen was a tomboyish girl of thirteen, who from Dorian's accounts, had as little time for the elder siblings and patriarch of the household as the boy had. It almost seemed like they may as well be two separate families: Eamon and his twin sons to one side, and his wife Jorette with young Dorian and Nareen to the other. By contrast, as demented as the twins were, their younger siblings seemed to be remarkably normal. Dorian's disappointment in his father's neglect aside, it was a gift that Eamon had done just that. Left alone, Eamon's youngest son stood a chance to grow into the fine young man his brothers could never hope to become.

Once Tryst had finished his meal, he took plate, cup and cutlery to the wash pit in the back of the kitchen, with Dorian following closely at his heels. The boy watched everything Tryst did with a look of admiration and that alone had become foreign to him. The last time Tryst had admirers they were the freshmen and sophomores of the University.

Since coming into the employ of the Lord Master Grenjin Howland the only emotions shown to him by those beneath the Lord Master's circle were equal parts fear and hatred. The stories woven and passed on to the folk and blindly accepted as truth depicted Tryst to be a blood thirsty killer capable of mowing down an army alone. Absurd notions to be sure, but those notions had a way of slowly slithering across the country and beyond, carried on the tongues of the heralds and the gossips.

Dorian though, being the son of Grenjin Howland's closest conspirator, knew truth from fiction. On every instance of the boy's visits to the manor, he had sought out Tryst, to follow and revere the swordsman.

Their walk back to the armoury was filled with Dorian telling Tryst about a cat and her kittens he and his sister had been caring for lately. They were nesting in the loft of the Hercalest mansion stable and the siblings were keeping it a secret from everyone but a stable boy they had bribed into silence. Tryst surmised that he must have made the confidentiality list as well. Their father forbade pets and the boy feared that the twins were likely to kill the animals for amusement.

Dorian's tales certainly weave a grim spectre over the reputation of the twins. Tryst thought, *I must admit that it gives credit to*

Marigold's desperation to be rid of them.

With the eighteenth birthday of the twins looming ever nearer, there was a definite change on the horizon. Granted, Grenjin Howland would not let power transition to the Palombs until he died, but the birthday of the twins marked their passage into adulthood. There were titles and responsibilities that they would come into after that - one of those being the marriage Marigold so sought to avoid.

Tryst and Dorian reached the armoury once more and the boy gave a despondent sigh as he knew Tryst was about to dismiss him for his own morning workout.

Before Tryst could say a word, the boy interjected, "Can I exercise with you? Everyone tells me I'm small and weak, but if I see how you exercise, I can do it myself back home. Maybe then I can get strong enough for my brothers to leave me and Nareen alone. Please? I won't get in your way, I promise."

There was an oddity in a Palomb asking for anything from someone financially below them. Everything was commanded, demanded and ordered. Although the boy had already shown he was less of a Palomb and more of a Morton, his mother's family from Weicaster Bay in the west. Looking at the young lad, desperate for a male role model, Tryst relented. "Today is the last day of the week. My routine today is Kav-Ma-Roe, that's an Elven combat art done for meditation. It's not really designed for gaining strength. However, I suppose you can follow along if you really want," Tryst said with a smile at the corner of his mouth.

"May I? That sounds great!" Dorian beamed as the two stepped back into the makeshift gym.

For the next hour, Tryst showed the boy the basics of Kav-Ma-Roe. The Elves had perfected the art of hand to hand combat and their key style known as Kav-Do-Roe, which roughly translated from Ancient Elven as "Strike Last". It was a style that required speed, intense focus and razor sharp reflexes to master with any proficiency.

The instructor at the University, an elf by the name of Jahiro, was impressed with Tryst's performance in the art. Given its Elven design, it was difficult for humans to become passingly proficient, let alone reach expert status, as Tryst had. Kav-Ma-Roe's basics, by contrast, only required mental concentration and the knowledge of how to make a proper fist and thus made for an easier learning curve. The elf Jahiro had explained to Tryst that the meditative art was how he introduced non-Elves to the combat applicable Kav-Do-Roe.

Tryst walked the boy through a basic pattern of movements, one that at least showed him how to throw a good, solid, forward punch. They went through the pattern together and on the first few attempts, Dorian stumbled. However, the boy showed a determination to learn and he improved quickly enough that by the end, Tryst altered the pattern slightly, adding a pair of extra steps.

It was surprising to Tryst how determined the boy was and there was never a second that Dorian asked to stop or reduce their pace. He was intent on bettering himself and gaining the skills and confidence to stand up to his older brothers. By the end of the training session, the boy's curly hair was matted with sweat, the white shirt of his suit was soaked and his jacket was lying atop one of the dummies.

Tryst patted him on the back with a laugh as the younger breathed heavy, trying to catch a breath. "You did well for your first time, young Dorian. Keep practicing what you learned here today and when next you return, I'll show you more of the way of Kav-Ma-Roe."

"Really? I would...most like...that...ser," the boy gasped as Tryst brought him a cup of water from the barrel he kept in the armoury for just that purpose.

"Certainly. In the meantime, I would ask that you keep that sword sheathed until your father assigns someone to show you how to properly wield it. Is that a promise?"

"Yes...Ser...I promise," Dorian replied, replacing the cup and picking up his jacket from where it lay.

After Tryst had shown the boy out, he returned to his quarters above the gym.

A busy schedule lay ahead of him that day in the city, but before it all he would need to take a bath and check in with Lord Master Howland.

The last day of the Parliamentary Sessions was known as the Summations. Usually it was only attended by the Lords of the Cabinet and a smattering of ministers. The rest took the day with their families to enjoy the city and even Tryst, on account of the Honourable Guard's presence, was excused from the duty.

This gave Tryst the day as his own, to do as he pleased without Grenjin Howland growing too paranoid in his absence. Of course, it wasn't a day spent in leisure, nor did Tryst ever feel such release from duty. There were tasks he must accomplish. The key would be in completing those tasks with enough of the day left to return and get a second bath before the evening feast began. It would not do to arrive smelling of the day's sweat at such a function.

Tryst took a small satchel filled with toiletries to hand and began to dig through a dresser for clothes. Along with his soaps and shampoos he gathered up a towel, underclothes, a black tunic, matching trousers and a simple leather belt. Upon which there was an Elven buckle emblazoned with an enamelled green leaf on silver.

Having locked his room behind him, Tryst departed for the public baths in the first basement, the location of them being the one inconvenience of keeping quarters where he did.

The rebuilt mansion contained bathtubs in both the master's quarters and the numerous guest rooms with water pumped in through a plumbing system powered by steam engine. Tryst's room, being the untouched remnants of a blaze, bore no such luxury. It was a minor issue in what was otherwise an excellent arrangement.

The basement stairwell lay in the belly of the Great Staircase that went to the second floor. As it was, it was a straight walk from the armoury, as both lay in the wide, expansive corridor that ran along behind the exquisite, marble stairs. A pair of guards named Raymund and Gerr manned the heavy steel doors this morning, greeting Tryst gaily as they swung the doors open for him.

Below the manor lay the duel levelled basement, standing as a testament to the true age of the building. The old walls were long gone and all outer signs erased, but the basement wouldn't lie: this was the palace of the family Valdarrow, who for three generations plagued the people who had lived in the Heroes era nearly a millennium ago. It was Segai, the namesake hero of the era and the original Master of Blades who had brought the last Valdarrow down and ended the madness at long last.

Until Tryst's spiritual ancestor had emerged, the Valdarrow family had lived in opulence and grandeur in a palace that had even eclipsed the manor that stood now. However, unlike the building Tryst called home, its constructors were the poorly qualified, enslaved folks of the old nations of the lands: Phaleayna and Amarosha. As such, it tumbled into ruin and decay after it fell out of use.

Several centuries after the fall of Valdarrow and the subsequent death of the last true King of Phaleayna, the government emigrated.

The Lord Master at the time decided that the capital city of Phaleayna was too remote in relation to the rest of its population to be effective. It was feared by the Lord Master of the day and his eastern lords that the Sealords in the coastal regions of the west wielded all the power within Illiastra. To bring a sense of balance back to the Phaleaynan government, Atrebell was named the new capital.

At the time, the town was merely a crossroad that served as a marketplace for the farming towns nearby, and the ruins of Valdarrow were overgrown and all but forgotten. A spare wall here and there that jutted up amidst more modern buildings of the time was all that remained of a briefly mighty empire.

Atrebell did have one feature that made it ideal, however, in that it was in the near exact centre of the continent. A Parliament house was erected and slowly, Atrebell grew from a small farmer's hub into a massive, sprawling city.

The crumbled ruins weren't made habitable until a century later, when an engineering team found the basement levels to be not only structurally sound, but to be affordably salvageable. Seeing an opportunity, the grandfather of the current Lord Master Grenjin Howland, quickly bought the land and established the original Howland Manor atop Valdarrow's ruins.

That was half of the exorbitantly wealthy Malcolm Howland's legacy. The other half was being a founding father of what would become the Elite Merchant Political Party, the name of which was thereafter shortened by dropping the word Political. Even Malcolm's manor was no more - a fire having consumed all but what was now Tryst's quarters. This manor was Grenjin's creation through and through, but the basements remained unchanged, regardless of who ruled above them.

Tryst descended the first flight of stairs made of smooth marble that showed signs of wear beneath his feet, yet still retained their original grandeur. The first flight and its landing were electrically wired for light and fairly airy, as the bathhouse was open for use by any who wanted to - guests and staff alike.

Beneath though, was another, longer flight of stairs that relied on the old stones put in place by Valdarrow's slaves. Crude wiring was tacked into the ceiling and dim, bare bulbs, dangled haphazardly to light the way down to a sizable guard room and Valdarrow's personal prison beyond.

The holding pens built to house those incarcerated by the long dead line of totalitarians was a rounded room, with heavy oak doors banded with heavy iron evenly spaced along the walls.

The Howlands had spared no expense to see that the dungeon remained open for business. Primarily it was used to make traitors from within the fold disappear. Malcontents, dissenters, spies for outside interests - if Grenjin found them out, then it has here where they spent their last days.

There was also one other whom the Lord Master sought to incarcerate in the subbasement. Her group was called the Thieves, a name bestowed upon them by the government to sully their reputation. In a case of pure irony, the Thieves took to the disparaging title and wore it with so much pride that the original intent was lost.

They were rebels and viewed as the most dangerous threat of all in the eyes of the EMP and the Lord Master. Despite being recognised as a dangerous threat, it wasn't for a violent reputation that the Thieves were so feared by the Lord Master: it was all due to their leader, a charismatic young woman known only as Lady Orangecloak. There was no other above her that Grenjin Howland sought to imprison in his abysmal pit of misery below the bathhouse.

Reports were steadily flowing in from the biggest cities to the tiniest villages with sightings of the woman with the red hair and the orange cloak. Wherever she went, she instilled dissent and rebellion in the youth of the nation, much to Lord Howland's eternal frustration.

What aggravated the Lord Master more than anything was that the reports claimed that Orangecloak appeared from nowhere, erupting in spontaneous displays of protest directed at the EMP. To anger him further, it seemed that despite every effort of the guards, her escape was always so well engineered that her evasion of capture was a foregone conclusion.

That didn't stop the Lord Master from ensuring that if she did get caught, he would be ready to make her life pure anguish until her last breath. As it was, any who would find themselves below the bathhouse were destined to a slow and painful death at the hands of the dungeon's lone permanent resident.

Grenjin Howland had dredged up a sadistic murderer from the bowels of the prison city Biddenhurst when Tryst had outright refused to be an executioner and torturer.

"I'm the Master of Blades, not a butcher," Tryst had firmly

stated in his first year of employment. "If you want someone to slaughter your enemies, you will need to hire another."

Following Tryst's advice rather literally, Howland sought out a convicted murderer dwelling in Biddenhurst who was known only as the "Carver of Capurnis" to be his indentured, morbid servant.

There was no justice for those dragged into the round room with that psychotic beast of a man. They were hidden there under heavy guard where there could be no argument brokered from the public. For the condemned, there was no trial or judgment, just the certainty of being plucked from darkness to die at the leisure of the Carver in his torture chamber.

Tryst had a secret purpose for even accepting the contract to work for the Lord Master to begin with. The knowledge that a psychopath like the Carver was kept on retainer to torture and kill innocents at Howland's insistence almost caused him to forsake everything and break his contract.

Pushing aside those past memories, Tryst reached the marbled landing, stepped through a whitewashed door and into the well illuminated bath house, which in itself was the very contrast of what lay beneath it. Ceramic tile walls with halved pillars set into it every six feet or so ran around the slate floors that outlined the bathing pool. The pool's surrounding area was wide and lined with lacquered wicker seats, with room enough for a grown man to walk quite comfortably between. On the back side ran a row of reclined chairs with feather stuffed, silk cushions complete with footrests.

To the right side from the entrance was a second whitewashed door that led to the steam engine that powered the manor. At all hours it elicited a constant purr that made one feel as though they were aboard some great steamship. Beside the door he came through were a series of brass pipes moored to the wall. Tryst turned a lever that brought the pool to a light bubble. That lever served as a junction between the mass of pipes that delivered the steam to the pool from the engine room. It was a wonderment of technology that ensured that the room and the pool were always warm and pleasant, no matter the season.

He adjusted the lighting in the room via a sliding handle. It was the only switch in the manor aside from one in the Lord Master's quarters that could be raised and lowered to give different levels of light. As usual, Tryst brought it to a low, relaxing din.

The sweaty silks he had been wearing this morning were slipped off and left haphazardly on the floor. With a quick tug at the ribbon in his hair, the long red mane fell loose about his body. From his satchel he drew his clean clothes, laying them neatly on a table built into the wall. The remaining items he took to the far end of the pool before making his way back where he began and stepping in.

The water flowed gently around his nakedness as he submerged himself down the few steps on the side of the bath facing the entrance.

The pool was five and a half meters square dimensions, with steps on three sides and a row of benches beneath the water of the far end and dipped just shy of a meter in depth. Tryst had found it to be just enough to make a stroke, something he took advantage of as he slid beneath the bubbling surface.

Leisurely, he swam his way across to the far side, breaching the surface an arm's length short of the stone benches. His nearly waist length hair slipped slickly from the waters behind him and a steady stream of rivulets ran down his shoulders and back.

With a heavy sigh, Tryst came to rest upon the lip of the pool behind the stone bench. His thoughts of the last day congealed at the forefront of his mind like the droplets of water the fell from his face to pool upon the tiles. They followed him as he reached for the satchel and drew the soap, and hung with him as he lowered himself onto the seat in the bath to scrub himself clean. All of them centred on Marigold and her plight with the Palomb family. The twins set a staunch fear in Marigold that Tryst could not deny. The two had crossed Tryst as cold and cunning, like their father, but they had a fear of Tryst that he knew muddied his perception.

Since his arrival four years ago, the pair had kept their misbehaviour to sniggering comments and remarks in his presence. Otherwise, they were wise enough to not cross a man known as the Master of Blades.

On the contrary, Marigold and her sister had known the Palomb twins long before Tryst's arrival. The Tullivan girls almost certainly would have an entirely different scope with which to view Eldridge and Pyore. They had grown up with the twins, had known them since childhood and had likely had seen the boys' amorality in raw form, something Tryst had only heard about in low whispers.

Am I the first she's spoken to? Tryst wondered to himself,

Perhaps her sister had joined her in pleading their case, and seeing no recourse fled into the night with her fisherman. The Tullivan girls' father was a browbeaten man and Tryst suspected that there was more to his forsaken courage than he probably knew. *Marscal is awaiting a meeting with death,* Tryst recalled. *Perhaps he doesn't care where his fortunes go when he dies. Marigold, Serephanie or Palomb, what difference did it make to a dead man who held the coin and the power? That could explain why Marigold seems to be keeping her schemes quiet for the nonce. Her father may foil the whole thing just to ensure there's no war, something Marigold is willing to flirt with to avoid the Palombs seizing total control.*

Once done soaping himself clean, Tryst exchanged his cream coloured bar for a vial of shampoo. Tenderly, he messaged his scalp until his mane was thoroughly lathered and the waters around him were a foamy layer of bubbles.

Embedded into the steps to his left and right were pipes that kept the water flowing, and constantly exchanged the old water with new, and before long the sudsy film was carried away.

Marigold, now she is a walking paradox herself, Tryst pondered. *Her sister disappears to avoid marital capture and yet she stays on. There is a queer sort of courage in that. She could leave and forsake her home, her lands and her people, and yet she fights to the last minute to change her fate. I have to admit that it certainly is admirable.*

Slipping again beneath the water, Tryst rinsed out his hair and rose once more when he felt it was thoroughly cleaned and returned to the bench. Tryst picked up the vial and exchanged it for a small mirror on a stand and a razor blade folded within a wooden handle.

Before he could clean his face of stubble, he heard footsteps from outside and turned to see the entrance to the bathhouse open. In the doorway Tryst's eyes befell the tantalizing frame of Marigold Tullivan, scantily clad in naught but a red satin robe that ended well above the knee.

"Oh, I see I'm not alone," she said in a lowered tone, a seductive, dimpled smile across her face. "I always liked bathing in this place. So much more room to move around than those cramped tubs in the bathrooms. Wouldn't you agree?"

"I wouldn't know, my lady." Tryst turned away, putting the razor back in the satchel, folding the blade as he answered. "My accommodations don't include a bathtub."

Light, soft footsteps brought Marigold around the room until she was above the submerged benches. Once there she lowered herself to the lip of the bathing pool, crossing and dipping her legs into the steamy water.

"My lady, I should leave you alone to bathe," Tryst said after a brief glance at the barely clothed beauty before him.

She gave a giggle at that and replied, "I'd rather you stay."

"As you wish. I presume you're here to proposition me once again, my lady?" Tryst asked in a tone of apathy, cutting straight to the heart of the matter.

The water rippled as Marigold moved her toes about, a playful smile across her flawless face. "You see right through me, don't you?" she asked rhetorically, eyeing his nakedness with a bite of her lip. "You know, it's strange. Most men would sell their first born to be where you are right now, yet you look like you could run across the surface of the sea just to get away. Do I make the Master of Blades that uncomfortable?"

Tryst wanted desperately to do just that. Not for the lack of desire for Marigold, for she was indeed a gorgeous woman to behold, but there was a game at play here. Until now, Marigold had not been able to get him in such a predicament before, as Tryst had been careful enough to ensure as much. Though, he had to admit that he was intrigued to see where this may go and more than a part of him was aroused by Marigold.

Despite his gut instinct, Tryst played along. "My apologies, my lady, I just thought I might cut to the point of your visit. That is what you've come for though, is it not?" Tryst moved to the benches, leaning an elbow beside where she sat.

"I have indeed, my brave knight." A manicured, soft hand covered his, caressing it ever so gently. "Evil gathers around me, seeking to use me as a puppet. Only the sweet, brave hero from the mountains of Drake can keep them from consuming me." Marigold said with a whisper as she leaned into his ear.

"I am but a man, mortal and alone. There is no love for me in these lands, nor do I command any armies and I can be killed like any other," he whispered back, looking her straight in the eyes. "What could I do against all the might the Palombs wield?"

"Marry me. What is mine will become yours to call before you. The Sea Lords will rise to your cause and their army will be yours to

command as my husband and the Commander of my armed forces."
The fingers of the right hand that caressed his left began to intertwine
with his as she spoke. "And Drake will surely marshal its might for its
Master of Blades, will they not? They alone could crush the Palombs."

Tryst sucked his teeth at the last notion. "I am but a Mercenary
Graduate of the University of the Combative Arts that happens to be
located in Drake. I am not of the Drakian Army, nor is there a drop of
Drakian blood in my veins. The Snowhairs will send no armies for my
cause." Tryst's own fingers had begun to respond to the advance of
Marigolds, though his were hard and callused from sword and guitar
play. But she still seemed to appreciate it as he went on. "Nor will my
true homeland, for that matter. To them I am but a disgraced and
disowned son, thanks to Lord Master Grenjin Howland."

"I know where you were born, Tryst Reine. You are the blood
of Gildriad, through and through. I hear it in your voice and see it in
those emerald eyes of yours. But you know all about eyes, don't you?"
Marigold cupped his chin to make him look right at her "Where was
the last place you saw eyes like your own, Tryst?"

"Why, I see them looking back at me, my lady," he answered.

Leaning on one elbow, Marigold brought herself in closer, until
Tryst could smell her minty breath. "They say the eyes are the
strongest feature of those of the ancient blood of the true line of
Gildraddi people. There are few outside of the royal family of North
Gildriad that even bear the mark and you are one such." Her voice
dropped to barely a whisper. "Gildriad courses even stronger through
my blood. My mother, Princess Farren was born and raised north of
the Karmourric Gates, in the majestic and ancient City of Kings. But
you already know all that, don't you?"

"Your mother was the youngest daughter of King Hector the
fourth, the reigning King of Northern Gildriad. Yes, I'm well aware of
your lineage," Tryst replied, knowing full well the history behind that
marriage, the short lived bond between the two nations and the tragic
end of that brief alliance.

She gave a single, slow nod, and Tryst saw the slightest tremble
in her lips at the painful memory she recalled to make her point. "She
was all that and more, Tryst, you have no idea." Marigold looked away
and swallowed before going on. "The reason I speak of my dear
mother is that her father, my grandfather, sits in his Kingdom with the
third largest army in the known world at his fingertips. We received a

letter from him some years ago, you know. It would seem that Grandfather had made a Captain of Guards of the other Master of Blades, a man named Myolas Himmato, whom I believe you're passingly familiar with. Should King Hector's granddaughter find herself embattled with foes on all sides and her life in danger, he would gather his army and cross the sea for her. With him would come Myolas, and I would have two armies and two men who own the title Master of Blades at my side."

"So you say, my lady," Tryst answered playfully. She had promises and dreams aplenty and knew exactly which names to say to him. "A whole army, combined with your own strength, which would be approximately a third of Illiastra's existing power. Why, I should say the odds of you succeeding to be incredibly good."

"You mean the odds of *us* succeeding." Marigold's eyes locked on to his with that word. She stood and untied her robe, letting it slide off her slender shoulders to puddle atop his satchel.

Her bare, lightly tanned body stood before him, beautiful in every way. Tryst's eyes fell to her perfectly rounded breasts above a deliciously curved waist. Below it was her womanhood, bare but for a small strip of hair and those silky smooth legs he had glanced the night before. There was nary as gorgeous a woman in all of Illiastra. Even her sister was not quite as comely as the brunette before him.

Tryst was still gazing upon Marigold when she lowered herself slowly into the pool, smiling ever so sensually as the water enveloped her shapely frame.

He knew he should move, that he should get out of the pool, yet he found himself entirely unable to move.

The water rippled as her fingers glided over the top of it as she slid up beside him. "I don't want it to be just 'I'," Marigold said again as she got upon him. Her hands slid across his chiselled shoulders and she traced her fingertips ever so lightly along his taut chest, down the rippling abdominals and below, where she found him hardened. "I want it to be us."

A hand wrapped itself around his manhood, stroking it with a light grip as Tryst's breathing became heavier with every caress.

Everything in Tryst told him this was folly, a fool's gambit that would lead them both to early graves. That spoke nothing of them being walked in on by anyone else seeking a bath at that moment.

However, instead of voicing his concerns a moan escaped his

lips when he tried to talk. His body shuddered, feeling as if it was coming alive at her touch. Tryst repaid the favour, working his way up her neck with his lips until they met hers where they stayed for some time. For a time there was no sound but their long kiss.

Marigold turned him around and pushed him back toward the benches until he felt his backside come to rest on them, the water rising to below his collarbone. Soon enough she was straddling him and Tryst did nothing to stop it as their tongues danced with one another. Her left hand was caressing his chest while the right worked his member into a frenzy he hadn't felt in a season.

The voice that told him to leave was silent, there was only passion now. Even if it was only a ploy to earn his loyalty, Tryst didn't care. It was too much and felt too good to walk away now.

His own hands had been on her legs, and he let the left slide up inside her thigh to work into her other lips. Marigold gasped, breaking away from their kiss to smile at him mischievously, as if he had found some secret treasure.

"You know your way," she managed to say before all but shouting with glee. Her forehead came to rest upon his and her voice dropped to low moans as he continued to stroke between her thighs. Marigold's hand tried to work his hardness, but she was overtaken by her own sensations, Tryst knew, and that was fine.

Her responses slowly grew louder, her breath quickened and Tryst could almost hear her heart pumping hard. There was a shudder and a restrained yell that she barely kept down and she threw her head back as he worked harder. Tryst put his free hand on the small of her back to bring her up onto his lap again. She reared her head back, bit her lip, removed his hand from where it worked and took his throbbing member inside her.

Tryst only hoped he would last. He had found no love since returning north of the Varras River in the late summer as there were no brothels up here to be found. Thanks to Grenjin Howland's tales, most women hated the ground Tryst walked on and the richest who knew better would never despoil themselves with a man of modest birth. Not to mention that one of the most beautiful women his eyes had ever beheld was currently atop him.

Her arms draped over his neck and one set of lips on his while he thrust inside the other. Tryst's hands gripped her perfectly rounded bottom as he thrust again and again, breaking the kiss to catch a quick breath before their tongues engaged in their dance once more.

Nails dug into his shoulders as he pushed harder and he heard his name in shuddered gasps in his ear as they broke away from their kiss one last time.

He spent himself suddenly, with no time to remove and little desire to do so. It was a folly he felt he would regret later, but not now, not with her. She moaned a little more as he let himself go inside her, leaving the rest to fate. The two were breathing heavy and Marigold stayed atop him for a while longer. She reached beneath the water to draw his member out from her so that she might sit sideways across his lap, her head resting on his shoulder above the water.

Both of them were spent, it seemed. Where the pool water started and the sweat ended, Tryst could not tell any longer, but he knew he would need to wash all over again.

There was nothing either thought to say to the other for a time, until finally Marigold slipped from his lap to her feet. Tryst reached over his shoulder, lifting the thin robe off his satchel and grabbing for the soap bar and a fresh vial of shampoo. "Would you like to wash off, my lady? The soap is plain enough, but I bought the shampoo while in Aquas Bay, from a merchant from Johnah. It's got a pleasant scent that he claims was made with vanilla plant."

"Isn't this water a little...dirty, now?" Marigold queried with that same mischievous smile on her face.

"It uh, the pool that is, it cycles water. There's a pump room that draws it fresh from the river and heats it, you can even feel a slight current at times," Tryst answered, his face a little flushed and feeling a little ashamed of having given in to her so readily. Somehow, he masked his feelings and cocked his head playfully. "Besides, you will no doubt be sitting in the gallery of the Parliament today and you shouldn't go there all damp and sweaty."

Marigold stepped up and took the small vial from him before sinking back to middle of the pool. "Actually, I won't be in the gallery today," Marigold answered casually. "Father is feeling poorly and it is only Summations to worry about today, so he is sending me to sit in his seat at Parliament."

"Is that so?" Tryst asked while he watched her intently as she emptied the contents of the vial into her hand before lathering up with the shampoo. "I don't think the Palombs will be too enthused about it when they find out."

"I know," she said with a wink. "It will give me no shortage of pleasure, I assure you. Anyhow, Eldridge and Pyore never attend the Summations, no more than you do."

The nipples on her perky breasts peeked back at him above the water line as she ran her hands through her luxurious, brown hair.

She dipped below the surface to rinse and rose just shy of Tryst with those soft, seductive, jade eyes of hers glowing at him even in the dim light.

An arm reached around Tryst lasciviously to switch the vial for the soap and before his eyes she began scrubbing herself clean, finding her voice all the while. "May I ask you a question?" she inquired curiously.

"Why of course, my lady," Tryst gave back, stretching his arms up to the pool's edge.

"Where will you go when the Lord Master perishes?" Marigold asked without looking at him, wasting no more time skirting her words. "Will you go back to Drake or Gildriad? Will you take employment with the Palombs?" She had turned side on to him and looked at him from the corner of her eye when she said that surname. "If you think Grenjin Howland has set you grim tasks, you will be eternally vexed when the twins make commands of you. But if you come with me..." Marigold turned towards him once more, bubbling soap running down between her breasts as she let Tryst soak in her raw nakedness once more. "There will be nothing more that could possibly vex you."

"How is it that you would know what vexes me?" Tryst queried lightly but sincerely.

"Because I know much about you, Tryst Reine," she cooed slyly, those seductive emerald eyes hard at work on him again.

Tryst couldn't fight the smile on his face. "Such as?"

From the way she scoffed at that, Marigold seemed amused by his testing question. "I know that behind the walls of your beloved University in Drake that they teach you the value of life before they show you how to take it. You wouldn't have graduated, let alone be called a Master of Blades, an equal of the ancient Hero himself, if you weren't a pillar of morality.

"The Lord Master thought he could break you of it and reduce you to a heartless killer to shut any mouths that opened against him.

That is what he wanted, that is even what he tells the world he has achieved. The truth is a different matter though, isn't it? Tryst Reine won't kill on command. If he did, why would the Lord Master seek out a savage imprisoned in the depths of Biddenhurst to do it for him?"

"I still capture his enemies, Marigold, and I still do his dirty work," Tryst explained in a flat tone, averting his eyes from her. "My hands are not clean. Though men may not die by them, they still die because of them."

"It pains you, doesn't it?" Marigold bluntly asked, causing Tryst's eyes to be drawn back to her. The girl cocked her head slightly to the side, regarding him with her sensual jade gaze. "It eats at you to know that you arrest those whose only crime is rebellion against an oppressive regime. Why do you do it? What has been your motivation to betray your own conscience for so long?"

The intimacy ended in that moment. Marigold had found her way back to stand before him, but her words struck Tryst deeply and took the lust from his loins. "I have my own reasons. That is all I can say on the matter," he offered.

"It says much," Marigold said as she came upon him again, using the excuse of replacing the soap in its satchel to sit upon him once more. Her soft hands, wrinkled from soaking in the pool, came to rest on his cheeks to bring his face to her. "I think you care about this place and its people. I think you want to see change but don't know how to bring it about." She kissed him again, tenderly. "You are just like me, Tryst. You are bound to this country now. We owe it a debt, you and I. We want to redeem ourselves and our names and give Illiastra the freedom no living memory can recall." She paused to touch his lips once more. "The freedom that the Hero fought so valiantly for and the EMP took away centuries later. We can restore it once more, Tryst. Come with me and let us save Illiastra together."

Tryst lifted her from his lap. There was no desire in him for any further bodily adventure and he felt the sudden urge to leave. He left her in the water, pulling himself up behind the bench and out into the coolness of the basement room.

"Where are you going?" she called to him, looking up with sadness in her eyes, Tryst saw desperation there, one that couldn't help but be sincere.

"The morning hour grows late. I have business in the city as you do in the House of Assembly." Tryst said in return.

"Will you do me a favour when you go to the city?" Marigold asked in a pleading voice.

Tryst towelled off while he considered his options. "That will depend on the favour."

"Eldridge and Pyore frequent the city as well on Summations day. Several times I have sent my steward or one of the other servants to tail them.

The twins seem to frequent a place called Hobbs' Tavern. I would like you to go and see for yourself what they are like out of sight of prying eyes."

"I know of the place." He sighed as he slipped his black shirt and trousers on and waited before finally relenting. "Very well, I would like to see for myself, actually. I have long heard of what those two are capable of, it is high time I saw it with mine own eyes."

"When you return this evening I want an answer, Tryst. I need to know if I can count on you." Marigold's voice echoed softly off the ceramic tile walls, equal parts sad and stern.

Her gaze followed Tryst as he dried himself with the towel in his satchel, his wet feet slapping on the tiles as he walked to his clean clothes. "You will have an answer before you leave tomorrow," he replied while running the towel down his mane and wicking away the dampness. "That should give me enough time to consider everything."

5

MARIGOLD

Actors, they were all actors. Marigold reflected to herself as she walked the hall to her room. She had been sitting in her father's seat the entire afternoon for the summations of the Autumn Parliamentary session.

Somehow, despite the plush comfort of the backrest and cushion of the chair, her bottom ached from it.

The whole thing was a farce, Marigold had concluded, and one she found herself lacking the taste for.

Up until today, Marigold had been in the gallery of the Parliament house for the entire week, itself a large, high-ceilinged room ensconced within the impressively larger Howland Manor. It had seemed trifling when she watched, though she quickly came to find that it was even more tiresome when she was seated among the lords and ministers.

For the duration of the day all she had done was nod her head and repeat, "Yes, Daol Bay consents," or, "Yes, Daol Bay agrees," when called upon. These were just summaries after all. For all intent, it was nothing more than an afternoon of pompous men with bloated egos issuing congratulations to one another.

Throughout the week, Marscal had stubbornly done his duty, fighting to maintain his strength and make sound decision from his vaunted position as Warden Lord of the West. She could see the pain plainly enough on her father's face, however, as could anyone with eyes. Beads of sweat had run profusely down his pale face every day as he vainly tried to mask his wincing. Marigold had been proud of his efforts all the same. No matter what men might say of Marscal Tullivan, none would say he ever faltered on the job. With the majority of the decision making completed, his latest decision was to spend the afternoon abed.

The family steward, Oire, had been coaching Marigold on the train ride to Atrebell of her responsibilities should her father fall too ill to participate. When Marscal made the decision that morning, it would have been expected of Marigold to inform her husband-to-be Pyore Palomb that he would be filling in for his future father-in-law. However, neither she nor Oire had deigned to tell the teenaged brat. Instead they let him and his brother run off to the city and feigned their dismay at the engineered turn of events.

A theatre troupe, that's what they are. As far as Marigold was concerned, it might as well have been a stage she stood upon. Everything that the ministers and lords put forward was a grand spectacle for the journalists in the gallery and cause for uproarious applause from the backbencher ministers. There wasn't a word spoken that didn't seem rehearsed and with no ministers of opposing parties, there were no questions asked of any of it.

Of course, Marigold had already known what her role would be today. To her credit, she had almost a decade as a spectator of the droll events from upon the second floor of the dual level gallery to her name. The lower floor, which was just a balcony of plain wooden chairs, was for the journalists and anyone of the working class who might choose to attend. On the upper floor, where she had been stationed all these years, were the male ministerial heirs and a smattering of wives and widows of the ministers.

It was a lavishly furnished affair, with cloth covered tables and ornate seats similar to the ones the Ministers themselves sat upon. Servants came and went with trays of finger foods, and hot beverages, and it seemed as though every attendee had personal butlers tending on them constantly.

Marigold had almost always had Oire at her side as both she and Serephanie would refuse to go to the gallery without him.

There was a time when the sisters had begged for a quad of guardsmen to accompany them, though Marscal had denied that request. "It would be both rude to our host and to the other soldiers on duty to have your own guards in the gallery," he had explained. "Furthermore, surrounding yourself with armed men in the gallery of the Parliament hall to protect yourself from two boys will just show them how much you truly fear them. You two cannot let them win so easily. I'll send Oire with you from now on. He won't let anything happen to you, not that I think the twins wold try anything in such public view."

The incident that inspired such fear was a memory Marigold shoved deep into the recesses of her mind and sought not to bring forth. As it was, Oire had proven he was more than enough security. Despite being a low born servant made steward, he took no affronts to the girls he regarded as nieces from anyone, regardless of birth rights.

Today though, she was out of the gallery and in plain sight. As such, she had given them quite the sight indeed.

Marigold had taken to dressing herself in tight, black breeches overlaid with an ocean blue, belted tunic of short, tapered sleeves and boots of supple leather almost to the knee. The long footwear was fastened with four buckles along one side extending from ankle to the boot top. To accent the attire she had decided on a velvet cape in cobalt blue. She had worn it to one side, covering her left arm entirely, clasping the cloak over the other with a broach of gold with a sapphire inlay. The cape was long, thick and heavy, and it had trailed on the ground behind her as she climbed the steps to her father's vaunted seat. Marigold had felt the eyes of malice and curiosity following her with every step.

Of course, it was neither the cloak nor tunic that grabbed attention. Rather it was the fact that a woman not only had the audacity to sit in a male dominated position, but that she was wearing trousers while doing so.

There had been titters and scoffs amongst the backbenchers when she was commanded to speak and recite a four word line. No matter how well Marigold presented herself, she was just a pretty dame to them. As far as the ministers and lords were concerned, she was not worthy of anything but scorn for being born with the wrong set of parts between her legs.

I hate the whole bloody lot of them, Marigold reflected hours later as she turned the key to her suite on the second floor of the manor. Once the door was shoved closed behind her, Marigold undid the clasp on her cape, threw it to the bed and slammed broach and key down upon the makeup table. Soon after that she found herself pacing angrily back and forth between the two, her hands curling into fists all the while.

There came the rattling of a slowly turning doorknob on the entrance leading to the servant's hallways and Marigold silently cursed to herself for forgetting to lock it.

A girl, a shy and diminutive little thing about Marigold's own age with a head of golden curls, poked in through the door. "Miss Tullivan, do you require help undressing and cleaning for the Ball later?" a tiny, timid voice asked Marigold.

"No, thank you," Marigold replied back, softening her stance, and feeling a little embarrassed, having been caught in such an angry and unladylike state. "If you would do me one favour though, go to my father's residence and let Oire know I have need to see him when the time permits. Tell him that if at all possible, I would like it to be before the Ball," Marigold gave back, as courteously as she could muster, given her level of frustration. The attendant nodded and closed the door once more.

These handmaidens were pleasant enough, but difficult to trust wholly, Marigold found. Being in Howland's employment, she was cautious to say anything in their presence. Not only due to the fear of her words reaching his ears, but also the ears of any other member of the EMP willing to pay for what the servants overheard.

With a great sigh, Marigold undid the belt that held her tunic tight. The blue garment fell open to reveal her bare stomach and the brassiere above it made of white lace.

With this image in her mirror, Marigold glared at herself. *This, this is what they expect a woman to be: a set of breasts for them to look at while they stick their dicks below and get me with child. That is the entirety of my role to them: a baby maker and a pretty trophy between making heirs. Fuck that, if I am heir to house Tullivan, than heir I shall be. If I get Tryst to join my cause, then fuck anyone who stands in my way. It's time for a real leader, I want real governance and I want real change. Those fucking fops just work on ensuring their own businesses and interests, and that has to end. We need a new Illiastra and it will have to be me to bring that to fruition. If not, I'll die in the attempt. What other option do I have? I will not be a wife to Pyore, nor will I abandon the populace and run like Serephanie. I'm better than that.*

Her mind went back to Tryst yet again, particularly what had occurred earlier that morning in the bathing pool. That was a gamble she had undertaken entirely on her own. Oire, her closest confidant, had not known she had done such a thing and would likely scold her if he found out. The steward might be surprised to learn that it had failed, however.

Tryst had given in to her advances and the two made a sweet love beneath the waters, but he had left any answers to her offers still lingering. *Silphium,* she reminded herself. *I shall need to acquire some silphium without anyone knowing to be sure I bear no seed of Tryst Reine.* Marigold knew her own body well and felt fairly sure she would bear no such thing, but she felt a little added insurance was in order.

After Tryst had left the pool and Marigold was alone she realized she had brought no towel. A wave of foolishness had washed over her as she walked back to her room on the second floor with only her robe. The short, thin covering had quickly become soaked, with dripping water trailing her as she went.

Marigold at least had the good sense to quickly duck into the servant's hallway as she surfaced on the main level of the manor. Though still, she had met a pair of maids and a butler who worked for the manor and later Steward Arthan, who served the Mortons of Weicaster Bay. The servants were not so worrisome to her, though they all had tongues that were far looser than she would like. Instead it was Arthan, known as an incorrigible gossip as it was, that gave her the most concern. The house he served was not only married into the Palombs, but was one of her father's wealthiest allies in the West. Once the Morton house found out, it was only a matter of time before everyone else did.

It was a topic Marigold would likely have to field during the course of the evening. Of course she would lie about it and say she simply forgot her towel after deciding on a whim to take her morning bath in the spacious basement pool. A trifle, an embarrassing incident she could play off and blush politely when brought up. *Let them have their laugh at my forgetfulness.* Marigold said to herself. It was mention of Tryst in her vicinity that was the real concern and one she would not want to have known, at least not yet anyhow.

This morning Marigold had been surprised with Tryst. Until then, he had given Marigold no reason to expect he would respond to her advances at all, considering how he had rebuffed her before. Instead, much to her consternation, he had taken her, all of her, there in the water of the bathing pool. Tryst had claimed to have visited brothels in the past but Marigold felt that she had not been his first that wasn't paid for. *He has loved and been loved, by some woman, somewhere outside of Illiastra, before he ever came into Grenjin Howland's employ most like.*

Marigold remembered her first time. Unlike Serephanie, Marigold's previous lovers had all been highborn. *All two of them,* she reminded herself. The first was clumsy as first times are like to be and she thought, in her misguided youth, that maybe Tarristane Morton could be the one to rescue her from the Palombs. *Morton and Palomb were already tied at the ring finger by then though, I was young and stupid to not realise how useless they could be to my cause.* The second time was all for pleasure. *Roland Daltis, he was handsome and pleasant, though none too bright. Not that he needed to be clever, just able beneath the sheets and in that regard he did quite well.* The Daltis family were neighbouring ministers located in the town of Galdourn, just to the south of Daol Bay.

Roland had been apprenticing for a summer as a manager beneath her uncle Rory Tullivan, councillor of Daol Bay and general manager of the Tullivan family fish processing facility. It was quite the summer of playful fun and adventure and those memories were as warm to Marigold as the days had been. *Serephanie hadn't yet met that fisherman, our father was in good health and the Palombs were a few years away from turning seventeen. Worries were few and far between back then.*

Now Serephanie was in hiding somewhere in the known world and had thrust everything onto Marigold's shoulders to deal with. The older sister had lost all hope, quite simply. Unlike Marigold, Serephanie saw no way out of being a puppet and a pretty, glorified slave for the Palomb twins, so she had run away from it all. As much as she would have liked to, Marigold couldn't fault her sister for that.

There were occasions when Marigold felt resentment towards her elder sibling for having left her on her own to fight, but Serephanie's selfish act had taught her a valuable lesson: that running and hiding would win no battles. This was not about saving herself any longer. Marigold's fight had become something bigger and more tangible than that. She knew that and sometimes she wondered if perhaps Serephanie did too. Some part of Marigold even wanted to believe that Serephanie had left it all knowing that the younger sister could do what the elder could not.

With things left to Marigold as they were, she and Oire had drafted a plan, the first phase of which was to sway Tryst Reine to their side.

Mercenaries had a different loyalty than military men, even mercenaries from the University of Combative Arts where Tryst graduated from as a Master of Blades. The universal truth was that above all, sellswords valued gold. Though Grenjin Howland had more coin to spend than almost anyone else in Illiastra, Marigold had reason to suspect that Tryst's loyalty stemmed from something more than gold. There was a reason Tryst was staying on at the manor that was beyond Marigold's knowledge at present. The man had an aversion to his employer's tactics as evidenced by the fact that he balked at the duty asked of him as an executioner and torturer. It also stood to reason that despite Grenjin Howland's wealth, there existed wealthier bodies in the known world that could pay above whatever price Howland may have potentially offered.

Furthermore, Marigold reckoned that a bladesman as skilled as Tryst could practically choose his own employer. Outside of Marigold's grandfather, King Hector the fourth, who already had a Master of Blades in his service, Tryst's options were many. Any of the Senators of Johnah could afford him as protection, as could the High Chieftain of Drake. Then there were the rulers among the Crescent Isles archipelago who were constantly fighting one another. The lot of them would start a war just to be the first to bid on having Tryst work in their service.

No, Marigold had to reckon that there was something else keeping Tryst Reine from entertaining other offers. One might think he was merely honouring a contract, were it not known that Expert Sellswords, as the University graduates were known, were prone to walking out on shady employers. Contracts meant nothing to them if it meant compromising their instilled code of ethics.

There was no doubt that in order for Marigold to sway Tryst Reine, she would need to find out what it was that kept him, the Master of Blades, working for perhaps the shadiest men of them all.

At best, Marigold was destined to be the Lady of Daol Bay in her sister's absence, as powerless and hollow a title as one could hold. As a woman, she could not rule by law, or even her inherit father's dynasty. Only males were permitted such rights. While she would technically be the next Lady of Daol Bay, it would be her husband who would be the Lord, to whom the right to rule would fall to.

To circumvent these laws, Marigold needed a man to support her claim. She had learned long ago that any man of high birth and Illiastran origin would be simply installed as the ruler and would bypass Marigold entirely. Tryst Reine, as he even he himself admitted, could not hold any lands or titles in Illiastra by law, nor did he have any interest in such positions of power. That, along with his skillset and the respect the man's mere presence commanded, made him the perfect suitor. As a man of modest, foreign birth, he would have no reason or cause to push her aside as ruler of Daol Bay.

Having Tryst – the Master of Blades – as her husband would also put a pause in the step of any who dared oppose her. Thirdly, it would also make it incredibly difficult for the Palomb family to enforce their marriage contract when Tryst Reine stood before them with an army to challenge their cause. Of course, to do that Marigold would need to convince her soldiers and civilians alike that Tryst Reine was a man worthy of their following. At the rate she was going, Marigold was starting to think that would be a far easier task than persuading him to marry her.

Quite obviously, all the plotting and scheming would not be needed were it not for that damnable marriage contract. That in itself was nothing more than a grand scheme hatched between the Lord Master and his Warden Lords to unite the most powerful factions in Illiastra.

It had all come to pass when Grenjin Howland's own wife had perished when the locomotive she was riding derailed in the wilderness between Biddenhurst and Atrebell. Despite pressure from his ministers to remarry, the Lord Master decided otherwise and opted to hand down his legacy to the first of his Warden Lords to bear a son. To the Tullivan name came Serephanie and soon after Marigold, but Eamon Palomb's first born were twin males, arriving four years after Marigold herself had come into the world. Upon their very birth, those two sons of Eamon became the tokens that would ensure Palomb became the most revered name in the land.

With only two daughters, it would have seemed that the Tullivan name was doomed to end. Seeing a golden opportunity, and to prevent another noble house from becoming Warden Lords, Eamon proposed that the Tullivan girls both be promised to the Palomb boys.

To his credit, Marscal had resisted at first, as Oire had told Marigold years later. Marscal knew the man Eamon was and who his sons would likely grow to become themselves, and he wanted no such home for his daughters. Fervently, he tried to get his wife with child again so that they might produce a male heir to inherit Daol Bay and the Tullivan legacy.

Lord Master Howland himself had eventually made a point of visiting Daol Bay to persuade Marigold's father towards the marriage contract, and again Marscal refused. This time, his refusal came with the announcement that Farren Tullivan was with child and Marscal reasoned that they should wait and see if she might produce a son. In such a situation, Marscal's daughters could be wed off without inheritance to any highborn without incident and the whole mess could be avoided.

Prior to Howland's arrival, Marigold's mother was sent back to her childhood home in secret, well before the news of pregnancy reached Howland and Palomb ears. Fearing that Eamon Palomb may bring harm to her if he knew she might produce an heir, Marscal and Farren both agreed that Northern Gildriad was the safest place. The Palombs could not reach her behind the high walls of Kingdom City's magnificent palace on the other side of the known world.

Months later, word came to Marscal that his heir was born, a son at last and a protector of Daol Bay for another generation to come. The announcement brought with it an end of any claim Eamon Palomb might have forged toward the Tullivan legacy.

Farren had named the boy Felixander, after her long, late grandfather and the previous King of Gildriad. She wrote that Mother and Son would return to Daol Bay when the boy was healthy enough for the journey.

Marigold recalled with clarity when Marscal had told her and Serephanie the news. Neither girl could wait for their mother and new brother to come home.

Their father put their wishes on delay and wrote back that the boy should stay in the Kingdom until he was past his fifth year. Reasoning that such a long journey would be arduous for a baby to endure and that Marscal would need time to smoothen out relations with Eamon.

One small concession Marscal did make though, was to spread the news that he had a son and heir at last. Marscal had even thrown a festival in honour of his newly born son in the town square. It was quite some time ago now, but Marigold still had vague memory of it. Mainly she remembered the smells of the food and the marvellous coloured lights of gunpowder being set off in the sky. She was only five at the time, her sister was seven and they hadn't been allowed to stay long. Years later though, Oire had told Marigold of how wine and mead had flowed freely until dawn and that her father embraced high and low born alike in merriment. Oire claimed it was the last time he had seen Marscal smile and laugh. Marigold had her own memory of the last smile of his she had ever seen and she held on to it dearly.

It was five years later when Marigold's mother finally sent a letter to confirm she was coming home via King Hector's fastest ship: *The Stormbreaker*. In response, Marscal had decided to send his own battle-ready ships ahead to meet the Gildraddi warship to serve as additional escort. Farren wrote that along with the Tullivan guard that had crossed the sea with her, there was even an additional compliment of Gildriad soldiers led by Knight's Commander Ser Galen. Neither Marscal nor King Hector were taking any chances with the safety of Farren and Felixander.

Marigold, Serephanie and their father waited and months went by without a sign of anyone. When at last word came from the lighthouse that a fleet was sighted, Marscal summoned a grand welcoming party to greet Farren and Felixander at the docks. Once the ships entered the bay, however, it became clear that the escort was without *The Stormbreaker*.

Marscal, Oire and Marscal's brother Rory were called aboard the Tullivan flagship, *The King of Tides,* to have an emergency meeting with Captain Tuff who had led the fleet. The captain reported that they had reached Gildriad's city of Berrisport without seeing any sign of *The Stormbreaker* along the way.

When the fleet reached the Gildriad port, Captain Tuff was informed that the ship bearing Farren and Felixander had set sail as planned, with a second warship named the *Wild Rider* in escort. The harbour master of Berrisport was told of their route in the event of an emergency and had been told that the captain of *The Stormbreaker* had charted a route outside shipping lanes to avoid unwanted attention. They had planned but one stop at a place called Tropuri: a small nest of islands that comprised the home of the water-breathing Aquatican folks.

The Tullivan ships had doubled back to search again and ask about in Tropuri and it was there that the trail went cold. No one in Tropuri had sighted either *The Stormbreaker* or *Wild Rider*.

Not even a third of the way into their journey, both ships had disappeared without trace.

Word was sent to the King of Gildriad, who later wrote to Marscal that he had organized a search of his own at no spared expense. The majority of King Hector's naval power was dispatched to search south, to the continent of Johnah and the Crescent Islands. Meanwhile, Marscal sent ships of his own to Drake. Every last ship among them returned empty handed.

The Stormbreaker and *Wild Rider* were missing and presumed sunk. At first, Marscal had refused to believe that his wife and son had perished. Instead, he pinned his hopes on the belief that they had been taken by pirates and he began insisting that a ransom letter would soon arrive. No letter came, no one sighted the ship afterwards and Marigold watched helplessly as her father, her pillar of strength, slipped into a deep depression.

Then the blackmailing started. Eamon Palomb promised in no uncertain terms that he would ruin the Tullivans if they refused the marriage pact any longer. Whether or not Palomb actually wielded the ministerial majority to pass such motions wasn't known at the time, but soon, Marscal found that Eamon's threats weren't without merit. Every piece of legislature that Marigold's father tried to pass during Parliamentary Sessions was turned down in great numbers, while everything Eamon requested was granted. It was a message, a flexing of Eamon's political muscle and soon it became an outright war of words between the two.

That was, until Grenjin Howland himself stepped in and put an ultimatum to Marscal: either agree to the marriage, or resign his seat. Grenjin told Marscal that one of Eamon's sons would inherit the Lord Mastership now, regardless of how Marscal felt on the matter. Lord Howland argued that as wives of the Palombs, Marigold and Serephanie would always have fortune at their fingertips and Marscal's line would be taken care of for generations. Initially, Marscal had declined that offer as well, but for reasons neither he nor Oire would divulge to Marigold, Marscal finally relented.

The contract was drawn up, and all parties converged on the Daol Bay Manor for the signing. The whole debacle was overseen by

Grenjin Howland, his steward and personal manservant, Hossle, the Tullivan's steward Oire, and Jorette, the wife of Eamon Palomb, pregnant with Nareen at the time.

The Palomb twins were barely five years old and already regarded as bratty and disobedient children and so were left to be watched by servants in the guest chambers.

However, Marigold and her sister had been allowed to attend. The two were aged ten and twelve at the time and it was a day that was carved into Marigold's memory. She could even picture the pretty yellow dress the handmaidens had picked for her to wear, with matching ribbons to tie her dark hair into pigtails. Serephanie was in light blue, to match her eyes, blonde ringlets neatly brushed but left otherwise untouched.

The two had sat on either side of their father, at his great oaken desk with its thick legs cut like the paws of some great, carnivorous beast. Marigold could still see the high-backed chair he sat with its marvellously carved letter 'T' on top, long since replaced with a more modest and cushioned seat. Until that moment, Marigold's young mind imagined that she might one day sit that chair.

To the mind's eye, it seemed that Marscal had read that contract for an eternity, saying nothing until it came time to sign. At which point, he spoke only to Oire, to ask that his feather pen and inkwell be brought to him. Howland and Palomb had watched him scrawl his signature eagerly from across the desk: the former merely wanting to make an end of this affair he was afraid would come to war and the latter finally seeing his grip closing on Illiastra.

Marigold and Serephanie had been told ahead of the signing what would be transpiring and the two had already had their tantrums and tears over the matter. Back in those times the Tullivan girls had dreams of marrying handsome princes that rode white stallions and saved the day, not awful, rotten brats like the Palombs.

It fell to Marscal to explain it to his daughters after they had cried themselves nearly sick over it. In hindsight, Marigold knew it had not been an easy job to try and convince the girls that the Palomb twins would grow up to be good men. Marigold didn't quite believe him, yet a little girl should feel like she can trust her father and so she and her sister finally gave in.

The Lords arrived, the deal was signed and for all intent and purpose, the fates of Marigold and Serephanie were sealed.

A quick rap on the servant's entry drew Marigold back to the present. She turned on her stool before the dresser to see Oire letting himself in quietly, closing the door as he slid into the room. "Good evening, my lady," the old steward said. "I don't feel I can stay long, your father requires me nearly constantly."

"Then we shall be brief, Oire. Father needs you far more than I." Marigold motioned toward the featherbed for him to sit before her. "Please sit, tell me how he has been today."

The greying man let out a sigh as he followed her gesture, sinking onto the mattress. "Marscal is failing, my lady. Doctor Garrick surmises he'll be gone before the first snows of winter arrive," he sullenly intoned. It wasn't new information to Marigold, yet it always laid a hard blow to hear it.

"What do you think, Oire?" she queried in a low voice. "Speak honestly: do you believe he has that much time?"

"I believe that if I can board him on a train in the morning, he may live to see Daol Bay one last time," the old steward said as he stared sadly at the hands he folded neatly on his lap. "Sitting in this session took the last of his strength reserves I fear. He might have made it through winter had he stayed at home like I suggested. But we both know your father enough to know he would do no such thing."

"It was folly to make this trip, we both said as much." Marigold exhaled, eyes going to the gold paisley pattern on the eider down quilt on the bed. "There are five healthy councillors that could have made the trip in his stead, one of which is his own brother. They easily would have substituted for father this session and even I would have sufficed alone. I have been to more sessions than anyone except Serephanie, for crying out loud, if anyone in Daol Bay could have sat in that high seat it is I."

"Of that I have no doubt, my lady, but it is already done. It is not wise to dwell on the 'could-have-been', we have to look at what yet can be," Oire said as he leaned forward, hands sliding up to his knees and eyes coming to lock on hers.

She raised a curious eyebrow. "You have news, I take it?"

"I do indeed." His old head bobbed affirmatively. "It would seem that your would-be-husband and his twin returned from their excursion into the city with a prisoner in tow."

"Not our friend, I hope?" Marigold's eyes widened in surprise and she fought to keep her voice low.

Oire shook his head quickly. "Nay, there was an incident at a tavern it seems. To hear it loudly, the twins heroically stopped two tavern wenches from becoming the victims of a beating at the hands of a brutish elf. When the city guard apprehended the surly fellow, the Palombs allegedly demanded he be turned over to their custody."

That's the lie the Palombs are going with, anyway. Marigold thought, before asking the question that Oire had left hanging. "What do you hear quietly?"

"There's a floating bit of gossip that seems to have originated from one of the city guardsmen that escorted the elf here. The city guard claims that the elf interfered in the boys having their own fun with the serving girls. The elf is to be held here, so as to be out of sight, until after the Sessions conclude. After that, the twins intend to imprison him in Hercalest. I think we both know that their father will no doubt circumvent that intention and have the elf expelled back to the Elven Forest."

"I also think we both know which of those two accounts has the truth of it." Marigold commented with her thumb and index finger pinching on the bridge of her nose. "I cannot fathom one thing we need less than another spitting contest with the Elven Forest."

"I agree wholeheartedly, my lady. It puts much tension on a line already about to burst, I fear." Oire glanced at the diamond shaped mirror above the dresser

Marigold brought him back from wherever his mind began to wander. "Has our friend returned from the city?"

"Mine eyes have not seen, nor have these old ears heard." Oire's eyes flickered as he returned their gaze to Marigold.

"I should have ventured to guess as much. I have no doubt he will be back for the Ball. In fact, our friend may already have returned. He's not one to make a grand entrance, after all." Marigold clapped her hands on her legs as she stood up. "I think that will be all, Oire. I shall see father before I go to sup, tell him that I encourage that he stay abed. I am more than capable of representing the house of Tullivan dutifully in his stead."

Oire stood with her and began heading for the door to the servant's entrance. "Verily on the first account and of the latter, your father has already decided to stay abed. He has no doubt you will do well by his name this evening. I will be staying with Marscal. He will have need of me when his own meal is brought to him.

"In the interim, I took the liberty of arranging an escort for you to the Ball. A particular man of the Honourable Guard we both took a notice of yesterevening. Is there anything else I can do for you before I take my leave?"

"Yes, if Father inquires after the day's summaries, inform him that I did as instructed to the letter," Marigold answered. "I will tell him the details when I visit in a while, should he ask at that time. Also, send two handmaidens, I'm feeling a little pressed for time to get prepared for the Ball."

"As my lady wishes," Oire said while holding the door in hand, already in a hurry to return to Marigold's father.

Shortly after, a pair of maidens arrived, one Marigold recognised as the same girl she had sent to fetch Oire. The second was blonde like the first but so pale she might have passed for a Drakian if her hair had been a few shades lighter.

It was the second one that spoke for them. "Milady, I understand you called for us?"

"I did, come on in now and close the door." Marigold urged. "I must look my best this evening and I would like your assistance if you don't mind, please."

"Yes milady, at once. I'll draw you a bath," the pale one answered quickly.

Marigold shook her head in reply. "I bathed this morning, that won't be necessary. Let's get to work. Time is not on our side."

As the two went about their duties, it was learned that the handmaiden who had arrived earlier was named Lilly, who claimed to be an expert with makeup. The girl with the lighter complexion alleged she was a hair specialist named Manda. Both let slip that they had recently been hired by the Palombs that day from the city and sent to the manor to wait on Marigold for the ball.

It was a gesture that soon repulsed Marigold as a thought crept in. *Doubtlessly they were sent with the intention of befriending me and would be expected to report whatever was spoken of back to the Palombs. If that is Pyore's intent, he and his brother will receive nothing but a mixture of lies and silence.*

There was no doubt of the women's talents as they promptly sat Marigold down before the dresser. Lilly was giving Marigold a fresh face of makeup while Manda set about styling her hair, working in close tandem with one another but never getting in either's way.

Soon, Marigold's lips shone blood red, contrasting against her own light complexion. Like Manda, Marigold had very light skin, though suitors often complimented her by saying her skin looked like alabaster and felt like silk. Manda they would just call pale.

With a line of black around Marigold's eyes and a touch of blush to bring colour to her cheeks, Lilly was ready to move on to Marigold's nails. Like her lips, they were given a shade of crimson red, fingers and toes alike.

Manda had coerced Marigold to try a new style for her hair, one that would suit the dress she had chosen for the evening. The bangs of the naturally straight, dark locks were pinned up, while the back was given free flow across her shoulders and down her back. It was a look Marigold took an immediate liking to and she couldn't wait to get the last piece of her outfit assembled to see it all together.

The dress Marigold had brought for just this evening was her favourite. It was black silk that fell to the floor and collected at her feet. The gown haltered, leaving her back open and bare. Silver linings ran down from the neck on either side and across her chest to converge into a brilliant, shimmering starburst in the low cut below her breasts. Her entire back was left exposed for all to see, coming together on her tailbone to give way to the flowing skirt below. To compliment it, she wore a silver necklace with a striking ruby inlay and black shoes with a spiked heel, though her footwear would be heard rather than seen.

Marigold stood before the half-length mirror atop the dresser to admire her attire for the evening with a smile.

As she looked herself over in the glass, she smoothed out the dress with her hands, exhaled a deep breath and felt satisfied with it.

She took a few dabs of her choice perfume: a lilac scent from her mother's homeland of Kingdom Valley in Gildriad. It had been Princess Farren's favourite and Marigold remembered Farren with every waft of the scent. Marigold knew she always would, even as the memory grew distant in time. The perfume was a reminder to Marigold of whom she aspired to be and that was a reflection of the strong, wilful, woman her mother had been in life. That will and assertive strength had been Farren's gift to her and Marigold wanted nothing more than to ensure that the gift was not squandered.

It was then Marigold realized the two handmaidens were still there, silently awaiting commands. Both wore the same polite smile, their hands folded neatly over their plain, white, cotton dresses.

Reaching for her velvet purse on the dresser, Marigold took a handful of silver coins. "My ladies, I thank you both kindly for your time. Here, this is but a small token of my appreciation," Marigold said with a warm smile, pressing four coins each into their hands.

Manda's eyes went as wide as saucers as she looked to Lilly, who seemed to be the first to find her own voice. "Miss Tullivan, we cannot accept this, it belongs to our guardians."

"I insist on it, speak nothing more on the matter and I will say naught to your guardians," Marigold replied, as she curled their hands over the coins, looking each of them in the eye in turn before pressing on. "Women have as much right to anything men do. You would do well to remember that."

The two glanced to one another once more and Manda began to quiver, nervously swallowing so hard that Marigold was about to ask if her tongue had gone down her throat. As Marigold thought to say something, the timid woman spoke of her own accord while staring at nothing in particular. "Miss Tullivan, thank you. Will that be all this evening?"

There was apparent fear in the two maidens. They had been bred to believe they were weak and useless compared to their male counterparts, just as Marigold and her sister would have been led to believe. If not for Princess Farren educating her daughters otherwise, they might well have.

It made Marigold simultaneously furious and sorrowful that women could think so lowly of themselves. "I have one more favour," she began, as a thought suddenly occurred to her. "Would you be so kind as to stay outside my room when I leave and inform my escort that I'm at my father's quarters?"

Lilly nodded nervously, managing to stammer out a, "Yes ma'am" in the process.

"I greatly appreciate that, ladies. Thank you very much," Marigold said before turning back to the dresser to take her key and give herself a last look before leaving the room for the evening.

It was then she noticed her ears to be empty.

The two maidens had let themselves out without another word and Marigold didn't notice them leaving until she heard the door quickly opening and closing behind her.

There were pangs of deep pity within Marigold for the maidens and their kin, they were terrified of their world and had come to be shackled by that fear. These women needed a champion. They had the Lady Orangecloak and her Thieves, true enough. Although as much as Marigold revered and respected the woman, Orangecloak didn't seem to be much more than a particularly charismatic rabble rouser. Marigold knew that many people within Illiastra needed a voice upon the upper crust of the controlling oligarchy to speak for them. If given the chance to see her work come to fruition, Marigold could well be that voice.

She reached for the small jewellery box she'd brought with her from Daol Bay as her mind drifted to the leader of the Thieves group. The red haired enigma known only as Lady Orangecloak, who had singlehandedly climbed her way to the top of Illiastra's most wanted list. Despite a great deal of effort and coin spent, the EMP had failed to apprehend her or even ascertain who she really was. It was all they could do to just react whenever Lady Orangecloak showed up in town squares and on rooftops to warn and rouse the populace to her cause. Try as the EMP might, the woman and her Thieves were always two steps ahead and out of grasp.

Marigold hadn't met the woman personally and had only seen her once, darting from rooftop to rooftop within view of the balcony in her chambers in Daol Bay. Up to that moment, Marigold had been enjoying her morning tea in relative quiet until the noise of feet clattering on the red slates below caught her attention. As Marigold turned her head, her eyes befell the woman known as Lady Orangecloak, her fiery hair and that old peach cloak catching wind as she ran by. There was a great haste, but also a pronounced grace to the way the woman moved, Marigold remembered. Every step and leap looked as though it was carefully calculated and weighed with due consideration. The strange woman's almost artistic movements had bewildered Marigold, but it was her disappearing act that was the most shocking.

It was so sudden and equally unexpected that it brought the red haired woman's pursuers to a full stop and caused Marigold to stand as straight as an arrow.

Without a misstep, Orangecloak had pivoted on one foot a mere dozen centimetres or so from the edge of a roof and faced the guards that had given chase. Two storeys beneath her feet was a cobblestone road filled with people coming to and from the market place. With nowhere to go, it seemed Orangecloak was cornered, yet her face was calm and relaxed.

A guard reached for her and caught only air as she plunged backward with her arms outstretched and disappeared into the mass of humanity below. The people seemed to engulf the woman and she was gone amidst the throng.

Marigold had later learned during an inquiry into the Thieves incident that no less than four Thieves had been waiting in the alley to catch their fearless leader. It was all an elaborate stunt, one of which that particular band of outlaws were becoming known for.

As quickly as her mind went to the memory, Marigold returned from it as she put her earrings in place. The light of the room caused the dangling silver bars Marigold chose to hang from her lobes to shimmer brilliantly. They were slender little things suspended in a grouping of five to an ear and varied in length, with the longest of each reaching just beneath the top of her jawline. Once they had been her mother's, made of pure silver that Marigold's maternal uncle Prince Claude had gifted to Farren to wear on her sixteenth birthday.

In that instant, peering at her own reflection, Marigold saw Farren staring back at her. It was in that mirror that she found her resolve once more, when for a moment she doubted it.

With a confident stride, Marigold crossed the small chambers, took a deep breath, and stepped into the hall, prepared now for whatever the evening may have in store.

6

TRYST

On an average day Tryst Reine would find himself lost in the history of the trail beneath his feet.

Nearly a millennium ago, those very roads were soaked with the blood of warriors on several occasions. The Valdarrow brood had repelled the dwarves here and even withstood an assault by the Amaroshan nation, itself now annexed into Illiastra. All their victories had only served to make the Valdarrows even more arrogant and they goaded the Kingdom of Phaleayna, the largest and wealthiest of the Illiastran nations, into open conflict.

Segai, Eleanor and Ruche, known better as the Teal, Maroon and Indigo Knights, had arrived here with their army. On the edge of their swords, three generations worth of Valdarrow tyranny had come to a bloody end.

This largely forgotten trail had once been known as Valdarrow's Highway: a road of flat rock and hard, packed earth that led from palace to city. Both had crumbled under the efforts of Phaleayna's armed forces and were lost to time and the slow, ebbing way it had of reclaiming everything.

A small creek that ran into the Perrion River bubbled noisily beside the trail and nearby lay the angry head of the first Valdarrow.

The carved boulder lay on its side, short a nose but still maintaining a cracked and pock marked beard. Moss and a small tree sprouting from a fissure on its cheek had begun to cover the disembodied cranium, but those empty eyes still stared angrily at the chattering brook.

The books of history said that Ruche Crenne had ordered the gargantuan statue that the head once sat atop torn down. The body was broken up and dragged off in bits and pieces, but the head remained, as vengeful and malevolent looking as ever.

The contrary face of the dead tyrant glared at Tryst as he made his way to where the creek grew shallow enough to cross. From the creek bed he walked uphill into a thick grove of bushy pine trees. Amidst them all sat a single, stunted redwood, gnarled and misshapen with a gaping maw at chest height. Tryst reached in and pulled out a sack suspended on a piece of rope. Inside was an old brown robe, faded and slightly threadbare. Wrapped within it were lengths of old linen to conceal his boots, more lengths of rope, a long, scraggly beard of grey and a small jar of adhesive paste.

Tryst upended the contents to remove the usual built up collection of acorns and walnuts accumulated by the resident squirrels and began to change into the costume. Parts of his standard, black outfit were removed for concern that they might be seen beneath the robe. When he was done, only his small clothes, the elven daggers strapped tightly to his thighs and his boots remained upon his person. The paste was applied over the stubble on his face that he had neglected to shave earlier in the pool and the beard was patted firmly into place.

Once he was in his new getup, Tryst drew the long hood of the robe down over his face to conceal everything above the beard. His black clothing was neatly folded, placed in the sack and lowered back into the lonely, mutated redwood for when he returned.

The squirrels will have to pick up their food on their own.

With his disguise complete, Tryst went about finding a good, heavy stick to use as a temporary staff and gathering some good kindling. It took only a little time for Tryst to gather a full bundle, which he bound with the extra rope and slung over his back. The sticks and twigs were one of the most important parts of his disguise: that of a reclusive hermit known as Old Man Sticks who peddled the kindling he gathered on his trail.

It was one of the few ways Tryst had of blending in with the common folk and hearing what the talk amongst them was. As Sticks, he was just a harmless old hermit that no one paid any mind to.

However, as Tryst Reine, he was the despised killer mercenary in the employ of Grenjin Howland, who had spurred on those wicked, false tales of Tryst to incite fear. The people believed the stories told in the Government newsprint and repeated loudly by the heralds around the country. Not one word of it was true, but that mattered little. All Howland had to do was ensure that the horrific tales were repeated and eventually it would start to default from legend to truth in the minds of the many.

The lies spread by his own employer weighed quite heavily on Tryst and he longed for a chance to one day find redemption. There were days when he doubted whether or not coming to Atrebell had been the right thing to do. The whole thing felt like one giant gamble with his reputation at stake if he lost.

When he had first decided to join the University of Combative Arts, Tryst had done so to forge a legacy his family would be proud of. The instructors had pegged him and his rival Myolas as the next coming of the Hero himself, a prediction that had placed a mighty burden of expectations upon his shoulders. Expectations which became nearly impossible to live up to since being cast vicariously in the role of a villain from nearly the outset of his time in Illiastra.

Four years on and what do I have to show for it? The only person who doesn't despise me seeks an affair that will ignite a civil war.

As the fallen leaves crunched beneath his feet, Tryst found himself toying with the ideas Marigold Tullivan had left him with.

I could join her cause before the Palomb Twins' birthday. Marry her out of sight of the three lords, and announce the deed when it was done. I might die for it, but at least I can say that I stood for something in this life.

It begged to reason that Marigold may well make a good leader. No one could doubt her willingness to learn or the amount of time she had spent at her father's side and in the gallery of Parliament studying for the role. She even had the wealth and birth station to stand amongst the elite.

Though, the old dogs of the EMP were not like to allow a woman to lead them. Even those who had served beneath Lord Marscal would have to be heavily coerced into it and some might even have to be removed from office entirely.

It would be a long road fraught with danger, but at least it would be a road to redemption.

Four years had passed since Tryst had decided to accept employment with Grenjin Howland and thus far, his other means of salvation had not yet arrived. Promises had been made to him when he had signed his contract and thus far it seemed as though they might not be honoured. In such a case, Tryst had to begin considering other alternatives, lest his good name be forever ruined.

Then there was the Lady Orangecloak. Tryst thought about her often, especially since his latest excursion to Aquas Bay. There he had seen a protest she had staged in the marketplace atop a merchant's booth in the dead of the summer's heat. Tryst could even remember what she had worn: brown leather boots, green, slim fitting trousers and a matching bodice over a sleeveless, white tunic. The trademark orange cloak was draped across her shoulders and her bright red hair had tumbled freely.

The woman was as animated as she was charismatic and used her whole body to illustrate the drama she wished to warn the marketgoers about. It seemed like she had been there for some time, yet in reality she might have been atop the booth for but a few minutes. The other members of the Thieves had drawn the guards from their posts, but more men in uniforms had arrived when news reached them of Orangecloak's presence in the market.

When the first guard made a grab for her, she kicked at his hand and was gone. Tryst recalled that it was almost as if she flew up over the old stone building that backed the merchant stand. How agile she had seemed, climbing a wall that had nothing that could count as a handhold, let alone enough room for leather clad foot. A broad shouldered fellow had helped her to the rooftop and she was gone. As she departed, her compatriots spread themselves out thin and dispersed from sight to reconvene somewhere safe and the people of the marketplace were left agape.

The memory of her visage was etched into Tryst's mind. Her face was so fair, with magnetic blue eyes that could pierce you to the bone. Since that time, Tryst had a desire to meet the woman veiled in a fog of mystery. No one knew her real name or where she had come from beyond the ruins of Phaleayna. Even those of the Thieves that were captured claimed they didn't know, withstanding hours and days of torture at the hands of the guards without altering their claim.

Not that it mattered who she had been or where she came from. She was Lady Orangecloak now, whose voice alone stood to turn the entire populace against the ruling class.

Tryst left the memory as he trekked from the forest to the main road. His charade began with his first step on the wide, cobblestone pathway that extended between the Howland Manor and Atrebell. Leaning heavily on the cane, Tryst began walking like his best years were long gone and that his body had betrayed him to time. Without looking beneath the hood there would be no way to see that he was just north of thirty and he continued the last portion of the trek in his guise. Even alone, Tryst made sure his gait was slow and feeble on the off chance he was passed by anyone coming to or from the manor.

Soon, the noises of the city met his ears and he looked up to see the barbican walls looming before him. The portcullis was down, more so to keep unwanted folk from taking the short route to the manor. If they wanted to get there, they would have to go out the south or west gates and walk around the long way. Only then to still be met by another wall and another gate in front of the Government house. But the man Tryst posed as was an exception, for he was just a harmless, old hermit from the deep forest, selling kindling to buy staple foods. No one cared if he came and went this way.

Beside the heavy, iron portcullis was a thick wooden door with a peephole in it. Tryst gave it a rap with his walking stick and waited for an answer. A minute or so later the door opened and a guard in a midnight blue jacket with white epaulets and gold buttons shining in the afternoon light answered. The man had half a sneer on his face as he leaned out to look at the old man before him. "Hello, Sticks, I haven't seen you in a while. You got your toll, old man?"

"Why of course, ser," Tryst said with a hoarse, aged voice while slinging the bundle of wood to the ground. Tryst drew a few choice bits of kindling, giving them to the guard gingerly.

"A pleasure doing business, Sticks," the guard nonchalantly said as he held open the door for him. "Here, come through the door, we won't be raising the bars for you alone. I don't have to tell you to stay out of trouble."

"Many thanks, ser, may Ios keep you strong," Tryst gave the guard as he passed through the tiny guardhouse and into the city.

The place was lively today and the streets teemed with people going about their daily routines. Tryst ambled about, asking the odd person here and there if they wanted to buy kindling. A few folks, all servants and staff of the upper class, would trade a handful of copper coins for a handful of sticks. However, most people simply ignored the old man and either walked around or pushed past him. Tryst wondered how forsaken he would be if this was his true form and not just a guise. It was a crude way to make coin, but there were many more who tried earnestly at the same task.

The further south he went the more coin he made, until there was just a fifth of his bundle remaining. That much he kept for a different purpose.

The two North districts were the opulent half of Atrebell. There were several taverns and inns on this side of the Yanxes River and almost all of them were luxuriously maintained and catered to the upper crust of society. Ministers, their non-elected associates and other members of their entourages attending events at the manor dropped their coins in these places for temporary residence. More permanent residences, offices and various other businesses lined either sides of the road around Tryst. Tall buildings with pristine paint jobs, immaculate lawns and tidy, stone sidewalks were the norm in these parts of town.

The upscale drinking establishments would not be where the Palomb boys would be at their most dastardly, for there would be too many important eyes upon them. According to Merion, they would seek refuge for their devious urges in the lone dive north of the Yanxes River. This same musty refuge for the impoverished and indentured was a place Tryst frequented. He knew the barkeep and in turn, the barkeep thought he knew the old hermit named Sticks.

Shuffling through the thick crowds, Tryst worked his way through the river of humanity and the buildings that were its banks until he found the hovel. Outside the door hung a simple wooden sign in black paint that just said 'Hobbs' to mark the spot. Sitting below the weather beaten lumber to either side of the door were two men in the easily identifiable, signature uniforms of Hercalest guardsmen: shining silver coats lined with black trim complimented with black trousers and tall hats, topped off with a silhouette of a boar embroidered above the left breast.

One stuck a boot in Tryst's path and instructed him to not speak or even approach the Palomb twins. In his best aged voice, Tryst promised to comply and the silent guard of the two swung open the door for him.

Someone had smartly decided that denying the patron's

entrance would raise too many eyebrows and instead opted to order their eyes and ears shut to what may be seen.

Inside was a dim and droll affair that Tryst knew only too well. Three walls were lined with worn, wooden-benched booths, only two of which were occupied. To one near the door sat an elf, flipping pages in a book with a goblet of wine beside him. While Tryst thought it strange to see an elf in these parts, it was the two he was secretly charged with following who garnered his attention.

He found Eldridge and Pyore occupying a corner booth between the entry wall and the back wall, hosting a pair of pretty damsels in flowing skirts and tight corsets.

To the right of Tryst was the bar. It was an old thing, with its varnish worn to nil and permanent rings of discolouration marring the pine top. The dark grey stone floor beneath it sported long cracks that seemed to run from every wall and its ceiling was bare save for the thick beams running through it. A pair of electric lights dangled in iron sconces, providing the only illumination to be found in the tavern.

Legitimate old timers lined the stools, mead steins clutched tightly in hand. These were the ones who had walked under Taves' eye of the law and had come out the other side with a measure of freedom still intact. They were a poor and destitute lot, but all alive and unshackled. Their final days spent reliving flickered memories as they drowned themselves in brew of yeasty comfort.

Tryst deserved no place beside them for these were men of the earth, hard workers who kept their noses spotless and played their parts to scrape by. Yet, this was a game he must play and so he sidled up in the dark corner on the far side of the bar. Upon his lap, he laid the remnants of the kindling and kept his head low to hide his face beneath the hood.

From behind the bar an old fellow in a patched red vest, a formerly white shirt turned yellow with sweat and a cloth apron marred with stains sauntered over. "A beer, Sticks?" the fellow rasped in the low smoky tones of a man who had spent a lifetime with a pipe clenched between his teeth.

"Hullo, Mont. A beer would be good. The regular rate, my friend?" Tryst gave back in his feigned voice.

"Aye, that will do," Mont replied, plunking down a stein of beer and a few coins.

That was Tryst's rate, his whole load of kindling for a beer and three coppers.

The man had his back to Tryst when he suddenly remembered something. "Oh, keep'er down tonight, Sticks. Fella's on the door must've told ya that we got special company."

Tryst gave a grunt back and glanced where Mont nodded his head. "Them two been here very long, Mont?" he asked in a whisper.

"An hour or so I figure, might be that they'll be on their way before long," the grey-haired barkeep replied.

The twins were bedecked in immaculately pressed Hercalest military uniforms, though neither had never truly served a day. When every exercise involves being flanked by men-at-arms who avert any real danger, it becomes difficult to assert such a claim. Yet they did just that with their undeserved medals pinned to their chest, the mere show of which Tryst found to be a display of repugnance in itself.

The women, a pair of brunettes in dresses that left everything above their nipples bare, were servers of the tavern. Tryst was familiar with the two, though names escaped him. He knew they were both of similar age and childhood friends. One was the niece of the barkeep and had a child out of wedlock with a gardener. The other claimed she still had her maidenhood, though the old fellows on the stools all disputed that claim.

The twins were entertaining the damsels with one each upon their laps. Tryst was able to pick up enough of their conversation to hear that the fellows were playing the women with the notion of taking them to the Parliamentary Ball. The women were giggling gleefully at the prospect and promising to dress in their finest gowns for the occasion.

The farce went on long enough for Tryst to nearly finish his stein of beer, despite the fact that he had taken his sweet time with consuming it.

It was all merely culminating toward their real pleasure though, and Tryst could sense that a proverbial pot was coming to a slow boil. Eldridge, the first born and more loquacious twin had a hand buried deep between the bosoms of the woman seated upon him, nodding and smiling as she spoke highly of him and remarked upon his handsome features.

The blonde-haired Pyore seemed decidedly less interested. His company grinned nervously and gave him sweet compliments as well, though her words seemed to lack the sincerity of her co-worker. It was hard to blame her, she was no actor and Pyore was homely where his brother was dashingly handsome. It was something Pyore looked to be painfully aware of as he sat quietly grinding his teeth, all the while watching Eldridge's companion chatter on flirtatiously.

The lass entertaining Pyore seemed unsure of what to say anymore. Hers was an unenviable task of eliciting a smile from a face too long accustomed to scowling. Finally, some words came to her. "Pyore, I saw the most gorgeous dress in the window of Laylord's store. It was the same shimmery silver of your coat, like your family colours. If you were to buy it for me, I could wear it tonight for you. Would that please you, milord?"

The blond twin merely nodded in return, looking across the floor as she spoke, as if for a second he might be contemplating her suggestion. Without a hint of foresight he put a hand to her stomach and pushed her out onto the floor. The woman in Eldridge's lap let out a startled gasp as her friend went tumbling.

Pyore slid from the booth to his feet, standing over the frightened woman crawling on her hands and knees.

"D-did I say something to upset milord?" she queried, fearful tears welling in her brown eyes.

"I should say so," Eldridge chimed in with a tone of nonchalance as the eyes of the lady on his lap went as wide as saucers.

The one on the floor began to sob. "What are you doing, milord? I'm sorry, I don't know what I said, but I'm so sorry. Please, forgive me, milord."

Pyore cupped her jaw in his left hand, lifting her to waist height until she was propped on her knees, tears running freely over her fair face. "You do not presume to tell me what to do. Do you understand me, wench?!" His right came crashing across her face in a backhanded slap. She fell backward and went sprawling on the floor as Pyore continued with his raving. "And do not insult me by calling 'my lord', I am not a lord, not yet and I don't require a lowlife whore like you to remind me," he growled.

Likely the two servers had not thought they had said anything potentially wrong. Not that any sane person would ever react so violently to being addressed by an erroneous, but otherwise innocuous title.

The old fellows on the stools kept their heads down and their eyes on their drinks in front of them, though none dared move enough to even take a sip. Tryst, being on the side of the bar that put the twins to his right, was the only one with view. Even the barkeep had his back turned and was ignoring the plight of his niece by running a clean rag through the freshly washed mugs.

The woman in the booth tried to get away, though Eldridge grabbed her roughly by her tailed hair, causing her to yelp in pain. She pleaded for help from the patrons frantically, even begging the Hercalest guard that had been standing sentry nearby. All ignored her pleas, even Tryst, who dug deep within to keep his poise and resist the urge to spring to the aid of the women and blow his cover.

The elf, who had been calmly reading his book, flipped it closed and stood up, stepping in between the frightened woman holding her sore cheek and Pyore Palomb.

Tryst was fighting every instinct that told him to join the fellow in what was sure to be an uphill battle. It was then that Tryst noted the elf was not an elven warrior, but an academic bedecked in a fine velvet suit of dark green. Long, dark hair ran straight down his back with a finely woven braid in the center and two to match that ran down to his chest from above his temples. The pointed ears, a regular feature of his kind, protruded through the elf's hair and his face was entirely hairless and looked as smooth as porcelain.

No race was as fair and beautiful as the elven folk and this fellow was certainly no exception to the rule.

"I say, good ser, is that any way to treat a woman?" The elf queried as he put himself between the enraged Pyore and his victim.

The guard moved in and grabbed the elf by the arm, but was shaken off and pushed back. "Unhand me, you knave. You have the audacity to grab me when it is this brute who strikes a woman. Have you no honour?"

"Who do you presume to be to speak to my brother?" Eldridge said as he jumped to his feet, casting the woman on his own lap roughly to the bench he had been sitting on.

"I presume to be a civilised elf with enough moral standing to treat a woman with more respect than to cast her to the floor. That doesn't even begin to speak for the blow you landed to her face," the elf answered quickly with a sharp tongue.

"You must not know of whom you stand before," Eldridge proclaimed in a show of puffery. "We are the twin sons of Eamon Palomb, Warden Lord over the Eastern Realm."

"I see who you are and I care not for any titles you or your sire hold," the elf hotly replied. "Your behaviour is utterly unacceptable, regardless of whom you are."

The guard that had been trying to stop the elf slowly stepped toward the door with a hand on the holstered pistol on his hip.

Pyore spoke up on his own behalf at that. "This whore tried to tell me that I should buy her a dress, as if I would even be seen with a filthy cock holder like her at the Parliamentary Ball," he said defensively, as if his reasoning held any value at all. "And she mocked me by calling me 'my lord' knowing full well that I am not yet a lord."

Tryst could have drawn the blades strapped to his legs then and there, took both twins with a single cut each and made do for all three guards. Though he dared not budge, for as vexed as the twins had made him in that moment, he could not abandon his cause yet. There was much to be done in the dark before stepping into the light.

Before the elf could speak again the guard who had stopped Tryst at the doorway had joined his comrade and had drawn his pistol. Of the third guard there was no sign, though Tryst had a notion of where he had gone.

"Put your hands above your head, elf. You'll not be touching these two." The one with the firearm grasped tightly in hand ordered.

The bewildered look on the elf's face spoke for how absurd he deemed that command to be. "How despicable can you get?" he asked, in a tone to match his facial expression. "You make no effort to reprimand these two, but mean to apprehend me? On what charges, might I ask?"

"Assault of a woman, I should say," Eldridge butted in, a contemptible grin widening across his face. "My brother and I were merely passing along and heard a scream. Being the *honourable men* we are, we responded to the call of distress to find this snobbish elf having demanded his way with these women. He had struck one and meant to strike the second before we and our entourage intervened. Isn't that right, Captain Geddrick?"

All of that drew a single, derisive scoff from the elf. "What is this nonsense you blather on about? You mean to blame me for your brother's transgressions? I wi-" The elf was cut off before he could continue when the door of the tavern flew open. The remaining Palomb guard marched in with four Atrebell guards in their midnight blue coats following.

"Sers, what appears to be the trouble?" the guard at the front of the pack inquired. He was a tall man of broad shoulder whose coat looked a size too small, though his attire was otherwise in fine order. The man's face bore an expression of indifference to the whole sordid affair and Tryst gathered that he might have been taken away from a more pressing task.

There was almost a full head in height difference between Geddrick and the Atrebell man, whom Tryst recalled was the captain of the Northeast district of the city guards.

In Atrebell, as it was in most of the major cities, there were four districts based on the compass directions of the town. Each district had its own guard station and was manned by an officer. One among these four officers was head over the whole city's defences and was titled the Major of the Guards. Overall he was chief, but had particular strength in one half of the city and direct command in his own district. In the case of Atrebell, Major Burnson controlled the South half and the Southwest district with its fortress of a station. The northern half of the city was overseen by a Commander, who held the Northwest district as his home base. This left the eastern districts to a pair of captains to enforce the letter of the law, one of which had been called upon to aid in this potential international incident.

Geddrick, himself a Palomb from a cadet branch, turned to look up at the Captain of Atrebell's Northeast district, retelling nearly verbatim the story Eldridge had spun just seconds prior. When the Palomb cousin finished, the bigger man looked ponderously from the elf to the twins and lastly to the women now huddled together on the edge of the booth.

The elf jumped to offer a defence from the levied accusations. "This story is entirely false. The only move I made toward these ladies was to put myself between that one and her attacker, the blonde haired fellow."

"All three of my men, the tavern keeper and even these patrons will attest otherwise," Eldridge stated, his brother nodding in agreement beside him.

"Arrest this elf, then," the guard said to the three to his rear without as much as a glance before adding to his orders. "And see to the hurts of the women."

The elf went into a defensive position Tryst recognized as a Kav-Do-Roe stance. He did not favour the odds of the guards, armed or not. The three bluecoats glanced nervously at their commander, who rolled his eyes in frustration at them and drew his pistol, barrel pointing to the ceiling. "Elf, I am ordering you to stand down. This will be your single warning," he commanded in a tone that brokered no argument whatsoever.

For a moment the elf weighed his options, his eyes darting to all parties in the room. The tension mounted until the big man lowered the weapon in elf's direction. The elf hesitated for but a second more before raising his hands in surrender, allowing the guards to move in and restrain him with a pair of shackles.

With the elf in custody, one of the bluecoat guards plucked a handkerchief from his coat pocket and knelt to the women. He swabbed at the drying blood on the face of the woman Pyore had struck, whose nose had bled like a faucet down over her lips and jaw. The blood continued to trickle toward her cleavage and congealed just shy of that. She had been so afraid that she hadn't even dared to wipe it away until the guard had swooped in to tend on her.

The twins straightened their clothes, feeling quite smug and satisfied in their selves. The Palomb guard and Atrebell captain holstered their arms and the captain uttered orders to remand the elf to a cell at the guard's station in the Northwest District.

Geddrick, however, intervened with alternative plans. "From one Captain to another, I would request that you add assaulting persons of first class to the list of charges. Given that he had the nerve to lay hands on the heroic twins as they separated him from his helpless victims."

The commander agreed to the charge and Geddrick continued unbidden. "As I am sure you are well aware, my good man, that charge would supersede the lesser charge of assault of lower class folk. Given that his victims in the greater charge are from my jurisdiction, of which I am a captain, I reserve the right to take the elf into custody."

"We can house him in the city just fine, if you'd like," the Atrebell Captain said with a sigh, having already grown tired of it all.

Alber Maldys, that's his name, Tryst suddenly remembered. *The Atrebell Manor guards named him Mopey Maldys behind his back.*

Eldridge spoke up. "Much appreciated, my good ser, but no, I think we'll take him back to the Manor. The dungeons there ought to hold him and we shall be taking him back to Hercalest to answer for his crimes on the morrow before our own courts."

"Whatever you so wish," Captain Maldys uttered with a flick of his wrist. "Take Arnold and Ched here to assist you in escort, I'll have a jail wagon brought around if you'd like as well."

"A fine gesture, ser and we'll take you up on both offers," Geddrick answered. "Osten, send for the Palomb's coach. Rall, pay the bill for the drinks, please."

One guard in a silver coat bowed out of the tavern while the other was reaching for a fat purse that hung from his belt as he made for the bar.

The twins straightened their uniforms and headed outside with Geddrick going before them and Captain Alber and his men following behind, an arm each linked around the now silent elf.

The noise began to die down as the armed men and the brats all shuffled out into the afternoon sun. The men on their stools, the women and the lone guard attending to them, the innkeeper and Rall of the Palomb's retinue were soon all that remained.

Rall, who Tryst figured was not quite thirty, looked along at the men that doubled his age, sitting as still as statues. "Fellows, you won't be bothered to answer in court to what you have seen today. However, we cannot have wild tales being told of the twins." He reached into purse and drew two coins he held in thumb and forefinger. "Could I buy your silence with a pair of silvers each?" No one stirred for a time, until the fellow closest to the guard looked up and gave a nod. Rall walked along the bar, placing a pair of promised coins in front of the five men who hadn't actually seen the commotion.

He came to Tryst and laid a pair more atop what he gave the others. "You had a view, old man. I would give you an additional payment for the holding of your tongue."

Tryst replied with a slow nod and Rall left him be.

Leaning on the bar, Rall drew two larger, golden coins from the purse and slid them across the bar to its keeper. "For you, ser, this should compensate you for the use of your establishment. Pay these women's guardians an extra day's wages and keep the rest as a tip for your silence and troubles." Finally, he turned to the Atrebell guard still on knee. "Will you see them home?"

"Aye," The guard answered dutifully.

"Good man. Ladies," Rall said with a bow. "My apologies on behalf of the Palomb brothers. We shall see the elf punished to the fullest extent of the law for his aggressions." When they didn't meet his stare he simply bowed again and departed without another word.

A few minutes passed and the still unnamed city guardsman began to herd the shaken women to their feet. Taking Pyore's victim by the arm as he led them out, promising to see them home safely all the while. The stool fillers began to whisper down the line to one another, silver coins disappearing off the bar to softly clink into their pockets, as if the Palomb guards might hear and return.

Tryst finished his stein. The beer had gone almost flat since he had last touched it and the yeasty brew went down hard. Once finished, he continued to wait a short time before pushing back his stool, playing feebly at getting his walking stick to make his own exit.

There were still things to be done in the city and he had his regular duties back at the manor for the Parliamentary Ball to attend to. He also had to speak with Marigold, he decided, and sooner rather than later.

It was an early autumn evening, brisk and cool. The cotton shift he wore provided little warmth against the chill, but Tryst scarce felt it. The sun looked ready to excuse itself behind the western hills and he had little time to waste in returning to the manor.

Across the high arching Crenne Bridge he went, named for Knight's General Ruche. According to the books of history, he had forded the Yanxes River over which his namesake bridge spanned and pushed Valdarrow's forces back to their palace.

From atop the highest point of the arch was a splendid view of both rivers that ran nearly parallel to one another in a diagonal line from east to west. Tryst figured that if Ruche Crenne were to stand atop this bridge now, he would not recognize the rivers he crossed in those ancient battles. The muddy banks that once ran red with the blood of Phaleaynan and Valdarronian fighters had long ago been replaced with manmade, stone canals.

Above the deep canals and all along the south shores of the Yanxes River were finely kempt homes. With their clapboard siding painted in earthy shades of red, green and blue with white trimmings around the edges, it made no wonder why the neighbourhood was referred to as Rainbowtown.

As Tryst crossed the bridge, he passed several maids on their way to their work in the last hours before dusk. They scurried past without as much as a look at the old man they presumed him to be.

The homes here were upper middle class dwellings and the

inhabitants mostly comprised of lower tier merchants and middle management staff, the majority of which were employed by the EMP. Modest homes they were and most were afforded their own parcel of land, complete with a green, lush lawn on the rear of the houses. They lacked frontage, though and were crammed together with barely any room to walk between the domiciles.

It was further south again that Tryst went, until he had trekked across a longer bridge that brought him into the heart of the southern districts of the city. This was Atrebell's ugly reality, despite the efforts of the city councillors to disguise it. The roadways that led to the train station and the front gates were all well maintained and the buildings fronting them were painted in bright colours regularly. Beyond that façade, however, was abject poverty.

The Southeast district was the worst of it, particularly the Batterdowns neighbourhood. The homes there were stone eyesores that were largely uninhabitable and hidden out of sight by the large warehouses operated by the Railways Division. Those who dwelled in those hovels were the families that worked the most menial jobs in Atrebell, their pay so low that they were little more than glorified slaves. Tryst need not go that far, however. Instead his trip took him just out of sight of the bridge he had crossed a moment before.

Nearby to where he shuffled, a group of the neighbourhood children had taken to playing a game involving the batting of a small ball with a stick. One of the huskier boys was tasked with knocking the ball down the street for the rest of the pack to run after and catch. Boys and girls alike dashed madly over the dusty, empty road as the ball rolled by. Tryst hobbled off to the side as the children darted past what they thought was just an old man.

When they had gone, Tryst reached inside the right sleeve of his robe to a pocket he had sewn in and removed all but a single piece of silver. It was a heavy handful of coins, coppers mostly, a silver coin he had brought with him for a purpose and four more that Rall had paid for Sticks' silence with. Tryst approached a closed barrel that stood against the outside wall of one of the brick houses and unfurled his fist upon it to deposit the coins. They would be worth a small fortune to these people and Tryst was paid handsomely for his real job as it was. As he left the small treasure behind, he tapped his walking stick a few times upon the barrel.

The batter looked in Tryst's direction but seemed to pay little mind at first, his attention squarely on the other kids tumbling and fighting over the ball. Tryst looked back one last time to see that the glint of the coins in the evening light had indeed caught the eye of the young fellow. The boy raced over to the barrel and swiped the coins out of sight before anyone else could see. With his joy barely contained, he called out to his friends to follow and ran out of sight with the rest chasing excitedly at his heels to see what he had found.

There is still kindness in Illiastra, one simply needs to show it and remind others that it exists, Tryst thought to himself as he turned a corner into a narrow alley.

The way he needed to go was simple enough to remember: fourth alley, third building and second door, once there he should knock once, then twice, then thrice, then four times rapidly.

Tryst found the door easy enough. All the buildings in these alleys were homes, albeit decrepit looking things. Their only signs of flourishing were the wooden doors painted with left over paint from the beautification siding jobs on the main streets. Much of it was mixed together to make odd hues of purples and browns and greens.

This particular door was a plum looking colour, but here and there were streaks of deep pink. He gave the appropriate knocks and sat back to sit and wait on a wooden box lain against the opposite wall facing the door.

The events at Hobbs' Tavern returned to Tryst's mind as he sat in wait. He had to wonder what that elf had been doing there at all. Elves were not permitted in the cities of human Illiastra. Even to reach the western ports to get to Elf-friendly places across the sea they had to take to the forests and stay out of sight. That was just to get within sight of the sea itself. From there it was a game of trying to book passage on a vessel of foreign origin without getting caught by the guards patrolling the docks. No ships of Illiastran nationality dared risk being found with an elf on board. The same could be said of most businesses inland also. None wanted to be caught with an elf buying from them or even on their property.

Old Hobbs was no doubt pressed for a bit of extra coin his usual patrons could ill provide and agreed to sell to the elf, provided he kept to himself in a booth. Even the Palomb entourage had been willing to overlook him at first, likely afraid that kicking him out would cause attention they ill desired at that point. But Tryst had to wonder why he would even risk entering the capital city of Illiastra.

The Palombs got their stir anyway, something much louder than simply arresting a trespassing Elf would garner. It would be known where they had been. They would lie, of course, though most would assume what they had been doing. It was likely that Eamon would still take the elf back to Hercalest. From there it would be a quiet trip north to the border of the Elven Forest for a quick deportation. A smart man would not risk punishing the elf. There was no doubt that news was already on its way to the Elven Council that one of theirs was in custody in Atrebell and the council would take great umbrage with it.

The other pressing concern was how accurate Marigold's prediction turned out to be. The two Palombs had done precisely what she said they would in seeking to get their sadistic jollies out on the two serving girls. Tryst had heard tales of their cruelty before, from serving staff and guardsmen mostly, but also from other, more authoritative sources as well. Not to mention the stories spun by their little brother, Dorian Palomb.

The amount of disregard the Palomb twins had shown for other fellow beings cast a grim spectre over them. By contrast, Grenjin Howland seemed to merely be a compulsive gold hoarder rather than the tyrant Tryst had thought he was. Where Howland was apathetic towards the plight of his people, Eamon's sons were downright antipathetic. Should the current Lord Master perish and the Palomb boys reach power, the people would be praying to Ios for Grenjin Howland to rise from the dead.

Better to have overseers that care not of your misfortune rather than ones who would derive twisted pleasure from it. Tryst told himself.

A noise from behind the door jarred him back to reality. The locking bolt was being slid back and forth, coming to rest after five slides. It was a signal and one he had been waiting for. A minute or two more passed before he slowly heard the latch slide once more.

He stood and hobbled toward it hastily, lest it be locked again. His hand wrapped around a simple wrought iron handle and he rotated it clockwise half a turn, as he had been instructed, in order to open the door. The level of secrecy in this task was daunting, but nothing Tryst wasn't accustomed to. The room inside was pitch black and he had to leave the last rays of light behind as the door closed at his back.

The clicking of a pistol's hammer being drawn reached his ears and with it a soft voice speaking through the darkness. "What does the heart seek?" It asked.

"A haven," Tryst replied back quickly.

"What has the heart found?" it asked again.

"A raven."

"Does the heart look upon it?"

"Aye, I am no craven."

"Good."

The Heart and the Raven were the code names given to Tryst and the owner of the voice and this little exchange was a routine they both knew all too well. A match raked across brimstone and a tiny flame ignited, producing a pocket of light. Bony, callused fingers held the long stick as it went into an oil lamp and caught the wick to give the room an orange glow.

"Ah, there you are, Heart," the owner of the soft voice said.

The man known as Raven was the same as he had always been: a thinning head of black, thin strands sprouted from a pale scalp and below that the fellow was no pretty sight. The man was rake thin and his skin weather beaten to the point of looking leathery. His face was gaunt, with two beady eyes set in deep sockets. Below that was a long, slender nose, perched above razor thin lips that always seemed a shade darker than lips ought to be. It made no wonder why he was known as Raven.

"Please, be seated," Raven said with an outstretched hand pointing to a ruddy chair pushed in to an old plank table, its wood splintered and grey with age.

Tryst shuffled quietly into the chair and laid his walking stick gingerly upon his lap.

"What have you come for, old Heart?" his host asked, a long, light grey, double breasted, woollen coat covering him from head to toe. It was an old military coat, worn by infantrymen a decade ago. They had since updated their wardrobe and their old coats were given over to the poor folk, once the heavy garments were stripped of their badges. There was still an outline over the left breast where the White Dove sigil of Howland's EMP party should have been.

"To write," Tryst gave as his only answer.

The one named Raven disappeared into the dark corner of the room and returned with a single piece of parchment, a black feathered pen and an inkwell. The items were placed in front of Tryst and the man took a seat across from him, elevating his feet to the table where he crossed a big pair of brown boots. Raven opened his coat just slightly, reaching his hand inside to produce brown wrapping paper, tied with yellow string. Nonchalantly, he untied the twine to reveal a piece of dried, pink ham and he began gnawing on it as he looked over his guest.

Tryst lifted the cover from the well, dipped the pen once and furiously began to write.

"Marken's meats have the best hams I've ever tasted. I've never been able to resist stopping there for a good, salty piece when I'm in town," the Raven commented while he gnawed on the meat with his yellowed teeth.

"It is certainly worth the price, I won't deny," Tryst gave back without looking up, dipping his pen in the reservoir occasionally. In the letter Tryst wrote of various bits of information he had overheard while in the presence of the Lord Master. Everything he wrote was of importance to the recipient, as it was all said during meetings the Lord Master had conducted with his city councillors, or visiting lords and ministers or other noteworthy men. Tryst had been there for it all and as was his duty, he was to report it to a man who sold such valuable information as a commodity.

When he had finished, Tryst simply addressed the letter to "The Nest" and signed his name as Heart. The deed was done for another third of a season and Tryst waved a hand over the paper to help the ink dry. Once it was read over once more to ensure it contained all that was fit to be heard by his associate, Tryst looked to his host. "Raven, I'd like you to carry this letter for me. Can it be delivered before morn?"

Raven waited a moment, staring at his prized snack lazily before putting his feet back to the floor. "It can. Give me a moment, please," he said as he disappeared into the black again, clomping away on his heavy boots. When he returned he carried a ball of white wax seated on a block of wood in one hand and in his other was an unsealed brown envelope.

The items were handed over to Tryst, who folded the letter and placed it in the envelope. The ball was held over the lamp until it began to grow wet so that the wax ran onto the seal and the small square block was pressed into it. When Tryst took it away, it left the print of a musical C-clef.

The single coin that remained to him was brought forth from his sleeve and he slid the silver piece across the table where it quickly disappeared into Raven's hand.

"For your haste, Raven," Tryst said as he rose from his seat and turned to leave. "I bid you safe travels."

Before Tryst could touch the door handle the room was enveloped in darkness again as Raven hurried to blow the lamp out.

The sun had fallen far behind the horizon and without a second look, Tryst left as fast as his disguise would allow, making his own haste to return to the manor for a feast.

7

MARIGOLD

There was no more denying the hard truth: Marscal Tullivan was dying. Nothing else could be as clear to Marigold as she stepped into her father's designated quarters in the Howland Manor and laid her eyes upon him.

Propped upright on down pillows amongst a bed that could fit five men, he looked like a sickly and shrivelled old man nearing his hundredth birthday. A white night shirt that laced from chest to neck hung limp and untied on the depleted frame of a man who in truth was shy of sixty. His face was the most striking feature now. Marigold had not realised how much makeup had been applied to bring life to the loose, clammy and colourless skin. One would barely notice his eyes: they looked as though they had fallen backward into the skull and had grown dark circles that made them look like pale moons in the night sky.

All through the Parliamentary sessions and even in the months leading up to it, her father had taken painstaking measures to conceal his illness as best he could. In addition to a wig and makeup, Marscal had taken to wearing thicker clothing to atone for the weight loss and dark rimmed spectacles to cover his face and eyes. It was seeing Marscal with his disguise removed that left Marigold no doubt of his rapid deterioration.

He's smiling. Marigold noted. *The last time he smiled Mother and Brother were coming home.* When the ship carrying them back to Daol

Bay from Gildriad disappeared, Marigold thought Marscal's smile had vanished with them forever. Yet, as Marscal sat in his bed, with the evening sun flittering through the tall, panelled window to fall upon his ill face, there it was: a smile and warmth in his eyes as they met Marigold's. In his hands sat a book, bound in leather that was coloured a shade of evening blue. A golden silk bookmark was laid into place by the paper thin hands that once had been so strong, before they closed the book, letting it come to rest on a tired lap.

"Good evening, my darling Marigold," Marscal beamed. "You look so splendid and radiant in your new dress. Please, come sit with me a moment, let me see it from up close. My eyes are going with the rest of me, I fear."

A grinding noise caught her attention and Marigold turned her head to find Oire on the opposite side of the room. His back turned to her as he worked something between mortar and pestle on a dark stained desk. "Good evening, Oire." She said to the steward as she strode gracefully across the room to her father's bedside.

"Good evening to you as well, my lady," he answered, still without turning to face her.

Marigold left him to his work and seated herself softly on the brown satin comforter trimmed in gold fringe that covered the twigs her father now called his legs. There was pain rapt across his face and beads of sweat running freely as he winced. The disease was sapping his strength and racking him with an incomprehensible misery. But in that agony there seemed to be delirium, as if he was drunk on it.

Tenderly, she laid a hand upon his, and sat there silently for a moment, unsure what to say as she forced a smile.

"You look even more gorgeous up close, Marigold," her father spoke first. "I always said you were the very image of your mother and she was the most beautiful woman these eyes have ever looked upon." His voice was still that gravelly tone Marigold knew so well, but a rasp coupled with heaving, laboured breaths made it harder for him to produce it. Yet, he pulled himself up higher on his pillows with a great effort expended and kept on. "You've grown to become just like her as well, you know, so spirited, strong willed and brilliant. Both of you were and are too good for this old country of old men and older ways. I should have taken your mother to Gildriad when Serephanie was born and raised you all there."

"You did what you thought was best," Marigold said,

wondering where these thoughts were coming from so suddenly. Her father was a man who kept his emotions hidden close and she felt this was all beyond strange for him to say.

"Did I, Marigold? Most days I feel like I made an incorrigible mess of things. In one stroke I signed away our home, my family's name, our hard earned fortunes and most of all, my only daughters. Then there was my wife and son. Both gone now and I blame myself for that too." Marscal's eyes watered as they looked away into a distant memory.

Oire, who had heard everything, turned sharply, almost dropping his tools as Marscal uttered the last sentence. Ever so quickly, he walked around the bed to his master, holding a curved, wooden pipe in his left hand and a box of matches in the other. "My Lord, I prepared your medicine, shall I light it for you?"

"Yes, please," Marscal said as his voice cracked. "Help me to dull this pain."

A match was struck on one of the high rising, ornately carved bedposts and Oire lit and took a few quick puffs of the Johnahweed to get it burning. The steward ran a handkerchief over the mouthpiece of the pipe to wipe any saliva from it before handing it over to Marscal. At once his grip on his daughter's hand was released so that he might smoke from the pipe.

That plant from the tropical nation halfway across the world was the only medicine they had been able to find that seemed to do her father any use. Usually, its effects served only to ease his pain and dull his senses with no detrimental effects to his cognition.

As the ill man in the bed drew from his pipe, Marigold turned to Oire. "Has father been given any new medication?" She cut straight to the point, a little perturbed by what Marscal had said thus far.

Oire exhaled through his nose and furrowed his eyebrows as he spoke. "That damn doctor that Lord Howland keeps paid a visit earlier. He claimed that Lord Howland himself had requested it." The steward stated in an annoyed, though hushed tone. "Lord Marscal had not permitted anyone but our own Doctor Bannington to know of his ailment, but I suppose your father could only hide it for so long. Doctor Garrick offered the Lord a tonic, one I was trained to use a long time ago. It is really only useful for killing pain and lasts but a short time, yet is highly addictive. I would not give it to anyone but the immediately dying to ease passing, personally. Your father refused it three times over but the doctor stayed quite a while. I couldn't prepare his Johnahweed and at any rate, Marscal would not have smoked it in front of him, given its illegality.

"Then that handmaiden of yours paid a visit to inform me that you had sent for me. I was about to send her back with a message to ask you to wait for me a little while longer, but your father insisted I tend to you first." Oire had walked back to his counter and returned with a towel to mop the sweat from his employer's brow as he spoke. "So, your father selflessly wallowed here in agony and endured the pain until I could return to him.

"And pain, as you well know, has a way of fogging the senses and can leave one as delirious as the drink. I wasted no time readying some of the herb from the tropical lands for him to smoke after I had returned. I don't think there's anything that fights the consumption quite as well as Johnahweed. It certainly has given your father quite an extension on his life where most would have already expired."

Marigold nodded at Oire's words, watching Marscal suck back the smoke from the burning plant. The room took on a pungent odour, one she had become accustomed to over the previous two seasons. It had become a familiar scene ever since Oire and Doctor Bannington both suggested the exotic plant be Marscal's medicine of choice to treat the consumption disease he had fallen victim to. The old steward slid quietly back to the counter, leaving the father and daughter to talk in relative privacy.

Her father lowered his pipe, holding it in the left hand. All the while his eyes took on the familiar pink hue they usually did when he smoked his pipe and they fell to the book still on his lap. That strange smile crept back on Marscal's face, just then and he tapped the book with a free finger before releasing his latest quarry of smoke. Coughing and sputtering a little before catching his breath again, he said, "I'm glad you came when you did, my darling daughter. I was just reading your mother's favourite book. She had taken our copy of it across the sea all those years ago and I never thought to replace it. Oire was able to find one in the library on the first floor. I hadn't read it in years, but it still makes me think of her with every page."

There was a yearning for Marigold to bring the conversation back around to his claim of responsibility for the death of her mother and brother. Yet, she went along with his current want. "What book is that, Father? You never told me she had a favourite."

"She most certainly did and this was it without a doubt. It is called *The Romance of the Two Knights*. A true story, though I think the author embellishes a little. It was one of the reasons she was so eager to move to Daol Bay with me, you know. She had wanted to see all the places in Illiastra that the knights in this book visited." Marscal coughed as his face warmed from recalling the memory. "They're gone though, the places, I mean and the knights too, for that matter. The world has changed much in eight hundred years, I am afraid."

This was the chance to change the topic and Marigold took it. "I would like to read that for myself when I return home now that I know it was Mother's fondest book. I will be certain to make a trip to the book store in our city to buy it." She said with a slim smile, clasping his free hand in her own again. "Father, I am wondering about what you spoke of a little while ago. Why do you feel responsible for what happened to her and brother?"

The book on Marscal's lap caught his eye again as he considered her question. A look of sorrow ran across his face as he tried to recall what was said just moments before in an agony induced haze. "I-I said far too much, my dear. This is not something that needs be discussed when the walls hear so well." Her father's eyes darted to the door she had entered through and then to the servant's door that led to their passageway. The dying lord was still full of pain, Marigold knew. It would be a time before he would sober from it, but at any rate, Marscal was suspicious of something or someone overhearing their conversation. Marigold was aware that the servants often reported to Lord Howland himself or to whichever minister was willing to produce the gold coins to pay.

There was little time to worry about the past for now, with too much else to currently deal with. Marigold would have to leave it as the ramblings of a man tormented with a cruel disease and move on. "Don't concern yourself over it then, Father. I'm sure we will talk when we are home." She patted his hand before continuing on and abandoning that particular train of thought. "I did you well today," she said by way of letting the topic switch to something more current. "Daol Bay's business with the Parliament is concluded for the year. We can leave for home on the morrow feeling resolved."

Marscal sank back into his pillows, relaxing once more. "I have no doubt you served the Tullivan name proudly. Likely, you could serve it far better than I ever have. I have done a lot of deeds I'm not proud of and I cannot alter that now, but you, my dear, can learn from my mistakes."

"I don't understand what you are saying, Father," Marigold said while shooting Oire a look of concern.

The steward had turned to face the pair, leaning against the counter in the corner of the room as her father carefully contemplated his words while puffing on his pipe.

"I am saying we cannot fool ourselves, my dear. I am dying and Serephanie has run off with that damnable fisherman." Spittle formed in the corners of his mouth, and the last word was tinged with contempt for a man he had never met. A coughing bout came over him for a moment, but he recovered, to continue on. "Everything named Tullivan will be yours and I don't want you to make the mistakes I made. Do what is right, for yourself and for everyone. I was too weak and craven to do as much myself after your mother perished."

"Why are you saying this now, Father? Why not wait until we were home safely?" Marigold uttered worriedly. Oire was standing behind her then, a gentle hand coming to rest on her shoulder.

Clearing his throat, Marscal gave her an answer in a lowered voice. "Because, my dear, as far as I'm concerned my record in Parliament finished yesterday and yours began today." Marscal reached for her hand this time, laying it meekly over her own and squeezing it with the bit of strength left to it. "There are many eyes on you now and they know I am as good as gone. I can tell you that those Palomb boys are starting to slaver at the thought of my death. You and I know I won't have time to turn cold before they try to lay claim to you and Daol Bay."

Marigold felt a welling sombreness within her as she found words to respond with. "You're still very much alive, Father. I don't want to even so much as think about a world without you in it."

"You must," he answered with a demanding voice. "You are the only child that remains to me now. Felixander is long dead and Serephanie has placed herself out of reach by all. But you, Marigold, you are what remains to hold the Tullivan legacy. The Palombs will come for you, or rather, for your hand in marriage, and they will claim everything of ours and erase our name entirely. They had foolishly thought you were but a key to the west, but today, you showed them you are much more than that. You showed them that you are a Tullivan of Daol Bay and a proud woman, not an object. You are the *keeper* of the keys, not the key itself."

A beaming smile crossed her face. "Thank you, Father. It gladdens me to know you have such faith in me. Might I ask how it is that you know all of this?"

"I had a visitor earlier, before the doctor," Marscal said with a content sigh. "Apparently you made a bold statement and you should know that it was hard for me to mask my pride when I was told of it."

"And might I ask who that visitor was, Father?" Marigold plied him, taking care to keep her tone hushed.

"The backbench minister from the Warrens in the Southlands. You know the fellow, yourself and Serephanie always had a certain name for him."

"The Vulture," she heard herself say aloud, even laughing a little at it. Marigold had called that long-serving minister by that name since the first time she had seen him as a child. He was perpetually hairless above the neck, with a long, hooked nose, a thin face and a wrinkled forehead. His facial appearance combined with the fact that he always wore a cape topped with a wide collar of feathers made him look almost identical to the scavenging buzzards. His real name was Minister Clay Harlowe, but the Vulture was what Marigold and Serephanie always referred to him as, though never in his hearing.

"The very same," her father pressed on, "You know how pious he is, always insisting on staying in the city during sessions so he can be near a Tower of Ios for morning prayers and such." Marigold nodded in reply and Marscal continued. "Well he was none too pleased when he saw you wearing breeches and sitting in my seat today. You broke quite a few of Ios' rules in Minister Harlowe's eyes, and he was quite offended at your slight of the god."

Marigold allowed herself half a smile and her father gave one back, a hint of pride glinting in his reddened eyes. "Surely he did not bring himself here just to complain to you?" she asked.

"Just so, he was quite adamant that I burn those breeches and any other traditional men's attire you might own to appease Ios." Marscal let out a scoff as he spoke, a wisp of smoke curling up before his face. "Clay also had the audacity to suggest that I hasten your marriage to the Palombs so that a male may sit in your seat and rule Daol Bay. Lest our name be cursed for offending and disobeying Ios, which will take down the entire parliament by association and all of that nonsense." He waved the hand that had just been over Marigold's dismissively as he finished.

'Your seat.' Those were the two words that stuck out the most to Marigold. The rest were the typical complaints of such a devout man of the Triarchy, which was something that Marigold had grown quite accustomed to.

The entire parliament had fallen silent when she was announced today. Their eyes had followed and judged her with every step taken up the red, carpeted stairs to the wide desk just below and to the right of Grenjin Howland's. The ire of the Lords and Ministers all stemming solely from the fact that she was a woman sitting in a man's seat in trousers. Such frivolity from supposed leaders was abhorrent to Marigold and the Vulture was striving to lead the pack of fearful men shivering before the female form.

'Your seat.' The words seemed to Marigold like it was a blessing and an acknowledgement of Marigold's intentions all at once. Her father could have said *'My seat'* or *'Your husband's seat'*, yet he clearly stated *'your seat'*. Marigold wondered if her father knew what her refusing to cower to the other men would really mean for Parliament and Illiastra. There was no doubting in Marigold's mind that the majority of the Elite Merchant's Party that currently held the nation would seek to remove her from her inherited position.

That would be pondering for later though, as there were things left to discuss. "Father, could you tell me what you said to the Vulture when he made his requests."

"Pheh!" He quite nearly spat. "Those were not requests. Thinly veiled demands, more like. I apologized for your behaviour and told him I would encourage you to attend sermons daily so that you may learn to be a proper woman of Ios." Marscal's tone was one of sarcasm. Neither he nor Marigold kept much stock in the Triarchy and they both knew Marscal had no such intention of enforcing anything he had told Minister Harlowe.

"Well, I would ask you what transpired today, besides every eye in Parliament following you around." He sighed. "Though we both know nothing of importance ever happens at the summaries. My dear, do enjoy yourself this evening. I know you will do me proud."

A knock came at the door, loud and quick that prompted Oire to hurry across the room to answer it.

"I'll see you on the morrow and we shall put this place behind us once more." Marscal added. "In the meantime, something tells me that your escort for the evening has arrived."

Marigold turned her gaze to see who it was and let her eyes fall to where Oire was showing a guest inside the room.

Clad in a captain's uniform was the resplendent form of Freyard Archer. His golden hair neatly combed to one side and that finely sculpted face freshly shaven. The uniform consisted of a double breasted, deep blue jacket with a shining gold trim and matching buttons up the breast, the cuffs and pinning down the gold fringed epaulets. The uniform was ornamented with a golden patch on either bicep denoting his rank and station. He wore white cotton gloves over his hands and black trousers bearing a gold stripe on his legs. To complete the ensemble were boots in black, shining, brightly polished leather to the knee. Hanging from his hips on a leather belt was a golden hilted rapier and a white, ornate pistol with an etching of a dove in the grip. "

"My Lord and Miss Tullivan, I bid good evening to you both," Freyard greeted them while taking a few steps into the room. "I hope I am not intruding, I was asked to escort Miss Tullivan to the Parliamentary feast this evening."

"Well met, ser," Marscal replied, trying his hardest to look and sound healthier than everyone knew he was. "I should say your timing is spot on, for my daughter and I were just saying our farewells."

Marigold turned back to her father and leaned in to kiss him on the cheek, a gesture he returned. "Goodnight, Father, I shall see you come morning." As she spoke, Marscal gave her hand a squeeze and gave a single, slow nod.

Rising from the bed, she smoothed out her haltered, black silk dress with its silver lined starburst and low, revealing cut and turned toward Freyard.

Who, from the expression he wore, clearly liked the sight before him.

The decorated soldier took her hand in his as Marigold approached and gently kissed it. "My lady Marigold, you look positively radiant this evening, as always you do. It is nothing short of an absolute honour for me to escort you to the feast."

"The honour is mine to wear as well, Captain Archer," Marigold felt her face grow flush as she replied to the compliment. "You are looking quite handsome in your uniform. It is far more suiting than the attire of the Honourable Guardsmen." Despite her cheeks blushing and giving her away, Marigold was ever the lady.

The Captain thanked her for the kind compliment and stepped back to hold the door.

With a final farewell and wave to her father and Oire, Marigold took Freyard's arm and the two departed the room for the evening.

Together they strolled down the long hallway to the marvellous staircase that rose from the manor lobby.

Marble columns with gold plated spirals roping upward sat in the dark brick walls at intervals. Brilliantly carved chandeliers of crystal lit with electricity illuminated their pathway, which was more stone lined with red, plush carpeting that muffled their footsteps.

The two exchanged pleasantries as they went, starting with Marigold asking Freyard how his day had found him. To which he mentioned that the biggest news to be heard was that some members of the Thieves had been captured in the night as they raided a farm house. The master-at-arms for Fort Dornett made no mention of Tryst, which told Marigold told that the two friends had not crossed paths.

A sparse few ministers, ladies and their offspring mulled about on the second floor, talking amongst themselves and exchanging pleasant greetings with Marigold as she passed by them. Eastern Lords mostly, she noted, like loquacious Minister Braggen, whom Lord Palomb wanted to replace with his younger brother.

The men all wore suits of dark colours, black, brown and blue mostly with a deep red as contrast here and there. It was evident to Marigold that the women had followed the men's pattern of blandness when it came to evening attire. They all had opted for wide, hoop-skirted dresses with modest necklines or high collars and sleeves that covered them to the elbows at the very least. Marigold's appearance was certainly a sharp turn from that of her peers. A notion that become apparent to Marigold when all eyes in the lobby fell upon her the instant she reached the balustrade.

The extravagant staircase began to either side of the railing, converging back into one long set of steps below a statue of a bare chested Ios. His massive, bearded head and shoulders emerged from the white marble with his giant hands pressed to the underside of the overhang, as if he were carrying it himself.

After a moment of pause, she was introduced to the gathered flock of ministers, families and loyalists below by a middle aged butler. "May I have your attention, my good fellows and ladies?" the servant began in a booming voice that echoed off the walls. "I give to you this evening a Lady of Daol Bay, daughter of Marscal Tullivan, Warden Lord of the West, Minister of Daol Bay and Lord of Fisheries and Seas for Illiastra: Miss Marigold Tullivan."

A smattering round of applause rose from the folks gathered below as Marigold and her escort descended the staircase. Marigold waved politely at the onlookers. Most of whom she knew by name such as Minister Mattersly, who held the lighthouse keep and surrounding seaside town of Tippard. The coastal town lay just north of the Tear, a vast waterfall where the Varras River, the longest and widest river in Illiastra, emptied over sheer cliffs into the ocean.

Mattersly was one her father's men and in the days before the rise of the Elite Merchant's he would have been titled a Sealord. The man was exorbitantly wealthy on account of being the latest family member to inherit one of the known world's foremost ship building facilities. The amiable elderly man with his round belly and cheery wife were the first to greet Marigold as she touched the lobby floor.

Elda Mattersly, a plump woman of sixty, patted Marigold's hand gently and congratulated her on a job well done earlier in the day in the Parliament. The minister echoed his wife's sentiments and if he felt that Marigold had slighted the gods, he made no mention of it.

For that much she was glad, Walter and Elda had always been kind to her and loyal to her father. It was that very same kindness and loyalty Marigold hoped she could come to rely on in the future.

The elegant, masterful musicianship of an orchestral band greeted her ears from inside the banquet hall. As was customary for the final feast of the Parliamentary session, Grenjin Howland had commissioned the Atrebellius Orchestra to perform. It had always been Marigold's favourite part of the sessions and she had long committed all of their regular performance pieces to memory.

Craning an ear towards the doors of the hall, she tried to discern the song they were in the midst of when she caught sight of Lord Taves. The salt and pepper haired Lord of Crime and Punishment was clad in a powder blue suit of satin with a pattern of golden filigree. When Marigold spotted him, he was hastily following a servant to the guardsman's office off the main entrance, behaviour that Marigold thought to be quite peculiar.

"Good evening, my betrothed," an all too familiar voice called to Marigold, making her forget about the curious behaviour of Mackhol

Taves for the moment. She turned to find Pyore Palomb standing to her right with a smarmy grin across his face. "You look as gorgeous as ever," he told her.

The boy of seventeen was bedecked in a tailored military uniform in the teal and gold colours reserved for the guards of the Tullivan household.

The whole ensemble was complimented with a tightly cinched belt containing a rapier and pistol nearly identical to Freyard's. It was a brash statement. Instead of the silver and black of the Palomb family, he'd gone out of his way to wear that of the Tullivan's. It implied impending possession over Marigold and the western realm. The whole display was incredibly distasteful in Marigold's eyes as it flaunted her father's terminal illness in her face as if he had already succumbed to it. It was no mystery what game Pyore was playing at here and she had to wonder how implicit his brother Eldridge was in the scheme. The twin sons of Eamon were always cooking up such cruelties, though rarely did Eldridge play a tangible role. Such brazen behaviour was left to Pyore, who seemed to revel in his own audacity.

Marigold knew that she must make every effort to not allow him to see how much his mockery hurt. "My dear Pyore, you look splendid as well. My, are those the colours of Daol Bay you're sporting? They suit you." It was quite taxing for Marigold to restrain her sarcasm, and even harder for her to restrain her hand from slapping his homely face.

"You're too kind, my lady," Pyore said in a tone that smacked of scorn as he gave a facetiously apologetic bow. "I had thought it would be best if I wore your colours, given that your father is so very ill and I was absent to take his place today. I did not want the good lords and ministers to forget who the heir to Daol Bay really is, after all. So consider it a token of my apology for leaving you to do a man's work, my lady. I assure you that it will not happen again."

Though few dared to look, all in the foyer were paying close attention to the spectacle before them.

Freyard stood silently, belaying no sign of what he may be feeling, though Marigold knew he heard the threat in Pyore's words as plainly as she had.

This was no apology. Pyore was relaying his anger toward Marigold for her decision to sit her father's place herself without informing him of such. In Pyore's eyes Daol Bay was his to inherit and in Marscal Tullivan's absence, the blond twin of Eamon Palomb felt it his responsibility to tend to the region's business.

This was precisely the response Marigold anticipated, and with such attention now cast her way, she proceeded forward cautiously. "It is I who should offer apologies, Pyore. When my father announced he was staying abed, I sent my steward, Oire, to find you, only to find you had already left with your brother for the city. I did only what I thought was right in such short notice and took the seat myself for today only," Marigold replied calmly, offering a curtsy where he had bowed. She noticed that Pyore's eyes were not on her, but on Freyard beside her, who was himself standing straight as an arrow to meet the hateful stare that the Palomb twin was shooting him.

"What's done is done, my lady," Pyore icily replied when he broke the gaze of the distinguished soldier. "I think we can both look beyond our misdeeds this time, can we not? I shall escort the lady from here, Captain Archer and I thank you for bringing her this far."

"As is your right, my darling," Marigold forced herself to say before turning to Freyard and letting go of his arm. "You have my thanks as well, ser. I promise you a dance after the feasting is done."

Freyard backed off a bow. "You are more than welcome, my lady. I would be glad to take you up on your offer later in the evening."

There was a glance of apology from Marigold to the dejected soldier, who met her eyes briefly before making for the staircase he had descended over not moments ago.

He understands how the game is played. Marigold told herself. *Still, I do hope he does not feel I have slighted him.*

Before she could wonder where Freyard was off to she was taken by the arm rather sharply by Pyore. The strength of the boy surprised Marigold and she had to step quickly to keep from stumbling over dress and shoes alike.

A pair of the Honourable Guardsmen stood to either side of the entrance to the hall, pulling open the heavy doors as the couple neared them.

The sounds from the orchestra greeted her wholly and she finally could identify the piece they were playing. It was one she rather enjoyed called *Springtime Prelude.* On another evening she might have even danced to it.

The music was the only thing she registered in the dining hall before Pyore painfully squeezed her arm and leaned in close to be heard over the band. "Don't you ever do that to me again, do you understand? His grip tightened to the point of pain, but Marigold refused to even whimper as he went on. "I'm your betrothed. I shall be the one who escorts you, not some ranger from the Southlands. Don't ever dare to embarrass me again or you *will* regret it."

"Whatever are you talking about?" Marigold feigned the fear in her voice, using it to mask her welling anger. "I had sought you earlier in the evening but you were nowhere to be found, whatever was I to do, darling?"

"That's another thing," he went on as they made the slow journey to the head table upon the dais. "Don't think I didn't hear about you having the gall to sit my seat in Parliament today." Pyore was visibly seething with a noticeable shade of red pouring into his cheeks. "If your father was too ill to sit, it should have been brought to my attention so I could attend his duties, as is my right as your betrothed. I am the man around here, need you not forget."

Marigold glanced at the other nobles that had already taken their seats. Proud families from both the eastern and western halves of Illiastra were now in attendance and even if their eyes were averted, they were watching. They had not heard, not over the music, but they observed the language of Marigold and Pyore's bodies and they knew what they saw.

Suffer the slights, if just for a few hours. Home beckons on the morrow and then Pyore's perceived rights end when I am safely behind the walls of Daol Bay. Marigold reminded herself. "You are correct once again, my dear. I should have consulted you." She said, fighting to keep the patronization from her tone of voice. "Please, forgive me for the slight."

Marigold thought it strange that Tryst Reine had not intervened by now and her attention went to his usual bench in the rear of the hall. *Empty.* She realised. *Has he not returned from the city?*

As she scanned the room for the swordsman, Marigold noticed that the scene had captured the attention of one Nathania Taves. Nattie, as she was known, was of the same age as Marigold and the eldest of three daughters of Mackhol Taves. Tonight she had opted to wear a scarlet, velvet dress that looked to be all skirts. The exaggerated garment was sleeveless, but it had shoulders on it like throw pillows. Tight about her neck was a velvet collar with a brooch dangling from it bearing the triangular symbol of the Triarchy.

There was smugness about her as she watched Marigold being chastised by the vain teenager. It was a predicament that Nattie was only too eager to point it out to the other ladies seated nearby.

In their youth Marigold and Nathania had been friends, though by the time they had blossomed into women that friendship had dissipated. Nattie had grown to be shrewd, greedy and entirely too quick to cast aside friend and foe alike to climb the social ladder. Those traits that had driven Marigold away had endeared her to Mackhol, a man Marigold had even less time for. If rumours of her cruelty were true, then she was all but a replica of her father now.

All of Nattie's work was largely for naught though, for she still was but a woman. Nathania's efforts had merely netted her the unenviable position of being the prize wife and child bearer for old Minister Barnan of Ravenkeep. The sixty seven year old man was the owner of a high yielding diamond mining operation in the foothills of the northern portion of the Illiastran Mountain Range.

Even Marigold felt poorly for Nathania in that arrangement, as the woman had been traded as an investment in Barnan's mining ventures. Left to make her own relationships, Nattie could have landed any man she chose with her curvy frame, golden complexion and matching golden ringlets falling past her shoulders. *Even for you, Nattie,* Marigold thought to herself. *I would even fight for your right to marry as you please. If only you could see that this is no way to live and rise with me. I fool myself if I think anyone beyond Lady Orangecloak and the Thieves share my vision.*

"Here we are, my dear, your table for the evening," Pyore said, breaking her thought. He had brought her alongside an empty table just shy of the dais, where she had been expecting to sit. The empty chair at the table head was decorated with an ornately carved letter 'T'. To either side of the letter was the pair of leaping codfish that were the insignia of the Fisheries and Seas office.

This was the table she and her sister Serephanie had ate at with Oire and any city councilmen that had tagged along to the sessions in the past. As a substitute for her father, her proper place for the evening should be at the long table upon the dais, where, beside her father, she had sat all week.

"I don't understand, dear Pyore, why have you brought me here?" Marigold queried lowly, taking into account that the band was nearly finished with *Springtime Prelude.*

"I've brought you here for a very good reason, woman. It has come to my attention that you've been displaying a rebellious streak," Pyore said, unsmiling and a little louder than Marigold would have liked. "It is beyond the time that you learned where your place as a woman is if you are ever to be a proper and obedient wife. You will sit here, alone and I will take your father's seat at the head table from here on out. Am I clear?"

That was a threat and an insult all in one. She was five years his senior and yet he scolded her like a child all the same. Her teeth grinded behind closed lips as she glanced to the head table where Eamon Palomb and Pyore's twin brother Eldridge had taken their places. There was no sign of Lord Master Howland yet, though a man dressed head to heel in black had taken a chair across from the Palombs. *Tryst.* Marigold knew at once. *That's where he's gotten to, but why? He's never been at the head table before.*

The music had stopped now, anything Marigold said would be heard by all, she decided in the moment that it might be for the best. "My dear, forgive me for correcting you, but my father still lives and we are not yet wed. It is his wish that I represent him until such time. I apologise, but I have to politely decline your request."

"You what?!" Pyore scowled, gaining the attention of the room. Marigold watched his fist curl and his face boil over with rage.

She stood her ground firmly and cast fear aside, waiting for him to do something brash. *Go on, hit me you lout. I dare you to try with your father so near at hand and every elected official in Illiastra watching. I wonder if you could land more than a single blow before Tryst Reine himself descends on you.*

Pyore's nails dug in to her bare arm sharply and she still gave him no sign of the pain as he leaned in closely. "You dare disobey me again? Are you daft, woman?"

A voice cut through the air. "Pyore, bring Miss Tullivan here, please." Marigold's eyes went again to the dais and to Eamon Palomb, who had now gotten to his feet. A sigh of relief came over Marigold while Pyore groaned with embarrassment beside her.

In a complete turn of mood, Pyore clasped her arm as gently if she were a flower and led her up the three short steps to the terrace and the dinner table upon it.

Eamon watched ashamedly as the two approached, he was still standing, taking the time to smooth the wrinkles from his finely pressed black suit. Beneath his jacket was a ruffled white shirt and over the whole outfit he wore a silver cloth sash.

Eldridge had matched his father in attire down to the last detail and looked every bit the heir he was destined to be.

Opposite of them in both placement and apparel was Tryst. His muscled frame was wrapped in a silk shirt and tight cotton trousers. The man had passed on a tie or even an evening jacket and seemed out of place amongst formally dressed males seated with him.

"Miss Tullivan," the middle aged lord began as his blond offspring approached. "I apologise for my son's outburst, you'll have to forgive him for being flustered. He had a harrowing encounter while in the city earlier today." Before Marigold could think of a response, Eamon had turned his attention to Pyore. "Now, my son, I want you to tell me what she said that led to that outburst. Keep in mind that Miss Tullivan knows what she said, so I would carefully weigh my words, were I you."

Pyore swallowed hard and told it truly from the moment they first met in the lobby. Either he was afraid of being corrected again by a woman or the teenager was sure he was in the right. Eamon, Eldridge and Tryst all listened intently, the former two nodding along as Pyore recounted it all. When he had finished his retelling, Pyore tugged on the bottom of his teal jacket with both hands and stood there looking smug and proud of himself.

The eldest Palomb took a deep breath. "Is what my son says the truth of how it happened, Miss Tullivan?" Eamon asked Marigold calmly with Pyore staring holes through her head, expecting another rebellious rebuttal.

There was nothing to correct though, he had told it true, and Marigold knew she had the wretched boy trapped. "It is as he says, Lord Palomb," she said, holding her head high and watching from the corner of her eye as both brothers registered the trap being sprung.

Their reactions were wholly contradictory to one another as Eldridge seemed to find some delight in his brother's misfortune that Pyore did not. As one side of the dark haired brother's face curled into a smile, he leaned his head onto his propped hand in amusement.

"Then she has the right of it, son," Eamon ruled decidedly on the matter. "That chair is hers, as denoted by my dear friend Marscal. It does not become yours by any rights until such a time that you are wed and her father bequeaths it to you. Now, I think a full apology to

Miss Tullivan is in order and you will show her to the chair beside
Mister Reine." Eamon's tone brokered no argument as he voiced his
commands. "Her father's usual place has been given to a special guest
of the Lord Master's for the evening. I do apologise on Lord Master
Howland's behalf, Miss Tullivan."

Pyore's lips curled inward in anger and he looked to Eldridge
for support only to find him trying vainly to stifle his chuckling.

"I won't," the blond twin said sternly, standing as tall as his
frame would allow. He came almost face to face with his father in that
instant. They were two faces of striking similarity as Pyore was the
only one of Eamon's offspring that bore any likeness to him. Eldridge
and his two younger siblings all bore the brown hair and sharper
features so common among the Mortons of their mother's side.

The gesture had caught Eamon off guard and he turned hastily
from Marigold to his son. "I will give you one more chance, Pyore,"
Eamon offered sternly. "Refuse again and you'll be seated with your
mother, sister and brother below. Further insubordination will leave
me no choice but to remove you from the dining hall entirely. What
will you choose?"

Pyore considered once more, silently keeping his father's stare
as he worked his jaw like a cow grinding cud. "My beloved, it has come
to my attention that I may have been in the wrong to correct you," he
said, finally relenting to his father's demands. "You have my sincerest
apologies for any boundaries I may have overstepped and I beg for
your forgiveness."

Though he tried to mask his tone, it was clear to Marigold and
perhaps the others that Pyore's apology was empty. The words were
dripping with bitterness and Marigold sensed that it gave him no
pleasure to be admonished before the entire dinner hall. Even if
everyone else had the decency to pretend they were unaware of
anything going on.

That sulking behaviour was a good enough victory for
Marigold. She had won and they both knew it. "Your apology is
accepted, my dear," she intoned with a grin that she hoped might
convey her satisfaction with how Eamon's judgement had unfolded.
"Would you be do kind as to show me to my seat?"

The last line was intended as a jab, despite its cool and poised
delivery. The wince on Pyore's face told her that both it and the smile
were received as she intended. If Eamon or the other two had noticed,

none showed and any sign of it, save for Eldridge, who could hardly contain his chortling at his brother's expense.

"Thank you for your forgiveness, your kindness knows no bounds, my betrothed. I would be glad to show you to your seat," Pyore stated, still in that forced apologetic tone. As gently as if he were petting a kitten, he led her around the table, only releasing her hand to pull back the heavy chair beside Tryst. Ever so graciously, Marigold curtsied before taking her rightful place. Pyore's new seat was beside his brother and directly across from Tryst, who made no attempt at false courtesy and ignored the boy entirely.

Eamon regarded Pyore again as he retook his own place. "You should be grateful that Lord Master Howland was not here to witness that," the old man started in as Pyore lowered himself into the chair beside his brother. "Though I have no doubts that he will be made aware of it come tomorrow. Fortunately, you will be on a train back to Hercalest by then and Lord Master Howland will have the remainder of autumn to forget about it."

"Yes, Father," Pyore said, seemingly defeated and daring not to even make eye contact with his sire.

Tryst still had yet to speak a word to Marigold and though she understood why, it didn't make the silence between them any more bearable and so she broke it. "Hello, Mister Reine, I trust you have had a pleasant day?" Marigold asked in a proper and friendly tone.

"Hello to you as well, my lady, it's been quite fine, thank you for asking," Tryst answered with full formality.

"If you don't mind my asking, ser, what brings you to the head table this evening?" she inquired, wondering what he was able to say in front of the Palombs.

He turned to face her and it was then she noticed the sword moving at his side. Not the standard, useless ornaments the guards and Pyore Palomb wore, but a fine looking piece in a faded, red, leather sheath. The light from the chandeliers overhead rippled on the worn leather like the waters of a creek. The hilt was wrapped in supple black leather with a fine linen ribbon of dark red encircling it, ending in a dangling knot. Marigold knew this was no ordinary sword. This was his master's blade from the University in the Mountains. It was forged of not just good steel, but the very best quality dwarven blacksteel and by the very best smith alive.

"I was invited by Lord Howland himself," Tryst explained. "I know no more about his reasons than you, my lady." Tryst was curt in his response, a little cold even, though he was a far better actor than the others would know and she made nothing of it.

"I see..." Marigold allowed her voice to trail off, and that ended their conversation.

Lord Palomb had fallen deathly silent, his hand occasionally going to a dish of hot pecans drizzled with honey before him. Each table had two bowls of them laid out for appetizers and between them a centrepiece made of a potpourri of colourful flowers.

Once things had quieted down, the servants began to approach with offerings of red and white wines, brandy and a hot, tomato based soup to whet the appetite. Marigold turned all but for the red wine away. It was a good vintage of blueberry sweetwine, the first taste running ever so slowly down her throat.

Footsteps and chatter preceded Mackhol Taves, who had returned from his impromptu meeting in the guard's office off the lobby. The minister had paused to speak briefly with the rest of the Palomb family before he climbed the steps to join Marigold and the others upon the dais. "Good evening, my lady Tullivan, gentlemen of the Palomb household and Mister Reine. I am so glad that I am permitted to join you all this evening for I have most splendid and exciting news to share once the good Lord Master arrives." His face was a wide, sly grin. As ominous a sign as any as far as Marigold was concerned with Mackhol Taves.

A servant appeared quickly and drew back the chair to Marigold's left, which had always been her father's, for Lord Taves to sit, to which he graciously accepted.

"Miss Tullivan," Mackhol spoke as he drew his chair in. "I want to congratulate you on a splendid performance today in the Parliament."

Marigold remained silent and waited for the slight she knew was yet to come.

His pearly teeth shone at her as his mouth widened in an arrogant smirk. "I must say, you did quite admirably for a woman. I believe you're the first to sit in parliament since the legacy of the Elite Merchants began."

There it is, as backhanded and sardonic as could be expected of the Taves family. Marigold thought to herself before framing a response. "Thank you, ser, you are too kind. I only sought to do my father proud," she replied courteously while watching Pyore twist in his chair.

Mackhol nibbled on a pecan as Marigold spoke, chiming in again when she finished. "Ah yes, how is your father feeling today? He was sorely missed at the summations. I had meant to visit him, though I am afraid I became occupied following the session's closing."

He wouldn't have wanted to see you anyway. "He is feeling better this evening." She lied through her teeth. "I should say he will be up and about before you know it. You know my father. He is not one to stay down." *And neither am I.*

The message behind Taves' words was clear enough. He was no more pleased with her presence in the Parliament than Clay Harlowe or Pyore Palomb had been. To Minister Harlowe's credit, he at least had the courage to say it forthright. Even that was far better than this game of thinly veiled insults that the Lord of Crime and Punishment was engaging her in. Although Pyore seemed to pick up on it, and from the expression on his face was clearly enjoying the verbal browbeating Marigold was taking.

Fortunately, Mackhol relented and changed the topic to the Palomb boys and to the events of their visit to the city earlier today. Eamon seemed none too pleased with the topic change and yet Taves insisted. Apparently, Lord Taves had a keen interest in a prisoner the twin's personal guards had arrested and brought with them to stew in a cell below the manor.

Marigold's ears pricked up at the sound of that, wondering what Eldridge and Pyore had gotten in to and if Tryst had seen it himself. The Master of Blades however was silent on the matter. He was content to stare at his hands folded on the table in front of him and relinquished no hint of what may be running through his mind.

After Eamon finished recounting the events in the city, he asked Lord Taves, as Lord of Crime and Punishment, for his counsel on the matter. "As you well know, Lord Palomb, I cannot take an elf as my ward." Taves began, only too glad to give his opinion. "That would be a nettlesome situation for one to find oneself in, given the Elven Forest's hostility towards human Illiastra. However, I do maintain and staff a small jail beyond my prison's walls to serve the town outside. I would be happy to keep him as my guest for a few days. The family and I are only returning home briefly, for you see, we are heading east to Ravenkeep to see our Nathania settled away and wed before the winter. The Almanac Sages are forecasting a rather harsh winter season in the east that could run well into spring. I decided that it would be better to wed her before that, rather than wait too long for the thaw." Mackhol took turns making eye contact with all three Palombs while he spoke. This was a man only too aware of the potential power those teenagers were destined to wield. He was taking every step to not give them any reason to dislike him before such a time.

It was Eamon who seemed to catch his meaning. "So I understand that you're willing to take our burdening prisoner and deposit him back to the Elven Forest on your route to Ravenkeep, am I correct? You would see to his deportation personally, on our behalf?"

"Why yes I shall, my lord, if you would give me the honour of undertaking this task." Mackhol sounded as humble as the lowly servants offering wine nearby when speaking with the Palombs. An all too noticeable contrast to the thinly veiled condescension he only offered Marigold.

Eamon gestured a hand, palm upwards toward Taves. "Then by all means, the elf is yours. I am indebted to you for relieving my family of this encumbrance."

I had almost forgotten they had arrested an elf until Mackhol brought it up. This was an interesting development indeed. Marigold pondered. *Any degradation by the Illiastran humans towards elves or their ancestral cousins, the amaroshan people, was an inevitable political nightmare if the Elven Forest caught wind of it.*

All of the animosity between Illiastra and the Elven Forest stemmed from the conflict concerning the amaroshans, or half-elves. When the EMP received a majority vote in the election, they sought total control and found heavy opposition in the amaroshan community to the Merchant's aggressive tactics. Subtly, the EMP began showing prejudice towards amaroshan people, which soon grew to a campaign of outright hatred against them.

In Marigold's youth, the level of fear and malice against the increasingly oppressed and marginalised race of half-elves came to an ugly conclusion known as the Amaroshan Exodus. The EMP had voted to expel all the amaroshans from Illiastra and gave a timeline for amaroshans to leave. Any found in Illiastra beyond that date would be arrested and transported to Biddenhurst. Many amaroshans fled across the sea to any nation that might take them, however most ran to the Elven Forest. The elves were quick to answer the plight of the refugees and voiced their outrage at the EMP's amoral actions.

That was before word reached the forest that the amaroshans who were taken to Biddenhurst were being executed by the dozen. A war seemed all but inevitable until the Elven Forest agreed to halt any plans of invasion on the basis that the remaining incarcerated amaroshans be deported to their borders. A treaty was later struck between humans and elves, though it was no true alliance, merely a tension filled armistice.

What now weighed on the mind of Lord Palomb was a particular clause in the treaty. It stated that any member of either nation caught trespassing was to be returned to their respective border without question. To help enforce this clause, a neutral ground of one hundred meters was maintained between both nations, with border outposts set up at intervals on the human side. The countries had remained isolated from one another and the Elven Forest made it clear that they would never negotiate with Illiastra so long as the EMP retained power.

A bitter childhood memory came to Marigold when she thought of the amaroshan people. As a girl she had innocently begged, as only a child could, for her father not to hurt the amaroshans, insisting that they had done nothing wrong.

At the time, Marscal's response seemed cowardly to her. "There is nothing more I can do, my dear," he had tried to explain. "I helped those Amaroshans who would leave my city to reach safer lands. If they choose to stay, then they force my hand. I have to follow the law, even if I voted against it."

"But, Father," Eldridge complained, breaking her away from the memory and back to the present. "We had intended to bring the elf to Hercalest with us."

Eamon grunted angrily at the notion. "What would you do with him, Eldridge? Incarcerate him indefinitely? Stick him in the stocks in the town square? Perhaps hang him for striking your brother's face?

"I'll be up to my armpits in letters demanding the elf's release. Then they will send envoys and ambassadors seeking to return him home, dead or alive. Those damn elves would follow that with requests for an inquiry into the incident. Not to mention their outrage should he actually die in our custody. Either way, the elves will seek proper trial for him in their nation. Following that, they will try to come for you and your entourage to have you tried for wrongful arrest if he is found innocent of wrongdoing. Which I assure you he would be, since neither of you would be present to defend your claims. It is a headache I am only too happy to avoid if Lord Taves can quietly deport him. You fools made enough of a scene today. I would dare say that you are both even bigger fools if you think word of this incident is not already on its way back to the Elven Forest."

"But, Father-" Pyore began to pout, before being cut off.

"No more, Pyore," Eamon declared sternly. "It is done and I thank you again, Minister Taves. I owe you a great favour for this, I assure you."

"You are the Warden Lord of the East, I am your subject and serve you as much as the man who brings the supper. Naught should be thought of the gesture," Mackhol said sickeningly with a sly, beaming grin. The man turned to face the dejected twins then. "My good fellows, take heart, I only had your own best interests in mind. Your father is absolutely right to say there is no alternative to this issue but to give the Elven Forest back their own. My apologies if I have caused you any grief, it was not my intention."

The two Palomb boys exchanged a look that screamed of malice, but beneath it was a hint of consideration. Scorned they were, yet they were not entirely without wit, Marigold had to acknowledge. There was no doubt the twins had a robust aversion to being corrected and reprimanded. In spite of that, they had to consider that even with his position beneath them in the hierarchy, that Mackhol Taves was not a man to be considered lightly.

He was quite cunning, with an underplayed, yet frightful disregard for humanity. Those traits alone made him quite possibly the most dangerous man at the table. Even when taking Tryst Reine and his combat skills into account.

The Lord of Crime and Punishment wore a wicked grin as he sat back in his cushioned chair and eyed the boys down. It was hard to say what Mackhol's specific game was here. Barring some extraordinary circumstances, the Palomb boys were destined to rule above him, however far away that time might be. Their father was a seemingly healthy man barely into his sixties, and Grenjin Howland, despite long passing his seventieth year, was of sound body and mind. As long as he possessed both, the greedy old miser would never abdicate any measure of his power.

Mackhol, by contrast to his current overlord's, was just pressing into his fiftieth year. So long as his health held up without sudden any deviations, then he could have decades left as the Lord of Crime and Punishment and Minister of Biddenhurst. It stood to reason that this future would be under the authority of Eamon's sons. If Mackhol did have a play in action here, it was to ensure that both generations of Palomb regarded him as an irreplaceable branch on the hierarchal tree of Illiastra.

That is a game he can afford to play as a man. If only women were perceived to be so necessary I might have a horse in that race. Marigold knew that neither she nor any other woman warranted such and so Mackhol Taves and his kin could freely cast their barbs and insults at her without fear of repercussions. *He is free to make that folly. Let him make his japes, for they shall not be forgotten.*

From outside the dining hall came the loud heralding of a pair of trumpets, signalling that the Lord Master was at long last ready to make his own entrance. The band abruptly ceased their playing, allowing a breath of silence to wash over the gathered guests and members of the Elite Merchant Party.

The wide doors leading to the lobby swung open with a whoosh and the band broke into *Ode to the Master and Lord*. The anthem of Illiastra and the Howland family since Grenjin's father rose to power a century ago.

The first to appear was an old sot draped in garish robes of maroon with a white shawl fringed in gold upon his shoulders. A ridiculous conical crown of gold set with amethysts sat upon a head of vanishing white hair that belonged to His Most Piousness of the Triarchy: Great Father Marburry.

The rotund Great Father waddled into the hall, mumbling prayers beneath his breath while tossing white flower petals at his own feet in blessing. To either side of the Crown Prince of Piety were men in simpler robes of matching maroon. Their heads were shrouded in long hoods and their hands clasped together at chest height, hidden in long sleeves. Silver hilted broadswords in jewel encrusted scabbards lay across their wide backs and the two men towered above the old priest to protect him from harm unseen.

Marigold had to wonder why a man who so astutely believed his god would protect him needed armed strongmen on either side of him. The thought lingered only briefly before everyone stood in unison at the sight of Grenjin Howland.

The old Lord had donned a lavish three piece white suit with a deep blue shirt beneath it. Upon his shoulders rested a cape in matching blue and embroidered upon it was a magnificent, shimmering white dove. To his side, acting as a surrogate cane was his faithful steward Hossle.

The procession began to slow to a near halt as the Great Father had taken to blessing the guests who ventured to kneel in his path. Chief among those seeking Marburry's grace was Nathania Taves, inviting the doughy hands of the great father to be placed atop her head for a few mumbled words. It took the urging of the Lord Master himself to get the Great Father turned and moving in the direction of the dais once more.

Applause went up from the back of the hall as the hungry lesser ministers fought greedily for every scrap of attention the Lord Master threw at them. Those backbencher ministers disgusted Marigold to no end. They were all only too eager to grovel at Howland's feet and agree with every word that came through his lips. What sickened her even more was that some of those ministers were westerners. Those supposed loyalists of Marscal Tullivan that should have rose to defend the honour of his daughter when Pyore nearly sullied it now stood in feigned adoration of Grenjin Howland.

Howland merely waved at them with his wrinkled hands, yet the applause continued until all the guests, save for Tryst and Marigold were applauding. She decided it best to politely put her hands together softly for appearances sake. Tryst, however, stood rigid and unmoving from beside his chair as the entourage drew close.

Following the blade master's line of sight made Marigold realize he was studying the two men-at-arms beside the Great Father. Analysing their weapons, checking for signs of armour or other weapons beneath the spacious robes they wore. Most would say he was as paranoid as Grenjin, though this was a man trained to be in a constant state of preparedness. By his own convictions, Tryst could allow no less of himself. Those were the tenets of the Swordspeople of the University of Combative Arts in Drake, at least as far as Marigold was able to find in her research of them. As it was, Tryst was among an elite group of only five men over the course of a thousand years to be given the title of Master of Blades. It only stood to reason that he followed stringently to their methods.

It took Marburry quite some time to climb the four steps to the dais. Making Marigold wonder how he managed the many steps of Atrebell's tall and opulent Tower of Ios on a regular basis. As it was, the Great Father was only capable of conquering the few steps presently before him while having the two tall guardsmen holding either arm for support.

Following behind, Howland fared only marginally better. He had grown overly arthritic in his seventy eighth year and for all his wealth and authority, arthritis would not yield for even him. Yet by contrast, Howland was by far the more nimble of the two.

Once the stairs had been mastered, Grenjin walked around the table to shake hands with everyone but Tryst and Marigold. The former received a pat on the shoulder as Howland passed and Marigold was subjected to yet another kiss on the hand, much to her chagrin. For a moment the Lord Master lingered on Marigold, silently judging her revealing attire. It was plain to see that he wholly disapproved and seemed on the verge of saying something until Marburry spoke up loudly above all other voices.

"Good evening, ladies and gentlemen of the faith." Started the Great Father on the evening prayer from where he stood atop the dais overlooking the room. As feeble as he was on his feet, the Great Father had a powerful voice that reached into the far corners of the banquet hall with ease. "I am most delighted to gather here with such fine people on this wonderful evening of the sixty second day of autumn. Tonight we shall celebrate, feast and eventually toast what Lord Master Howland has told me was yet another productive session of our Parliament. Yet before we begin the feasting of twelve courses, allow me to lead you in a prayer." The old codger waited until the room had fallen silent, his own head bowing as low as the multiple chins would allow.

He put his hands above his head in a steeple and waited until the majority of the room were following his lead. "By the grace of Ios, our glorious god and unto Iia and Aren to form the merciful Triarch that grants us life." Marburry's hands went from the steeple position to draw out a wide triangle that met with his two upward facing palms joining below where the steeple was seconds ago. All but one at the head table had mimicked the movement, even Marigold out of habit more than anything. Beside her stood Tryst, head bowed and entirely unmoving as the lone holdout.

"We gather this evening, oh dear Ios, to give you thanks for the bounty we have before us," the high clergyman droned in a singsong voice. Heads were bowed across the hall as everyone repeated the words in unison in a low murmuring that soon collected into a wave of voices.

Thank the farmers for their vegetables, the butchers for preparing their meat and the fisherfolk for the bounty from the sea. It was they who did all the work. Marigold thought to herself. *Your god only seems capable of feeding the mouths that already have the coin to pay for it. Would not a god of love and mercy see to it that the hungriest mouths are fed first?*

More prayers were said in the monotonous chanting fashion by Great Father Marburry. Marigold had drifted away into her own thoughts, particularly the unusual company of Mackhol and Tryst to either side of her at the head table. Something surely was afoot to warrant the presence of them both. Tryst had never been asked to dine at the head table before and had always taken his meals from the solitary bench in the rear of the room.

Then there was Taves. Unlike Tryst, he had been guested at the Lord Master's table on occasion.

Marigold recalled one such time when Mackhol had been honoured with a guest place at the table. It was an end of session feast such as this one. The Lord of Crime and Punishment and Eamon Palomb had together hatched new legislation that allowed Biddenhurst to sell off their low-risk prisoners when housing within Biddenhurst threated on overcrowding. The right of first purchase would fall to the Department of Natural Resources, overseen by Eamon Palomb. This is turn allowed the lord to make a single, miniscule payment for shackled, browbeaten labourers to replace his workforce of men requiring a living wage.

The act was viewed by Mackhol Taves as his crowning achievement. In a single stroke, he had made himself a far wealthier man than his father or grandfather before him. He was bestowed with further reaching authority, greater respect and a tight bond with the top tier of the EMP who sought to purchase his human wares.

However, Marigold's father had surmised that it would open a floodgate. Ministers and unelected businessmen would all be seeking to achieve their own roster of slaves with none of the rights and wages and Lord Marscal had not been wrong.

Soon, to fill the requests for prisoners, Mackhol Taves was having legislation passed in the Parliament to increase the sentences for the most petty of crimes. Of course, his outside demeanour indicated it was to combat a rising crime rate. This crime rate, of course, was such a manufactured work of hyperbole and fiction that no one could believe it, yet it was brandied about as if it were fact. The truth of the matter was that it was all in the business of laundering free people into slavery without them realising what was occurring.

With it came a foreboding and unified sense of fear amongst some and outrage among those courageous enough to wield that emotion openly.

Fear was the greatest commodity of this Government. Marigold said to herself. *Hand in hand with it came a sense of isolation. As long as the populace was afraid of their governing body and felt alone against it, they would stay submissive and passive to its activities no matter how nefarious. However, in the face of such oppression there would always be resistance, whether from the outside, like that of Lady Orangecloak, or from within, like me.*

"Now, my friends," the Great Father said in conclusion of his prayers. "Reap the rewards of this holy bounty. Praise the Triarchy."

The simultaneous reprise of "Praise the Triarchy" shook Marigold from thought just as Marburry concluded the prayers.

The old priest waddled toward the Lord Master's table while the others sat down to discover there was no place set for him.

Before the robed one could ask, Lord Master Howland answered. "My apologies, Great Father Marburry, a sudden matter has arose that could not be delayed until after the feast and must be discussed during it. I have taken the liberty of sending Hossle to have a place of equal honour set for you and your guardsmen this evening." Lord Master Howland was courteous, but blunt on the matter, which struck Marigold as an ominous sign.

The Great Father indeed took it as a slight, though, and Marigold could feel his eyes gazing at her while Grenjin spoke. When the Lord Master had finished, the pious one jumped at his chance for rebuttal. "What matter could this be that would see my trust and counsel looked over in favour of a woman's?" he injected quickly and bitterly, catching everyone off guard. "A woman, I might add, who not only dresses in a provocative manner but shows no symbols of homage to Ios on her person?"

Marigold noticed that even Tryst seemed taken by the comment and had craned his head to look up at the smug high priest.

The mannerly decorum of the Lord Master emerged above all to field the questions. "Miss Tullivan is here in place of her father, Marscal, who I'm sure you're aware of is terribly ill and abed. I require her to be his ears this evening and to bring the tidings of this meeting to him, as my vaunted Warden Lord of the West."

Before the clergyman could object again, Lord Eamon spoke up to dispel both further protest and an encroaching incident. "I would be most honoured to host you at the Palomb table this evening, Great Father. My lady wife and children would ever so much enjoy your company." The Lord of the East turned to his dark haired son beside him before Marburry could raise objection. "Eldridge, do the honour of seeing Great Father Marburry to our table, and inform Steward Crendle that he is to see to the Great Father's needs as he would our own for the duration of the feast."

"Yes, Father, I will deliver your commands at once." Eldridge stood tall and bowed to Eamon, Grenjin, and Great Father alike, catching the urgency of the situation quite clearly. *At least he has that much tact,* Marigold thought while stealing a glance at Pyore to find him grinning like an idiot at her from across the table. That was until he noticed his father staring at him with dagger eyes, instantly wiping the smile from Pyore's face.

The guards of the Great Father seemed none too pleased to be called back to duty to practically carry the old sot down the four small steps again. As the priest completed his descent he was met by Eldridge, waiting to personally escort Marburry to his new place with Jorette and the younger siblings Nareen and Dorian.

Servants began to bring the first course just as Eldridge retook his seat: a hearty soup of carrot, turnip, potato, asparagus and beef in an onion broth.

The sound of spoons and bowls clattering and people chattering in low voices filled the hall and the head table became no exception. The conversation remained light, with all waiting on Grenjin himself to turn the discussion to more serious matters.

Marigold's thoughts went to her father lying in the soft bed of his quarters, likely huffing on his pipe and sipping the same soup she was drinking. It would be all he would suffer and the other eleven courses would be turned away at the door by Oire. They were turned away by Marigold as well. She ate only a few nibbles of thickly sliced ham cooked in pineapples from the southern continent of Johnah. Of the honeyed capon she took the smallest among them to taste and the same from a serving of fresh halibut from Daol Bay, one of her favourites. The remaining courses came and went with barely a second glance.

The eleventh and twelfth courses were desserts. The first was a slice of pie made of cream and coconuts harvested on the Garja Isles of the southern stretch of the Crescent Islands. After that came a hearty piece of trifle. A dish layered in fruits from all around the known world, thick custard, sponge cake, flavoured jelly and fresh cream.

When the pie plates cleared they were issued teacups that were then filled from hot carafes of bold coffee or pots of black tea.

The Lord Master turned to face his steward, presently sugaring Grenjin's tea. "Hossle, my guests and I all have matters of crucial importance to discuss, ensure that no one disturbs us or even has the potential to overhear us. Instruct the conductor of the orchestra to resume his playing at a modest level and order the guards to permit no one under any circumstances. All matters of triviality can be dealt with either by yourself or one of my city councilmen below the dais until we have concluded our meeting."

Without a word further, Hossle departed in haste to carry out his commands, leaving those at the table to their meeting.

Finally, Marigold thought to herself. *Get on with it.*

Howland sipped his tea gingerly, watching until he saw the Honourable Guardsmen put themselves directly before the bottom step of the dais before beginning. "Gentlemen and lady of the houses of Palomb and Tullivan, as you know, we have two special guests with us this evening. Both Lord Mackhol Taves and my personal bodyguard, Tryst Reine, were called to sup with us and with just cause. Prior to dinner I received news that was brought to my attention too late in the evening to delay the feast for a meeting in a more private setting. Considering that it is Lord Taves at the centre of this revelation, I shall let him be the one to deliver."

"Thank you, Lord Master Howland, it will be my pleasure," Mackhol said, leaning forward with his forearms resting on the table below tented fingers. "In my role as Lord of Crime and Punishment, I have direct participation in not only the incarceration of criminals, but in capturing them as well. It begs to reason that the most sought after criminals would then naturally be my main focus. As such, I am always collecting information that could lead to the apprehension of these criminals and following the most promising of these leads through one of my task forces."

After a sip of black coffee and a clearing of his throat, the lord of Crime and Punishment went on. "With all that being said, I recently came into information that proved to be most fruitful and it fell to me to act upon it hastily. Failure to do so would have doubtlessly cost me a small, yet golden window of opportunity that I wasn't like to see again. That is why I had to keep the Lord Master and his Lords of the East and West alike in darkness on the matter. There simply was no time to bring them into things without risking the information going stale and for that I apologise and beg forgiveness. I also judged it prudent that I not risk my information getting intercepted along the way, potentially compromising the investigation. However, I think my work may atone for my misdeed in maintaining silence.

"With the help of our most gracious Lord Master, I have used the walls of Atrebell as a hunter may use the iron jaws of a bear trap to apprehend the most sought after prey of them all: the one they call Lady Orangecloak." Taves sat back upon delivering the last sentence, watching the Palombs, Tryst and Marigold soak in the information with a satisfied smirk across his face.

Marigold felt goose bumps rising on her arms as Taves said the name of Orangecloak and she looked across the table to see how the others had reacted.

Pyore was openly snickering, though his brother and father to the right of him were sitting sternly, neither of them looking surprised at the information. "Well done, ser." Eamon spoke up first. "You will be receiving commendation for this work, I assure you."

"There is more, my lord," Mackhol intoned with great excitement. "A unit of my finest soldiers led an ambush last night in Argesse, half a day's ride south of here by horseback. In that ambush, dear Captain Hoyt of Biddenhurst lost his life. I am proud to report that his courageous sacrifice was not in vain, however, for we captured four of Orangecloak's lieutenants and a score more of her footpads. Currently, they have been consigned to the jail in Atrebell's southwest district to await transport to my prison."

The gentle creaking of Mackhol's chair became the only noise amongst them and Marigold felt a queer feeling settling in the pit of her stomach.

Of all people, it was Tryst who asked the first question. "Do you know which lieutenants of Lady Orangecloak's were apprehended?"

"Why yes, as a matter of fact, I do," Lord Taves gleefully answered. "It was none other than the Three Sisters and Pretty Lazlo. Fine catches, if I do so say."

"Did one among them slay your captain or was his end met some other way?" Tryst queried on further.

"From what I am told it was the one among the Sisters they call, with all pardons for the language, the 'Red Bitch'." His smile faded on cue at the mention of his deceased officer. "It would seem that the good captain was assisting his men in restraining the members of the Thieves when she snuck up on him, as cowards are wont to do. Before he could mount a fair fight, she put a spear through his throat.

"The captain's own steward, one Corporal Cornwall, reported to me with this information just prior to supper. He has taken command of the unit in his captain's death."

Eamon chimed in then with a question of his own. "How many casualties were taken from our side in the ambush?"

"I was told there were seven, besides the captain. Apparently the pretty man and the sister called, forgive my language once more, the 'Blonde Bitch' are responsible for most of that damage. You should know, however, that our eight took two of their men to the grave with them," Mackhol intoned proudly.

Marigold had heard of those lieutenants before. The ministers and soldiers alike had named the three female lieutenants of the Thieves 'The Three Sisters'. After the Thieves had taken to that nickname themselves, someone had coined the more disparaging name of the Three Bitches. Eventually, individual sobriquets came with the umbrella term. The Blonde Bitch, also known as the Big Bitch, was reputed to be a greatly muscled woman of unbelievable strength. The Red Bitch was so named for her head of red curls. Apparently, she was of an age and size comparable to Orangecloak and her hair allowed her to serve as a decoy for the leader of the Thieves on several occasions. The last of the Sisters was the leader of that pack and as such, she was called the Queen Bitch.

If they had real names they were not known to Marigold and she had only known the pejorative aliases for them.

Despite being women, the Three Sisters commanded a level of

precaution from city guards. Marigold had heard it said the three either worked side by side or in close cohesion with one another. It was known that if you spotted one leading a party of Thieves, the other two were sure to be in close enough proximity with forces of their own. That, combined with the stealth tactics employed by the Thieves, made them dangerous foes when provoked and nearly impossible to ambush without setting oneself up for the same.

Apparently this Captain Hoyt had learned of their ferocity with fatal consequence.

The Pretty Man was a different sort of story. It was believed among the more superstitious that he was a shapeshifter, capable of altering his form from man to woman at the snap of his fingers. The more obvious explanation was that Pretty Lazlo was an incredibly convincing transvestite. There were also rumours that he bedded both sexes and even had both sets of parts. With those rumours came all sorts of wild stories of sexual prowess and a tongue that could seduce man and woman alike. Regardless of how unbelievable they seemed, the rumours only added to his reputation as the handsome man as skilled under the covers as he was in battle.

Marigold became morose to hear that such courageous members of the Thieves were apprehended. At one time she had thought that an alliance with the Thieves might somehow be possible if she rebelled. Now though, it seemed like the clan of outlaws might be at the beginning of their own end.

It was Tryst who jumped in again with further questions. "This trap you spoke of, it leads me to believe the Lady Orangecloak is within the city walls or will be soon enough?"

Mackhol addressed everyone when he spoke and rarely made eye contact with Tryst, as if the sellsword was not the man conducting the bulk of the questioning. "Why yes, as a matter of fact. We received word from an informer inside the Thieves that she was planning a protest in conjunction with our autumn session. The goal was to have this demonstration emanate from an unspecified rooftop between the Roghen plaza in the south east district and the train station we would all be boarding from nearby. Our information indicates that Orangecloak is hiding in the Batterdowns neighbourhood in the South East tonight. Hopefully the news of her lieutenants being taken will not reach her as I would not want her to be dissuaded from her protest. Atrebell is a big city. She could hide here for a whole season without turning up."

"What were her four lieutenants doing in Argesse with a considerable unit, do you know?" Tryst relentlessly plied onward with his line of questions.

"I am glad you asked." Mackhol seemed to have rehearsed the answers to such questions in advance. "It seems my little mouse squeaks through both corners of their mouth and let it be known to the Thieves that I was aware of the location of their leader. In turn they launched a counter move to warn Orangecloak and have her abort the mission. The little mouse squeaked that to me as well when I squeezed it hard enough. Afterwards, I sent my problem solvers to prevent any further information from going the wrong way."

"That is great initiative, Lord Taves." Eamon complimented, sitting back in his chair to fold his hands over his globular belly. "You have performed service above and beyond the call of duty for Illiastra. I will be glad when these Thieves cease plaguing us."

"Ah, but I have not gotten to the plan for tomorrow yet." Mackhol put in.

"Then by all means, elaborate, Lord Taves." Grenjin gestured towards the Minister of Biddenhurst, who was all too happy to continue talking.

"With permission from Lord Master Howland, I shall position a line of guards in both the plaza and the train station. They will be placed inconspicuously before she emerges from hiding so that it merely appears that there is an increased patrol presence. To most, the reasoning for that would be the obvious fact of Parliament being concluded and the members and their families returning home together. Her staging point, we have been told, is likely to be one of three third storey balconies in the plaza. Once the Lady Orangecloak decides to reveal herself upon one of them and attempts to start her protest, our men will form up and surround her."

The lord waited a moment to let that much of his plan process in everyone's mind before continuing. "As you all may well know, Orangecloak's preferred method of escape from city guardsmen across the country is a mad dash along the rooftops. In this instance, seeing the guards filling the plaza, she will have to leave by going east or west to continue. East leads to Hardnell Street and it is a dead end from the roofs. She will have to descend into the street from there, where my own task force that apprehended her allies last night will be lying in wait."

"Where will her friends be during this?" Tryst asked bluntly.

Taves winced at that before turning to Tryst to give him answer. "They will still be safely under the guard of Major Burnson, who has retained my prisoners until such a time that I can personally retrieve them. Now th-"

"What reason did Major Burnson give to claim possession of prisoners arrested by soldiers not of his command?" Tryst curtly cut in, taking Mackhol back by the sheer abruptness of it.

"Um...Well you see, Mister Reine," Mackhol emphasised the word 'mister', reminding Tryst that he was without a formal title in Illiastra. "I was told by Corporal Cornwall that Major Burnson had some complaints about the condition of the prisoners. What that condition was I cannot say as the corporal claims Burnson did not give him any reason. I will be filing complaint against the Major before I leave, to be sure."

Tryst nodded slowly, considering what he had heard. "I see, do continue, Lord Taves. You have my apologies for rudely cutting in."

"I accept your apology, ser," the minister cordially said before clearing his throat to continue on. "As I was saying, my own guards will occupy Hardnell street in the west and-"

"You mean the east, Lord Taves," Eamon said, correcting his subordinate minister.

Taves laughed nervously at his blunder. "Ah yes, thank you, Lord Palomb, I did mean to say the east, yes. That is where my men will be. West of the train station and the plaza will be, should he choose to be involved, Mister Reine and a party comprised of the Honourable Guardsmen of his choosing. This unit will be capable of giving a rooftop pursuit. The guards from within the plaza then break into two groups that will follow her from streets north and south of the row of buildings. That will further force her into one of two traps lying in wait to the east or west." Mackhol leaned back smugly as he finished, having recovered from his earlier gaffe. "I am confident that barring anything sudden to the contrary, the plan should lead to a successful netting of the greatest menace that Illiastra has seen in living memory."

Eldridge nodded in agreement, adding his own opinion. "This has been quite some time coming and I must say I'm quite excited to see our work paying off."

That caught Marigold by surprise. "Pardon me," she found herself saying. "Did Minister Taves not just say he accomplished this with no assistance from anyone outside of his own service? Why would you say 'our' work just now?"

Eamon recoiled when she said that, furiously looking to Eldridge and confirming it was not merely a poor choice of words.

Mackhol Taves leaned forward once more and took the lead on answering. "Well, you see, Miss Tullivan, the Palombs, as my direct overlords, were aware of my initial investigation, but not my latest progress, I assure you."

She eyed him curiously. "But the Tullivans, Overlords of the West, were not informed?"

"Miss Tullivan, I ask you to watch your tone." Grenjin stared her down and spoke in a tone that begged caution. "You are here to observe for your father, not to speak."

Pyore spoke up from across the table to Grenjin. "I apologise for my betrothed, Lord Master. She is but a woman and prone to a reaction that is purely emotional." He then looked to Marigold before she could muster a response to that insult. "As your husband-to-be and the heir to the West, I acted on your father's behalf in the matter. You will raise your voice no more whilst men are talking, woman."

"You overstep your boundaries, Pyore," Marigold cut back sharply, her patience with him having long expired. "The West has not become yours to rule yet, for if I am not mistaken, we are not yet wed and my father still lives."

"For now, we all know he won't make it through the winter," Pyore replied bitingly.

"How dare you?" Marigold kept her voice down, though she was seething. "How dare you speak of my father in such a way?"

Pyore was incensed. "The more apt question is how dare you answer me back? This matter doesn't even concern you, Marigold. You're just a woman, weak and simple of mind."

"Pyore, enough!" Eamon cut in sharply, slamming a fist on the table that caught the attention of everyone in the hall.

Marigold stood from her seat. "This matter concerns me greatly, for not only am I the voice, eyes and ears of Marscal Tullivan, but the issue revolves around a fellow woman. A woman I might add, that despite a weak and simple mind, as you so put it, has become 'the greatest menace in living memory'," Marigold repeated Lord Taves quote with much added gusto, pressing both hands firmly upon the table as she leaned over toward Pyore.

She had quite enough of the Palombs, Taves and Howland all looking down their noses at her on this night. "Tell me, Pyore, how does a woman like Lady Orangecloak become such a threat to this government if we are but simple creatures that are incapable of harnessing our emotions?"

"Miss Tullivan." All eyes turned to face the Lord Master, his face showing signs of frustration. "I think you are quite tired and you have had quite a long day. You are dismissed from this meeting. I will have Hossle find an Honourable Guardsman and have him escort you to your room." Grenjin spoke to her dismissively as if she were but a child throwing a fit.

Marigold turned to face Howland, trying with all her might to bury her anger and disarm the situation. "With all due respect, Lord Master, I do not feel tired. If I may, I would like to apologise to you all and retake my seat, as soon as Pyore apologises for his remarks."

"I will accept those terms, but I warn you I will take no further outbursts from you." The old master was quickly growing tired of the bickering, Marigold realized. "You are only here because of your father and it is the respect and friendship I share with him that has kept you here despite your behaviour. You will conduct yourself in a manner that will do no further dishonour and require no subsequent reprimand from myself. Is that clear, Miss Tullivan?"

"It seems more than fair, Lord Master. I thank you for your kindness in allowing me to stay and will heed your commands going forward." Marigold cast her eyes downward, accepting the lecturing in light of the Lord Master's leniency in allowing her to stay. Marigold cleared her throat and turned back to the disgruntled son of Eamon Palomb. "Pyore, would you care to apologise for your remark and allow our meeting to proceed?"

The young man stood and leaned in her direction, teeth gritted and face turning a deep shade of red. "Aye, I shall apologise." Pyore said with fury in his voice. A flicker of dread went through Marigold and the last thing she remembered was catching a glimpse of an open right hand cocked back over Pyore's left side.

8

TRYST

It was pure instinct that drove me to stop Pyore. Tryst reflected to himself briefly as he escorted Marigold Tullivan to her quarters following the incident at the feast. *And it was a great deal of control that kept me from dragging him across the table and slamming him to the floor.*

Pyore had attempted to give Marigold a backhanded blow across the face while she leaned in his direction. Fortunately for her, Tryst had caught the boy's wrist as he lashed the hand outward. There was a brief moment when the eyes of Tryst and Pyore locked. Pure terror had streaked the lad's face, but he did not scream, not even then. It wasn't until Tryst released his grip did the blond haired Palomb twin even gasp.

Old Lord Palomb had lost his patience with his son's temper by then and ordered him confined to his room for the remainder of the evening. He had even gone so far as to summon his own steward to escort the lad and post their own guards at the doors to ensure compliance. Tryst had moved to apologise for his actions but Eamon had refused it, declaring that no apology was warranted for preventing his son from making a fool out of himself.

It felt as though the air was sucked from the room by then. The gathered guests had already gone quiet when Marigold and Pyore had begun yelling at one another and Tryst's act only served to stifle them further. Even Marigold was left speechless, her eyes wide as the realization of what had almost come to pass dawned on her.

Now there was only the sound of Tryst's sword slapping against his hip and the click of Marigold's high heeled shoes on the marble vestibule floor.

The sword was his Master's Blade, worn as requested by Lord Master Grenjin Howland. It was a single-edged sword, the blade a scant few centimetres or so shy of a meter in length and forged from pure Dwarven blacksteel.

A few guards remained at the key posts in the Lobby: two on either side of the doors leading to the dining hall, a pair more at the front entrance of the manor and another pair to either side of the steps. Presiding over the guards was Lieutenant Raspen, seated at the desk in the little office beside the front doors. He had been given command of the watch while Captain Barrid stuffed his fat face and attempted to feel important in the dining hall.

"Tryst, my Lady Marigold, is anything the matter?" Tryst knew the voice of Freyard Archer and looked to the top of the stairs to see the man leaning on the balustrade above.

"Aye, Frey, there is," Tryst called back as they climbed the wide steps to meet the soldier. He was bedecked in his Captain's uniform instead of the Honourable Guardsman attire he normally wore during the Parliamentary Sessions.

"I noticed young Lord Pyore being escorted past me earlier. He seems to be confined to his room with his own house guards at the door. Now I see you're taking Miss Tullivan to her quarters as well and just as the band is about ready to switch to the dancing songs. I say, Tryst, what is going on?" Freyard asked, entirely nonplussed.

"Much and more, my good man, walk with us, for I have need of you," Tryst replied as he and Marigold made for the high ceilinged hallway. Freyard fell in behind them and the three quickly strode to the room.

As Freyard claimed, there were the Hercalest guards in their shining silver coats. One paced angrily while a pair more stood rigidly at attention in front of Pyore and Eldridge's quarters. Tryst noted that the pacing guard was Geddrick Palomb, cousin of the ruling Palombs and the same fellow who made the arrest of the Elf at the tavern earlier. Further down at the near end of the long hallway were a pair of men clad in the teal jackets of the Tullivan's house guard, manning the entrance to Marscal's residence.

From between her bosoms, Marigold produced a brass key to unlock the door. The lock clicked and Marigold was about to take the knob to hand when Tryst gently pushed past her. "What's the matter?" she asked as Tryst entered the darkened room himself, left hand going to the hilt of the sword on his right hip.

Once inside Tryst flipped the switch to illuminate the room. He scanned behind the main door, into the closet, under the bed and the hall outside the servant door before permitting Marigold to enter.

"What was the need for that?" she inquired while stepping through the threshold.

"A force of habit, but a good precautionary measure nonetheless," Tryst answered her before looking to his friend. "Freyard, would you do me the favour of guarding the main door? See to it that we're not disturbed and notify me if any of the Palombs or their people comes through."

"Certainly, though it will cost you a tankard of ale when next I am in town," Freyard answered with a thin smile crossing his lips.

"You have yourself a deal, ser," Tryst replied back as Freyard returned to the hallway, closing the door behind him to leave Tryst and Marigold alone.

Plopping down before the makeup table, Marigold buried her face in her hands.

There was much Tryst wanted to say, though he had no idea of where to start.

"That damn Pyore made a fool of me," Marigold began, saving Tryst from having to do as much himself. "He goaded me into yelling at him, Tryst. From the moment he heard that I sat for my father today in Parliament, Pyore made it his goal to ruin any measure of respect I may have earned." She began to tear up as she talked. "And the damn fool I am, I let him."

"I don't think you are a fool, my lady," Tryst answered, unsure of what else to say. "I witnessed how he treated you from the moment you both walked into the ballroom and I thought it was absolutely degrading." The dark makeup beneath Marigold's eyes was beginning to smear as she gazed up at him again while he stopped to clear his throat. "I also think you handled yourself gracefully for as long as you could, given that he insulted your ailing father."

"First, he tried to sit me below the Master table and he wore my family colours like we're already married." Despite the tears welling in Marigold's eyes, they shone with defiance and rage as she spoke. "Then he tried to scold and reprimand me in front of everyone like I was a misbehaved child."

"Even the Lord Master was appalled by Pyore's behaviour," Tryst said by way of consolation. "From my experience as a fly on the wall of political forums, I can say that this will reflect far worse on the Palombs than it will you."

"What reason do you have to believe that, Tryst?" she asked him morosely.

"Pyore was the instigator," Tryst explained with an easy shrug. "Howland will know come morning of what occurred before he arrived. For if no one else, I will tell him as much when asked. There is *nothing* the old Master hates more than someone knowingly causing such drama. It draws too much attention."

Marigold dropped her gaze to the floor. "It's not him I'm completely worried about, Tryst. If it came down to my ability to rally allies to my side, Grenjin Howland, if he wasn't dead and gone by then, would never be counted among them. It is the other lords and the ministers who need to see a strong, firm-handed leader in me. Not some fool of a woman being played like a violin by Pyore Palomb."

"There is truth in that," Tryst nodded in agreement. "Though Lord Howland may live with sound mind for decades more yet. He is in his seventh decade and riddled with arthritis, granted, but he is otherwise healthy. By the time you have to concern yourself with power, this indecency may be long forgotten."

"It is you who forgets, Tryst," she said with a sigh. "I am to be married to Pyore Palomb after his eighteenth birthday. Believe me when I say this: when my father is gone, they will come for me then. I cannot wait decades or even years for Grenjin Howland to keel over. I have to make a new marriage for myself before then or lose all my entitlement and wealth to Pyore."

"And you want this marriage to be to me," Tryst said, aware that he was perhaps a little blunt in his delivery.

"When you caught Pyore's wrist, did you not see the sheer terror on his face?" The corner of Marigold's mouth turned upwards as she reminded him. "If you held it a moment longer, I'm convinced the wretch would have soiled his trousers. Money is not the only key to the door of power. Strength is too and that is what you have, Tryst Reine. A young man who usually thinks himself invincible became aware of his own mortality because of your simple action. If I married you, do you think either of those Palombs would dare raise a hand to me again?"

Tryst resigned himself to the edge of her bed, to look her right in the eyes when he spoke. "Grenjin Howland might raise an army to your door, one that's short of only a few western ministers and their standing forces. Warships from Aquas Bay would be sent north to neutralise everything south of Daol Bay. Men bearing the colours of Palomb and Taves and the other ministers of the east will swarm over your walls like locusts and break down your doors.

"I could take a dozen to the dirt with me, perhaps more if I had your best swords and rifles at my side. Eventually though, I would die trying to stop the inevitable wave of humanity while our little lordling Pyore would be safely stationed in the rear of the assault. Then you would be wed to him, by force if needed, with some Patriarch of the Triarchy spewing words from his pious lips.

"By the end of it, you would be at Pyore's mercy while my rotting corpse is swaying in a gibbet for the entertainment of the crows and seagulls."

"What are you saying, Tryst?" Her gaze was hard as stone, "You are the fucking Master of Blades! There is supposed to be no man alive who can best you in combat."

"What I am saying is that I am just *one* man," he said doubtfully. "Am I proficient with a sword? Yes, I admit. Yet what is one man with a sword to an army? I am the low born son of a leather tailor from the town of Berris in the Gildriad Midlands. I hold no lands or manors or armies of my own, and my only strength is at the end of a piece of sharp steel. I may make a few men cower in fear of the sword, but a herd armed with rifles and bayonets would trample me."

"You would have my army, Tryst. You would be my husband to rule beside me." Marigold stood to face him as she spoke, her green eyes red from the tears. It was hard to refuse them, just as he could not deny Marigold's hands when they took one of his to hold. "It wouldn't be I commanding you, or you commanding me, it would be an equal partnership."

"A partnership…" Tryst let the words tumble from his lips as he felt her roaming through his mind with her piercing stare. She walked through the defensive walls he had spent years building as if she were a ghost, unbound by the constructs of mortal people. But he had to drive her out, for this was madness she spoke of. "What you would ask of me is to walk hand in hand with you through a nightmarish, political labyrinth. While I have no doubt that you could navigate that path, I am not who you need at your side when you decide to take that first step."

The frustration crept back into Marigold's voice at that. "You are the Master of Blades. Who better to stand with me? I will shine the light to carry us both through the maze. All you need to do is protect me, so that the light is not extinguished."

Tryst shook his head softly, denying her once more. "I am the Master of Blades, aye, though the only thing that title means, as grandiose as it sounds, is that I am an exceptionally capable sellsword. Not to mention the fact that my reputation is mired in the eyes of the public, the very public you need to back your claim to power. If you married me and foisted me upon the people, are you any better than those already in power?"

"It would only be temporary," Marigold countered with hope in her voice. "Once the EMP is overthrown, we ensure that the people have a voice and a vote in how this country is run. Marry me now and once our revolution is through, I know the people will come to respect and admire you as I do."

As much as Tryst would have like to believe her words, his good sense continued to thwart him. "That is a grim request, Marigold. A marriage should be a union of love between two adults, not a partnership to be consummated with war."

Marigold smiled at him sadly and reached up to brush away a red strand of hair from his face, leaving her hand upon his cheek to rest. "That too would be temporary, Tryst. I may have ulterior motives for our union, yes, but as I have said before, I do like you a great deal."

"I sincerely believe you do, Marigold," Tryst added with a sigh when her other hand joined the first in caressing his face.

She shrugged and began snaking her hands down Tryst's neck until they came to rest on his chest. "Then join me, Tryst Reine, for I am quite nearly out of time. If we do not strike now and stake our claim while the sun shines, we will be forever lost in the darkness."

"You have thought long about this, haven't you?" Tryst gingerly put his free hand to the small of her back that the dress left exposed. As he embraced her slender frame, Tryst saw a smile work its way across Marigold's face.

"I have," Marigold spoke singingly into his ear. "Almost as long as I've thought of you to be the one I share my life and legacy with."

Marigold drew his face down and caressed his lips with her own, slowly and sensually. With his will to resist entirely sapped, Tryst returned the favour and their tongues entwined as one.

"Ser and my Lady," Freyard called from without, interrupting before things could progress further. "I don't mean to disturb you, but there's a great commotion in the lobby. There's considerable shouting and I hear a woman in distress among them. I believe you'll be needed, Tryst."

"Fuck this night, at any rate," Tryst grumbled lowly before replying to his friend. "Yes Frey, give me a moment and I'll be right with you. In the meantime, take a gander and see what this disturbance is about."

With a groan, Marigold broke away from Tryst and sat upon the bed. "Will you return to me before the dawn comes?"

"I cannot say, my dear," Tryst lamented. "I do not know what awaits me at the bottom of those stairs."

"Forget the world outside the door for a night and stay with me," she all but begged in a longing voice. "There are a few hundred guards crawling about the manor and that fat fop Captain Barrid to tell them what to do. Let them handle this disturbance."

Tryst replied pointedly, "And risk us being found together when Grenjin Howland sends for me? No, I'll go do what's asked of me and with any fortune I'll be back before you know it."

"I shall be waiting," she said with a coy wink that Tryst reciprocated before going out into the dimly lit lobby.

Outside the room, Tryst found that the hallway's occupants, save for the guards at Marscal Tullivan's door, had gone to the balustrade to look at the lobby below. From within the dining hall Tryst could still hear the band playing. *Good,* he thought. *Whatever is going on out here may go unnoticed by the folks inside.*

Tryst estimated it to be some dust up between lesser ministers or their offspring, drunk and full of vigour. If so, he would quickly have them escorted from the manor for the night and be done with it.

The look on Freyard's face when he met the man near the stairway told Tryst that this was no mere scuffle between little lordlings. "Tryst, this is dire," he managed to say before a woman's muffled groans and the rattle of chains on the ceramic tiled floor rang through the halls. Tryst hurried to the railing to survey the scene without further comment, unsure of what he would find.

In the foyer below were a score of Manor Guards, led by Lieutenant Raspen standing in a semi-circle around a trio of men and a captive woman. One of the three recent arrivals had an arm across the woman's throat and shackled, pale white hands clasped the sleeve of the arm that held her in place. The captor's other hand clutched an expensive pistol pressed tight against the woman's temple.

The man holding the captive was a familiar character to Tryst. A bounty hunter by the name of Fletchard Miller, who was infamous for harassing the fugitives and immigrants that attempted to make use of Illiastra's port cities. A sinister reputation followed him, one earned by putting to use a deadly and extensive set of skills he had learned as a former Knight of Southern Gildriad. The revered bounty hunter now stood before them clad in brown leather boots, a suit of deep blue woollen trousers, a padded doublet and a shining steel cuirass above all. Atop Fletchard's head was a tightly cut flat of hair that looked coal black in the light of the dimmed lanterns with a well-kempt, matching beard on his face. The most distinguishing trait of all though was a thick leather patch that covered his left eye.

The man's compatriots by comparison were bedraggled louts, clad in cloaks of grey that may have been black at one time with torn and filthy tunics beneath. One was thinner than the other, with a mop of dirty, blond curls and a slack jawed face. The defining traits of the other man were a potbelly and a ragged beard that encircled his throat beneath a horseshoe of equally ragged brown hair.

A cloying stench of rum and sweat struck Tryst as he reached the scene, an odour Tryst traced to the flunkies of the bounty hunter.

It was the stout one of them garnering the attention as he waved around a rust-speckled pistol over his head and demanded payment for the bounty.

Raspen was bargaining with them to release the woman to his custody and in return the hunters would be compensated fully. However, the drunken sot was having none of it, repeating his demand to have the money in hand before releasing the woman.

Only one of the honourable guards remained at the doors to the dining hall. The other was no doubt gone to inform the Lord Master of what was occurring in the lobby. The guard left to hold the door had a hand on the hilt of his still sheathed, gold hilted sword.

If these men were pats of butter you might have a chance of cutting through them with that, Tryst thought sarcastically to himself.

As Tryst reached the floor, he realised that he had spent so much time analysing the armed men in the room that he had quite nearly overlooked the chained woman. She was thin, Tryst noticed as he joined the guards, with a head of long, damp, red hair that fell over her face and hid her features from view.

The woman was fair skinned, almost as white as snow from what was exposed of it and dressed in dark green leather trousers, matching jacket and boots of brown doeskin. It was elven-made clothing, finely tailored with impeccable stitching, though it showed signs of wear. Beneath the open jacket she wore a sodden, long sleeved tunic of white linen and a bodice of a similar green to the leathers. Its laces hung loose, though its make indicated it was a garment specifically made for her slim frame.

Her captors had taken all sorts of precautions in securing their bounty. Heavy shackles were locked on her wrists and ankles, with barely enough chain between her feet to allow even a hobbled shuffle, if she were allowed to move at all. The thick cuffs on her wrists were closely joined and bound to her leg irons with an even heavier chain. That thick string of rusting iron links no doubt made lifting her arms a difficult ordeal after a time. Hobbled hand to foot like that, Tryst was amazed that the prisoner had any strength left in her.

The longer Tryst gazed upon the red haired woman, the more he sensed a familiarity about her. Tryst had a suspicion of who she might be, but couldn't say with any certainty.

"Fellows, what seems to be the trouble here?" Tryst asked calmly when Potbelly stopped for a breath.

"This doesn't concern you, servant, piss off," Potbelly pointed his gun at Tryst, who ensured he gave no flinch.

Fletchard Miller cleared his throat audibly and beckoned the scruffy haired fellow to his side to whisper in his ear. "Boss says that fella there is Tryst Reine, Monty. That's the Monster of Blades," He said to potbelly fearfully.

"*Master* of Blades, if it pleases you," Tryst proclaimed. "I am the sworn protector of the Lord Master and the shield over his home. I demand to know your business here at once."

"We came to collect a bounty on this here lass. But this bloke's not so obliging to our demands." Potbelly thrust one of his stubby fingers in Raspen's direction as he spoke.

"I see. Just who is 'this lass' that you three feel the need to barge in on the Grand Parliamentary Feast to present?" Tryst asked as he looked over the three men cautiously. "Is she another member of the Thieves that the Biddenhurst men were seeking? There's a fierce bounty on all their heads, but nothing that couldn't have been taken care of at one of the city jails, or even at our front gate."

A tense silence underlined by the music of the orchestra within the banquet hall fell over them as the trio looked for one among them to answer the question.

Tryst craned his head upward to glance at Freyard, finding Marigold beside him and leaning on the balustrade on the second floor. The look on Freyard's face was one of grave concern as he met Tryst's eyes briefly and swallowed hard.

He knows who she is and he's quite sure of it, Tryst surmised before his attention returned to the bounty hunter and the unkempt men, both of which were now brandishing their pistols.

The scruffier one had a dinted knife stuck into the belt of his tunic as well, but otherwise they were lightly armed and entirely unarmoured. Apart from the gun already pointed at the prisoner's temple, Miller had that piece's twin holstered on his right hip, loaded, in all likelihood. Tryst also noted a rapier with a tooled leather grip and a narrow crossguard on a steel hilt beside the empty holster on his left hip. *Four shots between them and if the drunkards could hit the wall it would still be a fluke shot.* Tryst surveyed in his mind. *Miller's a problem though. If he doesn't shoot her, he could kill two guards in short order and cut a few to ribbons before I could even get to him.*

"Do you want to know who she is?" the scruffy fellow said while reaching a hand into an old, worn out satchel that was slung over his shoulder.

Raspen's guards drew back the hammer of their pistols as a precaution, raising them to eye level and drawing a bead on the drunk with the bag. "Easy now, lads." Lieutenant Raspen urged. "We will all stay calm and let this man slowly show us what he has in that satchel."

From the bag, the man with the wild mop of curls produced a folded square of cloth that looked at first like it might be a blanket. In the low lights it was hard to determine what it was until he held it at arm's length. "This is who she is," he said, letting it unfurl in his grasp before throwing it in Tryst's direction to pool on the floor.

It was an old, faded, peach coloured cloak. An embroidered, forest green shield with a bright, golden triangular shaped knotwork embroidered upon it.

No, not peach, orange, Tryst realised as he neared the cloak. At first, he did not believe what he was looking at to be real. For some time he had dreamt of the day when he might finally meet the woman who owned that cloak. *This could well be a forgery,* Tryst warned himself. *She matches the description and what I remember of her. Although without being able to see her eyes to confirm they are her rare shade of blue, I cannot be wholly certain.*

He knelt, gaze unwavering from the three armed men as he took the cloak in hand and stood again, clutching it tightly in his upturned fist.

It was thicker than he had thought it might be, with a sheep wool lining stitched into the fabric. Good enough for dry autumn weather, but still light and threadbare to make it useless come winter or a wet spring.

All the eyes of the room were upon on Tryst at that moment and he turned his head to meet them. He looked from Freyard and Marigold standing above to Raspen near at hand and finally coming to rest on the chained woman, her face still hidden behind the red hair.

Before Tryst could utter a word about the cloak, the doors of the hall swung open.

Leaning on Hossle and flanked by the honourable guards that had been in the dining hall was the Lord Master himself. Mackhol Taves, Eamon Palomb and his son Eldridge followed directly behind in his shadow.

Leading the wealthy throng that walked behind the men from the head table was none other than Captain Barrid. The robust officer made no attempt to usurp Raspen's authority on the matter, staying wide eyed and silent.

The brightness from within the hall bathed the bounty hunter and his female quarry in light. For the first time Tryst saw eyes of the most beautiful shade of blue he had ever seen staring back at him from behind strands of red hair.

It's her, I'm certain beyond doubt, Tryst said to himself as his heart all but leapt from his chest. *There is no fear in those eyes, nor defeat, just defiance and a glimmer of hope.*

Tryst made a move to speak as Grenjin Howland moved into

the room slowly, but the old Lord found words first.

"What in the name of Ios is going on in my lobby?" The Lord Master's voice was coarse, but it still bore considerable power when it needed to.

"Ser, the bounty hunter Fletchard Miller and his accomplices claim they have brought us Lady Orangecloak," Tryst answered, finally saying her name as he held the cloak out for Grenjin to see with his own two eyes.

"So it would seem." Howland didn't sound convinced, nor would he touch the tattered thing in Tryst's fist. "What evidence besides a ratty old cloak and a mop of red hair do you have to say that she is the delinquent known as Orangecloak?" The way he said her name echoed of revulsion and contempt and he would not grant her the decency of calling her 'Lady'.

Fletchard made a 'pssst' noise at Potbelly who stepped back to have his ear whispered in. "Boss says for me to tell you that we found the cloak on her when we took her in the old tunnels under the Batterdowns," the frumpy man answered as he stepped back to where he had been standing. "She had two men with her, bodyguards, like as not. We killed them."

There was a disgruntled moan from the bounty hunter, yet he made no move to speak for himself. Which struck Tryst as odd, but there was little time to dwell on it.

"Killed two men beneath the Batterdowns, is that the right of it?" the Lord Master said mockingly. He was still moving forward, albeit at a snail's pace, towards Fletchard and the woman. "It occurs to me that the one called Orangecloak keeps another red haired woman of similar appearance within high rank in her company." He stopped and turned back to his Lord of Crime and Punishment. "Lord Taves, what do they call that one?"

"That would be the 'Red Bitch', my lord, one of the 'Thee Bitches'," Mackhol answered diligently, catching on to the Lord Master's game. It was known to Tryst, Taves, the Palombs and Marigold that the Three Sisters were all locked up in the City Jail in the South West district. Whether these three and their captive knew that was yet to be seen.

"Yes, the 'Red Bitch'," Grenjin Howland said ponderously. "How am I to know that she is not who I look upon now? To be certain she is *a* red bitch, but is she *the* Red Bitch? Might be that she's some other member of the Thieves. Or is she even a member of the Thieves at all? Perhaps she's just some red haired prostitute who was pleasuring two men at once in a hole under the Batterdowns. What is there to say any different besides some orange rag you found on her person?"

"No, it's her! We're certain, milord. It has to be her," Potbelly spoke back to the Lord Master, his voice quaking with terror as Grenjin stepped up beside them.

Lord Master Howland turned his head sharply to let the drunkard feel his piercing, menacing gaze. "You *believe* she is Orangecloak, she doesn't have to *be* Orangecloak," Howland finally spoke straight to the man before leaving him to his trembling.

With surprising haste, the old man closed the gap between himself and the hunter still steadfastly clutching his bounty. "Tell me, Fletchard Miller, do you want to collect your bounty?" Grenjin asked when he was a mere meter from hunter and prey.

Fletchard swallowed hard, but did not dare to answer.

"You need only say 'yes' but I have to hear it from your lips," the Lord Master insisted.

"Y-Yes, he does m-m-m-milord. We wants the bounty on her head." Scruffy stammered, trying to answer for his employer. "H-h-he can't speak so well in front of lotsa people but –"

"Silence, you fool! I was not addressing you!" Grenjin shouted, giving the scruffy lad a taste of his stare as well.

The sudden shout made Scruffy drop his pistol in recoil, where it clattered to the marble floor. He was about to pick it back up but thought better of it and stayed still.

The head of the Lord Master swivelled back like an owl's to the bounty hunter. "Say it, Miller," he uttered through gritted teeth.

"Yes, my lord," the hunter said, barely above whisper. Tryst could see the sweat beading on Miller's forehead as he said the three words. It was no easy feat for Fletchard, but this was not a man to balk, no matter how much it pained him.

"That's all you had to say," the Lord Master said softly in a condescending voice before letting his glare fall to the lady in chains. "My men will take your prisoner to question her for themselves tonight. One way or another we will discover the truth of her identity, Orangecloak or no." He gestured toward Tryst in saying as much. The lie of the terrible monster Howland presented Tryst as coming back to haunt him once more.

The old man went on. "The guardsmen here will show you to the stables, in the meantime. The long one at the rear gate of the manor will do. We will have your mounts brought there as well and I shall have my steward see to it that the lot of you are fed. You may stay there and lodge in the spacious loft above the stable until we bring you word of our findings."

While Grenjin Howland spoke, Tryst's eyes were on the Lady's. When they met, the enrapturing blues hit him like a cannon blast. She knew what was waiting for her, and despite the look of desperation, there was no fear. Regardless of his Lord Master's playing at doubt, there was none in Tryst. This was indeed the same woman he spotted standing atop a low roof in Aquas Bay in the late summer. With the full light of the sun gleaming through her fiery locks and the wind making hair and cloak alike blow as wild as her heart. There was not a shadow of a doubt that this was Lady Orangecloak before him.

Fletchard hesitated, his breathing heavy and his grip on Lady Orangecloak tightening. Suddenly he exhaled. "Very well," he uttered meekly in defeat, lowering his pistol from the Lady's temple. He looked despondent, though there was little other option but to take the sole offer given to him.

"Lieutenant Raspen, take the prisoner and show her to the basement suites," the Lord Master began to command, his own tone softening slightly. "Mister Reine, wake the keeper of the vault. Inform him I'll have fifty thousand in gold counted up and boxed in the event that this woman should turn out to be who they say she is. Until such time comes, her and these men alike are in your charge."

"Understood, ser," Tryst replied back.

The dark haired, thick set, moustachioed Lieutenant holstered his pistol and stepped forward to collect the prisoner. After gesturing to the guard to either side of him to follow suit, Raspen took hold of the heavy chain linking the irons on the wrists and feet of Orangecloak.

Reluctantly, Fletchard released his arm from around her throat. At first it seemed the reluctance was his and it was then Tryst noticed it was in fact the lady who clung to the bounty hunter's arm.

The guards plucked Lady Orangecloak away from the bounty hunter in unison, eliciting a mighty rattle from her chains.

Tryst turned to walk away, feeling the stares of dozens of eyes upon his back as he walked beneath the marble staircase, still clutching the orange cloak.

The deep voice of Raspen bounced off the walls and to Tryst's hearing. "I require your keys, Mister Miller. I shall have Mister Reine return them with your shackles before you leave."

It was only a short while later that Tryst was back in his room at the end of the first floor hall, situated privately and cosily above the old armoury. The fine clothes he had worn at the party were neatly folded on his bed. In their place were his riding leathers, a cotton tunic that laced from chest to neck and a thick, warm, padded doublet, all of it in black. The trousers were tucked into a well-worn pair of leather boots in the same dark hue as the rest of his ensemble.

A million thoughts were running through his head at that moment and he had seated himself at the creaky table in the centre of his room to mull them over. His sword and its cleaning tools, along with a bottle of his favourite rum, a dark mix from Johnah called *Spiced Night,* rested before him.

Hossle had arrived and departed just moments before, bringing a written list of true orders from Grenjin Howland. The first order was that the three men were not leaving alive. Tryst was certainly in charge of them, but it was only to ensure they died. The second order was that old man Buchlan, the banker who tended the vault across the hall from the armoury, was not to be disturbed at all. There would be no reward going to Fletchard Miller and his employees. The third order stated that Tryst was to dispatch of the three hunters quietly, quickly and without trace. This was all anticipated by Tryst, having read that much between the lines when Howland was talking to the bounty hunter in the lobby.

There were orders pertaining to Lady Orangecloak as well, namely to get a complete list of names and the whereabouts of all her associates. From there he was to coax her into making false confessions for all sorts of heinous crimes. Some of which Tryst knew to have been committed by people in the fold of the EMP. There were letters he was to get her to write to the Ruins of Phaleayna, where the Thieves primarily resided. These letters would contain orders for the remaining Thieves to disband and for the impoverished people hiding in the ruins of Phaleayna to bow to Illiastran law and authority.

Not one word of any of these orders meant anything to Tryst any longer. These walls, the ministers, councilmen and the other schemers within, not one bit of it mattered now. Tryst knew that he was sitting squarely in his past. His present was locked in a cell in the dungeon, and the future lay somewhere out beyond the walls of Atrebell and the Manor.

This was never my home. It was a comfortable place to rest my head for a little while, nothing more.

His mind fluttered back to the quarters of the Chancellor of the University, nestled in the thick, brick and mortar walls that were built into the mountains of Drake. His lone peer, Myolas, also a Master of Blades, was at his side, their meagre things slung over their backs in heavy canvas satchels. They had come to bid their farewells before departing to the docks for their new lives.

"The Master of Blades is a heavy name to wear," the pale skinned, white haired, Drakian chancellor of the university said while sitting cross legged on a large, round, cushioned chair. "The title will swallow whole the lives and names you had before and soon it will be the only thing you know."

Tryst and Myolas had both reached that rank and were the only two Masters to ever live in the same lifetime. The pair stood proudly before the chancellor in new clothes they had bought for just the occasion from Fuwachita City, nestled at the base of the mountain. They were ready for the world, or so they had both thought, as they listened diligently to the seasoned mercenary dole out advice.

Of the great deal of wisdom the old fellow had shared, there was one thing that stood out poignantly to Tryst now: "You will walk this world looking for the homes you lost," the Chancellor had said with a longing sadness in his voice. "If you live to see the day that you are too old to swing your sword, you will find that home and discover it is not the one you had left. For Masters such as you are, this truth is even more so."

It was time to walk out of the past now, Tryst knew. This was not his home, it never had been. His search must yet go on. Taking the sword and sheath from the table, Tryst stood up. The blackened steel blade glistened in the lamp light of the room. It was freshly oiled and sharpened per his nightly routine and looked pristine. The sheath was boiled leather drawn taught over ash, bound with steel rings of enamelled black on top and bottom. A silhouette of the Drakian mountain range was pressed into its leathering, running the length of the scabbard. The stamping had been painted black, with one peak painted silver to mark Fuwachita Mountain, standing alone with its stone arms cradling the University of The Combative Arts.

The blade slid soundlessly into the sheath against the oily wool lining as he brought them together.

Tryst belted the sword onto his waist, took a deep breath and began the process of donning his other weapons and gathering his things. It was before his closet beside the door to his apartment that he began, taking his bag of toiletries and folding and stacking more black clothing and undergarments. After laying everything neatly on the table, he went beneath his bed and dug out the grey canvas satchel that he had arrived with in Illiastra.

While there he reached into a nook in the bedframe and came away with a wooden box he had hidden there long ago. The box was a finely crafted piece made of ebony wood, with a pair of hinges and a key lock hasp of matching gold plate. Tryst fished his small ring of keys from the pocket of his breeches and opened the wooden container. The interior was a soft, satin bed of violet and resting comfortably upon that was a fearsome mask. An old face in shining steel plate and black enamel from the past stared back, one Tryst hadn't seen in quite some time.

It was a traditional piece of equipment that had its origins several centuries ago with Tallen, the second man to earn the title of Master of Blades. Since then, with only one other Master emerging between Tallen and Tryst's time, the Mask of the Night was handed down to those who could obtain the rank of Expert.

Tryst recalled earning his to be as momentous an occasion as receiving his first true blades. Only his Master's sword, sitting nearby on the table, meant more to him as a possession. The plain face had one adornment: a single slash from the left eye that extended across the nose and halfway through the right cheek. The slash exposed the shining steel plate below and had been made by Tryst himself, just as every Expert before him had done. To the novices it seemed like the purpose of slashing was to mark the mask as their own, but that was only partly true. There was great symbolism behind the student wielding their chosen blade and taking it to the one piece of armour the instructors gifted to them. The shining steel was a scar, to show them that even with their skills that they were human, prone to mistakes and as able to bleed as anyone.

That lesson was one that Tryst dwelled upon every time he looked upon the piece of steel that had been moulded to the outline of his face from chin to forehead.

Eyeholes and a small hole beneath the nose to allow air through were the only gaps in the otherwise flawless mask. Thick leather straps that webbed into a cap held it in place over the head with a single strap running under the ears to keep it tight against the face. Tryst lifted it from its case, feeling the weight of it in his hand for the first time in many years. It too would be leaving with him and he ran the chin strap through his belt, letting it sit just below the kidney so it would be hidden by his cloak.

He next chose two of his heavy cloaks to take with him. The first was lined with the wool of a black sheep, which made it an expensive and rare garment alone. Its outer shell was the pelt of a black bear with high, padded shoulders that had an extra layer of fur atop it and the hood alike. A clasp dangled from one shoulder made of steel that was shaped like a bear paw and inlaid with tiny blue sapphires for the colour of the Elite Merchant Party.

That set of cloak and clasp had been gifted to him by the Lord Master himself during his first Feast of the Winter King. A festival steeped in tradition and superstition and celebrated by the followers of the Triarchy. The cloak was a size too small, a little short on Tryst to really be called a true cloak, but he had accepted the gift graciously anyway. *Now I finally have a use for it.* Tryst said to himself, holding the garment open for inspection with both hands before folding it on the table with the rest of his clothes.

His second choice was a better fit and he immediately slung the piece of outwear over his back, closing it with a silver and onyx Paladins shield clasp. The black fabric almost seemed to faintly shimmer in the light of the room and was lighter than the other cloak, despite the fact that it was longer. Unlike the first, which was made entirely of a fur pelt, this one was only trimmed with the natural dark brown fur of the wolves of the Elven Forest.

There was a third cloak to take, one that he had laid out on his bed and stared at for what seemed like several hours. That one too was folded and laid atop the bear hide cloak.

With all his clothes gathered, Tryst began to fill the canvas bag until it was half full, leaving it to sit on the table while he went to the weapons cabinet.

The first thing he reached for were the two slender elf blades. They were exactly thirty five centimetres in length, bound in black leather on the hilt and absent of a hand guard. Tryst took them down in hand by the pair of leather straps on either sheath and buckled them to his thighs. A fine yew bow hung above all on a leathern sash with a quiver of arrows lashed in between the curves of the bow.

Tryst had admittedly never been the greatest archer, but was proficient enough to make do and that too he took, slinging it atop the heavy cloak for easy access.

Behind the weapons rested a purple, velvet bag, heavy and bulging. What was inside was of great importance should things go as planned and so the bag was hung on his sword belt, directly behind the prized blade.

Standing neatly on a small shelf on the inside wall of the cabinet were small bottles and tinctures beside two rolls of gauze bandages. The bottles contained a serum to dull pain and a cleanser to keep wounds free from infection and to aid the healing process. The tinctures contained anti-venoms for critters big and small in the Illiastran wild that could poison a person. Another still contained a dose of syrupy medicine that could stop rabies dead in its tracks, were he to come in contact with an animal bearing that ailment.

Carefully, Tryst laid the medicinal kit out in the box his mask had called home and placed it between the layers of clothing and cloaks in his satchel for protection.

The last item he placed carefully atop it all was the faded orange cloak.

This was all Tryst could take, the satchel was full and any more would only weigh him down. Glancing about the room, Tryst looked upon the things he would have to leave behind, the most painful of which was his guitar. There was little doubt that he would miss that most of all and he hoped that Lord Howland wouldn't destroy it in his fury after Tryst had left. "May you sing long after I'm gone," he whispered softly at the instrument leaning in the corner, wrapped in its wooden case.

It was time to go at last. There was nothing left to do and little time to spare. Tryst uncorked the bottle of rum and took one last swig, replacing it in the middle of the table when he was done. *Let the guards have it. They will want it when Howland is done yelling at them,* he thought as he closed the doors of the cabinet, turning the key in the hidden lock on the right side panel. *At least this will keep them occupied for a while.* It pained Tryst to think of the old, antique cabinet being broken to splinters with an axe head when the guards couldn't open it by conventional means.

He slung his satchel over his back, letting it fall over the bow and arrows beneath it to obscure them.

With one last look at his old life, Tryst was gone, with the door to his past locked behind him.

The armoury was almost completely dark, with only a beam of moonlight filtering in through the far window to fill a long rectangle of pale light on the floor. *The clouds have broken and the rain has let up*, he noted. *And the wind is beginning to die out.*

The old heavy door to the hallway swung open with a whoosh as he pushed the iron ring that served as a handle. The dim lanterns in their sconces dimly lit the hallway behind the grand staircase, casting a low, yellow glow.

Six guards were calling the back hallway home at this hour. All were clad in the white coats and dark blue pants of the manor guards and Tryst knew them all by name. Two of which were guarding the rear exit of the manor when Tryst approached.

It was a man known as Ralph the Rascal that greeted him jovially. "Hello Reine, heading out to the stables to greet the guests, I would assume?"

"You assume right, Ralph." Tryst answered in a sombre tone. He bore Ralph and his brother Martos beside him no ill will, but a graduate of the University took no solace in killing and made no jokes about the matter.

"Well, I won't keep a busy man from his work, on with you," he answered as his tone went flat. The man was usually quick with a joke, though he seemed to sense the solemnity with which Tryst regarded his task and said no more.

Tryst gave him a nod. "Thank you, I won't be too long and I'll knock when I return."

"Certainly, ser," Ralph answered, reaching to open the door to the outer yard for him.

Before Tryst could walk through, Martus stopped him. "Where are you off to with a big, heavy satchel, ser?" the quiet brother of Ralph asked as he caught sight of what Tryst carried, either not seeing or ignoring the presence of the bow and arrows.

"They're rags and sawdust to clean up the mess, should I make one," Tryst explained while reaching a hand back to pat the bag on his back. "There is no need to bathe the stables in blood if I can avoid it."

"A wise call, I won't keep you," Martus said grimly, facing the long hallway once more and wanting no further explanation.

None of the guards wanted Tryst's job, and were all but happy to get out of his way when the Lord Master demanded heads roll. All that served to do was make it easier for Tryst to stay his blade and for that he was glad.

Tryst wasted little time once outside, taking the concrete stairs from the back entrance landing in quick fashion. Long strides took him across the stone pathway to the rear gate and the stables nearby.

The night air was crisp and the coolness in his lungs felt therapeutic, helping to calm him before the night that lay ahead. *I walk on the edge of a mountain here. One misstep will plunge me to my death, and yet, there is no other way.* The clouds above him sloughed eastward as he strode, taking turns blocking out both the pale and red moon as they headed east towards the Elven Forest and the impregnable Eastern Mountains beyond.

An owl hooted noisily from beyond the bailey wall of the manor and Tryst gave a glance in the direction it came from. Above him, the moons shone down onto the expansive and manicured lawn between the wall and the building. The pale light of the larger one made the rain soaked grass turn into a thousand blades of radiant, shimmering crystal. Maple trees dotted the landscape, shedding their dampened red and yellow leaves as they danced to the song of the night's wind. An elegant garden of shrubbery ringed the manor and divided the swath of grass in two, like a miniature green mountain range, looking snow-capped with its glistening layer of fallen rain. *There is no turning now. I accept the fate that awaits me.* Tryst reminded himself while looking upon the scenery.

The rear stable was a large thing in itself, built to house a small army's worth of horses. However, most of its occupants now were the pairs used to pull coaches and wagons to and from the city. They were supply wagons, mostly, though the ministers that were not afforded the luxury of accommodations in the manor during parliamentary sessions were also carted to and fro.

A lone guard with his arms folded stood before the front of the stables, between the tall double doors meant for horse and cart to pass through. Even those doors were decadent, made from thick, marvellous oak and banded and hinged with shining steel. Split between the wide doors was a massive, carved, whitewashed dove, its wings spanning as close to the edge of the frame as it would allow without inhibiting its ability to open.

"Who goes there?" the guard called out to Tryst.

"Tis I." Tryst called back.

The guard sighed with relief. "Oh, it's you. They're upstairs, an unruly lot, they are, but don't worry, we disarmed them."

Jorge Bickerington, Tryst knew at once. His father was a backbench minister from Tusker's Cove in the west, the most northerly region controlled by the human portion of Illiastra. The other guards called the man Bicker, a nickname immediately bestowed on him as a shortened form of his surname. Though, the man's consistently dour attitude played a part in helping him keep it.

"That one with the patch on his eye seems to be the dangerous sort," Bicker commented to Tryst. "Wouldn't see me trifle with him, no ser. I'd sooner stay out here all alone in the cold."

"You've been left alone to guard the three, is that the way of it, Bicker?" Tryst spoke softly to the squat man as he closed the gap between them.

"Stable lads are still around, feeding the horses that the bounty hunters brought. But I'm the only one that's armed, if that's what you mean," Bicker answered, running an ermine gloved hand through his dark, widow's peaked hair. He looked Tryst over while he spoke and inevitably caught sight of the satchel and bow slung over his back. "Um, what are you doing with all that, ser? The bow and stuff, I mean."

"Lord Master's orders, I'm afraid. I'm pressing you into service too, if you don't mind," Tryst replied with a firm pat on the shoulder.

Bicker jumped in his boots at that "Wh-what do you want me to, uh. I mean, to say, uh, what do you want me to do, ser? Edward and Joss are in the guard house on the rear gate, I can go fetch them if you'd rather. Big Ed swings a better sword than I do and Joss is a steadier shot, for certain, so, why don't I go get them-"

"Calm yourself, Bicker," Tryst cut in, before the other had a chance to run off. "I just need you and the stable lads to ready that wagon belonging to the guests so that it can leave in a hurry. I'm going to use it to move the bodies when I'm done, that's all. When you're finished, you and the lads go warm up with Ed and Joss until I lead the wagon through the rear gate. Can you handle that?"

The short fellow swallowed hard and wiped his brow. "Uh, aye ser, that I can do, that won't be a problem, I, uh, I'm just not good at killing, is the thing."

Tryst shot him a raised eyebrow at that. "I wouldn't say that too loudly or someone might question your decision to become a soldier in the first place. But no matter, we will fetch the stablehands and you can get on with preparing the wagon for me. I'll handle the killing." Tryst went to the standard entrance beside the massive double, barn doors, ushering Bicker through with his free hand.

The stables were illuminated by lanterns that hung from the posts separating the rows of stalls. Tryst let his eyes adjust to the low flickering glow of the oil lamps as he surveyed the quiet scene within.

Stepping ahead, Bicker glanced around worriedly. "Wickens, Gunter, where are you?" he called out in a voice that was all nerves.

No sooner had Bicker called out than two heads poked above a stall at the far wall, just before the wooden staircase that led to the loft above. "We're here, ser, what is it?" one called back. Through in the low light it was impossible to tell which it was.

Bicker walked halfway down the aisle to the left before returning a reply. "We got a job to do, where's the horses those bounty hunters came in with?"

"They're the pair of spotted rounseys near the front, ser. What do you need 'em for?" a different voice answered in an annoyed tone.

"Fetch 'em out and hook 'em up to that ruddy wagon they brought in, would ya?" Bicker said far louder than Tryst would have liked. There was no doubt that the three upstairs were hearing every word of it.

"What for, ser?" the second voice asked.

Bicker scoffed at that. "What for?' You're not to wonder the 'what for?' just get it done, lads. Do it quick enough and we'll sneak off to play dice with Joss and Ed for a bit."

"Aye, ser, we'll get it done," the second voice answered reluctantly once more as the noise of chairs scraping on the stone floor filled the stable.

Two lanky lads emerged before Tryst clad in flannel coats, with matching shaggy hair that fell almost over their eyes. They were young, little more than twenty at the very most, Tryst noted, as they went to work begrudgingly. One lad opened a single, wide door on the front of the stable while the other bridled the grey and black spotted horses. Neither one dared to even look at Tryst, or so much as speak to him, even when he thanked them as they left with Bicker in tow. The fear in Tryst ran deep amongst the common folk, even those who worked within the manor.

When the first floor of the stables was empty and the door shut to again, Tryst moved hastily to a stall in the right aisle. Inside was a chestnut stallion courser he had named Wildstar, for the white, star shaped patch on his forehead.

"Hello, old friend, it looks like we have a job to do tonight. Most likely it will be our last together," Tryst said morosely as ran a hand through the horse's mane. Metal pails were hung between the stalls at intervals, filled with varying levels of oats. Tryst reached a hand into the closest one and returned with a snack for Wildstar. When the horse had finished, Tryst reached above the stall and took down the brown saddle he had bought himself when the horse was given to him by the Lord Master.

In actuality, Tryst had been given his pick of the stables not long after signing his contract that put him in the employ of Grenjin Howland. There was a black destrier and several other prized horses that it was expected Tryst would choose from. Instead, to everyone's surprise he had picked Wildstar, then only a colt. Tryst had felt a bond with that horse almost immediately, finding a sense of similarity with the steed. The big destrier was like his friend Myolas, who was the beast everyone expected to grow into a strong fighter. But Wildstar, like Tryst, was the unexpected one. Tryst knew then that the colt would grow to be a fine stallion and he had not been wrong. The pair had become a formidable team in the four years since and the courser went nearly everywhere Tryst did. Oftentimes Tryst and Wildstar would ride for hours in the forest behind the manor. Together they explored the game trails and the broken old roads and ruins of what had been the Kingdom of Valdarrow centuries ago.

In quick time, Tryst had the horse saddled, with his bow, quiver and satchel shifted from his back to Wildstar's. "I'll be back soon, there are some things I need to take care of," Tryst whispered with a gentle pat before closing the gate on the stall and heading to the back of the stables. Each step of the stairs creaked loudly as he put his weight to it, giving the three men on the second floor ample forewarning of his arrival.

A voice thick with the brogue of the Knightdom of Gildriad called from above. "Will you be joining us tonight, Killer, or will you make us wait until sunrise for death?"

Without answer, Tryst covered the last few steps and stood at the top of the stairs. The second floor of the stables was sparse and windowless. A few spare rooms lined the wall above the front doors below, but there was little else. The remaining space was wide open with thick wooden beams in intervals. Amidst the rough, pine flooring was a round table with three of its four chairs occupied by the bounty hunter and his accomplices. A simple snack of bread and cheese had been served to them on a wooden platter along with cups and a flagon of cheap wine to wash it down with.

Fletchard spoke up once more as Tryst reached the landing. "The Master of Blades joins us at last," the bounty hunter spoke in a voice dripping with sarcasm. "Look, fellows, he comes without the bags of promised coin. Maybe we're going to be given a bank note. I only have one eye but I read better than my accomplices do with four, so I do hope it has the right sum."

Tryst was nonplussed with the sudden loquaciousness of the bounty hunter. "Odd, you let your bearded friend here do all the talking in the manor. Yet now you're positively chatty."

"Oh, you noticed that, did you? I don't speak well in front of big crowds and I knew I would draw an audience when I marched that bounty through the door. So, I decided to let Monty do my talking." Fletchard calmly said as he leaned back in his chair, intertwining his fingers across his chest as he reclined as far as the worn, wooden chair would allow. "That's enough about my communicative quirks, Reine. I know there's no money. That became clear when your boss started flapping those sagging jowls of his."

"You have the right of it, there is no money." Tryst said as he moved away from the stairs, taking a few small steps into the room. "However, I have a proposition for you."

"He's gonna kill us!" the thin, scruffy fellow said as he leapt to his feet, Monty not far behind. Tryst ducked the slender man's wild haymaker punch and drove a shoulder into his lower torso. The blow knocked the wind clear from his unfortunate foe and the forward momentum from the man's charge was enough for Tryst to flip him head over heels. With a loud smash, the fellow came crashing down on the floorboards.

Instinctively, Tryst raised his left forearm to his face, anticipating the one named Monty to be hot on his friend's heels.

What he found instead was Fletchard clutching a single leg of the chair that he had been seated on seconds before, with Monty groaning in a pile at Fletchard's feet. The other legs of the chair, the seat, backrest and countless splinters lay beside the dazed and bewildered form of Fletchard's potbellied employee, whose balding head was rapidly becoming a red, wet mess.

From behind Tryst came the gasps of air as the scruffy man struggled to fill his lungs again. Tryst took a step back to keep the three of them in view just as Fletchard came lunging. As Tryst readied himself to parry an attack, Fletchard ignored him completely, swinging the leg of the chair at the man trying to get to his feet. The sickening crack of wood on bone rang in Tryst's ears and the scruffy man's nose exploded in a blast of blood, sending the lackey to the floor once more in agony.

Tryst was careful to not give away his shock at Fletchard's hasty betrayal of his employees, though the silence spoke his surprise plainly enough.

"Both of you are fucking imbeciles!" Fletchard exclaimed as he threw the wooden chair leg across the room angrily and sat down hard in one of the undamaged seats at the table.

There was an awkward silence as the bounty hunter downed the last of the wine in his cup in an effort to calm his nerves. After a deep breath, he looked up at Tryst and gave an exasperated sigh. "I believe you were saying something about some sort of proposition, Mister Reine?"

9

ORANGECLOAK

She had lived with a dark thought tucked deep in the back of her mind. A thought that seemed to have taken a life of its own and would crawl from its hiding place to taunt her at the most inopportune times. When she greeted new recruits, new faces that were but masks and behind which may be moles waiting to sell her to her enemies, it mocked her. As she stood on the steps of town halls or on the porches of rural general stores and encouraged people to stand against the government, it pointed from the crowd and cackled. Even as she dispersed her gathered Thieves and walked alone save for her two loyal guards, it would not leave. That thought told her that despite her confidence and all her efforts, that she would likely find herself exactly where she was now: in the dungeon of the Atrebell Manor, waiting to die.

The guards in their deep blue coats had dragged her shackled and helpless form into the bowels of the building. Down a narrow, cavernous stairwell they went, to the waiting arms of more bluecoats in the guard room between the cells and the outside world. It was only then, with exits sealed and guards surrounding her, did they remove the chains and manacles from raw wrists and ankles and for that she was grateful.

It was her clothes they took next, which by this point were all she had left. Her doeskin boots, the prized Elven leathers and its matching bodice. They had taken it all save her tunic and smallclothes.

Two of the larger guards among those present had then seized her arms so tightly she was sure they were going to be torn from the sockets of her shoulders. Why, she could not say, for the fight was gone from her and she was too tired to resist. Regardless, they held tight and led her into the dim, circular room full of matching doors of thick wood banded in heavy iron.

There was at least one other inmate and he could be heard tittering from within an open cell that had a light of its own. There was no telling if any others were down here. All the cell doors had little windows built into them with an iron shutter for the guards to look through and all were closed tight.

A third guard was waiting, holding open one of the heavy wooden doors and the pair with her arms clinched tightly shoved her into the perpetual darkness beyond the threshold. Her feet came out from beneath her and she fell hard to the floor as the door slammed shut. The last noise she heard was the key turning in the lock.

At first she dared not to move from where she lay on the hard stone, having been robbed of sight and left unsure of her surroundings. After a time, she stretched out a hand cautiously and felt only more floor beneath it. The other hand followed, reaching a little further to find more of the same and after that came a slow crawl on her stomach.

The first thing she found was straw and a lumpy, scratchy blanket thrown atop it to one corner. Adjacent to that she discovered a pail for her leavings and naught else in the tiny space. The brick walls and the door had no weaknesses to offer, nor did the low ceiling when she got her wobbly legs beneath her to reach it. Defeated, she dropped to the hay and curled into a ball beneath the threadbare blanket, shivering as the cold coursed through her bones. *If only they had left me my cloak,* she thought forlornly. It was then she remembered that the cloak had not even come with her that far.

The man they called the Master of Blades was the last one to be seen with it, she recalled. It was as good as gone now and with it her very identity.

The cloak was who she had become and it was all she had left to mark her place in the world. Her real name, the one she had been born with, was etched into a stone to mark the empty grave of a girl whom the world believed to be dead. It sat in the forgotten corner of a cemetery to the south, overgrown with weeds and situated beside the final resting place of criminals and traitors of Illiastra.

From then onward, she had been known as Orangecloak and eventually she came into the title of Field Commander of the Thieves. The cloak on her back had been the symbol to which she rallied the people beneath and now it was in the hands of the Lord Master's paid killer. Without it, she was no one once more and the no one she had become cried into her straw pillow in a way Orangecloak had never allowed herself.

Memories of two lives once lived by one woman came flooding back. Before she was Orangecloak, she had a real family: a mother, father and sister, grandparents, aunts, uncles and cousins. For a moment she thought of them all and saw their faces flash before her in bittersweet recollection. Much of her family had passed on, though as far as she knew, there were several relatives still among the living. It seemed as if she had a tear for each of them.

The cruel ending of that life had shaped the woman she had grown into, the one who had been known as Orangecloak. Though the first life she had known had ended in tragedy, she was given the gift of a second chance and she had tried to live it well. In the years that followed she had made more friends that had become as close as family. So many of them had also been lost and now even her second life was drawing to its end.

As the most wanted person in Illiastra, she had woken every morning with the knowledge that it may all end at any moment. Though, with so much left undone and with so many still oppressed, she was not yet ready to die.

Who am I now? I am not the dead girl, nor am I Orangecloak. I'm a nameless body waiting on a noose.

Her limbs felt heavy from carrying the chain throughout the day and her wrists and ankles were terribly sore and chaffed. But for all of that pain, it was the shambled anguish of her mind that hurt more than anything.

In total darkness it was difficult to track time. The room seemed to swallow all sound and she felt as though she might already be dead. That was likely the purpose of these cells, she realized, to deprive the inmate of their own senses. However, there was one sensation that had slowly come creeping back.

Although she was not been given any food or water by any of her captives, she also hadn't been permitted to use a privy. Now, that she was alone and unrestrained, that urge had made its return. Rising from the hay pile she groped feebly to find the bucket they had left her and made her water.

Afterwards, while still standing, she decided to check the door for weakness again. There wasn't as much as a keyhole for her to peek through on this side of the door. However her fingers felt what could only be long, gouging and utterly vain scratches made by a previous occupant of the cell. Upon finding no give in the lumber or its iron holdings, she sank back to the hay and tried to close her eyes.

She lay there, curled into a ball beneath the rough blanket for what seemed an eternity. While thinking about the lives she had lost and everything she would never do, she began to hear again. Though they were merely muffled voices, she knew they were loud enough to be right outside the door. *Could a night have passed already? I hadn't slept. Or did I? Perhaps I dozed off after all,* she thought to herself, daring not to utter a word aloud.

The tittering prisoner was there. "Open it, open it, open it, hehehe!" it said with childlike excitement.

"Calm down, maniac, you'll get her," another, more rational and authoritative male voice said as the light from the circular room outside sliced through the blackness of the cell to fall on her face.

The sudden light nearly blinded her and she instinctively raised an arm to shield her eyes, glancing briefly to see a man standing before her. He wore a brown suit, complete with a black bowtie and a white, button down shirt. *Though, he wears no shoes,* she noted. Over the suit was a white apron, spattered in something red that she hoped was not blood. The strange fellow was plain of face with crazed eyes and teeth that ran the spectrum between yellow and brown. The hair on his head was cut by crude hacking, likely by a knife and his shaving regiment fared no better.

He cocked his head to one side and began to lick his lips at the sight of her. "It's been a long time since I've seen a woman," he said in a voice that grew soft and almost to a whisper. "Tell the man who brought her that I owe him a great thanks."

"I'll be sure to do just that," the guard that had opened the door sarcastically replied.

There was no heed paid to it by the bedraggled one kneeling before her and he kept his gaze fixed firmly.

"Are you afraid?" the mangy man said cooingly as she sat up, an arm still raised high in defence. The fellow went to one knee and leaned in close with a breath that stank of foul cheese. "Come with me, you must be hungry? Yes? Would you like some food?"

There was only the cold wall behind her, but she backed to it all the same "Get away from me, leave me be," she said, putting her other arm up to add to the shield of the first.

"Aww, come now, I'm not so scary as that, am I?" He clicked his discoloured teeth and cooed again, cocking his head to the other direction and giving her a grin. "I could take care of you. I'm so lonely down here in the dark, won't you be my friend?"

The guard let out an impatient sigh. "Take her already, you steaming sack of shit. Don't fuck with the poor thing like this."

"Fine!" the unkempt man snapped. His grimy hands grabbed for her by the hair and he yanked her roughly from the black cell into the circular room.

She screamed as loud as her lungs would allow and swatted feebly at the hands that clutched her red locks. They were quickly across the round room and into the lit cell she spotted earlier.

For a fleeting second, she found her feet, only to be violently shoved down to the ground, wailing out in pain as her knees harshly absorbed the fall. Before she could rise the savage had sprawled himself atop her, forcing her knees once more into the hard stone. She shot her hands out and tried to crawl away but the pain in her knees combined with the full weight of her captor's body made it futile. With no other alternative left to her, she resumed screaming, both out of pain and fear.

"Stop it! Shut up, you pox ridden slut, or I'll smash all your pretty little teeth to dust. I don't like screamers, no I doesn't," he yelled while clapping a pair of iron shackles to her wrists.

As she tugged on the chain, she realised the end of her new restraints ran to the ceiling and through a set of wooden pulleys. She traced the chain to the far side of the room where more pulleys angled it into a big wheel.

Searching desperately for anything that might help her she discovered that the walls were lined with shelves containing a wide assortment of bloodied tools and weapons. *This is a torture chamber.* It dawned on her and she began screaming for help again, hoping someone in the manor with a shred of compassion might hear her and put an end to this.

The maniac spun around while still atop her, keeping his weight on her body while pulling her bare ankles together to lock them in more irons.

When she kicked her feet, they brought up hard and she knew then that the chains were bolted to the floor. "What are you doing to me?! Let me go, please!" she shouted again, her voice breaking as terror took hold of her body.

She felt him get off her and she quickly made a jump to rise only to stumble and fall for a third time to the stone floor. The shock of pain that shot through her felt like someone had pushed swords straight through her kneecaps. There was nothing she could recall that had ever hurt as much and again she roared out.

The torturer spat and kicked her. "I told you, I doesn't like screamers, they makes me mad!" he yelled back at her as he left for the wheel on the wall.

The chain coiled around the apparatus as he turned it, yanking her arms and then the rest of her upward until she was hanging by the wrists from the ceiling.

There was a lone moment where she was dangling freely, then at once all the chains drew tight, causing her body to stretch out. She couldn't move at all and her knees and limbs were in agony, with every inch of her felt like it was ripping at the seams.

In the vain hope that someone, anyone might hear, she began to yell out once more. "Please, if anybody is out there, please help me!"

The pleading only seemed to frustrate the madman further. "See what you does? See what you makes me do when you gets me angry?! I only wanted to play a little before the questioner gets here, that's all. But you gets me angry and then we can't play, no we can't," the inhuman beast in a man's skin said as he grabbed her tightly by the jaw, forcing her to look upon his dishevelled features.

"Please, please, let me down! Please, somebody help me!" she cried out in his face. Though there seemed to be no one else to hear.

"No one's gonna help you! No one!" he said, jabbing a finger at her face. "All the guards runs up the stairs when it's time for me to play. They don't like to hear it, so they runs away, yes they does. There's an elf too, but he's locked up all tight and I'm not 'low'd to touch him, no I'm not, but he can't touch me neither."

The monster stepped out of the chamber into the circular room. "Do you likes hearing play time, Mister Elf?" he taunted. "Do you likes the sound of it? Filthy, vile elf, you're the worst things there is."

The monster began to laugh maniacally at the sound of what seemed to be a muffled voice from within one of the other cells. "If only they'd let me gut you, Elf. I wants to see if you bleeds green like they says, yes I do."

She struggled fruitlessly while he was away, but there was no slack in her restraints and the only thing it seemed to do was make the pain so much worse.

The monster came striding back into the chamber, slamming the heavy, wooden door behind him where it banged loudly against the frame and came to rest slightly ajar.

He looked like he was about to reach for her before stopping short and stepping back to go into a furious pace in front of her. "No, no, I can't make a mark, I can't make a mark or the questioner will lock me up. He don't like it when I makes marks, no he doesn't." Then the creature stopped, gazing up at her with his wild and emotionless eyes. "But I can stretch you." He began to cackle loudly at his own, sadistic compromise. "That won't make a mark, no it won't." He jogged around her quickly, bumping against her stretched frame roughly and causing her to helplessly spin.

When the chains unwound to bring her back to face the front of the room again she saw that another man had pushed the door open quietly and allowed himself in.

"That will be enough out of you, Carver," the new stranger's voice boomed.

"Noooooooooooo!" the monster shrieked and she heard the sounds of his bare feet slapping the stone floor behind her as he stomped about. "I didn't even get to play. You're not fair, question man. You're not fair at all. I hates you, I hates you so much."

The new arrival was clad in a black cloak, with its hood drawn over his head. His face was hidden behind a shining mask of black enamelled steel, a silvery slash running from the left eye and across the right cheek. The only part of the face the mask exposed was the eyes, and they saw what the monster's eyes could not. They were green as emeralds, glowing in the light of the lanterns and growing narrow as they stared down the monster that was still behind her.

"You will let her down this instant," the black-clad man commanded fiercely.

"I'll let her down when I feels like letting her down!" the one called Carver shouted as he stormed to the man in the doorway, pointing at the masked face that stood unwavering.

Before she could beg for his help the man in black had clutched the monster's outstretched right hand in his left. Pushing his thumb against the back of the monster's hand, he bent it backward at the wrist at a sharp angle, causing the man to yelp and fall to his knees.

"Lemme go, lemme go!" the fiend yelled, trying to jerk away.

There was a gasp from the vile creature as the man in black yanked him forward, releasing the wrist to ensnare the head in a lightning quick choke hold.

With the head of the monster in a tight vice, the man in black looked over his shoulder and called out: "Hurry, he should have the keys in the breast pocket of his jacket."

A second man bolted into the room and fished a hand into the monster's pocket to retrieve a small ring of jingling keys. "Be still, Miss. I'll have you down in a second," she heard him say as he went to work on the leg irons first.

The shackles fell away from her ankles and clanked to the floor. The tension on her body was relieved, though she was still left to dangle by her pain wracked wrists.

"I'm going to let you down slowly, try to stand." Her second rescuer spoke in a reassuring tone before dashing out of her sight to the wheel.

The monster opened his mouth, but all that came forth was a gagging noise as the first rescuer held him tight.

"You caused much suffering in your short, miserable life, Carver," spoke the masked man, as he walked the lunatic into the corner of the room and away from her seeing. "I could have killed you instantly. It would have happened so fast, you would never have realized you were dying. But I didn't, because I wanted you to see it coming, to know that there was justice for the innocent lives you took and punishment for the terror you caused." Then there was a loud snap, and the monster gasped for air no more. The only noise to follow was a soft thudding that sounded like a body rolling to the floor.

The masked man stood before her. "You're safe now, Miss Orangecloak, he'll harm you no more. I'm going to help ease you down." He placed his hands gently on her hips before looking to the man at the wheel. "I got her. Turn the wheel, ser."

The chains let out a groan, made a quick jerk and started to move, slowly lowering her to the floor.

"Easy now," the masked one said softly. "Be still."

She tried to put weight to her feet, but fell forward into his arms with a loud moan. The one in black held her firmly in strong arms and she was so thankful to be back on the ground that she almost forgot about her still manacled wrists. "Oh, thank you ser, whoever you are, thank you both."

"Hush, be still now. Lower your arms slowly, there you go," he coached as the chains gave slack. "Have you been up there long?"

"I-I don't know, it seemed so long, but I don't know, really." She felt helpless as the pain washed over her. "Is...Is he dead? The man you called Carver, is he dead?"

"Aye, he is dead and the world will not miss him," the masked man said as he gently held her upright until her arms were lowered to chest level. "Ser, that's low enough. Help me open these irons," he called to the other who been operating the wheel.

The man came forward at once and she looked upon his face for the first time. "You're an elf," she said in surprise. "You're the one that monster shouted at in a cell."

"I was, miss. This one freed me," he said with the lilting accent of the Elven people as he worked her wrists free of the iron bindings.

"Who are you two?" she asked as the chains came away from her limp hands.

"Sympathisers to your cause, my lady," said the masked man as he scooped her legs out from beneath her and turned to look at the elf. "Get the door to the guard room. Your things should all be there."

They hastily crossed the circular room to the now vacant guard quarters she had come through just hours earlier. She was set down on a chair at the head of a table that the guards took their meals from.

The masked one poured a cup of water from a nearby cask and passed it to her. "Here, drink up. There will be food when we're outside the walls."

Her hands trembled and shook so much that she spilled much of the water before it could reach her parched lips. "How are you going to get me outside the walls?" She asked between winces. "My knees, that...Thing in there drove me down on them and then stretched me out. I don't know that I can walk."

"You need not worry. I'm going to get you out of here," the one in black said before turning to the elf, clad like her in only smallclothes and tunic and rooting through a pair of chests against the opposite wall. "Find her things and prepare yourself to leave, I'll be back in a moment," he declared without waiting for a reply and returning to the dungeon.

The elf quickly donned a pair of fine, velvet dark green trousers and a matching jacket, leaving his tunic hanging loose as he garbed himself. "My lady, I gather this leather ensemble and matching bodice is yours?" he said while laying the outfit the guards had robbed of her earlier on the table beside her as she downed the cool water.

"They are, thank you, ser. I'm afraid I don't even know your name." She answered while trying to slide her aching arms through the sleeves of the leather coat.

He turned and bowed before her graciously. "My name is Tyrendil of the family Wildheart, if it pleases my lady," the elf stated courteously. He turned away again and shook out a grey cloak trimmed with brown sable fur and wrapped it around his shoulders. It was closed with a silver brooch shaped like a heart and slashed with three claw marks painted a crimson red. "I can sense the wondering in you, my lady and before you ask: I do not know the identity of our rescuer. His face has been hidden behind that mask of hardened steel since he sprung me from my cell."

"I see. Did he mention to you how he intends to take us from here?" she queried further as she painfully worked the leather trousers up her legs while still seated.

The elf stopped momentarily to consider that before answering. "No, yet I would rather take the risk than sit in that darkness any longer. Past instances of my kind being taken into custody in Illiastra would indicate that I would most likely be deported to the border of my country." He turned his back to her again while still talking, collecting a grey satchel that sat beside the chests to look through its contents. "Though, I can't recall any other occasion when one of my kin found their way into the Atrebell Manor dungeon and there's something off about those Palomb twins that arrested me. They seem rather...Wicked." Tyrendil gave the last word some consideration before turning to her to say it. "So, I decided my best course would be to take the masked man's offer. It couldn't possibly be the worst outcome of my arrest and it meant I got to lend a hand to the woman whose wails pierced the dungeon's walls."

"Thank you again for that, Tyrendil," she answered in a voice wracked with pain while trying to stand on her aching feet. For her efforts, she managed to hold herself upright long enough to yank her trousers up, sitting down quickly as the pain became too much. "I don't know how I could ever repay you for your assistance, Tyrendil."

The elf was before her then with a warm smile on his face. "You may call me Ren, my lady, as my friends do. As for thanking me, think naught of it. I am only glad I was able to render my assistance."

Her boots were brought to her next, doeskin and soft soled to help muffle her footfalls and rising to just below the knee. She tied one while Ren tied the other before he tended to his own footwear.

"My lady, I would assume by the name of the band you lead that stealing may not be below you," Ren stated as he crossed the floor to a pair of armoires, one locked with a heavy padlock and the other not. "Might I suggest a pair of these woollen gloves in the guards' inventory for your hands? The nights are dreadfully cold this time of year," he suggested while handing a pair over to her, stuffing a second in his satchel for himself.

"Thank you, that's thoughtful of you," she complimented as she tucked them into her waistband. She looked over to where he stood, finally taking the time to look him over. Ren's hair was light brown and stretched halfway down his back. So fine was it that each strand looked as if it were made of silk. He was fair skinned, lithe and tall, with eyes as blue as the ocean and full of life. It was known that humans could not dare compete with the beauty of elves and Ren certainly stood as testament to that claim.

He continued to shuffle through the cabinet before turning back to her. "If only there was a cloak or a warm coat here. Though perhaps it is best you're not walking about with a guard uniform on you," the elf commented idly while closing the doors of the armoire and turning towards a nearby shelf lined with equipment as another thought seemed to occur to him. "We could probably use a lantern. If my attempt to tell time is correct, night will have set in."

The slamming of doors from the dungeon drew the attention of both she and the elf and they turned in unison to see the man in black before them once more.

"Are we prepared to depart?" he asked as he drew the door between the guard room and the dungeon closed, locking it tight.

"I have gathered our possessions, meagre as they are," Ren answered the man in black, before turning to her. "How about you, my lady? Do you think you can walk?"

"I can stand, my knees are in agony and my ankles and legs are achingly sore, but I should be able to move, I think," she gave as a reply, trying to stand with the table as support.

"You should be fine in time. Though time is something we don't have at the moment, Miss Orangecloak. I shall carry you up the stairs, if you have no objection," the masked man answered as he held up a key on a thick ring for Ren to see before tossing the whole lot across the room to him.

The elf caught the keys and went to work on opening the outer door without a word. As it creaked open on groaning hinges Ren slid out into the darkness beyond and was gone from sight, leaving her alone with the stranger.

Before she could be scooped into his arms she held up a hand and resisted. "What of the guards, won't they stop us?" This all seemed too easy to her and she wanted answers.

The masked man's tone was equal parts reassuring and urgent as he replied. "Not to worry, they've been instructed to remain at the top of the stairs until called."

"How will we get by them, then, if they're waiting at the top?" she queried again, the last answer making little sense to her.

"Quite simple, we're not going all the way to the top," the man in the mask calmly intoned as he swept her into his strong arms.

Ren slipped back into the room in haste. "The way is clear. There are no guards on the stairwell whatsoever." He reported while grabbing his satchel and the last of their belongings, including the bodice belonging to Orangecloak from the table.

"Excellent," the masked man replied. "Go to the second landing, where the steps turn from stone to marble. There is an unlocked door and you should find a light switch on your left once insider. Oh, and mind the pool."

Once Ren had barred the door they began their ascent, with Ren slipping around them to climb as quickly as his legs allowed and keep watch.

They came to a landing and walked beneath a bare bulb and she chanced to glance upward at her carrier. From this angle, she could see a defined jaw beneath the mask and loose strands of long hair as red as her own beneath the cowl of his cloak.

"Stop!" She said loudly. "This is a trap. I know who you are, you're Tryst Reine. This is a trap, let me down at once."

The request was denied and Tryst Reine held tightly to her. "My lady, no, please, you have to trust me. If you call too loudly, you will bring the guards down here and doom us all." His voice was a desperate whisper as he replied and held her tightly as she squirmed in what was both a painful and futile struggle.

He laid her on the step above the landing, seated so that she could see Ren on the next landing above with an open door in hand.

The light fluttered out of the room to cast the elf in a silhouette as Tryst spoke softly, but hurriedly. "That's the bathing pool room just there. It's the top floor of the old basements, all of which are in fact the old fortress of the Valdarrow clan."

"What does that have to do with anything? What's in the bathing room for us? Are you going to drown me?" Her mind raced as she blurted out the questions as she was sure this was a trap of some kind. This was the Master of Blades, after all, the personal pet of the Lord Master who wanted nothing more than to make her suffer.

Instead he lowered the hood of his cloak and undid the leather bindings of his mask to reveal his face. There was only a single, dull electric light on the landing and yet she could see him plain enough. His face was stern, but not unkind, heart shaped with the greenest eyes she had ever seen and all framed by that long, red mane that made him look almost leonine. "I did not want you to know my identity until we were well away, for I knew you would not trust the lie the Lord Master has made of me. I am not the man you think I am. Please, give me this one chance to prove that. That is all I ask."

There was still too much doubt for her satisfaction. "Tell me where you intend to take me, and tell it true," she whispered through pained gasps.

Tryst Reine nodded and leaned in close enough so that his whispers could be heard clearly. "On the other side of the pool is a hidden door made of brick and mortar like the walls around it. Beyond lies a long passage of worn stone. It is unlit and hazardous, though it leads to the only surface ruins of the guard towers of Valdarrow's fortress. We'll surface well into the forest and away from here. There will be men waiting to lend assistance and the six of us will travel north, to the Dwarven Mountains. The Dupoire family of the Hotel Dupoire there are good friends of mine. You only need let me take you that far. I have friends in the West that share your goals and I would like for you to meet them. However, if you would go somewhere else before such meeting could occur, I would not stop you." He took a hand in both of his and looked her straight in the eyes. "I am not your enemy, Lady Orangecloak."

She took a deep breath, wincing as she did. *If he is playing me false, he has certainly taken lengths to ensure the charade accurately holds up.* Her eyes fell to the landing below and the stairs that led back to the dungeon and Ren's thoughts on the matter came back to her: *"I decided my best course would be to take the masked man's offer. It couldn't possibly be the worst outcome of my arrest..."*

With great reluctance, she met his stare. "Ruse or not, my alternative seems to be a cold, dark cell and a certain death. I guess that leaves me with little choice then, doesn't it?"

"I assure you this is no ruse, my lady," Tryst Reine answered in a relieved tone.

Her eyes closed, she exhaled and with little alternative, she accepted the offer and her fate simultaneously. "Your assurances give me little comfort, ser and I am sure you can understand why. However, against my better judgement, I will temporarily extend you this much trust. Let us be off."

"Thank you," he whispered as he tied his mask on the side of his belt and scooped her from the stone step and back into his arms.

Ren awaited them where the stone turned to polished marble, holding the door in one hand and the lantern in the other. Together the three slipped inside what unsurprisingly turned out to be a bathing room of great extravagance. The marble pool in the centre was filled with pristine water that was so still she might have mistaken it for glass. Smooth tiles of even more marble ran the entire floor and crept halfway up the wall.

Furnishing the room were chairs of some sort of soft wood lining all sides of the square pool and she even spotted benches carved into the pool itself to sit upon while bathing. Though she saw no sign of this door that was spoken of in the back of the room and that raised her suspicions.

She was set down upon one of the chairs as Tryst went to the rear of the room.

The elf looked over the wall and gave her a look that echoed her own worries. "I'm not seeing this exit you spoke of," Ren shot a hard stare at Tryst as he spoke. "This wall looks to be without any telling seams that would indicate false structure."

Tryst ignored Ren and turned his glance to a colour contrasted border running along the wall at chest level. It was comprised of small rectangular tiles that looked a reddish, coppery hue in colour, each one with a simple design of a fern leaf upon it done in gold paint. The border ran the entire length of the room and separated the mosaic of marble tiling that ran around the floor to the pool and the off-white sheeting that covered the ceiling.

It was these tiny tiles that she could fit two of in the palm of her hand that Tryst was most interested in. "It's here, but it's well covered. I took steps to ensure no one in the manor would ever know it existed and hopefully they still won't after we're gone." Tryst spoke without breaking his gaze from the border tiles.

When he found what he was looking for in them he slid a knife from within his boot and used it to pry a tile from its setting. The swordsman was careful and precise with his incision and the mortar scarcely fell away as the tile came loose. Behind it was a well cut hole, hollowed in an oval shape around where the tile had been. Tryst began prying at another tile a little further down until it too came away to show a hole that was identical to the first.

"We won't fit through those, I'm afraid," Ren said dryly.

In another time she might have found that comment funny, but she had no smiles to give right now, let alone laughter.

Tryst gave a look that indicated that he was no more inclined to laugh than she was. "No, but these will," he said as he opened his cloak to reveal a red leather sheathe that shone as it stretched from his hip to just south of the knee. Tryst reached behind that however, to a purple bag tied to his belt that looked near to bursting.

He took the bag in hand, untied it from the belt and opened it to produce what looked like a pair of brass doorknobs. The ends of which were an oval cut to fit the holes where the tiles had just been. Tryst slid one into either hole and pushed inwards forcefully until they could go no more and turned them until they heard a distinct pair of clicking noises. With a deep breath, Tryst gave a forceful heave and pulled at the wall with all his strength.

An entire, meter wide section of wall from the floor to the ceiling began to slide outward with a low rumble until it stood out half a meter from where it had been.

"That is simply amazing." Ren said in a fascinated tone as he approached the protruding section of wall and gazed beyond.

After a cursory glance into the darkness on the other side, Tryst returned to the bathing room. "Are you fit to walk, my lady?" he asked as he made eye contact with her. "I admit that it's quite a trek, but I won't be making it with you."

"Where will you be going then?" She asked worriedly.

"I have to go to the kitchens and obtain food and water for our journey and then to the stables to collect my horse. More importantly, I'll need to establish an alibi that will buy us more time to get further away." Tryst replied, bluntly and sincerely. "I shall be waiting on the other side of that underground path to retrieve you both. You have my word, my lady."

She still had her doubts of him and his intentions and couldn't purchase his promises so easily. "How can we be sure of that? You might seal us in there to die."

Plainly, that comment wounded Tryst and there was a pause while he stared at the ground, leaving her and Ren wondering what he would do next. He wheeled about, went to the wall, twisted the knobs and pulled them free from their settings. Once he had returned them to their holding bag, the drawstring was yanked tight and the bag tossed to Ren.

"What are you doing?" she asked, slightly puzzled.

"I can't open the door without those. So, if I were to seal you in, I couldn't retrieve this." Tryst explained while undoing his sword belt.

Holding the scabbard before her, Tryst drew the sword halfway out so that she might see it. It was Dwarven blacksteel, with a blade as dark as night save for its shimmering, silvery edge. If there was a finer piece of steel than this in the known world, her eyes had never seen it.

"This is my Sword of Mastery, my lady," Tryst explained. "I can think of no other possession in this world I value as much as this piece of steel. I offer it you to show the worth of my word. For if I want it back again after I push that wall into place, I will have to meet you on the other side of that tunnel." Tryst slid the sword back into its home before dropping to one knee and offering it to her in his open hands.

Taking it ever so gingerly, she felt its heft as it weighed down her sore wrists. "This is...You really want me to trust you that badly?" She desperately wanted for this escape to be genuine, though there was reluctance to side with a man who had been so loyal to her sworn enemy for so long.

It's a dark cell or a dark tunnel, at least the latter has a chance of there being a light at the end.

"This is a magnificent sword, and if you're willing to put trust in me to hold on to it, then that is the least I can do." She slung it over her shoulder, fumbling her tired hands with the buckle, but managing to pull it tight. "Ren, if you would be so kind as to light that lantern, I believe we have a walk ahead of us."

That elicited a brief smile from Tryst and he gently offered his hands to help her get to her feet. Pushing past her anxiety over the issue, she took them and let help her to stand.

Pain shot through her knees as she put weight on them for the first time since the madman had driven her to them on the unforgiving stone floor. She struggled to keep from falling and thought she was going to hit the ground until Tryst caught her. Her joints were the worst of it, but the muscles in her legs throbbed terribly from being stretched taut as they had. Yet, she knew she could walk, she had to, and she needed to.

She took a step, then another and a few more before she gently pushed Tryst away to stand on her own. Each footfall was a new, excruciating experience but she bit her lip and took them all the same. It was only when she came to the gap on the left side of the outcropped wall that she stopped, staring into the long, perpetual night of the underground. "Mister Wildheart, time is a wasting. Let's be off before the guards come down on us," she suggested while leaning against the wall.

Tryst turned and extended a hand to Ren. "Wildheart, is it? I never offered you my name yet, it's-"

Ren met his stare, but not his handshake. "Tryst Reine, yes, I heard the lady identify you on the steps below. Wildheart is the family name, my own is Tyrendil and I thank you again for the rescue, ser. Before we descend into that tunnel, is there anything we should know? A fortress as old and wickedly built as Valdarrow's is sure to be more than ordinary."

The look on Tryst's face showed surprise in the curtness from Ren. Tryst bore the slight well and shook it off to answer his query. "Aye, Tyrendil, there is a single route you must take, listen carefully: you'll have a few hundred meters of straightforward walking and then the crossroads begin. You see, these old tunnels were used by

Valdarrow's men to allow them unseen passage between the fortress and the outlying guard towers. It's a veritable maze down there by design and time has turned it into even more of a death trap. I've managed to shore up one path and it leads to the base of the last standing tower of Valdarrow.

"To get to where you need to be, you shall take your first right, then a left turn, a second right and then go straight through the next two intersections. After the second direct crossroad, there will be a cave-in that I have dug a hole through. You will have to move carefully there. Beyond that, it's one left, one right and you should come into a large room with layered stone walls. To the left of your entrance there will be a heavy stone slab door with a tower carved into it. Above the carving should be the letters 'N.W.' and the number two.

"Wait there in that room until I open the door. Do not come out beforehand, as I cannot guarantee that things won't go awry."

Ren called back the directions to confirm with Tryst to as he lit the lantern he had confiscated from the guards room.

She tried to commit all them to memory herself, though her screaming knees drowned out the whisper in her mind. The next thing she knew, Ren had stepped through the space on the right side of the moving wall and was waving the lantern to see the ground ahead. Tryst followed close behind and not wanting to be alone, she forced herself to take a few pained steps into the darkness until she was once again beside them both.

"My lady, please feel free to take your time, but try to not rest too much," Tryst spoke softly as she hobbled up beside him and leaned on the nearest wall. "I should be able to buy a few more hours by ordering the dungeon guards to wait at the top of the stairs until I give them further command. With any luck, it will be near morning before they realize that I won't be coming back, both of their prisoners are gone and the torturer is dead. The guards on the rear gate will think that I have left to make an arrest of the very men waiting to receive us. That should ensure that they won't come looking for our party themselves until the interior guards alert them that there has been an escape." He laid a hand gently on her shoulder to look at her with those green eyes that shone even in the low light of the lantern. "Hopefully, by this time, we will all be well away."

A thousand questions ran through her mind, though there were none she thought to ask before Tryst was out of sight. There was a soft groan as he leaned into the wall and the light from the bathing room slowly shrunk to a slit before disappearing entirely with one final shove. She could hear scrabbling and shuffling noises from the other side and before long that gave way to empty silence.

The pair stood for what seemed like an eternity, staring into the bleakness that lay ahead. "We should go," she urged Ren lowly while trying to walk toward him. Her knees buckled after the third step and she fell into him clumsily.

"Easy now," Ren said as he caught her with his free hand before she could tumble to the ground. "Here, wrap your arm around my neck and lean on me, we'll take each step together." It was less a suggestion and more of a command, as he draped her arm over his shoulder and adjusted his lantern and satchel to the opposite side.

The path was a difficult one and even if she were uninjured, she would have only dared step where the lantern cast its light. Broken bricks, uneven stones and scurrying rats made each footfall a calculated one and they moved at a snail's pace.

More than once she stumbled, with only Ren to keep her from falling flat on her face. "I don't think I could do this without you, Ren, in my shape. I'm sorry you are in such a dreadful place, but in the same breath I'm thankful that you are here," She told him after the second time he caught her.

"This is not a place anyone would want to be," Ren agreed assuredly. "Though, it is good to not have to face it alone."

It was after they had reached the second intersection that she asked to sit and rest. Once she had lowered herself to the floor, she began rubbing her haggard knees, trying to somehow massage the pain away. Ren paced the floor nervously, unable to settle at all.

"You could go on ahead you know," she suggested through laboured breaths. "Scout up along if you like, there's no need to stay here with me."

Ren stopped in his tracks and his face softened. "And leave you in the dark by yourself?"

"The darkness doesn't frighten me, Tyrendil," she replied, letting her voice trail off.

"Be that as it may, I think it would be better if we stuck together right now." He sighed while watching her run a hand through her matted and tangled hair. "I have a brush in my satchel, if you would like to use it."

For a few seconds she considered the offer before ultimately turning it down. "No, we should move on, we've rested long enough. But thank you, all the same."

The elf nodded at that suggestion and once he had helped her back to standing, the two of them got underway again.

As Tryst had described, the way beyond the second intersection was caved in. Only a small hole at the top of a pile of rubble remained to let them through and though it seemed daunting in her state, she offered to go first. The loose dirt rolled under her feet as she crawled up the embankment on her side, trying to avoid her knees making contact with anything. She felt her legs begin to buckle, but she dug her hands through and reached the gap. Tryst's sword on her back snagged in the small space and despite her efforts to protect her knees, she had to flatten to her stomach to get through. The lantern was handed through the hole to her so she could hold it high for Ren to see his way through to safety.

Once he joined her on the other side of the cave-in, it was fairly easy going by contrast.

The tunnel showed its age more visibly here. Thick roots poked through cracks in the ancient brick and fresh hewn logs stood in certain places while the rotted husks of their predecessors lay discarded nearby. It was clear that nature was fighting hard to take back the land from the architectural intrusion that took place nearly a millennium ago.

Their limping walk finally came to a conclusion when they entered into a spacious room. Dirt comprised the floor and vertically arranged planks made up all but one wall. Overhead sat sparsely spaced beams crossing to and fro to hold the clay ceiling at bay. The one wall not made of plank was comprised of rough stones and crumbling mortar.

In its centre was a stone slab door in a shade of yellow that was the colour of old parchment. A crude tower had been carved into it and the outline was painted in brown only recently. Above the drawing was the inscription they were looking for: *N.W.2.*

"We finally made it," she commented as Ren left her to lean on the wall and held his lantern before the exit. There didn't appear to be any handles, or any feasible way to open it like a normal door, but she supposed it could be pushed ajar. "The question now is: do we believe Tryst Reine or do we leave on our own?" she asked Ren, who was looking over the smooth door and running his free hand over the shapes in search of a handhold.

He hummed aloud a moment before answering. "That's a good question, my lady. Though, I'm not so sure we *can* leave."

Her brows furrowed as she looked upon the door. "What do you mean? Surely there's a latch or a handle somewhere here."

His shoulders rose in a puzzled shrug. "It's quite the conundrum. On one hand, I can't seem to see an obvious way to open this door." Ren turned to look at her as he continued on. "On the other hand, why would Tryst give us instructions to stay put if we could not let ourselves out without him?"

With a great deal of effort she managed to step up to his side, a hand on his shoulder for support. "Perhaps it is meant to be pushed outward?" she offered as a guess. "Either way, even if we tried to leave on our own, we wouldn't get very far while I'm in this state, especially if Tryst has a horse. I don't see any choice but for us to wait for him."

"It's hard to fault the logic in that, my lady," Ren agreed. "We should see if we can find you somewhere to rest while we wait," he added as he stepped away from the door to look about room with the lantern held high. The shining of the light into the adjacent corner to the door revealed a ruddy looking shape that turned out to be a low table. Ren put a palm down on it, shaking it and testing the weight. "This seems sturdy. Would you like to sit, my lady?"

"Aye, that would be nice for a spell," she answered wearily, shuffling toward Ren and the old table with its wood worn to a grey colour and light layer of fallen dirt atop it. The release of pressure from her legs felt down right alleviating and her whole body shuddered involuntarily.

The sword belt came loose as she hastily undid the buckle, tumbling from her shoulder to clatter loudly on the table.

Ren dropped his satchel and the lantern beside her and sat on the edge of the surface. "How are you feeling?" he queried lightly.

"Numb." She sighed. "This day has been a cruel nightmare come to life."

"I am so sorry for you, my lady." Ren gave her shoulder a light squeeze as he spoke.

The silence hung for a moment and before her mind could venture into the recent past, she spoke up. "Is the offer still available to use your brush?"

"Of course, my lady" Ren nodded, fishing the lacquered, wooden handled brush from his satchel and handing it off to her.

Tired hands fumbled to undo the knots in her hair, they felt heavy and clumsy and she barely had the strength to pass through the mass of red tangles.

Ren gently reached out for the brush. "Might I, my lady? As you can see, I'm well versed in taking care of hair."

With a nod she turned and gave him her back as best as the table would allow. It took some time, though soon he had her locks detangled. After a time she could feel the tender strokes working though her hair almost rhythmically.

"I have an extra ribbon if you would like me to tie your hair back," the elf suggested in a low, soothing voice.

A wave of exhaustion came over her and she had to shake herself awake to answer him. "Um, sure, yes, that would be fine, thank you," she managed.

The elf's smooth hands drew her long strands back in a smooth motion, wrapping the ribbon about the hair and tying it off in a simple bow. "Does that feel better, my lady?"

"Yes, it feels wonderful. Thank you, Ren, for everything," she said with a sigh, that he seemed to read.

He slid to the floor and drew the hood of his cloak up. "You're quite welcome, my lady. In the meantime, you should rest your eyes. I'll keep watch until Tryst arrives."

"Do you trust him?" she asked suddenly as she dragged her legs onto the table and nestled herself against the stone wall.

"I see little other choice. It's either trust him or take our chances in the cells." Ren answered from the floor below. "My odds of deportation were good, yet, it was no certainty and you..." He trailed off, leaving the obvious answer to hang in the air.

"I was headed for a noose," she uttered stoically. "Some part of me still feels like I am. Tryst Reine wishes badly for me to believe that his intentions are altruistic, though I can't help but think of the man he was reputed to be."

"You've been given no reason to trust me either, you know," Ren commented. "You believe I was your fellow inmate based only on what you observed."

There was a pause and she sensed he had more to add. "Go on."

And he did: "You never saw me emerge from a cell. All you saw was a half-dressed elf assisting a man in a mask who turned out to be Tryst Reine. You noted I was an elf and asked if I was the same one you heard the monster yelling at and I simply said that I was. You took my word on nothing more than that, my lady. I haven't given you any promises, or any assurances that I will stay with you after that door opens. Tryst Reine has and he held nothing back from the moment you saw his face. He told you his intentions, how he plans to go about achieving such and even gave you his sword in a show of good faith."

While Ren had been speaking, she had taken the sword in question to hand, sliding it halfway from its sheath. It slid out with barely a scrape, its blade shining with an oily sheen in the low light of the lantern. The black steel above the shining edge soaked the light up hungrily as she turned it in her hands.

"He has done much to win my trust," she admitted. "Yet all that has accomplished is to raise my suspicions all the more. But, I suppose you are right. There is nothing else for me to lose. I either see the light of day or the darkness of death."

She continued to stare at the sword, gazing at the naked, pristine steel. "I suppose my doubt of Tryst stems from the fear and hatred for him amongst the people," she started, wondering if Ren was listening or had dozed off to sleep, though deciding to talk regardless, even if it was only to herself. "The heralds and the bulletins all attribute some truly horrifying acts to him and have given him quite the dire reputation. I suppose my eyes have read and heard the tales so much that they defaulted from hearsay to truth in my mind over the years. They were simple stories that were easy to believe. The most oft repeated one being that Tryst Reine is a heartless killer who is only restrained by Grenjin Howland's command." She slid the sword back into its home and laid it across her lap. "But, for all that talk and for how skilled he supposedly is in the ways of combat, I have only ever seen him once before, at a distance."

Ren hummed ponderously from his seat on the floor below her table. "And where was this, might I ask?"

"In Aquas Bay, just this past summer," she answered readily. "I was there to deliver a speech in the marketplace. My lieutenants had set up Thieves near all the guard stations to act as distractions and lure as many of them as possible from the market square. When my decoys sprang into action, I climbed onto the roof of a merchant's stall erected on the side of a taller building and began my speech. It was right in the middle of the whole demonstration that I spotted him."

"How could you be sure it was him?" Ren asked again.

The memory came back vividly as she spoke of it and she could remember Tryst down to the last detail. "He was clad in black, from neck to boots, even in the putridly humid heat of the southern summers of Aquas Bay. He had red hair flowing to the small of his back and a sword, this sword, at his side," she said, tapping the scabbard. "He stared at me and I remember the eyes, how green they were. I should have realised it was him the second I saw those green eyes again through that black mask a few hours ago. They are like nothing I have ever seen before. I am told such a bright green is a common colour among those with the blood of ancient Gildriad in their veins, but until then I had never seen it myself. It seemed like a sure thing that he would try to chase and arrest me and yet those green eyes were the only things that followed when I bolted. When I looked back from the rooftops to wave at the people one more time, he was still there, still as stone and I remained free until now."

"It sounds to me like he didn't want to catch you," Ren observed. "A man of his skills no doubt could have given chase and by the Lord Master's decree you would be his primary target to capture, after all. Yet, as you say, you got away."

She nodded, having thought as much herself after the sighting. "There is still a part of me that is having difficulty looking beyond what I and everyone else have been fed in terms of Tryst's reputation. Let alone a man that I have been led to believe has spent four years hunting me," she added to her argument.

A point Ren seemed to agree with. "That is to be expected, though I have found that the wall of preconceived notions is rarely a good place to hang your judgement."

The poignant words struck a chord within her and she held on them for a moment. "You might be right, Ren."

The elf clambered to his feet and his body went tense. "I hear voices and footsteps," he whispered while taking the lantern from where it sat on the table.

"What? Are you certain?" she asked, sliding to the edge of the table with the sword clutched in her arms

A finger went to his lips to silence her and he turned towards the exit. "Listen."

At first she heard nothing but the sound of her own heart

beating wildly in her chest. Though soon the walls seemed to vibrate in tune with a heavy thumping that seemed to follow in a steady beat. "Are those hooves I'm hearing?"

Ren's answer was barely above a whisper and his gaze concentrated to where the ruckus seemed to be originating from. "Aye, there's a horse. I distinctly heard voices, too, though they seem to be quiet now. Two for certain, might be more. I'll take the lantern to hide you in the darkness. Get under the table, there's no telling who is out there. It is most likely Tryst, but I cannot say for sure."

It took her a frustratingly long time to crawl beneath the table and in her haste she had left the sword behind. Once she had accomplished what should have been a relatively simple task, she looked about for Ren and found him standing in the entrance to the tunnels. His hood was drawn low over his face and the lantern rested at his side, leaving her in total darkness.

The doorway let out a sudden groan that echoed throughout the room so loudly that she was sure the ceiling was about to cave in. When next she looked to the exit, pale light had begun to flicker in through a slit on one side of the stone.

The slim, low glow on the floor slowly grew to reveal a silhouette of a person in a long cloak. "Hello?" spoke the same voice that had left them on the other side of the ancient tunnel. "Tyrendil? Where's Orangecloak?" she heard Tryst ask as his gaze fell to where Ren stood clutching the lantern.

"Tryst Reine," replied Ren as he crossed the room to Tryst, illuminating the human in the light of the lantern. "The lady is safe, worry not. However, I have questions I need answering before I reveal her to you."

Tryst was eager to answer. "Certainly, what might they be?"

The elf stopped just out of arms reach of Tryst before he spoke again. "On the stairwell leading to the dungeon, I overheard you mention you were planning to take the lady to the Hotel Dupoire at the base of Graelin Mountain, then eastward to friends. Who lies in wait for her in the east?"

"No one," Tryst stated flatly. "For I said I was taking her west. My destination is the city of Portsward, where we will find a network of people with goals that closely align with hers. I'm bringing her to them, as per my orders."

A wave of fear came over her the moment Tryst uttered the

word 'orders'.

It was something that Ren had seemed to seize upon as well and his voice became tinged with curiosity. "What would these orders be and from whom do they come? I had thought you only took orders from the Lord Master."

Tryst bristled at that. "He is no Lord Master of mine."

"Then who does Tryst Reine swear loyalty to?" Ren threw out.

To that question, Tryst seemed only too ready to answer. "To we who call ourselves the Musicians." There was a measure of pride in his voice as he said it, as if he had been waiting to for quite some time.

"That's an interesting name." Ren was undeterred and kept his line of questions firing rapidly. "Who are the other Musicians?"

"We are men and women from Illiastra and beyond who play the song of freedom on the instruments of change." The answer seemed like one that was well rehearsed, yet the confidence and pride with which Tryst recited it was palpable.

It still looked as though Ren was unconvinced and he shrugged nonchalantly. "Yet another clever answer, Mister Reine. However, I need names if I am to trust you."

Tryst looked about uneasily, as if he were worried about being overheard. "The conductor of the Musicians is Greggard Simillon of Portsward, Lord of International Trade and Relations. The members of his orchestra are all in some way or another in the employ of the Illiastran Government save for a few foreign members."

Ren's tone began to border on sarcastic at that. "And your intention is to overthrow the Lord Master and the Elite Merchants?"

"Yes," Tryst said with a deep breath, his frustration audibly setting in. "If you have any other questions, ask them hastily. We have some time, but not so much that we can waste it standing around."

The elf raised a single finger in protest. "I have just one last question, if I may." When Tryst made no motion to deny permission, Ren continued. "After we reach Graelin Mountain, what is your intention for me?"

Exasperated, Tryst exhaled and ran a gloved hand over his face. "To be honest, my dear elf, having you captured by the Palomb Twins was a great twist of fortune for myself and the lady. I am indebted to you immensely for your assistance. What is it you want? You have only to name it and if it is in my power to grant, it shall be yours."

Ren jumped at the offer vociferously. "I was traveling to the

Elven Forest from Gildriad when I was taken. I have no wants other than to complete that journey. Going north and east from Graelin to the Northern Pass in the Snowy Lands of the Dwarves seems like my easiest way. So, I will travel with you that far at least. Before such time, if you prove to me your noble intentions for the lady, then I will decide what I want of you."

"I more than accept such terms, ser," Tryst said with relief, extending a bare hand toward Ren, who took it by the wrist and gave it a firm shake.

The elf turned her way, his voice going soft once more. "I hope these arrangements are sufficient for you, my lady."

She deigned to give an immediate answer as she dragged herself out sideways, daring not to put direct pressure on her anguished knees. It dawned upon her as she lay on the ground that getting up might be near impossible. Nonetheless, she gave it an attempt, fingers scraping uselessly against the wall for purchase that could not be found.

Tryst and Ren both seemed to sense she was stuck and the two came to her quickly enough, taking a hand each to help put her back on her feet.

"Ser Reine," she greeted him achingly. "I'm glad that you upheld your promise."

"I had no intention of doing otherwise," he replied ever so politely. "Also, if it pleases my lady, you may call me Tryst."

"Very well, then," she acquiesced with little more thought than that, focusing her energy instead on the effort to stay standing.

The slender shoulder of Ren was offered and she wrapped an arm over to help alleviate pressure on her knees.

With her free arm she reached for the sword on the table and handed it to Tryst. "You upheld your end of the bargain. I believe this to be yours."

Tryst had reclaimed his sword, buckling it back to his waist. "Many thanks for holding on to it, my lady. Shall we be off? We have a great deal of ground to cover before sunrise and I fear too much time has been squandered." With that he led the pair out into the night air and into a small pit ringed with steps.

Her eyes went to the sky and she breathed the cold fresh air hungrily while Tryst pushed the thick slab of stone that was the door back into place. The near, pale moon glowed brightly in the sky, streaked occasionally by the clouds that threatened to darken it.

It will indeed be a good night for trekking, she thought to herself. The wind seemed to be up, but it was blowing from the south, so it was not as sharply cold as it otherwise might be.

Turning back to Tryst, she noticed that the bedrock door blended nearly perfectly with the rest of the foundation. Above that loomed a crumbling, though still ominously tall tower.

Tryst picked up on her wonderment. "Impressive, isn't it?" he asked rhetorically. "The Valdarrow family had it built by the half-elves of Amrosha he had captured and forced into slavery. Those same slaves led Segai, the Hero of Phaleayna through these tunnels to cast down their oppressor," Tryst said as much with a sweeping gesture towards the decrepit tower. "I only wish that the people remembered *that* Master of Blades. If they did, they would know better than to believe what Grenjin Howland says of *this* Master of Blades."

With a despondent sigh, he turned towards the stone steps leading out of the pit. "But I digress. There will be time for me to regale you with history at a later time."

Ren had snuffed out the lantern while Tryst spoke. Reasoning that it might draw attention and pointing out that the moonlight would more than serve to show them the way.

To conquer the stairs, Ren suggested she climb onto his back and reluctantly, she accepted, knowing her knees would fight her on every step otherwise. Tryst went ahead of them, stopping briefly to look over the lip of the well and ensure it was still clear. When she and Tryst crested the top of the stairs she saw that they were indeed not alone and that Ren's earlier prediction of a horse was true.

"My lady, let me introduce you to my friend Wildstar, a fine chestnut courser." Tryst proudly beamed, petting the shaggy mane of the mount, which was saddled and carrying a full satchel on his back. "I know he would be happy to carry us both, if you would allow."

"I'm glad one of us still has a friend, ser, mine were both killed this morning," she said mournfully as Ren set her down.

"I apologise, my lady that was ill said of me." Tryst bowed his head. "If they were in your company, I am sure they were good folk."

"They are...Or rather, they were." She took a deep breath and fought to hold her composure. "Well, as it is, I can't walk. I shall take Wildstar up on his offer."

Tryst gave a nod and lifted her into the saddle. A gesture she allowed, knowing the effort of trying to haul her injured legs over the horse's back and into the saddle would have been arduous at best.

She hit a long object with her left leg as she swung in gingerly over the horse. Upon looking down she saw a sleek bow of silvery ash and a quiver of black leather, rimmed in shining steel lashed between shaft and string. It was full of arrows, all fletched in black feathers, likely from a crow or raven.

Tryst seemed to notice she was snagged in it and walked around the horse to help. "Tyrendil," he called to the elf. "How are you with a bow?"

"I am certainly not considered more than passably able amongst my fellow elves. In the eyes of humans, my skills may be seen more favourably though. Why do you ask?" Ren replied without so much as a look as he was busy staring at the crumbling walls of the old tower.

One loomed high above the others, coming to a point like some mountain made of brick and mortar. Though everything else was slowly losing a battle against nature, barely resembling what was once a mighty outpost tower for the army of a family of dictators.

Bow and quiver alike were unlashed from the saddle and presented to Ren by Tryst. "Then I lend these to your capable hands, Tyrendil. Use them well, ser, that's one of the finest bows crafted by the University. No doubt your own kin make superior weapons, but it should suffice."

Ren took the bow in hand to give it an inspection. "It is indeed a great piece. I shall wield it as best I can," the elf added as he gave it a test draw. He drew an arrow to see their make. "Bodkin head, they pierce deep and fly far, it's a good choice," he said as he turned an arrow in his hand. "I shall take good care of it while I have it."

The elf wasted no time slinging the bow and arrows over his shoulder to rest above his satchel and unlashing the purple, velvet bag on his hip. "I believe these are yours, if you would like them back."

"Yes, thank you," Tryst said, taking them to hand and placing them in one of Wildstar's saddlebags.

With a last glance at the tower, Tryst wordlessly turned and began to lead them away from the ruins and through an old path grown over with foliage. Wildstar followed dutifully at his heels with Tryst not so much as touching the bridle.

From where she sat atop the saddle, the lowest branches on

the birch trees reached out to gently claw at her face. In the night, with the tree tops hiding the two moons, it was difficult to see the limbs before they took a swipe at her. Ahead, she saw the moonlight gazing down on what she thought was another clearing, though as they drew closer she realized it was a road. It was worn from travellers though not rutted, which suggested that feet and hooves were upon it more than wheels. What she could see of this road ran north to south in bends and curves.

Ren fell in beside Wildstar, having brought up the rear while they were on the narrower, forgotten path. She heard a baying from another horse and her eyes followed the noise to see two large, moonlit silhouettes moving against the other side of the road.

Dirt grinded beneath Tryst's boots as he turned on his heels on the road, scanning as far as the dim light of the night would let him.
"Go back to the old path, my lady and stay just out of the line of sight, he instructed in a low, soft voice. "I'll be back for you once I find our companions."

Wildstar began to follow, taking her along until Tryst returned, having heard the hooves close behind. "My lady, take the reins. He's gentle and will go where you direct him," Tryst instructed before disappearing into the trees beyond the two hobbled horses on the opposite side of the trail.

Up until now she had just been holding the lip of the saddle, letting the horse follow Tryst. As it was, she couldn't remember the last time she had sat one. The Thieves had few of them, and they were used only by the group's couriers and the rangers that guarded the shores of Phaleayna.

It was my first life, she suddenly seemed to recall. *My father kept a tall, black warhorse and he used to take me riding with him in the countryside. That was back when I knew how to laugh, when I still knew what happiness was.*

She took the string of leather in hand and gently tried to turn Wildstar, who, much to her own surprise, actually turned. Ren came behind on foot and they went until she could barely see the road.

She sat quietly for a time, and started to feel the cold air of autumn sifting through her leathers and tunic to her skin beneath. Other sensations came to her as well, and soon she found herself in need of a certain relief. She softly called to Ren, who had taken a position behind a tree to remain out of sight of any potential travellers on the road.

"Yes, my lady?" Ren replied back from the darkness.

"I can't help but think that we have a long night of riding ahead with little chance to stop. Could you help me down?" she asked, a little bashful in her request.

"Of course, my lady," Ren dutifully said, coming up alongside the steed and lifting her down to the ground.

She hobbled off behind a tree, leaning against the trunk to take the weight from her knees while she dropped her breeches. When she finished, her knees were torturing her and yet she somehow managed to get back to standing without having to call for Ren. A small victory, given the effort it had taken from her.

While she tied the laces, she heard Wildstar trotting away from her through the trees. By the time she got back to where the horse had been there was only Ren, crouched low to the ground and staring at something in the road intently.

Ren turned to glance at her as she sidled up beside him. "Tryst has returned with his company and the horse went to greet him," he explained. "Are you okay to walk or would you like me to carry you?"

"A shoulder to lean on would suffice well enough, I think," was her reply and soon enough the two were back to the road's edge. Before them both stood Tryst, conversing in an angry tone of voice with another figure standing beside the hobbled horses in the shadows.

"I am telling you that it was ill done," Tryst barked. "If the wolves dig up those bodies, they will be found when the manor guards most assuredly sweep the area. Even if the graves stay undisturbed, they're beneath freshly dug soil. That alone will attract attention."

The other person scoffed at that. "And what odds is it if they are found?" Their voice was deep, gravelly and all too familiar. "Last time I checked, dead men weren't too chatty. If left alive those two imbeciles would have sold this whole thing out for a horn of ale at the first chance they saw."

She felt a wave of shock wash over her from head to heel as she suddenly realised just who the other person was.

Tryst turned and left the other fellow beside the horses and came upon her and Ren standing just off the road side.

The other man was still talking loudly to Tryst's back. "I should never have hired them drunks in the first place. They made a royal fucking mess of things today."

"Is this our other companion?" she heard Ren ask and she hoped it was not.

"It is, unfortunately," Tryst answered in a tone of frustration and she felt her stomach flutter as the words left his lips.

It felt as though a great force punched her in the stomach and she stumbled on her wobbly legs into Ren.

"What's wrong, my lady?" Ren seemed entirely confused and held her tightly as the pain coursed through her body.

Her attention went to Tryst. "What is the meaning of this?" she said with equal parts anger and bewilderment. "Is this some sort of sick ruse, Tryst Reine?"

Ren looked between the man in the road and back to her. "My lady, whatever are you talking about? Who is that man?"

"It is Fletchard Miller, the bounty hunter. He killed Myles and Coquarro, my dear friends, in cold blood and left them to die in the tunnels of the Batterdowns," she spat while looking only at Tryst.

"Is this true?" Ren asked Tryst, his voice full of shock.

Fletchard yelled an answer before Tryst could. "It was those fucking drunks that did that. I told you, they made a royal mess of things. I wanted to do this bloodlessly and take the three of you alive."

"My lady I-" Tryst tried to say, but she cut him off.

"No! Don't you dare to call me 'my lady', you have no right," she said with a shudder, fighting back the welling tears in her eyes as the image of Myles dying in her arms came flashing back.

He had collapsed into her after a rifle shot had been emptied into his stomach. "It doesn't end here, Orangecloak. It can't end here, not now," Myles had uttered in crimson coughs as she held him. "You'll find a way to keep moving on, you always found a way to get things done. That's why we followed you. I know you won't let my death be in vain." The blood was everywhere. Her tunic was stained with it, her hands and what seemed like every inch of Myles. There was no avoiding it.

She remembered running a hand through his short, wavy dark hair. "Don't talk so foolishly, Myles." Though she knew the wound was mortal, she tried to assure him otherwise. "You're going to be alright. I won't let anything happen to you."

"I'm done, Orangecloak. I'm sorry that I can't protect you anymore." Those had been the last words of Myles Stodden before his beautiful brown eyes had glossed over.

They had been her bodyguards, her dearest friends and the closest she had ever had to brothers. The pair had stood up to protect her as the door to the dingy room they were squatting in swung open, Myles asked the intruders what they wanted and they shot him for it. The tall, skinnier man of Fletchard's had panicked and fired, catching Myles in the stomach at close range. Fletchard started shouting at his dim witted employee, Coquarro saw an opening to charge the three men in the doorway and there had been another gunshot.

Afterwards, Fletchard pried her from Myles' body and clapped her in chains despite her protests to the contrary. It was only when they lifted her from that floor that she saw her other friend lying dead across a crate, a messy hole where his throat had been. She had screamed the whole way back to the surface.

Now, there he stood, the man whose ruffian employees had killed her dearest friends and handed her over to the Lord Master.

She wanted to leave, to run well away from all of them and away from the anguish in her heart. Her legs buckled and she began a descent towards the ground. If not for Ren holding her she would have collapsed entirely, instead she rolled into his lap on the gravel road. "What sort of cruel game is this, Tryst Reine?!" she roared at him. "Why is Fletchard Miller here?! Why am I here?!"

There was noise and footsteps, though she had turned away from Reine and Miller. It was all she could do, though one of them found her anyway. "We need him, my lady." Tryst reasoned in a pleading voice. "I do not condone what he has done, though there is no denying that he and his steeds have use to us."

She lifted her eyes to look at him. "Why would you need him? What use do you have for a heartless killer?"

The answer to her question came to her while Tryst fumbled for words. *He's going to make an end of it. The jape is up and let it be. Let him end my suffering, for this day is nothing but a nightmare,* she thought. *Let it be that sword, sharper than any other steel that I held for him in his false promise.*

Tryst lowered himself before her. "I will not allow any further harm to come to you," He said in a soft, sorrowful voice. "You have my word as a Master of Blades."

"Your word is little good to me," she said hatefully.

He turned away from her wordlessly and went to his horse.

Upon returning he dropped to his knees with a small bundle in his hands. "My word is all I have and I know that means naught to you right now, but I assure you it is true. I kept this to return to you, so that you might rise from the ashes of this tragedy and stand atop the world with it on your shoulders."

Her eyes fell to his hands and to the orange cloak, faded to the colour of a peach that they held out to her.

10
ELLARIE

For the past six years, Ellarie Dollen had found herself sorted under a collection of labels: rebel, member of the Thieves, freedom fighter, resister, emancipator, activist, protester, objector, and now all of it was gone, replaced with a single one. It was written on her back in white ink on a dark red, itchy shift in blocky letters that spelled it out for anyone that could read. It was a label she had never wanted and one that was hoisted upon her shoulders to bear. From now, until likely her last breath, Ellarie Dollen was a prisoner.

The other six women now forced to carry that same title shared what was called the 'Sobering Cell' with Ellarie. The space normally reserved for drunkards had been given over to the women of the Thieves in Major Burnson's meritorious effort to keep them together. It was a small comfort, though it was as much as they, as prisoners, could expect.

Those who were wounded were offered treatment by a medic, and all were given a simple meal of unsweetened oatmeal, water and buttered bread to break their fast. Afterwards, their ragged bits of raiment were taken from them in exchange for the long sleeved, hooded shifts they now wore. These made them look like crimson coloured druids of the Triarchy rather than members of the Thieves.

Outside of their cell hung a pair of bare bulbs, swaying gently with a slight draft that rolled through the room. A small but heavy wooden door sat to the left of the cell and sequestered the women from the rest of the world. On the other side of the entrance sat a pair of guards at all times. They entered on the half hour to give the prisoners a quick head count before leaving them be once more.

Ellarie did not trust the walls to keep silent and had instructed the others to keep their own chatter to whispers and never utter her name when addressing her. The guards still believed she was Bernadine and that Bernadine was she. It was the one arrow left in Ellarie's quiver and she planned to keep it.

Merion and Joyce had been cuddled together in one of the four cots suspended by chains from the wall from nearly the moment they had all been locked up. Hard, narrow planks lined with lumpy, rag-stuffed mattresses made for a poor bed, yet they made the best of it and suffered no complaints. Joyce held the seething, silent Merion in a tight grasp and led the others in a solemn remembrance of the three friends they had lost the night before.

Ellarie had paced the cell, taking the time to test the door, the bars, the bricks and everything else she could get her hands on as she did so. Finding no weaknesses to exploit, she resigned to sharing a cot with both Allia and Coramae, tucking her knees beneath her chin to keep her feet off the cold floor. There was little room on the cot, and most of it had been given over to Coramae, who tried to find a comfortable position to rest her bruised and swollen bottom.

They had all surmised it to be about noon when they were next fed. Their meal this time consisting of baked beans in a tiny bowl and a refill of their tin water cups. Ellarie could recall having worse meals and going longer between them, especially when she, Merion and Joyce first went on the run.

The sisters had fled first to Joyce's home, located on a little farmstead just east of Atrebell at the time. As it was, Merion's lover was living in the barn loft of the farm, all under the guise of being a man. Merion had selflessly urged Joyce to let her go and continue her own life as a delivery driver, but Joyce had refused. "I've been running since I was fifteen years old, Merion," Joyce had begun her argument. "I'm nothing more than a vagabond. I go from job to job under different names, pretending to be a man so I can work, and leaving in the night when the ruse runs its course. There's no place for me to call home anymore and I have no family. Besides, if you and Ellarie are on the run and your little brother knows what I look like, then they're going to come after me next. My time at this farm is done and I'm going with the two of you."

That next day, Joyce snuck Ellarie and Merion away from the farm and into the forest to wait for her. When she returned to them at daybreak, she was carrying her things in a rucksack on her shoulder and the three departed together for Phaleayna.

Together they stowed away on trains, walked the dirt roads and camped in the forests. They had no hunting supplies, but Joyce had brought a fishing line and they did manage to catch trout whenever they happened upon a body of water.

We even managed to catch a big salmon that one time, Ellarie recalled warmly. *That was a great day.*

She remembered standing on a rock overlooking a river, the line in hand as she gently swirled it about the water with a big, wriggling worm on the hook. Next thing she knew, one foot was knee deep in the water and the rest of her was wrenching the line and running towards the shore.

Joyce had jumped the fish while it was flapping on the shallow edge of the river, and before long the blonde was soaked to the bone. All the while Merion had laughed fitfully at her lover's colourfully flavoured language in her struggle to wrestle their dinner ashore.

We laughed so hard about it afterwards that Joyce practically shook her clothes dry around the fire.

Ellarie wished they were back at that river once more, just to hear Merion and Joyce laughing again, even for a few minutes.

Three wanted runaways they were, violating gender oppressive laws that reduced women to possessions to be owned by men. But out on the road, with only the stars for a ceiling, they felt free, they felt alive, and most of all, they felt happy. They had only a few coins, their clothes and little else, but neither did they need anything more than each other.

Joyce became like a sister to Ellarie in that time and she came to think more of the woman than she did for all her full-blooded siblings back in Atrebell.

As for Merion, she was madly in love. Ellarie couldn't recall a time when her sister had been as easy to smile as she had been on that journey to the Southlands.

It was the rangers of the Thieves that came across Ellarie, Merion and Joyce on the shoreline near the voluminous Great Valley

Lake. The Rangers of the Ruins were the guardians of the island home of the outcasts, patrolling the shores for intruders and refugees alike.

The three of them had been quite apprehensive of the rangers who so casually strode into their camp on the beach. One among them approached the trio of tired travelers, pushing back the hood of a faded, peach cloak to reveal a woman with hair the colour of fire. "Welcome to Phaleayna, friends. You need not be afraid of us, for we are merely the Thieves and we will not hurt you."

After exchanging silent glances, it was Ellarie who finally stepped forward to speak for them. "My name is Ellarie Dollen and this is my sister Merion and her companion Joyce Keena. We have come seeking refuge here. It was our understanding that the island was a haven for runaways and outcasts like us."

The woman had smiled and nodded at that. "You have heard right, Ellarie Dollen, and you three would be most welcome here. Come, I'll take you to our encampment. There should be some meat and vegetables on the spit for you to eat and mead to drink if you would like it. You all look famished, where did you all come from?"

"We made the journey from Atrebell and we would much like to take you up on your offer, uh, ma'am," Ellarie answered, unsure of how to address the stranger.

"That's quite a distance and I would love to hear all about it over some warm food." The woman raised her hood over her head once more and gestured back the way her unit had come. "Gather your things and follow me. I'll be your guide for the day."

A male of the unit spoke to the redhead from beneath his own hood. "Shall we continue on without you?"

The woman, who looked to be of the same age as Ellarie, answered the fellow quite authoritatively and confidently. "That would be fine, Chade. Check the shores as far as the Nook for others and return to camp for your lunch." She turned back to her new guests, suddenly remembering something. "It seems I have forgotten my manners and have yet to introduce myself. Everyone here calls me Orangecloak and you may as well."

"Are you one of the Thieves?" Merion had asked curiously. "You look too young to be, if you don't mind my saying. But you sound like you could be."

The Orangecloak of those days still smiled and she had in that instance as she answered Merion's question. "You're right. I'm not a member, not yet, anyway. But thank you for saying I could be. Come on now, follow me."

It was Orangecloak who eventually took them to the island. Rowing across the lake in one of the many little, yellow dory boats that they hid amongst the reeds and paddled back and forth to the ruins. The entire trip was spent with her inquiring about their journey in the thick accent found commonly amongst the Southlanders.

Upon arrival at the thriving town on the island, they were brought before Yassira Na-Qoia, leader of Phaleayna and the proclaimed 'Mother of the Thieves'. The ebony-skinned woman from Johnah welcomed them with open arms and insisted she hear their story of how they became runaways.

The three took turns recalling the events, speaking truthfully and honestly of everything that had befallen them. Both Orangecloak and Yassira listened attentively and spoke nothing until their guests had finished.

"You ladies have been through much," Yassira had said to break the tension that had fallen over the former throne room of the last King of Phaleayna. "We have heard many stories like yours and they have all led me to know for certain that the Triarchy is poison in the well of the mind." She had stood from her seat as she said that and taken Merion's hand in both of hers. "You will be safe here from the Triarchist law for we permit no proselytising. People are free to believe in whatever gods they will, but it is not their place to force others to live by the rules of their own beliefs."

"Thank you," answered Merion for all of them. "We simply seek a chance to make a life for ourselves here, in a place where we might be accepted."

The beaming smile on Yassira's face was still a vivid memory for Ellarie and she recalled the relief that washed over her when the woman had replied, "And you shall have it, my new friends."

The wooden door separating the cell from the rest of the guard station creaked on its noisy hinges and Ellarie's eyes fluttered open at the sound.

I fell asleep, but for how long?

She glanced at the others, finding Joyce to be snoring softly and still holding tight to Merion, herself wide awake and curiously watching the guard that had entered.

He had come with a lantern and stood with it held aloft,

lingering and inspecting the prisoners silently.

That's a different guard. Had I slept through the shift change?

Ellarie kept her head down as the guard stepped close to the bars and shone the oil lantern in on them.

That's a new habit too, the others just did a head count and left. This one's actually looking *at us, but what's he looking for?*

"Merion?" the guard whispered in a strikingly familiar voice.

Her sister detangled herself from Joyce, waking her lover in the commotion as she stood and approached the bars. "Dolph...Is that really you, brother?" she answered nervously.

"Aye, tis me, the other guards said they had you and Ellarie and I had to come see for myself. There's something going on at the Atrebell manor and they called in whatever guards we could spare to aid the manor guards and the Honourable Guardsmen already posted up there. So this is my one chance to slip in here and see you." Dolph glanced around at the others in the cell sadly. "This isn't how I wanted us to be reunited, but somehow I knew it would be the only way. Where is Ellarie?"

From the far cot Ellarie saw Bernadine rise, ready to play her part faithfully, though Ellarie was on her own feet before she could. "It's alright Bernadine, this is my brother. He can know our secret." she said as she slid to the edge of the cot and approached the bars. "I'm here, Dolph, they think Bernadine is I and we're not correcting them." She wrapped her fingers around the bars and pressed her body to the iron to get as close as she could. "It's good to see your face again, you've grown up quite a bit."

"I wish I could say it was good to see you as well. Truth be told, I thought the best fate you two could have was if we never crossed paths again," Dolph sighed

Merion smiled sadly at him and reached through the bars to caress his clean-shaven face. "I didn't think I'd ever see you again. I've missed both you and Mother so much. Tell me, how is she?"

"She's fine," Dolph answered quickly.

"You're lying," Ellarie said flatly.

Amidst such a sombre reunion in the worst of places, somehow Dolph found that amusing. "I never could get one past you, Ellarie. I missed you both and I'm sure our mother and the rest of Clan Dollen have too. The truth is that I haven't seen Mother in nearly as long as you have. Yeoll banished me from coming near his house and forbids our mother from seeing me. She has a grandson now that she has never met because of that bitter prick of a husband."

"Congratulations Dolph, this is most wonderful news. I'm so happy that you have a son of your own," Ellarie said excitedly, with Merion echoing her sentiments.

"Thank you both, I'm sure Buchlan would love to meet you as much as you would like to meet him." Dolph beamed with pride as he spoke of his son. "Because of Janie and him, I finally have a family of my own, a Clan Farhart, as it were. It's a good life, apart from Bucky not knowing his grandmother or his aunts. He just reached his fourth year just a few weeks ago and he's growing like a weed nearly every day. Janie is sure he looks like me and he has the same dark hair as you and I, Ellarie. We've been letting it grow out a bit and I think he actually looks a great deal like you."

"I'm sorry we couldn't be there, Dolph," Ellarie said sadly as she laid a hand on his arm.

"What choice did you have? Yeoll is insufferable and only growing worse as he ages. I wish there was more I could have done for you at the time and I wish even more that I could do something now," Dolph said as he disentwined from Merion's hand.

"You're going to leave us here?" Merion asked despondently.

Dolph's eyes dropped to the floor. "I have very little recourse. Please understand... If they even found out we're related... I have a son now and Janie is expecting another child. Please, don't ask me to do something that could put them in jeopardy."

Merion's voice quite nearly broke. "Dolph, they're going to hang us in Biddenhurst."

"They'll hang me too if I'm caught aiding you and my family needs me," he replied in a voice that was equal parts stern and sorrowful. "I have to think about Janie and Bucky first, I'm sorry. I just wanted to see you one last time, my sweet sisters.

"Be strong, be brave and I promise you that Bucky will grow up knowing who his eldest aunties were. He will know that they were the best sisters I could have asked for and my only family before Janie. My son will know that he shares blood with great warrior women who fought bravely for the rights of all."

From behind Merion came Joyce's strong arms, wrapping around her waist and squeezing tight to comfort her.

"You must be Joyce," Dolph inferred of the woman holding the younger of his sisters before him.

She nodded as she leaned in over the redhead's shoulder. "I am indeed. It is good to meet you, Dolph. Merion and Ellarie have always spoken highly of their older brother. They have both told me countless times that you are their favourite sibling.

"Don't worry about us, ser, we'll look after ourselves. You take care of that boy of yours and make sure he grows up to be as fine a person as these two aunts of his. Because I can tell you that I've known no better people then they."

There was sobbing from a few of the others seated on the cots and Ellarie felt a single tear rolling across her cheek as she locked eyes with her brother. "She's right, Dolph. We understand. I wouldn't ask you to put you or your family in harm's way for us. I'm just glad you came, I had wanted to see you again so badly."

The eldest sibling nodded silently, loosing tears that had been welling in the process. At last he released his grip on his sibling's hands and stepped back. "Farewell, my sweet sisters," Dolph stammered as he vainly fought to keep himself from breaking. With a quick turn of his heel, he was gone, back through the wooden door to the station and out of their lives.

Merion lingered at the bars, still in Joyce's embrace and watching the door as if waiting for him to come back once more. When at last they moved, it was only so Merion and Joyce could recede to their shared cot once more. As they lay back, Joyce held her love tight and buried her face into Merion's manse of red curls.

The visit and departure of Dolph had been a dagger to the heart of Ellarie's hope. Somehow she had thought that he might be able to help as he had when she and Merion had first escaped Atrebell.

It was merely wishful thinking, nothing more, Ellarie told herself as her head came softly to rest on the bars of the cell.

"I'm so sorry, Ellarie," she heard from her side, turning to see that Bernadine had slid up beside her. Bernadine was too quiet by half and easily the stealthiest among their ragged party. Like Ellarie, the woman would never admit as much. From the time they first met, Ellarie had always thought that she and Bernadine were much alike, in more than just hair colour.

The younger member of the Thieves was without confidence and thought of herself as worthless, requiring the other women to lean on in order to bolster the value she perceived in herself.

"If only she knew how strong she really was," Ellarie had once commented to Joyce after regrouping with their party following a burglary job the two dark haired shadows had completed together.

The two had been tasked with sliding in to a tax collection agency owned by Councillor Davens of Weicaster Bay. It was reported that he was overtaxing and pocketing the difference for himself, an action that Orangecloak thought warranted correction.

She had given Ellarie command of the operation and she in turn chose Bernadine to accompany her. The two had done such a clean job of it that no one could tell that anyone else had ever been there that night. The guards on duty had reportedly taken the blame for the loss.

Ellarie recalled just how deft and limber Bernadine's fingers were as they picked the lock on the vault while Ellarie had kept watch. The woman had precise control over every limb and digit, moving about as silent and nimble as a housecat, yet Bernadine possessed no confidence in any of it. Now she was before Ellarie, those same deft fingers caressing her shoulder.

"Thank you, Bernadine," Ellarie answered lowly. "And thank you for so quickly responding to my name. It's a small thing, but it's the only gambit we have left to us."

Bernadine shrugged in her typical, aloof way. "I just thought it was the right thing to do, you're chief lieutenant after all. If giving you my name and I taking yours helps in some way, then you're welcome to it." It amazed Ellarie that despite their previous day's toil, Bernadine was able to maintain her outward stoicism. Ellarie could look right through those smoky grey eyes and see the whirlwind within though. The widow from Layn by way of Wyford could go stone cold save for her eyes. They spoke louder of her emotions than her voice was ever like to.

"Knowing what they could very well do to whomever they thought was our leader, it's nothing short of a great sacrifice to bear my name, don't forget that. I owe you my life for this," Ellarie added.

"Think nothing of it," Bernadine said with another shrug as she began to turn back towards her cot.

Before she could get two steps, Ellarie spun Bernadine around by the shoulder and drew her into a hug. "We will overcome this I assure you. This is just an obstacle, not the end," Ellarie declared before she let the younger woman go.

Whether or not Bernadine believed that, Ellarie did not know, but it seemed to reassure her in some way and that comfort alone was all that Ellarie could offer now.

Hours crept by after that. Ellarie had retaken her spot on the cot with Allia and Coramae and everyone either slept or whispered quietly to one another. The guards came and went about their business four more times that Ellarie counted, jarring her awake from loose slumber every time the wooden door opened.

On the fifth time, the door opened queerly, almost softly, as if someone was trying to sneak in. Staring above the top of the knees she was cradling, Ellarie watched the slender form of the blond steward of Major Burnson slip into the cellblock. The long, golden braid running down his back shone in the glow of the low burning lamps as he stepped inside, keeping close to the far wall. He seemed to just stand there wordlessly for a time, staring down the women hidden in almost complete darkness.

"Excuse me, ladies?" he timidly asked just when things were on the verge of growing inordinately uncomfortable. "I-uh, I have some news I thought you should hear."

The man who had been so confident earlier in the presence of his Major was sorely lacking for those same traits here. It was Merion lying nearby in Joyce's arms that cut to the heart of the matter. "What is this news? May we have it?"

"I-uh, that is... Um." He cleared his throat and tried again. "I felt you should know that your friend... er... boss I should say, that one Orangecloak, well, she's been captured."

An audible gasp went through the prisoners in unison and a few whispered curses. "Captured by whom?" asked Joyce as she propped herself up on an elbow.

"Not by we, at any rate," the steward answered. "Or else she would be here, but as you can see, she's not."

"Is there anything else?" added Bernadine from the corner she'd been sitting in,

The steward took a step back "Oh, uh no...That's it. I just thought that you should know that. I know she is well loved among her own kin. My condolences to you all, for everything, I'm sorry, truly I am...This world is, uh, it's a cruel place and I'm sorry for the things that happen to nice people like you." He turned to leave with a slow pivot on his heel toward the exit.

"Wait," said the voice of Coramae to Ellarie's left. A voice Ellarie didn't know she would ever hear again.

"Yes?" the steward asked almost fearfully.

"How is Donnis?" Coramae inquired, her voice trembling.

"Oh the, uh... Thieves men? They're as comfortable as our cells allow. We tended to their, um, wounds as best we could, but they were badly beaten, I'm afraid. Again, I'm sorry for what happened to them. My fellow guardsmen would never do such a thing, but the Biddenhursters... They're a different sort... They're not like most folk, they don't, um... Feel. Lord Taves likes them that way I hear, but that might be just a rumour. Oh shit, forget I said that. I have to go."

He departed quickly, pulling the door to with an audible thud and leaving them alone in near darkness once more.

"Damn the man that did the deed," Ellarie heard Joyce mutter from behind Merion. No one else could seem to find any words to say on the matter for some time.

"Is it true, do you think?" Bernadine asked to the rest of the party after a time. "Perhaps that young man played us false?"

Ellarie shook her head in the dim light. "I don't think he was lying, he seemed sincere enough in the way he spoke. In another life, he might have even been one of us, the way I see it. He truly felt sorry for our predicament, but was no more able to help than Dolph was."

"Then they have Orangecloak... It's over, we're over..." Merion stated in a heart wrenchingly sombre tone.

Two eyes weary from their ordeals begged for sleep, but the mind was too busy to allow Ellarie any sort of luxury. She leaned back on the cot beside Coramae and Allia once more in deep thought.

If the steward to the Major has told us true, then Orangecloak, Myles and Coquarro had been captured.

Not taking she, Joyce, Merion and Lazlo into account, that left only three other leaders in the field. That number didn't consider Old Bansam and his middle aged men that battled the raiding gangs of the Southlands of their own accord as associates of the Thieves. Between the other lieutenants, they would command only a small number of fully fledged Thieves between them in Rillis Vale. Of course, Phaleayna had their Rangers of the Thieves, though they were mostly comprised of those too green or too old to take to the field. As it was, they were left to guard over an island refuge full of children, the elderly and those who otherwise could not fight. But those numbers mattered little if Orangecloak was gone.

The Thieves would dismay, despair and ultimately disband in the wake of such a loss. It also stands to reason that if Orangecloak has been arrested, that we are as good as dead. The EMP won't waste time, food or resources keeping us alive. It would be a sure trip straight to Biddenhurst to be fitted for nooses.

The others in the oblong cell seemed to realize as much as the sound of sniffling and weeping echoed all around the room.

"We're going to die, Joyce," Merion said from the next cot as they lay cuddled in tight to one another. "It's all but guaranteed if they have Orangecloak."

"Maybe…" Joyce said. "But whatever they do to us, I want you to know one thing: I love you. I love you as the sun shines bright and the stars twinkle at night. I wouldn't change a thing we did, not one minute of it. I would sooner die with you beside me than live one day without having loved you. Do you hear me, Merion Dollen? I love you and nothing they can do to us in Biddenhurst will change that."

"Always… I'll love you always, Joyce Keena," Merion replied.

"Loving you is worth whatever they do to me in Biddenhurst," Joyce added between soft kisses Ellarie could hear through the darkness. "I regret nothing because it all brought me to you, Merion and you're worth everything to me."

11
TRYST

It was a sullen, sombre morning in the forest. Beyond Tryst's directional commands, no one had dared speak since climbing into their saddles.

There was a collective exhaustion between the four of them and the first rays of the sun only served to remind Tryst of the sleep he had missed.

It was fairly easy going here, as Tryst and Wildstar both knew these trails well. Though the path had become covered in the fallen leaves and was spotted with fresh mud, the courser and the pair of rounseys maintained a steady, surefooted pace.

The sun had begun to rise on what would surely be another chilly autumn day. It was cloudless, with a light wind gusting through that was barely strong enough to move the heavy cloak on Tryst's shoulders. Tryst felt his bladder jabbing him for relief and his eyes were fighting to remain raised, though he pressed forward a little more. The four riders and their three mounts had not stopped and Tryst reasoned that by now they were likely far out of the radius of any search party. Still, it would not do to halt out in the open, Tryst knew, and when the opportunity arose, he steered the group towards a secluded clearing nearby.

There was no telling if Ren or Fletchard had slept in their saddles, but Tryst had no doubt that Orangecloak was still wide awake. Her nearly tangible hatred had been burning holes in the back of his skull all night. Fletchard's mere presence further angered her beyond measure and was coupled with the grief she felt for the loss of her two friends during her bungled capture.

The grey jays among the trees chirped excitedly at one another as they followed the travellers with hopes of food to steal, entirely oblivious to the misery below. A sniffle cut through the chirping and Tryst knew it belonged to Orangecloak. She had been crying softly to herself all through the night when she thought no one was listening. Since seeing Fletchard before they had gotten underway, any semblance of trust Tryst had been able to build with her had evaporated instantly. Only Ren had been able to convince her to come along with them and that came with the assurance that she would ride with him atop one of Fletchard's horses.

Tryst pointed off the beaten trail to his right and led the party down a narrow path and through a thicket. They emerged in a little clearing that overlooked a wide, round pond that was fed by a noisy waterfall in one corner.

It was here Tryst dismounted and took a good look at the trio he had been leading. From the rear of the pack, Fletchard let out a loud, apathetic yawn as he stirred from the sleep he had managed to find while in the saddle. The man seemed entirely unbothered by the whole ordeal, seemingly more annoyed by the fact that he had lost out on the bounty than by anything else that had occurred. The same could not be said for the elf and the redhead sharing a horse, or Tryst himself, for that matter.

Ren drew back his hood and scanned the clearing that Tryst had brought them to before turning his gaze to Tryst. "Might I ask where we are?" the elf asked in a tired voice.

"This would be Gomy's Pond, or rather that body of water over there would be," Tryst answered while tilting his head in the direction of the pond further below. "We are atop Gomy's Lookout. This should be a safe point to rest for an hour or so. We have a several hour head start before the guards even think to go looking and longer again before they send anyone straight this way."

Tryst slid from the saddle and gave Wildstar a pat on his mane as the horse began to munch the grass in the clearing. "We won't light a fire," Tryst declared. "It's too risky for that just yet. We'll stop to let our rides catch a breath and a drink from the river and be off again."

He glanced up to where Orangecloak remained in the saddle of one of Fletchard's grey horses. She had reluctantly accepted the black bearskin cloak that Tryst had brought for her after the cold began to bite and had wrapped it over her trademark orange one. The hoods of both were down over her face in an effort to conceal the softly falling tears she had shed in the darkness of their journey.

Tryst didn't know what to say to her, but he knew he must try. "Would you like a hand down from the saddle, my lady?"

She raised her head just enough so that Tryst could see her eyes, red and puffy and full of loathing as she looked upon him. "Ren can help me," she said in a low voice barely above a whisper and tinged with disgust.

The elf climbed down to the ground from behind her and softly lowered Orangecloak to her feet. She winced and gave a groan as her legs touched the ground but managed to hobble off on her own.

"I'm going into the woods to be alone for a few minutes," she announced to no one in particular, grimacing with every step she took.

Fletchard sighed as he walked off to relieve himself in the opposite direction. His lackadaisical nature towards the entire situation ground on Tryst's nerves but he tried not to let it show. There was tension enough amongst this motley crew of fugitives.

"She's been through quite an ordeal," Ren commented when he was alone with Tryst.

"Aye, I feel for the poor woman," Tryst agreed with a sigh of his own. "Something tells me she has seen much and more in her short life." The burlap sack of food that Ruggard the chef had prepared was unbuckled from Wildstar's back by Tryst as he spoke. Once unburdened, the courser wandered off to find the stream on his own.

Ren followed Tryst as he ventured toward a pair of old logs surrounding a long forgotten fire pit. "I won't argue that," the elf replied. "However, I was referring more so to recent events. Her wounds are raw and painful to the touch, and I don't mean her legs. The hurts of yesterday will take a long time to become even scars."

"This is true, and I am not faulting her for that," Tryst added as he dug out one of the two loaves of bread he had. A chunk of which was broken off for Ren and a second handed to him for Orangecloak.

"Aye, you are not, though I sense that you resent how she feels about you. Might I offer a word of advice?" Ren asked as he chewed his bit of food.

"I would welcome it," Tryst answered affirmatively.

Ren hesitated with an answer and Tryst glanced to where the elf was looking to see Fletchard emerge from where he had gone.

It wasn't until the bounty hunter took his horses by the bridle to lead them to the stream that Ren began talking once more. "Leave her alone," he suggested. "At least until we get to the Dupoire's hotel. Let me talk to her and only speak directly to her yourself if she addresses you first.

"Until she can see the truth in your altruism, you will only see a wall of ice from Orangecloak. She needs to rest, physically and mentally, and around yourself and Fletchard, she will try to stay vigilant and alert."

Tryst took a deep breath and nodded slowly. "I see your point. Believe me when I say I wish I didn't need Fletchard for this, but I did then and I'll have use of him once more should we be set upon."

"You're a fool if you think he will fight for us if we're caught by human soldiers," Ren answered quickly.

"What choice does he have?" Tryst argued in a low voice so their subject wouldn't overhear them. "He's an outlaw as much as we are. Even if he sells us down the river to Grenjin Howland, the old man will hang him for the trouble or send him to Mackhol Taves to make a slave of him. One way or the other, his fate is as sealed as the men he buried. Even if he takes off with his mounts, he can't go anywhere. Everyone knows Fletchard Miller, the one-eyed bounty hunter, or at least the guards and soldiers do. If he wants to leave Illiastra and get out of this jam, he knows I'm his ticket to do just that. If the man is fighting for his own selfish reasons, at least he's fighting with us." Tryst took a few mouthfuls from his water canteen as he spoke to Ren, looking for either of the other members of their ragged band as he did.

"Besides," Tryst added, "were he to turn on us, he would have me to deal with."

"I only wish I had your confidence on the matter, Tryst," Ren sighed as Fletchard returned to the clearing with the mares in tow.

Sensing the intense dislike between the two, Tryst leaned in to Ren in a whisper. "You should check on Orangecloak, she may need your assistance."

Ren wordlessly agreed and was gone before Fletchard hobbled his horses.

"Hungry?" Tryst asked Fletchard in a tone that could well be taken as rude.

The bounty hunter slumped down exhaustively on the log beside Tryst. "Aye, I could eat," he answered as Tryst tore him a chunk of bread. "Are we staying here much longer?" Fletchard asked with a surprising amount of concern before taking his first bite.

"Not if I can avoid it," Tryst gave back.

"Good to hear. We shouldn't linger on these rests very long." Fletchard seemed eager to talk and Tryst sat quietly and listened. "We have a good lead on the guards, but the longer we rest, the more we allow for them to close the gap between us and them. I say we take two more breaks: one just past high noon and the other with the last light of day and neither one longer than what we've got going right now. We'll set camp long after dark, when we have put some more hours on the road."

That drew a slow, contemplative nod from Tryst. "I agree, we'll keep our camp stay short too, be gone before the light of dawn gets through. If by some chance we are being pursued, the guards will have to stop and rest as well. The task then becomes a matter of just keeping short rests and we should maintain any lead my measures have given us."

"Aye, we're on the same page then." Fletchard smirked. "So if I might ask, Reine, what do you plan on doing with me?"

Tryst turned his head quickly in surprise at the brashness with which Fletchard asked him the question. "I beg your pardon?"

"What? I know you don't plan on keeping me about for very long," Fletchard said with a nonchalant shrug. "The woman hates the very ground I walk on, for a start. That elf is of the same mind and you don't give much of a shit for me either, which still makes you my biggest supporter here. I'm a spare sword to you, that's all. You might as well not mince words about it for we both know that to be true."

The bounty hunter paused to stretch his limbs briefly before going on. "I reckon when we get to the west coast you'll have no more need for me. Then what? Are you going to turn me in to be tried for killing those Thieves in the Batterdowns, is that it? Because I can turn my horses back to Atrebell and get fitted for a noose there. It's quicker, easier and I get the luxury of knowing I might possibly be taking you down with me."

Tryst kept his gaze on the pond as he gnawed on the heel of bread he had picked for himself. "I can't say for certain, though it is quite likely that the Conductor will have you shipped out of Illiastra."

"Well that's kind of you," Fletchard responded sarcastically. "Is it just I or are we all taking a journey across the sea together?"

He turned to face Fletchard and look him in the eye. "I think you know the answer to that. When we spoke of a deal in the loft of the stable you told me that the Conductor sent you. That you even knew that much tells me that he wants you returned to him."

The incredulous look on Fletchard's face was plain, though he articulated it into words anyhow. "You mean to tell me that you didn't know I was coming?"

"The Conductor communicates in subtle ways," Tryst gave as a reply. "Your simple message of 'The Conductor sends me to carry the tune' told me everything I needed to know when I formulated my plan. That plan going forward is for you to go with me to Portsward. Odds are that if the Conductor wants to see you again, it means he has further use for you. Would you be interested in further work?"

Fletchard rubbed his jaw in contemplation. "That depends, what will the job pay?"

"Your freedom, for one." Tryst glanced over his shoulder to see Orangecloak leaning on Ren as they returned from the woods.

"No good, sellsword." Fletchard stood up with a groan. "You'll have to pay me in hard coin. If you put me on a ship, I'm not coming back. That will be my freedom from this cesspool of a country."

"I have no doubt of that. Don't worry, you'll be compensated for any work the Conductor might have for you," Tryst offered to the bounty hunter.

"You would pay the man who killed my friends? Is that how you expect to earn my trust?" Orangecloak asked rather loudly in a tone of sheer disgust as she limped into sight while leaning on Ren.

Tryst stood before her and gave a bow. "You have my apologies, my lady. Fletchard here was just asking what my intentions with him are once we reach the West." Vainly, he attempted to change the subject. "Are you hungry?"

There was no deterring Orangecloak though. "What *are* your intentions? For what will you have need of a blackheart killer?"

"You'll be thankful for this blackheart should the Atrebell guards catch up to us," Fletchard shot back before Tryst could answer.

Orangecloak's mouth turned into a scowl and she spoke scornfully through gritted teeth. "I'd be thankful to have Myles and Coquarro here, not a despicable monster like you."

Fletchard began sauntering towards her cockily. "So what would you have done to me?"

In short order, Tryst had laid aside the remaining two thirds of the bread and was standing between the bounty hunter and the pair of elf and woman.

Despite Tryst standing directly in his path, Fletchard continued on uninterrupted. "Perhaps you'll get Tryst to nick my head off? Or tie my hands and feet and sling me over my own horse like a sack of spuds?" He mockingly offered his hands to her for binding as he made the sarcastic suggestion. "No, you don't know what you want to do with me, do you? You're the high and mighty pacifist who hopes her pretty words will move everyone to ask the EMP to leave nicely. You can't get it through your little, red head that men like that won't answer to niceties when they can pay men like me to enforce their will by the sword."

"I've heard quite enough!" Tryst bellowed loud enough to wake the whole forest. "Leave her be, Fletchard."

A ball of phlegm was hawked up by Fletchard and spat on the ground at Orangecloak's feet and he turned away to his horse without another word.

Disconcerting looks were exchanged between Tryst and Ren, though Orangecloak's piercing, angry gaze was fixed solely on Fletchard.

She took a step away from Ren, so that she could stand on her own legs, shaky as they were. "If you think the Thieves are weak, then that's your mistake. The EMP made that same error themselves once. Now I'm the most wanted person in Illiastra. I didn't find my way to the top of that list with bloodshed either. I did it by engaging the people and showing them that they are not alone, that we are one and that together we can defeat the EMP."

Fletchard scoffed in amusement at that. "Aye, you want peace and equality and all those nice things and you shout about it all the time, but it's not the shouting that's made old Grenjin Howland so nervous. He and the EMP are worried that the shouting will stop and be replaced with action. That they might wake up some morning and see a united army of the downtrodden at their doors with sharp steel and rifles in hand and you at the forefront. That's the only kind of protesting the Elite Merchants are afraid of, not you and your little band of mewling outlaws trying to play nice."

"Shut your filthy mouth, you vermin." Ren threw out of nowhere, his voice full of fury. "Tryst, might it be possible that we get underway? I'm finding I miss this morning's silence."

"Aye," said Tryst in agreement. "I think that would be best." He scooped up the bread from atop the satchel and offered Orangecloak her share. "You should eat, my lady. It must be a day or so since your last bite. You need your strength."

The food was accepted by Orangecloak timidly and only after she finally tore her gaze from Fletchard. For a moment she stood motionless, clutching the bread and saying nothing until Ren stepped in to help her towards their shared mount.

Tryst wrapped the bread in its brown parchment and stowed it back in the sack. "We shall rest just before dark, but only briefly," he said to the three of them. "Though I suggest we ride well through the night and stop for our sleep at about midnight. Let me retrieve Wildstar and empty my bladder and we'll get going."

The remainder of the day fell back to the reticence of the morning's journey.

Orangecloak ate her bread in the saddle and drank her fill of water from Ren's canteen. It wasn't much, especially for one as famished as Tryst knew she must be, but it was better than nothing.

I'll make us a small stew tonight. We should be well enough away that lighting a fire wouldn't harm us. I have a carrot, a pair of potatoes, dried salted meat and a small crock of flour. It's little, but it will be hot nourishment and Orangecloak needs that. Perhaps I'll boil some tea too. I do have the leaves for it, after all, he thought to himself after looking back at her and the elf sharing a ride while they navigated a winding, uphill turn.

They made good progress through the old dirt pathways, wending around tall sentinel trees and clusters of alders that seemed to grow wherever their roots could take hold. It was a northwest trail that gently inclined every so often as they closed the gap between them and the Dwarven Mountains. Until a millennium ago, that very mountain chain had been the home of the proud dwarven people, before the heinous Valdarrow family had drove them out.

The attacks and subsequent sacking of Dhalla, the former coastal city of the dwarves, had been the bloody precursor to war in Illiastra. When the surviving dwarves finally retreated and gave up the city they did so in two groups. The first was led by Axel the

Goldenhair, who left on the last of dwarven naval fleet and settled on a large island off the coast of Drake. Those who didn't cross the sea went north at the heels of the wise Dorrhen the Frostbeard. There they settled at the edge of northern Illiastra, in a barely hospitable stretch of barren, frozen, rocky realm aptly called the Snowy Lands.

Deep beneath the ground, the great city of Frostbeard's people stood as a monument to the will of survival and as the last bastion of the once powerful dwarves of Illiastra. For all the underground city of Gondarrius had given the dwarves, their access to the rest of the world had always been at the mercy of the humans. With the rise of the EMP, that connection was lost and the dwarves remained largely isolated and allied with only the Elven Forest to the southeast of the Snowy Lands.

South of the Snowy Lands and hidden amongst the Dwarven Mountains there remained only a handful of frontier outposts. There, small mining and harvesting operations occurred in the more fertile regions around the mountains.

Among them there was only the Hotel Dupoire as lodging for travellers. Its current owner, and the latest in the Dupoire name to do so, was Kevane, an ally of Tryst's and a fellow member of the Musicians.

Kevane and his daughters will help us. They have known that a day such as this might come from the moment I crossed the sea.

The treeline on the right of the party began to descend as they trekked further, until it opened a view to the forest below. Their path left them a little open, but it could not be helped while on horseback as the trees here were too close to lead their steeds through safely.

Tryst tuned in his saddle to face Ren and Orangecloak sharing the mare in the middle of the pack. "Ren, do you see anything down there the rest of us might miss?" Tryst called back to the elf.

There came no immediate answer at first as Ren scanned the horizons. It was known that the eyes of an elf could see further than any humans might and Ren would not be an exception.

"No," he replied back after a time. "If there's anyone down there, they have hidden themselves well."

"Thank you for that, Ren," Tryst answered, bringing Wildstar to a stop and turning the courser so that he was facing the other three riders. "This place is called Raskin's Point. That we are here at this hour shows that we're making good time."

All while Tryst was speaking, Orangecloak had sat with her head down and both hoods drawn. Tryst felt horrible for her, knowing she was living in a world of agony over her lost friends. Despite it all though, she still had a fiery spite to her when she had argued with Fletchard earlier. There was life in those eyes, a will to exist. Even if she was bombarded with grief and mistrust, she was still fighting through it all. It was a spirit that Tryst had a profound respect for and though he had wanted to say as much, he thought better of it and left her alone.

Tryst gave a flick of the reins and turned Wildstar about, letting the afternoon lapse into silence once more.

Evening came and went and with it a small, grassy grove secluded from the road that was their second resting place.

Orangecloak hobbled off to herself again and Tryst shared up more of the bread between them when she returned. During the stop, Orangecloak spoke to Ren and Ren alone from the moment they dismounted until they were back in the saddle. Even Tryst's offer of food was met with only a meek thank-you.

Before they knew it the night had crept upon them and the sky glittered brilliantly clear with the light of a billion stars and both moons to guide them.

"Do you see how Gallick the Red looks pink this night?" Tryst overheard Ren asking Orangecloak as they passed through a wide, grassy field that left the sparkling ceiling of the world open to their view. "That is an indication of good weather. Our journey shall be cold, but dry for the nonce."

"Gallick the Red, I had heard that name before," Orangecloak commented, the first words Tryst had heard her say in some time. "We humans have only ever called it the Red Moon. It admittedly doesn't have the same ring as the elven name." She waited a beat before adding to her thoughts. "I hope you're right Ren, good weather would be appreciated."

The moons moved halfway through the sky above their heads before Tryst came to the place he expected to find. He guided Wildstar off the path and onto a small game trail. The others followed his lead into the deep woods, well out of sight of the road. They came to a clearing before Tryst brought the party to a halt and turned to face them. "We'll make our camp here for the night."

"It's just as well. This seems like as good a place as any to light a fire," Fletchard tiredly observed.

Tryst gave him a nod as he slid to the ground. "Aye, we can afford a small one. I'd like something warm in my stomach and we're not like to be found here. We're up high and well sheltered by trees." The food and supplies were unloaded from Wildstar and Tryst pointed to a small stream. "Wildstar, water, go that way."

By the time he turned to the other two horses, Tryst found that their occupants had also dismounted and were going separate ways. Now it was just he and the two hobbled steeds left in the clearing.

A circling of small stones of various sizes sat in the centre of the field, just waiting to be used. Despite the urge to make water, Tryst decided it would be best if he got the fire going first and he set to the task of gathering kindling and timber. Soon enough, he had the fire quietly crackling while he built a makeshift spit strong enough to hold small copper kettle and pot that Ruggard had given him.

Fletchard had since returned and had taken his horses to the stream to drink without a word to Tryst. It was only once the bounty hunter left that the elf and Orangecloak showed up together from amidst the trees and seated themselves beside the fire.

Tryst was carefully stirring the contents of their dinner and spared Orangecloak a glance. "Do you like stew?" he asked her to break the silence.

"Yes," Orangecloak answered quickly.

"What are you making it with?" asked Ren as he folded his legs beneath himself and sat beside the wincing Orangecloak, trying vainly to find a comfortable place for her aching legs.

The wooden spoon came to a rest and Tryst sat back to peel a potato with a knife from one of his boots before answering. "I have a potato to spare, a few strips of our dried meat and a carrot. It will be a little thin, I confess, as I don't have anything to help thicken it. Though, if nothing else, it should be edible and flavourful and will fill our empty stomachs, which is as much as I ask."

Fletchard came back through the trees still lacing his breeches with a face of pure apathy that Tryst could sense irked Orangecloak to no end. "Your courser is by himself at the stream," he remarked to Tryst as he settled himself across the fireplace from Ren and Orangecloak.

By now, she had taken to laying her head on the elf's lap to allow her knees to lie straight for once. Once she got comfortable,

Orangecloak blanketed herself with her pair of cloaks for warmth and relaxed as much as she could.

Tryst let out a shrug at Fletchard's observation. "Wildstar goes where he will. I try not to dictate to him. He'll venture back to have his fill of the grass here before long, I do imagine." He cleared his throat and stood up and turned to Fletchard. "Would you mind tending the fire for a moment while I retrieve some water for tea and stew?" he asked as he stood with the pot and kettle in hand.

"As you wish," Fletchard replied nonchalantly before Tryst went off to the stream without waiting for such.

Wildstar was found to be still lingering beside the water and crunching grass in his teeth as he lazily watched Tryst approach. "There you are." Tryst said to the horse, giving him pat on the neck in passing. He knelt to the stream and filled the kettle, pouring its contents over the meat and vegetables in the pot before filling it once more for tea water. As he turned to leave, the horse was on his heels and they returned together to the clearing.

The campfire Tryst returned to was a place of quietude, with solemnity hanging in the air like smoke. Everyone was just where Tryst had left them, staring at the fire and lost in their own thoughts. After setting the kettle and pot back on the spit, Tryst seated himself on a raised mound between the bounty hunter and the injured redhead whom clearly wished they were a thousand leagues away from one another.

The four let the silence blanket them as the boiling water and crackling flames dared to utter noise through the darkness. A slight breeze picked itself up, giving the trees carefree whispers to carry amongst one another. Orangecloak let out an audible shudder and pulled her cloaks about her chin tightly as rather chilly gust of wind swept over them.

The stew began to grow warm and Tryst sat on his knees over the fire, stirring and watching it, growing hungrier by the second.

Everything Tryst had before him had come on account of the chef at the manor, who was only glad to be rid of the Master of Blades he so loathed. A gleeful smile had even crossed his bearded face when Tryst had told him as much after freeing Orangecloak and sending her and Ren into the tunnels. "I would be lying if I said I was going to miss you," the tall fellow declared.

"I understand, Ruggard. Would you care to help me prepare

some foodstuffs to take? You know your kitchen far better than I do," Tryst had asked him.

The chef had looked him over several times, unsure if he could be believed. "Fine then, but only for the lady. If you've told me false of your intentions, I shall hunt you down to the ends of the world myself to strangle you with my own two hands," Ruggard told him with his thick arms folded across his barrel chest, judging eyes looking downward intimidatingly at the Master of Blades.

Tryst had cautiously extended a hand toward Ruggard at that. "I would expect no less."

Ruggard could have killed me right there if he wanted to, if he could have caught me, Tryst reflected.

He had never known anyone as tall as Ruggard and the man carried his size remarkably well. Most men Tryst had known that were even near his height had a gangly disposition that nearly made them look like they were on stilts, but not the cook. The man looked as though he could snap trees in half and Tryst had no doubt that it would take little effort for Ruggard to wring the life out of him.

After they had shaken hands, the two walked together to the kitchens from the server's quarters. "How far are you planning to go before you reach fresh supplies?" Ruggard had probed along the way.

"I have friends in the north," Tryst had admitted quietly, aware of ears that could have been everywhere in that yard. The cook seemed to understand and let it rest at that. Together, the pair went through the pantry and cupboards, compiling essential foods and the tools to eat them with to last for the journey. A few potatoes, a couple of carrots, a small burlap bag of dried fruit and nut mix, bread, a small jar of butter and dried meat were given for food. To eat it with, Tryst was given a pair of wooden bowls and two each of spoon and fork to go with them.

Tryst thanked the man immensely for all of it, though Ruggard was disinterested in his thanks. "I'm not doing it for you, Master of Blades, just for Orangecloak," he corrected Tryst. "Get her out and get her to safety. Poor girl does not deserve to die down below the manor. You two should stay off the roads, even the back ones see use from time to time."

"I believe there will be six of us, actually, we have to make haste," Tryst said while lifting the burlap sack to his shoulder.

The Chef's bushy eyebrows rose at that. "Six? I only gave you supplies enough for two."

"Indeed, but this is as much as I can carry anyhow. I'll ration it out as best I can and hunt along the way. I have a bow and a good quiver of arrows." Tryst hadn't known then that Fletchard had already cut those numbers down by two.

"You could fish too, you know. You do have a fishing line, right?" the Chef inquired.

Tryst admitted he did not and Ruggard gave him a sigh before leading him to a small storage shed off the servant's apartments.

"Here, line and hook." Ruggard had said while pushing a small cork reel wrapped in hard twine with an embedded hook into his hands. "If you can dig up a worm, you have bait. The rivers north of here are usually teaming with mud trout and with even a little luck you could catch a few meals out of it. Enough to maybe stave off the hunger before you eat the dwarves out of house and home."

The big man saw Tryst out. As the two were about to part, it was Ruggard who stopped Tryst and extended his massive mitt of a hand for a last shake. "If you save the girl I'll be the first one to say I was wrong about you, Tryst Reine." The chef squeezed Tryst's hand, letting him feel a taste of his strength. "But play her false and I will fulfil my promise, be sure of that."

"I will give you no cause to want to do so, Ruggard," Tryst answered him gratefully. "I thank you for your help."

"It sounds like dinner is ready," Ren commented, drawing Tryst back from his memory of the night before.

The pot and kettle had both begun their rumbling from their place over the fire and Tryst went to work serving everything up. The four scraped the pot clean of its contents in turn. The stew, while watery, as Tryst had forecasted it to be, filled their bellies and the tea chased it down well. Ren offered to take the utensils and containers to the river to wash them out, his elven eyes allowing him to see where the other three would only see darkness.

"Wait," called Fletchard, scrambling to his feet before Ren left the clearing. "Might I follow? I'd like to let the horses get another drink and you see the way better than I can."

"Come along, then," Ren aloofly replied over his shoulder, slowing up to allow Fletchard time to undo the reins of his mounts, but not stopping entirely. Fletchard hurried to catch up and soon there were only two sitting beside the fire.

It dawned on Tryst that this had been the first time he and Orangecloak had been alone together. From the moment he had sprung her from capture, Ren had been with them every second and having Fletchard about only served to stifle Orangecloak further.

Tryst glanced at her as she lay near the flickering flames, bundled up beneath the two cloaks and trying to make a lumpy pillow of their hoods.

Unsure of what he might say, Tryst decided to leave her well enough alone and instead produced whetstone and oilcloth to clean and sharpen the knife he had used earlier.

In the glow of the fire, Orangecloak's naturally wavy hair shone radiantly red and Tryst could see the flames dancing in the reflection of her sad eyes.

Sad or not, Tryst thought she was quite the beauty. With slender pink lips and a cute little nose sitting perfectly amidst the lightly freckled complexion of her face, all of it scarcely disturbed by dimple or line, she made for a welcome sight.

Gorgeous, Tryst said to himself. *Any man so fortunate to earn her affection would be a fool to ever let those affections ebb.*

Tryst put his attention on his sword, drawing it nearly noiselessly from the sheath and taking stone and cloth to its edge. The tired eyes of Orangecloak went wide as the black blade came forth and Tryst noticed her watching him work as the blade and whetstone made their one note song.

"Might I ask you something?" Orangecloak inquired in a low voice that bordered on a whisper.

"Most certainly, my lady," Tryst replied, masking his surprise and delight that she had even spoken to him.

She audibly cleared her throat before proceeding in a melancholy tone, "How many people have you killed with that thing?"

"With this?" Tryst said as he thought about the answer, looking the blade over earnestly as it soaked in the light of the fire. He wasn't sure if he should be honest with her, unsure of how she would react. Yet, he did not want to start off on a false foot. "I've killed six men," he answered her.

"Do you feel like they deserved their fate?" Orangecloak continued the questioning.

"Five of them did," Tryst echoed her sombre tone with his words, looking directly into those deep blue eyes. "They were terrible men who made horrible choices and harmed innocent people."

Her gaze went back to the fire as she weighed his words before coming to her next query. "What of the other one?"

Tryst shifted in his place on the wild grass. "He left me little choice, it was either I kill him or risk unveiling my true self too early. If he hadn't engaged me in the middle of the Northeast Square in Atrebell, I could have allowed him to quietly live, but he would have none of it. So I made his passing quick and painless."

Orangecloak looked to him once more. "Who was he? Anyone I might have known?"

"A former servant of the Lord Master, Adlan was his name," Tryst recalled sadly. "He was wanted for stealing silverware from the Atrebell Manor. A minor offence in reality, it's not like the missing forks and knives would even have been noticed if Adlan hadn't been carelessly caught in the act. The problem was that the man made a point of continually boasting about his thievery and evasion of the city guard. So, the Lord Master demanded I deal with him personally and send a message to other would-be bandits who dare to mock him."

"He challenged you to a duel, I remember now," Orangecloak said with sudden realisation. "That story made its way to us. Some thought he was one my Thieves, but we never had anyone working under guise in the Atrebell Manor."

Tryst nodded at her slowly. "Aye, he did. The man was a bit of a bravo and thought he could best me and I had my own orders from Grenjin Howland to kill the man. With no chance to offer Adlan a silent disappearing act, I was left with little recourse. Many say I won that night, but the only winner was Grenjin Howland," Tryst added as their eyes met for the first time since he had removed his steel mask on the steps of the dungeon.

"So you have killed six with your sword and one more last night," Orangecloak offered after she broke the brief stare. "Is seven as much as you have killed, Mister Reine?" she asked while pulling her cloaks tighter around her chin.

"Counting the monster in the dungeon, I have killed seventeen in total," Tryst gave back willingly, entirely honest in his answer.

"Seventeen..." Orangecloak let the word hang there for a moment. "I have a favour to ask you, Tryst Reine," she said, meeting his eyes again.

"What would that be?" Tryst probed.

Her expression belied the inquisitiveness in her voice as she laid her favour at his feet. "I was told once that to know a swordsman is to know those who have died by his sword. Before we get to Portsward I want you to tell me of some of the other fifteen lives you have taken. Can you do this for me?"

Upon taking a brief moment to consider, Tryst nodded in return. "Very well, if that is what you would like, then I shall tell you. Would you have me start now?"

She sighed sleepily. "No, I would rather not start tonight. I'll ask again in time, to be sure."

12

ORANGECLOAK

Several days had passed since her nightmare in Atrebell began and Orangecloak had to wonder if it might ever end. Even sleep was no good, for she dreamt of Myles and Coquarro and before she woke, they vanished.

The waking was always beside a smouldering fire pit in the company of strangers, one of whom was responsible for the death of those very friends she mourned. There were times when she felt like screaming at Fletchard, at Tryst Reine and even Ren, who had been so kind to her. They didn't understand what she felt or the pain her mind was racked with.

Just days ago, Coquarro and Myles had been by her side, and had been since the day she had been declared the Field Commander of the Thieves. The three had crossed Illiastra together so often that it felt wrong to move at all without them.

Coquarro, with his easy smiles and sage advice, who had been the big brother she never had. From the moment her second life had begun in Phaleayna, he had been her guide and protector. His aunt, Yassira Na-Qoia, known as the Lady of the Ruins, had raised the both of them as her own amongst the island ruins she presided over.

Then there was Myles, who had loved her once. Fleeting though it was, he had been her first and he had stayed true to her as a friend, long after the flame of their love had gutted out. He was a charmer and a joker, reminding her that without love and laughter, the world was a place of sordid darkness.

They had been her bodyguards, strategists, councillors and most importantly: her dear friends. Losing them had left a great hole, one that Orangecloak thought might never be filled.

Fletchard's presence only exacerbated that pain, though Tryst Reine insisted there was a need for him, especially once they reached the west coast. Between now and then, Tryst claimed that Fletchard would be a valuable fighter who would stand with them should they be set upon. No matter how many times she repeated Tryst Reine's words in her mind, Orangecloak had a difficult time accepting Fletchard. The only thing that made it easier was his placement at the rear of the pack, not out of her hearing, but out of sight at least.

Camping was another beast entirely. She had found herself rendered mute by her anger and frustration when Fletchard was present at their little campfires. It was only when the former bounty hunter would swagger off on his own that she would speak, and even then it was mostly to Ren.

Despite her request to hear of Tryst Reine's deeds as a killer, she had yet to ask him to elaborate on any of them. There was still little desire to speak with Tryst and Orangecloak kept any exchanges with him short.

If there was one thing she admired about Tryst Reine though, it was his confidence. Most people she knew would be cowed and fearful in the presence of cold hearted rouges like Fletchard Miller, but not the Master of Blades.

Men like Fletchard relied on intimidation. It was their token to getting what they wanted in life and Tryst Reine had robbed him of it entirely. Fletchard had apparently been relieved of his pistols after turning Orangecloak over to the Atrebell Manor guards and Tryst ensured he stayed that way. The man was armed now with only a sabre procured by Tryst prior to leaving the Atrebell Manor.

Orangecloak wouldn't have given him even that, but she soon saw the sense in it: armed with a sword, Fletchard could fight if they were set upon by ranging guards of Atrebell or marauders. Amongst their own party, Fletchard's blade would do him little good should he attempt to turn against the Master of Blades.

Under the normal circumstances of her life prior to a few days ago, it would be Orangecloak who was making such decisions. She was powerless now, being pulled forward to Portsward and no more in control than the steed beneath her. In her current predicament, Orangecloak had to wonder if that was not for the best.

My decisions as Field Commander of the Thieves resulted in the deaths of Myles and Coquarro. Perhaps it is good I am gone and the others think I am dead. Better they don't see me as the broken, wounded thing I have become.

"Whoa!" Ren said with a sharp tug on the reins of the horse, returning Orangecloak's attention to her surroundings. She raised her head and drew back the hoods of her cloaks to see that Tryst Reine had brought the party to a halt. He was focused on a grassy clearing nearby, a puzzled look on his face.

"Isn't it a little early for a rest, Tryst?" Ren asked, his body twisting in the saddle as he looked about. "I don't see anything amiss, why have you stopped?"

Tryst turned Wildstar about to bring horse and rider to face the rest of the party. "We're well behind schedule."

"What makes you say that?" Fletchard queried with that almost lazy tone of his, the words practically sloughing off his tongue.

To that Tryst directed the gaze of the three of them to a rounded rock below the elevated path that wound about it. "That's the Stone Egg landmark right there. We should have come upon it this morning. We're behind by half a day by my reckoning."

Upon inspecting it, Orangecloak thought that the boulder did indeed look like a moss covered egg lying on its side. As the others looked upon it and pondered the implications she turned her line of sight back to Tryst. "Then we will have to make haste," she proposed with a shrug. "We can't risk being caught out here."

A disparaging hum from Ren gave away his disagreement. "That would be hard on the horses, ours in particular. The poor beast is already carrying two."

Fletchard spurred his horse and brought him up beside the others, much to Orangecloak's chagrin. "There's also the matter of our food supplies. Last night we ate the last of the meat. We have bread to do us, though only if we ration, along with a pair of potatoes and half of that bag of nuts and raisins. It's not going to be enough to last us to the hotel. We will need to hunt."

"Did you not just hear Tryst Reine?" Orangecloak interjected bitterly. "We're already behind by half a day. There simply is no time for a damn hunt."

Before Fletchard could utter some snide retort, Tryst quickly intervened. "I'm afraid my lady is right. There is no time for us to stop and have a proper hunt. However, I do have a solution." His eyes fell on the elf. "Ren, if you would be obliging, I was wondering if you would ride ahead with the bow I've given you and see if you can find us something to eat."

There was an apprehensive moment of silence before Ren reluctantly answered the request. "I think it would be easier if you went ahead, given that I have the lady riding with me," Ren countered.

Tryst shook his head. "Mine eyes can't see what yours can, Ren. If it's okay with Miss Orangecloak, she may ride with me. Fletchard can go on ahead as well, if he would like. Up further the hill peaks and we descend into Long Bend Valley, the natural divide between the Dwarven Mountains and human Illiastra. There's a lake and rivers that should be directly in sight for you to fish from. I have line, hook and bobber in my satchel I can give you and the soft ground should be teeming with worms for bait."

"A little time away from you mopey lot? Where do I make my mark for that deal?" Fletchard answered sardonically, spurring his horse and guiding it around Ren and Orangecloak on the narrow trail.

Tryst declined to respond to the slight and wordlessly slid from his saddle to dig through the food sack to find the fishing supplies he spoke of. From within the bag he produced a thick piece of cork wrapped in black line, a steel hook shining from where it sat in the soft wood. A light toss from Tryst to Fletchard and the bounty hunter was out of sight around the bend, his horse already up to a steady gallop.

Orangecloak sighed with relief at his leaving and almost forgot about the other matter at hand until Tryst reminded them. "What do you say Ren?" Reine broached the question with a relieved sigh of his own once Fletchard had departed.

"If my lady has no objection to sharing a saddle with you, then I shall see about finding us our dinner," Ren said with a hand on Orangecloak's shoulder, putting the choice entirely on her to make.

As much as she rued the thought of riding with Tryst, she felt it would seem selfish if she kept Ren back. It was true that elves had sharper vision and averaged above all in terms of archery skill. Even their hearing far outmatched any others. If anyone among the party had a chance at finding wild game, it was Ren.

In truth, her hunger made it an easy decision for her. "I suppose I could ride with Tryst Reine, if this lake he speaks of really is so nearby."

"Very well, then." Ren swung a leg over the saddle and hopped to the ground in one fluent motion, offering a hand to help her down.

Orangecloak's knees were slowly healing and she found that when she woke this morning that walking on her own had improved to a laboured shuffle. Considering that in the days prior, walking on her own was an excruciating exercise in endurance, she practically welcomed this lesser, dull pain running through her.

After the initial shock of being back on her feet again, Orangecloak began walking the few slow, scuffling steps to where Tryst stood beside Wildstar.

For once, Ren left her completely alone and remounted, his mind centred on his task ahead. He adjusted the quiver of arrows until they hung by his left leg for easy access, moved the bow to the left hand and the reins to the right. Sitting as he was, Orangecloak thought he looked somewhat like an elven warrior of legend, ready to loosen an arrow on anything ahead that moved.

"Alright then," Ren said with a tinge of nervousness in his voice. "Let's see if I can find us some sustenance."

Once Ren had left, Orangecloak stood quietly for a moment, warily looking over the remaining horse and rider beside her.

Tryst seemed to sense her discomfort and spoke in a comforting voice. "I know it's not ideal for you, but I assure you it will be little different from traveling with Ren."

"No, it's fine," she answered while tucking her hair behind her ears and taking a deep breath. "Like you said, Elven eyes and all that would make Ren the best hunter among us. I just need a hand getting into the saddle."

Tryst nodded, lifted her up with ease and allowed her to sling a leg over the chestnut coloured beast. He waited patiently for her to get comfortable before speaking up. "Would you rather I sit ahead or behind, as you had been doing with Ren? Either way is fine with me."

"Whichever is suitable for you, you're the one holding the reins." She shrugged yet again, not sure how else to mask the slight bit of discomfort she was having with the situation.

"Right, slide up then, and hold the saddle if you need to," Tryst added as he put a foot into the stirrup and swung himself into place.

His muscled arms came slowly around her waist and collected the leather reins in hand. A pair of clicks of his tongue later and they were underway once more.

Wildstar was a bigger horse than the dappled one she had been sharing with Ren and he seemed to bear the weight of two people easier. Even though Tryst himself easily outweighed Ren by at least half a dozen kilos. After a time, she even began to think that the riding was easier and she figured it was most likely on account of Wildstar being familiar with the trail.

They rounded the turn in the hill and the valley came into view just as Tryst said it would. To the other side of where they rode were the rising foothills of the Dwarven Mountains beyond.

This was the first time Orangecloak had seen them and though she had been born in the shadows of the Illiastran Mountain chain, the Dwarven Mountains were a sight to behold in their own.

Six neat peaks they were, with the tallest standing the furthest north, guarding the realm from the howling, cutting gales of the Snowy lands and the frozen tundra beyond. Before the Old Giant lay what were called the Giant's Five Children: Burelin and Montagen looking west to the ocean, barely visible off in the distance. Orangecloak knew that cradled between them was the abandoned dwarven city of Dhalla. The peaks of Graelin and the comparatively tiny Shorreck stood in the southerly reaches and east of them stood the last mountain, the name of which she could not recall.

"So these are the Dwarven Mountains," Orangecloak said as a means to spur the conversation as she beheld the natural splendour of the landscape that had unfolded before her. "If I recall correctly, they're known as the Old Giant, Graelin, Shorreck, Burelin and Montagen and...I believe I'm missing a name."

"Aye, the easterly mistress." Tryst pointed it out, his tone slightly wistful at the prospect of any amount of banter. "That's the Elven guardian: Maratova. Between her and the Illiastran range sits White Canyon Pass, which acts as a natural gateway between the Elven Forest and the Snowy lands."

Orangecloak was impressed. Tryst certainly knew his Illiastran geography, for one only here a few years. "You know the lay of the land well," she commented idly.

"Why, thank you." Tryst chuckled lowly in response "There's more to being the Master of Blades than just being apt with a sword, my lady. I spent many nights in the Academics buildings in the Drakian University with my nose buried in books, scrolls and maps. Always trying learning as much as I could of this world we live in. My peers and I studied history, biology, astronomy and medicine, among other fields. Above all, I had a love for geography. The professor used to say, 'If you know the land, you'll know the people that live off it.' And he was certainly right about that."

"I agree with him," Orangecloak answered with a slow nod. "As that is a lesson I have certainly come to know as well in my own travels." Her eyes scanned the horizon as she spoke, taking in the snow-capped peaks of the mountains. A ring of clouds wrapped themselves about the nearest peaks like the brim of a hat. Further below that was the divide between the perpetual snows and the bare, grey-blue rock of the mountainsides, standing sheer and majestic in their rugged beauty.

"I see no sign of Ren," Tryst observed. She could feel him shifting in the saddle behind her, craning about in an attempt to find the elf in the foliage between them and the mountain range. "I spot Fletchard, though. He's near the lake already."

Orangecloak cast her gaze to the lush valley below, itself putting on a splendid colour show beneath the autumn sun. The browns, reds and oranges of the leaf trees shedding their yearling foliage cascaded with the rich hues of the evergreens, making a scarf of many colours to wrap about the glittering lake in the centre of the valley. Amidst it all was Fletchard, sitting almost lazily in the saddle and navigating the dappled grey mare where the declining forest path opened around the body of water.

It pained her to look at him from even this distance and she turned her eyes away after only the briefest of glimpses. Worse than anything she felt in her knees was the pain of the memory that the sight of Fletchard conjured. It was as though she was reliving the last minutes of Coquarro Lo-Qoia and Myles Stodden time and time again.

The main path wound slowly down the south side of the valley wall, amongst the soft hills and tall trees. Somewhere down there she knew Ren was sitting astride the horse, bow and arrow at the ready to bring down their evening meal. As much as she tried to scan for the elf, she found her eyes wandering back to Fletchard, her nostrils flaring angrily with every second she held sight of him.

He's going to be in my view for some time. I should find some other way to occupy my attention, lest I drive myself insane, she thought to herself before an idea came to her. "Tryst, I think I would like to hear about your first kill now, if that would be acceptable."

He seemed taken aback by the sudden request "Why certainly, my lady. It was your wish after all."

"Indeed, I thought now might be a good time to begin," she replied quickly.

Anything so that I might get my mind away from my own pain, even if for just a moment.

Tryst cleared his throat from behind her before he began. "To hear my first one is to hear my first two, which leads in to three more. I'll start with those, see where that takes us."

"That's fine, at your leisure, ser," she shrugged, just eager for him to start.

"I was an Expert at the University at the time, just turned twenty and proudly bearing a live steel sword as only a young man can. Not this blade, mind you, that wouldn't come for several years later." They rounded a turn and continued the descent, the view, while lower, gave sight of the wide river that sprouted from the lake.

Tryst continued on once he helped Wildstar navigate a tricky rut. "Junto, the Chancellor of the University, had received a request from Yohei, the High Chieftain of Drake for an escort for his son Gedo to the Jinku Prefecture. I'm not sure if you are familiar with Drake, but in any case, Jinku is in the far northwest corner of the country. There had been a recent judicial case that could not be resolved at the regional level and had been sent to the High Chieftain for judgement. Gedo was to deliver that judgement on behalf of his father to the region's capital of Kushika, it being as rustic and backwater a town as one can get in the known world."

An elk bellowed out a warning cry, breaking the tranquillity of the forest and bringing Tryst to a silent stop.

Orangecloak looked all about and saw no disturbances. "That was an elk if I'm not mistaken. I'm not seeing any signs of it though."

"Aye, that's what I was thinking as well," Tryst said, shifting from behind her to try and catch a glance of anything moving below their position. "My guess is that Ren spooked it, though I have no idea where he is at the moment. Shall I continue?"

Convinced there was nothing further for her to see besides Fletchard lounging on a rock beside the lake, she urged him on.

"Alright then, where was I?" Tryst pondered aloud for a moment, before finding his mental placeholder. "Ah yes, Kushika City. Chancellor Junto had sent a snow haired Drakian named Keo Gunpai and I as the escorts for Gedo. At the time, I was still an Expert of the University and not yet a Master of Blades, as was Keo. Two swordsmen may not seem like much for protection, granted, but we were not alone for the High Chieftain sent a retinue of guardsmen as well. Keo and I were simply the added insurance wearing the instantly recognisable black, white and gold uniforms that instilled respect wherever they were worn.

"It was a simple job: escort Gedo through the hills, stand beside him when he delivered the edict to the elders of Kushika and return home. Both Keo and I agreed that it would be easy work for good pay and we were quite excited for it."

Orangecloak nodded as she absorbed the backstory. "I've never been to Drake. It seems like such a mystical place. Is it true they have no trains there as of yet?" she probed Tryst while she looked all about for other signs of life amongst the valley, besides the terrible man casting his fishing line into the pristine lake, of course.

"They had none, at least up until I left four years ago. Can't say for sure if they've started laying down tracks since then," Tryst answered. "They get about by donkey primarily. Horses are fine for the city dwellers, but anyone going beyond that usually relies on mules, given that they're much surer on the hilly terrain."

That explanation sated Orangecloak's curiosity on the matter and she apologised for interrupting and asked Tryst to continue with the recollection.

"The journey to Kushika City was uneventful," Tryst began again. "As expected, we encountered snow, as anyone going north in Drake is well accustomed to, and little else. Within a week of leaving the south, we had arrived in Jinku, tired but unharmed. We lodged at the inn and Keo and I began our second task of escorting Gedo to and from the Elders' Lodge day after day. As I said, it was boring, uneventful work. Just standing about, listening to the elders and the chieftain's son bartering back and forth for days upon end."

That struck Orangecloak as odd and she inquired about it. "I thought you said that Gedo was only delivering a judgement, what was there to barter over?"

"As to that," Tryst said, wearily exhaling. "One of the elders had been found guilty of embezzlement and fraud. Apparently it had been going on for over a decade and had resulted in an exorbitant amount of tax money going directly into one man's pocket. His fellow elders had found him guilty, but couldn't decide on a sentence and that's why it was deferred to the High Chieftain in the first place.

"While the elders were debating on how hard of a figurative slap on the wrist to give the guilty elder, the High Chieftain had levied a much more severe punishment: every ill-gotten coin was to be paid back in full and the elder would be relieved of duty. Should he not be able to repay the fines, he would be forced to forfeit personal assets valued at the amount stolen.

"Predictably, the elders thought this sentence too harsh and it was left to Gedo to find some balance. By the time it was done, Gedo had secured a lump sum to cover almost half of the embezzled money and obtained all of that particular elder's lands. It was nearly enough to pay for everything and the rest would be garnished from the elder's wages, including the expense of Gedo's trip to settle the matter."

"That seems like a fitting punishment, I suppose," Orangecloak commented, despite not knowing the full details of the nature of Drakian government and their taxation system.

She could feel Tryst nodding from behind her as he went on. "We all seemed to agree, and I have a feeling it was what the High Chieftain expected he would get. He knew aiming high on the punishment scale would mean he could bargain the elders for what he really sought."

He shrugged at that. "When it was settled, we returned to the inn for one last night before beginning the trip home and found the place strangely full and bustling. Gedo's other guardsmen informed Keo and I that a corsair ship from the Crescent Islands had landed in port while we were at the Elder's Lodge. The general word from the townspeople was that the crew were hiding out in Kushika while they waited for a bounty on their ship to settle down. Despite the activity they brought, the corsairs kept their distance from our party, but Keo and I kept an eye on them all the same.

"Meanwhile, Gedo got too drunk, his tongue got loose and they got word of just who he was and a taste of his wealth. We whisked Gedo away to his room and hoped the corsairs would be wise enough to not make an attempt to rob or kill the son of Drake's High Chieftain before sunrise."

"Wait," Orangecloak said before raising a question. "Why didn't you just have the corsairs arrested if they were wanted men?"

"They had a full crew of morally bankrupt seamen on the run," Tryst answered with haste, indicating it was a question he had anticipated. "We had six guards, me, Keo, and a town marshal with three deputies to counter that. The ship wasn't wanted in Drake and we didn't want the whole town to be razed to the ground over it. For their part, the corsairs were trying to keep out of sight as well. An incident in Kushika would not only give away their location, but it would add the Drakian navy to their list of pursuers. So, we were all in agreement to leave everyone else well enough alone."

"I can understand that," Orangecloak said. "Please, pardon my interruption and go on."

"Nothing to pardon, my lady, it's a fair question," Tryst replied, picking up his story once more. "Morning came and everyone saw daylight unscathed. The staff of the common room told us that the corsairs had left port as quickly as they had arrived in the wee hours of the morning. We headed for the road with the first rays of the sun and had covered quite a bit of ground before sunset, thinking no further of the corsairs."

After a deep breath, Tryst's voice went grim. "It was the next day that brought trouble. We were riding through the relative safety of Dochen pass when we were approached from the east path by two men on mules. They seemed innocent enough at first, looking merely like two travellers bundled in heavy furs. As we got closer though, Keo recognised them as being among the corsairs at the inn.

"The rogues were armed with muskets and short swords and with their furs I had no way of knowing what armour they might be wearing. Before anyone could utter a word, the two became five as three more emerged from atop an embankment with muskets trained on us. Their demands were to the point: we were to trade Gedo and any valuables for a ransom note to be taken to the High Chieftain or the five of them would open fire."

An audible sigh escaped Tryst. "Gedo panicked. All the grace and poise he had put on display with the elders vanished in the face of armed thugs. He bolted back towards Kushika and the corsairs emptied their muskets at the rest of us. Two guards were killed in the barrage of shot. We were now two experts of the university and four guards against five corsairs.

"Gedo's stunt had forced the corsairs to use their shot and three of them missed, they had lost their advantage and they knew it. It became apparent at that point that the corsairs had no contingency plans. A notion they proved when one of the two on the mules loudly commanded the others to contain us while he chased Gedo."

"You mean to tell me that he told you exactly what he was going to do?" Orangecloak asked in disbelief.

She could feel Tryst scoff at the memory. "Aye and that went about as well as you might expect. Keo cut him off and killed him in a single stroke of his sword as he tried to charge through us. As that plan evaporated before their very eyes, the corsairs broke and tried to run off. Fearing they might have reinforcements lying in wait, we decided to give chase and hunt them down. We quickly broke off in pairs. Keo and I followed the three riflemen, two of the chieftain's guards went after the surviving mule rider and the other two went to find Gedo.

"The runners didn't get far. Keo and I found them hopping downhill through knee deep snow and on our mules we were able to close the gap in short order. One turned, sword in hand as I got near him and tried to swing for the donkey, the beast flinched and threw me into soft snow. As quickly as I could get up, the corsair was trying to take my mule and was paying no mind to me. My sword had gone flying from my hand when I fell, but I still had a dagger. I yanked it from the sheath and I drove it into his ribs as he tried to grab the reins of the mule."

His voice went flat. "That was my first. I would later find out that his name was Jeppo."

A quiet fell over them that risked growing uncomfortable and Orangecloak tried to think of something to say to disrupt it. "Something tells me that was not your last for the day."

"No," he answered in the same flat tone, pushing forward toward the story's end. "The other two had decided to attack Keo together. By the time I had found my sword they had killed his mule from under him. He came up swinging and managed to push them back long enough for me to join him.

"The cold had weakened the corsairs. They simply weren't accustomed to it like Keo and I happened to be and it wasn't much of a fight in truth. One turned his attention to me and made a desperate cross slash at face level. I ducked it and plunged my sword through his heart. As quick as that, he was dead and upon sight of it the other dropped his sword and begged for mercy at Keo's feet."

"Did you spare his life?" Orangecloak asked quickly.

"But of course," Tryst replied. "He had yielded and dropped his weapon. There was no need to kill him as we had the others."

That led Orangecloak to the defining question she had been waiting to ask from the start. "How did killing make you feel?"

"My feelings were mixed, to be honest," Tryst answered ponderously, as if he were still thinking about it years later. "On one hand, these were blackhearts who made their living raiding and pillaging any shores of the known world where they could drop anchor. On the other hand, it felt like a terrible waste of life."

Orangecloak thought about it herself for a moment. "Five men and a mule killed in what sounds like no time at all, two of them guards you fought beside. All for a folly of a plot to take this Gedo fellow for ransom. Aye, I find that quite sad."

"Six," Tryst corrected her. "The one who tried to flee on his own mule was run down by the guards before he got too far away. By the time the four guards, Gedo, Keo and I had all returned to the place where the attempted ambush was to take place, the day was nearly done. Instead of pushing on any further we all agreed to rest there and give the slain guards a proper burial. We built cairns, buried those in the snow and Gedo spoke of the men at length."

"Do you remember the names of the guards?" Orangecloak asked, trying to dig a little further into his memory.

"They were Ito Kamesiro and Mikku Takisa," Tryst answered without missing a beat. It meant something to her that he remembered not just those he killed but his fallen comrades besides. "Our prisoner told us his name was Uvat and that the other man I killed was named Zamak. He told us a great many more things about his shipmates and their intentions before we got Gedo home to Shatoya. All of it in foolish, vain hope that his cooperation might earn him mercy for his crimes."

Orangecloak waited for Tryst to follow that up and when he didn't, she broached the question. "What became of this Uvat fellow?"

"His information proved valuable," Tryst explained. "However, informing on a corsair ship in Drakian waters was not enough to erase his deeds. His mercy came in the form of a quick death at the hands of the High Chieftain himself."

The ground had levelled out beneath them as the story came to an end and Orangecloak realised they were nearing the lake she and Tryst had espied from above. She looked about for Ren but saw no sign of him through the trees and wondered where he had gotten to.

A soft turn later revealed the body of water at the end of the continually narrowing pathway. The bushes and trees loomed closer on either side and she had to brush away the leaves and branches that came close to her face. Soon enough, the path fell away to the marshy shores of the lake. Here, one of the grey mares was grazing restfully on the tall grass that grew out in the open. The windless day left the water still, its surface reflecting the tree line and Graelin's mountain peeking above that. The silence and serene beauty of the scene before her left Orangecloak captivated.

It was then Fletchard emerged from the woods noisily, baring the naked sabre Tryst had given him, its blade half coated in the crimson hue of blood. Her eyes went wide at the sight of it, though she stayed quiet and let Tryst ask the question they were clearly both thinking. "What's all this Fletchard? I sent you off to fish."

"Why don't you ask the elf?" Fletchard shot back as he flicked the blood from the sword. Before she had any time to wonder what he was talking about Ren stepped forth from the same place as Fletchard, looking a little ashamed as he did. Of his horse there was no sign and his suit, getting dirtier by the day, was now blood spattered as well.

"Ren, what in the world is going on?" Tryst asked with a slightly befuddled tone. "We heard a beast cry out earlier and discover you and Fletchard bloodied and he with a half reddened sword. Would you care to explain?"

The elf glanced around sheepishly, trying not to make eye contact with the two sharing a saddle. "Right, that, well…I came across an elk and I thought it would make a filling meal, so I loosed an arrow at it. I was aiming for the spot just to the rear of the front legs, as is recommended." Ren made a circling motion with his hand over his ribs as he spoke, to indicate his intended target area "But uh…I guess my aim was a little off, I hit him right in the shoulder and he sort of ran off with the arrow in him."

"Ran right into me that is," Fletchard chimed in, apparently not as content to let Ren do all the explaining as he would have led Tryst and Orangecloak to believe. "I heard it bawling over yonder. Damn thing ran itself over a bank in its panic and broke a leg, so I put it out its misery quickly." Fletchard made a motion of drawing his thumb across his throat to indicate how he did the deed.

A grunt came from Ren as he folded his arms. "I'm an engineer, not a hunter. I spend my days behind a desk in Gildriad, lecturing students. Last time I wielded a bow I was a boy in the Elven Forest and believe me, my childhood is much further in the past than yours."

Tryst took a deep breath behind her before responding. "Don't worry too much about it, Ren. Here's as good a spot as any to stop for the night. Don't mistake me, I had wanted to cover more ground this day, but that's all that can be done about it now. Let me find a dry spot to set camp. Orangecloak can take a rest there and the three of us will get that elk cleaned up and ready to cook."

Night had fallen by the time they feasted on the roasted elk. The four of them all shared their fill of meat as it slowly roasted over the flames of their campfire. For the first time in as long as she could remember, Orangecloak felt full. It was one less pain she had to deal with for the time being and for even that bit of relief, she was grateful.

The settled upon place for the campfire was in a clearing of soft ground and yellowed grass, situated a few meters above the waterline on the north side. Tryst had found some fallen logs to press into service as benches and the foursome sat in considerable comfort as the fire sent embers into the night sky.

The wobbling call of a solitary loon who had decided to call the lake home for the night could be heard off in the distance. Orangecloak sat sullenly with her back against the log, listening to the sad tune. *I know your song, little bird,* she thought to herself. *And I hope you find your companion someday.*

Her own companions were all ripped away from her and not just Myles and Coquarro. Somewhere out of her reach were all her fellow Thieves, being led by her lieutenants, who would find out one after the other that she was captured and likely dead. Despite Tryst's promise that he was freeing her to do as she pleased once they reached Portsward, she still harboured doubts. There were still hundreds of kilometres to cover before they reached the ocean and more again once they turned south towards the port city. The northern forests near the Dwarven Mountains were known for being inhospitable and dangerous and she was still certain that Fletchard could turn on them at any time.

Look at us, an elven engineering professor, a repudiated bounty hunter, the Master of Blades and the broken Field Commander of the Thieves. What a motley crew we make. How can anyone expect us to survive a journey through the north to the west coast together?

"I'll take first watch." Tryst announced as he stood up, bringing her out of her train of thought. He brushed himself off and adjusted his clothes and sword belt before walking off toward the lake to patrol the perimeter.

Ren leaned over from where he sat and she turned her attention to him. "My lady," he said in a low voice. "Would you care for another piece of elk?"

"Yes, 'my lady'," Fletchard said the last two words with implied sarcasm and the rest with noted derision. "Would you like more of the elk that *I* killed? You're welcome, by the way."

She ignored Fletchard's comments. "No thank you, Ren."

"Funny thing how *he* got thanked for providing a filling meal and *I* didn't." Fletchard prodded again, his eyes on the dripping meat clutched in his fingers. "All he did was torment the poor beast. I'm the one that killed it."

"Shut up, Fletchard," Ren scowled.

But it was Orangecloak who had taken enough of the bounty hunter's morbid sense of humour. "I'm well aware of who and what you have killed," she answered through gritted teeth, working hard to contain her rage.

Fletchard snorted through the mouthful of elk meat he was still chewing. "Well, well, you've finally spoken to me. That's good, for I was starting to think I had died back in Atrebell all along and was just an ethereal vessel that only men could see and hear."

"It should have been you that died back in Atrebell, but instead it was two good men that paid the price for your folly," Orangecloak spat back at him.

"And two drunks, you mustn't forget them. I know I won't. Those bloody idiots cost me everything," Fletchard said while waggling a filthy finger in her direction.

Her tone had turned to unfiltered venom and for once she no longer cared. "It was *you* that cost me everything, Fletchard Miller, not the louts. *You* hired them, *you* came looking for me, and *your* employees opened fire on my men. Myles and Coquarro were good, brave men, and you killed them both because you were stupid enough to believe that Grenjin Howland was actually going to pay you fifty thousand gold pieces."

"Oh fuck off, you cantankerous little bitch. What do you want me to say?" Fletchard threw the bit of gristle he had left into the fire forcefully. "Yes, I killed one of your friends. I told the drunks to just aim the rifles I gave them, force you three back to the corner and let me come in behind and do the talking. That's all they had to do, but the dumb sots got spooked when your two men jumped up. The black man in your company lunged at me with that curved knife of his and yes, I shot him in the face. I did it, I confess, it was kill or be killed and I decided that I didn't want to die and I'm not sorry for that."

Fletchard stood up and paced on the opposite side of the fire from her. "It was a poorly executed plan on my part, I admit. The drunks were a mistake to hire, yes. But, by that point it had all gone to shit. I was facing a big, tall, angry lad who looked like he wanted to gut me like a trout and I made a decision in the moment. He died, the other one died, the drunks died later and now it's just you and me left to tell the tale."

At that, Fletchard threw his arms wide and began talking far louder than Orangecloak would have liked. "As I see it, we both need to get far away from Atrebell. Grenjin Howland has decided he would rather kill me than pay me. As for you, he is going to be pushing even harder to get at you now that you've gotten away from him once. We have a need for each other at the moment, you see. We both need to get the fuck away and it's better to travel with numbers. Furthermore, I don't have the supplies to make it to the coast or the money to afford that dwarven hotel. When we get to Portsward, we can go our separate ways and never look at one another again. I, for one, plan to get on a ship and go to any place not named Illiastra. Then I'll be out of your sight forever. Until then, perhaps we can learn to work together a little so that we can reach the coast without dying."

Her jaw dropped as she stared at him incredulously. "You killed my two closest friends before my eyes. How do you expect me to treat you with anything more than animosity?"

Fletchard groaned. "What is it with them, anyway? Was one of them your lover, is that the way of it? Which one did you belong to?"

"I belong to no one," Orangecloak angrily shot back.

"That's entirely enough." All heads turned to see Tryst standing at the edge of the camp, holding all three horses by the reins. "You two can spit at one another later, for now we have to get moving at once."

Fletchard turned his attention from her to Tryst, giving her a reprieve from his nastiness. "There's someone out there?"

"Aye, I heard male voices. I can't tell if they're dwarf or human though." Tryst craned his head in the general direction of the lake. "They're coming from the east and I'm fairly certain they're up near the Stone Egg. Not much reason for dwarves to be around there these days, nor most men, so chances are we're dealing with soldiers."

Scooping up his scabbard, Fletchard turned back to Tryst excitedly. "Then what are we waiting for? Let's go deal with them."

"Gods, you're so eager to kill aren't you?" Orangecloak said vehemently, the corner of her mouth turning up into a snarl.

Tryst cut off what was likely a nasty retort from Fletchard. "Now's not the time for that, my lady." He turned his gaze to Fletchard. "And unless you intend to use that sword on us I suggest you put it away. I have no reason to believe that we've been spotted. If we had, they would already be on us. So we're going to snuff out this fire and ride long through the night. Ren," Tryst added while putting his gaze on the elf, "leave your mount hobbled here and go uphill on foot. Find out what they are and who they are if you can. We can't take any risks in being seen, one way or another, so we're pressing on, regardless. However I would like to know who else is on these trails."

"I understand," Ren said in a calm voice as he stood up and reached for the bow Tryst was lending him and the quiver beside it. As he adjusted the bundle on his hip he looked at Tryst and Orangecloak in turn. "What of the rest of you?"

"The three of us will pack up as much meat as we can in the food sack and douse the fire. If you're not back by the time we're done, look for us down the trail." Tryst pointed to where the old road winded north and west towards Graelin Mountain.

"Alright then, that sounds like a decent plan," Ren said with a nod toward Tryst before turning back to Orangecloak. "My lady, I hope to see you soon."

"Wait," Tryst called over his shoulder before Ren could depart. "If they are soldiers and you are taken, tell them nothing."

He was back before Tryst then, with a hand on his shoulder and a solemn tone. "If I have not returned by sunrise, presume me dead and don't come looking for me." With that, the elf disappeared into the night.

13

ELLARIE

ight of them had paddled out into the lake in a pair of yellow dories. Ellarie, Orangecloak, Merion & Joyce sat in one, Myles Stodden, Coquarro Lo-Qoia and Lazlo and Donnis Arbor in the other. They headed around the back of the island, steering for the ruins on the south banks of Great Valley Lake.

The Crypt of the Kings of Phaleayna rose tall, clinging proudly to existence as their crumbling towers poked the remnants of their heads above the treelines. Therein lay the final resting home of the last monarchy in Illiastra and their closest kin.

This was a rite of passage for those would join the Thieves: to visit the tombs of the last men and women to be knighted by King Malleon the Seventeenth.

There in the crypt lay the brave warriors that had quelled the rouge dictatorship empire of Valdarrow, one that had quite nearly plunged the entire continent into chaos.

Four girls and two boys had descended that day, and by nightfall they returned as men and women imbued with confidence. Together, they braved the dark and gloomy chambers of the ancient dead, now merely brittle, speckled swords and rusted, colourfully enamelled plate armour encasing the bones of the Knights Generals.

"The Woman Knight: Ser Eleanor Price of Upriver," declared Myles as they looked upon a skeleton bedecked in what once was a fine suit of plates in a shade of deep red. It lay in the center of the room, bony fingers clutching a dried out piece of curved wood that once might have been a bow. On the walls to either side of her lay more knights, each identified by a brass plate engraved and mounted before the shelf that each pile of armoured bones lay upon.

Ellarie had committed the names to memory as she read them: Ser Roy Donnell, who had been the commander of Ser Eleanor's knights, Ser Kenneth Warbridge and Ser Evelyn Voch, also a knighted woman. Ellarie considered them to be her ancient brothers and sister in arms at that moment.

The naiveté of youth, I was never a knight, not like they had been.

Two of Ser Eleanor's five were missing, but that was not unusual. There were knights who died in battle far from home and were buried near their place of death and others grew old and were interred in their places of retirement.

Turning to say as much to the others she saw that Orangecloak lay upon Eleanor's burial plinth, wrapped in her famous cloak, her hands clutching a bloody dagger. The empty shelves that were made to hold the absent knights were now claimed by Coquarro and Myles, their eyes open and staring with faces rapt in agony. She looked about for her sister and Joyce, and found they now occupied the resting place of Ser Roy and Ser Kenneth. Beneath them both, lying behind the plate that marked Lady Evelyn's berth was Ellarie herself, dead eyes looking mournfully up at her.

She screamed and ran back into the corridor, searching for the way out only to stumble across the threshold into another tomb bearing Lazlo Arbor in its center. About him lay Allia, Coramae, Bernadine, Nia, Jorgia, Ami Rosia, Bernarian, Errol, Haris, Etcher and Donnis lying in the cavities of the wall around the plinth. Pale light shone down on them from some unseen source, illuminating ghastly, horror stricken faces of those she had known and cherished.

This isn't right, these women and men served beneath me, we're no knights and only Nia is really dead. This isn't right.

"How do I get out of here?" she screamed into the darkness.

"How indeed?" a voice echoed off the walls over Ellarie's shoulder. Back in the hallway stood Orangecloak, her back turned, hood drawn, the orange cloak slashed in ribbons and bloodstained.

"We're not dead!" Ellarie shouted at her friend. "Wake up!" She grabbed the field commander of the Thieves by the shoulder and spun her around.

"No, we are not yet dead, though the world thinks we are," Orangecloak spoke to Ellarie, though her eyes were looking beyond, wincing and reacting to some tragic sight unseen. "No one out there knows or cares which of us served whom, or even all of our names. They don't know what happened to us or where we are going, they only think that we have collectively shuffled off this mortal coil. Some of us have and more will before this is all over. Though you and I and ours don't give up so easily, do we Ellarie? This wrong will be righted." Orangecloak produced the blade she had been holding on her stone plinth. "And this bloody dagger will be returned to its rightful owner. It has only begun Ellarie, we shall meet again."

Orangecloak left her there, walking into the dark depths of the halls of the dead. "Wait! I don't know the way back, don't leave me!" Ellarie called out as she tried to give chase. She was alone then, in complete darkness, calling out for Orangecloak, her sister, Lazlo, anyone to hear her and find her. Somewhere, a door opened.

"I am not pleased to have to be dragged here, Major Burnson." The voice was that of a man and one Ellarie did not recognise. "You dare to waste my time with this foolishness."

I was dreaming, she realised. *But the waking is almost worse.*

Her eyes groggily opened, taking her from the darkened tomb in her mind's eye to the dimly lit cell she currently shared with her captured unit. Two men stood a few steps from the bars of the cell, peering in at the seven prisoners huddled on the cots. Bedecked in his finely pressed suit with its chest of medals was indeed Major Burnson.

"I see only women here, where are the men?" spoke the same man who had woken her. He was dressed in an expensive looking, three piece indigo suit. His hair had receded far from his forehead, leaving only a white, neat ring around his head and a shining, bare dome on top. The man's face was lined and aged and he stared at the women with dark, apathetic eyes above a round nose and long moustache. His mouth was turned in a sneer and Ellarie had to wonder if it had ever known a smile.

Is that who I think it is? Ellarie wondered to herself.

"We put the three of them upstairs in the single cells, Lord Taves," Major Burnson said, answering both Taves' question and Ellarie's in one stroke.

The Minister of Biddenhurst scanned the prisoners silently for a moment before addressing the Major again. "They look fine to me.

Tell me again why you claimed them from Corporal Cornwall?" he said in a tone that sounded equal parts annoyed and disinterested.

Burnson grunted at that. "They look fine because *my* men cleaned them up and dressed the wounds *your* men caused. The flesh wounds anyway. One of the Thieves upstairs told my steward what your savages did to the skinny, little blonde one there. I can't fix those wounds, I'm afraid." The Major was seething as he said it. Ellarie could sense he tolerated no such behaviour and was appalled by what he had heard of the night of horrors and the aftermath he had witnessed personally.

Unperturbed and rather indifferent to the accusations levelled against his men, Mackhol Taves went on in a sly, calm tone, "Aye and a good job you did cleaning them up. Though I must say, Major Burnson, I am shocked and dismayed that you would take the word of a thief over that of a soldier. It says much about your character. By all means, let your complaint spread its wings and take flight through the courts, let us see how long it stays aloft."

"That was ill done of your men, at any rate," answered Burnson, agitated by Taves' arrogance. "No soldier under my charge would ever do such an unconscionable deed. Your men abused her and abused their power, Lord Taves. I would lock them up for such abhorrent behaviour if they were mine to command."

The lack of intimidation Mackhol Taves was able to instil in the decorated veteran clearly irked the Lord of Crime and Punishment. "But they are not yours to command, are they? They are mine and I am the law in Illiastra. If I say no crime was committed, then that is the way of it. You would do well to remember that, Burnson. I answer only to the Lord of the East and the Lord Master above him. You, like this lot," Taves said with a point toward Ellarie and company, "are only an ant beneath my feet, to be crushed at my discretion. Do not give me a reason, Major Burnson. If I went to great lengths to get these waifs, I will certainly waste no time going after a man seeking to besmirch my good name."

Taves turned back to the women. "That goes for all of your kind too. Do you think that little island in the lake is a refuge? No, it is a mercy I allow. If I so chose to sink that island to the bottom of Great Valley Lake, then that is where it will go. Someday, when I require the filth and abominations of Illiastra to fill out my indentured workforce, I may well do that."

A glance from Ellarie toward her sister saw anger and fury welling up in Merion. Joyce held the fiery redhead tightly to keep her from making a grab at him through the bars.

Taves pivoted on his heel and turned towards the door to leave. "Burnson, come with me. We have some paperwork to fill out so I can get this load of human waste stored away properly in *my* city."

"Aye, my Lord," Burnson called back in a voice that rang of defeat. He gave the women one last regretful glance before following Taves back into the heart of the guard station.

Merion exhaled and relaxed in Joyce's arms as the door closed once more behind the lord and major. "You didn't need to squeeze me so tight, Joyce. I wasn't going to jump him."

"I know you too well to believe that. You would have tried to strangle him through the bars," Joyce answered firmly. "I could feel you getting angry."

"I think I know why Mackhol Taves hasn't crushed Phaleayna." Bernadine said from where she sat on the furthest cot.

Ellarie nodded. "Something tells me it's the same thing I've been thinking."

"I think that whoever sold Orangecloak and us out didn't do it for coin. They did it to save the island," Bernadine uttered in a voice full of sorrow, which was exactly the thought that had crossed Ellarie's mind as well.

"Aye, the price of freedom was Orangecloak and us," Ellarie agreed "What I want to know, is how Taves managed to get someone to pay. That island has been a den for the Thieves for decades and all of us have been roaming the countryside for a few years now. How did Taves come to get a death grip on it?"

"Our numbers were growing too large, I would say," Joyce hypothesised. "Before now we weren't really a threat. The more Orangecloak talked to the people, the more they joined or at the very least sympathised with us. So the EMP decided to squash the bugs before they became an infestation."

"Or it was a bluff," Merion added from where she laid.

"That could be," Ellarie considered. "We have no reason to believe what he says. The person who sold us may well have done it for personal gain and Taves may not have the means to march all the way to Great Valley to siege an island full of refugees. Not without risking the entire nation revolting at once. Sacking a refuge of women and children would even raise the ire of the other nations too. The Elven Forest up north might ignore it, but Johnah, Drake, and all three nations in Gildriad would all condemn it. Furthermore, we all know the dwarves would align with anyone willing to overthrow the EMP.

"No matter how insulated Taves feels in his power, he is well aware that any two of those countries working with the Dwarven Nation could invade and overrun Illiastra if they chose."

"Indeed." Bernadine added. "He may be the law in Illiastra, but he's not the law in the rest of the world and even he has to be careful not to overstep. Though even still, we cannot say for certain that he would not go through with it. He might well be arrogant enough to believe he is just that untouchable."

Everyone seemed to be in agreement with that much and their conversation tapered off. They spent the next little while milling around in their cell and stretching their aching limbs, too anxious to attempt sleep again.

The other women talked amongst themselves and Ellarie allowed her mind to drift off, playing back the events of her bizarre dream and the words of Mackhol Taves.

Roughly an hour passed before the door opened for the second time that morning. From without came a line of Atrebell guards, all dressed in the uniform of a deep blue jacket and black trousers. A pair holding a wooden platter and a tin pitcher came first and behind them came a bearded sergeant-at-arms with auburn hair, distinguished by the single silver shield on his collar.

"Morning, ladies," he said to them in a soft tone. "My name is Sergeant Akers and I have been tasked with seeing you all readied for transport. Until the moment you are loaded into the wagon out front, you are in my care and I hope I can have your full co-operation on the matter. I can understand that you would want to resist my men and perhaps mount an assault in some last ditch attempt at freedom. However, it is my hope that we can avoid such a grievous mistake. Neither I nor my men want to have to hurt you. Please remember that we are only here to do a job, nothing more." The sergeant, who looked to be just above his thirtieth year paced as he spoke. His voice was gravel on stone but his words were as softly doled out as possible.

Ellarie ran over a thousand scenarios in her head that saw her and her unit making a mad dash for freedom. It was only in the wildest of them did they actually succeed. The others were nothing more than added woe to their strife.

When none of the prisoners answered, the Sergeant took that for understanding and ploughed ahead with his instructions: each of the women were to take a piece of folded, buttered bread and produce the tin cups they had been given the night before for fresh water. The prisoners would be given time to eat while the guards working beneath Akers this morning prepared to ready them for transport.

Beneath Ellarie the cot was rattling on the chains it was suspended from. A glance to her left revealed the reason behind it being Coramae, the woman no doubt shivering at the thought of being restrained and vulnerable again. Rubbing the terrified woman's shoulder was Allia, trying to calmly reassure her that these men weren't going to harm anyone. It was a lie, of course. The guards working for Akers were only holding them long enough for the Biddenhurst men to take custody.

Finishing his little speech with a plea for order once more, the Sergeant asked politely if any of them had any questions they would like to ask.

Bernadine spoke up from the furthest cot into the cell and asked what hour it was, to which it was revealed to be the seventh hour of the morning.

Next to ask of the sergeant was Allia, inquiring of the condition of the men. Akers claimed they were doing as well as could be expected of men who are locked behind bars. Their wounds seemed to be welts, bruises and abrasions for the most part, though one of them was bleeding at the mouth from having lost teeth. Ellarie suspected that was Etcher, whom she recalled taking the hard toe of Corporal Cornwall's boot to the face while slung over a horse like a burlap sack.

A moment of silence lapsed and Ellarie could sense what many of them wanted to ask the sergeant. When no one else dared, she spoke up herself. "We caught snippets of conversation between the guards posted at the door last night and they seemed to be talking of a commotion at the Atrebell Manor. We also heard the name Orangecloak being mentioned. Would you be able to shed light on that?" Ellarie was careful in her wording, to not get the Major Burnson's young steward in any trouble for his good deed of telling them that little bit of news.

With a nervous clearing of his throat, Akers replied, "From the reports we have received, it would seem that the one you call Lady

Orangecloak was apprehended by bounty hunters in the Batterdowns neighbourhood. The hunters produced her at the manor, directly to the Lord Master himself and collected their bounty. That is all I am at liberty to divulge."

An audible gasp went up in unison from the women as thoughts swam through Ellarie's head.

No wonder Taves was so upset this morning, it wasn't coming here to collect us that pissed him off. It was a bounty hunter getting to his prize before he did. We're a small consolation next to Orangecloak.

What was even more surprising to Ellarie was that the hunter not only got by the gates, but was successful in getting the Lord Master to pay the bounty.

Given that she is the most wanted person in Illiastra, anyone able to capture her would have a guaranteed, immediate audience with the Lord Master.

Other questions soon followed, mostly from Jorgia and Bernadine. They queried Akers on whether or not the captured men would be riding with them and how they were to be transported to the train.

Akers kindly took the time to answer all the questions while simultaneously encouraging the women to eat their meagre breakfast. It was explained to the women that they and the men would together be transported by wagon to the train station in time for a departure to Biddenhurst by noon. There they were to be moved onto a train car made specifically for prisoner transport before the train departed at the first hour of noon.

While Ellarie and the other prisoners ate their buttery brown bread and tepid water, the guards went to work setting up. A table, two chairs and a large chest were brought into the room with a ruckus that Akers had to raise his voice to be heard over.

With her breakfast finished, Ellarie had nothing else to do but clutch her tin cup and watch the guards arranging the ugly, linked irons that her unit were going to be forced into soon enough. The others in the cell were of similar mind, with even Merion and Joyce staying put on the cot where they had slept, their bodies held tight together in embrace.

This bunch of macabre servants takes no joy in arranging the 'poor man's jewellery'. No more than those on this side of the bars take at the prospect of wearing them.

When the terrible assortment of iron chains and cuffs were laid out, one guard departed in search of another man they referred to as the Writer.

After a few minutes, an older man bearing a worn and faded yet spotlessly clean military jacket over civilian clothing shuffled into the room. Behind him came the same guard, clutching to hand a thick stack of paper with an inkwell, feather pen, a jar of white paint and a small brush atop it.

The Writer looked like a man who should be retired or near enough to such a point that they had reduced him to the task of just putting ink to paper. As it was, there were very few among the poor that knew how to read and write, meaning that those like the old man, were highly valued in their fields.

The soft-spoken elder politely nodded and greeted everyone, guard and prisoner alike, as he entered. The thing Ellarie noticed the most of him was his bearing of a cup and saucer of tea to hand as casually as if he were sitting for breakfast. His jacket was hung on the chair and he sat down to the table and thumbed through his papers. "I seem to have everything I need," the older man declared, while opening his inkpot. "When you are ready, Sergeant, you may begin our unenviable task."

The sergeant responded wordlessly with a nod of his own while turning a key in the door of the cell, pulling it open on its moaning, rusted hinges. "Let's do this peacefully with one person at a time." When no one moved, the Sergeant sighed audibly. "Can someone please step forward? I don't want to have to send my men in there to drag you out by force."

Remembering who she was supposed to be without prompt, Bernadine leapt from her place on the floor, striding on her wrapped feet to the sergeant holding the door. Akers admitted her through the threshold before slamming and locking the door behind her unflinching body. Instructions to kneel on the chair were relayed and Bernadine followed, placing her hands flat on the table for support.

With a dip of his quill, the old guard gently bid her a good morning and asked for her name. Dressed in plain clothes, one would easily just think of him as a kindly grandfather rather than a guard in service to the Elite Merchant Party. Much like his co-workers, he was quite likely pressed into service and was just trying to make the best of what life had paid him. Ellarie sensed no more desire in him to be here than she possessed and she bore the man no ill will.

While the writer asked Bernadine the standard questions of her name, place and date of birth, the uniformed men went to work snapping the iron restraints closed on her wrists and ankles. The force and speed with which they did so was pushing Bernadine about so much that Ellarie thought she was about to tumble over.

It took a moment before Bernadine was able to regain herself and answer the old man. Patiently, he repeated his line of basic questions again for the now bound woman. Bernadine gave Ellarie's information, getting the year and season of her birth correct but having to make a guess on the specific day.

Close, she was only a week ahead. Ellarie thought. *It was the sixty-third day of spring in the year fifteen thousand and seventy five, by Elven reckoning.*

That was the standard measurement by which the entire known world, besides the staunchest of the Triarchy's adherents, went by. To them it was the year seventeen hundred and ninety on a two thousand year calendar that supposedly prophesised doom after that point.

The guardsmen backed the woman they thought was Ellarie off the chair and back to her feet, her new adornments rattling all the while. Two of them held her arms in vice like holds while a third wrapped a chain around her waist. Feeding it through a wide hoop at the end before cinching it so tight that Bernadine looked about to break in half. They attached a lock to moor the chain between her hands to the belt of iron links they had just given her.

When it was all done, the old man stood with his white paint and brush to mark Bernadine's new prisoner number on the shoulder of her shift. With that, she was gone through the wooden door before Ellarie could blink, whisked away to the waiting wagon.

It was Jorgia they took next, followed by the separation of Merion and Joyce. What the soldiers lacked for empathy in general, they more than made up for with their energy. Ellarie thought they would tire of their unnecessarily egregious approach to handling the prisoners, but with four down and three remaining, the guards showed no signs of slacking.

Then, the turn fell to poor, little Coramae and she began shivering violently when Akers called her forward.

"Go on, Coramae, I'll be right here," Allia spoke softly. "Just keep your eyes on me the whole time. These men won't hurt you."

"They're giving us back to the ones who hurt us. Don't you see that, Allia?" Coramae's voice was broken by her weeping as she turned towards the Sergeant-at-arms. "Please ser, I beg you, don't let them take us." Akers sent one of the guards in to fetch her out and she continued the fruitless pleading as the uniformed man tried to gingerly take her under the elbow. "Please, I'll stay here, I'll be a good little prisoner in here, just don't let the Biddenhursters get me. I beg you, please!"

"By the gods," the Elder gasped, watching her over his spectacles "What did they do to her? She's positively petrified."

"I would rather not say it aloud, Garr," Akers answered in a low voice with a sigh and a nervous swallow before addressing Coramae. "Come on, miss, you'll only make it worse on yourself if you make the Biddenhurst fellows late. Just come on out of there, keep quiet and hope for the best. The pleading with us will do no good, we can only follow orders."

"He's right, Coramae, we have to get on with it or we'll all suffer worse." Ellarie added, "You'll see Donnis soon, think of that, he'll be riding with us to Biddenhurst."

With a little more prodding, they got Coramae out of the cell. "Please be gentle with her," Allia put in as Coramae hobbled to toward the chair she was to kneel upon. "Keep your eyes on me, Cora, it's nothing, just chains is all."

"My dear," the elder man Akers called Garr said with a light tap on her hand. "I'm so sorry for what the other guards might have done. These good fellows aren't like that, I can assure you. I have a few questions I would like to ask you if that might be okay. You can look at the other girl if you want or close your eyes. But talk to me, please. First question, what is your full name?"

"Your 'good fellows' are giving me and mine over to terrible, cruel men, ser. That makes yours as bad as the Biddenhursters to me," Coramae muttered.

"They're just following orders, my dear," the older man stated before moving back to his question. "Now, might I have you name?"

"My name...It's..." She turned to Allia before answering, who nodded back reasurringly. "Coramae Chandler."

Garr followed with getting her age and place of birth while Akers gave the cue to his men, who went to work applying the restraints. Coramae tensed up at their touch and tears rolled freely down her face. Every snap of a shackle locking in place came with an audible sob from Coramae and it took two guards to keep her steady when it came time to leave.

"I'll be right behind you, Coramae. Keep an eye out for me. I'll be with you in just a moment," Allia called after her.

Before Akers could call her out, Allia had already stridden to the exit of the cell and was gone shortly after. She answered the old man as quickly as he could ask his questions and departed with a thank-you to the Sergeant for his compassionate treatment of the traumatised Coramae.

It was down to only Ellarie then and she stood when called, approaching Sergeant Akers with her eyes downcast and the hood of her shift drawn. She knelt up on the chair without prompting, opting to accept her immediate fate with as much dignity as she could. If not just for her own sake, then for the woman whose identity she was about to assume.

"It would seem that you're the last one. Well, let's get this over with. What is your full name?" Garr seemed tired of the activity, or perhaps was more stirred by Coramae's words than he let on.

Ellarie answered, "She's right you know."

"I'm sorry?" The old guard looked at her with furrowed brows, pushing his eyeglasses back up his nose.

"Coramae, she said that your men are no better than those Biddenhursters and she's right," Ellarie stared him down as she spoke.

"We have orders," Garr started to say as Ellarie cut him off.

"You have choices, ser. One man may issue an order, the choice to follow that order is on you. Power is founded in the choice of the many to acknowledge and follow the will of the few. If a lord or an officer gives a command and there is no one to carry it out, is he any more powerful than the beggar huddled outside your door?" The guards all paused and Ellarie could see the few ahead of her looking to one another with chains and iron cuffs in their hands as befuddlement washed over them.

Akers slammed the cell door shut with a loud bang.

Ellarie maintained her poise, acting as though she barely heard the noise as Akers approached the table, standing between young woman and old man.

"I'm sure Orangecloak delights in telling you all that same line," he commented. "Yet, here you are, having followed her orders and it's my good men that have to clap you in chains and deliver you to the terrible men of Biddenhurst."

"I choose to follow through with her wishes because I agree with them." Ellarie met Akers line of sight, courage welling in her voice. "We of the Thieves don't follow a leader blindly. If we don't approve of what our superiors ask, then we're under no pressure to oblige them. If Lady Orangecloak or Lieutenant Ellarie asks me to carry out a task for them, I do so because I freely agree to, because I concur with their purpose for doing so. Can you say the same, ser? Or are you merely a trained dog?"

"You may call me a dog, but you're the one on a leash being led to her slaughter. That's the difference between you and me. You chose rebellion and played with death, where I chose servitude and survival." Akers put his knuckles on the table and leaned in, his patience clearly wearing thin.

"To me, that's no choice at all." Ellarie's tone went defiant as she brought herself to within mere centimetres of the Sergeant's face. "Some of us just can't live with following the orders of tyrants."

"And some of us have four children at home waiting for their father to put food on the table," Akers cocked his head to the side in saying. "As nice of a thought as it is to run off and save the world, some of us just happen to have responsibilities to tend to first." It was then he noticed the guards still standing about with their eyes wide. "What in the fuck are you all waiting for? Get on with shackling her."

The guards all jumped into action at once, the chains in their hands rattling loudly as they hobbled Ellarie at wrist and ankle.

The old man regained his composure and once again went through the process of gathering her personal information, to which Ellarie gave Bernadine's when prompted. "I'm Bernadine Voyer, born in Wyford, down in the Southlands on the seventh of autumn in the year fifteen thousand and seventy nine," she said spitefully at the old fellow. The assuredness with which she gave her answers seemed to suit him well enough as he scrawled out her words on the parchment in the black ink. As he had with the others, he traded the dark tipped quill for the brush and wrote the prisoner number he had given her on the shoulder of the shift.

"I have all I need here, Akers. Let me retrieve my writing board and I'll join you upstairs to speak to the men," Garr said as he stood up and stacked the paper. "I'll have to make a copy for the Biddenhurst records too. But I'll have no time to do that today, let them know I'll mail them forward at a later date."

"I'll tell you what, Garr: go copy what you have while we get the men ready. I'll write down their name and birthdate and we'll mail that information forward later. There are only three of them, after all. I think the Biddenhursters know which one is which."

"As you wish, Sergeant," Garr said as he stood up, turning back to Ellarie briefly. "Miss...Voyer, was it? Heed my advice: our fellows are a far more amicable than the louts of Biddenhurst. You would do well to keep quiet once you leave here. You've got a very pretty face, but they won't let you keep it that way if you open your mouth."

"He's not wrong," Akers added after Garr had left. The sergeant's demeanour had calmed down once again in the interim. Noticing his guards waiting on his command, he turned back to them. "Take the box of chains and go ready the men."

Once his charges were gone, the Sergeant returned his attention to Ellarie, pointing towards her legs, still kneeling on the chair. "Your feet are showing and it will be cold outside. Might I at least fix your wraps?" Ellarie put her head down and gave a slight nod, letting the man named Akers slip behind her and retie the ragged strips of old cloth they had given the women to cover their feet in place of boots.

The Sergeant looked quite nervous, glancing at the door to look for others before turning back to her with a low voice. "You don't remember me, do you?"

Ellarie felt the fear running down her spine. She didn't know anyone from Bernadine's former life and felt sure she was being led into a trap, though she tried to play along anyhow. "I'm sorry, where have we met?"

"It's alright, Ellarie, I wouldn't expect you to." Akers shrugged. "It was a few years ago since last we've seen each other. I've filled out a little since then and grew a beard that I didn't have in those days."

"You have me mistaken, I'm Bernadine Voyer," she answered quickly while trying to place the man.

"You can relax. I know who you really are. Dolph came to me this morning on his way home and told me everything." He put his hands on her shoulders softly and looked her straight in the eyes. "It's me, Roch. Dolph nicknamed me 'Rowdy' if you remember."

The more she looked at him, the more Ellarie began to think that he did indeed look familiar, but she still couldn't be sure if this was some trap. "I don't know what you're talking about, ser. I'm Bernadine, not Ellarie."

"Oh come now, the others might not know one dark haired girl from the other, but I know Ellarie Dollen. You're Dolph's half-sister, the closest one in age to him. You might not know this, but before you left, I was quite smitten with you." He seemed to blush a little at that. "Dolph was going to try and get us together, on account that it would get you away from your father, who was treating you and Merion quite poorly. Dolph's my best mate, Ellarie. Don't you remember?"

He does know a lot about me, things only the family might know.

"What happened to your hair?" Ellarie asked to test him.

"They made me cut my shaggy curls off. I couldn't tie them tight enough for regulations, so I had to get rid of them altogether," Akers said resentfully.

"Why did Dolph tell you what was going on?" she finally relented, dropping the charade.

Roch breathed deeply and took the chair across from her. "Dolph's worried sick about you and Merion, as I'm sure you can appreciate. He asked if I would oversee your shackling and turnover to the Biddenhursters. I told him I'd take care of it if I could and he told me about your little disguise. You need not worry, Ellarie. I won't spill your secret. I'm just looking out for you as best as I can for Dolph's sake."

"Dolph wanted us together?" Ellarie said with a sad little smile. "He never told me that."

"We tossed around the idea just about the time Merion was sneaking out with that blonde girl. Poor Dolph was so afraid that your father was going to find out and give Merion up to the Triarchy or worse. I was quite taken with you back then, so Dolph was going to set us up, to get at least one of his sisters out of Yeoll's grasp anyway. But then you two left the city on your own and I found a wife not long after that." A smile crossed his face at the mention of her, Ellarie noticed. "We live near Dolph over on the east side of town now."

Ellarie gave a long, slow nod. "I'm glad for you, Roch. And I thank you, for looking out for us here, it means a lot to Dolph, I know, but it means much to Merion and me too."

"Think nothing of it, Ellarie, it's the least I could do." Roch stood up and checked the door again. "We should get moving as I still have to go upstairs and get your friends. Come on, I'll escort you out." With a hand in the crook of her elbow, Roch eased her back off the chair to the racket of her clanking chains. "Those will take some getting used to, I'm afraid," he said apologetically. "Before we go, I should tell you a few things about where you're going."

"You mean Biddenhurst? Have you been there before?" Ellarie queried with a glance at him from the corner of her eye.

"I have, a group of us escorted a convicted murderer there." Roch's face was grim, his tone stoic. "The things I saw have stayed with me like some waking nightmare. Whatever you do, give them no cause to hurt you for they beg for such a chance. Speak if spoken to, stay silent otherwise. Those guards – many of them were former convicts themselves. Rapists and killers mostly, but word is that Lord Taves will put a uniform on any man he believes will follow his orders, no matter how sadistic those orders might be. So, whatever you do, heed my advice: don't give them the satisfaction of hurting you."

Ellarie nodded back at him. "I'll do that, thank you again, Roch."

The station's main foyer was practically empty as Roch led Ellarie in by the arm. Apart from one or two guards lingering about and minding their own work stations, it felt practically deserted. It was a dark room, even with the daylight trying to force its way through the converted arrow slits and as unwelcoming a place as she had ever been. In that moment though, the thought of leaving it seemed a worse fate. At the main entrance stood a young fellow with sad eyes that followed Ellarie as she was brought before the pair of heavy doors that led outside.

"How's the crowd?" Sergeant Akers asked the baby-faced fellow in a uniform that looked barely worn.

New to the world and newer to the force, Ellarie thought as she looked him over.

"Ser, the guards outside are keeping them on the far side of the street and there's a wide berth around the wagon, ser," the boy worriedly replied with his gaze on Ellarie as she stood beside Akers.

Akers turned to her. "Keep that hood up and your eyes down. Don't look at the crowd, they're fairly peaceful, but some have been hurling rotten fruit and dead rodents. There's a Patriarch and some Brothers of the Triarchy out there stirring them up by reading loudly from *The God's Gift.*"

Ellarie gave him a "Yes, ser," to both acknowledge his advice and let him know the ruse was back on. From here on out they weren't acquaintances from their teenage years, rather they were Sergeant Akers of the City Guards and Bernadine Voyer, his prisoner.

"Open it," the Sergeant commanded the youthful guard.

A pair of vertical bars were slid in opposite directions and the handle of the leftmost door turned to let them pass.

To call what was gathered a crowd was a kindness. *This is a mob,* Ellarie realised, and they looked like they might devolve into chaos at a moment's notice.

She understood then why the inside of the station was nearly empty. It seemed as though every bluecoat in the city was out there keeping the frenzied folk at bay.

Standing shoulder to shoulder and bearing batons, the men in the uniforms kept the shouting men and women to the other side of the street. A wagon had been pulled up to the bottom of the stairs and was already occupied by Ellarie's fellow Thieves.

A booming voice could be heard preaching above the noise of the crowd. "Here they deliver yet another whore of the forest!" it heralded to the masses.

Ellarie followed the voice until she found its owner: a plump man in the bright red, white and gold robes of a Patriarch of the Triarchy, who was standing atop something that put him a head above the crowd. One hand pointed at Ellarie with an index finger of judgement, the other waved a black, leather-bound book she knew must be *The God's Gift.*

"They fornicate wantonly with man and woman alike amongst the trees and bushes, out of sight of decent men like us," the Patriarch proclaimed. "Though Ios bears witness to their sins and he puts it to us to judge them."

The crowd let out a roar of approval at the Patriarch's accusation and that gave him all the encouragement he needed to plough forward. "This cage full of whores should be brought to the town's centre and strung by their unholy necks until they are as dead as their kin. So sayeth *The God's Gift,* chapter twelve, paragraph eight, verses two through four."

Shouts of "Kill them!", "Give them to Ios!" and "Hang 'em high!" from the most religiously devout males echoed the Patriarch's sentiments. Ellarie ignored the barbs and insults and instead glanced about to see if her parents were in attendance.

"Pay him no mind and watch your step," Akers spoke into her ear as he nudged her forward.

With her head down and eyes on the concrete steps ahead of her, Ellarie began her descent. The chains binding her ankles clanked noisily on each step, playing a tuneless elegy for the damned woman.

The caged wagon that waited for her was indeed larger than the one she had been transported to Atrebell in. It was tall enough for proper benches and long enough to hold at least a dozen prisoners, more if there was no issue against crowding them. The wooden benches were positioned in the center of the wagon, with a backrest between them which forced the passengers to face outward towards potential onlookers. The caging was also divided between the two benches, with separate doors for the two sides. One side was closed already with tightly wrapped chains and heavy locks and within Ellarie could see Joyce and Bernadine bookending Jorgia, Allia and Coramae. Opposite of them sat Merion all to herself. Her head was down, but even from upon the steps Ellarie could see her sister's head moving about, scanning the faces shouting for her immediate death.

At the second step from the ground the guards had erected a pair of planks to stretch the gap to the wagon's doors. The guard manning it opened the one Merion sat behind upon Ellarie's approach.

"This is the last of the women." Sergeant Akers told his charges as he walked Ellarie across the planks to the guards.

"Aye sergeant, we tried to keep the Three Sisters apart, ser, as we were told. We put the Queen Bitch and the Tall Bitch on opposite sides of one bench and the Red Bitch all to herself on the other."

"Good job, lad," Akers replied, before adding to it. "I don't care what order you stuff the men in there, one's a lieutenant of the Thieves, but the sisters are apart and that's all that was asked of us to be done."

The guard nodded. "Understood, Sergeant Akers." As Akers was about to turn back to the building the same guard stopped him once more. "Ser, the Biddenhursters sent a man to tell us to not make them late for the train, ser."

Akers spun around to face the guard. "Fuck the Biddenhurst cunts," he groaned wearily. "Let them wait. They'll get this lot when I'm good and fucking ready to let them have them and not a minute before. I don't like being rushed, especially not by savages dressed up like men. The next time a Biddenhurster shows up here, politely tell him to fuck off. Am I clear?"

"Ser, yes, ser," the guard answered quickly, averting his eyes to the ground as he slammed shut the cage door and secured the latch.

Ellarie sidled up next to her sister as she took her seat behind the iron bars of the wagon. "Do you know who that is?" she whispered to Merion, inclining her head towards Akers before he disappeared inside the building.

"Sergeant Akers, the guard just said so," Merion responded in a hushed and disinterested tone of her own.

"No. Well, yes, he is, but he's more than that," Ellarie gave back. "How many men do we know named Akers?"

"I don't know, quite a few I would think. It's only the most common surname in Atrebell, after all," Merion answered, evidently in no mood for making any further guesses.

"He's Dolph's best friend, 'Rowdy' Roch." Ellarie said, cutting right to the point.

"Good to know, though something tells me that he can't do anything for us either," Merion gave back despairingly.

"No," Ellarie sighed. "Dolph asked him to oversee the transfer as a favour to him. However, he's in no more of a position to spring us than Dolph was." Beneath her shift she tried to stick her fingernails into the keyholes of the shackles binding her hands and felt every link of chain and hinge for weakness. When that failed, she tried fruitlessly to slip her wrists through the loops. The iron refused to yield in any form and she sat back, resigning herself to her current predicament.

"Be sure to remind me to send Dolph a thank-you note," Merion sarcastically intoned, her line of vision scanning the crowd all while she spoke.

"Any sign of Yeoll?" Ellarie queried her sister. There was no doubt that Merion was looking for him.

Merion's lip curled up in disgust at the mention of the name. "That shit won't show his face here. Every time Yeoll hears there's a member of the Thieves in the lockup he stays far away, I bet. Afraid it might be us and someone will figure out that we're his offspring." Neither sister referred to him as their father anymore, they had decided long ago that he had lost any right to such a title.

"These women are the temptresses of Aren himself, come to seduce you to his army of the underworld!" the Patriarch suddenly called out louder than his previous chants. "I shall lead a petition on behalf of us holy people so that we may see that these vile creatures are sent back to Aren from whence they came! In Ios' name we should cast them down before they tempt our good men! Let them hang in this life to descend into the darkness of the next!"

"Hang them! Hang them!" the crowd took up the chant.

Merion eyed the middle-aged man in his robes with his bushy, light brown beard. "If I had a free fist I'd use it to smash that fucking bulbous nose of his," she said, as fiery as ever.

The steel doors of the station swung open together and a cavalcade of guards poured out. No less than seven, led once again by Sergeant Akers, all flanking the three men of the Thieves that had been captured two days past.

With a noticeable shadow of stubble on his normally smooth face was Lazlo Arbor, chained hand and foot like the women who waited on his company in the wagon.

"And here come the perpetrators of sodomy! Aren's most wicked creations in the flesh!" The proselytising holy man called at the top of his lungs. "Feast your eyes on he who would lie with another 'he' in absolute sin! Ios sees you, Ios judges you and by his own word we should take the head from your shoulders and the manhood from your loins! It is written! To Ios I pray that our benevolent leaders heed your words, o' mighty lord, and punish the heathens as is your will!"

"You shouldn't mock sodomy until you try it, preacher man!" Lazlo taunted while trying to navigate the steps in his leg irons. "In fact, why don't you come on over here and I'll shove that book up your arsehole and see if I can make you smile!"

"Shut up and keep moving," Akers ordered while turning to face Lazlo one step above.

The preacher seemed ready for such a spitting contest. "Your words have no bearing here, in the hearing of holy men! Your foulness shall not deter the will of Ios!"

"But I am a holy man, Patriarch. Every night when I lie with one of my men I'm shouting 'Oh Ios! Oh Ios! By the good god Ios, YES! RIGHT THERE, IOS, THAT'S THE SPOT!'" Lazlo roared at the top of his lungs, his head cocked back as if he was in the middle of the act.

It was all Ellarie could do to contain her smile as the Patriarch grew increasingly incensed at Lazlo's lewd display.

The cage door was flung open and the three men shoved hastily inside by the guards.

"I told you before I opened that front door to keep your gods damnable mouth shut," declared Akers quite angrily, leaving without waiting for any sort of reply. He turned his attention towards the guards holding the mob back. "Shove them off, we're leaving immediately." He looked to the men standing near the steps. "The rest of you, saddle up and form rank about the wagon."

Above Sergeant Akers' bellowing, the Patriarch could still be loudly heard preaching to the remaining crowd, even as the guardsmen holding the line ordered the gathered folks away.

"Hello, Bernadine and Merion," Lazlo said with a sly smile as he slid in next to them, before dropping his voice low. "The good sergeant filled me in on your little ruse, quite clever if I do say so. It might just be the one bit of leverage we have left, we should be careful with it."

"I intend to do just that, Laz," Ellarie gave back, thankful that Roch had told Lazlo. Having not being able to tell him had worried her. However, as she looked over the three men her worries grew tenfold. "Your poor faces, you must be in terrible pain."

The three were showing the marks of their beating. Out of the six eyes between them four were swollen, both of Donnis' and one apiece of Lazlo and Etcher. Etcher had lips that were thick and purple and all three bore various cuts and scrapes on their cheeks and foreheads.

"We've been better," Etcher said from the end of the bench.

From beside him, Donnis turned in his seat as best as his restraints and injuries allowed and called Coramae's name. Upon sight of him and despite their dire predicament, she began to cry with joy.

Ellarie let them have their moment and turned her attention back to Lazlo. "Did you hear any news?" she asked him flatly as the ramp was pulled away from the wagon and the horse's reins cracked.

"Aside from your little ruse, I don't know a thing, my dear," Lazlo replied lowly.

Reappearing from around the corner of the stations was Sergeant Akers. He had saddled a brown destrier and was hollering commands to the other guards and leading a line of horsemen that flanked the wagon as it turned to the east.

"They got her, Lazlo," Ellarie stated solemnly as Akers passed. "They have Orangecloak."

14
ORANGECLOAK

espite an overcast sky that blotted out moons and stars alike, Tryst and Fletchard kept their steeds at a steady canter and had made a surprising amount of progress. Although, by the first welcoming rays of daylight, the lot of them, people and animals alike, were thoroughly exhausted and in dire need of rest.

The bounty hunter had been quiet all throughout, which was as much as Orangecloak could ask for. At his usual place at the rear of the pack he was alert and on guard for whomever may have been at the Stone Egg.

Though Orangecloak abhorred violence in all its forms, she felt it queerly comforting knowing that Fletchard and Tryst were ready to go to battle against any potential captors. This feeling came in spite of the fact that Fletchard's decision to fight was purely in the interest of self-preservation.

Regardless of everything, there was a certain sense of helplessness she couldn't help but feel. She had spent the entire night clutching the mane of the horse, with hoods drawn and her head tucked against its strong neck to avoid any outcropping branches or limbs that may take them unawares in the dark. There was no other recourse, nothing else she could do but hold on and stare at the ground passing before her. It bothered her to have had so much control over her own life stripped away so quickly. She had been a free woman one moment, plotting a protest in Atrebell with her friends and in shackles the next.

What am I doing now? Orangecloak reflected. *I'm being transported to Portsward to meet a man I'm told sympathises with my cause. A man that until now I've had no reason to believe was anything more than another enemy of mine. I have no say in the matter and I feel as much a prisoner as I did when Fletchard bound me in iron. My knees are still swollen and painful to walk with for any measurable distance and I'm dependant on Ren, Tryst and these horses to help me along. If I tried to go on my own I would get nowhere. I have no choice but to trust them and to hope that Tryst Reine's intentions are as altruistic as he would have me believe.*

The sound of hurried hoof beats came thundering from behind the party. Both riders brought their steeds to a halt and turned them about. "It's a lone horse by the sounds of it," Orangecloak observed. "Perhaps it's Ren."

"Might well be," Fletchard agreed while still drawing his sabre from its sheath. "I'll not be taking chances, though."

Behind her, Orangecloak could feel Tryst shifting himself until he had a hand on the hilt of his blacksteel sword, ready to draw it in a moment's notice.

At last the horse and rider slipped into view, a grey, dappled beast carrying a brown haired elf.

"Just the elf after all, shit on that," Fletchard cursed, shoving his sword back where it came from. "I'd been itching for a fight too."

By the time Ren slowed the beast down, Tryst was already off the roadway and leading them on a game trail. They emerged at a babbling brook where Ren all but fell from the saddle, exhausted and out of breath.

Orangecloak and the others dismounted and waited for Ren to collect himself before asking him of what he saw. "Bluecoat soldiers," he said at last after drinking his canteen dry and refilling it from the brook. "I counted six, with as many horses. One man among them wore the wide hat of an officer. They were camped on the eastern side of the Stone Egg and I was not detected insofar as I could tell."

Tryst rubbed his jaw as he processed the information and he seemed to have a thousand questions, but so did Orangecloak and she beat him to it. "How were they acting?"

Ren looked a little befuddled as he answered. "That's the queer thing," he started in. "They didn't seem like men hot on anyone's trail. In fact, they were oddly relaxed, laughing and carrying on and such. They were even passing a bottle of some sort of alcohol around."

"Seems like they might not know we're on this road," Tryst surmised. "Something tells me that there's another search party heading on the eastern trail, it leads into the grasslands and the town of Falsamere. I would say there's another group heading south towards Argesse. There might even be a third walking through the forest towards Barnam and Obalen. I would have to imagine that yet another would be covering the old roads leading to Biddenhurst and on to Farmourd. That would be the quickest route to the Great Valley Lake and the Phaleaynan Ruins, if we had gone that way."

"You think so?" Fletchard queried. "Why so many?"

Tryst squinted and inhaled as he explained his working theory to the three of them. "The men in Atrebell have no idea which way we went, the only thing we left them for evidence was your wagon."

Fletchard scoffed at the last two words and Tryst cut his story to ask him what could possibly be amusing. "It isn't my wagon. Not my horses either. I rented them both when I got off the train in Atrebell. I live, or should I say *lived,* in Daol Bay and I didn't bring wagon and horses all the way out here. So yes, on top of everything else, we're horse thieves." Fletchard turned to Orangecloak. "Not like that should bother the lady, though. Given that she's the leader of thieves already."

Orangecloak shot him her daggered stare but wouldn't give him the satisfaction of an answer, allowing Tryst to press on.

"Not much we can do about that now," he said with a shrug. "Anyhow, as I was saying: odds are they have no idea how Orangecloak and Ren got out of the dungeon as of yet. The Lord Master would have to know that if the lady and the elf are gone that they couldn't have done so without my help. By that extension it's also dawned on him that I have turned my cloak. If I've come to know that old codger at all in four years, then panic should be setting in. I'd wager that he's got soldiers going in all directions looking for us.

"However, if Ren's assessment is correct, those men back at Stone Egg are as relaxed as they are because they're fairly certain we've not come this way. Our efforts to cover our trail may well have worked. I would say that no one's heading into the little groves off the beaten trail to look for fire pits. If they had uncovered even one of those they would be much more vigilant. No, by Ren's account they're just enjoying their diversion away from life and responsibility and expecting to find nothing. Why would they? If I were the man who organised that hunt, I would be thinking south is where we would go. Orangecloak isn't one to run across the sea and hide and neither am I. Everyone is probably assuming that we'll be trying to cross the Varras River, not running towards the Snowy Lands."

"Somehow I don't think you're about to let us go back to our previous pace, though." Ren commented between hurried breaths.

"No. Our pace is what allowed these six to close the gap between us while they languidly strolled along." Tryst turned his head to Graelin Mountain, basking in the morning sunlight. "We're in the shadow of the mountain now, we'll have to make a small deviation from our path and I can't say it will get us there any quicker. Yet, I think it should serve to keep our trail aptly covered."

Something seemed to occur to him and he abruptly stood up and turned his gaze to Ren. "How were the six armed? Could you tell?"

Ren shrugged in answer. "They had muskets lying nearby, and most also had swords on their hips, some didn't or they were possibly obscured from my line of sight."

"Riflemen," muttered Fletchard from where he stood.

"Rifles indeed..." Tryst's eyes darted as he pondered aloud to himself. "No, the Lord Master would not send his most able protectors. These are most likely city guards, rather than the Honourable Guardsmen."

"Is something the matter, Tryst?" Ren seemed nonplussed by the comment, which echoed Orangecloak's own sentiments. She was curious to know who he could be talking about.

Tryst shook his head slowly after a time and gave them an answer. "I was just thinking that perhaps the leaders of these units might be members of the Honourable Guardsmen. They're a unit of elite soldiers, typically riflemen, who are called up to preside over Parliamentary functions or to escort the Lord Master when he leaves the city. At the moment they're all gathered in the Atrebell manor, but no, Grenjin Howland won't send them out. Not when he isn't sure I won't come back to haunt him."

Fletchard looked between the other two men mischievously. "So the uniforms who are most likely on our trails are the standard city guards and they might not even know we're out here," he pointed out. "As I see it, we could ambush them and end the threat on our heels. The odds are six to three, but we have an elf that can *almost* kill an elk in one shot and the fucking Master of Blades himself on our side. We can take them by surprise quickly without them ever knowing what hit them and be on our way."

"If I have any say, I won't allow it. No violence if at all possible," Orangecloak intoned sternly. She was not letting this turn into a bloodbath over her if it could be avoided.

"Aye, that would be a poor move," Tryst agreed. "We need those men to ride back to Atrebell with no sighting of us. If they don't come back, the others in Atrebell will know which way we went for sure. The lady is right: we leave those searchers well enough alone unless they get upon us."

"What a stupid plan." Fletchard snorted derisively with his hands on his hips, alternating his condescending glare between Tryst and Orangecloak. "Your efforts to ingratiate yourself to her will get the four of us killed, Reine. If we let them get upon us, we're the ones going to get ambushed. Do you think for one second they won't find a hoof print here or there in the muddier parts of the road? Do you think they won't come across the hastily covered fire pit back there by the lake? Or the remains of that elk we dumped in the bushes? You can't be that dense to believe all of that will escape their notice."

Orangecloak was loath to agree with Fletchard, but he raised some points that she couldn't help but foster doubt over as well.

She looked to Tryst to see what he thought of Fletchard's statement and he seemed to be considering what the one eyed bounty hunter had said. "We're taking a risk, aye, I won't deny that. However, the road runs far away from all our resting points. It would be highly unlikely that they diverge from the main path, though I won't say that it's entirely improbable. The truth of the matter is that it's a better gamble than hoping we can ambush six men and have all three of us come away unscathed. That's not to mention the fact that if we kill those men and they can't return to report to their superiors, more will definitely come looking.

Fletchard was ready with a counter for that. "We'll be well away from here by then, what's it matter if a thousand soldiers march up this road once we're gone?"

"It matters because I have close friends and allies up ahead at the Hotel Dupoire." A frustrated Tryst closed the space between him and Fletchard as he spoke. "If you haven't noticed, this road will lead right to that hotel. Should more men come marching through here looking for the ones that we've killed they will arrive on the hotel's front porch.

"I shouldn't need to tell you what Grenjin Howland would do if he found out that the Dupoire family harboured us in their place of business. We have made a fool of old Howland as it is. He had Orangecloak in his clutches and I took that away from him. I know the man enough that I can tell you with near absolute certainty that what I just told you is figuratively eating him alive. He will hunt all four of us down to right the perceived wrong against him until the day he dies. We need the protection the Dupoire family can offer and in return we have to do right by them and ensure that they are protected too."

Another scoff, a throwing of hands in the air and Fletchard gave up his argument.

Orangecloak was satisfied with that, having no desire for slaughter and bloodshed. She shared Tryst's frustration and knew it well from her time as Field Commander of the Thieves.

"Ren, is there anything else to report from your scouting trip?" Tryst asked, cutting through the tension that had fallen over them.

"No, that's everything," Ren replied while still catching his breath. "Tryst, I can't help but ask if I might have something to eat? I'm starving."

"Aye, by all means." Tryst unslung the food sack from Wildstar's back, handing it over to Ren. "Eat the cooked elk meat first," Tryst suggested. "We have a short window of time before that turns inedible. I fear we've exhausted all but a potato and half of that bag of trail mix otherwise and the lot of it will have to do us for at least another few days. The hotel is on the western foothills of Graelin and we have a long trek ahead to close that distance. We also shouldn't dally much longer lest our progress through the night be in vain."

With meat and water serving to satisfy Ren's hunger for the moment they were back in the saddles and underway once more.

The elf offered Orangecloak to ride with him but she opted to remain upon Wildstar with Tryst. She felt sorry for Ren's poor horse, which still looked exhausted from the hard run Ren had put it through to catch up with the rest of the party.

The sun was warm and the air mild and windless as they returned to the road and brought the horses up to a brisk trot. With her pair of cloaks pulled tight and both hoods drawn, Orangecloak grew comfortable and within minutes found her own weariness from the sleepless night in the saddle catching up on her. At first she tried to fight it, her eyes struggling to stay open, but it was too much and she nodded off.

The dream that awaited her was wild and fitful. Visions of Myles and Coquarro hovered before her in near darkness, asking her where she had gone and why she had left them to such a miserable rest. Orangecloak tried to tell them it wasn't her fault and that she had no choice. However they could not hear her and disappeared into the black void, their voices growing fainter until at last, Orangecloak heard nothing at all.

There was a brilliant flash and the darkness gave way to the glittering, luminous caverns that she and her Thieves called Rillis Vale. She was home, her eyes first befalling the natural caves cut into the side of the vale's walls where they slept. Below, she saw the glimmering, natural pool with its shores alight with the luminous plants, looking bottomless as always. High above, near the entrance was the jutting plateau that loomed above the waters and they jokingly called the stage. In truth, it was stage, courtyard, marketplace and town hall alike.

Upon it stood her lieutenants, standing motionless or shuffling aimlessly about, giving no notice of her approach. One by one she turned them to face her: Edwin the Raven, Garlan Vahn, the sisters Ellarie and Merion Dollen, Merion's lover Joyce and Lazlo Arbor. They looked lifeless, their flesh pallid and drawn tight to their faces, but it was their eyes that stuck with her. They were all whitened, blank and completely sightless to the world around them.

"This is your life's work," Orangecloak heard from behind her in a deep, wise old voice. She turned to find a rugged, familiar face of nearly sixty winters sitting at the base of the tall stalagmite beside the entrance in his dinted cuirass and faded doublet. "All of them were good, young fighters," Old Bansam growled bitterly. "And now they're all gone, Orangecloak."

He was sharpening the nicked bastard sword he always bore and looking at her through those dark pits of eyes nestled beneath a forehead bearing a long scar. "All you have left now are Mell the Huntress and me, Old Bansam, neither of which you ever gave the satisfaction of calling a friend. The same Old Bansam whose men you thought to be foul brutes." He stood to face her, sword still in hand.

Beneath his greying mop of hair and matching beard he cut a fierce figure, despite his age. "Don't dare deny it, Orangecloak, we all knew what you thought of us. You didn't think we were fit to be Thieves on account of the fact that we fought with steel."

Orangecloak shook her head quickly. "I told you my terms and you refused to follow them. What choice did I have? I couldn't force you to follow my rules, but I could determine who followed me," she explained, standing as tall and proud as she once had. "No killing, that was what I asked and yet you took your unit and ran into the Southlands to do just that."

"Yes, I remember," Bansam said in his gravelly voice. "Look about and see what your terms have won you." The sword was raised to eye level and pointed at the shambling remnants of Orangecloak's lieutenants. "You insisted they fight with words against an enemy that abides by no rules. As a result, the only people left to you who are capable of being lieutenants are the two who were not afraid to meet the enemy on their terms." Bansam turned the sword horizontal in his hand, for her to see the scarred steel on the flat of the blade.

She cast her eyes to the floor sombrely, unable to look at either Bansam or her lieutenants. "You don't understand. If I fight and kill, I am no better than the Elite Merchants."

Bansam sheathed his sword and turned to leave her. "And if you're dead?" he called from over his shoulder. "Are you better than the Elite Merchants if you are dead?"

Something softly shook her and suddenly everything was gone. "My lady?" she heard Tryst calling her, feeling his hand on her shoulder as she woke from the dream. "You've been mumbling and trembling. Are you alright?"

For a moment she forgot she was still riding and reached for Wildstar's mane to steady herself. Tryst's left hand went firm to keep her from falling. "Easy now," he whispered soothingly from behind her. "I got you."

"I must have dozed off," Orangecloak surmised as she shook her head clear of the dream. "How long was I asleep?"

"By my reckoning I would say two hours, judging by where the sun is sitting now," Tryst replied with a wistful hint in his voice. "Are you thirsty?"

"I could drink," Orangecloak gave back as Tryst brought his canteen forward to her. She took the canister in hand and drank deeply. When she had her fill of water she sat quietly for a time and took in her surroundings.

She noticed that they had climbed quite high into foothills of Graelin Mountain while she napped. Up on high as they were, Orangecloak could make out the hillside path leading to the Stone Egg and the valley that lay between that they had crossed through. From here, the lush, green grass and blue shimmering lake looked absolutely resplendent in the afternoon sunlight.

Coquarro would love this, no one appreciated the beauty and splendour of nature like he, she thought to herself, immediately inviting a wave of guilt that stabbed at her like a thousand knives. *I shouldn't have gone to Atrebell. I had not been there since I was a young girl. Why now? How many other sessions of Parliament did I stay away from? I was a fool to bring myself, Myles and Coquarro there.*

With a despondent sigh, she gazed up at the mountain, from where their horses strode she had to crane her neck at an uncomfortable angle to see the top.

Now I'm alone, in the company of three strangers whom I must blindly rely on to reach what one of them claims is a safe haven somewhere in the west.

Still, she had to consider that Tryst had been very forward with his intentions and the true purpose for his employment in Atrebell.

It does sound a little farfetched that a lord and several ministers would conspire against the man that keeps them in wealth. However, if this were a lie, I would have to think that he would surely concoct a more believable tale than that. There must be some honesty in all of this if we are indeed going to the Hotel Dupoire. If nothing else, if I meet Tryst's friends and am still unsure of his intentions, I'm sure Ren will allow me to travel with him to the Elven Forest. From there I can make my way back to the Southlands alone. I know those roads well enough. In the meantime, I suppose I can delve further into Tryst's past and learn more of his deeds.

Orangecloak handed the canteen over her shoulder and turned her head as much she could to look upon him. "How are you feeling?" she asked, trying to gauge if he was even in the mood to tell her more of his past.

"A little tired, I admit," answered Tryst through a yawn. "Why do you ask?"

After a yawn and a stretch of her own, she replied, "If you feel up for it, I would hear of your third kill. I understand if you are feeling too tired to talk about it." Orangecloak tried not to come across as prodding, but she felt the need for the distraction and indeed wanted to know more about the man who so wanted to be her rescuer.

"My third, fourth and fifth are all tied into one. I can tell you, sure. It should help to pass the time and keep me awake," Tryst obliged her and began. "Remember who I said the first two men I killed were?"

She nodded slowly as she remembered. "Aye, corsairs named Jeppo and Zamak."

"What do you know of corsairs?" he asked, testing her knowledge.

Orangecloak searched her mind before answering, "That there are three distinct levels of unaffiliated sailors on the sea: privateers, pirates and corsairs. Those who identify as privateers are the most pliable and agreeable lot. Essentially, they are mercenaries of the waters and can usually call on most ports. They take on work supplied to them by private high payers or even from governments, but pledge no loyalty, unlike sailors of the various navies.

"Then there are pirates." She went on. "They're outlaws, but not outlawed everywhere. They pillage, plunder and ransom to make ends meet, but can be contracted for less reputable jobs. Depending on the ship, they can call at a number of ports, but Illiastra is generally hostile towards them. I was often told that if I was born on one of the island nations that I would be a pirate rather than just a common outlaw as I am."

That made Tryst chuckle lowly. "You're an outlaw alright, but there is nothing common about you, my lady, if you don't mind my saying." He steered the subject back to the topic at hand. "So you know about privateers and pirates, what about the corsairs?"

"I know only little about them, to be honest. I've never met one as far as I know, nor do I think I would want to. They're pirates, from what I'm told, but they're so void of honour that even other pirates have little to do with them."

"Have you met pirates before?" Tryst asked.

"Coquarro's father was a pirate," Orangecloak exhaled sadly. "Though, I never met him. Coquarro claimed he had died at sea when he was just a boy. All I know of the seafarer's ways came from him and his aunt Yassira."

She could feel Tryst shifting nervously and hear him clearing his throat, seemingly sorry for having made her mention a man she still mourned. "That's a fairly good assessment of what a corsair is," he said affirmatively. "In the Gildriad Midlands, where I come from, corsairs are known as the 'Forsaken men of the Sea'. The reason being because corsair ships are crewed by two distinctive types of men: the wanted criminals destined for a noose and the slaves bound to the ship by threat of death. The captains of their ships hold power by brute force and the smallest signs of weakness can lead to mutiny. No port will willingly allow them and even most pirate vessels stay well away from a ship that's been designated a corsair, lest they risk being branded a corsair as well. Instead, the corsairs rely solely on what they can take from other ships or what they can scavenge and steal when sneaking ashore in uninhabited coves."

Orangecloak remembered something then. "Yassira told me that a privateer can be seen as a pirate to some and a pirate can align himself with a nation and become a privateer. Once either of them is labelled a corsair, there is no returning."

"Yassira is not wrong," Tryst said in agreement. "The corsairs we killed outside Kushika City were no different. They saw the High Chieftain's son as a big payday, figuring that they could ransom him for enough to retire on and couldn't resist attempting to capture him. With no one to return to the corsair ship, we had thought that the other corsairs would consider the mission a failure and sail on before any of their pursuers from the south could find them. The survivor would stand trial for murder of two guards, attempted murder of the rest of us and attempted kidnapping of Gedo. Everyone had figured that we had seen the end of it."

Orangecloak stated the obvious that Tryst had left unsaid, "Yet it wasn't the last of it."

"Indeed not," Tryst confirmed. "Uvat, the surviving corsair, plead guilty immediately to all charges when the High Chieftain read them aloud. For admitting his guilt, the High Chieftain granted Uvat the mercy of a swift death by beheading. As witnesses and victims of the assault, Keo and I were summoned to Shatoya, the capital of Drake. Initially, it was to testify. But when Uvat avoided a trial by pleading guilty, we were asked to stay and witness the execution. Before they brought him into the execution chamber in the city prison, Uvat asked to speak with Keo, myself, the High Chieftain and Gedo. He didn't ask to be spared or for forgiveness, instead he simply wanted to tell us that his captain was waiting in a cove on the south shores. If the kidnapping party didn't return with Gedo, the corsair captain had told his subordinates that scouts would be sent to find out what befell them. Should the corsairs be killed or captured, the captain would seek recompense for the loss."

"That makes no sense," Orangecloak said, puzzled by it. "The corsairs attacked your party without provocation, why would he think he has any right to compensation?"

Tryst's tone went deathly serious. "It made no sense to us either, until Uvat told us the name of his captain: Rorsted the Revenger, one of the more infamous corsair captains to sail in our lifetime. As it was, he had been a wanted man since you and I were but children. Any corsair captain who could hold a ship for two decades without capture, death or mutiny had to be begrudged some measure of respect.

"The Revenger, as his name implies, was keen to take any action against him as one warranting immediate vengeance. If Uvat was telling us true and Rorsted's ship was hiding on the south coast of Drake, then his men may already be sacking any lightly garrisoned settlements down that way, seeking that vengeance."

"It seems like Uvat only told you of Rorsted as a final threat rather than as a genuine warning," commented Orangecloak flatly.

That elicited an amused scoff from Tryst. "You couldn't be more right. He was laughing and ranting about our supposedly impending doom even as the guards bound him to the headsman's block. I still remember him prattling on about the Rorsted's wrath until the very moment that the High Chieftain brought the axe down.

"That very evening, the High Chieftain gathered his war council, of which Keo and I were permitted to be a part of. Together, we narrowed down the potential hiding places of Rorsted the Revenger to two locations in the south west corner of Drake. Both of which happened to lie only a day's journey from Fuwachita City. Of course, the University itself was in no danger. The corsairs could never hope to assail our warriors atop the mountain, but they could burn the city to the ground before we could reach them.

"A message was sent by snowy owl to the University to alert them of the danger and Keo and I set off for Fuwachita. At our heels was a sizable force of Drakian soldiers mobilised by the High Chieftain to assist in fortifying the city against a potential situation. I say potential, because we couldn't take a corsair at his word. There was doubt amongst us that his captain was Rorsted, or even if it was, that the ship was still in to be found in Drakian waters. Though, we had to take the threat seriously."

Tryst stopped his story as they crossed a small wooden bridge that extended over a shallow stream and glanced about quickly.

Orangecloak followed Tryst's line of sight but could see no issues. "Is something amiss?" she asked curiously.

Tryst turned Wildstar towards the Mountain and called a halt back to the others before answering. "No, my lady, I just felt it was ample time for a rest. We won't find much more water beyond here for the horses." He swung a leg over the horse and dropped to the ground below. "I'll tell you everything you might want to hear once we're back in the saddle."

The stop was brief and quiet, with Fletchard choosing to hold his tongue for once. Even Ren seemed too tired to talk and looked as though it was taking all his energy just to stay awake. Before anyone could get too comfortable, Tryst got the party underway once more to continue what was becoming an exhaustive journey.

It was still midday when they returned to the road and the sun was high into the sky and leaning westerly. Despite the brisk autumn weather, there was warmth to the sunlight that was undercut only by the scattered gust of wind rolling down Graelin Mountain. Orangecloak had decided to lower her hoods and soak in the mild weather while it lasted.

Once the road was beneath the hooves of Wildstar and the grey rounseys, Tryst resumed the recounting of his encounter with Rorsted the Revenger. "Fuwachita was on alert before our arrival," he said, picking up where he left off. "It turned out the condemned corsair had decided to use his last minutes of life to inadvertently turn the tide on the captain he thought would avenge him. Expert level students from the university had been sent to scout as soon as the owl had arrived bearing the warning. All the townsfolk that could fight were waiting in their homes for a call to action and armed with whatever weapons they owned. The elderly, the children and their parents were invited to take refuge in the Academic building of the University, located at the base of the mountain. There, they were protected by the combat instructors and their most capable pupils. Fortunately, the scouts returned from their task just ahead of the arrival of our party from Shatoya. All of us then convened for an emergency war council in the conference room of the Academic's buildings below the Combat University.

"The corsairs were easily found by the scouts and were just where we had anticipated them to be. Our scouts were even able to confirm that the ship was *The Bludgeon*, whose last known owner was in fact Rorsted the Revenger.

"Chancellor Junto decided that Instructors Sheo and Himmato would lead a group of experts including myself, Keo and my friend Myolas Himmato, son of the instructor of the same name. Our goal was Kunokishi Cove. The ship was moored just off the shore and a ring of tents had been established in the shelter of the beach. From what the scouts could see, Rorsted the Revenger was staying aboard his ship with a skeleton crew. It put the bulk of his men in a natural trap between the steep, tall cliffs of the cove and the freezing ocean waters of Drake, a strategic advantage for us.

"Kunokishi Cove is difficult to access from land as well, though it does bear a single, narrow path. It was there that the High Chieftain's soldiers were stationed, lying in wait in the darkness of the night for any stray corsairs that may leave the cove. Meanwhile, our unit comprised of instructors and students from the university had moved into position on the western cliffs.

"An expert level student by the name of Yahmina Windleaf, a name you may recognise as both female and elven in origin, was brought with us. She was one of the few experts who specialised in archery and, due to her elven origins, was unmatched with a bow and arrow among our ranks. Armed with a longbow, a bushel of fire arrows and an apprentice to light them, she was left overlooking the ship and campsite.

"The rest of the unit moored rope to the cliffs and lowered ourselves slowly down the rock face to the beach below. Once there, Instructor Sheo signalled Yahmina with three sharp tugs of his rope and seconds later a single burning arrow pierced the night sky, coming to rest on the largest tent of the encampment.

"The corsairs on the beach became frantic and their own noise and chaos provided distraction enough for the soldiers hidden on the path to descend on them quickly.

"While the Shatoyan men engaged the louts on the beach, our

party stole the rowboats and made for the ship. The crew left aboard with Rorsted realised their shipmates on the beach were under siege and had opted to abandon them. As we approached unseen, the anchor was raised and sails were unfurled in a desperate attempt to make for open sea.

"Yahmina was prepared for that very thing and sent enflamed arrows high above with her longbow. The mainsails began to burn and the flames spread quickly with the blowing wind. As we boarded, we were faced with a crew and captain that were prepared to die and take as many with them to a watery grave as they could."

Orangecloak chimed in with a question. "Was there none that could be spared?"

That took Tryst aback and he seemed genuinely at a loss for words. "You would spare men as vile as corsairs?" he finally asked.

She was quick with a response to that. "You even said that not all among the corsair ships chose to be corsairs. There are surely people among them either enslaved or otherwise pressed into being aboard those ships."

That softened Tryst's tone. "Of course we would spare slaves and captives. However, in the heat of battle there is no time to sort the willing combatants and those fighting against their will. Among all of the men we encountered among Rorsted's roster we found two in chains and they were saved. One was a Johnan man left shackled to a stake on the beach and the other was an Illiastran fisherman who Myolas found in the brig of the ship. They were the only ones shown mercy that night."

She was glad for that and let Tryst know as much. "That's good to know. If there's one thing I have learned in my time with the Thieves, it's that in any sort of conflict there is no such thing as absolute right or absolute wrong. There's good and bad on either side in some capacity. Even if it was just two men kept prisoner aboard a corsair ship in this case. At any rate, I apologise for interrupting. Please, continue on."

"Those are very wise words, my lady," Tryst commented in earnest. "It is no wonder why you were chosen to be Field Commander of the Thieves."

Despite the comment being delivered without sarcasm, Orangecloak didn't find it to be complimentary, given where her decisions as Field Commander had landed her. "Please, do go on with the story," she said as a means of changing the subject.

Tryst seemed to sense that his words had inadvertently hurt her and did as suggested. "Right, where was I? Yes, of course, we had reached the dilapidated old galley that Rorsted called a ship without detection. Fortunately, the burning sails served as ample enough distraction to keep the men on the ship from noticing a rowboat approaching. The rowboat's oars were already muffled, as corsairs are like to do, and we slid quietly across the waters like a fog.

"Instructor Sheo and Keo were the first over the gunwale and they were discovered almost immediately by the crew dashing about to put out the blaze. By the time the rest of the corsairs with the desire to fight answered the call, Myolas, his father and I had reached the ship's deck. We were slightly outnumbered and that was all it took for the corsairs to descend on us. Being the shortest and youngest looking made me an inviting target, for I was the first one to draw blood. I was rushed by a bloke wielding a cudgel of some kind. The man swung for my face with it, I ducked and drove my sword into his heart. He was dead when he hit the deck."

She shifted in the saddle so that she could look him in the face. "What was his name?" she asked flatly, eyes locked to Tryst's.

"I remember it as Culder." Tryst answered without delay. "Whether it was his first or last name or even a nickname I don't know. Perhaps it was not even a name but some word from one of the old languages. It was shouted by a corsair who foolhardily charged me with a cutlass he swung downward like a cleaver. It dug into the railing as I sidestepped him and I opened his throat while he tried to pull his weapon free." Tryst let the word hang on the air, as if his own kills caused him pain to remember. "That was my third and fourth..." He trailed off.

"I thought you said this story would bring us up to your fifth kill?" Orangecloak wanted to know now. As gruesome a tale as it was, she had to hear it to the end.

There was a hesitation from Tryst, but with another clearing of his throat he went on. "The crew were all dead, insofar as we knew. Myolas and his father went below decks to check the hold for prisoners and left Keo, Sheo and I above. There was crashing and banging coming from within the captain's quarters and we approached it to try and apprehend Rorsted. As we neared it, a pistol was shot and we went for cover. When next I looked, the light within the cabin was gone out and a lumbering, gunshot brute was on deck, bleeding and raving.

"It would seem in the chaos he had turned on Rorsted, whether to kill him or rob him we never knew. Regardless, he was belligerent and swinging his sword wildly at us. Sheo and I engaged the crewmember and Keo darted into the darkness after the captain. The large corsair pressed Sheo and practically ignored me. I got behind him, hamstrung him and let Sheo finish him off.

"I reached the cabin and found everything eerily silent, save for the door swinging open on its rusted hinges. As I got beside the threshold and glanced inside something came over me. It was this sense of what lay ahead, as if some innate ability that had lain dormant had suddenly become active within me. I could see through the darkness of the room with alarming clarity and there lay Keo, dead on the floor not a few metres away. I saw Rorsted too, huddled to a corner, bloodied and wounded, but still alive and holding Keo's curved sword.

"One of the lines holding the sails snapped loudly and caught Sheo's eye for a second and I dove forth into the room before he saw me. Rorsted stayed in the corner, confident that I could not see him. I approached as if I was indeed blinded, to lure him into making a move and he did not disappoint. He was vicious, but wounded and desperate. I kept well clear of his reach as he stabbed at the air and waited, leading him where I wanted with the noise of my footsteps. From the doorway Sheo shouted, Rorsted looked his way and I buried my sword clear through his chest, ending him the same way I had ended Culder before him."

"And that was your fifth, a captain of a corsair ship," Orangecloak filled in the rest for him. "Might I ask what happened to the two men you said the others spared?"

Tryst seemed surprised in her request. "The Johnan and the Illiastran you mean?"

"Aye, if they were spared, were they free to go? Did they go home?" she followed up his question with questions of her own.

"The Johnan man's name is Loio Ma-Telhys. I only remember that because he still lives in Fuwachita City by his own accord. After he was brought there he refused to go near the sea again, understandably terrified from his ordeal. He begged the Elders of Fuwachita to let him stay in the city and they made him a citizen then and there." Tryst paused ponderously. "As for the Illiastran man, he went home as soon as he was healthy enough for travel in search of his wife and children."

Orangecloak followed her question with another. "What of the men on the beach? Did they succeed in putting down the corsairs?"

"Aye, they did, at the price of six of their own." Tryst's voice dropped to barely above a whisper. "As for the university mercenaries, we had one loss and that was Keo."

The mere mention of his friend's demise seemed to put a pause in Tryst's speech, but he went on. "Despite the fact that we accept the risk that comes with enrolling at the university, we still mourn our dead. I lost a mentor and a friend that day and I miss him dearly. The man was a natural leader who specialised in warfare and military tactics, but his knowledge ran far deeper than that. There was a stern nature to him, but those who he took a shining to saw the other side of that, to the kind man beneath the hard shell. I was fortunate to be one of those few and I strive to live up to that honour in everything I do."

Minutes seemed to pass then with nothing said between them. Orangecloak was short of words and unsure of what to make of Tryst's revelation, though one thing came to mind for her to say: "I'm sorry for your loss."

"Thank you, I have no doubt he would have allowed you to know him as well." Tryst said, letting his words trail off into the wind.

"I highly doubt a specialist in warfare and military tactics would have had much to say to me," Orangecloak stated doubtfully. "I am, after all, a pacifist."

"It wasn't whether or not you're willing to go to war that Keo used to determine the worth of a person," Tryst explained. "Keo respected dedication, tenacity, determination, humility, selflessness and empathy. You have all of that in spades my lady."

The conversation lulled once more, leaving them with a melancholic stillness between them. Orangecloak was dwelling on Tryst's story, turning the pieces of it over in her mind. The elven woman, with her longbow raining fire down atop the camp, the five swordsmen rowing to the ship and the four that returned. It seemed an elaborate story with far too many details to be just conjured up so quickly. That was before Tryst talked of the effect losing Keo had on him. Orangecloak had nothing else she could think to ask and left him alone with his memory.

Instead, she focused her attention back on the roadway ahead. Their trail seemed to run downhill and into a deep woods that ran tight along the foot of Graelin's Mountain at a sudden turn. It was a foreboding sight, yet one she apparently wasn't going to face right away as Tryst turned Wildstar towards the mountainside.

"Good timing for a rest I think." Orangecloak said to Tryst as he swung out of the saddle first. "That forest looks to be quite thick. If we can clear through it before nightfall it would do us better than to have to stay within it. The men on our tails could catch us easily in there if they got upon us."

"All good points, my lady," Tryst agreed. "Though, we're not going through that forest."

"Then where?" Orangecloak asked, entirely confused and scanning her surroundings for another route. "I'm not seeing any other way," she added while sliding from the saddle slowly on her own. Her knees throbbed, but she was walking and for once standing upright. Almost involuntarily, she let out a single audible grimace as pain shot through her knees upon contact with the ground.

Tryst looked her over as he started undoing the clasps on the food satchel on Wildstar's back. "How are your legs?" he asked with a concerned look from the corner of his eye.

"They're recovering. I think being in the saddle helps. Are you going to answer my question?" she queried through gritted teeth as she struggled to stay standing.

"It will be easier to show you than to explain, follow me for a moment." Tryst slung the bag over his shoulder just as Ren stepped out of the saddle to the ground.

The elf gingerly laid a hand on Orangecloak's shoulder as he neared her. "How are you?"

"I'm feeling better than I have lately, though I'm worried. Tryst says we're taking an alternate route." Her eyes went to the ominous wilderness that wrapped as far as her eye could see around the mountain. "I see nothing but the one road that leads through the forest below."

He thought about it for a moment. "Now that you mention it, I thought I saw a southward path not too far back, perhaps he means to backtrack to it."

There was a low rumbling that caught the attention of everyone and all eyes turned on Tryst as he rolled a large, circular stone away from the otherwise vertical rock face. "Over here," he called to them, pointing at a small hole that the stone had been hiding. "We'll go through to the other side. Beyond here there's an old parapet walkway the dwarves made centuries ago. It will take us to a rear entrance in the hotel, but it will mean that we will be on foot from here on out."

"On foot? What about the poor horses?" Orangecloak asked with great concern. "We can't leave them behind."

"There's little else we can do. We have a potential tail, and this will ensure we lose them." Tryst pointed above to indicate where the walkway lay unassuming along the stony side of Graelin "They have to go through that forest or turn back. We have another way and it's a straight walk along the mountain's face."

"Aren't you worried about Wildstar?" she added.

Tryst was unyielding from his position though. "I am, undoubtedly, yet we have to rid ourselves of pursuers."

"Do you know that they have even followed us this far?" Ren wondered.

"I don't, no more than you do. However, the fact remains that even with our best efforts, there will be tracks." Tryst pointed along the path they had already traversed to illustrate his point. "It will be impossible for the guards not to notice at some point, so the tracks have to end here. If we go through the forest we'll be leading them directly to the front door of the Hotel Dupoire."

While Orangecloak and the other two had been talking, Fletchard had been kneeling before the small crawlspace. "So, we go on foot, is that the way of it?"

Tryst nodded affirmatively at Fletchard. "Aye, take what you can carry and unburden the horse entirely. If our pursuers see no saddles, bridles or satchels they might think we just turned the horses loose. If all works according to plan, our searchers will continue to believe that we might not be this way and that they were just following our freed horses. However, a suspicious trail of hoof prints ending at the hotel would leave no doubt of our whereabouts."

"I feel terrible for the horses though, what will happen to them?" Orangecloak asked sceptically, still not convinced that this plan of Tryst's was the right way to proceed.

"The greys will likely linger around here," Tryst answered while unbuckling Wildstar's saddle. "If the guards on our tail find them, they'll most likely bring them back and they'll be returned from whence Fletchard rented them. Wildstar, on the other hand, knows how to get to a safe haven. He'll serve to take the guardsmen further off our trail if they happen to follow his tracks. Though I think they'll be satisfied with the other two."

Orangecloak shrugged. "You seem to have thought this through. Who am I to argue?"

The other two reluctantly resigned themselves to the plan and went about unloading saddles and supplies from the horses. Tryst sent Ren through the small hole in the rock face first and passed him their food sack, the satchels the three men carried and Ren's borrowed bow and arrows. It was decided to haul the unneeded equipment of the horses' through as well, to safely hide it all from sight of pursuers. Orangecloak had helped as best as her legs would allow, removing the bridles from the three beasts and passing the gear along to Tryst.

Soon, the task was complete and only the three horses remained to be dealt with. "Ren," Tryst called through the tiny entryway. "Climb the steps to your right and have a look over the parapet. I'll be back in a moment."

The swordsman turned directly into Orangecloak standing behind him.

"I'm coming with you," she declared boldly. "I want to see the horses run free for myself, lest it be something else weighing on my mind. I need to see it with mine own eyes."

"As the lady so wishes," Tryst replied with a sad smile. It was clear he didn't relish the task and perhaps even welcomed the company.

Sitting idly on a rock nearby was Fletchard, having done little besides tend to his personal items since stopping.

"I was going to have you come with me to set the horses free," Tryst said to him. "Orangecloak's elected herself for the job, so feel free to proceed through the tunnel to the passageway."

The bounty hunter shrugged aloofly at them. "You'll get no argument from me."

They left Fletchard on the rock and turned their attention to the horses. With a hand on the mane of one of the rented rounseys each, Orangecloak and Tryst walked the way they came, with Wildstar following close behind.

She found herself more so leaning on the horse rather than leading it, but the mare that had been carrying Ren hardly minded.

Before her lay a splendid scene of trees waving in unison as a soft breeze worked its way through their branches. The clouds above cast moving shadows on the landscape of green foliage and softly lapping, blue waters. The only variance in the scenery was the speckling of red and orange leafed trees that worked to shrug off their summer growth.

After what seemed to be at least ten minutes of their slow trek they came to a crossroads she scarcely recalled them passing before.

"This is the place," Tryst called to her.

The roadway ran along the edge of the forest, serving as a border between it and a small, grassy plain. Tryst put the two horses that Fletchard had acquired on the gravel and gave them a slap across the hindquarters to send them darting away one after the other.

She watched them from a few steps behind Tryst. The pair of rounseys bolted down the roadway and into the field, galloping away as quickly as their hooves would take them.

"Run far and be free," Orangecloak spoke under her breath as they disappeared out of sight.

There was nothing to note in that moment besides the overwhelming serenity. The wind rolled down the mountainside, stirring the long strands of Tryst's hair as he stared southward to the far horizon. The tension hung heavily as horse and rider stood as still as stone, side by side. At that moment she felt as if only the three of them in the world and they were standing at the edge of all existence.

"I guess this is it, old friend," Tryst finally said in a solemn, hushed tone. He glanced over his shoulder at her quickly, as if suddenly realising she was still standing behind him. "My lady, would it be alright if I had a moment alone with Wildstar?"

"Certainly, I'll start walking back to the passageway and leave you be" Orangecloak said. "I'm sure you'll catch up with me before I make it back." With that she nodded and hobbled off a ways, until the pain became quite nearly too much and she sat upon a loose rock against the hillside.

"This will likely be the last time we'll see one another," Orangecloak heard and she glanced down the road and noticed that Tryst was speaking to Wildstar, with his back turned to the rock where she was seated.

He thinks I've gone on, she realised as she continued watching.

Tryst sighed and turned to face Wildstar. "I suppose I always knew a day like this would come. You know, I told myself I wouldn't form a bond with those I met in Atrebell, but I made an exception for you, my friend." He reached up and began to stroke the courser's mane. "It's been a good run, these last four years. There were times when riding through the forest with you was the only peace I knew. When I was sure I had reached my limit of patience with the Lord Master and his kind, I had you to rely on. I can sincerely say that there's been no greater friend I have known in Atrebell. You've been a loyal confidant and a reliable companion to me, and I'm forever grateful to you. So, you know that it's not easy for me to say this, but, this is goodbye. I'll be going west from here and it's uncertain if I'll ever turn east again. It's not up to me if I do, in any case. If Orangecloak doesn't fight, I'm leaving Illiastra."

Tryst seemed to chuckle a little at the mention of her name. "You like her, don't you? I could tell the minute I carried her out of the tower and you let me put her in the saddle. I trusted your judgement on the matter, you know, and it put my mind at ease when you accepted her. So you know what we must do is for her and for this country and you know she's worth it. You stay safe, Wildstar, I'll be thinking of you."

Orangecloak kept her eyes on Tryst, watching as he stood there with his head lowered. "You know where you have to go," he said at last. "The stable keepers there know us, they know you, and they will look after you." From where she sat, Orangecloak could see Tryst taking a long, deep breath. "Obalen," he said loudly and clearly in a commanding tone, repeating himself once more.

And then Wildstar was gone, trotting briskly down the same road the two grey mares had taken not too long ago.

She watched the horse for a moment longer, looking back just in time to see Tryst turning towards the nearby woods. There was the sound of tree limbs cracking and whatever he was doing, she knew it was a good chance for her to move further down the road. It would do no good for Tryst discover that Orangecloak had eavesdropped on his entire conversation with Wildstar.

From the moment Orangecloak had met Tryst in the dungeon, he had been working diligently to earn her trust. That sort of kindness was nothing new to her and she was wary of anyone so eager to please her. In an effort to discern for herself, Orangecloak had asked for stories of Tryst's past, listened intently for the things unsaid in conversation and gauged his actions and choices. Despite the honesty and transparency he promised, Orangecloak still fostered doubt.

Until now, some part of her couldn't shake the feeling that all of this was just another mask worn by the Master of Blades, the mercenary of Grenjin Howland. However, it wasn't until overhearing his farewell to his horse that Orangecloak knew she had finally seen the naked face of Tryst Reine.

15

TRYST

It had taken three days. Three days of Fletchard and Orangecloak squabbling, three days of little food to be found and diminishing supplies, and three days of straight walking. The lone bit of fortune they had was that the weather had been mostly favourable aside from an afternoon of softly falling rain that had left them dampened.

After the arduous trek that had taken its toll on them physically and mentally, the sight of the hotel in the early evening of the third day brought them all relief. The high rock wall that had hidden them from sight and shielded them from wind gave way to the dwarven ingenuity that was the Hotel Dupoire. The pathway ran behind the building, leading them into an unremarkable alcove containing only a short door. The structure loomed high overhead, and from where they stood, one could look above and see the sky through a web of thick, wooden trusses that moored the building to the mountainside.

Tryst remembered from a previous visit that viewed from the front, the hotel looked to be a glass wall built into the mountain itself. It was an elaborate architectural illusion and made the hotel one of the most unique buildings Tryst had ever seen.

Approaching the varnished, oak door, Tryst gave it a few raps with his knuckles.

Behind him, Fletchard dropped his pack roughly and began

pacing tiredly, rubbing his face and groaning to himself.

Orangecloak stood to the opposite side of the alcove, with Ren close at hand. She looked equal parts exhausted and nervous and was still encumbered by the injuries dealt to her knees by the torturer in Atrebell.

Soon you can rest, my dear. You deserve no less than that, Tryst thought as he glanced at her.

It took two successive bouts of knocking before an answer was finally made from within. A young dwarf, who looked no older than his eighteenth year, poked his beardless face out beyond the threshold timidly. "Uh, hello there, how can I help you?" he apprehensively asked them.

"We come as friends of Kevane Dupoire, my good fellow. Would you be so kind as to let us in?" Tryst replied with a smile.

"Umm..." the dwarf said while looking the four of them over cautiously. As Tryst watched the young man's eyes scanning, them it dawned on him how suspicious they all must look.

I would be on my guard at the sight of this foursome too.

Aside from hair and tooth brushes, they had little else in the way of maintaining hygiene. Their clothes were filthy, their hair greasy, and all but the elf surely stank of body odour. That didn't even speak for the general intimidation factor Tryst and Fletchard posed, with their armour and armaments about them. Even Ren had Tryst's bow across his back in plain sight.

After looking over the dishevelled party, the boy finally gave them an answer. "I uh, I don't think that's a good idea. Could you go back the way you came and go 'round the building to the front entrance, maybe?"

Fletchard threw his arms in the air. "Oh, for fuck sakes," he grumbled. "Three whole fucking days of walking through a trench cut into a mountain only to be stonewalled by some little shit who tells us to walk all the way back."

The youth's eyes went wide with fear at Fletchard's cursing and he looked to retreat back within and shut the door in their faces until Tryst grabbed the handle. "Wait lad, we're not here to hurt anyone. Could you deliver a message to Kevane Dupoire for me? If you can't find him, get one of his daughters. Tell them, 'The heart has awoken.' Could you do that for me? We'll gladly wait out here in the meantime," Tryst asked the young dwarf in a soft tone to counter

Fletchard's frustrated grumbling.

The lad nodded quickly and Tryst released his hold on the door and let the dwarf close it behind him.

"Well done, Fletchard, I think I can smell the shit in his trousers from here," Tryst said frustratingly, staring hard into the lone eye of the bounty hunter.

Fletchard put his hands up mockingly. "My sincerest apologies, Mister Reine, I'll be sure to contain my outrage the next time. It's just that it's not every day some twit suggests we walk back the way we came with no food and little water for three whole fucking days to find a front door." The sarcasm in his voice was palpable as he sneered in Tryst's direction.

Tryst decided to let Fletchard be, too tired to quibble with him further. He exhaled his frustration and turned to face Ren and Orangecloak. "Most of the staff knows me on sight. I'm willing to bet the young fellow is a recent hire."

With a shrug, Orangecloak spoke up for the first time in hours. "It's hard to blame the lad, I don't know that I'd let us in either if I were he. We're not exactly in a presentable state."

"Agreed, I would be suspicious of us too," Tryst added with a nod. He was happy just to hear her talk. In close proximity and on foot, she and Fletchard had been exchanging verbal shots any time one of them spoke. A ceasefire would only arise when the lady would go silent and ignore Fletchard entirely, opting instead to shoot him hateful looks. Both Tryst and Ren had tried to negotiate a truce between the beleaguered Field Commander of the Thieves and the bounty hunter, though to no avail. As much as Tryst would like to say Fletchard was the instigator, Orangecloak had hurled insults on her own and prolonged the sparring of volatile wits. It was only her continued silence that bought them reprieve, as the lack of a willing opponent made Fletchard eventually relent as well.

When at last the door opened, they were greeted by a portly dwarf in his late fifties with a jolly face. "Hullo, Tryst, tis good to see you again!" the fellow greeted Tryst warmly upon recognition, before calling back over his shoulder at the same dwarf who had answered the door. "Yes, I'm sure it's alright, Gelmin, I know this man."

He shook his head quickly before turning back to the party waiting outside. "Come in, come in, you must all be exhausted. I don't know the rest of you, but any friend of Tryst Reine's is a friend of mine. I am Kevane Dupoire and this is the hotel that bears my name," the dwarf said through a beaming, inviting smile as he stood back and held the door open.

His beard was long and naturally a light shade of brown, though the years had seen it streaked with white. Atop Kevane's head, his short hair matched his beard, poking out beneath a floppy cap commonly seen among sailors. For his attire he had donned grey slacks, a white, button down shirt and a black vest that he left open.

Kevane eyed Orangecloak with a look of curious excitement as she stepped through the door, exchanging a telling glance with Tryst.

To Orangecloak's credit, she gave her best effort to not look as injured as she was, hobbling only slightly and masking her pain as she stepped inside ahead of Tryst.

Once all were within, the guests looked about their surroundings, finding themselves to be standing in a labyrinth of hallways. From a previous visit, Tryst knew that back here were the offices of the management, quarters of the staff and all the storage areas for the sustenance and supplies. It made for an inadequate introduction to the grandeur of the hotel, but the privacy the back entrance allowed for far outweighed the need for first impressions.

As he shut the door and joined his guests, Kevane cheerfully ushered the awestruck young dwarf off towards the front of the hotel. "Gelmin, quit shaking in your shoes and go fetch Tinnia, lad, on the double. Oh, and be sure to tell her that our new guests and I will be in my office." Kevane turned back to the party of four with his arms open wide. "If the rest of you would be so kind, would you follow me?"

Around a pair of corners he led them and down a long hallway with a dozen different doors, all marked for different purposes. It was bright and airy, even in a corridor used primarily by staff and management. The walls and low ceiling were white plaster, with finely crafted trim and mouldings. Beneath their feet, the floors were teak wood, stained and varnished to a dark shade. Potted plants and wall-mounted lamps adorned the hallway, and here and there was a scenic oil painting. It was at the end of this hallway they were led, arriving at a door marked 'Kevane Dupoire: Owner' in gold painted letters on a black plaque.

Once inside, Kevane ushered the guests to one of the several seats around the small space. "My apologies, friends, I don't usually host so many tallfolk at once," he said while sliding in behind a modestly sized desk and the plush chair behind it. "Please, take a seat wherever you may find one. Don't be shy now."

Orangecloak opted to seat herself in one of two leather chairs directly in front of the desk, sitting quietly and exhaling with relief as her legs finally gained reprieve.

It was Tryst who ended up speaking first for the group as he took the seat beside her. "It should probably be I who apologises, Kevane. My arrival was unexpected, not to mention with so many in my company."

That yielded a nonchalant wave from Kevane. "Nonsense, Tryst, we have both been preparing for this day for some time. Though, neither of us could have predicted when it would come. Still, here we are and I must say that this is an incredibly exciting moment to be a part of. While we wait on my eldest daughter, might I be introduced to your traveling companions?"

"Why certainly." The chair groaned beneath Tryst as he turned to face the remaining two, who had taken to standing behind Tryst and Orangecloak. "Back here we have the former bounty hunter, Fletchard Miller, who was the catalyst of the events that led us here. Beside him is Tyrendil Wildheart of the Elven Forest, who has been an invaluable asset these last few days. Finally, seated to my right, as I am sure you are aware, is the Lady Orangecloak, Field Commander of the Thieves."

"I was aware of who she was the moment I laid eyes on her standing in the porch," Kevane said with a solemn nod before turning his gaze to Orangecloak, wrapped in her cloaks and seated beside Tryst. "Allow me to say, my lady, that my hotel and its entire staff are at your service. I am duly honoured to host you and your party beneath my roof."

"I thank you for your generosity, kind ser," she cordially responded. "There is no need to give me any special treatment."

"Don't be so modest, my lady. Your legend is renowned, even here in the north." Kevane insisted with a warm smile that resonated in his eyes with a twinkle. "It is said that while Grenjin Howland may be the controlling head of human Illiastra, it is the Lady Orangecloak that is the heart. The will of the people flows through you, my lady."

Orangecloak answered politely, though her exhaustion was bleeding through in her tone, "Your kind words flatter me, ser. I had never heard that claim before."

As Kevane was about to speak again, there was a quick knock from without, followed by a dwarven woman in her thirties letting herself inside.

"Good afternoon, everyone," she spoke as she stepped within the office and closed the door.

As Tryst pivoted to face the woman, he couldn't help but grin at the sight of her. "Hello, Tinny, it's a pleasure to see you again."

"Tryst Reine, it is indeed good to see your face. It's been far too long since last I have," she gave back with a smile of her own to match.

Kevane rose to meet her. "Folks, might I introduce you to Tinnia, my eldest daughter. She and her sister Tyla manage this hotel," he said before running through introducing her to Fletchard, Ren and Orangecloak in turn. The latter of which was clearly impressed with the sight of Kevane's eldest offspring.

Folding her hands over a grey, knee length skirt, Tinnia addressed Tryst and the other guests. "It's good to meet you all, I'm sure. Any friends of Tryst Reine are more than welcome here." Her outfit was completed with entirely black attire, starting with a blouse with rolled sleeves to the elbows and a neck open to her ample cleavage. A wide belt with an ornate buckle wrought with flowers and knee high, leather boots complimented a curvy frame in an undeniable way. Completing her appearance was her long, dark hair flowing over one shoulder in waves that outlined an appealing face.

The elder dwarf returned to his seat and gestured towards his daughter. "Tinnia, my dear, I was wondering what suites we had available to accommodate our guests?"

"We have nothing vacant until the fourteenth floor, Father," she answered him. "It's been a busy autumn. I think number sixteen should more than suffice, if you would like."

Kevane stroked his beard while he thought on it. "Can we make it number twenty? It offers a more commanding view of the slopes."

"Suite twenty can certainly be arranged without issue," Tinnia agreed before casting her eyes back to the guests. "Are any of you in need of medical attention? I'm a highly trained medic and would be only happy to offer my services."

Tryst raised a hand to get Tinnia's attention. "The lady injured her knees on the night of our escape. She's recovered greatly, but she still walks with a noticeable limp. I'm sure she would appreciate it were you to have a look at them."

"Is this true, Miss Orangecloak?" Tinnia queried.

The redhead was coy in her answer. "Oh no, I couldn't bother you like that."

"Nonsense, my lady, allow me to grab my medical bag and a key to your suite and I'll meet you on the top floor to see you in." The dwarven woman turned quickly and left without another word, leaving her father to lead the guests.

Kevane slid out from back of the desk at that. "Well then, we had best not dawdle or Tinnia is like to have my hide," he chided. "Follow me once again and I will be only glad show you upstairs to your accommodations."

Following behind the dwarf, Tryst and his party went back the way they came until they could see the rear exit at the far end of the hallway. At this intersection they instead turned toward the front of the hotel, meeting other guests milling about.

To the dwarves, the bedraggled, filthy group of tallfolk lugging old sacks and satchels and sheathed weapons made for a startling sight. Several guests let their manners get the better of them, gaping and gazing at the strange visitors on the heels of the hotel's owner.

They emerged on the second of the two levels of a sprawling lobby on the left side of a massive oaken staircase. On the first floor sat a long reception desk encapsulating nearly the entire right hand side of the steps. Opposite of that was a common sitting area furnished with chesterfields, deep, comfortable chairs and low tables. Between them all stood an ostentatious bronze statue depicting a parka-wearing dwarf on skis, in the act of manoeuvring down a slope.

Tryst noticed Orangecloak tapping Ren on the arm as she looked over the bronze depiction of the dwarf in the centre of the lobby. "Ren, that statue there, is that the skiing thing that dwarfs like to do?" she asked the elf innocently enough in a low voice.

"Just so," Ren answered with a chuckle. "That's what this resort hotel is dedicated to. Well, that and serving as a resting point for miners coming south to the mountains from the dwarven city of Gondarrius."

"Interesting, I've always wondered what skiing looked like. I had heard it was a very popular pastime amongst the dwarves," she commented attentively.

Seeing his chance to insert himself, Kevane turned happily to jump in before Ren could say another word. "That there is my grandsire, Modo Dupoire, a founding father of the second sport of the dwarves: skiing." He beamed. "Have you not tried it, my lady?"

"I'm afraid not, I have only heard of it," she replied. "It was never something that we were allowed to practice when I was a little girl and when I grew up I had neither the time nor the coin to afford such activities."

Kevane stepped up beside her then, making a wide gesture in the direction of his grandfather's likeness. "I'm sure you'd love it, my lady, it's such a graceful sport, such as your Thieves are reputed to be. It requires great control of one's body and lightning quick reflexes to master, but is so simple that a child could learn it. It's quite exhilarating, if I do say so, though I might be biased on the matter."

"Ah yes, I recall it being described similarly," Orangecloak surmised "Though I always thought it seemed dangerous for an activity done for leisure."

Kevane shrugged slowly as he considered what she said. "It can be, certainly. There has unfortunately been a death or two. But those are few and far between. It's mostly safe, and I take great care to ensure the safety of all my guests using my slopes."

As Orangecloak seemed about to ask another question, Tinnia appeared from the other side of the second floor of the lobby. "Hello again," the dwarven woman greeted as she approached the party. "Are we still waiting on the elevator?"

"No, my dear, I simply decided to wait on you," Kevane answered quickly. "Would you be a dear and ring the bell to let Baltar know we're ready to go up."

"The alla-what?" Fletchard asked out of nowhere. "I thought we were taking the stairs?"

That gave Tinnia a hearty laugh. "No, no, we don't need to take the stairs here," she stated while turning their attention to a sliding steel door located directly in the wall behind them. "We take the elevator." With that, she pulled on a velvet rope overhead that caused a bell to ring.

A machine within the wall whirred to life, giving Orangecloak and Fletchard both a startle. Tryst noticed Orangecloak looking at him nervously and he gave her a reassuring smile, hiding his amusement at her wonder in the dwarven technology. The steel door was pulled open from within by a red cheeked, rotund dwarf about Tryst's age in the uniform of a double-breasted, burgundy jacket and matching slacks. "Hello there, Mister and Miss Dupoire, I hope that I have not kept you waiting?" he said cheerily.

"Not at all, Baltar," Kevane replied to the young fellow. "Will there be enough room for all my friends here?"

Baltar bowed and gestured a hand towards the inside area of the box. "Why certainly, ser. Yourself, Miss Tinnia and all the tallfolk can fit at once with their things if you like. Come on in, don't be shy."

The dwarf stepped out when he was finished to allow them all in first. Kevane and Tinnia led the way, with Ren and Tryst following close behind.

Orangecloak and Fletchard both remained where they stood, sharing an unspoken, mutual disdain of the contraption.

"Don't worry, it's perfectly safe," Ren said to the both of them. "You have my full assurance as an engineer."

The two stepped on, the three eyes between them scanning the tiny space while Baltar slid the door closed once more. Tinnia gave instructions to take them to the fourteenth floor and Baltar turned his attention on the controls beside him.

The elevator came to life with a rumble and a jolt that caused the red haired woman and the one eyed bounty hunter to flinch simultaneously. Tryst sympathised with their apprehension, as he had been equally suspicious of the elevator the first time he had rode it.

Slowly, the box began to lift upward, a small bell dinging within the lift with every floor they passed. After the thirteenth floor, the lift gave a final jolt and came to a stop. Tryst felt a hand grab his forearm and glanced to see Orangecloak holding it tight. Their eyes met and she noticed what she had done, letting go of Tryst's arm as quickly as she had clutched it.

"This is it, ladies and gentlemen," Baltar happily stated as he swung open the steel doors and stepped out to let them exit. "Will there be anything else?" he asked while holding the door in hand.

"That will be all for now, Baltar," Tinnia answered. "I've taken the liberty of calling on the launderer and the kitchen staff. Be sure to bring them right up when they come around."

They left Baltar to his work and Tinnia led the way down the hallway to the far end and a white door with a brass plated number twenty mounted upon it. Tinnia produced a key ring from a front pocket on the black, leather bag she carried, unlocking the door and stepping back. "Here we are, folks: your accommodations."

Orangecloak was the first to step within, her eyes going wide at the majesty of the apartment that lay before her bathed in the sunlight shining through tall windows.

"I think this will suffice, don't you?" Tinnia asked rhetorically.

"This is a very nice room," Orangecloak replied as she shoved back her cloaks and looked about. "It all seems quite odd that you would bestow this on a perfect stranger like me, though," she commented while running her bare hand over the blue, upholstered chesterfield that was the main piece of the sitting area furniture set to the left of the door.

Kevane took the compliment as his cue to chime in. "I'm ever so glad it is to your satisfaction, my lady," he answered, shuffling by the table and chair set of the dining area toward one of the windows along the wall as he did. It seemed as if the elder dwarf wanted to say more, though Tryst sensed reservation in Kevane's voice and understood why. The Musicians hadn't survived for so many years by speaking liberally in front of others, and Kevane had no reason to trust neither Ren nor Fletchard.

It was Tinnia who took up where the silence left them off. "This suite is more than this living area, my lady, might I show you about?"

"That would be lovely, thank you," Orangecloak answered as Tinnia led the way around the table and chairs to a pair of doors to the right of the entrance.

"Here are the bedrooms," Tinnia began, her eyes curiously watching Orangecloak's limping gait as she worked to keep up. "There are two single beds in the windowless room and a couple's bed in the master room."

As Tinnia gave Orangecloak a tour, the men were left to themselves. Fletchard had already flopped down on the chesterfield and moaned as his feet left the floor. Both Tryst and Ren opted to join Kevane at the window to take in the splendid view of the vast lands that lay before the mountainside.

The women emerged from the bedroom area and Tinnia gestured toward the opposite side of the room. "And over here is the bathroom facility, complete with draining privy." Tinnia stepped back, her vision falling to the faltering steps of Orangecloak once more. "If you would like, we can adjourn there and I can take a look at your knees. You can get out of those filthy leathers and into a nice, hot bath afterwards. We even have a launderer who will gladly have your clothes cleaned and mended for you."

Orangecloak shook her head. "Oh no, I couldn't part with my clothes, this is all I have."

"We have some very warm, plush robes you could wear while your current outfit is being washed. It wouldn't be much good to take a bath only to climb back into grimy attire, now would it?" Tinnia countered, wrapping her hand through Orangecloak's elbow and casually leading her across the suite and beyond the sitting area.

A knock at the suite's entrance stirred the four men from their thoughts and Kevane all but jumped across the room to answer it. "Hullo, Yancey, do come in," he said by way of greeting whoever was waiting without.

Kevane stepped back out of the way to allow entry to a trio of dwarves, two males and a female, who made their way into the room.

The woman, a fair blonde looking no older than her early twenties, pushed a trolley bearing a numerous covered platters above lit candles, several flagons, steins and wine glasses. As for the men, one was of comparable age to the woman and the other closer to Kevane in years, they bore nothing save for a canvas bag.

"Allow me to introduce Dellah, Yancey and Harbrecht," Kevane said to the three men who were all standing about. "Tinnia called on them before she joined us, it seems. Dellah here works in the kitchen and has a platter of fresh, chopped vegetables and dipping sauces for you to whet your appetite before dinner. The young fella with the sack is Yancey, who runs the laundry and beside him is Harbrecht, our resident tailor."

The other three said their hellos and Dellah was about to invite them to partake of the food when Kevane stopped her. "Not yet, we'll let it sit until the lady is finished with her bath, elsewise there may be nothing left for her." The owner of the hotel turned to Tryst, Fletchard and Ren. "You have my apologies, gentlemen. However, if you would rather not wait for dinner, the dining room is at your service, my compliments, of course. There is also the tavern, the bar of which is open to you all if you would take a drink or several."

"Open bar, you say?" Fletchard's ears pricked up at the mere mention of it. "Could someone be so kind as to show me to this tavern? I'll gladly take you up on that offer, ser."

Kevane seemed anxious for Fletchard to leave and happily obliged. "That can be arranged, certainly. Dellah, be a dear and escort

Mister Miller here to the tavern."

"As you wish," Dellah bowed politely. "Follow me, ser."

Something caught Tryst's eye and he called out to Fletchard, "You should leave the sword. Furthermore, if anyone asks, you shall tell them that you are a trapper from Tusker's Cove. We shouldn't have to worry about our whereabouts being leaked by the dwarves, but being cautious doesn't hurt."

Without a word of argument, Fletchard undid his sword belt and left it hanging it on the one of the dining room chairs. "If I'm given an opportunity to be away from my usual dour company, I'm seizing upon it. If you wanted me to, I would tell the dwarves I'm the jester to the King of Gildriad if it means I'll get some peace and a stiff drink. Suffice it to say, I'll rather enjoy an evening without a certain red haired woman trying to kill me with her venomous stare," Fletchard commented with relief before leaving on the heels of the blonde dwarf and out of sight for what Tryst surmised would likely be the duration of their stay.

"He won't be back tonight," Ren commented flatly, not the least bit sad to see Fletchard going. "Though, I suppose I should follow suit. I gather we'll be staying in the room with the pair of single beds?"

"Aye, we'll give the lady the large bed all to herself, I think," Tryst answered.

While Ren changed into whatever other clothing he carried in his satchel, Tinnia made her return, closing the bathroom door as she emerged. "The lady is taking her bath and none among you will disturb her until she is good and ready," she declared while crossing the room to the others, redoing a buckle on the medical bag slung over her shoulder as she did.

"Good, if anyone here deserves a little rest and relaxation it's her. How are her knees, Tinny?" Tryst inquired, airing his concern for the injuries obtained at the hands of the man known as the Carver.

"From what I observed, the damage doesn't appear to be anything permanent," Tinnia stated matter-of-factly. "Though, I should remind you that I am a medic, not a doctor. Based on all of that however, I see no reason why she won't make a full recovery. There also doesn't seem to be any tears in the musculature or tendons of the knee, or fracturing of the bones and kneecap. Those, of course, would be the worst case scenarios and she would not be walking if she had done something so serious, in any case. The most likely injury she sustained is severe bruising and more so to the right knee than the left. She's very fortunate, in that regard. Given what she told me of how she obtained the injuries, it could have been far worse."

After delivering her prognosis, Tinnia turned to the two remaining employees. "Ah yes, Harbrecht, I'm glad you could come." She glanced about quickly. "We're missing some people. I see a food cart, but no operator and Mister Miller is gone."

"Fletchard decided he needed a reprieve from our company," Tryst explained. "Dellah escorted him to the tavern downstairs."

"I see," Tinnia nonchalantly replied. "That shall likely suit him better than staying cooped up here." Her tone indicated to Tryst that Tinnia wouldn't miss him any more than Orangecloak would. It made him wonder if Orangecloak told Tinnia of anything else that happened on their journey.

Ren's emergence from the smaller of the two bedrooms got everyone's attention. He had changed himself into a dark green, long sleeved, cotton tunic tucked neatly into a pair of brown trousers. Bundled in his arms were his suit and cloak, of which Tryst figured both were surely ruined by now. After discussing the matter with Harbrecht the tailor, however, Ren was charmed to hear that his clothing was entirely within the realm of repair. "I work with leather too," Harbrecht hinted with a look towards Tryst's muddied armour.

"I appreciate that, but my leathers need no mending. I'll send them downstairs for a cleaning after my bath, though. Thank you," Tryst answered.

At that, Tinnia began herding the other dwarves towards the exit. "Well, you heard the man. I think we should all be on our way. They need rest, and they won't get that with us hanging about. Yancey, leave the laundry bag, they'll fill it themselves and have it brought down for washing later. Harbrecht, you can get to work on Mister Wildheart's suit and Father, you and I are late for dinner with Tyla."

"Tyla will have to wait, my dear," Kevane responded, standing still while the others shuffled towards the door. "Tryst and I have a deal to talk about. Send my apologies and explain the circumstances."

Tinnia pointed a stern finger at her father at that. "If you're planning on skipping dinner with Tyla, you can explain yourself to her. I refuse to face her wrath on your behalf."

"She's right." Kevane sighed. "Tyla is going to be displeased as it is that she's not been informed of your arrival. I had best go and explain what is afoot. If you would like to catch up later, by all means don't hesitate to seek me out."

"Mister and Miss Dupoire," Ren spoke up before the father and daughter left, prompting them to turn in his direction. "I think I would like to see this tavern as well, if you would show me the way."

That grabbed Kevane's curiosity. "Why certainly, my good elf, but if you don't mind my asking, what would be in the tavern for you to so urgently find?"

"I have to find a way home to the Elven Forest and it would do me no good to let a day slip by," Ren replied casually. "I must make the best of it and begin searching for fellow travelers to make such arrangements with."

"Why don't you join us for dinner first?" The invitation was floated by Tinnia and Kevane grasped at the idea immediately.

The older dwarf all but leap as he embraced his daughter's offer. "Yes, yes, a splendid idea, Tinnia! Mister Wildheart here should join us for dinner. Tyla would love to meet you and afterwards she can show you to the tavern. She's performing tonight with her violin. I may be biased in saying so, but she's by far one of the most revered violinists in all of the Snowy Lands. You simply must hear her play, I insist on it."

Ren smiled warmly at that. "That sounds just wonderful, I'll gladly take you both up on that. Shall we?" he said while strolling towards the door. "I shall be back sometime throughout the night, Tryst. Have a pleasant rest," the elf said, closing the door behind him.

With the room emptied and seemingly alone at last, Tryst allowed himself a deep breath. He unclasped his thick black cloak with its brown furred shoulders and draped it over the same dining chair supporting Fletchard's sabre. Upon retreating to the room with the pair of single beds, Tryst noticed first and foremost that Ren had claimed one already, laying his things on the bedspread. Not that it mattered to Tryst, who was content to just have a bed to sleep in.

That's one way I've gone soft, he thought to himself. *Having spent so much time sleeping under Grenjin Howland's roof, I've forgotten what it is to live and sleep off the land. If Orangecloak keeps me in her service, that's likely one thing I'll have to get accustomed to in short order. For tonight, however, I will rest my head on a soft pillow.*

His leather jacket, the elven blades strapped to his legs and his sword belt were all removed and hung from the ornate post at the foot of the bed. After a bath, he would change the rest of his attire, but for now it would have to do, despite the odour.

Back in the sitting room, his attention fell to a fireplace along the same wall as the entrance. It sat empty, with a stack of dry firewood, a neat pile of kindling and a box of matches. Tryst went to work and got a little fire going in no time, welcoming the flickering, gentle orange glow it produced.

In that time another young, male servant had allowed himself into the room. The young lad informed Tryst that he was delivering dinner, replacing the untouched trolley with a new one. Arranged neatly atop the cart, Tryst espied steaming platters with lit candles beneath, flagons of wine and more plates, cups and cutlery than two people could possibly need. Tryst thanked the lad kindly and he left as quickly as he arrived, leaving Tryst to himself once more.

With the crackling fire working to warm the room and dinner at the ready, Tryst contented himself upon the cushioned bay of the window nearest the dining table. Along the way he took the liberty of pouring himself a glass of white wine and contented himself to watch the encroaching sunset.

The most pressing part of this journey is behind us, he thought to himself while gazing out at the last skiers of the day winding their way down the slopes. *The escape was the worst of it. The more distance we put between ourselves and Atrebell, the easier things become. The lady's knees have nearly healed, and though the loss of her friends will leave a scar within, that wound too will mend itself.*

Movement in the bathroom caught his ear and he listened as he heard the water being drained from the tub and the sound of limping wet feet on ceramic tiles.

After a time, the bathroom door opened, slowly creaking on its hinges as Orangecloak peeked out to see who remained. "Has everyone gone?" she said to Tryst when she stepped out.

"Aye, the dwarves left us alone for the evening to rest and our other companions decided to visit the tavern," Tryst answered as he turned to face her. Inhaling deeply, he gazed upon her freshly bathed form and felt himself greatly enticed by what he saw.

The dwarven robes were cut a little short for a human, leaving her porcelain skin exposed several centimetres above the knee. The robe was quite thick, made of a fluffy, towelling material and belted tight across her fine frame. Across her slender shoulders fell the long, damp, locks of her hair he had become so fond of. The way it framed her gorgeous face and shone brilliantly red in the light of the fire as she stood before it was a sight to behold.

"I will never consider Fletchard my companion and Ren is leaving us." The melancholy tone of Orangecloak was palpable as she stood before the fire, a small jar clutched closely to her stomach. "As far as I'm concerned, we have no companions after this day."

Tryst gave a slow, thoughtful nod at that. "I suppose you're right, my lady," he said before changing the subject. "You look refreshed. How are you feeling?"

She shrugged in response, her gaze on the fire before her. "I'm feeling clean for the first time in about two weeks and I feel like I should be relaxed and at ease. In truth, I feel like I should be feeling a lot of things right now and yet all I feel is despair." She sighed before turning her eyes to the crock in her hands and held it out for Tryst to see. "As for my knees, soaking in the hot water seems aid with the lingering swelling and soreness."

"Tinnia is a sage medic. I would trust her as much as any doctor on the matter," Tryst said, letting a thin smile cross his face as he stood and gestured towards the trolley of untouched food. "If nothing else, you must be hungry. Come, the dwarves left a meal for four."

Her eyes befell the covered trays of food and Tryst could see the hunger plainly on her face. "I certainly am starving," She admitted. "Give me a moment, I'll put this cream on my knees and be right with you." Orangecloak added before disappearing into the master room.

After stoking the fire once more, Tryst went to the job of revealing the dinner beneath the lids of the platters to reveal a cacophony of dwarven cuisine beneath. Sautéed deer, served with black pepper and salt sat stewing in its succulent juices beneath the first, boiled turnips served soaking in butter beneath another. There were baked potatoes, sliced down the middle and stuffed with a sour cream and green peppers and small, roasted chickens that had been marinated in a sweet, red sauce.

Tryst placed the trays in the centre of the table, laid the lids aside and began digging beneath the trolley for the plates, cutlery and wine goblets. When everything was in place, he set the long table for two, arranging it so they would face one another with the food and wine between.

Before long Orangecloak returned, finding Tryst had a chair

pulled out for her. "This all looks quite delicious, the smells alone are making my stomach growl," the lady said while seating herself across from Tryst, who had finished his glass of wine and was moving on to his second while filling hers for the first time.

The white wine was sweet and tangy with only a slightly tart aftertaste. Tryst had not been able to identify what it was during either glass he drank, but Orangecloak knew straight away.

"It's Frostberry. Oh, I do like frostberries. This is remarkably good," she said with what Tryst almost thought was a smile, but it came and went so fast it was hard for him to be sure. "Hard to come by in the south, both the berries and the wine, but the Thieves have procured both from time to time," Orangecloak explained after a few more sips.

From there the two of them ravaged the feast. The deer, which they both seemed to enjoy most of all, was made quick work of and a tidy dent was made in the buttered turnips. Two of the undersized chickens were reduced to bones and a third was left limbless. To finish it off, Orangecloak nibbled on a baked potato slice and its sour cream and green pepper filling.

Throughout the meal, they spoke little beyond standard table courtesies and comments on the courses. Neither Tryst nor Orangecloak gave much consideration to anything for the time being but filling their empty stomachs.

When she had her second goblet of wine downed and was filling the third, Orangecloak seemed to find her tongue at last. "These dwarves seem like very nice people. I think it would be hard to not like Tinnia and Kevane, they're very generous."

Tryst nodded in agreement. "They are indeed, I consider them all friends."

"Is that why they're so kind to me? Is it only a favour extended to me by being in your company?" she asked plainly.

"Not at all, my lady, you're quite famous in these parts. The dwarves see you as someone to be admired," Tryst answered truthfully.

She seemed mystified by that. "Now why would the dwarves give two figs about me? How am I, a human rabble rouser, of any interest at all to anyone outside human Illiastra?"

"You underestimate yourself my lady," Tryst replied casually. "You may not realise it, but there are many eyes from around the known world on you and many of them want to see you prevail. Not the least of which are the dwarves and elves that share this continent."

She shook her head, the damp red locks moving about her shoulders. "My people and I are merely protesters, not opposition to the state. I don't see how the rest of the world can cast their eyes and hopes on me."

Tryst had to laugh a little. "My lady, you are the *only* opposition to the state."

"Now I know you're being facetious, Mister Reine," she scoffed in return.

"You truly underestimate yourself," Tryst said while turning sideways in his chair, propping a leg on the armrest lazily. "The Elite Merchant Party made you their official opposition on the day they acknowledged your existence."

She reached for another flagon of frostberry wine as she phrased her next question. "I garnered attention, aye. I'm the most sought after person in Illiastra, I know that too. What I don't know though, and perhaps you can answer me this: how much of a threat does the Lord Master really see me as?"

"You're enough of a threat to him that the Lord Master bought into the idea of hiring me in the first place," Tryst spoke confidently, catching her glance as she slowly sat back again.

"I'm the reason why Grenjin Howland hired the Master of Blades?" she asked with a hint of satisfaction in her voice, trying to believe it could be so. "You mean to tell me that I inspired that much fear in him?"

"For that you have Greggard Simillon to thank as well. It was he who planted the seed in the old man's head and nurtured it to bloom." Tryst stood up, placing his cup on the table while he added another log on the fire. "As I'm sure you know, my lady, Greggard is the Lord of International Trade for Illiastra," he said while glancing to her, noticing her attention rapt to his every word. "It's a position that allows him to travel the globe without suspicion and through this he has developed connections with men and women of all stations outside the country.

"For a long time Greggard sought to have a reliable man not only inside the Atrebell Manor, but one that might hear the Lord Master's every word. Once you started your rebellion, that opportunity appeared. Lord Simillon convinced Grenjin Howland that you were going to lead the people to toppling his regime and Howland believed him. The old man is paranoid as it is, so it wasn't too difficult of a notion to sell."

Tryst returned to the table to collect his goblet, walking about the room as he continued to talk. "From there it was a matter of Greggard convincing Grenjin that he knew where to hire the very best protection that money can buy. Once the Lord Master believed he was safe from any threat you posed, he pushed forward with his plan to snuff out yourself and the Thieves once and for all."

"What you're saying is that Greggard used the perceived threat I posed to bring you into the manor. That's interesting," Orangecloak pondered aloud before pushing forward with another question. "So am I to assume that you blew the whole plan out of the water when you sprang me from the dungeon? Is that the way of it?"

"On the contrary, my lady," he began as he returned to the table. "You *are* the plan."

Orangecloak didn't seem to believe him. "The dwarves knew that you would come trotting up the road with me in tow someday?" she asked, gesturing around the room. "And Greggard Simillon anticipated you showing up at his door, his inside ear in Atrebell deafened, just so he could meet some impoverished rebel?"

"An ear within the Lord Master's hearing is a valuable thing to have, granted," he replied as he came to sit on the edge of the table directly beside her. "However, both Greggard and I agreed that *you* were top priority. In fact, we came to a consensus that losing an ear in Atrebell was but a small price to pay for even a chance of working with the Thieves."

For a moment Orangecloak seemed content and Tryst was about to excuse himself for a bath when he saw her pause and dwell on a sudden realisation. "What of Fletchard?" she inquired, with flashes of anger in her voice. "Was he part of the plan?"

It was a question Tryst expected at some point and one he was only happy to answer. "My lady, I can assure you that Fletchard Miller was never a part of any plans of mine."

"That is good to know," Orangecloak replied, her voice trailing.

Tryst exhaled and returned to his feet. "My lady, if it's alright with you, I think I'll go give myself a bath now. I'm becoming more and more aware of my own odour."

She shrugged. "By all means, do as you wish, it's not for me to order you about."

Upon heading to the second bedroom, Tryst retrieved his set of clean, black clothes, his hair brush, soap, shampoo and the shaving kit he hadn't been able to use so many days ago in the bathing pool of the Atrebell Manor.

That romp with Marigold seems a lifetime ago now, he thought to himself while looking at the razorblade.

Flicking off the light in the bedroom, he re-entered the sitting area. Upon return, Tryst discovered that Orangecloak had taken her goblet to the bay window that he himself had earlier been occupying.

Wordlessly, Tryst left her to her own thoughts and retreated to the bathroom for a much needed cleaning. It was while fumbling with the belt of his leather pants that he heard what sounded like crying. Tryst paused where he stood and listened to what he definitely discerned to be soft sniffling.

Do I leave her be, or see if she's alright? She wasn't crying when I left, he thought to himself briefly, before redoing his belt buckle and making up his mind. "My lady?" Tryst asked in a soft voice while stepping back into the main room. "Are you alright?"

He found her sitting with her head against the glass pane of the bay window, a goblet still to hand and tears running freely down her face. She didn't answer him and he couldn't be sure if she even heard him. "My lady, is anything the matter?" he asked again after he had closed the distance between them. The fierceness was gone from her deep blue eyes and what remained was a broken heart that looked about to break in a thousand brittle pieces.

"I...I'm alright," she stammered, averting her gaze to the drop of wine left in her glass.

"Are you sure?" Tryst sat himself down slowly until he came to rest on the cushioned seat.

As much as he wanted to look her in the eyes, she would not meet his. "It's just the wine, nothing more," She offered by means of explanation. "Please, go on and take your bath."

Gently and cautiously, he laid a hand atop hers. "My lady, if it was something I said, I sincerely apologise."

"Oh no, it's nothing you said. If anything it was my own fault for bringing up Fletchard. Even talking of him brings back the sight of what happened to Myles and Coquarro. They were my family, they were my friends and now they're gone," she finally relented, staring into the eternal darkness of the night.

Tryst shook his head gently. "Orangecloak, I never got a chance to say this to you, not without Fletchard being in our hearing: I am so sorry for what happened to you and your friends in Atrebell."

"Thank you, Tryst," she gave back, her speech slightly slurring. "I miss them both terribly. It's unbecoming of the Field Commander of the Thieves to be acting like this, I apologise."

He shook his head and gave her hand a sympathetic squeeze. "We should never apologise for missing those we lost."

"Tryst…" He heard her swallow as she wiped away the last of her tears. "Why have you done so much for me? You've forsaken wealth and fortune and comrades for some stupid fool trying to save this doomed nation without so much as a sword to her name."

"Because I know you're worth it," Tryst stated, sliding a finger on his free hand beneath her chin to raise her to eye level. "I have since the day I saw you standing on the merchant's stall in Aquas Bay. Do you remember that?"

She glanced at him a moment and he could see the recognition of the memory. "I do remember. I couldn't believe you wore all that black clothing in that heat. To be honest, when the guards got through the crowd and made a grab for me, I thought I was done for. As I ran away I kept looking back expecting you to follow me and you didn't."

"I didn't follow you then, but I would gladly follow you now," Tryst told her earnestly.

Their eyes met, those sad blues still wet with tears. "Tryst…" She put a hand behind his left ear and pulled him close, bringing their lips together before Tryst knew what she was doing. The taste of her in his mouth was intoxicating and he returned the kiss. It tasted of frostberry wine and sadness, with a touch of passion hidden beneath it all. A hand on his chest pushed him back and suddenly her face was flushed, as if she didn't know what she had done. "I…I'm sorry. I shouldn't have done that," she said in a whisper.

"Don't be sorry," Tryst whispered back, their faces barely a breath apart.

Her eyes went wide and she was on her feet quickly. "No, that was wrong. Please, don't think anything of it, it was just the wine. At any rate, I should get to sleep, I'm exhausted." She sounded embarrassed in herself as she thumped the empty goblet on the table.

Tryst decided it would be best if he pressed the issue no further. "Goodnight, Orangecloak," he said as she shuffled away as fast as her drunken, sore legs could take her.

The door to the bedroom began swinging closed behind her but stopped short of closing. "Goodnight, Tryst," she said in a whisper, the words floating to him across the room.

16
ORANGECLOAK

The morning's light shone through the slanted windows of the suite, throwing warm rays across the floor before it.

When was the last time I slept in a bed? Orangecloak wondered as she lay atop the feather stuffed mattress.

She had wrapped herself tight in the soft, white eiderdown quilt before falling asleep and had slept quite well for the first time in what seemed an eternity.

I was comfortable in my hammock in Rillis Vale, though I never slept peacefully. Perhaps it was the wine that helped last night, but the last time I slept like this I was still living my first life.

She released herself from the quilted cocoon, rolled onto her back and stretched her arms out across the span of the bed, emitting a groan as her muscles and joints woke up with the rest of her.

A painting on the wall caught her eye just then. She had noticed it the day before when Tinnia had shown her the room, but until now hadn't looked upon it. It was a portrait landscape, done in watercolour paint on a large canvas on the wall to the left of the bed. The subject was a large stone, located in the middle of a field of wild, tall grass. For a moment the stone looked like any other she had seen in her life, until she picked up a shape in it.

That's the Stone Egg, she realized at once.

The painting was done in a warmer season. Lush greens in the fore and background and blooming wildflowers made it barely recognisable from what Orangecloak had seen. The autumn weather had taken the life from the stone's surroundings when she and the others had passed it by. The stone still looked the same though. While everything around it ebbed and flowed, lived and died and went through the cycle of time, the stone never changed.

How much has changed since last we were before that rock? she pondered while staring at the canvas. *I was consumed with hatred, for Fletchard most of all, though I had hatred enough to go around for Tryst too.*

It was more than those two though, she knew. Orangecloak had been mourning for Myles and Coquarro, longing for them and the other Thieves that she was suddenly torn away from. When she was seated on that horse with Ren, she had felt so consumed by her own enmity that she had barely even seen the stone.

I remember Tryst saying the name of it and all I could think about was my own pain. I didn't see the stone and I didn't see Tryst. All I saw was selfish angst.

Her gaze returned to the painting. *What do I see now? A beautiful painting of a strangely shaped rock in a green field, hung on a wall in a lavish hotel room.*

She looked away to the sky beyond the window, overcast with patches of blue poking through the white blanket of clouds. *I was in the hands of my enemies, facing death for the second time with everything I knew and everyone I loved taken away from me. Tryst could have left me there and went on with his comfortable life tending on Lord Master Howland. He sacrificed the life he had known so that mine could go on and for that I gave him my loathing. I didn't see the field or the odd boulder in the middle of it. I was blind to everything.*

Sitting up, she stretched out her limbs again, running a hand through the mess her hair had become in her sleep. The blankets were pushed away and she spun her legs to the edge of the bed, standing on knees that hurt less with each passing day. Today, there was but a little discomfort.

I'll be sure to thank Tinnia for that cream, she made note while standing with considerable ease for the first time in quite a long while.

A full-length mirror stood beside the open door of her room and grabbed her attention. Upon looking at herself, she suddenly remembered that prior to falling asleep she had shrugged out of the plush robe she had been wearing after her bath.

It had been some time since she had seen her whole naked form reflected at her. Orangecloak considered herself thin, but not rail-thin. Years of running, climbing and toiling had built a sinewy and noticeable layer of muscle atop her frame. She didn't think her breasts were very big, certainly not what men seemed to like and she thought her body shape was a little too straight. A sideways turn showed a behind that was not the most ample she had ever seen either.

Tryst seems to be attracted to me though. She shrugged to herself as she put her hands to her hips and inspected herself a little more, trying to ascertain exactly why that was.

One of the things Tinnia had offered the night before was a razor, and Orangecloak was glad to have taken the offer. When she had finished with it, Orangecloak had wicked away all of the hair on her body save for a little mound of red above her womanhood.

For the moment she gave up trying to find a reason why Tryst Reine might take a shining to her and went in search of her robe. It was at the foot of the bed in a ball that she found it and she slid her arms into it and tied it over her light flesh.

Once more her own reflected visage caught her eye. *I'm a pale, skinny redhead with barely a breast or an arse to my name,* she thought after leaving her reflection behind to relieve herself in the bathroom. *He's the Master of Blades, who could have nearly any woman his heart so desires and yet, for some reason he seems to desire me.*

The fire was still crackling away in the main room. The wood splits upon it looked to have been burning for no more than an hour or so at the most. At first, she thought that odd, until she noticed Tryst sleeping soundly upon the chesterfield nearby. Save for a pair of undershorts that tied tight about his taut hips, he was naked and uncovered by blankets.

I kissed him, Orangecloak recalled, suddenly embarrassed by what she had done while under the influence of the white wine several hours ago.

I kissed him and I stopped at that. She looked him up and down from where he lay, and found herself not turned off by the bare body of the sleeping man as he rolled from his side to his back. With his abdominal muscles looking like chiselled granite as they rose and dropped below hardened pectorals, it would be hard to not find him attractive.

Orangecloak left him there and turned for the privy, scolding herself for even raising that question.

The first thing of note in the bathroom was that the laundry basket was piled higher than it had been the night before.

Tryst must have bathed after I went to sleep, she deduced from the added towels.

After her business was concluded, she stood before the washbasin to clean her hands and face and discovered Tryst's hairbrush sitting nearby.

I doubt he will mind if I use it, considering mine was left behind when Fletchard arrested me, she reasoned to herself, taking brush to hand. Mounted on the wall was another mirror in an ornate frame, encapsulating a once proud face and an intimidating look capable of making grown men quake in their boots.

I am Lady Orangecloak, she sternly reminded herself while running Tryst's brush through her red locks that had become tangled in the night.

All I had to do was don the cloak and city guards from Aquas Bay to Ravenkeep chased it like slavering dogs eying a steak. That cloak, with I beneath it, commanded respect from my peers and fear from the most powerful men in Illiastra.

The face staring back in the mirror surprised her in that moment. It wasn't as tired as she recalled it being as of late, rather, it bore the strength of a fearless leader she had once known.

Having drained the sink and replaced Tryst's brush, she turned to leave and moved back into the main room where Tryst still slept, looking upon him from a distance.

This is the same man who spoke so sweetly to his horse on their parting. No matter what doubt I could harbour, I know that man can't be who he was believed to be. I know that in my heart of hearts as surely as I know the hands in front of me are my own.

Yet as much as she felt she knew, there was still a little dark spot in that knowledge. It lingered there, keeping her from feeling too safe and secure. It had been with her since her first life, and had kept her alive to see a second. Now, she was on her third life, still fostering that cloying pang in the back of her mind that kept from truly trusting in anyone.

What good has it done me? For all my mistrust in everyone I've ever met, I should be dead, twice over. The Thieves saved me the first time and I never gave them my whole trust for it. The second time, it was

Tryst Reine who saved me from a sure death in the Atrebell dungeon. He's done everything I've asked of him and sought nothing in return but that I meet his friends.

Orangecloak crossed the room silently, her stiff knees cooperating fairly well for once. Along the way she opened the drapes, filling the room with the morning's light that poked in from the east on a sharp angle.

These dwarves are three of Tryst's friends, and the two I met are genuinely good folks. They've gone out of their way to ensure we've been well looked after and bestow me the same sincere respect that I shared with the other members of the Thieves. How much more can I ask for?

Staring at Tryst from across the room, she let her thoughts roam again. *I can fight him, I can hate him and I can drive him far away from me. I can even run now, if I wanted. Or I can take what's given to me, which is the fucking Master of Blades himself. What's left to happen to me if this is all an elaborate betrayal? I die for a third time, for true? The world thinks the girl from my first life is dead, they probably believe the woman from the second life is dead, who will mourn me should I lose my third? No, I have to perish that thought, it's only foolish paranoia. This can't be a sick ruse any longer. This is too far for it to go, even for a man once employed by the EMP.*

She stepped softly across the floor, careful to maintain her silent steps as she made her way back to the dining table.

On the side nearest the bay window sat Tryst's dwarven blacksteel sword resting in its sheath and beside it sat the elven dirks that had been strapped to his legs.

She had seen the sword before, but never had a chance to look at the smaller blades. Quietly, she slid one from its scabbard and felt the weight of it in her hand as she took it by the hilt – what weight there was, anyway. Elven weapons were known for being light and slender and Tryst's elongated daggers were no different. The edge of the blade she held was arrow straight and looked dauntingly sharp, with but the slightest curve near the tip.

I was wrong, tis no dirk at all, she suddenly realized.

Despite the slender nature of the blade, it was in fact a short, single edged sword meant for rapid slashes rather than being purely a thrusting dagger.

The blade cut through the air with a slight, whispering whoosh as she made a slice with it. The hilt bore no guard, and a less experienced handler would easily find their hand nicked and bloody, but not someone like Tryst Reine. Even Orangecloak was no stranger to handling a knife, despite her own moratorium on using weapons against people.

In Phaleayna, it was part of the training for upcoming Thieves and protectors of the ruins to learn the ways of bow and blade. The training was mostly for personal defence and hunting, at least when it came to Orangecloak's own ranks. The guardians of Phaleayna and anyone willing to join Old Bansam or Mell the Huntress were outside of her jurisdiction.

With it having been so long since Orangecloak had to either bear a blade or even so much as string a bow, she imagined her own skills had grown quite rusted. Ever so gingerly, she slipped the blade back into its sheath and laid it back where she found it.

It was then she noticed that despite Tryst sleeping on the chesterfield nearby, the door to his room was closed.

It's Ren, Fletchard or both of them, having come back throughout the night, she thought, hoping for it to just be the former of the two within the room.

Tryst had also taken the liberty of laying their plates, goblets and dinnerware back on the trolley and putting it off beside the door.

He's tidy, I'll grant him that. She sighed as she glanced about once more, seeing what else she had missed after going off to sleep.

The fireplace was down to hot embers as she came before it and she bent slowly, cautiously buckling her knees to retrieve the last junk of wood they had. Carefully, she laid it atop the red hot remnants of the fire so as not to burn herself. Despite her best intentions, it started to roll back out and she caught it, albeit by making more of a racket than she would have liked.

"Good morning, my lady," she heard over her shoulder, turning to see Tryst leaning on his elbow and looking at her with a grin on his face. Before she had looked his way, he had taken the time to cover his waist and legs with a blanket he had tossed aside in his sleep.

"Good morning to you too, Tryst," she said in a whisper so as not to stir anyone else. Anything above that would surely wake at least the elf, given that their hearing was far greater than most humans. "My apologies, I didn't mean to wake you."

Tryst groaned a little as he stretched, rubbing sleepily at his face for a moment before returning to his smiling self.

He smiles with his eyes as well as his mouth, Orangecloak noticed before Tryst spoke.

"It's nothing to worry about, my lady. I should have woken anyhow to keep the fire from getting so low. That and I'll need to get more wood delivered, lest it get cold in here." He blinked a few times in quick succession, trying to knock the sleep away. "You're awake bright and early. Did you sleep well?" Tryst asked, having lowered his voice to match hers.

She shoved the log back into place before answering. "Aye, I certainly did, thank you. Ren or Fletchard might be in the room and whoever it is are still asleep, so keep your voice low." Orangecloak stepped over to the chesterfield and sat on the edge, beside Tryst's midsection. "What about you? How did you sleep?"

"I'm afraid my time in Atrebell made me soft for a bed," Tryst replied casually "I've missed it since leaving, so I relished the chance to lie on something other than cold ground." He stifled a yawn with his hand. "I ended up here when Ren returned, I kept getting up from the bed to stoke the fire and every time I did, I inadvertently woke him. So, I decided to just sleep here and let him rest. As for Fletchard, he never returned at all."

As for Fletchard, I couldn't give a fig, Orangecloak thought to herself but left unsaid, steering the conversation back to the first topic. "I had not known a real bed in well over a decade myself. Nor have I slept deeply without worry in half as long," she spoke in a relaxed tone, but couldn't match his smile. "Perhaps it was the wine, perhaps it was sleeping within comfortable walls, but when my head touched that pillow, my eyes closed of their own accord."

The long haired swordsman sat up to come face to face with her. "That's good to hear, my lady. Though, I have a feeling you want to talk about something, am I right?"

"Well yes, I want to talk with you about many things, but mostly...Last night." She swallowed as she spoke the last words, feeling her heart beat a little faster.

Tryst relaxed at that and let himself lean back on the armrest of the chesterfield, giving her full view of his ripped upper body. "Don't concern yourself with it. I'm sure that was most certainly the doing of the wine. You have nothing to be ashamed of."

"It's...Well the wine did have much to do with my emotions and my impulsiveness...Yet, I don't know that I'm ashamed," she answered with a shrug, trying not to look him in the eyes.

Tryst seemed taken aback by that revelation. "Oh?" he said with his tongue going to one corner of his mouth teasingly. "Might I ask why that is?"

"I have been through much lately. I have been through much throughout my lives to be sure, but as of late there's been drastic changes happening quite rapidly. It's overwhelming to say the least and I want to trust you, I sincerely do, though it's not easy for me as I'm sure you can appreciate. I thought..." She searched herself for the right words. "I thought that everything you had been doing for me up until now was... A sick game of some sort. I know that's foolish of me to think and I'm sorry if my words wound you. However, I'm sure that you can understand that all I've known of you since you came to Illiastra is that you were Grenjin Howland's sadistic pet and I'm sorry to say even that." She cringed as she spoke, regretting her choice of words immediately.

Upon glancing at Tryst to see how he reacted, however, she found herself surprised to see him nodding in understanding.

"I fully expected that you thought of me as such," Tryst answered almost sadly. "I am not deaf to what the people say of me. I tell you truthfully that it's all lies spread by the Lord Master himself to invoke fear. Despite how close I guarded him, he and I had our differences early on. He wanted me to be exactly what you thought I was and was disappointed when I was not. As such, when I refused to kill on command, he did the next best thing and made the people believe I would. I don't blame you for believing the tales. I just hope I can prove to you that they are only myths."

Orangecloak sighed at that, feeling silly for even having believed the lies spread by the EMP in the first place. "You have, I feel quite daft for letting myself even think that this could be some sort of awful ruse. I feel even worse for being so selfish and childish these last few days. I'm the Field Commander of the Thieves, for all sakes, my behaviour was unacceptable. I mourned for my friends and I'll miss them until the day I join them in death, but I let my grief carry me away. For that, I am sorry Tryst. I think in my drunken state, I thought a kiss would be a good way to make up for that and show you that I want to trust you."

"You have nothing to feel daft for, though I thank you for the apology all the same." Tryst slid a hand onto her knee and let it sit there, exhaling loudly before he continued on, "There is something else I need to tell you. Information I have been sitting on since Atrebell, but I think you're ready to hear it now and it's going to come up later when Kevane arrives."

Swallowing hard, she fearfully asked, "What is it?"

"The night before your capture, there was an ambush in Argesse," Tryst started. "It was led by men from Biddenhurst under directives from Lord Mackhol Taves himself. In the resulting skirmish, four of your lieutenants and their unit were taken and some killed."

"No..." she said breathlessly, feeling as though she had been punched in the stomach. "Do you have any names?"

He was direct in his answer to that. "The Three Sisters and Lazlo Arbor, and they were all taken alive. The names of their subordinates I do not know, but Mackhol claimed that two males among them perished." Tryst took her hands in his, garnering her sorrowful gaze. "I'm so sorry. I would have told you sooner, however I felt you were already burdened with pain enough as it is."

"It's alright, I understand why you waited," she said in a tone burdened by grief. "I have questions though, if I might ask them."

"Absolutely, my lady, ask at your leisure," Tryst offered back.

"What were they doing there? How did Mackhol know they were there?" Orangecloak began, asking quickly.

He waited a beat before answering. "They were there to stop you from going through with your protest. I have reason to believe that Mackhol Taves has a mole within the Thieves. He knew you were not only in Atrebell, but in the Batterdowns. The Thieves tried to counter this leak with an operation led by your lieutenants to extract you before daybreak, but somehow he found out about that too. This information was brought to light mere hours before you were brought to the manor by Fletchard."

"Are you inferring that I was betrayed by one of my own? Did Taves confirm a mole?" she asked frantically, her eyes locked directly on his and burning with fury.

Tryst met her gaze. "Aye, he stated specifically that he had an informant, though he did not give a name. This mole knew you were going to Roghen Plaza in the morning when the lords, ministers and their families were boarding the trains. You were sold to Lord Taves."

"I think I'm going to be sick," Orangecloak gasped, her lips quavering. "Who would betray me like that? Who within my own fold would sell me out to my enemies?"

"I wish I had that information to give you, but I do not," Tryst added, he was about to say more when the door of the smaller bedroom creaked open.

Her stare fell to the fireplace and she paid little mind to the opening of the door. "He's taking them to Biddenhurst, isn't he?" she asked sombrely.

"That was his plan and he wanted you to go with them, but Fletchard had other ideas," Tryst explained to Orangecloak. "Had that not happened, Taves had bigger and better things in mind for you and your lot. Nothing would have cemented him as irreplaceable in the eyes of the EMP like taking down their biggest threat, after all. Lord Taves wanted to hang you all in the courtyard of his prison city from atop that monstrously large gallows he's so proud of. I, however, fully intended to see him choke on that wish."

"You've only partially succeeded, I'm sad to say," Orangecloak gave back to him, noticing Ren standing behind the chesterfield. "Taves now has Ellarie, Merion, Joyce, Lazlo and a score more, and he'll still kill them."

Tryst spoke softly and assuredly, "Alive they're hostages, valuable in their own right, to be used against you. Dead, they're worthless to Mackhol's cause and he's well aware of that. I don't envy your friends, it's the worst possible place to be, but they'll live so long as you do."

"I hope you're right, Tryst." Her eyes went from the human to the elf standing behind the chesterfield, quietly waiting to speak. "Good morning, Ren. I was wondering if you had come in last night."

"Good morning, my lady and Tryst, is something amiss?" Ren curiously inquired.

She caught a glance from Tryst that told her that he was going to leave that to her discretion, though she saw no reason to withhold the information from the elf. "I found out that some of my fellow Thieves were arrested while attempting to thwart an ambush on me. They're being taken to Biddenhurst, the prison city. Likely they're already within its walls."

Ren bowed his head. "I'm terribly sorry to hear that," he said through pursed lips.

She looked the elf over, noticing he was still wearing the same outfit from last night. Though the tunic now hung loose over his hips, the laces at the neck dangling open and loose. "How did you fare at the tavern?" Orangecloak asked him, to take her mind off her own matters for a moment.

"Quite well, thank you for asking," Ren returned while stepping around the chesterfield to take a seat on the matching chair across from it. "It turns out two of my pupils named Radmer and Edwin from the University of the Midlands of Gildriad were here for a skiing vacation on their honeymoon. As it were, they had intended to seek me out for consultation on wind turbines they intended to install to help deliver electrical power to the dwarven city of Gondarrius. We since came to an agreement that I would give them my undivided attention on the project in exchange for travel companionship as far as White Canyon Pass."

"It looks as though you'll be leaving us, then." Orangecloak sighed despondently. "I won't deny that I've grown fond of you during our time together, Ren, but I would not dare keep you from home."

Ren smiled sadly at that. "Thank you, my lady. I must admit that I've become fond of you and Tryst as well. I shall certainly miss your company. Not to fret though, we won't be leaving for three days yet. We'll have plenty of time together before then."

"Aye, so we shall…" Orangecloak trailed off, her gaze on the licking flames of the fire that were starting to shrink quickly as the last log was turned to ash.

With silence falling over them, it was clear that Ren was becoming increasingly uncomfortable and looked to be elsewhere and Orangecloak gave him a way out. "My dear Ren, would you be interested in fetching breakfast and firewood for us?"

The elf all but leapt from the chair. "Why yes, I'd be glad to do that." He started for the main door and had a hand on the knob when he turned back. "I forgot to ask: what would you like to eat?"

Orangecloak shrugged. "I don't know what the kitchen offers for the breaking of the fast. Tryst, do you have any suggestions?"

After considering it for a moment, Tryst spoke up. "I'll take coffee for certain, a full urn at that, with cream and sugar to the side. Seek out Kevane or one of his girls for the rest. They'll know what's on the menu. Also, could you tell them that we'll meet with them over the meal if they would prefer?" Tryst looked back to Orangecloak. "Of course, if that's alright with you, that is. We can put it off until dinnertime or supper, if you would prefer."

With a wave and a word, she agreed to the meeting for the morning. She felt that by the time Ren returned, she and Tryst would have discussed everything they needed to in private. The elf left them then, closing the door as he departed for the elevator and the main floor beyond it.

Once they were alone again, she turned her attention back to Tryst. "I have to know something, Tryst and perhaps you can provide an answer," she asked when they were alone.

"By all means, ask away," Tryst replied warmly.

She looked him in the eyes. "My Thieves engaged the Biddenhurst men, didn't they? You claimed two of them died, I would think if they ran as I would have directed that there wouldn't even be that many losses."

"Aye, according to Lord Taves his men engaged in combat," Tryst answered her straight. "They took about a half a dozen losses and reported killing two men of yours. Among their own losses, though was a Captain Hoyt, felled by the red haired woman of the Three Sisters, armed with a spear no less."

"Oh Merion..." Orangecloak said with a sigh, remembering her comrades. "She and Ellarie are close companions of mine. They have such vigour and I love that about them, though they were advocates of fighting. I worried about them and Joyce and for good reason."

"Do you think they were entirely wrong to counsel you so?" Tryst cautiously suggested.

She considered him incredulously for a moment. Orangecloak knew where he was directing the conversation and she didn't know that she was in any mood to hear more of it. "If you're going to offer me the same advice, you might as well send me on my way now, Tryst. I have others in the Thieves who counsel the same with aggravating regularity." The words were spoken in a way to ensure she was seen as stern on the matter.

Violence wasn't about to become Orangecloak, she saw it as lowering herself to the standards of her enemy. If the other Thieves couldn't change her mind, there was slim chance of Tryst doing so.

Tryst swung his legs out beside her and stood up quickly. "I understand, my lady. I bring it up only because I know Kevane will upon his arrival. As is the general way of dwarves, he's not one for subtlety. I'm merely preparing you for this ahead of time, that's all."

"Is this to be my life now?" she asked, unable to withhold her frustration any longer, reminding herself of what he was suggesting. "Dealing with obstinate men who want to fasten a sword to my hand and push me into battle? If it is, I'm not sure I have the stomach to listen to all these aspiring warlords who seek nothing more than to make me the face of their war."

Tryst was pulling his black tunic over his head while he listened to her, responding once he had pulled the garment down over his chest. "My lady, I should think that you of all people would know that Illiastra has been a dry tinderbox in need of only a single spark for some time." He fetched up his trousers and hauled them over his legs as he went on, "I can tell you from my time in Atrebell that the grasp of the Lord Master is tenuous at best." As he spoke, Tryst pulled the long mane of flame red hair from within the tunic and let it flow out over his shoulders, tumbling nearly to his waist. "The Lord Master tries to rule by fear and intimidation, but there's only so long one can push before someone begins pushing back. Though it may seem like it's just you and the Thieves doing the pushing, there are others in the shadows ready to shove for themselves. The Elven Forest grows less amicable with humans by the season and the Dwarves outright despise the Elite Merchants and they make no qualms about it. Then there's the internal power struggle *within* the Elite Merchants Party and I'm not referring to Lord Greggard and the Musicians."

This was not entirely new information to Orangecloak. "You're referring to the western lords and ministers, aren't you?"

For that she got a nod from Tryst before he went on to explain further. "Indeed, little is said of it, but then again, anyone paying attention to the highborn folks can easily see that the men of the west are growing discontent. It's more than that, though. Lord Eamon Palomb has a marriage agreement with the Tullivans that will see the Palomb family assume control of Illiastra. There are several in the west that oppose this, but none more than Lady Marigold Tullivan, heir apparent. As we speak, she is trying to change her fate by any means necessary and the marginalised ministers may yet answer her call. Barring the Elite Merchants suddenly evaporating into thin air, war in Illiastra is practically inevitable."

"So then we won't partake. I'll pull all the Thieves back to Phaleayna and we'll stay on the island until rich old men stop sending poor young men to slaughter each other in their name," Orangecloak replied quickly, feeling satisfied with her answer.

Though Tryst was just as quick with a counterpoint, "And one set of rich old men will win and things will go on as they have been. Your opportunity to mobilise the poor young men who just died for the rich old men will have passed and with it, your chance for change.

"You know I want change, but not by violent means," she shot back, not appreciative of Tryst's tone that threatened to venture into condescension.

"Then how, I ask?" Tryst queried, gesturing with his arms wide, his voice still in the same calm volume. "I've seen you speaking of change and I'm sorry to have to say this, but Lord Master Grenjin Howland isn't swayed by speaking alone. He fears you because he believes you will convince the people to revolt against him and oust him by violent force. You know yourself that he will use violence against you quite readily, regardless of whether or not you will reciprocate. It's not the words themselves he fears, it's the potential those words have to inspire and motivate the people." At that, Tryst buckled his belt in place, strode across the room and retrieved his weapons from the table to put them away before company arrived.

Alone for the moment and left to dwell on what Tryst had said, Orangecloak made for the same bay window she had been seated at the night prior. Outside the sun was falling over the valley floor, shining off lakes and rivers alike as the awe inspiring view was illuminated before her. Along with the shimmering blues of the waters, there were yellowing, wild fields and green forests speckled with orange and red leafy trees.

Craning to look as north and west, she could see there was an almost perfect delineation where the snow line began. Behind that line was Graelin's mountain, which the hotel sat upon. The mountainside angled toward the corner of the hotel where her room was located ever so slightly, allowing her a view of the skiing slopes. At this early hour, there were only a handful of dwarves using the snow covered hills. Orangecloak watched them curiously as they wound back and forth on long, wooden skies to the bottom of the various slopes.

From behind her, Orangecloak picked up the faint footfalls of Tryst, having returned from the shared bedroom. "Quite interesting, isn't it?" he asked, gesturing his head towards the skiers outside as he joined her.

"Indeed, it looks like great fun," she returned.

"My lady," Tryst started with a touch of remorse. "I don't want you to feel as though I'm forcing you to the front lines of a war you don't want. I'm more than willing to help you explore other options."

It was all she could do to subdue a scoff as she let him see the blues of her eyes. "And what are those options you feel I have, if they do in fact exist?"

"For instance, I could help you leave Illiastra. In Drake or the three nations of Gildriad, a woman can follow whichever path she so chooses, especially one with such a skillset as yours," Tryst offered. "It's your life to journey as you want and I won't dictate to you how you should go about it. My counsel is merely suggestion."

She shook her head quickly at that, giving it little consideration. "Running away and leaving the cause behind is no option." Her intonation was firm as she delivered the line.

"Yet, running from your foes in the face of aggression is? Harsh words are no match for sharp swords and those Grenjin Howland has in great supply," Tryst pointed out just as a knock came at the front door. He left her by the window to answer it.

"Tryst," she called to him before he could reach the other side of the room, causing him to spin on his heel to face her. "Therein rests my problem, does it not?"

"I beg your pardon?" he gave back with a raised eyebrow.

Orangecloak went on to explain, "Even if I wanted to seek change by steel rather than by words alone, I lack the steel."

"Well then, this day might be in your favour." Tryst placed a hand on the doorknob. "For you are about to break your fast with one of the very men who is willing to provide you with that steel."

The breakfast came on a full trolley pushed by a maid with another behind her and a footman pulling a wagon of firewood. The latter tended to the diminishing fire while the maids went about clearing away last night's dishes and washing down the table. Behind the staff came Ren, amiably chatting with Kevane, Tinnia and a second woman that Orangecloak surmised must be Kevane's other daughter.

A beautiful dwarven woman with full hips, a modest bust and honey blonde hair with sun kissed, natural highlights stepped forward at Kevane's beckoning. "Folks, I give you my daughter, Tyla Dupoire. She shares managerial duties in the hotel with Tinnia and is the band leader of the musical troupe that regularly entertains in the tavern."

Tyla took Orangecloak's hand to shake and cut her father off before he could reverse the introductions. "You are the Lady Orangecloak and if I may say so my lady, it is nothing short of an honour to meet you." Her voice was soft and sweet and her tone one of admiration. She looked quite the lady in her white, short sleeved blouse and violet, knee length skirt.

"I assure you, the honour is mine as well," Orangecloak answered her, attempting a smile that would not materialise. "I'm very grateful for your family's boundless generosity."

The young dwarven woman seemed barely able to contain her excitement as she responded, "I wish I could have met you yesterday, truly, but I was with my beau, Gerard, on the slopes when you arrived. However, I'm so glad you felt up to having breakfast with us, I simply couldn't wait to make your acquaintance."

"Yes well, I have your sister to thank for that. Her salve did wonders for my knees. They haven't felt this well since before my capture," Orangecloak replied politely, watching the two maids hastily exchange dirty dishes with steaming plates of food.

There was a thin, freckled red haired woman who reminded Orangecloak of a more demure version of herself and an even thinner blonde with a sharp nose. They wore their hair in buns with white caps and aprons over plain black dresses. The dark haired footman working beside them wore a black suit with a long tailed jacket, his beard neatly trimmed and his hair slicked back. Neither of the three even made eye contact with Orangecloak.

Tinnia stepped forward, dressed in black slacks with a white, short sleeved, silk blouse. "Think nothing of it, my lady. I'm only glad the cream was effective. You certainly do seem to be walking with less of a limp."

The footman and the two maids completed their task and stood beside the two trolleys with their hands behind their back, waiting for further orders. The red haired maid took the gap in conversation as a chance to speak up. "Mister Dupoire, we have finished setting your table. Might there be anything else you would like of us or shall we take our leave?"

Kevane, clad in a cream coloured three piece suit turned his attention to them. "Yes, thank you, Gayle. That will be all."

"Won't you be joining us?" Orangecloak asked the servants before they could leave, catching them by surprise. The three exchanged looks and seemed to perspire immediately.

"Um… You see, my lady," the footman started "We've um, already eaten our breakfast and we couldn't possibly eat any more. Not to mention that we have work of our own to get to. I offer my sincerest apologies, my lady."

"I'm sorry to hear that," Orangecloak responded. "I thought we might all dine together."

Kevane stepped in for his servants, trying to relieve the tension Orangecloak purposefully brought into the room. "Well, my lady, as they've said, they have work they should be getting to. It would be impolite of us to keep them from it."

"You have my apologies as well, my lady," Tinnia spoke courteously of the matter. "The servants don't typically dine with us," she said before gesturing to the table. "Speaking of eating, shall we?"

The response of Kevane and his employees bothered Orangecloak, though given all her hosts had done for her so far and the look Tryst was giving her, she let it go. "It is I who should apologise," she spoke directly to the servants. "I shall not keep you from your duties."

Once the servants had taken their leave, the Dupoire family and the three guests took their seats at the table.

The meal that had been delivered was nothing short of a smorgasbord. Amongst the food were a heaping plate of crisply fried bacon and a platter of boiled eggs still steaming in their tiny cups and topped with pepper and spices. There were fluffy, moist pancakes with powdered sugar, maple syrup, honey and fresh sweet cream to side. A large carafe of coffee and a pot of tea sat side by side with cream and sugar between them.

Flagons of freshly juiced apples were the first thing Orangecloak found herself reaching for. Apple juice wasn't something she had tasted since she was a girl in her first life. The taste was savoured on her tongue for a few seconds before she helped herself to the rest of the feast.

Tryst dove in hungrily, taking a heaping portion of bacon, four boiled eggs and a slice of toasted bread for himself quickly. To top it all off was a tall mug of coffee, taken with cream and a pinch of sugar. Orangecloak, Ren and the Dupoire family ate more modestly, taking small servings from each offered.

It was the pancakes Orangecloak found herself enjoying most of all, with a dash of powdered sugar and a gob of honey atop them.

The tea on hand was a black variety that Kevane identified as a breakfast blend popular among the dwarves. When everyone else had passed on a second cup, Orangecloak decided she would finish the rest of the pot herself.

After the meal, with her second cup of tea to hand, Orangecloak was asked by Kevane to recount her escape. The prospect of which brought Tyla to the edge of her seat, where she seemed to hang on Orangecloak's every word. It wasn't a story Orangecloak relished telling, but it kept them from asking about events of the more distant past and for that she was glad. Those were memories she didn't think herself prepared to divulge with this audience yet.

When Orangecloak had finished, the bewildered Tyla took the chance to sing her praises. "You may not realise it, my lady, but amongst the dwarven women of the snowy lands you are seen as something of an icon."

She was taken aback by that and relayed as much. "You flatter me, Miss Tyla, I had no idea I had achieved such levels of celebrity outside human Illiastra."

"Indeed, my lady," Tyla went on. "It was not so long ago that we fought the battle for equality ourselves. Not Tinnia and I, granted, but it was the fight of our great-grandmothers to be certain, my lady."

"I'm given to understand that dwarven women share equal rights with men?" Orangecloak asked inquisitively of both women. "They're permitted a say in matters of rule in both house and state? Their wages are the same as men and they're given equal opportunity in the work force?"

It was Tinnia who took the lead on the answer to those queries. "Yes to all of that, although it wasn't granted overnight. Those things all came in their turn, but eventually we achieved the equality we so spiritedly sought."

"I find this all to be both incredibly interesting and inspiring," Orangecloak commented incredulously. "You don't find there to be resistance from your Triarchy figureheads?"

That drew a hearty laugh from Kevane. "Not at all, my lady, for we don't worship the gods here. For that you can thank your human Triarchists. They did such a marvellous job of casting the old dwarven god Aren in a villainous light, after all. Even the Valdarrow line used it as their war cry for trying to eradicate our kind from the known world. After that, my ancestors that moved into the Snowy Lands, where they formed close ties with the Elves, who, as you may know, also have no use for the gods. We learned at their feet and cast blind subscription to deities aside. What your adherents of the Triarchy call religion, we refer to only as myth."

"I was not aware of any of that," confessed Orangecloak, feeling a little embarrassed at how ignorant she must seem. "I admittedly know very little of the dwarven ways. So few of you are seen in Illiastra and the Elite Merchants maintain an embargo on your country and the Elven Forest. It's as though we are totally isolated from one another and yet all that lies between us is swaths of easily traversable land."

Tyla was quick to chime in helpfully. "That is perfectly understandable, my lady. We would only be glad to teach you of our culture and history."

"There is one thing I would certainly like to know," Orangecloak stated, giving Tryst a sideways glance as he refilled his coffee cup.

"Of course my lady, feel free to ask," Tyla happily offered from across the table.

"Tell me, how much blood was shed by your women to achieve equality?" Orangecloak defiantly put out there, her eyes firmly on Tryst while she asked it.

Tyla and Tinnia exchanged a look of sheer surprise and for a moment it seemed like no one was willing to take the question until Kevane himself spoke up in answer. "Why, none, my lady, is there a reason you ask?"

Orangecloak knew she was too far now to turn back and forged ahead with what she had to say. "It's been brought to my attention that my quest for equality is one that can't be won without a bloody conflict of some kind. I would simply like to know what dwarven women did to achieve their rights."

It was Tinnia who took the reins on that request. "The battle for women's rights in the Snowy Lands was never one that had to be fought, my lady. It happened a century ago. My great-grandfather Modo, whose statue is in the lobby, was minister in caucus for the First Minister at the time. He wrote in his journal that things were turning poorly in human Illiastra, which was then still called Phaleayna. The reason for this was that the Elite Merchant Party had just risen to power hand in hand with the Triarchy and the two were implementing Triarchist Law. The former, on demand from the latter were effectively regressing the rights of everyone that wasn't a heterosexual, human, Illiastran-born, male. My great-grandfather was part of a group of ministers that called for a study to compare quality of life among humans to that of the much more progressive Elven Forest. The results are as you see today. We strived to be more like our elven neighbours than our human ones and saw to it that equality was achieved for the betterment of our nation as a whole."

"That's quite fascinating," Orangecloak commented in earnest when Tinnia finished.

Kevane interjected before anyone could say another word edgewise. "Tinnia summarised the events a little. It was far more laborious than that, as is the nature of bureaucracy. The study was incredibly comprehensive. They composed it into a very large book, so thick and heavy that my grandfather used his copy as a footstool in his reading den. However, it did boil down to burying of stubborn dwarven pride and tradition and doing what was best for everyone."

He stopped to clear his throat before going on. "I should point out though, that the Elite Merchant Party and the Triarchy are both deeply entrenched beasts. Then there's the matter of their shared piety and it goes without saying that these are all men who feel their power is willed and backed by their supposed god, Ios. Any who feel so righteously empowered will not be led to think they could be wrong or unjust.

"Before all that though, goes greed, as Tryst bore witness to on uncountable occasions. The Elite Merchants are hoarders of wealth and power, they want everything and the thought of sharing with others sickens them to no end. These aren't men to be reasoned with rationally and they will leave you no alternative but to use force."

Orangecloak let out a despondent sigh as Kevane finished his lecture to her. "You make it seem as though my capture and subsequent rescue have put me on an irreversible path. That my new found freedom comes at the price of a bloody war that Illiastra can ill afford to wage."

"Not at all," Kevane replied nonchalantly, leaning back in his chair and hooking his thumbs in the buttoned vest of his suit. "I am just counselling you on the reality of things. We have been watching you from afar for quite some time, my dear lady, and we see your intentions for Illiastra quite clearly. All that I and the other Musicians seek to do is support those intentions with gold, steel and counsel."

"And if I reject your support? You'll let me walk off with the knowledge that this group exists? That would be foolhardy given the levels of subterfuge the Mùsicians have taken to keep their identity hidden," Orangecloak pointed out confidently.

"I was the first to say to Greggard that trying to ally with you and the Thieves was a great risk. I said it the first day that Tryst here landed on Illiastran shores, I said it when Tryst first paid visit to my hotel and I'll say it again before you," Kevane spoke wearily, exhaling when he was done. "You are, if nothing else, a rogue and rouges make for poor allies, no matter how much one might have in common with them." Kevane refilled his teacup while he spoke in his morose tone. Orangecloak could sense that he knew she wanted to speak and he gave her no grounds to do so politely. "However, beyond Greggard's ambitions in the west, there is only you and your Thieves with the potential to overthrow the Elite Merchant Party and the Triarchy. That much I acknowledge and admit while still being a proud member of the Musicians.

"I am honour bound to help my dear friend Greggard in his mission to aid you, my lady. I do all of this for him and yourself in spite my well-founded doubts in you."

It was with those last words that Orangecloak realised how much she wounded her gracious host with her ungrateful behaviour since his arrival to the room. "I should apologise, ser. You and your daughters have been most kind to me, as has Tryst and all I can seem to do is repay all of you with mistrust and suspicion. Know that I will forge no excuses for my behaviour. I merely ask that you forgive me so that I may make an honest attempt to curb these poor, long ingrained habits of mine."

At that a brief silence fell over the table, cut by Tyla, who was quick to take Orangecloak up on her attempt to make amends. "Worry yourself not, my lady. We all understand that trust is not easy for you. I see no reason why Father should deny your apology, right Father?"

Orangecloak turned her eyes to Kevane, who was stroking his beard and staring at nothing in particular. "The thing troubles me the most, my dear lady, is not your evident mistrust in anyone outside your faction. It's that you so fiercely assume that anyone else with even the slightest interest in changing Illiastra must be war mongers." Kevane stood up and pushed his chair into the table. "Alas, what you don't seem to realise is that like you, we would like nothing more than a bloodless removal of the EMP. The difference between the Musicians and yourself is that we accept that war may well be the only viable option for what we both seek. With that said, Miss Orangecloak, my daughters and I all have work ahead of us that must be completed. You'll excuse us, I'm sure."

Tinnia and Tyla stood from their places, silently agreeing with their father's decision to leave. Ren stayed seated, having said nothing since the conversation began. This was his room too, after all and he was free to stay. The disappointment on the face of the three dwarves was palpable and Orangecloak felt poorly about how she had treated them, but thought better of saying any more.

As they reached the door, Tyla stopped in her tracks and spun back to Orangecloak. "My lady, if you are feeling up to leaving your room later, I would much love to see you take in my band's performance tonight at the tavern."

"That may be just what I need, Tyla, thank you for the invitation," Orangecloak answered quickly, eager to extend them some form of kindness. "If my clothes are returned by then, I shall certainly take you up on that offer."

Tyla smiled prettily at that. "That's fantastic news, my lady, I'm sure you'll enjoy yourself. In the meantime, I'll see to it personally that your laundry is returned."

With another thank you from Orangecloak, the Dupoire family left her, Tryst and Ren to themselves.

After a few tense minutes had passed, Ren excused himself from the table and announced he was taking the bath he had skipped the night before.

Tryst, on the other hand, seemed to be mildly upset.

He rose from the table and threw another junk of wood on the fire, staring into it for some time before deciding to utter a word. "That didn't go quite as well as I had hoped it would," he finally said in a monotone voice while twirling a toothpick in his fingers and watching the flames lick at the log.

On that point, Orangecloak readily agreed. "All I can seem to do since escaping Atrebell is repay kindness with venom. If Kevane turns me out to the cold winds, I will not hold it against him."

"I had figured it would take time for you to warm to the Musicians, if it were to happen at all. So, we shall not dwell too much on it. Besides, I know Kevane is not one to take your defensiveness to heart," Tryst stated in a lethargic voice before changing the subject. "I noticed there was no mention of Fletchard whatsoever. I wonder where he got himself to."

"Quite frankly, Tryst I couldn't care less," Orangecloak said, aware of how bitter she sounded in saying it.

That garnered a nod from Tryst, who looked disinterested in further discussion on the matter. "Very well, my lady, if I may excuse myself, there are things that Kevane and I must need talk about."

"What sort of things might those be? Anything I should be concerned with?" Orangecloak queried, still seated at the kitchen table and finishing off her latest cup of tea.

Tryst shook his head while slipping into and lacing his boots. "No, these are things pertaining to the Musicians that Kevane would not discuss with anyone outside of our group. It's nothing personal." He was at the door then, looking back over his shoulder at her. "I should be back in a few hours. In the meantime, you should take this opportunity to get all the rest you can. We will be back on the road in just a few short days."

17

ORANGECLOAK

eft to her own devices, Orangecloak took her tea to sit at the bay window she had come to like so much. The events of this morning replaying in her mind while she watched the happy dwarves on the slopes outside. The skiers were taking full advantage of the sunny day, taking to the slopes by the dozen in their thick parkas and woollen scarves and mittens.

With her tea finished and the pot empty, Orangecloak decided to retreat back to her room, where she slinked her way beneath the thick, white bedspread.

Can I really be this foolish? she thought to herself as she felt her whole body relax and her eyes grow heavy. *They're offering me a way back home, showering me in food and comfort, and all I can do in response is snap at them over a war that may never happen.*

Daylight had nearly faded when she was woken by the creaking of the door. Her room was bathed in the red glow of the evening sun as it struggled in its futile fight to keep from slipping beneath the horizon. Orangecloak rolled over to see what had moved the door, her eyes falling on the freckled maid that had set the table earlier in the day.

"My lady, I was asked to wake you," the young dwarven woman spoke in a timid, hushed voice.

"By whom? What hour is it?" Orangecloak asked sleepily as she sat up in the bed.

The maiden stepped into the room bearing the leather jacket, pants, bodice and smallclothes that Orangecloak had been wearing since her capture. "Mister Reine sent me," she explained. "He asked that I bring you your clothes so that you could dress for dinner at the seventeenth hour, it's nearly the sixteenth hour at present. Do you need any assistance?"

"I appreciate the offer, but I can get ready on my own, thank you," Orangecloak answered kindly as she threw back the covers and slid to the edge of the bed. "Who is attending this dinner?" she asked while reaching for the nearby lamp.

"It's in the tavern, my lady. The Dupoire family have invited Mister Reine, Mister Wildheart, his new traveling companions and you, of course," the maid replied quickly, laying the clothing out neatly on the end of the bed. "I was asked by the launderer to give this to you with his sincerest apologies." In her hands was a new white tunic that laced to just below the breastbone. "He said your own was beyond salvage on account of all the dried blood. He sent to the tailor for this one and Mister Dupoire is bearing the cost. It is made of very fine, double woven linen with a cloth-of-gold fringe. It's very nice if I do say so and I think it will compliment your bodice well."

Myles' blood, there had been a lot of it, she remembered.

"That's very kind of him, do give him my thanks," Orangecloak commented while taking the tunic in hand to give it her own inspection.

The maid folded her hands over her smock, standing in wait of a command.

"Might I ask your name?" Orangecloak asked of the patient, little redhead.

"It's Gayle, if it pleases my lady," she answered politely.

"Gayle, thank you for everything thus far. I can manage my clothes on my own though," Orangecloak said, attempting to dismiss the handmaiden.

The young woman was not so easily sent away though and wringed her hands nervously before speaking up. "My lady, might I speak freely?"

Orangecloak nodded. "Of course, you are a free woman and that includes your tongue."

Seeing no way to politely get the privacy she sought, Orangecloak shrugged out of the robe in front of the maid, who didn't so much as blink at the sight. Instead, Gayle went to the pile of clean clothes and returned with Orangecloak's lace underwear while she was pulling the tunic over her head.

She was clearly nervous, but there was a queer courage in how Gayle spoke. "Well...I'm a Lady's Maiden, my lady. This is my job and I would be very honoured to tend on you."

It was impossible for Orangecloak to not admire Gayle's persistence and she decided against sending her away. "Do you not mind serving rich people who treat you like you are lesser than they, Gayle?" she asked in return while pulling up her trousers and lacing up the fly.

That drew a shrug from the maid. "Some might say we all serve, my lady. There are those of us who serve the people, like yourself and those that serve only a few, like I. I don't feel like the Dupoire family thinks I am beneath them. They're very kind to me and pay me quite well."

"This morning they didn't want you or the other servants to eat at our table," Orangecloak pointed out. "Forgive me if I'm wrong, Gayle, but that certainly seems to me like they don't feel you worthy of their company."

The Lady's Maiden shook her head quickly to dismiss that notion. "No, no, that's not it at all, my lady. What they said was true: I and the others had other work to get to and had taken our breakfast already. I am assigned to overseeing the maintenance of this entire floor and I have other maids and footmen to direct. Not to mention that the other two, Marcha and Shaul, would have fallen behind on their own duties. Please don't think poorly of Mister Dupoire and his daughters for that, my lady."

"You're a free dwarven woman," Orangecloak said while reaching for her bodice to slip it on. "Why would you subject yourself to a life of service for anyone? You can hold any job you like here in the north."

That free dwarven woman didn't seem to mind the questions and didn't balk when asked. "I just like my job, I guess. I take great pride in it and it pays very well. I'm also permitted to ski at no cost for the slopes or the skis on my days off, I get generous yearly vacation time and plenty of other benefits. The Dupoires pay for any medicine I might need, they even set up a retirement fund for anyone working for them longer than a year.

"As the bastard daughter of an absent trinket peddler and a barmaid, I think I'm doing quite well."

All the while that she spoke, Gayle was watching Orangecloak as she constantly readjusted the laces on her bodice and made an offer to assist. "Might I tie that for you? It laces from the front, but I'm quite good at tying corsets and you won't have to fiddle with it all night."

Orangecloak sighed and relented. "Fine then, you may have at it," she said reluctantly while putting her hands atop her head. "What did you mean by mentioning your parents and their occupations, if you don't mind my asking?"

"Oh that," Gayle said, pausing for a moment while she worked on the bodice. "It's just that I come from poor parents. I don't have the same chances that say, Miss Tyla and Miss Tinnia do in life. They were born into a prosperous hotelier family that they were destined to inherit the legacy of. It gives them the money to be or do whatever they want. I simply never had those advantages, so to reach anything that's outside of the impoverishment I grew up in is a great thing, that's all I meant."

"That right there is exactly the problem, Gayle. How can you say you are a woman, free to pursue any lot in life you want when so much is closed off to you on account of your birth station?" Orangecloak rhetorically questioned. "Yes, it's leaps and bounds ahead of human women in Illiastra. We're nearly entirely without any rights at all, regardless of parentage. Yet, it's still prejudicial behaviour and I would hardly describe it as equal," she added as Gayle finished.

The maid stepped back and looked Orangecloak over. "There, that should do it. Would you like the leather jacket?" Gayle said, satisfied with her job.

"No, that's fine. I'll forego the cloaks too. I would imagine the tavern to be quite warm anyhow," Orangecloak decided, looking herself over in the mirror with Gayle at her side. "I'll need to brush my hair," Orangecloak pondered aloud.

At that, Gayle all but jumped. "I could do that for you my lady, would you also like a ribbon to tie it back, or perhaps I could braid it for you?"

"I think I'll leave it down. As for a brush, I don't have one of my own anymore. It was left behind in Atrebell when I was captured. Everything I owned, save for the clothes on my back and my orange cloak were lost on that night.

"Although," Orangecloak said, suddenly remembering. "I know both Ren and Tryst have brushes, are either of them still about?"

Gayle snapped her fingers. "Yes of course, they both have fine, long hair, they would have to have brushes," she agreed. "Mister Wildheart is here, he's reading a book he borrowed from the library. Shall I ask him for you?"

"If you wouldn't mind, I would appreciate that," Orangecloak replied reluctantly, still not warm to the idea of someone tending to her wants.

Despite her lofty position as Field Commander prior to her capture, Orangecloak had always insisted on tending to herself. There had been offers of service from former slave servants of the upper class, looking to apply themselves at tasks they were familiar with. Orangecloak had refused them all under the notion that free folk don't wait on others. Gayle was challenging that idea simply by her attendance this evening, let alone her words on the matter.

She is free to be whatever she desires and willingly chooses service, Orangecloak thought to herself as she heard Gayle asking Ren for his brush and their footsteps as he went to fetch it for her.

It was different with the liberated human slaves. They had been void of freedom for so long that they had lost all notion of what the word meant. Gayle, on the other hand, was born and raised with rights and freedoms so many in Illiastra had only dreamed of. Though, despite it all, she still felt limitations on account of her inherited social standing and had accepted a job waiting on the affluent.

Almost as quickly as she left, Gayle returned with Ren's fine hairbrush to hand. As much as she tried, Orangecloak once again had to relent and let Gayle dote on her.

The woman began the task of brushing the tangles from the red locks of Orangecloak with long, gentle strokes. The two were quiet while Gayle went about her work, with Orangecloak seated on a low chair to bring her to the height of the dwarven maid.

"There you are, my lady. I think that should do it, unless my lady has changed her mind in regards to leaving her hair down," Gayle said with a pat on the shoulder when she finished.

Upon looking herself over in the mirror and being quite satisfied with the result, Orangecloak turned back to the maid. "Thank you very much, Gayle. I suppose I should make my way to the tavern. I would like it if you joined us for supper at least, surely your work day is near finished now? It would please me to share wine and cheer with you."

"I appreciate the generous offer, my lady, but I have a few things left to do that will keep me until after supper, I'm afraid," Gayle replied politely, placing the brush on the dresser that stood beside the full length mirror.

"Then after supper, perhaps? Tyla will be performing and I hear that she and her band are quite good," Orangecloak said, holding steadfastly on the matter.

Gayle was even more stubborn in her declination. "Once again you flatter me with your offer, my lady. Though once again I am afraid I will have to turn you down. I am quite exhausted and would prefer to retire to my quarters and read a book. I'm reading a most delightful romantic tale by the elven author Cheltay and I would much like to get back to it, begging your pardons. Besides, I've been working here at the hotel for nigh on six years now and I have seen Miss Tyla performing many times. Thank you, though. I am flattered by the invitation, my lady."

Something Gayle said surprised Orangecloak and she stopped in her tracks. "You can read?" she asked uncertainly.

The question seemed to baffle Gayle. "Why of course, my lady. I don't understand your confusion. If I might be so frank to ask, do humans not read? I had thought they did."

"Those of the upper classes of society generally know how to read. I myself was taught at a young age, but I am the exception amongst those born poor," Orangecloak answered, growing despondent as it dawned on her why Gayle found her question so confusing. "Among human women there's even less who know how to read, I'm afraid. Education is something of a privilege and only children of parents who can afford the schooling ever learn to read and girls are not permitted in school. There are some, like me, who learn to read by less conventional means and girls of wealthy families are usually tutored, but most never have such an opportunity."

Gayle put a hand to her chest empathetically. "I can't imagine a life where I could not read. My goodness, just to think of all the wonderful knowledge and stories they are all missing out on. I think there is something profoundly wrong with a nation that doesn't see the value in ensuring that their people have a fair chance at learning."

"I agree wholeheartedly. It is one of many things I would

change in Illiastra if I could." At that, Orangecloak acquiesced, "I shall leave you to your book, Gayle. Enjoy every word of it and take it not for granted."

With a last glance at herself before turning to the door, she looked back to the maid once more. "Thank you for everything, Gayle. I'm not sure how I'll ever repay you."

"Worry not about that, my lady," Gayle said as she followed behind, turning off the lights and collecting Ren's brush to return to him all the while. "Mister Dupoire pays me kindly and it is honour enough to be able to aid you. You're a heroine among the dwarves. Girls and women alike want to be you and men simply adore you. To think that I, Gayle Bopherson, may say that I got to wait on *the* Lady Orangecloak, oh I'll remember this day until I die. I feel it is *I* that should thank *you*."

That gave Orangecloak a pause in her step and she turned back to Gayle with a hand on her shoulder. "Oh Gayle, never think so little of yourself that you should grovel for anyone. People should aspire to greatness in their own right rather than simply seeking to worship at the feet of those they perceive as great."

"Most of us have no choice but to live vicariously through people like you, my lady, given that so few of us will ever reach such daring heights," Gayle gave in return.

"Fewer still if we don't try," Orangecloak countered melancholically.

It was there that Orangecloak left Gayle, who insisted she finish cleaning the apartment before retiring for the evening.

Ren was waiting in the sitting room for Orangecloak and joined her for the brief trip to the tavern below and they chatted while waiting for the lift to arrive. There was evident joy in Ren's voice at the prospect of traveling with his dwarven friends. Despite the fact that she would miss his company, Orangecloak was genuinely happy for the elf.

The bright and airy lobby was nearly empty at this hour, save for a single woman behind the front desk who was tending on two miners checking in. When Orangecloak had seen the lobby last, it was lit by the natural sunlight filtering in through the magnificent glass windows. Now though, it was bathed in the glow of a pair of ostentatious chandeliers that gave the room an entirely different, albeit equally wondrous, appearance.

For a moment she lingered, looking over the polished bronze statue of Modo Dupoire and the expansive lobby in which he stood.

The tavern she was led to was lowly lit, as most taverns she had ever seen were. Unlike most taverns though, its ceiling was high and airy, allowing air to circulate rather than grow stuffy and odorous with the smell of perspiring people.

Two of the walls were lined with semicircle booths upholstered in leather with dark wooden tables of a reddish hue. Above each table hung an electrically lit chandelier on ornate iron chains, casting light for the diners of the tavern to see their plates. The last walls were given over to a long bar and a short stage, standing adjacent to one another.

The bar was lined with stools, most of which were occupied by dwarves of all walks of life. Miners in dungarees were chatting with skiers in knitted wool sweaters with colourful patterns. Mead, ale and wine were flowing as fast as the barkeeps could fill the cups and merriment was alive in the air.

Upon the stage sat a variety of instruments but no musicians to play them, leaving Orangecloak to surmise that she had arrived early.

Of her company she saw no sign at first until a stout, middle aged, beardless dwarven servant approached to get the attention of her and Ren. "Good evening, Milady Orangecloak and Mister Wildheart," the dwarf said with a polite bow. "Mister Dupoire bid me to wait on your arrival so that I might direct you to the table he has reserved. If you would follow me please, it is right this way."

The fellow turned quickly on his heel and strode off to Orangecloak's left, leaving her and Ren to follow behind to an expansive corner booth and familiar faces enjoying wine and ale.

"Ladies and gentlemen," the serving dwarf spoke up upon reaching the rounded table and the guests seated behind it. "I present to you Her Lady Orangecloak and Mister Tyrendil Wildheart."

"That's Professor Tyrendil Wildheart, Carlin," said a voice belonging to one of a pair of unfamiliar dwarves seated to Orangecloak's far right.

The servant turned red in the face and bowed in apology before Ren. "Please accept my sincerest apologies for the error, Professor, I had not known."

"Not to worry, my good man, it's not your fault for I had not spoken of it myself." Ren said with a polite bow of his own.

Until now it had not dawned on Orangecloak that Ren was such a renowned person in his own right. Ren had made mention that he was employed by the Midlands University of Gildriad. Though, in Orangecloak's defence, Ren had not once had he asked to be called by his title or corrected anyone for calling him *Mister* Wildheart.

The dwarf that had corrected the waiter and another beside him slid from the upholstered bench and insisted the standing guests be seated beside them.

Orangecloak sat first, bringing her shoulder to shoulder with Tryst Reine, his extensive red mane tied into an elaborate trio of braids. With one to either side of his face and the thickest braid running down his back, he looked to Orangecloak like a painting she had seen of a dwarven warrior of ancient days.

"Good evening, Tryst. How fared your day?" Orangecloak greeted him.

"Good evening to you as well," he replied gaily. "My day was quite productive, thank you for asking. What about you, my lady? How was your afternoon?"

Orangecloak was thrown off by his suddenly jovial nature, but she answered him anyway, sensing a reason behind it. "It was an entirely relaxing afternoon, I admit. Once you left, I slept it away in the absolute comfort of my soft bed," she spoke amiably to Tryst as Ren and the two dwarves took their places beside her.

"Goodness!" Ren said from Orangecloak's left, loud enough to nearly startle her. "Where are my manners this evening? My lady, might I introduce you to Radmer and Edwin Pylas. They are former pupils of mine who graduated from the Midlands University to become Power Generation Engineers in their own right."

Reaching across the table, Orangecloak shook their hands in turn. "It's a pleasure to make your acquaintance." The conversation threatened to stall for a moment until Orangecloak thought of a question that might spur it on. "You two have the same last name, are you brothers or cousins by chance?"

The two dwarves chuckled to each other at the question. "Neither, my lady, we're husbands," Radmer answered while laying a hand lovingly atop Edwin's.

Upon looking for herself, Orangecloak saw matching wedding bands. "That's absolutely wonderful. I had known that same gender marriage was legal in both Gondarrius and the Elven Forest and I must say I'm delighted to meet a wedded couple. Would it be presumptuous of me to ask how long have you been married?"

"Not at all, my lady," Edwin spoke up. It had been he who corrected the waiter moments before. "We've been married since we were students of Professor Wildheart in Gildriad. It's legal there too, after all. Yes, it's been almost five love-filled years for us now."

She nodded and for the first time in as long as she could remember, Orangecloak even felt herself smile. "I couldn't be happier for you both. I wish only that my fellow humans of Illiastra could love so freely. We've been fighting for it, I and the Thieves, that is and quite a number of them are openly gay." Orangecloak sighed and shook her head sadly. "The Triarchy deems homosexuality a crime though, on account of their scriptures, and the Elite Merchants upholds the Triarchy's ridiculous laws."

Ren clicked his tongue off his teeth as Orangecloak spoke, his gaze off somewhere in the distance. "The Triarchy is a potent poison in the well of knowledge." Looking at Orangecloak from the corner of his eye, he went on. "Why else do you think they hate elves, amaroshans and dwarves so much? They've always hated us, to be sure, but until the Elite Merchant's took power they had no hand with which to flex against us. Once the EMP was squarely in place, they wrapped that hand about the Forest and have held it there since, choking off our contact with the outside world.

"We will not give in, though," Ren said, quite vociferously. "Not then, not now and not ever. The elves and our half-blooded brethren will persevere, as will the dwarves, who are as figuratively garrotted as we are by the theistic fanatics that hold Illiastra. You may not realize it, or perhaps you do now, but both nations here in the north have been rooting quite heavily for you, my lady. I dare say that when I return to the Elven Forest, I shall be reporting to the Council of the Nine Realms of the Forest to let them know that you live and to advise them to lend you support should you so ask for it."

"I was not aware I had such supporters." Orangecloak stared at her hands folded on the table in front of her as she talked. "Then again, until a few days ago I had not known that I had any supporters at all outside of the Thieves. It would seem a network of allies was in arm's reach but I could not see a hand before my face with which to grab onto them."

"That is through no faulting of your own, my lady,"

Orangecloak heard from across the table, looking up to see the Dupoire family seated opposite of her and Tinnia doing the talking. She was clad in a sleeveless, samite dress of bright red to match her ruby lips. With her dark brown hair tied up, it left her slender shoulders bare but for the straps of her gown running to meet at the back of her neck. "Just as the EMP and the Triarchy have made a point of making the dwarves and elves feel isolated, they have done the same to you. It is only natural that you feel so alone in this world save for those directly in your presence."

"This is known, my lady." Tyla took up her sister's reasoning, with her warm eyes and pursed lips, still basking in Orangecloak's presence. The younger sister had opted for an orange dress, no doubt done in a tribute to their vaunted guest. Tyla's gown was entirely strapless and studded around the breasts with tiny, white and silver gemstones. "It was our hope that we could show you that your Thieves are not so different from the Dwarves of Gondarrius and the Elves of the Forest. We all seek the same thing, albeit for slightly different reasons."

It was Kevane nodding along with them, speaking up when the younger had finished. "My daughters are right, my lady. We and the Elven Forest would only seek to work alongside you, not through you, as you suspected. The entire continent of Illiastra would benefit greatly from the removal of the Elite Merchants and the Triarchy, and to do that we need cohesion between elf, dwarf and human alike. The first two we have had for some time, now we just need a united contingent of the last. To that end, we firmly believe it is you who can unite the human populace against our common enemy."

"I owe you all a great deal," Orangecloak bowed her head in saying. "If not for Tryst and Ren, I realise I would be dead beneath Atrebell. Then, the Dupoire family graciously opened their doors to me and aided in getting me back to full health, at least physically. I feel I should apologise for my behaviour this morning, to Kevane especially, you did not deserve to face the wall I put up nor will I make excuses for it. It was a poor move in light of all that's been given to me freely by all of you. I don't know exactly what you want me to do nor do I believe I am such a prophetic hero as you make me out to be. Yet, I will make every effort to listen to your offers and meet them to the best of my abilities if I can."

"That is all I have ever asked, my lady. I accept your apology and I thank you for it," Kevane said with a final, approving nod. "I'm growing famished. Tyla, seeing as how you're on the outside of the booth, would you be a dear and tell Padraig to bring forth dinner?"

The others began talking amongst themselves as Tyla went off to do as her father bid and Orangecloak leaned in to Tryst to speak quietly to him. "You don't suppose Kevane was withholding food just for that apology? Surely he had no way of knowing that I would come forth with it so quickly?"

She heard Tryst stifle a laugh as he reached for the mug of ale resting before him. "No, my lady, merely a pleasant coincidence, I assure you. Kevane is not a man to stave off dinner for any reason." Tryst leaned in close. "By the way, I couldn't help but notice that you were talking to Ren's friends a few moments ago, my lady."

"What of it?" Orangecloak turned her head sharply to face him, having been staring at her hands once again.

"You should smile more often, like you did then. It really suits you, if I do say so," Tryst said with a coy little smile of his own smattered across his face.

She answered him with a shrug, not sure what he wanted her to say, and she steered the conversation away from the scarcity of her smiles. "Your hair looks quite nice braided like that, what made you decide on it?"

"This was Tyla's notion and she did it herself. She's interested in all things pertaining to the Musicians and is a candidate for future membership, so she sits in on meetings. Today, with it just being Kevane and I, it was a relaxed environment. Tyla started braiding while she listened to us and here we are." There was amiability in how Tryst spoke about the whole thing and Orangecloak noticed he continually met eyes with Tyla across the table while he talked.

"Yes, they're both lovely women that Kevane has raised," Orangecloak started to say, until a dark shape in the corner of the bar started to move from the lump of a position it had been in. She felt the hatred that had ebbed over the last day or so come welling up in her once again and tried to choke it down to keep a civil tone. "So that's where he ended up," she said in a low voice for Tryst's ears only.

He glanced over her quickly to see who Orangecloak was referring to before answering. "Fletchard's been in a drunken stupor since he found the tavern. When they closed up the place last night, he refused to return to our room and decided he would rather sleep on a chair in the lobby."

"For once he and I agree on something," Orangecloak spitefully commented, before Tryst went on.

"As it were, Tinnia happened to disagree with the both of you," Tryst explained. "She decided they couldn't have a drunken, human lout becoming a fixture in what is the face of the Hotel Dupoire. Since he wouldn't return to the room where we are, they gave him his own on the second floor. Well away from us and out of sight of the guests."

Orangecloak added to that thought, "And here he is, back in the tavern once more and entirely inebriated. Do you plan to sober him before we depart?"

"I shall speak to him about it tomorrow." Tryst nodded as he reached for his mug of golden ale. "I plan to leave two days from now and he'll need a day to deal with his hangover. I'll also have Tinnia cut off his service at the bar if he refuses to comply. However, I don't think Fletchard will give us any grief on the matter. As luxurious as the roof over his head is, he's a prisoner. There is no place in Illiastra for him to go. Gondarrius and the Elven Forest will give him no sanctuary and any place south of here will arrest him immediately and mail him straight to Biddenhurst. No, that man needs to leave this continent and the only way he'll do that is through me. That fact alone shackles him in a way that iron fetters cannot."

A line of dwarves in white, button down shirts, black bowties and slacks came through a door behind the bar, all carrying trays bearing multiple plates of food. Kevane clapped and rubbed his hands together at the sight. "The food has arrived at last and not a moment too soon, I might add," He exclaimed.

Orangecloak reserved further comments on the sullied bounty hunter as the servers arrived. The Dupoires' table were given priority over all the others, getting the first three trays of food delivered directly to them.

A hearty soup in a dark broth was the first course of the evening, which Kevane explained to Orangecloak and the others, was called Muskox Soup. Having only heard of muskox, they being a species of oxen found only in the Snowy Lands and Drake, Orangecloak had no idea how it would taste. However, with the first spoonful, Orangecloak was pleasantly surprised with it. The soup, which she noticed only Tryst, Kevane and herself drank entirely, was followed by the main course of peppercorn black duck served with a mixture of spiced and fried vegetables.

Having seen the face of hunger personally, Orangecloak couldn't allow a morsel of the food on her plate to go to waste and stifled her own displeasure at those who did. Upon noticing as much, Tryst ensured his plate was also empty, complementing the Dupoires' on a fine meal only when he placed his used, linen napkin on the barren porcelain.

The others left their plates half full and Tinnia and Radmer seemed to have barely touched theirs at all.

Wastage is the price of opulence, Orangecloak said to herself.

Once the last course was cleared away, black tea and blacker coffee were brought forth in urns and a desert of blackberries in sweet iced cream was served along with it.

The iced cream brought a wave of old memories for Orangecloak that dated back to her childhood and she dwelled within them with every taste.

Iced cream was father's favourite treat and it became mine too, She remembered sadly. *I tried so hard to be like him, to not let the fact that I was but a girl restrain my ambition. Most would heed the lesson to be found in his fate and abandon such pursuits. Yet, here I am, and despite the fact that I should be dead twice over in my own right, I'm still trying to be like him. Would he be proud of me right now, sitting here with powerful allies eager to help me while I push them away? Would he tell me to forsake nonviolence and take up arms against the foe or encourage me to stay true to my methods? If only I had such knowledge, it would make this all so much easier.*

With the dish of cream and berries now empty, she pushed it away and turned her attention to an urn of black tea.

Excusing herself and bowing out, Tyla retreated to find her band members so that they might prepare to take the stage. Her sister, on the other hand, had engaged herself in conversation with Ren and his former pupils about their windmill-generated power project, a subject the husband dwarves were quite eager to speak of.

Tryst and Kevane were both watching a swaying Fletchard, who was now in a heated battle against both gravity and inebriation to stay seated on his barstool. No matter how much pity Tryst tried to throw Fletchard's way, Orangecloak could only feel hatred for him.

For as long as I remember Myles and Coquarro, nothing will alter that river of contempt.

"Ladies and Gentlemen!" the singsong voice of Tyla boomed from upon the stage where she stood with her violin to hand, catching the attention of Orangecloak and the remaining company at their booth. "It is with my pleasure that I present to you our band, *Children of Graelin,* for your evening entertainment." The gathered audience gave applause as a quartet of dwarves joined Tyla on the raised, varnished, wooden platform beside the bar. A blond, longhaired male with a beard tied in elaborate plaits was first out, taking a position behind a set of five drums lined in a semicircle. Behind him came another male, dark of hair, slender of frame and bearing a flute and lastly a woman that looked to be the flautist's sister bearing a stout, little guitar. As the applause died down, the blond man began thumping his drums with the palms of his hands to an uplifting beat.

The crowd, recognising the song, all rushed the dance floor at once before Tyla and the other two could begin to play their own instruments. Edwin grabbed Radmer by the hand and the two disappeared into the throng as the tavern came alive with the cheerful music and merry dancing.

"This one's called *The Harvest Dance,*" Tryst explained, as he leaned in close to be heard over the music as violin, flute and guitar became one together with the beat of the drums. "It's a standard for Tyla's band and I love their rendition of it," he said joyously while his right hand tapped along on the table in time with the drums.

"I think I have heard it before, though played only with a lute and not so well," Orangecloak commented. "There was a bard that lived in the Phaleaynan ruins for a time and this sounds like one of the songs he would play for us."

Tryst leaned in again to reply, his eyes squarely on the band dancing about to their own music. "Ah, so you're familiar with it, then. I wasn't sure."

Playing her violin in the middle of the stage was Tyla, directly in front of the drummer, her feet tapping away beneath her to the rhythm of the song. Occasionally she would add a spin to the routine, making the orange, chiffon dress gracefully swirl about her.

Ren, who had his back to Orangecloak since the music began, slipped from the booth and turned to face her. "My lady, would you care to dance?" he asked with a beaming smile.

"No thank you, Ren, I don't quite think my knees could bear dancing to such a lively song. I appreciate the offer, though,"

Orangecloak said, thinking to herself that perhaps her answer came a little too quickly. The elf nodded and turned his attention instead to Tinnia, who gladly accepted the invitation.

Before Orangecloak could blink, Ren had the dwarven lady out on the floor and the two of them were dancing up a storm happily. It wasn't until minutes later when the song came to an end that either elf or dwarf seemed to stop and take a breath.

The crowd broke into applause and the lads and ladies at the bar thumped their steins and mugs and demanded another song. "Dancers, stay to the floor and take your partner close to hand!" Tyla spoke excitedly above everyone, biding time while the other female on stage exchanged her guitar for what looked like the same instrument with a thicker body, a longer neck and four strings instead of six.

"That's an odd looking guitar," Orangecloak commented aloud to no one in particular as the band began playing a waltz led by notes of the flute and a simple drum line.

"Not a guitar at all," Tryst replied. "That there would be a bass."

"Now I'll certainly have to call your bluff on that one," Orangecloak responded sceptically. "A bass is a large instrument that has to be stood on the floor, she's wearing this one with a leather strap like a guitar and it's not near as cumbersome."

Tryst's tone was light and whimsical as he responded again. "Indeed, we are both right on that account. The dwarves found human basses to be unwieldy things and made some innovations to it. The result is that hybrid of guitar and bass that Quail is playing."

Orangecloak found herself nodding curiously at that information. "Is that so? Her name is Quail, you say? She's certainly quite pretty, isn't she?"

"Yes and the fellow with the flute is her brother Qarl. On their own they're the *Sallard Siblings*. Together with Tyla and Alton Standish back there on the drums, they're the *Children of Graelin*," Tryst explained readily, eager to be talking of the band. Orangecloak could tell that music was of great interest to him and she let him go on without interruption. "Now this song is called *Lovers by the Brook*. It's a classic, I'm sure you must know it."

"Why yes, now this one I know quite well," Orangecloak answered amiably as she turned to face the musicians, watching as they swayed softly to the sounds emanating from their instruments.

Behind her, she heard Tryst clear his throat tellingly and she waited for him to speak.

Orangecloak already had an idea of what he wanted to ask and was wrestling with the answer as Quail began plucking out a slow tempo beat on the bass guitar.

"I was wondering, my lady," Tryst began to ask, his voice oddly nervous. "Could I have the pleasure of this waltz?"

There it is, she thought to herself quickly while trying to find a reason not to take him up on the offer. "Well..." Orangecloak started in while turning in her seat to face him. *I have no reason to refuse. What do I say?* When no reason to deny him came to her mind, she had nothing left but to accept. "Very well, though I'll give you fair warning that I'm no dancer."

"That's quite alright, my lady. I'm quite comfortable leading," Tryst said as he slid from the booth and took her hand in his.

She waited for Tryst to step out onto the floor, whereupon he gently took her hand and led her out amidst the sea of dwarves and the lone elf.

Tryst took her through the steps easily at first, guiding her through the pattern until she caught on to it quickly. "I knew you would have no trouble picking up on it," he complimented her. "You're known for your footwork when it comes to running and climbing after all. I had a feeling that it would translate well to the dance floor."

"So you say," Orangecloak answered as she leaned in close and followed his steps.

There was an effort on her part to not let herself get lost in looking upon Tryst, but Orangecloak just couldn't resist.

It's those emerald eyes of his, they pierce deep and hold tight, she tried to convince herself as he looked back at her fondly.

Tryst leaned in close to her ear. "You see, my hunch was right. You have not missed a step thus far, my lady."

Orangecloak found herself almost laughing at that. "It's not me, Tryst. I'm merely following your lead."

"I'll take that as a compliment," answered Tryst with a beaming smile from ear to ear.

They lapsed into silence after that, letting the music guide them as they moved about in close step with one another. Orangecloak began to recall the lyrics, picking up into the last verse and singing along with it.

She realised suddenly that she wasn't the only one putting

lyrics to the song that the band omitted from their performance. "If I were to hold your hand and touch your lips, out where the entire world could see. If our love was given wings and allowed to soar above the trees," Orangecloak heard Tryst quietly sing.

His voice is as sweet and golden as honey, Orangecloak thought while she listened intently to the words as they passed his lips.

"Then no more would I go a-wanting, no longer would this pain come a-haunting. Until such day as my love is free, unsaid lovers by the brook are what we'll be." Tryst finished the song softly and in perfect timing with the lonesome wail of the flute.

As the flute faded out, Tyla picked up the outro with the delicate dance of her bow upon the strings of the violin.

Orangecloak let her eyes wander back to Tryst's, and allowed their green glow to whisk her away to some distant place where pain and worry were things unknown.

For the first time since her world collapsed in Atrebell, she was able to forget everything.

18

ELLARIE

or the briefest of moments, Ellarie had felt relieved to be in Biddenhurst. Before she could even fathom how queer a thought that was, it evaporated and gave way to a sickening dread in the pit of her stomach.

The last few days had been one nightmare after another that began with their being paraded through Atrebell in the wagon with the iron bars. All the while, that fat Patriarch of the Triarchy and his fellow clergymen encouraged the many onlookers to hurl curses of condemnation at them. Curses soon turned to small stones and rotting produce and had it ended there, Ellarie would have let it go.

The procession had been intercepted by Lord Mackhol Taves and an entourage of suits and guardsmen in the southeast square of the city. The scorn and contempt they had rained down upon the captured Thieves was matched only by the sheer malice Ellarie and her company felt for them in return. After the fop was done with his little speech, he had pointed to something overhead. Ellarie hadn't thought to look, not at first, until she heard Merion recoil in horror.

Someone had taken the time to gibbet the bloody corpses of Myles Stodden and Coquarro Lo-Qoia, who had been their friends and Orangecloak's bodyguards in life. Until that moment, Ellarie had assumed them to be alive and merely locked away in the Atrebell manor with Orangecloak.

Their bodies were in a grisly state and Ellarie could only look for a few seconds before turning her eyes away in equal parts sorrow and disgust. Poor Myles, she could still his lifeless form swaying there, tempting the crows and magpies that had taken to the gloomy, overcast skies above.

There was squabbling then, between Lord Taves and Sergeant Akers, who was in fact an old friend of Ellarie and Merion. The latter was as stubborn and unfazed as Major Burnson when it came to retaining the prisoners until the last minute and Taves had begun to grow irate.

The exchange had only come to a halt at the doors of the train car, and with it came the last Ellarie saw of daylight for several days. One by one they had been led from the barred wagon and stuffed into cages so low that rising higher than one's knees was impossible. Even lying down was reduced to a state of curling into a ball. She had tried to lie that way as much as possible, listening to the clacking of the train as it rolled along the rails, everyone's chains harmoniously rattling along with it. Her elbows and knees were cramped and aching within hours of being crammed into her tiny space and did not relent until she was removed from it.

For the duration of the ride, she had been caged up between Lazlo and Merion, and at first they had tried to talk in the pitch black car. The guard left to stay in the rolling wooden box that reeked of human waste had not appreciated that, and started kicking at the cages until they quieted down. He had promised beatings if he had to return to them again, so Ellarie gave him no further reason to have to be disturbed.

The cage was decrepit and she felt filthy for having to lie in it. By the time they had pulled her out by the chain between her feet, Ellarie had felt relieved to be anywhere outside of that inhuman entrapment. Once on the barren, gravel ground of Biddenhurst though, that feeling of freedom fled.

Upon being unceremoniously booted off the train, the band of ragged Thieves were immediately assembled in a row and fitted with heavy collars that linked them to one another. At that juncture, they were reunited with Corporal Cornwall, who somehow had become even more cross than he had been before. He shouted and spat upon them, trying to elicit a response and give him reason to inflict more punishment.

Ellarie had refused to give him so much as a wince and for their part the others held out admirably too. Even Lazlo, much to Ellarie's surprise, had remained quiet. She had expected him to protest Cornwall's treatment of them, yet he had kept his head low from where he had been positioned directly behind her.

After a slow trek, the prisoners were ordered to stop before a row of buildings that to Ellarie looked like a military barracks. The Corporal began to call out to those who might be within and encouraged them to come out and gaze upon his captives. Men with uniforms in various states of dress stepped out through the doors or leaned out the windows and looked upon the macabre display. Some even came close enough to touch and inspect the sorry lot, judging them silently or commenting disparagingly to Cornwall and the other men-at-arms in his command.

The Corporal finally made a move to end the showcase and continue the slow journey to what Ellarie could only assume was a cellblock. Prior to the first step being taken, the sound of a rattling chain cut through the low chatter of the gathered guards.

"What in the blazes is that?" Ellarie heard Lazlo mutter from over her shoulder and she turned her head in the direction of the noise to see for herself.

From within the barracks emerged a woman in a torn and dirty dress. She was shackled at the feet and moving along as quickly as her restraints would allow. The Corporal's face immediately turned beat red with rage as he watched the prisoner approach.

In years gone by, Ellarie had supposed that the woman might have been pretty to look upon, but now she was the definition of unsightly. Her nose was bent at an odd angle, clearly having been broken and improperly set back, if it was set at all. There were but a few, yellowed teeth left in a mouth fixed in an awkward, terrified smile and her long, dark hair was limp, greasy and stringy. One eye even seemed to droop lower from the other.

I have seen pit fighters with faces in better shape, Ellarie noted.

"Milord, you've come back alive, I had been praying for you since you left," the strange woman spoke in a voice that was brimming with apprehension as she neared.

"Billie, what are you doing?" Cornwall addressed her sternly, trying to repress the palpable anger displayed across his face.

"I...I thought you might like it if you had a woman to greet you upon return is all, milord. I had missed you so terribly," she answered, apprehension turning to dread.

A vicious backhand caught the poor thing in the face and she tripped in her shackles into the dirt. The corporal dragged her back to waist level with a handful of hair and gave her another taste. "You do not presume to do anything, you dirty whore. I told you to never be seen with me in any capacity, did I not?"

"You did, milord, I'm sorry, I swear," Billie pleaded.

Cornwall began to kick at Billie from where she lay and Ellarie closed her eyes rather than watch as he spat and yelled. "Do not call me, 'milord' you wench! How many times must I remind you? Get up! Get up on your miserable feet!"

"Is this her?" asked a particularly tall guard as he grabbed Merion by the face and turned her to face him. "Is this the Lady Orangecloak?"

The Corporal scoffed and rolled his eyes. "Does that look like Lady fucking Orangecloak to you, you dumb shit?!"

"Aye, she got the red hair, pale skin and freckles and she looks about the right size," the guard answered indignantly while cracking the knuckles of his free hand with his thumb.

"That's the Red Bitch, not Orangecloak, you imbecile," Corporal Cornwall shot at the towering guard with blatant condescension.

The guard spat on the ground and released Merion from his grasp. "I reckon that if a certain nitwit doesn't address me with a little more respect, that I'm going to make *him* a red bitch."

The colour drained from Cornwall's face and he looked everywhere but back at the big lad. "I didn't mean to say that, Corporal Hill, I apologise."

"I'm glad you have the sense enough to apologise, I would hate to have to do to you what you've done to our poor washerwoman," the tall guard commented in a voice that was calm, yet underlined with a subtle rage.

Ellarie never thought that she might not hate a guard of Biddenhurst. However, at the moment she was willing to forgo loathing the tall guard named Hill as he stared down Corporal Cornwall.

"Now, why don't you be a good little shit and get this lot to where they are supposed to be without delay," Hill ordered Cornwall. "Or a superior officer or two might just hear that you've been housing a slave in your quarters to fuck and beat bloody. Do you hear me?"

"Very well, Corporal Hill, is that all?" Cornwall replied, still refusing to meet the other guard's eyes.

"Aye, now get out of my face and take the washerwoman with you. I'm not to find her in your quarters again. In fact, I want a new, better looking washerwoman and if I so much as see a nick on her face, I will ensure you get the same. I've tolerated you long enough and this was the last straw," Hill said, giving no room for Cornwall to argue and leaving him standing there, browbeaten before his spectating peers.

As much as Ellarie wanted to find it amusing, she sensed that Cornwall would direct his anger at his prisoners before they reached whatever cells awaited them.

"Move, you flea-bitten bilge rats," Cornwall growled at the lot of them. "I've got to get you idiots to the Gallows Hotel before someone deems you all late and you're punished for your tardiness."

The shuffling march of the rattling chains continued on, with Cornwall muttering curses under his breath all the while. The joy he had found from showcasing his captives had gone from him and his subordinates were careful to not worsen his mood.

The prisoners were led down gravel streets in feet covered only in linen wraps. They moved past ominous stone buildings two and three stories tall with iron bars across every window and heavy wooden doors in iron bands.

In this world, down here behind the high walls of what was once said to be a beautiful city, there seemed to exist no other colours but brown and grey. Just looking about was enough to sap the hope from even the most optimistic of people. Everywhere that Ellarie cast her eyes she saw a place built solely to snuff out the human spirit and instil misery and despair.

They passed an emaciated woman chained to a post by a heavy, iron collar. She was lying face down in the dirt, freezing and shivering in the chilled autumn wind. The poor thing stirred as they walked by, though only briefly, indifferent to the marching prisoners and their own suffering.

Further down, they encountered a man who was left to dangle by the feet from a wooden beam structure. Whether or not he had been alive when he was suspended was unknown, but there was no doubt the life had left him by the time Ellarie had spotted his body.

The count of the suffering and the dead continued to rise and

Ellarie began to feel more eyes upon the group. From behind the iron bars of the windows in the buildings they passed, she saw those eyes, as dead as the dangling man.

Hope has fled them, Ellarie realised as she espied a haggard man peeking from his cell window at her. *That is how Biddenhurst breaks its prisoners and that is why no one escapes. The walls may be tall, but they might as well be only knee high when the prisoners feel that all hope is lost.*

Ellarie could only wonder what was in store for her and the others, they being of the Thieves, after all. It seemed to reason that whatever was normally inflicted upon the average citizen would be done tenfold to a member of the rebellion.

The washerwoman had been sobbing during the entire trek, her fettered ankles forcing her to match the hobbled steps of the Thieves beside her.

Ellarie only wished she could be so free. *If I had my hands loose like she does, I wouldn't be crying like a hungry babe. No, I'd find a way to get a sword and I would make a few men bleed.*

A bespectacled and freckled guard in a neatly pressed uniform came striding up the street hastily toward the morose march. "Corporal Cornwall," he began in a voice that sounded well educated. "I have just finished putting your paperwork in order. I seem to have everything I need aside from your signature. As I recall you are literate, so, if you would like to read everything over, I would appreciate you doing it now rather than later. My office is quite nearby if you wouldn't mind following me."

A huff escaped Cornwall as he glanced back over his prisoners. "I really should see them to the Gallows Hotel."

"At the pace they are walking, you will be back before they even catch sight of the building," the man stated, gazing over his glasses at Ellarie and the others apathetically. "It would be prudent to get this done sooner rather than later, Corporal. So please, come with me."

"Fine," Cornwall relented before turning to his men. "Keep walking them and keep that unsightly whore with you too and see that she doesn't wander off. This shouldn't keep me for long."

One of the guardsmen, the largest one that had beaten Coramae outside Atrebell, stepped forward to take the Corporal's place at the head of the pack.

If I had a sword, it would be you I'd kill first, you vile savage, Ellarie thought to herself as she heard the brute usher them forward.

They had trekked for some time, though managing to cover but a little ground by the time the Corporal returned, with the guard in the glasses on his heels.

"I'm telling you, Staff Sergeant, that I am not missing anyone. You may count for yourself," Cornwall was saying as they approached in a hurry.

The second man walked along the line and counted the prisoners audibly, starting with Lazlo in the rear and ending with Bernadine at the very front. "I count ten for the second time, Corporal. Your manifest claims there should be eleven. It would seem that you are missing a prisoner."

"How can that be?" Cornwall fumed as he looked over the sheaf of papers in the Staff Sergeant's hands. "We'll do a roll call right here and figure this out," he said, lifting his head and looking upon the prisoners. "Listen up, you wretched maggots, when you hear your name, raise your right hand as much as you can and declare yourself. Let's start with Jorgia Creakly, where are you?"

Shyly, she raised her hand as much as her chains would allow and the exercise commenced.

When the name Bernadine Voyer was called, Ellarie claimed it and the real Bernadine dutifully claimed Ellarie's.

Corporal Cornwall had only three names left to call when he reached the inevitable snag that Ellarie knew was coming. "Nia Hedgewall," he called, his eyes running up and down the line of Thieves. "I said, Nia Hedgewall, raise your filthy hand."

"It seems that Miss Hedgewall would appear to be the missing piece," the man in the spectacles said, stating the obvious.

The corporal grew irate at that. "How the fuck could she possibly have escaped?!"

"She slipped out just before we reached Atrebell." It was Joyce who spoke up from where she stood near the front of the line. "When you were beating the men and Coramae, she was able to escape through some loose floorboards in the wagon. I would say our Thieves have found her by now and that she will tell all of what you did."

It was all a lie, of course. Poor Nia had died along the road to Atrebell from a blunt head wound taken in the chaos on the night they were all captured in Argesse. The Biddenhurst men had taken no care of their prisoners and Nia's fate was only discovered by the Atrebell guards. That was, of course, *after* Corporal Cornwall and his men had been relieved of caring for the prisoners. Her body was placed in a pine box by the Atrebell guards with a solemn promise that she would receive a proper burial.

Ellarie had to figure that either Akers or Garr, the old writer, had added Nia's name and likely improvised information to the prisoner manifest and let Corporal Cornwall go home thinking he had eleven people in chains.

"That fucking shit of a sergeant that turned them over to us probably set this racket up," Cornwall ranted to no one in particular. "Him or that Major Burnson, those Atrebell shits are all the same. They look down on us Biddenhurst guards and treat us like filth."

The staff sergeant adjusted a black military hat on his head, revealing him to be smooth and bald where Ellarie had expected a head of red hair. He wore an irritated look on his face as he inserted his own voice between Cornwall's ranting. "Regardless of your feelings towards the guardsmen of Atrebell, there still exists a problem of us being one prisoner short. We can try to blame the Atrebell guards, but the word of a corporal versus a major or a sergeant won't get very far."

"I don't need to go that far," Cornwall answered, his eyes falling on the washerwoman.

"Billie, come here please," he called in a soft, cooing voice.

The woman dutifully obeyed as quickly as her chained feet would allow, coming to stand before him.

"You love me, don't you Billie?" he said while petting her stringy hair. As Ellarie took a wary glance at Cornwall, she caught him whispering to one of his guards who trotted out of sight for a moment.

"Yes, ser, I really do. I would do anything to make you happy," the woman answered between sniffles, trying to smile for him with her mouth of broken teeth.

A wicked sneer crossed Cornwall's face. "That's good to hear Billie, because I need you to do something for me. Go ahead and take off that dress, right here in the middle of the street. You see, it's all torn up. You'll need something new to wear in the nice place that I'm taking you to."

"I can't just take off my dress in the middle of the road, I'll get cold and people will stare at me," she feebly countered.

"Now Billie, you're a whore, remember?" The tone he took with the poor woman reeked of condescension. "You were charged with prostitution. That means you would take off your clothes for anyone that had the coin. So why wouldn't you do as you are instructed for the one you say you love?"

"I suppose so, ser," Billie acquiesced, dropping her long sleeved, ragged purple dress to the dirt in seconds, exposing her rail thin, naked form to the autumn air.

The guard returned and handed off a bundle to Corporal Cornwall. "Oh my, it would seem that Private Thatch couldn't find the new dress I had in mind for you right away. He brought you this to put on while you wait, just to keep you warm. Isn't that nice of him?"

"Yes, that's nice of him, thank you, Private Thatch," she agreed as she slid into a long, hooded red shift much like the ones worn by the captured Thieves.

Ellarie caught another guard sneaking up on Billie with an iron collar in his hands. As the woman stared longingly at the corporal, the guard wrapped the collar about her neck and snapped it shut roughly.

"Wait, ser, what's he doing? I don't understand," she answered in a desperate tone, trying uselessly to pull the collar off. "Why did that guard do that, ser, why?"

"Hush now, Billie. You're doing me a favour, remember? I need you to pretend to be one of the Thieves for me for just a little while, okay? All you have to do is tell the guards in the cell block where the Thieves are going that your name is Nia Hedgewall. Let's try it together: what is your name?"

"My name?" Billie didn't seem to be grasping what the Corporal was telling her and looked about blankly at everyone before landing back to Cornwall's sneering face. "My name is...Nia Hedgehog."

"Hedge*wall*. That's Nia Hedge*wall*. Let's try it again," he corrected Billie while leading her by the arm to the back of the line. Ellarie could hear shackles and chains being secured to the woman's wrists as she repeated the name of the slain member of the Thieves she was to impersonate. When at last Cornwall was satisfied that Billie could remember the name she was to give, he called out to the staff sergeant. "How many do you count now? That looks like eleven by my reckoning."

"It's almost good enough to work," the officer snickered in response. "You just need some white paint so you can mark a prisoner number on her sleeve and I'll look the other way."

When that last step had been done, the group were sent on their way once more down the gravel streets. The going was slow and arduous and there was nothing to see but dun browns and lifeless greys of the buildings and the inhumane agony inflicted upon the incarcerated. The atmosphere the management of Biddenhurst so desperately sought to instil clawed at Ellarie with every painful step.

The Thieves passed men and women alike, some bound, others shambling aimlessly and all of them with an expression on their faces that seemed to lament their very existence.

I will not become this.

She cast her eyes downward to raw ankles, chafed bloody by the iron that ringed them, determined to look no further upon the personification of death that was Biddenhurst.

They walked beyond the edge of a street of holding cells and a sharp wind began to blow at the ugly shift that Ellarie had been made to wear. There were voices here, all male. They seemed jovial and excited in their tone and that alone made Ellarie nervous.

From the front of the pack Corporal Cornwall began cackling loudly. "Oh, you boys really know how to plan a welcoming party for my prisoners." The line was brought to a halt, though Ellarie was steadfast in her determination to not look further than her feet. "Gaze your eyes upward, maggots and behold the fate of the Thieves in Biddenhurst!"

Against her better judgement, Ellarie tilted her head back and came to regret that decision almost instantaneously.

She counted fourteen people in total, nine men and five women. They had been strung up to either side of the road in crude wooden frames. Chains held their arms tight in a V shape and their legs were bound together and moored to the ground in a second chain that was pulled bar tight. All of them were kept aloft quite high off the ground and held outward on an angle that forced them to loom over the arriving Thieves. At first Ellarie wondered how they were able to keep their heads up, then she noticed that all of them had a plank lashed to them that ran from the tailbone to the skull. A leather strap around the forehead ensured they remained in a rigid stare.

Ellarie made a point to look at them all individually, looking over their features to see if she knew any of them. Every last one yet lived, though some were hanging on by only a thread. A woman with pallid skin and tightly shaved red hair loomed above and her desperate eyes locked on Ellarie. For a moment, she thought it was Orangecloak looking back at her, but the eyes were brown and the girl was about half a decade too young.

This one knew Ellarie, quite well from the way she fiercely held her gaze and at last it dawned on her who the poor creature was: a young woman by the name of Larissa Degrant, who, for a brief period of time, had been under Ellarie's command. A fresh face who hailed from Norvale in the Torrento Region, she had made her way to Phaleayna on her own to become one of the Thieves.

Like Merion before her, Larissa bore a passing resemblance to Orangecloak and she found herself being used as a decoy for Orangecloak's protests and demonstrations. It was Ellarie who had pushed her into the role, and in hindsight it had been a mistake. While the girl was quick, she lacked the agility and experience that Merion and Orangecloak had when it came to evading capture.

It was two years ago during an operation in Geise, a large town on the northwest side of the Varras River, that Ellarie had last seen Larissa. They had lost her in the chaos when the guards had descended upon the protest. When there had been no sign of her at the meeting point and she failed to turn up at Rillis Vale or Phaleayna, they had presumed her to be dead.

Unfortunately for Larissa Degrant, she had found a fate worse than death.

Ever so cautiously so as not to be noticed, Ellarie leaned forward slightly, towards her sister Merion situated directly in front of her. "Look on your left side, nearly directly above you. Take a gander at her face."

Slowly, her sister raised her head and studied that of the overhanging woman. Ellarie could almost sense the recognition setting in before an audible gasp confirmed it.

"Larissa?" Merion whispered over her shoulder.

"Aye," Ellarie answered lowly after a deep breath. "I failed her."

"We all failed, best get used to that feeling," Merion replied in a defeated tone, putting her head back down so as to avoid having to look at the rows of tortured former Thieves' members.

Ellarie could not look away so easily, she looked upon every face strung up overhead and tried to commit their features to memory. Some she knew – if not in name, then in appearance. There were two men well beyond her in years that she recognised from Old Bansam's roving band. Another she placed as briefly being the right hand of Edwin the Raven, whom Ellarie had left as castellan of Rillis Vale when she departed. Three more of the women had been long serving members of the Phaleaynan Rangers, who guarded the shores of the lake that the island sanctuary sat amongst. Their names escaped her, but she had seen them before, in what seemed like a lifetime ago.

The last woman had served beneath Mell the Huntress. One whole half of her body was marked in the dark, heavily lined tattoos similar to those that Mell bore across her arms and chest. They served as a stark reminder of the women's days among the raiding gangs before finding their way to the Thieves.

A sickening, malicious smirk stretched from ear to ear on the Corporal as he exchanged pleasantries and congratulations with the other gathered guards. It took a while for him to grow content with the duration with which he forced the shackled Thieves to look upon their lashed up compatriots.

I will not become this.

"So, what do you think?" Cornwall asked rhetorically, his arms outstretched before the horrid display. "Your friends up there had to be evicted from their cells, since there's not much room at the Gallows Hotel after all. So, my friends here thought this was as good a place as any to put them while we got things ready for you lot. Maybe you should thank them all for being so generous as to give up their luxurious accommodations? No, your browbeaten faces say thanks enough."

"Ser, we should get moving," urged one of the guards.

Cornwall slapped his leg in his mocking, jovial façade and turned to the guard. "Oh darn, you are right. I would love to let our new guests stay and commiserate with their old friends, though. Since I'm in such a good mood at the moment, I'll make you all a deal: if you're on your best behaviour, I'll let you all come on out to say farewell before they are sent on their way. How does that sound?"

When no one answered, he clapped his hands together. "Good, I knew you would all enjoy my generous offer. Say goodbye for now so that we can move along and get you settled in to your new home."

The march proceeded and the faces of the agonised former Thieves fell out of view behind Ellarie and the others.

They were led across a wide, sturdy, reinforced wooden bridge over a dry moat filled with tall, iron spikes looming several meters below. Ellarie dared to glance down to either side of her and saw a lone corpse tangled amongst the sharp stakes. It had been there quite a while and was little more than bones and rags now. It was likely left to lie there and serve as a reminder of what happens to those who attempt to escape.

Beyond the bridge was a building, ringed by the moat and isolated. A pair of guards watched them approach from a single tower atop the stone structure, eyes fixed firmly on the rattling, red parade. "Afternoon, lads," Cornwall called up to them upon approach. "Who is running the hotel today?"

The pair exchanged a glance before the one on the right leaned out to answer. "Lieutenant Crispin, ser."

The Corporal threw his arms up happily. "Fantastic, would one of you mind running and fetching him to let him know that his new tenants have arrived?"

"Aye, ser, we'll be right out," said the same man before the pair of them disappeared down a hatch.

A silence fell over the group, one that Cornwall was not content to let stand. "Crispy is an old friend of mine, we're like brothers, even. I'm glad he is here to see my moment of triumph over such menaces to decent society."

Footsteps could be heard in the dirt and at the sound of them the Corporal went quiet and stood to attention. From around the side of the building came a man with a neat haircut, a tidy uniform and a drooping, light brown moustache. He stepped into sight with half a dozen armed guardsmen following behind in an orderly line. To Ellarie, the officer looked to be nearing forty or perhaps a little beyond that. He bore a face that had not been spared from the wind over the years, which perhaps made him look older than he might have been.

"Lieutenant Crispin, ser, it is good to see you again. I trust you have been well?" Cornwall started, suddenly full of formality again.

"I have, thank you, Corporal," the Lieutenant answered flatly in a smooth, bass deep voice. "How many do you have?"

"Eleven: three men, eight women, four among them are, or rather were, lieutenants within the Thieves, ser."

"Good. Lord Taves doesn't like having his cells empty for long, even here." As Crispin uttered the sentence, he gestured to his guards who took up positions on either side of the shackled line. "Corporal Cornwall, you and your men are dismissed to take their rest, I will take the prisoners from here."

"Ser, would I be permitted to stay?" Cornwall asked nervously.

The lieutenant considered the question for a moment. "You and you alone may stay, your men are dismissed. I will keep you here for debriefing from our superiors afterward. That will have to be done sooner rather than later anyhow, so it might as well be now."

"Yes, ser. Thank you, ser," the corporal answered with a sheepish bow.

Ellarie was beginning to think that perhaps Cornwall overstated his relationship with Lieutenant Crispin.

Cornwall thanked his superior officer and the guards were swapped, with the Corporal's men going back the way they came over the bridge.

"Take them around the corner," Crispin ordered to his men. "We shall let them see where all things shall start and end for them within these walls."

A guard near the head of the pack produced a short whip and let it crack against the backside of Bernadine at the front of the line. As the woman flinched, so did Ellarie. The strike would have likely been hers to take had they not been playing at their ruse.

"Move it along or you'll get another taste," The guard ordered, getting everyone underway once more.

They circled the building, walking between a long wall of barred windows, cold, grey stone and the open trench of sharp death.

In the distance, Ellarie saw the largest collection of scaffolding she had ever seen. It was three rows of stepped, semi-circular platforms raised into the sky, plateauing on a forth, with beams stretching across from end to end on every level. Before the whole wooden monstrosity were rows of bench seating, each one separated by rails equipped with iron rings set every half a meter. Far to the side of the benches there sat a second seating area, high up and covered with a roof trimmed with colourful bunting, its individual chairs of varnished wood and cushioned seats.

"Welcome to the Gallows Hotel, ladies and gentlemen," the Lieutenant declared proudly, sweeping his hand out in the direction of the large, wooden setup. Behind him, Corporal Cornwall began to chuckle delightedly under his breath and the Lieutenant pressed on.

"As you can see, we offer a marvellous stage show to all our residents and you lucky folks will someday get to stand on that stage yourselves and dance on air. Until that day comes, I must insist that you reside here in the hotel, where my staff and I will see to all of your needs and cater to you around the clock. Gentlemen, let's see our newest performers to their luxury suites, shall we?"

Bernadine was lashed again and this time she groaned in pain before being herded towards a tall, imposing door of darkened wood. One of the guards unlocked it and gave a yank on the large, cast iron handle. It swung open loudly, creaking all the way on hinges left without oil, likely to prevent anyone from sneaking out without making a racket.

Within they were led through a spacious living quarters and dining hall for the guards, through which sat the only means of egress from the building.

Yet another measure to prevent escape, Ellarie surmised.

The prisoners soon found that beyond that there were two back-to-back doors, one made only of steel bars and the last one of thick, solid oak. There was little light back here and the room reeked of human waste, sweat and other odours that Ellarie could not identify. The further into the long, cavernous room they walked, the more Ellarie's eyes adjusted until she saw nothing but cells to either side of her. They were tiny and unfurnished outside of some damp looking hay to one corner.

A guard stepped out and stuck a key in the first cell to the right and held open the door. Another unlocked the collar around Bernadine's neck and gave her a hard shove into the cell. She stumbled and somehow caught herself from falling headfirst into the wall. "Careful now, Private Grose, we can't have our guests getting hurt before their big performance," the Lieutenant added, eliciting a loud chortle from Cornwall.

Unabated, he continued on while Allia disappeared into a cell opposite of Bernadine and the line moved forward. "As you can see our suites offer nothing but the best for revered guests such as yourselves. You have the finest straw to sleep on and a small hole with which to do your business. Do be courteous to your fellow guests though, we only run water through the pipes once in the morning. Keep that in mind if you decide to make use of the facilities."

Coramae and Jorgia went next, doors slamming shut loudly as

they were shuffled into their confinements.

After them came Etcher, the first of the men. Joyce was released from her collar but sent further down, to the far end of the cells. "Good, let's keep the Big Bitch to herself," Lieutenant Crispin commented. In Joyce's stead they went to the back of the line and took the washerwoman standing in for Nia. She began to sniffle and sob as they locked her into the cell and looked longingly to Corporal Cornwall, who acted as he didn't know her at all. Next were Ellarie and Merion and lastly Donnis and Lazlo.

Ellarie stood still in the tiny space as the banging of her cell door rang loudly through her ears. There was some small measure of comfort knowing her sister would be across the walkway from her and within sight. Though, she quickly came to realise that her sister would be the only comfort to be found within the enclosure of brick, dirt and iron.

"Make no mistake." The Lieutenant's voice lost all the mocking tone and went deathly serious. "You will die out there on my gallows. Every last one of you will hang from the neck until the last of your life drains from your sorry corpses. This is the end of not just you, but all of the Thieves. Now that Atrebell has Orangecloak and we have four lieutenants, your band of misfits will soon be but footnotes in the history books. I recommend you come to terms with your fate, for this will be the last chapter in your sorry lives."

No, Ellarie told herself. *I will not become this.*

19
ORANGECLOAK

From where she stood atop a hill with a name unknown, the Hotel Dupoire looked like a part of Graelin's Mountain that was cut from shimmering glass. The eastern facing windows reflected the mid-morning autumn sun while the rest of the hotel slumbered beside the darkened ski slopes beside it.

After four days within its walls, Orangecloak had found herself a different woman than when she had first entered. When she had arrived, it had been through a rear door off the kitchens with battered knees, dirty clothes, wounded pride and a mournful heart. In leaving, she was clean, healthy and proud once more and the wound left by Myles and Coquarro, while still fresh, was surely healing.

The last two days at the hotel had seemed but a blur in recollection. She had slept heavily and long for much of it, having relished the short time she had a real bed to lie in.

The rest was spent with any combination of her new friends discussing a wide variety of topics that seemed to interest them all. Radmer and Edwin had visited with her and Ren, showing her blueprints and sketches of different devices for generating electrical power, particularly Ren's windmills. The elf had beamed proudly as he explained how they now dotted the hillsides of the Elven Forest and were responsible for almost all of their electricity.

Tinnia and Tyla had continued to take their meals with her, exchanging between their own commodious apartments in the hotel and Orangecloak's suite. Tyla had even invited her band mates to one meal and Orangecloak had wondered if they thought her a queen with all the fawning they had done.

The drummer alone offered to write "A hundred songs and one" about me, Orangecloak reflected genially.

Below where she stood, Orangecloak could hear Tryst and Fletchard debating the best way to navigate the road ahead. The entirely-too-loud, rough, rasped voice of Fletchard grated on Orangecloak's every last nerve as it bellowed in protest of Tryst's refusal to cross a nearby river. It was only Tryst's calm, measured tone of reason cutting through the inanity that gave Orangecloak any reassurance in where her life was headed at this juncture.

Of all the people I have met since leaving Atrebell, I'm given to travel with the only one of them that happens to be an incorrigible, amoral, alcoholic killer.

Argue as Fletchard might, Tryst was headstrong. There was a strict path Tryst planned to stay to. They were looking for a member of the Musicians named Jack Paylor, who was apparently a fifty-seven year old trapper. Allegedly, he patrolled the roads between Portsward and the Hotel Dupoire, running news and mail between the two locations for the secretive group.

Tryst had also convinced Fletchard to abstain from alcohol long enough to get himself in a good enough state to hike in. At first, Orangecloak was glad for that, although now she was debating with herself if there would be more peace with a drunken Fletchard.

That was one of the things she truly had relished about her time in the Hotel Dupoire: the space it gave her and Fletchard with which to avoid one another. Aside from the first moments within its walls, and the one occasion they were both within the tavern, the two had been able to dodge each other entirely. For that kindness alone Orangecloak felt herself forever indebted to Kevane Dupoire. Despite a tense start to their acquaintance, Orangecloak and the dwarf had come to a level of great mutual respect. By this morning, she had found herself melancholy at their parting.

Of course, leaving Ren had been harder for her to do, and Tyla was tearful during the entire farewell. With Kevane, however, Orangecloak had genuinely felt she had been unduly harsh towards the old dwarf who had offered her shelter beneath his roof.

While Ren and the Dupoire daughters had sat in the lobby and conversed with Orangecloak, Kevane had been holed up in his office with Tryst. Amidst pleasant snippets of chatter her mind wandered, thinking of what the two could be meeting about and feeling some part of it was about her. When at last they emerged, Kevane was smiling warmly at the sight of Orangecloak and the others. After their goodbyes he had hugged her tightly and wished her all the best on the roads ahead.

Tyla and Tinnia had then presented Orangecloak with an expensive gift on behalf of all the Dupoires, in extension to a replenished and extended inventory of supplies.

Lastly, Orangecloak had to bid a solemn goodbye to her elven saviour. "I'll always remember you, Professor Tyrendil Wildheart. You gave me trust, friendship, counsel and aid when you owed me none of those things. For all you gave there was nothing asked in return, and in any case, I don't know what I could give to repay you."

Ren had chuckled heartily at that, embracing her for a long hug. "Your friendship and thanks are payment enough my lady, but if I might be so bold, could I ask you a favour?"

"Of course," Orangecloak had replied hastily as she stepped back from their embrace to look him in the eyes. "If it's in my power to do, you may consider it done."

A hand as soft as silk cupped her chin to raise her face to his. "If you will give to me eternal friendship, ensure that we meet again so that your gift is not empty."

"Aye, I'll come back to the north someday, I promise. We will meet again, my friend." That vow she had spoken with determination and the words came easily and assuredly.

She now stood upon a knoll, staring at the hotel and hoping that the road she was about to embark on would bring her back to see it again. *No more looking back,* she told herself. *I'll cast my eyes ahead and hope this place comes into view once more.*

Clomping footsteps preceded Fletchard Miller, covering the softer footfalls of Tryst Reine behind him as they climbed the hill to catch up with Orangecloak from where she waited.

"Looking back at that fucking place again?" Fletchard scowled. He had been scowling the whole morning, expressing his disdain at having to walk such a long distance.

Orangecloak blamed that partially on the poor timing of the party of dwarves Kevane had sent in search of the horses that the party had been forced to abandon. The searchers had returned just as they were leaving with two of the three steeds, famished and exhausted. Of Wildstar there was no trace, as she and Tryst had both expected there wouldn't be. That courser, if it was alive still, was undoubtedly heading for Obalen. How it knew to get there, Orangecloak didn't have the foggiest idea, but Tryst claimed without reservation that it did.

Fletchard grunted at her as he passed close. "No point in looking back at that hotel. Odds are that none of us will ever live to see it again. So, get a move on, let's not stall this fool's march any more than we already have."

Instinctively, Orangecloak found her hand wrapping about the slender, deep green leather hilt of the gift given to her by the Dupoire family. An index finger weaved through a ring at the pommel and she squeezed tightly upon it until she could hear the leather of glove and hilt groaning upon one another in her grip. The blade within the sheath on her hip was dwarven blacksteel, a few centimetres longer than her hand from the base of the palm to tip of her middle finger. It was fiercely sharp, as blacksteel was wont to be and light, even for a blade so short. A slender curve gave it the appearance of a knife, but dual edges made it a dagger. An exquisite weapon and incredibly expensive, Orangecloak only accepted it upon remembering that her previous dagger was left behind in the Batterdowns of Atrebell.

Upon Orangecloak's acceptance of the gift, Kevane had gone into detail to explain why its form was the standard blade used by the dwarves for centuries without change. According to him, few daggers or knives existed that were crafted from blacksteel, as it was thought to be too precious of a metal to be wasted on small blades. So to see one was a rare occurrence in itself, to own one was rarer still.

The ring hole for the index finger, Kevane told her, made it more difficult for the dagger to be taken away from the wielder. When held with a closed fist and the blade on the pinkie finger side of the hand, the ring also gave the finger a steel knuckle of sorts, to make a punch that much more effective. There were no doubt the dwarves had spent considerable effort crafting such a useful combat tool and Orangecloak promised she would wear it proudly.

Though I never said I would use it in combat, she reminded herself as Fletchard's lone eye fell on her. *No matter how badly some people try my patience.*

She let him pass her by without comment, opting to fix him with her steely gaze instead.

"Fine then, by all means stay silent, I prefer you that way anyhow," Fletchard shot over his shoulder at her before disappearing into the thick forest beyond.

As Tryst's footfalls reached her hearing, his words did too. "Ignore him. He's projecting his own distaste for trekking on foot. Not to mention the fact that he's still battling the aftermath of a diet that has consisted almost entirely of rum."

Orangecloak felt and heard the arrows in the quiver on her left hip rattling as she turned quickly to face Tryst, who was still talking. "It's not personal, at least not that last barrage of barbs. However, I can't speak for what he might throw at you next." A gentle pat on the shoulder from Tryst accompanied his affably spoken words as he passed. "We can't waste the daylight, especially this time of year when there is so little of it. If we keep a good pace, we'll reach the Sluiceway by tonight. It will mean a rudimentary roof over our heads versus the rain that I suspect is coming. Take a moment to have a last look if you like, but you shouldn't dawdle too long, my lady."

Without answer, she gave the Hotel Dupoire a last glimpse and turned her face to the west. Orange and black cloak alike caught the westerly wind and blew away from her, allowing a gust to creep up her leather-clad body. With an adjustment of the pair of straps running from left shoulder to right hip, holding bow and satchel in place, she strode after Tryst and Fletchard.

Carrying the bow and arrows had been Ren's idea, one Tryst endorsed readily and one Orangecloak was not wholly opposed to herself. The elf had pointed out that since he was going north to Gondarrius, he would not be able to hold on to Tryst's bow. With Tryst already carrying a sword, elf blades and two satchels, he was quite nearly overburdened for a long hike. So, at that, Ren had suggested that Orangecloak should be the one armed with the fine yew bow and arrows. From there it was Tryst who carried the notion, even offering to show her how to use it if she was interested.

Orangecloak had omitted telling Tryst that before being given the title of 'Lady' she had been a highly respected archer and hunter amongst her peers in Phaleayna. Nor was she telling him or Fletchard any different now.

Better they think I don't know how to use a bow. It gives me the element of surprise should I have to brandish it, she had told herself upon agreeing to carry it.

In truth, it was an impeccable weapon made of first rate yew primarily, with a composite of sinew and rams horn. That was the Drakian style, one that emulated and came second only to elven bows in make and durability. The elves had a patented process for making bows, with access to high quality softwood that Drakians could only dream of. As a result the Drakian bows were close replicas, but could never hope to surpass their elven counterparts.

Of course, on the impoverished island she called a home in the center of Great Valley Lake, handmade self-bows were all to be had. Orangecloak had learned the craft on them first and had become quite good with it.

She had only seen a Drakian bow for the first time amongst one of Old Bansam's men and once she had seen it, Orangecloak was determined to own it. Before Bansam and his fighter with the Drakian bow had left the island for the more volatile regions of the Southlands, Orangecloak managed to barter for the weapon. When the trading was done, it had taken a good quality steel axe and two bottles of whiskey to get what she wanted.

That bow, which was still inferior to Tryst's, had become her primary hunting weapon. She became one with it, bringing down deer, elk and boar alike, providing many a meal for her kin in Rillis Vale. After becoming Field Commander of the Thieves and having the title 'Lady' added to her name, she had passed the bow on to Mell the Huntress as a peace offering.

It took my good bow and a considerable amount of concessions to bring her to my side. Now though, if she believes me to be dead and the Sisters and Lazlo are gone, I have no doubt that she will claim Rillis Vale for her own. That is of course, if Old Bansam doesn't make a claim for it himself. Garlan and Edwin the Raven are the only Lieutenants I have left and either of them would fold before the old soldier or the Raider's Daughter. If Lazlo and the Sisters remained, I would be far less worried. Those four are fearless and would never concede Rillis Vale to Mell or Bansam.

It had been known for some time that if something happened to Orangecloak that it would lead to a potentially bloody power struggle. Though from where she was right now there was little she could do to prevent it. An idea came to Orangecloak then: *perhaps when I reach Portsward, I can contact the recruiter in the West.*

Charl Summerton was a man of near seventy, who made Old Bansam seem youthful and vigorous by comparison. In her years as Field Commander however, Orangecloak knew of no better person to evaluate the worth of potential Thieves. Though long retired from active duty, the elderly military veteran maintained membership within the Thieves and served as the recruitment officer for the entire region west of Obalen. Anyone who sought the Thieves out would have to first find Charl if they wanted in and the finding was far easier than gaining the vote of confidence.

The recruiter lived in Portsward and spent a select few nights at an inn where recruits could find him if they knew where and how to look. Orangecloak had been there before and she knew the way.

He'll have news of Rillis Vale and Phaleayna, he always does, she told herself while navigating an overgrown descending path.

Below her stretched a lush, vibrant valley teeming with life. Brooks and streams crisscrossed every which way, converging into a larger river that flowed north east to south west. The view was breath taking to behold, with Graelin Mountain falling further away and the westerly peaks still looming ahead in the distance.

Down the path ahead of her was Tryst, carrying his satchel of belongings and supplies and further beyond she could see Fletchard, laden with the replenished food sack. The two of them were walking in the same direction and in close proximity to one another but Orangecloak didn't feel like they could be called a travelling party.

After a time, Orangecloak wended a turn to find Tryst stopped and waiting for her. "My lady, here, have a look at this," he called while brushing away the long red strands of his mane as they caught the wind and fell over his face. In the hand not currently reserved for hair removal was a map Kevane had given them, flapping noisily with each gust that slapped at it.

Orangecloak waited until she was at his side before answering. "What is it?"

Tryst pointed a finger at a tree on the map, directing his gaze at one before them all the while. "There's one tree here that's not like the others, a crab apple tree to be exact. It's a landmark on the map Kevane gave us." The swordsman offered her a side of the map so they could hold it up together against the competing high winds. She saw nearly right away what he was referring to. A single tree had been drawn bigger than the others with a drawing of apples upon it and inscribed with the dwarven words that she guessed were 'crab apple'.

"This must certainly be it, then," Orangecloak agreed as she glanced at the tree before them, its branches heavy with the small, round fruit. She pointed at the next landmark on the map. "This is the Sluiceway on the other side of the woods marked here then? It doesn't seem so far, we might even make it before sundown."

"That's the thing with dwarven maps," Tryst said as he took the thick, long sheaf of paper back, folding it up neatly. "They always make light of the forests. Complete opposite of elven maps, really. The dwarves spend more time pointing out rocks, odd trees and other obvious landmarks. They just draw rough green blobs for full forests and leave the size of it to the user's imagination. Not to mention they never outline pathways. It might be a simple, straight trail like the map says, but the better odds are that it's a maze in there."

Letting his eyes fall to the crab apple tree again, Tryst went on. "Elves though, they'll go into great detail to outline every possible pathway in near perfect scale. The downside is that there's so much detail on such a close scale that you need a train of mules with saddle bags to carry all the maps." He fixed her with a half-hearted grin, attempting to illicit a laugh from her.

Orangecloak nodded to show her amusement, even going so far as to lift her eyebrows, but a smile, let alone a laugh was not to come. "That's quite good," she even tried to offer, to show appreciation for the jest before quickly moving the topic along, lest it become an awkward encounter. "I assume Fletchard has gone on ahead, with our food no less. Shouldn't we catch up with him to ensure he doesn't gorge on it?"

"Aye, we should find him, though the worst I suspect he'll do to our food supply is rummage through it in hopes of there being a ration of rum amongst it." Tryst winked at her again, to show yet another attempt at witticism. "There's not, don't worry. I wouldn't dare think of allowing him another drop now that I know the hold the creature has on him."

The two of them took the time to pick as many of the ripe, low hanging apples as they could reasonably carry and made for the woods ahead. The trail before them was wide at the mouth of the forest, allowing them to walk side by side for most of it. There was little said between them as they noisily munched on their bittersweet snack and yet, that was perfectly fine. Orangecloak appreciated silent company and Tryst either respected that appreciation or liked the solace as well.

Of Fletchard she saw nothing and bore no complaints on the matter. Either he had gone on much further ahead, which got him out of her sight and gave the party a scout or he had gotten lost somewhere. In the case of the latter, aside from taking the food sack with him, Orangecloak wasn't like to miss the man.

The forest closed in around the pair as they moved through it, until it seemed as though it was the only place in the world. Here and there it was dotted with light where the sun managed to poke through cloud and canopy alike to find the forest floor and penetrate the shadows. Above their heads, a fat, red squirrel readying for the winter slumber seemed startled by their appearance and squeaked at them as they passed beneath the thick branch he rested on. All about were songbirds chirping and singing noisily to one another. They were the last of the southbound stragglers coming from beyond the Dwarven Mountains and the cold weather holdouts that stayed on after the frost fell. As foreboding as the forest seemed to be from without, Orangecloak felt it was strikingly beautiful and calming all at once within its embrace.

With the sun hanging high and gracing them with an extended visit, they came upon Fletchard, having seated himself on a fallen log along the pathway. The rogue sat with his head in his hands, staring forlornly at the ground and moaning loudly.

It was Tryst who spoke as they neared him. "What seems to be the matter, Fletchard?"

"My bloody head feels like it's going to come apart," the bounty hunter growled in reply. "If I could, I would strangle every one of them little birds that keep squawking. Is there any need for such an incessant racket?"

"You need water, alcohol is wet but it doesn't quench thirst, it'll only dry you out," Tryst advised him calmly. "That's all you're feeling now: your body is crying out for water, heed the cry and drink deeply and often."

"Oh, fuck off already," Fletchard groaned at Tryst, ignoring Orangecloak entirely to continue his complaining. "You act so smug about it, but what do you know about the drink?"

Tryst's tone fell flat and he grabbed the food sack from where it sat by Fletchard's leg. "I know well enough about it. Can you eat at the very least?"

That morning they dined on a simple meal of juicy ham and fresh cheddar cheese on sliced bread. It was plain fare compared to how they had dined at the hotel, but filling and satisfying all the same.

Orangecloak and Tryst had both taken to sitting on the opposite side of the path from Fletchard, on a mossy knoll that offered some comfort. It was as peaceful a meal as Orangecloak could hope for and she relished the relative tranquillity.

The bounty hunter was the first to finish, swaggering to his feet lazily when the last morsel of bread went down his gullet. "Right then, I'll get a move on. I would sooner be ahead of you two than behind where I can see you," he said while reaching for the food sack.

His hand was centimetres away when Orangecloak grabbed the sack first. "I'll carry it, you can go on. You've had it all morning, take a rest," she spoke in a tone that belied the generosity of the offer.

With a flick of his filthy brown cloak over his shoulder, Fletchard stomped off down the path without protest. Curses were mumbled curses at both of his traveling companions until he fell out of both sight and hearing.

Having wrapped the unsliced ham, cheese and bread back in their parchment papers, Tryst put them back in the satchel and pulled the drawstring tight. "There's no need to carry that my lady, your knees-"

"-Are nearly healed, thank you," Orangecloak cut Tryst off curtly. "I don't trust him with our food, so I would sooner carry it myself. As it is, I'm only carrying the light pack that Gayle gave me and your bow. I can manage the food sack just fine."

"Very well then, if it gets too heavy just say as much and we'll stop to rest," Tryst relented, putting his hands up in surrender.

The two got back underway themselves shortly after that, following the old pathway as best as they could. The trail winded through the forest like a river of dirt and gravel lined with a layer of fallen leaves.

The afternoon wore on, with no sighting at all of Fletchard, indicating he was keeping a faster pace than they or had veered far off the road. It was after the sun had started to slip into the west when Tryst craned his head around them, seemingly searching for the bounty hunter. "Keep a low voice," he said to her, himself barely above a whisper while he reached inside his jacket and pulled out a letter in a dark brown envelope.

"What is this?" She asked, matching his low volume as she took it to hand when offered.

She could see a smile playing at the corner of Tryst's lips as he explained. "You won't be able to read it, it's written in the dwarven alphabet and even then is encoded in a manner that only members of the Musicians would understand. However, I want you to pay attention to the signatures on the bottom, they're written plainly enough and void of our usual codenames."

The words on the paper she drew from the unsealed envelope were indeed written in dwarven letters and she didn't understand any of them. The signatures were in the human, cursive alphabet. The first in a heavy hand to match the body of the letter above it and the other beneath it in a light, but sharp manner: Kevane Dupoire and Trystavius Reine.

"Are you going to offer me an explanation as to what's on this paper, Trystavius?" Orangecloak asked lightly as she handed the letter back, having replaced it in its envelope.

"Please, just call me Tryst. There are four people in this world that have ever referred to me as Trystavius and that's too many as it is." A low chuckle escaped Tryst as he spoke and tucked the envelope safely into a pocket inside his jacket. "This letter I've signed as witness and been entrusted to carry and deliver to Greggard Simillon concerns you, my lady."

That much seemed obvious to Orangecloak and she told him so. "I had gathered that, I doubt you would have shown it to me otherwise. What are you and Kevane saying about me here?"

"Kevane is giving you a letter of avouchment, my lady," Tryst smiled brightly as he explained. "He has decided to throw his support behind you and will give you an investment of gold and steel to pursue your cause. As far as endorsements go from the Musicians, that's as much as one can ask for from a First Chair. As you know, Dupoire is a man of great wealth and the amount of money he will invest in you is substantial. The weapons and armour alone would be enough to arm the current members of the Thieves with ease."

"*If* I decide to arm them," Orangecloak jumped in. "This investment hinges on whether or not I decide to raise my banners for war, do they not?" She made no qualms about showing her apprehension on the matter.

Tryst nodded with a sigh. "Of course, that ever present *if*, I'm not long to forget it. The thing to note with this letter is that despite your performance after our first breakfast with the Dupoire family, Kevane saw what I see in you: hope."

She stopped in her tracks as the word left his lips and stood still. "Do you really think that?" asked Orangecloak when Tryst looked back at her. "I've heard it a lot over the past few days. From Kevane, his daughters, Gayle the handmaiden, Ren's friends Edwin and Radmer, Tyla's band and just about anyone else that's spoken to me. But I have to wonder if anyone really believes what they say or if they're just echoing the general consensus."

"My lady, everyone has heard the stories, they know-"

"They know the stories, aye," Orangecloak cut him off. "Let's be honest, Tryst: I'm just a protester. There is no reason for anyone to put such stock in me, especially not the dwarves or the elves."

He laughed at that, turning away down the path again and forcing Orangecloak to move quickly to catch up with him.

"What is so humorous?" she asked as she got up beside him.

"You're just so damn humble, is all," Tryst answered with a shake of his head. "Here you are, the very woman who brought the Thieves back from certain extinction after the Yaelsville incident and you don't see yourself as anyone special."

Orangecloak was in tight beside him then, her heart beating furiously in her chest. "What do you know of Yaelsville?"

There was a look of regret on Tryst's face for even bringing up the name and he looked her over cautiously before finally responding. "I've read the reports made by the captain of the soldiers sent out of Hercalest by Lord Palomb," he admitted with a tinge of nervousness in his voice. "You weren't Field Commander then, it was a man named Marros Delauren."

"I might not have been Field Commander, Tryst Reine, but I was there and I survived the Yaelsville massacre," Orangecloak said through gritted teeth. "You merely read *papers* about it, I *lived* it."

Tryst swallowed hard and looked away. "I'm sorry, my lady, I had no idea. Your name was never mentioned in any reports."

"And why would it be?" she angrily asked the rhetorical question. Yaelsville was a painful memory and dredging it up was never easy for Orangecloak. "I was nothing worth noting back then, just a young follower of Field Commander Marros."

The remorse on Tryst's face was palpable just then and he looked at her forlornly. "You're right, my lady. There would be no reason for your name to be on any reports. I should never have mentioned it and I never would if I knew what talking about it would do to you."

Orangecloak pointed at a nearby downed log. "Sit, Tryst Reine and tell me what those reports said. I would like to know how those bastards rationalised their senseless killing."

"My lady, I don't know if that would be best. Are you sure?" Tryst asked hesitantly.

She fixed him with a stare and pointed again at the log. "I'm positive, Tryst."

After Tryst removed the satchel from his back and lowered himself down to the moss covered, fallen tree, he gestured for Orangecloak to join him. It wasn't until she was seated did he start in. "If this is what you want, I shall not deny it. Though know this: we don't have a long time to spend here. This forest is not a place to be caught after dark and the rain is surely coming."

"I understand, now out with it." Orangecloak quickly nodded, urging him on.

He took a deep breath and began. "The captain compiled the reports of all the officers in the field for the operation into one omnibus report and it was that one that I read," Tryst explained. "He, or rather, Captain Tinderman, stated he was given orders to arrest Marros Delauren, Field Commander of the Thieves on the charges of common banditry. The truth... The truth was something else that I learned from the mouth of Grenjin Howland himself: Marros Delauren and his people were, until then, agents of the Elite Merchant Party. I suspect you know this already."

After Orangecloak nodded solemnly, Tryst went on. "Marros was not the first Field Commander of your gang. The history of your group is rooted in events that lead to the EMP's rise to power. But what Marros will always be known for in the history books is being the first Field Commander to lead your group after they took the Thieves as a name. That is his written legacy. The story that won't be written in ink is the one of how he broke a long standing contract with the Elite Merchants."

Orangecloak shrugged. "You're not telling me anything new,

Tryst. I know what we were, where we came from. The group is a century old, in truth. Though we've only been the Thieves for about five years or so. At first, the group was merely a unit from a secretive sect of the Illiastran military. A small number of that group were sent into the Southlands under the guise of being traitors to Illiastra. The mission was to assume control of the ruins of Phaleayna, drive the raiding gangs from its shores and further control their numbers. That group aligned with an armed militia of Southlands residents that were already trying to fight off the raiding gangs. What would become the Thieves was born from that merger."

From there, Tryst bridged the story back to more recent history. "Ever since then, every leader of the ruins has answered to the EMP. Including the present leader, Yassira Na-Qoia, the woman from Johnah."

"And the Field Commander of the ranging group answered to the Leader of the Ruins," Orangecloak added plainly, knowing full well of the history of the Thieves. "Until Marros decided to go rogue on the whole operation."

Tryst turned to face her. "Who can blame him? For years the whole purpose of his group was to control the raiding gangs and manipulate them into sacking innocent towns on both sides of the Varras River. The whole thing was done so that the EMP could send in their men in uniforms to play hero whenever they felt like it. This was in order to give the people someone to fear and make the reigning government look like the saviours of Illiastra.

"How could anyone think of starting a revolution against the only people who could protect you from the mean raiders in the Southlands?" he asked rhetorically in an exaggerated tone. "The sad part is that it worked for decades without anyone suspecting a thing. However, Marros risked exposing everything and everyone because he wanted to kill off the raiding gangs entirely. He was done with letting innocents die to preserve the villains that the EMP needed to make them look heroic."

"You know," Orangecloak began to comment. "That was why I looked up to Marros so much. Once I learned the history of our organisation I was appalled, but by then he was already laying the groundwork to rid ourselves of the EMP and making a group I could be proud to be associated with. He was such a charismatic, charming man and a natural leader in every way. We devoted ourselves to his cause with little thought on the matter."

Tryst ran a hand over the growing beard on his face, his gaze on the ground ahead of him. "All the previous reports I had read of Marros certainly do reflect that. Even the EMP approved of him, or at least in his ability to command respect from his followers."

He waited a beat before bringing the subject back around to the Yaelsville incident. "The last reports though, they speak of a man who refused to bend his knee to his government any longer. Captain Tinderman stated that he found the Thieves holed up in Yaelsville with the citizens as hostages. He claimed the military tried to negotiate a peaceful surrender and Marros attacked without provocation, forcing the soldiers to put down him and his entire armed unit. While the main fighting force of the Thieves held back the soldiers at the north gate, the remainder of the Thieves led the hostages out through the south gate. From there the groups split. Some were caught and it is reported that those groups, in their panic, executed their hostages and attempted to flee. I would venture to guess that you were among one of those very groups, my lady."

A tear came unbidden and Orangecloak wiped it away before Tryst could see it. She collected herself and waited until Tryst had finished before speaking up, "I suspected the EMP would lie about the whole thing and try to shirk responsibility for what they had done. However, what they've fabricated to cover for their horrors is just as abhorrent as their actions."

"My lady, perhaps we should speak no more of it. I can see how much it hurts you to reflect on the incident. There's no need for this," Tryst offered gently while laying a tender hand upon her knee.

She laid her own hand atop his and looked him square in the eyes. "I feel like I should, I feel that if I hold it in any longer I might burst. I want to trust you, Tryst Reine. It's a daily struggle within myself to give you that much and I know you understand why that's so hard, especially now. I keep thinking that maybe, if I let you know things like this that, I'll feel like I'm giving you a little piece of my trust every time that I do."

Tryst shook his head ever so slightly. "That's not necessary, my lady. I'm aware of your trust issues and you have no reason to relive such painful memories to please me."

"It's not you I'm trying to assuage, it's me. Will you let me finish, if for no other reason than my own benefit?" she asked him plainly, still meeting his eyes.

When Tryst made no further protest, Orangecloak continued on. "Things seemed so hopeful and positive when Marros first announced his intentions. We all felt so renewed, like we had found a purpose in life once more. That feeling lasted so very briefly, though.

"As soon as word reached the EMP of our betrayal we soon found ourselves the enemies of both the raiders and the government. When we approached the river forts, we were fired upon and the raiding gangs seemed to grow even more aggressive. We were trapped between the territories of the raiders and the Varras River, with Phaleayna too far out of reach.

"You have to understand that we didn't have Rillis Vale back then, just makeshift camps that provided little defence. By the time we learned of the coming force of soldiers aiming to put us down, it was too late to run to Phaleayna.

"With nowhere left to go, we holed up in Yaelsville, one of the few towns in the Southlands with stone walls for protection. The residents there were so kind to us. They sheltered us all in their houses, barns, sheds and stables. Wherever they could find a roof, we were welcomed.

"Our scouts reported a large contingent of armed soldiers from Hercalest crossing Barrows Bridge by Fort Layn and we knew our time was done. We begged the people of Yaelsville to leave, but they insisted on staying and fighting by our side. They argued that for so long it was the Thieves who protected them from raiders, so now it was their turn to stand and fight with us."

It was there she halted the story, taking a moment to compose herself before going on. "So, Marros engineered a plan: he knew it was him that the EMP forces wanted and he was prepared to sacrifice himself for the cause. To that end, he and the adults of the Thieves agreed to surrender on the condition that the EMP let the residents of Yaelsville and the junior Thieves members go. I remember how much we protested that decision, especially Lazlo Arbor. He was adamant that we all stand together and that we had a chance to win if we did."

A lump began to form in her throat and she swallowed to clear it. "I can still vividly see Marros looking directly at Lazlo and saying, 'A victory today will only bring more battles tomorrow. I have to preserve the cause and to do that I need you, the youth of the Thieves, to carry on in our stead.'"

She stopped briefly, reflecting sadly at the memory of the man. "By the gods, Tryst, even in the face of death Marros was gallant. By the time the soldiers arrived, some people had already evacuated, though most had stayed, deciding to support us to the bitter end. While Marros and his elite unit, the Fearless Forty, stood upon the walls of the north gate and negotiated, the rest of us were herding people out through the other.

"A shot rang out and one of Marros' lieutenants fell from the wall, ending negotiations abruptly. After that, the Fearless Forty came down from the walls and marshalled their might to go out and meet the enemy so that the rest of us could escape.

"I can see Marros in my mind's eye, standing on a box, his sword drawn and hair blowing in the wind. 'Men and women of the Fearless Forty,' he had said. 'Know that we will not live to see the sun set. Today we fight only so that the people of Yaelsville might have a chance to see the sun rise tomorrow. I am sorry for the mistakes I have made and please forgive me for making you pay for those mistakes with your lives. Go into this fight and know that our sacrifice is not in vain. We will give our lives so that the rest of our people can continue on. If we are thieves as they so call us, then so shall we rob them of their wish to destroy us. Stand with me, my Fearless Forty! Let us die together and take as many of the Hercalest scum as we can!'

"The north gate crashed open, Marros and his forty fighters rushed forward and the rest of us slipped out with the last of the Yaelsville residents who would run."

Orangecloak paused there and braced herself for the harsh truth that she knew she must say. "Not one of those who stayed in the town lived. Even the townspeople, like the elderly who were too frail to leave and those who fought beside the Fearless Forty, the Hercalest men slaughtered them all. I remember there was also a small group of residents who foolishly believed that if they pledged fealty to the EMP that they would be spared. They were wrong."

"I am so dreadfully sorry, my lady," Tryst said with earnest empathy. "I had no idea of the extent of what truly happened. Grenjin Howland had declared the incident classified and forbade people from speaking of it. All I had to go by were the few written records I could find in the manor's library."

"Wait, I'm not done," interrupted Orangecloak before Tryst could go on with his apology. "You mentioned that the report stated that the soldiers from Hercalest regrouped after the slaughter of Marros and his Fearless Forty and pursued the rest of us. Where do you think I was for that?"

He shook his head but dared not give more of an answer than that, allowing Orangecloak to continue once more. "We were in the forest just south of the town. The last Thieves to leave closed the south gates behind them and the very final one to squeeze through the gate was Mell the Huntress. In one arm she carried a crossbow and on her back was a young girl who was almost left behind.

"I'm sure you've heard wild stories of 'Half-Mad Mell' before and most of them are probably true. While Mell the Huntress is perhaps the closest thing to a real name she has, many more call her the Raider's Daughter. Most would probably think that her erratic behaviour is on account of the cold, cruel life she grew up with in the raiding gangs, before her time in the Thieves." Orangecloak turned to face Tryst at that and meet him with her stare. "I can tell you that they are wrong. The Mell I knew before Yaelsville and the one in Rillis Vale right now are two different women entirely. She saw something inside those walls and it broke her mind. Whatever it was, she won't speak of it. Not to me or anyone else in the Thieves. But those who knew her before Yaelsville all attest that any madness within her was born on that day. I could see it in her eyes when she dropped the girl into my arms. It was in her voice when Myles asked her what happened and she merely told us, 'Run and don't you ever look back. Do you hear?'

"The girl was seven at the time and wouldn't stop crying long enough to tell me her name or where her parents were. An older boy recognised her and he told me that her name was Molly and that he knew her family, but he didn't see them amongst the survivors."

She shook her head and sighed at that, letting the unspoken fate of Molly's family sink in to Tryst.

"The Thieves and the remaining Yaelsville folk had a brief meeting," Orangecloak said, to continue on with the grim story. "We decided to split into three distinct groups composed of a mixture of Thieves, Yaelsville adults and children. One group went east, to the town of Layn or onward to Phaleayna if need be. The next group went west, towards Aquas Bay. I was with the last group. We turned south, towards the Warrens."

Orangecloak saw the look of dread on Tryst's face as he knew where her story was going. "The Thieves amongst that group were

Lazlo, Coquarro, Myles, a girl named Andra and myself. There wasn't one among us older than twenty-five at the time and a resident in his forties named Breggen or Bargen or something like that took charge of the group. Not that anyone minded. He was one of the few adults who weren't part of the Thieves, he seemed to know the forest and the rest of us had other things on our mind. What did we care who was at the front of the pack? I was busy enough trying to take care of Molly. With no relatives and no one that seemed to care if she lived or died, I decided that I couldn't abandon the girl and I kept her with me."

At that point Tryst spoke up. "When I read the reports, I couldn't understand what made any of you think that Minister Harlowe would help you when you reached the Warrens. The man has only ever been a pious mining magnate and a slaver. Those aren't exactly qualities that would endear him to the Thieves."

"As to that," Orangecloak began in answer, "before the soldiers had ambushed Yaelsville, Marros had informed us that Harlowe was indebted to him and was bound by the tenets of the Triarchy to honour said debts. It turned out that Marros had already sent a bird to Clay Harlowe ahead of the fighting to ask that he repay the favour by sheltering us. Minister Harlowe had either forgotten his faith or found a way around the scriptures, because he clearly had no intention of repaying Marros."

Tryst hummed ponderously at that. "That's as good a reason as any, I suppose. Go on, what happened next?"

This was the part of the memory that was the most difficult for Orangecloak to speak of. She closed her eyes, took a deep breath, exhaled and began for the last time. "The walk took us several days. Along the way we lost a few who had been wounded in the battle. There were others who just couldn't endure the walk and just refused to go on or strayed away on their own.

"When the collection of amalgamated, walled mining towns they call the Warrens came into view, I remember having this great feeling of dread come over me. I had never been inside before, but I had travelled to the gates when following Marros and the place had always seemed so foreboding and ominous. I tried to chalk up my feelings to that and pushed forward with everyone else. There was something else, though and I felt as if it was more than unnerving past experiences.

"We got close enough that we could make out the men walking

the walls and there were a lot of them, more than I ever remembered seeing there. I warned our group leader, but he would hear none of it. All he wanted was to get everyone to safety, fearing that the soldiers from Hercalest might be hunting us down. Andra sided with him, but I managed to convince my close friends to keep a distance.

"We hid just out of range of the town in a thick forest. Molly and a few of the older children stayed behind with us. The few adults, Andra, the leader of the group and the rest of the children went on ahead to the gates.

"Lazlo and I snuck close to hear what Harlowe was saying to the group leader and we left Coquarro and Myles behind to protect Molly and the others.

"I can still see it all so plainly, Tryst. I can see the look of contempt on Clay Harlowe's face and the ugly burgundy cape with all those feathers, all of it. The most striking thing of all though was the way he just stood there, straight as an arrow on the wall, staring down at the refugees below. All while he spoke, his riflemen were at the ready, their rifles pointing at the sky. Then, he said the only words Lazlo and I had heard plainly, 'May Ios be merciful in his judgement.'"

Orangecloak bowed her head and hastily wiped another single tear with her old, faded cloak and turned to face Tryst again. "The men on the walls lowered their rifles in one great wave and opened fire in a loud, thunderous bang. Some standing below had tried to run, though most didn't have the chance. They were children, Tryst. Minister Harlowe ordered the murder of children."

A look of shock covered Tryst's face as he took in that information. "That is unconscionable. I never knew anything about it. Not from the Lord Master or even Lord Greggard or in any report from the incident."

"It is likely that Greggard never knew either," Orangecloak reasoned. "The ministers and military officers of the east and the Southlands clearly did their very best to cover everything up." She stood up and brushed herself off at that. "Or maybe they made sure to keep you in the dark for fear that you would back out of your contract. I don't know and frankly, it doesn't matter. You know now."

20
TRYST

The forest had fallen behind them in the last light of the overcast evening. The macabre memories of Orangecloak had drawn a pall over both she and Tryst, and the sight of the Sluiceway and Fletchard's small campfire beneath it was a welcome sight.

Alongside all the tension of the afternoon, a feeling had lingered within the pit of Tryst's stomach, one that his training gave him no room to ignore. Yet, he had pushed it aside as a trick his mind was playing on him in the dense woods and refused to let it get the better of him. The foreboding sensation had still prevailed long after they had cleared the woods and three chilling words from Orangecloak confirmed what Tryst had feared.

"We're being watched." Her voice had been low and full of apprehension when she said it and her eyes scanned the horizon from beneath the overhanging, natural bedrock waterway they were nestled beside. "I felt as much earlier in the forest and I feel it now."

Tryst let the volume of his voice fall to a whisper as he stoked the tiny fire with a slender junk of wood. "Aye, I feel it too."

"You don't suppose..." she started to ponder aloud as she craned about from where she sat, peering into the darkness. "Kevane said his rangers found only the two horses and no sign of anyone else coming this way. Still though, it's a large wilderness up here, perhaps our pursuers found another way west?"

"It's not something that can be entirely ruled out," Tryst answered her. "I can't see them following us this far. Though, if they didn't find or disturb the horses in any way that says they likely didn't even go far enough to discover them."

A groaning Fletchard leaned forward from his resting place. "I have to agree with Reine," he offered in a rare tone that held no biting aggression. "These are city boys from Atrebell we have been dealing with." Fletchard gestured to the great outdoors around them. "This is far outside their element and they're not like to stick around if they don't have to. If they've found a few hoof prints, then that's all they've found and they clearly didn't follow that trail far enough to find the horses. No, those lads are safely home in Atrebell right now with a clean report and all eyes for us are pointed to the south."

Orangecloak nervously pulled her pair of cloaks tightly around her frame from where she sat on the opposite side of the fire from Fletchard. "If the both of you are right, then that makes me wonder what exactly is out there watching us."

Aside from the prevailing sense that something was looking down upon them, Tryst had, for once, general peace within the walking party. While he and Orangecloak had been dealing with a haunting piece of her past in the forest, Fletchard had cleared through the woods. With his head clearing of its alcohol-induced fog, he had found the Sluiceway and spent the late afternoon with the fishing line Tryst had left with him. By the time Tryst and Orangecloak came upon the Sluiceway, four mud trout were gutted, cleaned and sitting on spits over a growing campfire.

"I'm taking the bigger two for myself," Fletchard had proclaimed as they approached the encampment he had built. "Do what you like with the smaller two trout, but the two big fat ones are mine alone."

Given that it was uncharacteristically generous of Fletchard to give them even that much, neither Tryst nor Orangecloak brokered any complaints. They took their supper in near silence, the three of them each losing themselves in their own thoughts as the rain began to softly fall outside their stony shelter.

With the trout reduced to bones, dinner came to an end and the trio sat still and quiet around the fire. The symphonic sounds of the crackling sticks, tumbling raindrops and the flowing river kept their ears entertained while the flickering flames mesmerised with their arrhythmic dance.

There was no abatement in the air of unease over the party as the night wore on. Any noise outside of the usual caught the attention of all. Even something as trivial as the creaking of trees or the hoot of an owl was enough to turn heads quickly.

"Whatever is out there seems content with keeping its distance." Fletchard sighed from where he lay with the hood of his cloak down over his eyes, "I would say it's a pack of wolves. They probably picked us up in the forest and followed us all the way here. They won't come near the fire. So as long as we keep it burning and stay near it, we'll be fine. Wake me when you want me to take a shift, for my eyes have declared it won't be the first one." With that, he rolled his back to them and the fire to wrap himself in his dingy, brown cloak and drift off.

A thought entered Tryst's head then as he unbuckled his sword belt and got comfortable beside the fire. "How would you like first watch?" he asked Orangecloak coyly.

"You're allowing me the watch?" Orangecloak answered sarcastically. "That's an improvement from our journey from Atrebell to the Dupoire place. What's the reason? Is it my knees being healed or the fact that we're short a man now?"

Tryst was careful in how he worded his answer, making sure the right for her to refuse the offer was in place. "It's a bit of both, admittedly. The option is yours, of course. You don't have to take a watch if you don't want to."

"I'll gladly take it," she answered hastily before Tryst could consider rescinding the offer. "Get your rest for I'll be waking you in a few hours," Orangecloak added, scooping up both bow and quiver in her hands as she stood.

The narrow stretch of eroded bedrock they called a campsite provided sufficient shelter from the rain and westerly winds. It also offered the defensive advantage of limited access across the riverbed that the sluiceway emptied into from above.

Despite all that, Tryst still felt caged and cornered should anything come down on them and the look on Orangecloak's face seemed to match his gut feeling.

Even in the low, shifting light of the fire, there was a radiant beauty about her. It was etched into the outline of the determined, fierce face of a warrior woman and highlighted by the fiery hair that fell in dangling, loose curls over her back. Orangecloak had taken to braiding and tying off the front half of her red locks again and letting the back fall where it may, as she had worn it before reaching the hotel. *This is the woman I saw in Aquas Bay,* Tryst told himself. *She is strong once more, in body and mind alike.*

Tryst rolled himself in his dark, fur cloak and stretched out beside the fire, groaning contentedly as his muscles relaxed.

Orangecloak had taken to patrolling the campsite with an arrow lying across Tryst's bow, ready to draw and loose at a second's notice should something emerge from the shadows. The light of the fire was her boundary, a precious line of safety she dared not take more than a step or two beyond. Through heavy eyes Tryst watched her stalk about silently, holding the bow nearly as skilfully as an elf might, each step taken with awareness of the weapon in her hands.

There was indeed an archer in her, at least insofar as Tryst could see without her actually using the bow for its intended purpose.

With no more of the campsite to patrol, she resigned herself to sitting on a rock, bow across her lap and her gaze on the surrounding blackness across the riverbed.

That was where Tryst's consciousness left him, and at long last he drifted off.

What tried to pass for sleep was a restless dream of fire. The flames were all about, surrounding him at every turn and grasping an unseen ceiling above. Beyond sat only darkness and amid it all stood Orangecloak, staring directly at Tryst, those radiant blue eyes now just dark orbs as black as night. The hair, as bright as the flames themselves, seemed to lift and blow with an unseen wind in a thousand directions. She was wearing her orange cloak, leathers, bodice and tunic, but everything was in tattered ribbons and her face was streaked with blood.

Her mouth opened to speak but the voice that came forth was not hers. It was deep and garbled, but loud enough to shake a mountain. "You desire this woman, she who wears the orange cloak." Tryst knew whatever this was before him was not Orangecloak, not in truth. This was like some sort of demonic thing with a terrible power.

To his horror, Tryst discovered that the scabbard on his hip was empty of the blacksteel sword and this thing posing as Orangecloak was gaining on him quickly.

Every step it took sent flames shooting into the air and Tryst shielded his face from the heat as it spoke again. "The ground burns where she walks. Let her scorch the world on her own, Tryst Reine, for you do not need this in your life. You are a great man, a talented man and you do not need to follow this doomed soul to the grave."

The thing was within reach, carried to him by long strides that seemed slowed by some force. "Come with me, Reine," it offered, beckoning him forth enticingly with the wave of its right hand.

There was a way the creature mimicking Orangecloak called him Reine, the way the word seemed to entangle in its tongue as it fell forward that was unnerving. "Leave her to this vacuum of pain she has created. Come to me."

"Tryst wake up, it's your shift." His eyes fluttered open to see Orangecloak, the real Orangecloak, crouched over him with a look of worry as her brilliant blue eyes scanned his face. "Is everything alright?" she asked him as he sat up and glanced around.

As the night air hit him, Tryst realised he was sweating and breathing heavily. He turned back towards Orangecloak to answer her concerns. "Yes, I'm fine. I was having a restless sleep I suppose, nothing more than that. What hour is it?"

She shrugged and looked towards the sky. "I'm not entirely sure. There are no moons by which to gauge it. The rain has mostly abated, though." Tryst flinched as she said the word rain and she recoiled in tandem with him. "Are you sure you're quite alright? I'm not too tired if you want to sleep some more."

"No, I'm fine, go ahead and lie down, my lady. You need to rest too," Tryst said reassuringly as he clambered to his feet, taking his sword and its belt with him as he stood.

He could feel Orangecloak's concern as she considered his behaviour warily. "Would you like your bow back for your watch?" she offered as she returned the ready arrow to its quiver and unbelted it from her hip.

"I feel more secure with my sword and blades, you may hold on to it," Tryst declined.

As Tryst was replying, Orangecloak had removed the dagger from her hip. "Should you change your mind, you won't be leaving me unarmed as I have my own blade for protection if I need it." She spoke of the short, curved piece of sheathed blacksteel clutched in her hand.

"Are you sure you're alright, Tryst?" she said once more, throwing out another apprehensive query.

"Aye, a poor dream is all it was. I'm sure you can appreciate that there's been quite a bit on our minds lately. My imagination was just reacting to it all," Tryst answered back calmly, forcing a smile as he looked about into the wet wilderness beyond the river.

Orangecloak resigned herself to rest at that. "Very well then, wake me when it's my shift." She chose Tryst's sleeping place for her own and wrapped herself and the dagger snugly in the pair of cloaks she wore.

Even after she had settled down to sleep, her eyes remained open and curious. "That's strange..." Orangecloak said quietly from where she lay on the ground, the hoods of her cloaks nearly hiding her head entirely.

"What's strange?" Tryst responded while stoking the fire with sticks and branches to get it burning well once more.

"All while you slept I continued to feel like something was watching us. However, I no longer feel it," she spoke through a sleepy yawn. "It's like your waking drove it off. That's odd though, you were awake all day when I had this feeling of being watched, save for the last few hours. Why would that feeling subside now?"

A shake of the head from Tryst was all the answer he could come up with at the moment. "I don't know, my lady, I don't feel it anymore myself. Perhaps it was nothing all along, or maybe it was wolves as Fletchard suggested and they have simply given up on making a meal of us."

"It's so strange..." she said with a sigh as her eyelids sleepily fluttered shut.

The remainder of the night ebbed away slowly into dawn. The fire remained lit and Tryst patrolled the camp by himself, leaving the other two to enjoy the rest that his nightmare ensured would elude him. The image of Orangecloak with those black eyes and the ethereal voice played back vividly in his mind throughout the night. By the time the morning's light crested the eastern skyline, Tryst was no closer to an answer and still tormented by it.

There was something about that voice that had an unsettling, sinister quality to it, almost as though someone else was in my dream with me and the voice was theirs.

The first to awaken from slumber was Fletchard, rubbing his lone eye as the darkness of the night receded and glancing about in surprise when he sat up. "It's daylight already?" he said loud enough that Orangecloak was woken by his voice. "I can't help but notice that you didn't wake me for a shift."

"Nay, I couldn't sleep after my brief nap so I left you two alone," Tryst said to the back of Fletchard's head while the latter quickly shambled off to expel his nightly fluid.

Fletchard called back over his shoulder while in mid-stream. "You'll get no complaint from me on the matter. Stay awake all you damn well want."

Tryst turned his attention to Orangecloak, still curled up where she had been sleeping. "I'll get us something to eat before we get underway again, I think some tea would go nicely too. How does that sound, my lady?"

"That's just fine, would you like some help?" she yawned.

"It's nothing that requires much work. You can stay comfortable for now." Tryst answered with a smile he hoped she would buy as sincere.

The breakfast of oatmeal and black tea came and went without much in the way of conversation, as any length of time that Orangecloak and Fletchard had in each other's company was generally spent. Tryst accepted that, knowing the alternative was the two of them hissing at one another like housecats.

The three of them had enough bowls and spoons to go around now, courtesy of the kitchens of the Dupoire hotel, and soon they had only dirty dishes to show for their breakfasts. Tryst gave Fletchard the task of taking them to the river for washing and left the dismantling and cleaning of the campsite to himself and Orangecloak.

When Fletchard was out of earshot, Orangecloak opened up again. "You dreamt something terrible last night, didn't you?" she asked while taking apart the sticks used to make the spit over the smouldering fire pit.

Tryst answered with a wink and the same smile he wore before. "Aye, I had an unpleasant dream. I think it was just due to an overactive imagination, nothing to worry about."

"Won't you be tired today?" she followed with another question, seemingly unsatisfied with his initial answer.

He laughed off her worry. "I appreciate your concern, my lady, but I've managed to do more on less sleep than that. I'll rest better tonight for certain. We should have an extra pair of eyes to share our watch anyhow as I'm hoping we find Jack Paylor today." Tryst hoped the mention of the man might spur Orangecloak to change the subject.

"Oh yes, this mysterious Jack Paylor, the hermit trapper that brings news and parcels to the Dupoire family from Portsward. You mentioned we were looking for him," Orangecloak recalled. "From what Kevane said of the man, he seems like the sort of fellow that will only be found if he wants to be found."

Tryst gave her a jovial nod at that. "Indeed, no one knows the wilderness at the edge of the Dwarven Mountains quite like he. The man could be anywhere between the Hotel Dupoire and Tusker's Cove by now and if he didn't want us to come across him, we wouldn't. However, he has a few shacks and a cabin between here and there that he frequents. If he's willing to meet with us, then one of those places is where we'll find him."

The return of Fletchard rendered Orangecloak mute once more and the cleaning went as quietly as breakfast.

When everyone was loaded up with satchels and weapons and ready to resume the journey, Tryst unfurled the map, showing them where he intended for the daily trek to take them. "The forests from here on out are sparse and spotty and most of our journey will take us over rocky grasslands full of rolling hills as far as the eye can see." Tryst pointed out with a finger on the map he had spread across a rock large enough to sit upon. "It's in three of these larger patches of forest that we'll find his sheds. The cabin is much further along and when we reach that we'll be less than a day's walk from Tusker's Cove, in an area called Sama's Meadows." Tryst tapped the place on the map. "We'll walk a trail that takes us to these shacks and the cabin in turn. Should we not find him by the third shack, then I suspect that we'll have missed him entirely."

With no further questions, the party agreed on the route and began their day's march.

Surprisingly, Fletchard stayed close to Tryst and Orangecloak until their first break in the shadow of a large, lonely boulder overlooking the barren, treeless landscape that lay head. Fletchard had barely sat down before getting underway again, eager to leave the other two behind and be on his own. Neither Tryst nor Orangecloak were opposed to letting him go on alone and they sat together to give the bounty hunter time to get well away for the rest of the morning and afternoon.

Not too much later, the remaining pair got moving once more.

The rest of the day went by with little incident and nothing of consequence was discussed between them.

Orangecloak had decided with the clear weather and low winds that she was going to hunt should they come across any game. To aid this effort, Tryst spoke only when necessary so as not to alert any potential targets. Unfortunately, there was nothing to be encountered but squirrels, ravens and songbirds, and they remained empty handed by sunset.

The first of Jack Paylor's shacks was found by Fletchard in the early evening and he was none too impressed with it when Tryst and Orangecloak came upon him. It was a tiny thing, made of unshaved lumber and big enough for one man alone, as Jack Paylor preferred it. A bunk, a table and a seat, all built into the walls made up the sparse furnishings and while it protected from the weather sufficiently, it provided little in the way of warmth.

To remedy this, they lit a fire in a wide pit outside. That did little to help inside the shack though and the three of them opted instead to sleep beside their pit. Of Jack Paylor there was no sign, and they convened sleeping and guarding in their three-person rotation to keep the fire burning and perimeter protected. When not on watch, Tryst slept heavily to make up for the lost sleep of the night before and felt fairly well rested when the light of the day came.

Another breakfast followed, eaten beneath a sky that was overcast with heavy clouds that looked like they might spill their watery burden at a moment's notice. High winds blew in from the northeast to send a harsh chill through them and the three braced themselves for what would surely be a miserable walk.

It was just before midday when the rain began, dampening their spirits as much as their clothes. The trek had started as it had since they left Hotel Dupoire, with Fletchard scouting ahead on his own, well away from Tryst and Orangecloak. Once the rain came down, they caught one more sighting of Fletchard running over a hill, presumably for cover, and lost track of him. The wet weather did little to spur conversation and served only to get them moving quicker than they had ever been on this leg of their journey.

They even ate while walking, with Tryst reasoning, "We should really get out of this weather before nightfall. We have no lantern and it would be dreadfully hard to hold a candle in this cold rain."

The second shack was similar in size to the first they had

encountered, bare and windowless, with a crude bunk, chair and table made for one. Fletchard had reached it first, his soaking wet cloak hanging from the stump of a branch on the horizontal logs used in the construction of the walls. "We'll freeze to death in here tonight," he said by way of greeting.

"First and foremost, we should get out of these wet cloaks or we'll surely fall ill," Tryst suggested while shaking off the rainwater.

The frustration in Fletchard's voice was palpable. "There's no fireplace and everything outside is saturated. We need fire or the cold will take us in the night."

Tryst kept a calm demeanour as he responded to Fletchard's complaints. "Our bodies will generate enough heat to keep this place moderately warm. Jack Paylor sleeps here, in all seasons, I might add. It is survivable."

"It's going to drop below freezing. I can feel it in my bones." Fletchard complained.

The only thing Tryst gave him in return was a nonchalant shrug. "What do you suggest I should do about that? Despite what my last name might infer, I cannot manipulate the rain."

"This bickering is getting us nowhere," the voice of Orangecloak broke through the back and forth exchange. She had made her way to the bunk and was inspecting the bedding when she had spoken up. "Look, there are several warm pelts here, I'm counting five. We can share these up and stay warm enough."

Fletchard scoffed. "All cramped up in this shack with you two, wrapped in a bear pelt and freezing my arse off. That sounds like a magical evening," he commented, the words oozing with sarcasm.

His smarmy quip was met with the icy stare of Orangecloak. "Then by all means, feel free to go outside and sleep in the rain."

There was no further issue from Fletchard and the three ate a modest meal of buttered bread and dried beef for their supper without a word.

Orangecloak had taken to wrapping a pelt about herself and sitting on the bunk, sharing the bed with Tryst while they ate and listening to the falling rain.

Night came on quickly, costing them the little light that managed to make its way between the vertically arranged logs that made up the walls. Tryst was quick to retrieve the pair of candles and box of matches Kevane had put amongst their replenished supplies and got to work procuring them some light.

It was quite some time later, hours by Tryst's own reckoning, when the sound of heavy footfalls could be heard coming toward the hovel. "Someone's out there." Orangecloak was the first to say it, sliding to the edge of the bunk with her hand wrapped tightly around the blacksteel dagger on her hip.

The door swung outward on the old pieces of rope serving as hinges with a loud bang. Outside was a stooped, cloaked figure standing in the threshold, bearing a lantern in one hand and a large, heavy pack upon his back. His eyes were hidden beneath the dripping wet hood of his cloak that hung low and his mouth and nose were buried beneath a long, dark beard.

"Good evening, Jack Paylor," Tryst greeted him warmly, rising to extend his hand. Behind him, Tryst could feel the uncertain eyes of Orangecloak watching nervously.

Jack Paylor laid the lantern upon the table, freeing his right hand to firmly and tightly shake Tryst's before he answered at all. "A good evening to you as well, Tryst Reine. It's good to lay eyes on you. I was told I should be expecting six, but I count half that number."

"Two perished and one parted with us at Kevane's," Tryst said bluntly, knowing Jack Paylor was not one for roundabout explanations.

The hermit pulled back his hood to reveal the weather beaten face beneath. He was only in the middle years of his fortieth decade but looked to be well into his fiftieth. The bald head and thick beard were largely responsible for that image. The life in the wild had taken care of the rest.

"No elf," Jack Paylor stated as his grey-green eyes looked over Fletchard, surmising who he was. "That's unfortunate, I like elves."

There was dislike sowing between Jack Paylor and Fletchard already as the two eyed one another down. "Get up, bounty hunter, that's my damn seat."

"And if I don't?" Fletchard shot back defiantly.

In a flash, the heavy, pea green cloak of Jack Paylor flew back and his right arm shot up over his head bearing a hatchet. With a mighty smash that sent splinters flying, he sunk it deep into the top of the table. "It's my shack, my rules. You can get out of my seat or I can feed the wolves with your dead carcass."

Fletchard stood so fast that he almost tripped in himself as his back went against the wall and his right hand darted for the scabbard on his hip. "Tryst Reine guaranteed me safe passage out of Illiastra," he said quickly and even a little fearfully.

"I'm not Tryst Reine," Jack Paylor growled through gritted teeth while ripping the hatchet from the splintered tabletop.

The two men were at quite a height difference, with Fletchard having half a head on Jack Paylor. The thick, hard muscled frame of the hermit more than made up the difference though. A betting man would have a difficult choice trying to pick a potential winner if it came to a skirmish.

Tryst stuck an arm between them, eying both men down as he attempted to deescalate the situation. "Fletchard, we're guests here. Don't forget that. You will have to sit somewhere else if our host wants his seat."

"Then where am I to sit?" Fletchard growled towards Tryst.

"On the floor, as a dog like you ought to," Jack Paylor answered before Tryst could suggest the same in more eloquent terms. "And be glad I give you that much."

Fletchard yanked his cloak from where it hung and pushed past Tryst and into the damp night without as much as another word.

"Was there a need for that, Jack?" Tryst asked rhetorically, turning back to the bunk he had been sharing with Orangecloak.

A sigh escaped Jack Paylor as he removed the heavy pack from his back, letting it thump loudly to the dirt floor. "Don't worry, he won't go far," he said casually as he lowered himself down onto the seat he had reclaimed before turning his attention to Orangecloak. "My lady, it's an honour to host you in my spacious abode. My name is Jack Paylor. I'm formerly a soldier and currently a trapper and an admitted recluse."

"Why thank you, ser," she slowly began to answer before Jack Paylor cut her off again.

He nodded towards her hip. "Are you planning to stab me with that knife, my lady?"

Orangecloak gasped, suddenly remembering she was still clutching the sheathed, blacksteel knife. "Oh no, my apologies, I put my hand on it when I heard you coming from afar. I guess I got caught up in the sudden tension with Fletchard and just kept a grip on it."

Jack Paylor spoke softly to Orangecloak, in sharp contrast to his brusque manner with Fletchard. "That's quite alright, my lady. It's a pleasure to meet you, if you don't mind my saying." He shrugged off the sodden cloak and hung it where Fletchard's had been moments before, revealing the tunic and trousers made entirely of animal hide and pelts beneath. "You have my sympathies for the loss of your comrades in Atrebell."

That drew a single, solemn nod from Orangecloak. "Thank you," she said almost timidly.

"Do you vouch for her?" Jack Paylor asked Tryst, inclining his head towards Orangecloak.

The hand of Tryst went inside the leather jacket to bring out the letter before sliding it across the table and stating, "Aye, that I do, as does Kevane."

Jack Paylor opened the envelope and scoured its contents. "Very well, if you and Kevane are sure, I'll stand by the judgement for now. However, you and he will be the ones responsible if you've judged wrongly, not I."

"I accept that responsibility, Sparrow," Tryst replied, calling him by his codename within the Musicians. He picked up the letter once more and returned it to the safe place beside his chest before following up with a question. "What was the word from Portsward?"

With a brief glance in Orangecloak's direction, Jack gave answer to Tryst. "There are things the Heart should know," said the woodsman, making sure he got Tryst's sobriquet in there as well. The Musicians could only talk about matters pertaining to their own after referring to one another by their codenames, which acted as a password system.

"The Fox and the Raven returned to the Nest two days after you fled," he informed both guests.

Tryst couldn't help but smile at the thought of the Lord Master fretting and shouting over his lost prize. "The Atrebell Manor was in panic after I sprung Orangecloak, no doubt."

Jack Paylor reached for a jug hanging on a leather thong around the large satchel he carried. It was clunked onto the table, its cork popped off and a large swig taken. With a burp and a contented sigh he finally saw fit to answer. "There are two stories: one is the truth that the Fox uncovered and the other is the official lie being issued as fact by the EMP.

"The truth starts as plainly as the nose on your face: you and she are here, having escaped the Atrebell manor with Fletchard, his cohorts and an elf that the Palomb boys had arrested over some scuffle in Atrebell city. From there it gets a little more difficult as the Fox could only learn so much before he was sent back to the Nest.

"What he did learn, was that you, Tryst Reine, are now the most wanted man in Illiastra. All soldiers and guards have orders to kill you on sight with no deals offered. There's an added charge of death or lifetime incarceration for anyone found to be in cohesion with you. Fletchard, on the other hand, is just to be apprehended for questioning, as it was so put to them. Though, he is to be taken by whatever force necessary to Atrebell for this questioning. You and I both know what that means."

The beige, ceramic jug was slid across the table to Tryst. "We certainly do," he agreed before taking a taste of it for himself. "A fine, wheat grain whisky, if I do say so. Did you brew this one yourself, Jack?" Tryst complimented of the beverage burning its way down his throat, offering the jug to Orangecloak who politely declined.

"That I did." Jack Paylor proudly beamed at his homemade alcohol. "You're drinking from a batch I made when I first built my cabin almost twenty years ago. I like to call it 'The Welcome Wagon'. Are you sure you won't try a shot of it, my lady? It'll warm the bones far better than my old lantern."

Reluctantly, Orangecloak took the jug in both her hands and took a swallow, her face showing no signs of distress over the fiery drink. She hummed appreciatively of it and swigged again, plunking the jug down firmly when she finished.

A bellowing laugh burst forth from Jack Paylor as the whisky was slid back to him across the table. "Not a sputter or a wince out of ya, my lady!" The strongman grinned broadly, holding the jug aloft to toast to Orangecloak. "You're made of tougher stock than most men, I can tell ya that!"

"Not my first taste of the hard stuff," Orangecloak commented dryly with a wink.

"Aye, now that I believe to be no lie." Jack Paylor laughed again following another swig, the whole thing eliciting a chuckle from Tryst.

When the laughter died down, Tryst politely turned the conversation back to the matters at hand. "Now, Jack, you said a moment ago that there were two stories. You have told us one, which is what the Fox had learned. The other I suspect is the Lord Master's cover story."

The bearded man nodded quickly, going back to briefing them on the latest news. "Aye, the Manor is trying to contain the truth and relay their personal brand of false information."

"What information would that be?" Tryst asked.

There was amusement in the tone of Jack Paylor as he explained the lie the EMP was trying to sell as truth. "The official word that the government is putting forward is that Lady Orangecloak is dead. They're claiming you, Tryst, refused to do the deed, turned traitor and fled into the night. Fletchard Miller, still at the Manor, was dispatched with his employees to hunt you down along with a full contingent of Atrebell guardsmen."

Apparently, Orangecloak didn't share Jack's amusement. "That doesn't sound like a typical statement from the Merchants." She furrowed her brows and leaned forward on the bunk, putting her closer to both men. "They would never admit fault in their own and until now, Tryst was one of their own. To add to that, admitting Tryst had betrayed them would show weakness in their own ability to hire loyal subjects. Also, what if I am seen? That would prove the claim of my death to be a lie. This whole thing reeks, if I do say so myself."

"He'll claim you're an imposter in your own cloak," Tryst surmised while turning his gaze to Orangecloak. "It will put doubt in everyone's mind that who they see before them is really the Lady Orangecloak, should you turn up. Grenjin Howland is desperate to regain the prize he so briefly had in you and sow doubt should you elude him again.

"As for me, I know enough to bring down his empire and he wants me dead before I can sell his secrets. The only cost to him to accomplish both of those tasks is allowing a little fault to show. Above all, I think the Lord Master is going to try and bait Fletchard and the dim-witted accomplices the EMP likely thinks to be alive. He hopes they will turn us in rather than risk being caught abetting a traitor and a woman impersonating Illiastra's formerly most wanted woman."

"Do you think Fletchard would take the bait?" Orangecloak asked worriedly.

Tryst spoke confidently in his answer. "Not Fletchard, he's smart enough to see it for what it is. Had his accomplices lived to hear about it though, they would have turned on us the first second I turned my back to them. For their trouble they would wind up swinging from a gallows' pole as soon as they squealed and a small army would be barrelling down towards Kevane's hotel."

Jack Paylor started in with a question of his own. "Those men you speak of, Fletchard killed them, didn't he?"

"Aye, he opened their throats and sunk them in a bog against my orders while I was freeing the lady." Confirming such was a sombre experience for Tryst, he had never intended for those men to die and the callousness with which Fletchard carried it out had shocked him.

"That is a fell, foul thing you keep in your company," Jack Paylor commented after Tryst had finished speaking, his old eyes locking on him.

"He's lost everything he's ever had," Tryst commented in a low voice. "The man has been tricked out of it by greed, both his own and that of Lord Master Grenjin Howland. He's reduced to taking an offer of exile further than he's already known or death. I prefer just to leave him be and not antagonise the man."

That didn't seem to sate Paylor. "It's more than that, young one. Let me tell you a thing or two about me and maybe you'll understand. Before I became a recluse, I was a soldier in the Illiastran Military. That was a different time, when there was still a shred of pride to be found in serving kin and country.

"We had no wars on Illiastran soil in that time, but the Island Nations brawl with one another like drunken sailors from dawn to dusk. Thrice I crossed the sea to those isles and once more as a peacekeeper during the civil war between the Johnan coasts and the Manobius Empire in the interior of the continent.

"In that time, we had men in our ranks that would drop their duty and desert the army. Some of them we found alive, others we found perished and some not at all. Every last one that was taken alive though, I could only use one word to describe them: Broken."

A nip was taken from the jug by Jack Paylor before he went on. "These were men that had forsaken their vows and their duty and stranded themselves in a foreign land with no allies on either side. It leaves them with not a friend to their name and no family for thousands of leagues. These men had nothing and therefore had nothing to lose but their miserable lives. They became desperate savages, capable of the most inhuman atrocities. Execution was the only option for those we captured. These broken men could not be mended. They had become unscrupulous and nearly feral and needed to be cast down. It was a mercy we gave them, for them and those they would have come across. A quick, clean death with an axe across the neck, they deserved that much for their service. You would be wise to give Fletchard Miller the same, before he turns on you in your sleep."

Tryst heard what the older man was saying, feeling Orangecloak's disgruntled gaze upon him as he did. "He helped me save Orangecloak. For that I promised him safe passage from Illiastra and I intend to fulfil that promise."

"You would set that walking pox upon the world?" Jack Paylor asked incredulously. "I admit not having much good to say of the Island Nations and Johnah, but what have either done to deserve you inflicting such a broken wretch upon them? What do you think will be his fate henceforth? I'll tell you what: the man is a former Knight's Commander of the Knightdom of Gildriad. He has the skills of a leader but the only men who will ever follow him are other oathbreakers. Fletchard Miller will be a corsair, captain of a full ship at worst, a minion at best."

Tryst was adamant that it was not the case. "I have to disagree with you, Jack. He's a man with a hard lot in life at present, aye and I admit that he is unhealthily apathetic toward others. Would he fall to the level of a corsair though? No, I can't fathom it."

"Can't, or won't allow the thought?" Jack Paylor countered quickly, as if he expected Tryst to say as much.

That drew an audible sigh from Tryst as he glanced toward Orangecloak briefly to gauge her thoughts on the matter. The look he got in return spoke of the same heavy uncertainties he was having and he hoped she agreed with his words. "It's not logical to kill a man on the off chance that he may become a corsair captain. By that matter he may fall back on his skillset as a bounty hunter when he reaches the islands and hunt down corsairs as a privateer. I could be killing a man who could bring about peace to the Island Nations."

"Highly unlikely," Jack Paylor retorted with a scoff.

"As unlikely that he'll become a scourge of the known seas." Tryst fixed Jack with a stare. "All I can go by is the fact that I promised the man safe passage out of Illiastra and I intend to see that through. What he does with the chance at another life that I give him is up to him entirely. We can sit here and wonder what that chance will amount to all night and we'll be no further ahead."

Jack relented, turning his attention instead to Orangecloak.

"What do you think, my lady? It was your friends he killed, after all. What are your thoughts on what should be done with him?"

"I don't believe killing to be a solution," Orangecloak stated with pride and integrity in her voice. "He is responsible for the death of Myles and Coquarro and for those crimes I would see him punished, though not with death."

Paylor pressed her further. "What sort of punishment would suit him then?"

Tryst watched as Orangecloak's eyes fell to the floor, her mind seeming to go back to that haunting memory. "I would see to it that he lives a long life and that every day of it he is reminded of Coquarro and Myles. If his mind withers and he can't remember his own name, I want him to still remember theirs." Her tone was deathly serious with a fire in her eyes. "That would be punishment enough for me."

"Very well, then." Jack Paylor shrugged. "I can only advise. It is not my place to carry out my will. I only hope I am wrong about Fletchard, for it would grieve me greatly to have to bury you two."

The pattering of the rain outside coupled with the occasional gust of wind became the only noise to be heard for a time after that. Jack Paylor dug into his heavy pack and produced a pair of bundles wrapped in brown paper and tied with string. The first proved to be a stack of sandwiches, all appearing to be roasted meat, likely wild game of some sort and further filled with tomatoes, lettuce and butter.

"Is there any more news?" Orangecloak put in hastily while Jack Paylor ate. "Did you hear anything about other Thieves that were captured in Argesse and brought to Atrebell? There would be four for sure, about a dozen at most."

Jack munched on his sandwich noisily while he thought about what she said. "I've been trying to find the words to tell you, my lady. I suppose going straight to the point will have to suffice." He swallowed the food in his mouth, took a pull from the whiskey jug and went on. "The Fox told me that he saw a contingent of Thieves bound in heavy chains being boarded onto a train while he was waiting for his own. Their train was bound for Biddenhurst. By now they're within its walls, my lady. I'm so sorry to have to tell you that. I too have lost friends to that cesspool and I remember the knowledge of their arrests hitting me as hard as if they had died."

Orangecloak was quick with a response to that. "Mine are not dead though, not yet. Tryst, you said yourself that you're sure Mackhol

Taves will keep them alive as long as he can use them against me. The longer I live, the more time the Sisters and Lazlo have to escape."

Jack Paylor's voice was full of doubt. "My lady, Biddenhurst is inescapable."

"You don't know my Thieves." She was hopeful as she made the statement and Tryst felt a pang of pity for her.

"You don't know those walls and the men guarding them." Jack Paylor replied, seemingly reading Tryst's mind on the matter.

She recoiled as Jack said the words, flinching visibly and dropping her gaze to the floor. "I have to say, Mister Jack, you talk an awful lot for a hermit. I thought the men of the wilderness sought it for the solitude and to avoid human contact."

While gently folding up his paper full of sandwiches and tucking them back in his satchel, Jack Paylor gave her a response. "I'm far from a typical hermit, my lady. I didn't choose the solitary life, it was offered as repayment for the saving of another."

Tryst and Orangecloak exchanged a glance, but there was nothing Tryst could tell her about Jack. Whatever the man was speaking of was not information he had offered to Tryst before.

Orangecloak turned her attention back to Jack. "Might I ask if you would elaborate on that?"

"Why certainly. We have mutual friends that you have helped. I know my story is safe with you," Jack began as the look of puzzlement on Orangecloak's face grew more apparent. "As I told you before, I was a soldier, having fought overseas in the ongoing Island Nations conflicts. The unit I was stationed with was captained by Vernon Simillon, father of Greggard, the current Lord Simillon. We found ourselves dispatched to Vellick Island which was in the midst of a civil conflict with the Calaran Rebel Army."

There was a weight in Jack's eyes as he spoke of his wartime life. "Vernon, unlike his son at the same age, was very much of the opinion that men of his class were made only to rule over everyone else. There was a condescending nature to how he ran the unit. In those days, the men of low birth like I were less than human in his eyes. He didn't see our lives as having value and as such placed us in dangerous situations where death was almost certain. I kept coming back from whatever damnation he dispatched me to, often dragging my dead and dying comrades along with me.

"That all changed when the Calaran Rebels came down upon

the beach we were holding and Captain Simillon froze in the face of the enemy. I took charge and led the men in holding back the Calaran rebels long enough for a message to get to the Vellick forces to come to our aid. The Rebels cut and ran when the Vellick soldiers answered and Captain Simillon lived to see another day. He thanked me for my work and told me that if we lived to see Illiastran shores, that I was free to ask anything of him that he could grant."

There was a lapse as Jack Paylor took another drink from his jug. "I came back from that war, the last one I fought in. I felt, having seen so many tours of those dreaded isles and lived through all of them, that I could go home at last and be at peace. It was as if there was a reason I had come back and that reason was waiting for me with open arms and all the love in the world."

A deep breath later and Jack went on. "A pox had swept through the poorer districts of Portsward while I was in Vellick, it took hundreds and my love was one of them. It was in a hospital where last we saw one another. My love had fought off death just to see me one more time." The weight of the emotion in that little shack was something Tryst had rarely felt before. Tryst and Orangecloak shared a quick glance, both feeling the emotional weight that the telling of this story brought upon Jack Paylor's shoulders.

"There were only us in that moment in time. The others faded away from my mind's eye. They didn't exist and that was my mistake. Our hands were holding to one another tightly and I could feel the strength slipping, so I spoke the words I wanted to say: 'The thought of seeing your face was all that brought me back home. It was all that kept me alive and fighting. We fought so hard for our love and I fought to come home and now you have to fight this.'

"I still remember the last words my love ever spoke: 'I'm all out of fight, Love. I could only hold on this long, just long enough to see your face one more time and tell you that I love you, Jack Paylor. You were the best thing to ever happen to my life and I can die happy for having you at my side for the best and worst of it.'"

Jack Paylor swallowed hard, his eyes on the lantern on the table, letting the flame take him back. "That was when Nathaniel Parrigrin died in my arms, these big, strong arms that for all their muscle couldn't do anything against that pox."

"I'm so sorry, Mister Jack," Orangecloak started before Jack talked over her.

"Not as sorry as I was for telling my dying lover that I loved him," he said mournfully. "There was a Patriarch of the fucking Triarchy ready to give last rites when I said it. We had spent our entire relationship hiding who we were and in Nathaniel's death I wasted our efforts. I don't regret it, not to this day do I regret it, but I was sorry for bringing forth what we had worked so hard to conceal.

"I ran to the Simillon Manor after I left the hospital and I asked Lord Vernon Simillon for that favour. I asked him to get me out of Portsward and out of the reach of the Triarchy before they came for me. That is why I am here, that is why I am loyal to the Simillon family until my last breath. They gave me life where the Triarchy would have only given me death. Sure enough, the big blokes with the broadswords and the burgundy robes broke down the door of my home the next day. By then I was on a ship headed for Tusker's Cove."

Sad eyes went to Orangecloak, glancing over the face that reflected the heartbreak of Jack Paylor. "My fighting days are behind me, I fear. My will to bear a blade and a pistol has ebbed away to nothing. You though, Lady Orangecloak, you are an ally to men and women like Nathanial and I. Men and women that still have a future in this world if they are willing to fight and as long as there are people like you willing to help. Please, consider them when you meet Greggard, this is all I ask of you."

Orangecloak met his eyes with her radiant blues, her voice shaking as the weight of the request came to rest upon her. "I promise you that I have never forgotten the plight of your kin, nor shall I. Everything and everyone will be considered in Portsward, of this you have my word."

21

ORANGECLOAK

It had been a tiring hike since leaving Jack Paylor's second shack. The terrain was boggy, the weather wet and the mood dour. What had kept Orangecloak putting one foot before the other was the thought of a warm shelter and a hot meal at Jack's cottage. Now, with a satisfied appetite, she sat in that very cottage upon a wooden rocking chair, staring into a brick and mortar fireplace as the logs upon it crackled and burned.

They had left Jack to go on his own way to the Hotel Dupoire, delivering news and information to Kevane and his daughters of the human world. Orangecloak's own company had talked very little since that night, speaking only of immediate matters pertaining to their journey and naught else.

There had been no tales of the men Tryst had killed or sarcastic retorts filled with contempt from Fletchard, just a sombre hike beneath an unyielding dome of clouds. The silence had afforded Orangecloak time alone with her thoughts, though two days since meeting Jack Paylor she still felt quite perplexed.

The cottage home of Jack Paylor was a fine little abode and spacious in comparison to the three shacks he had built between there and the Hotel Dupoire. It had a proper fireplace with iron cooking tools, a handmade kitchen table that could comfortably seat four, even a separate bedroom and a rudimentary lavatory for convenience.

Tryst was currently catching his slumber in the bed large

enough for two, his watching of the fire having ended. Stretched out across the floor on a bear pelt rug in the centre of the main room was Fletchard, contentedly wrapped tight in his brown cloak and snoring audibly.

The fire began to wane and Orangecloak rose to feed it another log. As she did so, her eyes fell to the portrait painting above the fireplace for what seemed the hundredth time. In it a bright eyed, handsome man with a beaming smile and a nice suit posed proudly in an ornate chair. A name engraved on a brass plate embedded in the frame confirmed what Orangecloak had all but exclaimed when she had first seen it earlier that evening. *Nathaniel Parrigrin, the late lover of Jack Paylor.*

Orangecloak stood on the shoreline of the sea of her memories, reflecting on what the woodsman had told her of his life and how he had come to live it solitarily. The morning after, he had placed a hand on her cloaked shoulder and told her, "If I were ten years younger, I would sling my axe across my back and venture with you. Alas, my will to go warring has long passed."

Orangecloak had answered that accordingly. "I have not decided to pursue war and on the contrary, I abhor the very notion of it, Mister Paylor. I have sincere doubt that Greggard Simillon will alter that position."

"No matter what road you choose after Portsward, you will find no easement, my lady," the hermit trapper had said of that, his voice utterly melancholic. "The EMP will continue to hunt down you and your fellow Thieves until the end of days. If you will be cornered into a fight, you might as well fight back. If nothing else, you will be able to say you went down bravely."

Orangecloak waded out further into the waves of recollection, recalling the day the gates flew open in Yaelsville. Marros and the Fearless Forty had brandished their steel and ran to meet an enemy numbering over five hundred, just to give the innocents of Yaelsville time to escape. Forty-one Thieves and scores of civilians slaughtered like sheep, for all the good it did them trying to fight back.

I would be dead too if I had followed their example.

She dove deeper into the ocean of her past, diving until she came face to face with her father. Iron bars separated them, a mere girl of eleven and the man that had given her life and had protected her. This was her last visit, the last time they spoke but not the last time she saw him. Orangecloak's uncle, by then the guardian of her and her little sister, had arranged for the visit. The younger sibling had refused to see her incarcerated parents, but not Orangecloak. She was her father's daughter, stubborn and determined to a fault.

That determination led her to sitting on a cold floor, her little hands reaching through the bars to hold the larger, callused mitts of her father. His face was rough to look upon as his captors had beaten him fiercely, rendering one eye grotesquely swollen shut and knocking out several of his front teeth.

"My darling daughter, you shouldn't have come, this is no way to see your father." His voice was drowning in sorrow as he spoke.

"I wanted to see you, Father. I heard Uncle talking with some other men and they said they're going to kill you. They're lying though, aren't they? They're not going to kill you, are they?" She was young and still so naïve to the world. Even so, some part of her knew the answer all along.

She could still hear him as if she was sitting outside that cell. Even in such a dreary, forsaken place, with his poor, beaten face, he was brave and strong. "Sweetheart...I'm sorry. I won't be here much longer. You deserve to hear that from me."

Orangecloak remembered that her own resolve was not as strong as her father's and tears had been streaming down her face by this point. "No, that's not fair, Father! You can't let them kill you, because you were only helping those poor people in Phaleayna."

Even with his death looming near, Orangecloak's father was a voice of measured calm. Somehow, even in a dark and gloomy jail with a door of iron bars between them, he had tried to soothe his daughter's worries. "I broke the law, my dear, now the men who enforce that law are going to punish me for it."

"How come you always tell me I have to follow the rules and laws, but you don't have to? Why was it okay for you to break the law?" she had asked him next, full of questions as she had been known to be back then.

"It wasn't okay, now I am going to be punished for that," her father had explained. "Just as your mother and I would punish you or your sister when you broke the rules at home, that's how the law works."

That had only frustrated Orangecloak further. "So then why did you break the law if you knew it was wrong?"

The answer he gave was one she had carried with her as a reminder of what the cause was really all about: "You know how in your history books there used to be a King in Illiastra?" She had nodded as he said that, not sure where he was going with his explanation. "Well, when a King is in charge, he would make the rules and his people had to follow them. We don't live in a Kingdom anymore, not since the last king died hundreds of years ago. Today, we are supposed to be living in what is called a Democratic Republic. What that means is a voice for every man and woman in the say of how this country is run. Do you understand?"

"I think so," she had answered between tearful sniffles.

He went on, "In Illiastra today, we don't have that anymore. The EMP alone tries to decide what is right and what is wrong as if they were kings. They give no one outside of the EMP a voice and that is not how this country is supposed to work. The EMP has used their place of power to hurt and control innocent people. Your mother and I and our friends stood up for what we believed was the right thing to do and we helped those people that the EMP would have hurt. Does this make sense to you?"

"Sort of," Orangecloak had replied to him uncertainly as her young mind had tried to comprehend it all. "So the EMP tries to tell everyone what to do, even if it's not the right thing to do. So you and mother and the others decided to disobey them and do what you thought was the right thing do?"

His callused, yet gentle hand had reached through the bars to wipe the tears away from her face as he spoke. "Very good, you're a very smart girl and I don't think I've told you that often enough. It is a lot for me to try to make you understand at your age, but if I don't explain myself now, then I'll have no other chance to do so."

She had tried to deny it could happen, tried to bargain with fate. "You'll have lots of chances, Father, because I won't let them kill you. I'll find your friends from Phaleayna and we'll get you and mother and the others out of here and we'll all go live in Phaleayna together and be happy."

"No, my sweet, I'll not endanger the lives of you and your sister again," her father had whispered in an empathetic tone. "Freeing me would not only endanger your lives, but the lives of all the other girls and boys in Phaleayna. That's not fair to them to have to maybe lose their mothers, fathers and their own lives just to save me. I am one man and a whole island of people should never die to save one man.

"I'm sorry I won't be there for you and your sister, and I'm sorry I tried to be a hero when I should have been your father. Your uncle and aunt will take good care of you and your sister. They will make sure you grow up away from mine and your mother's shadow."

Orangecloak had been adamant in her efforts to save her father. The thought of trying to accept a world without him was simply not one her young mind had any interest in comprehending. "It's you that don't understand, Father. You were already my hero for helping all those people and I want to be just like you when I grow up. I don't want to be like Auntie Florice, wearing dresses and letting men tell me what to do," she had argued.

Her father had been quick with a counterpoint to that. "Your Auntie Florice is going to be alive and free next week and all that's asked of her is to get dolled up in a pretty dress. Meanwhile, I'll be dead and your mother will be somewhere far worse. My dear, don't strive to be like me, this is what it will get you."

"Why would you tell me about right and wrong and all of that if I can't pick what's right and wrong for myself?" she had loudly queried. Orangecloak had been argumentative at that age, not that there had been much change in that regard, she had to admit.

In retrospect, Orangecloak realised how calm her father had been at that point. While she was trying to find every reason to deny his fate, he had already accepted it. His soft, hushing voice at that moment was clear indication of that. "Because, darling, I don't want my daughters to end up like your mother and I. You deserve better than to spend your last hours in a dingy cell waiting for a noose."

Red curls had bounced all over her shoulders when she shook her head in protest of that. "How is it better to be like Auntie Florice if I'm not happy?" Orangecloak had asked defiantly. "You told me a long time ago that 'We only get once chance at life and we should spend it doing what makes us happiest as long as it doesn't hurt anyone.' That's what you said and now you're saying I should be sad if it means I can live to be old. Which is it?"

She would remember her father's laugh until she drew her last breath. "You really are too smart for your own good," he had said. "I see your mother in you. You have her face, that same stubbornness and best of all her mind. Your mother always had more sense than me. Though, I couldn't talk her out of doing what she wanted either, you know. Just, do me one favour, Sweetheart, just this one thing I ask."

"What is it, Father?" she had inquired.

His hand had cupped her face then, a smooth thumb caressing her cheek. "Promise me that if you follow your heart and do what makes you happiest that you won't throw your life away as easily as I did. We only get one life, my sweet daughter, don't squander it."

It was at that moment that Orangecloak breached the surface of that sea of memories, bringing her back to Jack Paylor's cabin and the dwindling fire. While her mind was far in the past, she had absently wrapped herself up in the orange cloak that her name derived from.

It had come to symbolise everything the Thieves and I stood for. It rallied the downtrodden and gave the oppressed a banner to marshal beneath. Yet, before it was all of that, it was Father's cloak.

When Fletchard ordered his minions to take the tattered garment from her, she had barely noticed. Amidst the violent deaths of her friends and her own capture, the taking of her father's cloak had been the least of her worries.

It wasn't until the cloak was in the grasp of Tryst in the lobby of the Atrebell Manor that she remembered it had been taken from her at all. Once he had it, before Orangecloak knew who he really was, she had considered it lost. In the face of her life ending in that dungeon, the fate of the cloak meant little. Then Tryst had sprung her and Ren and once outside she had come face to face with the man who had cost her everything in the first place. When the sight of the one-eyed bounty hunter had convinced her it was all a ruse, Tryst had gifted her with hope. The same hope that the faded, orange garment with its embroidered golden knotwork sigil upon a green shield had instilled in many others when it was upon her shoulders.

In her younger days, the cloak had dragged behind her on the ground, though as she had gotten taller, the cloak had become frayed. Now, as she made her way to stoke the flames in the fireplace, the ragged ends only brushed the back of her calves.

The fire had begun to burn low and the most recent log she had recently placed atop was already nearing its end. She stirred the hot embers with an iron poker laid nearby and stacked a pair of logs atop the flames that began to lick upwards once more.

Orangecloak found her eyes growing heavy and was relieved that her watch was almost over. When she had the fire back to full strength, she stretched, yawned and began scanning the room for her own place to rest. There were corners to choose from or she could curl up in the rocking chair again, but neither option looked comfortable. Fletchard's watch was next, meaning Tryst would be staying in the bed and Orangecloak was left to fend for herself.

Her body felt heavy, her eyelids began to flutter and she knew that if she didn't decide soon, she was like to fall asleep standing up. With a socked foot, she nudged Fletchard a few times to wake him from his place on the floor. "Wake up, it's your watch," Orangecloak told him flatly.

He rubbed his good eye and adjusted the patch on the other. "What hour is it?"

"The second past midnight provided that Jack Paylor's pendulum clock isn't wrong," Orangecloak shot back while staring down at him, thinly veiling her contempt. "Now get up, we can't let the fire go out."

Fletchard rolled over and turned his back on Orangecloak. "The door is locked, there's likely no one is chasing us and no wild animals are going to bother us. We don't need a watch to be set, so if you want that fire to stay lit, either do it yourself or fuck off."

"No, I won't fuck off. Now, get up, you lazy sot," Orangecloak answered him with equal parts defiance, impatience and exhaustion. "You're the one who has been complaining about the cold since we left the hotel. If anyone should want to keep that fire going it's you."

A groan escaped Fletchard as he sat up. "Fine, I'm up."

Orangecloak gave him no chance to add to his insulting tirade and left him on the floor. Her options for reprieve from him seemed to be limited to the lavatory and the bedroom. As she stood there, wrapped in the cloak Tryst had returned to her during the escape from Atrebell, an impulsive decision came upon her. She lifted the latch on the bedroom door and slipped inside, deciding she didn't want to spend any more time in the same room with a conscious Fletchard than necessary. The door creaked ever so slightly on its iron hinges as she closed it behind her and she stood still, letting her eyes adjust to the blackness of the room.

No sooner had she secured the latch than she heard Tryst moving about. "Orangecloak?" he asked as he stirred from his slumber, reaching for the oil lamp and box of matches on the table beside the bed. "Is something the matter?" The man was evidently a light sleeper and even the rattling of the door had woken him, despite her best intentions to not disturb him.

Orangecloak found herself to be nervous at the sudden urge she was following through with. "No, nothing is wrong. It's Fletchard's shift and I wanted to get some sleep. The floor is not comfortable and Fletchard is insufferable, so I thought I would perhaps lie in the bed."

"Very well," Tryst threw back the bear furs serving as bedding, revealing his ripped, nearly naked torso beneath. "I'll take the floor instead then, could you pass me my tunic?"

She stopped him before he could swing his legs out. "I was thinking that we could both take the bed, perhaps?" Orangecloak suggested. "No need for one of us to be out on the cold floor, there's room enough for two beneath the furs."

"That would be fine, if my lady wants." Tryst slid to the side of the bed beside the wall, gesturing to her to join him. There was calmness to him, likely due to his tired state. Though, all the same, Orangecloak sensed Tryst was not opposed to the idea of them sharing the bed.

This was just the two of them sharing a sleeping space, nothing more, yet Orangecloak felt strangely foolish about it. *I'm Lady Orangecloak, Field Commander of the Thieves*, she reminded herself while approaching the bed in an effort to steel her resolve. She hung her cloak upon the bedpost and removed her leather trousers and jacket until she was wearing nothing more than her tunic and smallclothes. A deep breath escaped Tryst as he looked upon her in the low light of the lamp and Orangecloak took the opportunity to slide in beside him.

It was a snug bed, just large enough for the two of them, and once under the covers their bodies came into contact. "This is nice and warm," Orangecloak said with immediate regret, feeling like a silly girl with her first love.

"Aye, it's quite comfortable. Jack Paylor did well in making it," Tryst answered, revealing his own nervousness. "Could you get the lamp?" he asked sleepily.

Orangecloak obliged the request and snuffed the light source, casting them in darkness once more. She found herself facing away from Tryst and thought it the best place to lie. This wasn't an encounter that was intended to be romantic. She was simply tired and wanted a warm, comfortable place to sleep.

An arm taught with muscle snaked its way over her side and across her stomach, tugging her close in a tight grip.

"What are you doing?" she asked him in a whisper.

Tryst explained himself in a tone of slight embarrassment, as if he had been caught doing something wrong in the middle of the act. "I'm finding a comfortable position as my back is to the wall and it's quite cold. I thought if we lie closer together that it might be warmer. I can let go if you would prefer. You need only say the word."

"No, that's quite alright, Tryst, I wouldn't want you to be cold," Orangecloak replied, unsure of what else to suggest.

With a yawn and a contended sigh, Tryst drifted off into slumber, his strong arm still holding tight to Orangecloak. She pulled the furs to her chin, adjusted the down pillow beneath her head and closed her own eyes in hope that sleep would find her.

As much as she tried, her mind was still racing, running a marathon through recent events.

Illiastra has apparently been watching me more closely than I thought. There are many like Jack Paylor whose hopes rest upon my shoulders while others, like Kevane, are willing to invest in me as if I were a commodity. They all think I am a saviour and until lately I had convinced myself I was just that. Now though...With my own Thieves away from me, all I am hearing from these other supporters is the drums of war. I had not heard their beat before, yet now they sound loudly, ringing in my ears and asking that I go before them and lead them in their march. I wanted to be the catalyst of change, but not like this. I am Field Commander of the Thieves, granted. That I hold the title of commander, however, does not make me a war commander, nor do I desire to be.

I cannot fathom Illiastra requiring war to change its ways. Not even to oust the Elite Merchants, as consumed by greed and void of compassion and empathy as they are. I would have to believe that even they wouldn't want to see the nation reduced to blood and ashes. If they saw that they couldn't stop the will of the people, they would have to capitulate. Otherwise, they would stand to lose all. On the contrary, Tryst, Ren and the Musicians that I have met thus far all seem to think the EMP would take that risk rather than yield the slightest bit of power.

Would Father have been so ready to go to war if he were faced with such? Or Mother? Would Yassira if she was not still trying to keep the EMP from her door? Father and Mother knew that if they were caught smuggling supplies and weapons on behalf of Phaleayna that the price to pay for that would be death. They were prepared to lay down their lives for their cause, so would it be so different if they had died fighting? What of Yassira for that matter? Would she have waged war and challenged the EMP if she was given a fighting chance?

How can the Thieves even fight a war? The last war fought on Illiastran soil was fought by hardened warriors in plate armour swinging greatswords, not a scraggly band of leather clad outcasts skilled at acrobatics and stealth. Who are we to wage war and who I am to lead them into that? We are not knights or warriors or soldiers and I am no one to command those people, nor do my Thieves possess the discipline to be successful in battle.

Her left hand brushed against the rough arm coiled about her as she adjusted her position. *Tryst could, though. What he lacks in wartime experience he would have to more than make up for with knowledge alone. The Combat University teaches more than single combat. These are men and women that have been readied for war of their own free will. Of those, lying beside me is one of only five in their thousand-year history to have been declared a Master of Blades.*

Orangecloak stopped herself short of pursuing that thought further. *No, regardless of who is on my side, it is madness to consider attempting war. For war is merely chaos under the guise of change. There is another way and I will find it.*

Tryst adjusted his position behind Orangecloak and in his sleep nuzzled in closer to her. By the time he settled, his face was practically buried in her hair and his breath rolled over her cheek and neck. The air flow felt odd, though working her head out of Tryst's breathing space distracted Orangecloak from her thoughts, allowing her exhaustion to finally catch up to her wandering mind. At long last, she felt her eyes close down and sleep took her unaware.

Orangecloak couldn't recall if she had dreamt, or what those dreams may have been about by the time she and Tryst were woken by Fletchard. "The dawn is breaking, get up," he said as a waking call before breaking into a snort of condescension and derision. "Fucking lovely, it looks like you two are getting nice and chummy."

In their slumber, she and Tryst had shifted. By the time Fletchard discovered them, Tryst was lying on his back with Orangecloak facing him from her side, an arm visibly draped over his chest. "Good morning, my lady, how did you sleep?" Tryst greeted her more warmly, looking upon her with a thin smile playing at the corner of his mouth.

Orangecloak spoke in a low voice as she met his bright green eyes. "I slept well, thank you for asking. It's quite the cosy bed and in truth I wish it wasn't yet morning."

"Aye, I echo that sentiment. The dawn comes too soon," he said with a sigh. "I suppose we should meet the morning though, some food will do us good and then we'll get underway. With any luck we'll reach Tusker's Cove before nightfall."

Orangecloak detangled herself from Tryst and slid to the edge of the bed. "It will be good to clear these wilds and get back to some semblance of civilisation," she began to say until the frigid air hit her and nearly drove her back beneath the furs. "Fletchard must have gone back to sleep and let the fire die out, it's freezing in here."

"That would explain why neither of us was woken to take a watch." Tryst surmised insouciantly as he sat up, his rippling body stretching out before her. "Nothing to be done about it now and we would have to greet the cold soon enough once we step outside. We'll merely be braced for it now."

He was right, she supposed. However, that didn't stop her from being ever so slightly annoyed by his carefree attitude towards Fletchard's failure to maintain the fire. She got dressed hurriedly, yanking her leather trousers over her legs and flinging her arms through the sleeves of her leather coat. Her dagger was still on the belt she had left hooped through the pants and she adjusted it accordingly. The toggles of her coat and her orange cloak were fastened quickly and soon she had herself warm again.

Outside the room the air was chillier again and her black cloak was added to her layers once she retrieved it from where it hung beside the sadly extinguished fireplace. Fletchard hadn't waited for them to rise and was seated at the table, riffling through the food bad.

"What hour is it?" Orangecloak asked him as she glanced about the room barely lit by the first rays of the morning sun.

"Half passed the sixth," Fletchard mumbled in return without so much as a glance.

"It's barely daybreak," Orangecloak began to suggest. "I'm thinking we could light the fire again and have a warm meal before we get walking."

A hand was waved in the general direction of the fireplace by

Fletchard as he disgruntledly answered, "Be my guest."

The sound of footsteps preceded Tryst Reine as he joined them in the main room. "I think that sounds like a wonderful idea," he agreed jovially. "We'll have hot tea, toasted bread and boiled eggs if it would suit my lady," Tryst added as he stepped from the bedroom, clad once again in his black leathers and tunic. "Jack Paylor was kind enough to allow us access to his cellar and his winter stores after all, he would probably be insulted if we didn't."

Orangecloak snapped her fingers and jumped into action. "That would be excellent, Tryst. Leave the fire to me. You can get the food from the cellar," she decided while already stacking kindling in the fireplace and searching for the piece of flint they had used the night before to ignite the fire.

Fletchard closed the satchel and shoved a hand under his jaw while Orangecloak and Tryst went to work making breakfast. Enough was made for the three and they dined contentedly on the meal. Orangecloak felt the warm food and hot tea coursing down her throat and relished every bit of it.

From the corner of her eye, Orangecloak saw movement from the window outside. "My goodness," Orangecloak exclaimed as she glanced in its direction. "It's snowing outside."

Sure enough there were large, fluffy flakes tumbling down outside the glass panes.

"It looks as though our hike just got interesting," Tryst observed as he rose from the table with his dishes. "We shouldn't delay any further. Let's get this place cleaned up and get on the trail."

Fletchard let out a despondent groan. "Surely we can stall our journey long enough to let this weather pass."

"We could, but it's only a day's trek to Tusker's Cove and the snow won't collect beneath us as the ground is not yet frozen. So, it is only the falling flakes we'll have to contend with. In my experience with snow, which living in Drake gave me in spades, walking in falling snow is preferable to walking in the rain," Tryst argued while filling a pot with water from the cask to boil for dish washing. "In the meantime, Orangecloak, could you go shake out the furs on the bed and fix that? Fletchard you can grab that broom beside the door and sweep the floors quickly."

"I could, but I won't." The bitter tone of Fletchard was palpable.

Tryst shrugged in response. "Suit yourself."

The act served to disallow Fletchard the opportunity to goad either she or Tryst further and for that Orangecloak was grateful. The two of them set to work, leaving Fletchard to brood at the table.

Admittedly, Orangecloak harboured similar feelings as Fletchard on the matter of trekking through the snowfall. The counterpoint to that was her desire to not spend any more time than need be in his presence.

In short order the small abode was in better condition than when the trio arrived. The fire was soon snuffed and when the last of the dishes were stacked away, the three of them collected their belongings and set out into the chilly weather.

It was an uneventful morning, which in comparison to Orangecloak's recent past, was welcome. The snow continued to fall softly, accumulating on the hood of her black cloak and the light rattling of the arrows in the quiver on her hip kept a steady beat.

The air was crisp, with a slight wind coming from the north east and the sun considered emerging through the cloud cover to throw its light upon them in spurts. The trail became barren of trees after a time and small ponds and clusters of stones dotted a vast landscape of rolling, yellowing grasslands.

They stopped at high noon for a cold meal of water, hardtack and a handful each of the granola, almond and dried fruit mix that they had gotten from the Hotel. Orangecloak never had a taste for tack, but forced it down anyhow, gnawing on it as she sat beside Tryst, overlooking a marshland that lay ahead. Fletchard was staying near, though not so near that he could be considered sitting beside them.

In the days following their encounter with Jack Paylor, Fletchard had grown even more insufferable than previously on their journey. Spending his time moping and glowering about, his only words to be spoken being done so when asked a question and always in a sarcastic or scathing tone. Orangecloak left well enough alone, though she had to wonder if Tryst had picked up on as much. If he did, he made no mention of it.

An end was called to their break and for the first time it was Tryst and Orangecloak that were out in front, leaving Fletchard to finish his food alone. Once they were back to moving, they walked the edge of the marsh, finding it be a marked area on the map and deciding to stay near it.

The tall, westerly peaks of the Dwarven Mountain range had

grown even taller and Graelin's peak was but a distant point. The terrain was barren and indistinguishable from what they had trekked through already and Orangecloak found herself just so slightly lost. "What is the next landmark we should be looking for?" she asked Tryst for no other reason than to give her something to seek amongst the grassy plains.

"You should keep an eye out for a pair of gargantuan heads." Tryst answered in a whimsical tone with a grin across his face.

Orangecloak looked upon Tryst in disbelief. "I beg your pardon, did you say we're searching for 'a pair of gargantuan heads'?"

The laughter in Tryst could be contained no longer and he chuckled at her response. "Aye, I certainly did. I assure you that you will know them when you see them."

It was mid-afternoon when they crested a rolling hill. The view below stretched for miles, with the Burelin and Montagen mountains serving as a backdrop, the former looming closer than the latter. Here, where the hills began a slow ascent towards the mountains, there was forest for the first time since leaving the cabin. A dense, red, orange and yellow mass of it fostered in the protective embrace of the westernmost of the Old Giant's Children.

Tryst and Orangecloak lingered for a while to take in the view, their cloaks and loose strands of hair blowing in the strong gusts of wind that rose. From their rear, Fletchard approached on heavy feet, grunting with every step. "I'm calling a stop soon," he declared upon approach, leaving them behind as he started his way down the hillside. "Near that forest, preferably!" he shouted back at them over his shoulder.

When Fletchard was well beyond them, Orangecloak turned to face Tryst, "I've noticed that his temperament is getting worse."

"Indeed, my eyes have seen the same," Tryst spoke to be heard above the wind, giving her a quick glance before moving on. "He's gone now, you can let go of your blade."

Just as it was when she met Jack Paylor a few days prior, Orangecloak hadn't even taken notice of her hand wrapped tightly about the dagger on her hip.

I'm getting too reliant on this thing, she observed of herself as she took her first steps down the rolling slope of the hill and released the hilt from her clutch.

The forest proved to be almost entirely oak, with here and

there a fir tree. It was widely spaced and airy, giving indication of its age. There were no discernible paths, but a forest as spacious as this one didn't require marked trails to navigate. Despite that, they stayed near the edge of the woods, using the leafy canopy to keep the still tumbling snowflakes from falling on them as plentifully as they had.

The leaves that had made their fall to the forest floor crunched noisily beneath their feet. Orangecloak remembered a time when she liked that sound, when she liked this season in general. That had been her first life, when she had a warm home to retreat to from the cold nights. Her eyes caught sight of an odd shape and she turned quickly to face it, finding Tryst already with his gaze upon what looked to be a boulder the colour of onyx.

Tryst offered her the map to look upon, his finger on the place he wanted her to see. "Here, have a look."

"The heads again, though this doesn't look like a head and there's only one," Orangecloak pointed out.

"Is there?" Tryst asked rhetorically, fixing his gaze further along to where a dome shaped rock lay buried in the ground and covered with leaves.

She shrugged, unimpressed with the large rocks. "They don't much look like heads to me," Orangecloak began to say, then she walked to where Tryst stood and at once she could see carvings in the larger of the two. There were outlines of a nose and eyes, a mouth and a defined chin. It was indeed a gargantuan face staring back at her. Its buried brethren looked to be peeking above the ground as she got closer and saw it was little more than two eyes and an ancient looking helm. "I stand corrected," she finally admitted as Tryst smiled broadly.

"I must say that I'm impressed," Tryst stated. "They're in far better shape than I expected them to be in, given their age."

Orangecloak shot him a sideways glance. "You know the history of these fellows?"

"Aye, they're the carved likeness of two dwarven brothers, each one sculpted the other." Tryst ran a hand on the scarred and beaten jawline of the taller brother while he explained. "Though I don't know which one is which, you are looking upon the faces of Torgus and Vargus of Clan Spearsmasher. There were supposed to be bodies to match, in equal proportion to the craniums. However, neither was able to complete their work."

"War befell them, didn't it?" Orangecloak surmised, swallowing hard in anticipation of the tragic tale to come. "They were in the old dwarven city of Dhalla when Valdarrow's Army sacked it, no doubt."

Tryst gave a nod in answer. "Indeed, they rallied beneath the banner of the legendary Axel the Goldenhair and helped him hold the pier while the children and the weak were loaded onto dwarven naval vessels. Neither one survived the onslaught, as was the fate of all but a handful of the Goldenhair's men."

"I have to wonder why they were placed here," pondered Orangecloak as she reached out to touch the half buried of the two heads. "It seems like a random location for Dwarven statues. Isn't the old city much further to the north?"

"They were to mark a road that was to be built leading to the city," Tryst replied in a melancholy voice. "Like these fellow's bodies, it was never built. As it was, they had the existing coastal road that ran through the heart of the city allowing passage north to south through the dwarven lands in the west. That road could be followed along the north coast. It began in Tusker's Cove and ran all the way through what is now Gondarrius and into White Canyon Pass and the Elven Forest. However, the dwarves desired a closer link to the former Kingdom of Phaleayna and the friendly humans therein. This road was to be that link, with the two mighty statues to mark it for the world to see. Now they're no more than ancient, unfinished work."

Orangecloak stepped back and pulled her cloaks tight as a hard wind blew through. "You wonder why I don't want to go to war, Tryst," she said as she nodded towards the statues. "This is why, right there. All war breeds is ruination. The dwarves never recovered their city, Valdarrow set out to eradicate them and he nearly succeeded." Her body trembled as she glanced from brother to brother, looking in their blank, sad eyes.

"Do you know why Valdarrow sought to wipe the dwarves from existence?" Tryst asked to gauge her knowledge of her own nation's history.

Orangecloak was not one to disappoint. "It had to do with the Triarchy faith. The three gods of it are Ios, Iia and Aren. The latter was supposed to be the dwarven God and he was the enemy of Ios, the God of Man. Valdarrow thought he was fulfilling prophecy by destroying Aren's creations and sending them to him in his underworld lair. I remember reading that much."

That elicited a sigh and a click of the teeth from Tryst. "That's about the long and short of it, alright. All three generations of Valdarrow were insane religious fanatics. They thought they were infallible scions of Ios and that their destiny was to fulfil the prophecies in the *God's Gift* scriptures." Tryst began to leave the heads behind as he carried on explaining what Orangecloak could only guess was a point he had yet to make. "Once they finished with the dwarves, Valdarrow sought to move on to Amarosha and the half-elves therein. They were Iia's people. Well, half of her people anyhow and reckoned to be abominations in Ios' eyes for being hybrids of human and elf. Therefore, the Triarchy claimed, they needed to be cleansed from the earth. Does this remind you of anyone?"

It did, but Orangecloak thought the comparison was a bit of a stretch. "The clergymen of the Triarchy today are nowhere near as horrid as those of Valdarrow's empire, though. You can hardly make that comparison."

Tryst disagreed. "Indeed I can. They sought to force their religious beliefs on everyone else, regardless of the beliefs of those they condemned and oppressed. Is that not what the Triarchy seeks to do with so many humans that disagree with them?"

"It is, but..." Orangecloak said while seeking a counterpoint to Tryst's claim. "The difference back then was that Phaleayna was a secular Kingdom. They had the original Master of Blades, Segai, as a Knight General and an army behind him that could ride out and fight Valdarrow. Phaleayna today is an island of downtrodden and impoverished people who ran away from the rest of the country. We are no army, I am no Master of Blades or a Knight and furthermore I have no desire to be any such thing."

Tryst shrugged and folded the map. "You *have* a Master of Blades at your disposal if you so choose." They moved on from both the disembodied stone heads and the conversation with that and Orangecloak gave the morose, lonely faces a last look before they left the forest.

A question came to her then, as she moved quickly to catch up to Tryst. "Let me ask you something, Tryst. You're from one of Gildriad's three nations, right?"

"Aye, I was born and raised in the Midlands Republic. Is there a reason you ask?" Tryst answered question for question.

"I've heard that nearly everyone there is a nonbeliever in gods. Is that true?" She would know now where Tryst stood on the Triarchy.

He turned to face her as he responded. "That's a tricky question. You see, all three countries in Gildriad have adopted similar stances on religion in that they view them as claims of scientific measure. If the Triarchy or any of the other faiths want the right to preach publically, they have to be willing to submit their claim to scientific scrutiny. So far, none of them have done so, and therefore, the Midlands Senate, the King's Court in the North and the Knight's Council in the South all grant them no standing. There is no tax relief for religious entities, they can only build temples and towers on privately owned land and they cannot preach in public places.

"The Triarchy sends Brethren and even Patriarchs from time to time to try and make inroads. However, all three countries ask for scientifically verifiable, peer reviewable evidence and send them all home empty handed to whine to their superiors when they cannot deliver. They cry persecution, hypocritically I might add, yet they have nothing to present to the University of Gildriad's scientists, for their claims are but philosophical arguments." Tryst's tone was dismissive on the matter. He clearly had little time for the Triarchy, but skirted speaking of his own beliefs.

So she asked him bluntly, "What of yourself?"

That drew a chortle from Tryst, but he did not balk at the question. "The Patriarch's tried to get me to subscribe to the Triarchy faith when I first took my position in Atrebell and they all failed miserably. There is a reason why religious beliefs are pressed upon the impressionable minds of children. That is because it is much harder to convince adults of such nonsense. Do you have any idea how ridiculous it looks when grown men in coloured robes tell an adult a wild tale then threaten eternal damnation if they don't believe it?"

"I do know," Orangecloak answered the rhetorical question quickly. "You're a male that moved to Illiastra in adulthood, I'm a woman that was born here. A girl in Illiastra grows up being told by the Triarchy that she is nothing more than a servile being, second to men in every conceivable way." The forest gave way to the open, grassy plains again while she told Tryst of her outlook on beliefs. "So, no matter what you think you *know* of the Triarchy's methods of oppression, I've *lived* them, Tryst.

"You think I don't know about ridiculous men in garish robes spouting outlandish stories? I've seen them shove my friends in cages, whip them bloody, lock them in pillories or worse. What grand crimes and schemes did my friends commit you ask? Oh, things like loving another adult of the same gender or for being a woman who was not blindly obedient to a man or for even questioning the faith.

"Yet those are the laws they hold us to all because a bunch of old, dead men wrote an ancient book and claimed a god dictated it to them." Her voice had grown fierce the more she spoke of the Triarchy. "I don't know if there are gods, or if it was Ios, Iia and Aren that made us or even something else. I know this much though: if the Triarchy have it right and I was made to be a wench for some man then when I die, I will walk right up to whatever that god calls a face and say, 'Fuck you. Fuck you, Ios, for making a whole gender servant to another and fuck you for being such a malevolent psychopath that you would command death and enslavement for the crime of being born.'"

Tryst stopped her with a gentle, reassuring hand on her shoulder. "I can see why even if it was all somehow real that you would be filled with anger toward the gods. I see no reason to believe any of it is true, though. Until such time that the Triarchy can present evidence to verify their claim scientifically, I shall continue to withhold that belief."

Orangecloak felt Tryst was eager to let the subject slide. At any rate, she felt Tryst had the right of it and she was in agreement with his assessment of Illiastra's governing religion.

They found Fletchard minutes later seated on the ground with his back on a fallen log. He had chosen a hilltop for his resting place and was seemingly marvelling at the landscape ahead, entirely unconcerned with his approaching companions. The sound of his teeth gnashing loudly concerned Orangecloak as against her wishes, Tryst had entrusted him with the satchel containing their food provisions once more.

"I'll carry it, I'm only carrying a bow and quiver and this small shoulder bag the Dupoire sisters gave me, so it won't burden me," she had argued, but Tryst was adamant that Orangecloak not worry her knees so badly after their recent recovery and she had eventually capitulated after a time.

Now, Fletchard was devouring their dried meat, at least what was left of it. If there was anything else he might have helped himself to she couldn't say, but the bounty hunter seemed more than content with his meal. "Oh, there you are. I thought you might have gotten lost. What a shame that would have been." The words dripped with sarcasm as Fletchard eyed the dark piece of salted, cured and smoked deer in his hand.

Orangecloak disallowed his words a chance to harm her and burrowed to the root of the problem. "How much have you eaten?"

"Worry not. I left myself enough food get to Tusker's Cove." Fletchard grinned mischievously at his own retort. "I think that's far enough to travel with you two anyhow. Tryst can fulfil his promise and put me on a ship right there. I'll find my own way after that."

Tryst interjected bluntly, shutting down Fletchard's attempt at humour. "You're with us until Portsward. There are no ships calling port in Tusker's Cove that can get you out of the country. I'm ensuring you leave personally and that means you go to Portsward with us."

"I'd rather not," Fletchard put back to him.

Orangecloak grabbed up the sack of food on the ground and looked within. "Tryst," she called out to him. "We're down to hardtack, oatmeal and the nut and berry mix. He's eaten all the meat and bread."

Fletchard waved the remnants of his food at them. "It was delicious, my compliments to those dwarven cooks."

"How could you?!" Orangecloak shouted at Fletchard, dropping the bag to the ground.

"Fletchard, we needed that food. Tusker's Cove is a poor little village and we won't get much to restock our supplies with," Tryst said in a calm voice, clearly trying to keep the tension from growing further than it already had.

"I declare that to be bullshit," Fletchard spoke disconcertingly, making no eye contact with either of them. "There's going to be another of them Musician chums of yours there and Greggard Simillon won't see them go poor. I'd wager they'll have a full pantry."

After he ran a hand over his face and collected himself, Tryst spoke up again. "Have you no regard for the snow falling upon your head? Winter is fast approaching and the residents of Tusker's Cove have to ration their own provisions until spring. If they can offer us a meal, then that is all I would expect of them," Tryst tried to explain.

The anger began to grow with Orangecloak. She knew Fletchard was purposely trying to antagonise them and she fought with herself to not give in. "This is unacceptable, I can't fathom why you would do this to us."

"My apologies to the man who only values my life as far as his promise extends and a woman who loathes the very air I breathe."

Fletchard snorted derisively. "What? You didn't think I heard what you and Jack Paylor spoke about? You thought I couldn't hear you on the other side of that rickety pile of sticks serving as a shack? I know Jack Paylor thinks I'm some sort of broken man, unworthy of living in this world and that you agree, Tryst Reine. You let me live solely for your own selfish reasons of keeping your precious word. It would just eat at you if you broke that promise and did me in, wouldn't it? It has nothing to do with me and everything to do with your own selfish satisfaction."

Tryst maintained his calm and collected demeanour in his delivery. "That's not true. I gave you my word that I would see you out of Illiastra alive."

Fletchard spat on the ground at that notion and turned his attention back on Orangecloak. "Then there's Lady Orangecloak here, can't kill a person, not even I, but she wants to see that the names of her dead friends get shouted at me on a daily basis. That's her idea of justice, or so she claims."

"You killed my friends, why do you think that act should not be punished?!" Orangecloak loomed over him and shouted at him through gritted teeth.

"I only killed one of those pox ridden whoresons!" Fletchard roared at her.

Orangecloak couldn't say what came over her as she leapt on top of Fletchard. He fell over sideways with Orangecloak straddling his torso and pinning his arms to his side. She coiled her right hand and lashed her fist into his face rapidly. "You murderous bastard!" she screamed between blows to Fletchard's reddening nose and lips. "How dare you speak of Myles and Coquarro? You have no right!"

She wailed on him long after she had grown too exasperated to speak. Reeling back, Orangecloak inhaled deeply and tried to regain her breath. A right hand shot up and took hold of her throat before she could draw any air at all. A panicked gasp escaped, but she could not refill her lungs. Fletchard sat up and forced her back easily with the hand on her throat, his left grabbing at her hip. There was a hard slam against them and suddenly Orangecloak was free of Fletchard's grasp just as quickly as he had grabbed her. She collapsed to the ground coughing and sputtering to breathe, struggling to get up as her head spun with every attempt to put her feet back on the ground.

When at last she was upright again, Orangecloak scanned for

the two men and found them having gone over the softly sloped hill. Fletchard was crawling on his knees from the bottom, groaning in pain with every movement while Tryst descended toward him slowly.

Tryst's cloak and satchel lay in a pile between he and Orangecloak and he moved carefully, watching Fletchard with caution.

Orangecloak fumbled with the buckle of the belt that kept Tryst's bow firmly attached to her back until she felt it start to fall away. The bow, arrows and the bag she had been carrying tumbled to the ground and away from her and she stumbled forward to peer down at Tryst and Fletchard.

From where she stood, Orangecloak could hear Fletchard's raving quite well. He was still on his knees, one hand supporting him, the other clutching his ribs. "Of course, Tryst Reine is to the rescue in the nick of time, just as I predicted you would be. I see that you'll let her take her shots at me, but as soon as I get my chance, you spring into action to save her pretty red head."

"You have no right to lay a hand on her, Fletchard," Tryst answered him loudly.

Through broken teeth and bloody lips, Fletchard kept hollering at Tryst. "I ought to have finished off that cunt when I did in her tall brute of a man that rushed me with a knife. As far as I knew then, there was still a reward for her corpse. I tell you, going after her was the worst decision of my life. It's my own dumb fault, I should have known better than to get involved with all of this bullshit."

Tryst had reached the bottom of the hill by then, his voice was fury but his body was loose and limber. "I've put up with your sour mood, I kept peace between you and Orangecloak and I even kept Kevane from tossing you out of the hotel entirely. You repay that by goading the lady into a fight. You are a man with neither honour nor integrity. Perhaps Jack Paylor was right about you."

"Fuck Jack Paylor!" Fletchard roared, standing up tall and spitting blood and teeth. "Fuck that old codger in his queer, old arsehole! That man knows nothing of my life or the hardships I've fought through. What right does he have to say whether I should live or die?!" As he spoke the last sentence, his hand went to the hilt of the sabre on his side, pulling it loose from its scabbard clumsily.

"Drop the sword, Fletchard," Tryst commanded him sternly. "I warn you now that you don't want to fight me."

"No, I assure you I do. Fuck your promise, Tryst Reine. I'm

either going to kill you or make you break it." Fletchard let out a bloody ball of phlegm on Tryst's boot as he maliciously spoke. "I was handling a sword when you were barely old enough to handle a butter knife, that's got to count for something. I don't care if you are a Master of Blades. My experience trumps your title. Come and give me that quick death Jack Paylor prescribed for me."

Orangecloak felt her heart leap into her throat as Fletchard lunged at the still empty-handed Tryst. The blacksteel flashed from the red leather sheath just as Fletchard made a roaring slice at Tryst's face. The sound of steel on steel echoed through the evening air. The blow had nicked Fletchard's sword deeply, but not Tryst's, at least not that Orangecloak could see.

Through the falling snow, Fletchard pressed his attack, slashing and slicing hungrily at his younger foe.

There was little Orangecloak could do but spectate as Tryst parried and dodged everything Fletchard could throw at him. No matter how fast Fletchard moved, or how hard he swung, Tryst seemed two steps ahead with his sword in place to parry and his body out of harm's way before Fletchard's blade could land.

Never had Orangecloak seen a fighter like Tryst. His face was a blank slate, giving nothing away to Fletchard that might tell of his next move. The Master of Blades moved as agile as a dancer, as if every muscle and tendon was individually controlled in one fluidic motion.

By comparison, Fletchard's ability seemed to derive from brute force and pure offense. It seemed to Orangecloak that he would be more at home battering his foes with a mace rather than trying to stab and hack with a sword.

A wide slash to Tryst's midsection was met with a counter blow that sent Fletchard's arm high and his feet stumbling. As he recovered, Fletchard came back with an overhead slice that Tryst sidestepped at the very last chance, leaving Fletchard's blade to touch ground with Tryst's coming down atop it. A loud snapping sound rang out and Fletchard stumbled forward into the rising elbow of Tryst.

Fletchard landed on his back and Orangecloak saw the longer portion of his sword's blade lying in the grass. The rest of it and the now useless hilt were still in his grasp. As he rolled to his knees and realised his weapon was ruined, Fletchard cursed and tossed it away. He tried to stand only to be met with a hard side kick to the diaphragm, knocking the wind from his lungs and sending him back to the ground.

Orangecloak breathed a sigh of relief knowing Tryst seemed to have the fight in hand. He sheathed his sword and stepped toward Fletchard, now lying on his side, his left arm propping him up and his right tucked beneath him.

Fletchard was still backing away as best he could, dragging himself on his backside while mumbling something unintelligible.

"What are you trying to say?" Tryst was asking as he covered the ground between Fletchard and he, whose back was now to Orangecloak and the hill.

There was another mumbled response from the breathless swordsman that Orangecloak couldn't understand from her viewpoint, though her eyes caught something: the distinct glint of blacksteel in Fletchard's right hand, tucked beneath his left side on the ground. She patted her right hip for her dagger and to her horror confirmed that the blade in Fletchard's hand was indeed her own.

"I can't hear you," Tryst called out again, no more than half a meter from where Fletchard lay with the small blade ready to strike.

Orangecloak looked about the pile of possessions strewn about where she stood for something to aid her and saw the bow lying where she left it.

She worked the leather straps that had lashed the bow to her back free, grabbed a handful of arrows from the quiver and began sprinting down the hill. It had been some time since last she had wielded a bow, but her body remembered what her mind had allowed to slip. Her feet planted firmly a half a dozen meters from the combatants and she drove all but one of her arrows into the ground.

"Drop the dagger, Fletchard!" she shouted while nocking an arrow to bow.

A cackle burst forth from Fletchard. "Or you'll do what?" he mockingly replied.

She gritted teeth her teeth and pulled the bowstring to full strength, her voice deathly serious. "Drop it or I'll feather your pathetic carcass."

Fletchard kept up his goading. "Tryst Reine promised me I'd get out of Illiastra alive. You wouldn't kill me and make the Master of Blades break that promise."

"I'm not Tryst Reine," Orangecloak retorted.

The taunting continued. "No, you're Lady Orangecloak, the

woman who has built her reputation on being the benevolent saviour of Illiastra. You won't kill me. You wouldn't give me the satisfaction of a quick death."

"You're absolutely right, Fletchard. I'm not going to kill you." Orangecloak slackened her grip and lowered the bow.

Fletchard pushed off his left arm to rise up.

Orangecloak held her breath, made a fresh draw and let the arrow fly.

22

TRYST

letchard Miller, bounty hunter of prolific repute and former Knight's Commander of an entire nation, lay in a pile before Tryst. His groans and cries of pain would be enough to lead any foes or predatory animals down on them had any been about. Tryst stood there silently, allowing the man to roll about in agony and clutch his bleeding left bicep.

The familiar creaking sound of his bow being drawn reached Tryst's ears. Glancing upon the hillside, his eyes befell the image of Orangecloak with another arrow nocked, its feathered fletching resting against her creamy white cheek. "Get up, Fletchard," she called unsympathetically, caring not for his pain. "Get up or I'll strike the other arm too."

"You fucking miserable cunt, I loathe you with every fibre of my being!" Fletchard screamed at her.

Though she spoke through gritted teeth, Orangecloak was strangely calm and focused as she spoke with a stern tone that brokered no argument. "The feeling is mutual, I assure you. Now, get up." Seeing little other recourse, with Tryst to one side of him and the fiery, red haired woman to the other, Fletchard began to comply with her orders.

Tryst had been genuinely surprised when she had loosed that arrow and even more surprised at her accuracy. The arms were hard points to hit, small targets in comparison to the torso and legs, yet her arrow pierced clean through the center of Fletchard's bicep.

Judging from her stance, Orangecloak was clearly comfortable with the bow and more than able to hold the draw weight. It was an impressive sight to behold, one that Tryst even found alluring in a way. There she stood: orange and black cloaks billowing to her side in time with the free falling hair running down her back. A fierce look was fixed upon her beautiful face, unflinching, despite the wind and the large, tumbling snowflakes still falling about. She had lowered the bow and released the tension, though the arrow was still nocked, ready to be drawn again at a moment's notice. It was an image of a strong, confident, enticingly attractive woman that Tryst would remember forever more.

This is indeed a Field Commander before me, a born leader with an unbent knee for her oppressors.

When Fletchard had collapsed upon himself after the arrow's strike, Tryst had taken the opportunity to disarm him of Orangecloak's dagger. Admittedly, Tryst knew of its whereabouts the moment Fletchard had grabbed for it in the scuffle atop the hill. The murderous intent burning in the bounty hunter's eye was truly frightening, but Tryst would let that dagger draw not a drop of Orangecloak's blood.

From the second he saw the blacksteel reflecting the light, Tryst had kept tabs on the dagger. When he had smashed Fletchard in the face and knocked him over the hill, the blade had gone flying and man and dagger had landed close to one another. As Tryst had closed the gap between them, he saw Fletchard crawling over the blade and tucking it into his belt in the small of his back.

The duel between Tryst and Fletchard had been a predictable bout, the hacking methods of the latter proving entirely ineffective against the former's precision. The entire time, Tryst had been waiting for the blacksteel dagger to make its appearance. It wasn't until after Tryst had destroyed Fletchard's sabre and drove him to the ground that Fletchard had produced the dangerous little weapon.

Now, whatever Fletchard's intentions were, they had turned to ash in his usually loud, unyielding mouth. The beaten form before Tryst was all out of fight. His face was a bruised, bloody and broken mess and a stream of crimson ran from the wound on his left arm over the fingers on his right hand and to the grass below. "Can you pull this thing out of me?" Fletchard asked Tryst weakly.

"I could, but there's a better than good chance that if I did, you would bleed out." Tryst surmised as he looked over the pierced arm. "I'll wrap the arrow to keep it from moving and we'll get you aid in Tusker's Cove. They have a skilled medic there that I know will be able to mend that wound nicely." Tryst turned his attention to Orangecloak, still upon the hill, unmoving and unwavering. "My lady, could you be kind enough as to gather our things? It's imperative that we get moving at once, both for the sake of nightfall coming upon us and for treatment of Fletchard's wound."

A nod was all Orangecloak felt to give Tryst before she turned and supposedly followed through with his request.

"What do you plan to do with me now?" asked the defeated, trembling Fletchard from where he stood, almost looking ashamed.

Tryst looked him over, masking his outright contempt he held for the man. "I told you I would see you out of Illiastra alive, I intend to do that. What you do beyond that is your choice. However, I would recommend staying out of my path for as long as your miserable life might extend."

"Aye, I suppose I can do that." Fletchard kept his lone eye downcast while both being spoken to and in his response.

With Orangecloak came their possessions and a veil of silence. The bow, quiver and the travel bag were once again belted across her back, the food satchel and Tryst's bag to a hand each and his cloak across her arm. Tryst's things she laid at his feet and the bag containing the food she added to her own weight. In return, Tryst gave her back the dagger Fletchard had taken from her.

Orangecloak looked over the blade, giving it a visual inspection before returning it to its sheath on her hip. "Patch him up and let's get to Tusker's Cove, we have little light left to walk by," she requested flatly, leaving the pair of them behind for a nearby rock and helping herself to a few handfuls of the almond and berry mix.

Tryst broke open his bag, retrieved the box of medical supplies and went to work on Fletchard's arm. The shaft of the arrow was snapped off with a loud grunt out of Fletchard, producing a stream of fresh blood. What remained was covered in bandages and tied off tightly to staunch the bleeding.

"That should hold you until Tusker's Cove," Tryst stated while closing up his things once more. "In the meantime, you've threatened the life of Orangecloak and wasted our evening with this tantrum.

Given all of that and knowing that Orangecloak no longer has any qualms about putting arrows in you, I suggest you keep your mouth shut and walk quickly."

The last rays of sunlight disappeared beneath the western horizon mere minutes into their renewed hike, and night descended sooner than any of them would have liked. Even if they had a lantern or candles, they would be useless against the persistent snow and winds. As it was, the three of them resigned themselves to a nearly blind walk aided only by intermittent moonlight.

Orangecloak had taken to walking out front, keeping lead to maintain distance between her and Fletchard. The open grasslands made the trek easier and most obstacles remained easily spotted, despite the encroaching darkness of the evening.

After what felt like an hour passed, Tryst brought a halt to the party. "I smell smoke," he announced in a foreboding tone that caught Orangecloak and Fletchard alike off guard.

"That shouldn't be out of the ordinary," Orangecloak queried in befuddlement. "I would think most people in Tusker's Cove would have their fireplaces working tonight."

"That's not wood smoke you smell, this is different," Tryst explained worriedly. "This is the scent of a burnt building. I hope nothing dire has happened in the cove."

It was only a short while later, that they began to see the lights of the town. Tusker's Cove was still in the shadow of electricity, relying on oil lamps for all illumination after dark. The glow of the lighthouse on the southern hills was the most discernible light source, with its flame burning brightly and brilliantly in the night sky. Below it, they began to make out the twinkling of the lamps on the town wharf and roads and the dimmer lanterns within the houses.

They were upon a high hill overlooking the tiny town when Tryst finally caught sight of the destruction. "The Tower of Ios," Tryst pointed to the smoking rubble on the north side of town, atop a cliff that matched the lighthouse's home. "That's what we smelled."

"You've been here before?" Orangecloak asked as she looked upon the rising tail of smoke from the indistinguishable pile of rubble.

"Just once," Tryst answered. "I remember that tower standing out quite plainly as it was taller than the lighthouse on the south hill. It was built that way by the Triarchy intentionally, to show that even in a tiny town like Tusker's Cove that Ios still stands high above all."

They descended the hillside path into town without further discussion. Here they found no roads of stone, but narrow dirt trails that weaved around picket fences and alongside a babbling brook. The dozen or so homes were two storeys tall and nearly square in shape and from upon the trail Tryst could see life within nearly all of them. Candles, fireplaces and oil lamps provided the light, which most of Illiastra had given up for electrical power.

"Here I thought that everyone outside the Southlands had electricity," Orangecloak commented as she glanced about the houses.

Tryst knew the reason for that: "It was never brought here on account of the wiring company's notion that the north was too far to run electrical wires to serve too few people. The dwarves could provide it, but despite it being too remote for wires to be run, the EMP would have no trouble sending armed soldiers to run the dwarves off. What you see before you and indeed along the entire north coast is the last bastion of the candle and lantern north of the Varras River," he said, giving the explanation while leading the exhausted party to the largest of the houses, nestled in a corner of town and upon a knoll.

It was a modest home, barely any bigger than the others in the village. Its shutters and trim were painted white and the clapboard siding was a bright shade of red. The house was the same basic, box shape of the others, albeit with extensions on the first floor that looked to have been added well after the original structure was built.

A horseshoe hung from the panelled wooden door on a rusted hinge and Tryst grabbed it, rapping it several times off the door.

From within, he could hear a gravelly voice calling out, "Sheila, we have company!" It declared, following that with hard, clomping footsteps. The door swung open wide and on the other side of it stood a thickset man in a blue, collared shirt, black trousers and suspenders. Curly, sandy hair slowly fading to nothing and a shadow of a beard speckled a lined face and warm eyes. "Who's at my door at this hour?" he asked amiably of the three of them.

Tryst flung back the hood of his cloak. "It's good to see you, Oldstone," he said, calling the man by his Musicians codename first and foremost, out of habit.

"Tryst Reine!" the man bellowed. "You old dog, I told you to come by again sooner than this. I haven't seen you in an age now. Come on in with the lot of you and get warmed up. It's a frosty night out there and you'll catch the death of cold, come now."

"Were you expecting me, Harold?" Tryst asked as he, Orangecloak and Fletchard crossed the threshold into the cosy home.

Harold patted him on the back as he came through the door before taking his hand to shake. "Aye, we were, lad. We had a visit from Jack Paylor a few nights past who was told by Greggard that you were heading this way through the north pass."

Tryst sighed with relief at that. "That's good to hear. I was hoping you wouldn't be caught unawares, I know your food must be going into ration right now and I wouldn't want to press you too badly for a meal."

"Nay, don't worry yourself about that," Harold reassured him. "Sheila's been baking since Jack Paylor left. You will not go hungry here." His eyes went wide suddenly. "Oh, but I forget myself, we have a bloody code after all. Heart! There, I said your codename, now we can dispense with that."

Tryst had to laugh as he set his things down. "A minor detail, Harold. In the meantime, I have introductions to make," he said as he turned to his companions. "This here in the rear is Fletchard Miller, former bounty hunter and before you is the Lady Orangecloak, Field Commander of the Thieves. My lady, and Fletchard, might I introduce you to Captain Harold Bickerington, the Honourable Minister of the Tusker's Cove Region."

"I would sooner you introduce me as Harold Bickerington, Captain of Illiastra's North Sea Fishing Fleet and Ship's Captain of *The Myra*," the captain corrected Tryst politely. "It means much more to me than any title as a minister for the EMP."

A woman had entered the room quietly while Harold spoke, her hands folded over a white smock and a long sleeved, flowery blue dress. She was middle aged, with a friendly, round face, a pleasant smile and greying blonde hair tied into a bun and Tryst recognised her immediately. "Sheila, there you are," Harold said before Tryst could utter a word. "Look who is guesting in our home for the night."

"Hello, Tryst, it is good to see your face again," she said in a small voice, barely containing her elation. "Please, tell me true, is she who you said she was? I mean, is it really the Lady Orangecloak standing in my porch?"

Orangecloak spoke, stepping up beside Tryst as she did. "Hello, ma'am, thank you for taking me into your lovely home. I am most certainly in your debt."

"Nonsense, my dear, you are in no debt to us," Sheila said with a curtsy. "It is my pleasure to host a proud, fighting woman such as yourself here. We've all heard of you in these parts, though we've never been graced by a visit before now." She caught herself gushing and turned back toward the kitchen. "Oh, would you listen to me fawning on over you. Please, take off your wet boots, get your toes into some knitted slippers, take a seat at the kitchen table and I'll get you all something to eat."

"You're too kind, ma'am," Orangecloak said with a polite nod, moving into the inviting kitchen beyond the porch and allowing Fletchard to step into the light.

Sheila gasped upon seeing Fletchard clutching at his punctured arm. "For goodness sakes, this man is gravely wounded!"

"If it wouldn't be too much trouble, madam, I would like this looked at before supper," he said pitifully. Had Fletchard not attacked Orangecloak, Tryst might have even given him that pity.

"Harold, close your big maw and go get Arthur already," Sheila said while shoving her big husband out of the room and beyond before gently leading Fletchard in by the uninjured hand. "My word, that's an arrow head poking out of your arm isn't it? Were you assaulted by ruffians or Elite Merchant soldiers along the way? Don't tell me the army is coming towards Tusker's Cove. Oh, gracious me, that's just terrible."

"Please calm yourself, Mother, you're being melodramatic," a voice said from the doorway where Harold had disappeared seconds before. Standing in the threshold was a slender, bespectacled teenaged male in tweed trousers and vest and a white, collared shirt buttoned to his throat. He had the eyes and slender face of his father, the small features of his mother and short, light red hair like neither of them. The lad turned towards the guests with his hands casually resting in his pockets. "Hello again, Tryst. Miss Orangecloak, it is a pleasure to meet you, I am sure." He turned his gaze to Fletchard lastly. "And you must be my patient."

Fletchard eyed him sceptically. "I don't think I'm *your* patient, *boy*. Where is the medic?"

The lad produced a handkerchief from the breast pocket of his vest and removed his glasses to wipe them of something unseen. "If you are looking for the medic, then you will look no further, as I am he," the red haired fellow shot back with an air of confidence.

"How is it that a boy of only fifteen be a medic?" Fletchard dubiously retorted.

The lad returned his spectacles to his face and put his hands to his hips before giving a reply. "I will have you know that I am sixteen years old and I have been the closest thing the Tusker's Cove region has had to a proper doctor in several years. Now, you may come into our living room, which in times such as these is pressed into service as a treatment centre, or stand there staring at the hole in your arm. The choice is entirely yours. However, my recommendation is that you waste no more time arguing over preconceived notions of me as that wound is at a great risk of festering and becoming infected."

"That's my Arthur," Sheila beamed proudly. "He's an absolutely brilliant boy. Let him have a look at your arm, ser. I promise you that he'll have it fixed right up in no time. In the meantime, Miss Orangecloak and Mister Tryst, please take a seat and I'll bring you some tea and supper. Harold, you should go rouse the other men, there might be trouble on our doorstep come morning."

"Mother, please, there is no reason to believe the arrow wound was caused by outside forces," Arthur spoke in a tone that bordered on condescending. "Father, you need not go outside for I feel I shall have need of you right here."

Fletchard gave the adults in the room a wide-eyed look and receiving no indication that he shouldn't trust the young man, sheepishly followed him from the room.

Once Harold, the teenager and the bounty hunter had gone, Orangecloak removed the bow, quiver and satchels and then her damp outer cloak.

The sight of her in her signature garment drew a look of awe from Sheila. "My goodness gracious, you'll have to forgive me, my lady. We don't get any people of such reputation here, besides Lord Simillon, of course. I'm simply taken aback to see you in person, my lady and if you don't mind my saying, you're every bit as beautiful as they said you were."

"You flatter me, ma'am, I don't feel I am worthy of all the praise you shower me with." Orangecloak blushed slightly as she took her seat at the bench before the kitchen table.

Tryst removed his own satchel and cloak, even taking the time to remove his blacksteel sword and elven blades before putting himself beside the red haired heroine on the long seat.

As they settled, Sheila got to work cooking dinner while she gushed over her special guest. "Nonsense, my lady, you have put up a good fight against the Elite Merchants for the rights of everyone. We think very highly of you here in the far north, you should know."

Tryst watched warmth arise behind Orangecloak's eyes and the hint of a smile cross her lips. "I had no idea I had such supporters in Tusker's Cove as I've never gotten a chance to visit. Now I wish I could have come sooner."

"Don't worry yourself about it, your fight isn't here, you would have no reason to grace us with your presence," Sheila commented with her back to Orangecloak and Tryst, the peeled skin of potatoes flying to one side of the long counter and the sliced taters to the other. "We're just honoured to have you under our roof on this leg of your journey back to that fight."

The conversation tapered off as the moaning of Fletchard began to reach them. There was a scattered command from Arthur to his father to be heard and requests from both Bickerington men for Fletchard to be still that went unheeded.

"Do you not have a drop of ether about?!" Fletchard shouted. "If you're going to butcher my arm, at least numb me before you do it!"

"This is going to hurt and I'm sorry for that, ser. However, if you don't let me work on your arm, it will become gangrenous and in need of removal by the time you reach Portsward. Barring that it doesn't kill you before then. Now, please stop wriggling about," Arthur answered sternly.

There was more grunting from Fletchard peppered with vulgar words as Arthur attempted to go back to the unenviable task of removing the arrowhead.

Dinner was evidently going to be boiled potatoes, drawn butter and freshly fried halibut fillets and the smell of the salt water fish soon filled the kitchen. A basket of fresh tea buns and a fresh butter pat were placed before Tryst and Orangecloak by Sheila, who sat and joined them while the fish sizzled on the iron pan behind her.

Sheila had just begun to tell them of Jack Paylor's visit when they interrupted by Arthur.

"Excuse me, Tryst." All heads turned at the urgent tone of Arthur's voice to see him standing in the doorway. He had put on a long, white mackinaw over his suit, tied a white bandanna about his nose and mouth, another around his head and donned long, cotton gloves. His hands and the coat were streaked with blood and his eyes spoke of impatience with his patient. "I hate to be a bother, but could you by chance help us hold Fletchard down in the next room, please? We require strength that my father alone seems to lack."

"Yes, of course, Arthur," Tryst said as he slid his chair back and left Orangecloak and Sheila alone in the kitchen.

Within the living room the scene was fairly chaotic. Fletchard lay upon a long table draped in a beige sheet, his body trembling and his forehead a river of sweat. A girl Tryst knew to be Arthur's sister sat nearby in a short sleeved, red dress and white smock. Her mouth and head of dark curls covered similarly to her brother's and a tray of medical tools on her lap as she curiously eyed the arrow wound. At the head of the table was Harold, his thick arms and meaty hands were trying to hold the shoulders of Fletchard down, but he was clearly growing tired of the exercise.

"Have you two come to watch me wallow in pain after what you did to me?" Fletchard slurred in his delirious state.

Tryst looked over his shoulder to find Orangecloak standing behind him, her face stern and hardened as she looked upon Fletchard's pain-wracked body. "Perhaps you should tell the Bickeringtons what you did to warrant your wounds," she uttered spitefully at him.

Arthur returned to a wooden stool beside his sister, her attention focused to her brother before she caught sight of Tryst and Orangecloak standing in the room. The girl's eyes went as wide as saucers and she began moving her hands about frantically in different formations before Arthur, who began to speak as the girl's fingers and hands became a blur. "Louisia says, Hello to the both of you and that she is very excited to meet Lady Orangecloak and would like to speak with her later when we are done sewing Fletchard up."

"Tell her I said hello as well and that I'm glad to see her again," Tryst replied, watching Arthur move his own hands and fingers for his sister in response.

Orangecloak watched the scene with a look of puzzlement. "What is going on here?"

"Louisia is stone deaf," Tryst explained. "She and Arthur developed a language so that the two of them might communicate that is derived entirely from hand signals. They have hundreds of words and the human alphabet made into hand signs and memorised."

The raised eyebrows of Orangecloak indicated just how impressed she was. "That's incredible," she commented. "I've seen signing languages before, nothing quite as complex and never anyone who could gesture as quickly as they could."

"My sister is every bit as brilliant as I am," Arthur jumped in while signalling for Louisia to hand him one of the instruments on the tray. "The only limitation she faced to expanding her knowledge was the ability to communicate with the world and the two of us remedied that with our signing language." Arthur leaned back on his stool for a moment and Louisia diligently leaned forward and dabbed a dry cloth to his forehead to mop his sweat. "Alright, Fletchard, I have prepared your arm for the extraction of the arrow," he stated. "This will most certainly be painful, but when we are through the entire arrow shaft will be removed."

His dark little eyes glanced to Orangecloak knowingly. "Luckily, your assailant happened to be an archer of such sufficient skill that the arrow head penetrated clear through muscle and tissue and avoided the bone completely. Tryst and my father will hold you down and I will need you to remain as still as possible so that this might go smoothly. Do you have any questions before I begin?"

"Just get it over with, already," Fletchard barked impatiently between deep breaths.

Arthur nodded at that and leaned forward again. "Excellent. Now, let's position your arm so that I have a good view of the underside, like so." Arthur gently adjusted Fletchard's limb while he spoke until it was where he wanted it.

"Now, Tryst, stand beside Father and restrain Fletchard's wrist and forearm to keep him from flexing away from me. Father, I need you holding his shoulders." The two men stepped into place as instructed while Arthur signed instructions to Louisia beside him. She signed back quickly and handed him an object that looked like a shiny pair of pliers. "Alright, here we go."

It took less than a minute of grunting, cursing and straining to pull the arrow free. Fletchard cursed and jerked with every movement that Arthur made of the wooden shaft, but Tryst and Harold managed to hold him tight. From the entry and exit points of the wound came a fresh pouring of blood, but the shaft was soon free of the arm.

Fletchard began to relax almost at once, panting and moaning, but otherwise no longer resisting. Both Tryst and Harold released their hold on him at Arthur's command. "Thank you both for your assistance, Tryst and Father. Louisia and I can handle things from here," Arthur said while speaking to his sister with his hand signals.

With that, Harold rose with a nod and ushered Tryst and Orangecloak from the room as his offspring began treating the arm.

Upon returning to the kitchen, Sheila was only happy to inform them that supper was on the table and waiting for them all should they be interested. It was an offer her husband and the two present guests readily accepted.

Fish and boiled potatoes beneath a simmering layer of drawn butter were the evening's offering. It was a tasty meal and the long dinner table was soon fully occupied with the entire Bickerington family and their guests. Even Fletchard came to sit amongst them, trying awkwardly to eat with only his right arm while his left, to keep his stiches from tearing, was in a sling.

Through the course of the meal, Tryst told Harold and the family of the intense escape from Atrebell, leaving out Fletchard's cohorts and their deaths at their employer's hands. He instead spoke of Ren and his efforts to aid and comfort Orangecloak, the Hotel Dupoire and the parts of their stay that Tryst was at liberty to speak of. The recollection ended short of meeting with Jack Paylor and the fight that erupted afterwards. Sheila and Orangecloak ate in silence, the latter stealing glances at Tryst as he spoke. All while Tryst talked, Arthur translated the conversation to Louisia and was last to finish his meal as a result.

"So, you came across Jack Paylor after that, I take it?" Harold finally asked after Tryst abruptly ended the story with the departure from the hotel.

"Aye, we did, he's doing well and on his way to see the Dupoire family," Tryst answered hesitantly.

Harold continued to push the story along. "I'm to guess that what happened to Fletchard came *after* meeting Jack Paylor, then?"

"Aye, we had an incident." Tryst nodded.

Sheila began to grow a little impatient. "What sort of incident? Bandits? Soldiers? Who came after you?"

"No one came after us." It was Orangecloak who spoke up from her place at the table beside Tryst. "Fletchard drove me to attacking him and took my knife before Tryst could come between us. They fought and Fletchard was going to use the knife and I put an arrow in him to prevent that from happening."

"I see..." Harold's voice trailed off as silence overtook the room. Tryst could almost feel the Bickerington's perceptions of Fletchard tangibly changing.

Orangecloak swallowed audibly and lowered her eyes back to her plate, as if she was ashamed of having loosed that arrow.

Louisia's fork clanked to her plate as she hastily began to sign back to Arthur following his translation of the incident.

It was while the two of them conversed in their noiseless language that Sheila attempted to steer the subject away from the violent events outside town. "Tell me, Tryst, did you happen to see our eldest son before you left Atrebell?"

Tryst took the cue and ran with it. "As a matter of fact, I spoke to Jorge on the night of our departure. He was guarding the rear stables when I went to liberate Fletchard. He's doing quite well, complaining as always, but keeping his nose clean all the same."

A humorous scoff escaped Harold. "He wrote to us once and said the lads had taken to calling him Bicker, you included. When we wrote back, we told him if he didn't complain so much they might not call him that."

Arthur chipped in on that. "Louisia and I both agreed that it was an apt sobriquet for our elder brother. Jorge is not like to do anything without first complaining about it."

"That does sound like the Jorge I knew in Atrebell alright," Tryst added lightly.

Sheila stood up from the table and turned to Arthur. "Could you ask your sister to help me serve some tea?" She asked her son, earning an annoyed look from him.

"Mother, you really should practice speaking to Louisia yourself," Arthur scolded with a folding of his arms.

"It's easier if you do it. We have guests, Arthur, now is not the time to watch me fumble my hands about trying to talk to Louisia," Sheila countered.

His father furrowed his brows and crossed his own arms, themselves thick with muscle and coarse hair. "Boy, you do as your mother tells you and don't answer her back."

"Fine, but Mother, you know how to sign simple words and sentences to Louisia now and you know how much it would mean to her if you tried. At least Father makes an effort." Arthur huffed in a fashion that highlighted his annoyance clearly. He set about asking the favour of his sister and she nodded quickly and signed back to Arthur before going off to help her mother. "You see that, Mother? Louisia agrees, she said she wishes you had asked her yourself."

An exasperated Harold sighed from his place at the head of the table. "Let it go, Arthur," he said before turning to his wife. "Can we just have some tea please and perhaps a hot raisin bun and a spot of butter to go with it, if it's not too much to ask?"

"It's not too much at all, dear," Sheila said from where she stood over the stove while Louisia fetched the teacups from the cupboard. The dessert was served up and the tea poured, though the tension began to linger noticeably.

Sheila and her children both avoided eye contact with Fletchard and Harold seemed to have only glares for him. Soon, Fletchard grew too uncomfortable to stay seated. "Thank you very much for the meal, I think I might take my tea into the next room and sit quietly for a while if no one objects," he said morosely. Harold gave him a nod and the wounded man walked off with a wince, clutching teacup and saucer in his good hand.

"That's a real shame what happened," Sheila commented as she sat down slowly with her cup of tea to hand.

"It was indeed." Tryst sighed. "Jack Paylor said some very forward things about Fletchard and unfortunately it was the spark that set off a slow burning fire."

"Speaking of fires," Harold interjected. "I don't suppose you have noticed the smoking ruins of the Tower of Ios."

"I did, we were all quite curious to know what happened," Tryst replied politely.

Sheila set her cup down quickly with a loud clatter, her eyes darting from person to person. "Arthur, you and your sister should leave the room."

"Nonsense, Mother. Louisia can't hear them talking and anyhow, the both of us know the matter to which you are speaking of," Arthur added in a frustrated tone, clearly frustrated that his mother had attempted to shoo him and Louisia away.

Harold laid one of his thick hands gently on his wife's arm. "Sheila, you call the two of them brilliant in one sentence and treat them like children the next. Let them stay."

"Very well, Arthur," Sheila relented before turning to her son.

"Be careful what you tell Louisia, there's no need to scare the girl."

"I assure you she can handle the retelling of the strife we've dealt with for the better part of a season," Arthur replied, disgruntled at the treatment of he and his sister.

"That's enough, Arthur. Let me get on with it," Harold said in an exhausted tone while raising a free hand, palm outward, in a gesture to silence him. The hand that had been upon Sheila's arm was now wrapped in her slender fingers as Harold started. "It began when Patriarch Feldham became too feebleminded to deliver the weekly sermon any longer. We sent him with Brother Lomery, the Hand of the Tower, as escort to a hospice in Daol Bay that serves the elderly Patriarchs in their last days. What the Triarchy sent back as replacement for both men was..."

Harold let his voice trail off as he ran a hand through his balding head of dark curls. "We didn't think much of the new Patriarch from the start, he was always smiling, but it wasn't a pleasant smile and it never faded. It seemed eerily phoney, as if he thought it masked who he really was. Though, what was more surprising was that with him came a new Hand of the Tower. After all, Brother Lomery was a young, able man not quite forty. It crossed all the townsfolk as odd that Lomery was replaced. He was born and raised in Tusker's Cove, for the sake of all things. We couldn't even begin to reason why they wouldn't send him back here."

Arthur interjected in his confident tone, speaking both aloud and signing to Louisia beside him. "It was clear to Louisia and me from the outset that Patriarch Hussman and Brother Durne were foul."

That garnered a nod from Harold. "Indeed, the two of them were the first to raise concern, but the townsfolk tried to at least give the new men a chance. After the first sermon Hussman delivered, he began asking the young girls to stay behind. It was never more than one and never with their parents or any other townspeople around save for Hussman and Durne."

"The first girl, a little one of ten, came back telling strange tales of foul touching and groping," Harold told them regretfully. "No one could think that a Patriarch or a Brother of the Triarchy could do the unspeakable things she spoke of and we didn't believe her. It wasn't until another one and another one after that, all near the same age, came back telling of increasingly worse stories that we did anything about it, much to my shame."

The room grew deathly tense and Tryst felt the bile rising within him as he surmised what was to come.

His eyes fell to Orangecloak, her teeth grinding and her own eyes locked on the tea in her cup. "Mister Bickerington, when you finally believed what they were telling you, what did you do about it?" she asked, trying to contain her anger and nearly failing.

Harold cleared his throat before going on. "The parents of the three girls came to the house together and asked me as Minister of the Region and Captain of the Fleet to do something about it and so I did. I went to the Tower with my first mate, Kerrell Greenlee, at my side and we approached the two Triarchy men with the stories we were hearing. They denied it all of course, but neither Kerrell nor I bought their lies, not anymore. We told the two of them that they were not permitted to leave the Tower for any reason nor hold any sermons. Two of my crew were posted in the tower as guard and I declared the Triarchy men under arrest by my authority as Minister of Tusker's Cove. Our plan was to take them to Portsward so that they could be formally charged with the crime of child molestation."

"Yet, that wasn't the end of it," Sheila spoke up, soft tears rolling down her cheeks. "That very night, they killed Thom and Martin, who were the two men guarding them, and they came down from the hill to kill the girls that had spoken out. They broke into the home of one of the girls, took her at knifepoint and stabbed her father repeatedly. He would have died had Arthur and Louisia not seen to him so fast."

Arthur added to the horror story that was unfolding. "That girl's brother is a friend of mine. He escaped through his bedroom window and came running to our house straight away."

Harold picked up from there. "I gathered Kerrell and the rest of my crew and we all went to the tower with whatever we could find as weapons as fast as our feet could carry us. While we went to the tower, Arthur and Louisia went to the girl's father to treat his wounds. Sheila woke the rest of the townsfolk and we came together in the face of the crisis with every able man and woman taking torch and makeshift weapons to hand. By the time myself, Kerrell and the other crew got to the tower, they had the poor girl tied hand and foot to the altar and were saying a ritualistic prayer over her with a knife to hand. They were going to sacrifice her to Ios for besmirching their names based on old laws in the *God's Gift*."

Arthur cut in on his father, who seemed to want a break to catch his breath anyhow. "Laws that she didn't break, I might add. They sullied their own honour and befouled themselves as men. She was just the first one to speak of their heinousness."

"Aye, luckily for us and the girl, the pre-ritual prayer happened to be long winded," Harold added, resuming where he left off. "We knocked down the door and my men grabbed the Triarchists before they could do anything. In the melee, Kerrell took a slash across the chest from Brother Durne's knife, but there were no other injuries and the Triarchists were quickly tied up. The girl was freed and her uncle took her back down the hill."

Orangecloak asked quietly, "What did you do with the Patriarch and the Brother?"

It was Sheila who spoke up with an answer. "They're dead now. We dealt with them ourselves, as a community."

Harold confirmed as much with a nod. "That all happened three weeks ago. The Tower sat empty after that and I called a town meeting to decide what was to be done. A vote was held and three quarters of the townsfolk decided to burn the tower to the ground.

"As far as anyone concerned outside of Tusker's Cove are going to know, Durne and Hussman died in that fire. I had put off burning the tower, but I knew the deed must be done before I left, so, I torched it yesterday morning. I'm beginning the gathering of the fleet tomorrow. We sail along the north coast as far as Portsward gathering the other fishing ships from the other northern ports and we head for the fishing grounds. It keeps us away for a long stretch of time and while in Portsward I intended to let Lord Simillon know what happened and look into finding Brother Lomery."

The middle aged man turned his attention to Orangecloak, seated beside Tryst. "My lady, I know you speak out against violence. However, my only regret over the incident is that I didn't prevent the Triarchy curs from hurting those girls to begin with."

Tryst glanced at Orangecloak, still staring at her tea. She moved to speak, but was cut off by another voice.

"Hussman and Durne are dead, are they?" Fletchard interjected with a rhetorical question from where he had come to stand in the kitchen, laying his empty teacup beside the wash basin gingerly. "This is good to know, I shall remove their names from my list."

All of the Bickeringtons seemed befuddled by that and it was

Harold that asked what they were likely all thinking. "What do you know of Hussman and Durne?"

Slowly, Fletchard lowered himself into a chair on the opposite side of the table from Tryst and Orangecloak, putting him between Arthur and Sheila. "Allow me to explain: I had been looking for those two for some time," he began. "There's a whole ring of their types within the Triarchy fold. They stick together and the whole, corrupt organisation shuffles them around from town to town to cover up their sinister crimes. It's too bad I hadn't found them myself. I might have been able to squeeze the location of a few of their kin from them. Not that it matters much now, anyway," he said, his eye falling on Orangecloak. "This one and others like Jack Paylor loathe me because I make my living hunting down wanted people like themselves. It pays my bills and my taxes and gives me the funding needed to dole out justice to this vile ring of molesters that would otherwise get away."

Orangecloak found her voice at last. "Fletchard, I didn't know."

"No, you wouldn't," he answered quickly, before going on. "I've been very careful to make sure that no one does. Even the Triarchy and the EMP have never been able to figure out who has been picking off the Patriarchs and Brethren. It doesn't matter now. I have to leave that job unfinished, as much as it pains me. However, you got to Hussman and Durne before I did, Captain Bickerington, and for that I applaud you. Tusker's Cove was only one in a string of towns they brought their sickness to. Those remorseless beasts deserved no less than death." His lone eye fell to Orangecloak again. "I think for once even *you* can agree with me on that."

A single tear was glistening on Orangecloak's cheek in the glow of the oil lamps in the kitchen. She raised her stare from the plaid tablecloth and for once, Tryst saw her looking at Fletchard with something that wasn't hatred. "Aye, Fletchard, you and I most certainly do agree on that."

23

ELLARIE

She had been dreaming of Phaleayna again, and sleep, as sparingly as it came, was her only release from the unending drudgery her life had become. Lately, Ellarie had seen much of Orangecloak in the fluttering moments when she managed to nod off. Alongside Merion, Joyce and Lazlo, the former Field Commander of the Thieves had been among Ellarie's closest friends. They were all condemned to die now, with four of them stored away in Biddenhurst and Orangecloak consigned to the dungeon of the Atrebell Manor.

I will never see Orangecloak again. The feeling gnawed at Ellarie as she stood up in the tiny space she was given to occupy, brushing off the hay that clung to her dirty shift. Normally one could push such thoughts away and focus the mind elsewhere. In here, all there was to do was stew and let the mind wander where it wanted while the body had nowhere to go.

Her eyes fell to her sister, still asleep in her own hay pile. Their cells sat opposite of one another, so close that if they reached a whole arm through the bars that their fingers almost grazed. Yet, to Ellarie, locked in here with guards overhearing their every word, she and Merion might as well be kilometres apart.

Not that any of the guards spent much time in the cellblock. Every half an hour, one would bestir from the comfort of their heated room and patrol the corridor briefly, if only to ensure that everyone maintained a state of misery. Any signs of anyone finding even the most menial of things to occupy their time were grounds for punishment.

Poor Jorgia had found this out when one of the guards discovered her to be making a wreath from her sleeping hay. That incident had happened only a few days into their stay and, according to the whispers from cell to cell, she still couldn't stand. After the straw ornament was confiscated, the guards manacled her to the bars on the outside of her cell and had given her ten lashes with a long whip. The crack of the leather still rang in Ellarie's ears. The auburn haired woman from Prive had sworn loudly that they would not make her scream. To her credit, she endured four hard blows before breaking.

It consumed the entirety of Ellarie's willpower not to beg the guards to stop, willpower that neither Joyce nor Lazlo possessed.

Another lesson learned: don't protest with the guards. When they were done with Jorgia they left her where she was chained and gave both Lazlo and Joyce the same punishment in their turn. Only Joyce had managed to not bawl out. Though Ellarie was far from surprised, even among the Thieves, Joyce was considered to be extraordinarily resilient.

Then there was Merion, sitting on the floor the entire time, hands over her ears and her eyes shut tight, waiting for it to end. Joyce had known that if she screamed, Merion would lose her resolve and have pleaded with the guards to stop, which would have led to her being whipped as well. No doubt that notion had helped stay Joyce's resolve to not even so much as whimper.

That was how lessons were learned in Biddenhurst it seemed, through a cruel means of trial and error. Most of the guards Ellarie had encountered were only too happy to inflict punishment and if prisoners didn't know the rules, they were sure to break them.

There was another trial too, or so Lieutenant Crispin told them, anyhow. He had arrived one afternoon in a freshly pressed, spotless, formal uniform with a shit-eating grin on his face and Ellarie knew something was afoot. Rather gleefully, he informed the prisoners that after a brief trial, they had all been found guilty of a multitude of crimes. It was quite the list: rebellion against the governing body of Illiastra, theft of over one thousand gold pieces, vandalism of government property, murder of Illiastran guardsmen and apostasy being the most notable. The trial had lasted but an afternoon and the defendants had not been permitted to even attend, let alone speak in their own defence. The judge rendered a verdict of guilty on all accounts and had condemned the lot of them, including Billie, still pretending to be the late Nia Hedgeworth, to death by hanging.

Not that there was any doubt that they would be sentenced as such, given that they were being housed in the death row cellblock to begin with. The trial was merely a formality for the sake of appearances. Justice was but an illusion in Illiastra and such farcical displays in the courtroom were a part of maintaining that illusion.

A moan from Merion garnered Ellarie's attention. Her sister had woken and was sitting up in her hay pile by the time Ellarie's gaze fell upon her. She rubbed her eyes and released a depressed sigh when her dreams gave way to reality.

"How are you?" Ellarie whispered as she pressed her face to the bars of her own cell.

"Still alive, that's about as much as I can say," whispered Merion in response, rolling over to her side and propping herself upon an elbow to look upon Ellarie's face. Almost immediately, Merion's line of sight went from Ellarie to the tiny window behind her sister. "Is it snowing outside?"

Ellarie wheeled about to the window and glanced outward. Heavy flakes were tumbling down and looked as though they had been for some time, collecting about the ground in windblown tufts. "Aye, winter is here, I suppose."

"Good, maybe we'll all freeze to death before we can be hanged. Wouldn't that just stick in Lord Taves' craw?" Merion mused.

Since being locked away in the dreary little dungeon, they had all forgotten what it was to feel warm. There was a wood stove in the building, but it only pumped heat into the guards' room. Whatever warmth managed to seep through the walls was merely enough to keep death at bay. Of course, that seemed to be the overall goal of the jailers: to keep the prisoners in a torturous state on the cusp of grave, but never quite within it until they were ready for burial.

"Have you been talking to anyone else?" Merion piped in. She was of course asking if Ellarie had been whispering to the other cells. From her own cell, Ellarie could see Lazlo and Billie to either side of Merion if she went to the furthest reaches of either corner of the bars. The former was barely moving from his hay pile since being flogged and the latter was taciturn at best.

"No, we both know that's best left to you." Ellarie answered despondently.

"Very well, I suppose you're right." Merion sat up with a heave and looked to Donnis' cell. "Donnis, are you awake?" she called in as loud a whisper as she could manage.

After a brief moment of silence, Merion called again, almost daring to let her voice creep into a dangerously audible level. Before Ellarie's heart could leap into her throat, she finally heard Donnis stirring from atop his hay, grumbling and groaning all the while. He said something in reply to Merion, though it was indecipherable from where Ellarie was.

Merion shook her head quickly to answer a question he had asked. "I don't know. Neither Bernadine nor I have spoken to anyone else yet." She was careful to always call Ellarie by the name she bore falsely and never her real one. There was no way they could trust Billie to keep the secret, especially should Corporal Lance Cornwall happen to visit. Beyond that, there was also no way they could know that they weren't being listened to by the guards.

"How are Lazlo and Joyce?" Merion asked, and another answer Ellarie couldn't discern came back, the tone of which sounded despondent.

Her sister turned her attention back to Ellarie while Donnis started trying to rouse the whipped and wounded lieutenants. "Donnis says that Lazlo's sleeping hay looks dark, like he's bled through his shift. He can't see Joyce, but last time he did, she was scarcely moving. We need to do something."

"Do what, exactly?" Ellarie replied exasperatingly.

"We have to tell the guards," grunted Merion, now pacing about in her cell. "Someone has to have a look at them. Their wounds are likely infected. They will need a salve for that and proper bandaging or they'll die."

"I don't think our overseers are going to care enough to do anything. We are condemned to die, after all," she replied to that, feeling equal parts hopeless and helpless. "Check the other way and find out how Jorgia is doing."

Merion didn't seem to care too much for that response, but stifled her frustration for the moment. "I doubt she's doing much better, but I'll see what I can find out."

From the corner of her eye, Ellarie saw Billie walking about in her cell, arms folded across her chest and trying hard to not to look at any of the other prisoners. The woman had taken to ignoring any questions Ellarie might try to ask, answering only with, "I'm not one of you, don't talk to me." Her hateful glares this morning said that she would be no more conversational.

"Jorgia has been lying on her stomach all night and she seems to be in a lot of discomfort," Merion reported before long. "According to what Etcher has been told, she's been doing a lot of convulsing and shaking, too."

The door to the guard room swung open suddenly and Ellarie looked to Merion quickly. "Be quiet, I'll think of something."

The sound of slow footfalls on the stone floor outside the cells echoed off the walls, growing louder with every step. Ellarie pressed the side of her face to the bars to try and see which guard had been sent in to make a round, but could see nothing of whoever it was. Nervously, she walked about, trying to come up with some sort of plan to get her friends some much needed medical aid.

"What are you trying to do, walk a hole in the floor?" a young voice asked her curiously. Ellarie looked up to see a youthful looking guard staring back at her with an eyebrow turned upward in curiosity.

She ran with the first idea that came to mind. "I'm glad you came, the three who were flogged the other day are in a very bad way. I think their wounds are festering."

He scoffed. "What do you think I can do about that? Do I look like a doctor to you?"

Ellarie tried to contain her irritation with his apathy. "You have to go get a doctor, they need help or they'll die from the infection."

Somehow he found some sort of humour in all of this and was chuckling as he spoke. "What does it matter if they die of an infection? You're all supposed to be executed anyhow."

"You were here when we were brought in." A thought came to her as the young man spoke and she pounced on it. "Your last name is Grose, I remember you, and I remember that you shoved Ellarie Dollen headlong into her cell. Do you remember what Lieutenant Crispin said when you did that? 'Don't hurt the guests before their big performance.' If we die in here, then that means Lord Taves can't hang us out there," Ellarie added while pointing in the general direction of the inordinate gallows beyond the cellblock.

"Something tells me that Lord Taves would be downright furious if he found out that two lieutenants of Lady Orangecloak's have perished from wounds induced by Lieutenant Crispin's men," Ellarie said to Grose in a ponderous tone. "If I know Lord Taves at all, I know he won't give two shits about who actually did the whipping. He'll blame the lot of you for not having the combined sense to get them well enough to be killed at *his* command. In fact, there's a good chance that he would also feel robbed by his own subordinates for having the pleasure of executing us taken away from him."

"You know what I think?" he snarled while puffing out his chest. "I think you talk too much and that I ought to have *you* flogged."

An intimidation tactic Ellarie thought laughable considering he was plying it on an unarmed, caged woman smaller than he. Regardless, she let him feel like it worked and padded her voice with what she hoped would pass for fear. "That's one thing you can do, sure, but then you'll have four dead Thieves that someone will have to explain to Lord Taves. I think you're smart enough to know that's a piss-poor idea."

"Like I said, you scrappy little wench, I'm no doctor and you don't want our doctor to come look at their wounds." He leaned in a little closer and dropped his voice low. "He likes to experiment on patients and he especially likes fiddling around with open cuts and sores. Even the hardest men I know in here shy away from guard duty at his clinic. So, listen to me when I tell you that you don't want him coming here."

"I can tend to them, I have some medical training," Ellarie pressed on. "They teach us how to tend to lesions and stave off infections in Phaleayna. If you get me supplies and put me in their cells, I can take care of them. Please, let me help my friends, they're as much of a family as I have. Would you not want to do the same if it were your family?"

The guard turned away from her and walked to the back of the cellblock, stopping at Joyce's cell to peer in at her a moment. A hopeful glance was passed between the sisters while the guard contemplated Ellarie's request in silence. On his way back, he took the time to check on Lazlo as well before returning to Ellarie. "I'll have to bring this to Lieutenant Crispin's attention. The only way I'm going to do that is if you play along with me and let them all think it was my idea to save these people, am I clear?"

"Yes, absolutely, whatever you want, just please let me help them," Ellarie readily agreed, not caring who got the credit as long as aid was rendered.

He lowered his gaze to the floor and held it there for some time, letting Ellarie's ideas mull in his head. "*If* the Lieutenant agrees to this, what supplies would you need?"

"To start, I'll need a large basin of hot, clean water. It will need to be freshly drawn for each of the three of them. I'll need clean washcloths, a cleansing salve and lots of bandages as well. I would say that I'll have to wrap their whole torso to cover the wounds. They'll need clean shifts, too and some fresh hay to lie on."

"You push it with the hay, the rest I might be able to manage," he said while pointing a finger in her direction. "You'll get your food in half an hour, I'll be back sometime after that."

Ellarie sighed with relief. "Thank you, ser, this means a great deal to all of us."

"Save your thanks until I return as I have no bloody idea how this is going to go over with Lieutenant Crispin." Grose said over his shoulder as he departed. There was a pause in his footsteps and Ellarie guessed it was so he could look upon Jorgia.

When the door to the block opened and shut at last, Merion audibly exhaled and locked eyes with her sibling. "Well done, now we just have to hope he doesn't lose face when he presents what you told him to his Lieutenant."

"Aye, he may well, but this is our only chance to do something for Lazlo, Joyce and Jorgia," Ellarie answered as she lowered herself back down to her straw bed, such as it was.

They remained relatively quiet after that, listening for the others to send word up the line of cells to them and answering back with whatever information they could offer.

The door swung open after what felt to Ellarie like half an hour, as Private Grose had promised. Judging from the number of boots Ellarie heard on the floor, she guessed there to be a trio of guards entering the cellblock.

"Feeding time, maggots, get on your feet and get your tin cups out," one of them called out loudly to the inmates.

The sound of simultaneous shuffling filled the air and Ellarie found herself joining the chorus of the hungry.

It would be a poor time to rebel now, might as well line up at the trough like a good little sheep this morning.

Breakfast was tepid, smelly water in a poor shade of yellow and a single, wisp-thin slice of bread she could practically see clear through. It was better than nothing and Ellarie swallowed it all quickly, slurping down the terrible water before the taste could make her spew up what little was in her stomach.

Across the floor, she espied Merion nibbling on the bread and laying her tin cup of water off to the side for later. The redhead had her own eyes trained on the guards, studying their movements, watching them for weaknesses and tells. By now, Merion had nicknames on them all to help her remember them. She had told Ellarie that one of the very guards present right now had a poor left knee that aggravated him endlessly. An injury of some kind that never healed properly and Ellarie now saw it as she looked for herself. That one Merion had aptly named Gimpy. The one pushing the wheelbarrow she called Greenboy, as he was new, young and largely unskilled. Most likely he was a relative of an officer and given a position based on nothing but nepotism.

As for the last guard, both sisters agreed he was a threat. Icicle, as they had taken to calling him, was a cold, hard piece of work and one of many in Biddenhurst.

Analysing the guards had been one of the few ways the sisters could pass the time and Merion had a gift for it.

By now they had also run through hundreds of escape scenarios. Almost all of them involved battling their way out, and every one of them ended in abject failure. While Merion had a knack for figuring out the traits and weaknesses of their foes, it was Ellarie who had the mind for organising and executing their delicate operations. She was realistic in her approach and never let her wants and desires cloud logic and sense, unlike Merion. The younger sister optimistically saw all of their escape plans to some grandiose, successful conclusion, which Ellarie knew were fantasies and little more. Fighting their way to freedom would only get this ragged and weary band as far as the moat outside the cellblock. After that, there were too many guards armed too heavily for the group to get very far.

The creaking wheel of the barrow resumed once more and the guards began to make their way out. Icicle fixated on the red haired woman for a moment, watching her take tiny bites of her meagre morsel of food. "Better eat up, you've got a busy day." The square shouldered man scowled before leaving without further explanation.

"What do you suppose he means?" asked Merion in a hushed whisper when the guards were gone at least.

Ellarie shrugged. "I haven't the foggiest idea. We know Lord Taves is back in Biddenhurst, perhaps he's coming by to see us with his own two eyes."

"Or something decidedly worse…" Merion added, not finishing the thought and not needing to. They both knew what that something worse was. It was something they felt looming over their heads with every passing minute.

After another hour had passed, marked by two more guards patrolling the cells, Private Grose returned. Along his travels, he had commandeered the wheelbarrow used for bringing meals and laid it down before Ellarie's cell with a stern face. "I have kettles of boiled water, a basin, a handful of the whitest rags I could find, rolls of bandages and a crock of salve. I think that's everything you asked for."

Not only was Ellarie surprised that the guard had come through, but she was thoroughly impressed as well. She almost felt remiss to point out what he had forgotten, but it was intrinsic to the hygiene of the injured. "You've done wonderful, ser and I hate to mention it after all you have done, but what of the clean clothes?"

"I hadn't forgotten," Private Grose answered thoughtfully, even bordering on a tone that might be mistaken for friendly. "I looked through the stores we have available and we have nothing I would ever dare to call clean. Besides, I also remembered that your shifts have your prisoner numbers painted on them. Meaning that if a new shift was issued, I'd also have to track down white paint and a brush and destroy the old ones."

"Thank you all the same, for everything you've gathered and taking the time to even search for the shifts," Ellarie said, relenting.

"You're welcome," he returned while reaching to the back of his belt and returning with a pair of irons. "I'm hoping that will make this a little less awkward. I'll need you to turn around, place your hands on your back and put your back to the bars."

She hesitated for a moment, wondering if this might be some sort of trick, going so far as to cautiously question the request. "You need to shackle me to go between cells?"

"A thief is still a thief." He shrugged. "I cannot give you any trust no more than you would for a man in a Biddenhurst uniform.

Please, turn about."

Reluctantly, Ellarie complied and allowed him to restrain her in the tight chains. When she was out of the cell, Private Grose led her by the arm to Lazlo's cell. "Start with him."

From the matted down straw, Lazlo sprang awake suddenly, groaning in pain as he glanced upward at the sudden ruckus. "Ellarie, what's going on?" he mumbled as the cell door slammed shut.

"It's not Ellarie," she corrected him quickly, before he could say any more and cost them the ruse. "It's me, Bernadine. I've been given permission to patch you up. Come now, let's get that shift off of you and we'll clean your wounds."

"I don't...Feel...Everything hurts..." Lazlo mumbled, seemingly trying to say several things at once while trying and failing to get up.

With a stumble, he fell into her arms, his body trembling with the agony that was going through him. "Shh, don't talk. I'm going to take care of you now, okay?" Ellarie said in a comforting voice, careful to keep her hands from touching his back. It was then she realised she had nowhere for him to sit. "Private Grose, do you think we could have a stool or something similar for him to sit on?"

"There's a bucket at the other end of the room, will that do?" Grose asked, accepting a quick nod from Ellarie as an answer and dashing off to retrieve the makeshift seat.

Ever so gently, she ran a hand through Lazlo's long, curly hair to try and relax him, dropping her voice to a whisper. "It's going to be alright, just remember that I am Bernadine."

The guard was back and opened the cell door just wide enough to lay the stool, basin and a kettle of water inside. The other things he left in the wagon, setting it against the bars of Lazlo's cell where Ellarie could reach them.

"Thank you again. You've been most helpful, Private Grose," Ellarie said while slowly lowering Lazlo onto the overturned bucket. "Let's get that shift down and see what we're dealing with here." Gingerly, she opened the shift up from the front and began the arduous task of sliding it down to his waist. Lazlo shuddered as the cold air hit him and grimaced as the scratchy fabric grazed his raw back.

There was a pungent, sharp stench in the air suddenly and the guard recoiled as it wafted his way. Grose returned his sight to Lazlo and audibly gasped at the ghastly sight, seemingly forgetting about the smell.

Wounds and injuries were no new sight to Ellarie, but even this shocked her. She kept her composure to keep Lazlo from knowing the full extent of it and tried to reassure him. "It's not so bad, just a little pus. We'll clean it off and get some soothing ointment on it and you'll feel better in no time, I promise." The truth was that his back was oozing the light green fluid from every lash and whatever flesh was left to him was bruised and stained with dried blood. As much as she tried, Ellarie couldn't think of a worse injury she had ever seen.

Without delay, she poured the steaming water into the basin and soaked a rag. Using soft, tender dabs with the rag, she began to wipe at the wounds, though no matter how lightly she touched him, Lazlo shuddered and flinched. The more Ellarie dipped and wrung out the rag, the darker the water got.

"By the gods, what have they done to me?" Lazlo finally stammered out.

"It's nothing," Ellarie lied. "They're just a few cuts that were left a little long without attention. I've seen worse." She had only sopped off the upper half of Lazlo's bloodily striped back when she discovered the water was too dirty to use further. A glance at the remaining stock in the wagon told her there would not be enough for Joyce and Jorgia too. "Private Grose, I'm afraid I'm going to need a lot more water boiled up, if that would be possible."

"Oh! Yes, certainly, I'll be back with more water and a bucket for the dirty rags straight away." There was no doubt that the guardsman was simply glad to have a reason to not look upon Lazlo's tortured flesh any longer, fleeing at the chance Ellarie gave him.

The door to the guard room swung open and shut quickly.

After a few breaths without hearing further footsteps, Ellarie spun about to face Lazlo. His face was milk white and he could barely keep his eyes open as she looked into them. "Lazz, I need you to pay attention to me."

"We're done, Ellarie, it's over for us," he said, the words tumbling clumsily past his lips.

"Don't say that Lazz, not now." Her hands cupped his jaw to keep his vision at eye level. "Just listen to me: I'm going to get you better, but you have to promise me that you'll keep your damn mouth shut. No matter how hard that is for you to do and despite what they may throw at you, do not give them the satisfaction of an answer. I know it's against your nature, but please, Lazz, you have to endure."

His voice was full of pain as he mustered an answer. "Okay, for you, Ellarie, I'll try, that's all I can promise."

"Thank you, Lazlo." Ellarie laid her forehead against his and stayed there in silence with him until the noise of the far door being opened reached their hearing. "And remember, call me Bernadine," she said as she broke away and returned to washing his back clean.

A single kettle and a bucket were in the guard's hands as he returned at a striding pace. "Here, I even got more rags, they're in the bucket. How is he?"

"He's nearly clean. Once I finish with his lower back, I'll just need to cover him with the salve and wrap him up tight in the bandages," Ellarie answered studiously.

When Ellarie was at last finished with tending to Lazlo, she drew his shift back over his shoulders and tied it closed for him. He had to be helped from the bucket to lie down on his side in the musty hay pile and it was there she left him with simple instructions. "Try to lay still and get some rest, and for the love of all things, be sure you eat when they bring you food. You need to keep your strength up, even if it is only a bit of bread and dirty water."

Gritting through the pain, Lazlo reached out to Ellarie and squeezed her nearest hand. "Thank you, for everything."

"I'm only glad to do what little I can for you. Now, rest," Ellarie answered, rising back to her feet when she was done. "I'm finished with him, I'll need to redress his back tomorrow and onward until the infection clears up and the open wounds heal."

"I don't know if I can do that," shrugged the Private while holding up the shackles and gesturing Ellarie to turn around. "The Lieutenant may not allow me to use any more supplies on prisoners. It was fortunate enough that he gave permission for all of this."

That frustrated Ellarie and she tried to reason with him over the sound of the cuffs clicking shut. "I understand that, but their wounds won't heal so easily, especially in terrible conditions like this."

There was another shrug from Grose as he led her from the cell and locked it behind them. "The most I can promise is that if Lieutenant Crispin's mood isn't too dour tomorrow, I may run the idea by him again."

"That's all I ask," Ellarie acquiesced reluctantly. It dawned to her that Private Grose was leading her away from Joyce's cell and towards the front. "Where are we going?"

The guard stopped before Jorgia's cell before replying. "The underling that was flogged needs your touch far worse than that one Joyce does. I'll take you to her last, but I really think this poor thing needs to come next."

It was hard for Ellarie to argue as she looked at the pallid, shivering form of Jorgia lying on the other side of the bars. "By the gods," Ellarie sighed pitifully. "There's not much time to waste, let me get to work."

She was released from her bonds, kneeling beside Jorgia and reunited with the supplies within minutes.

Poor Jorgia had become so delirious with suffering that at the mere touch of Ellarie, she thrashed violently and no doubt painfully. Before even trying to get her seated, Ellarie had to calm her. "Jorgia, it's me, Bernadine. I'm just going to take a look at your back and get you all fixed up. Be still and relax, I won't do anything to hurt you."

A short time later, the scrappy scout from Prive was disrobed to the waist and seated unsteadily on the upturned bucket. The shift had become matted to the bloody lesions crisscrossing her from shoulders to tailbone and it took quite a while just to expose Jorgia's whole back.

"It hurts...Please, it hurts so much," she managed to mumble.

"I know, dear, just be still. This will feel hot and it will sting, but it will be over before long," Ellarie cooed softly as she soaked a rag and went to work. By the time she finished cleaning and dressing Jorgia, Ellarie had nearly emptied the crock of salve and had sent Grose for yet more water and rags. The only part of the inventory that she seemed to have enough of for all was bandages.

Having left Jorgia lying as comfortable as possible and with the same advice she had given Lazlo, Ellarie was bound once more.

"Just one more for you to look after," commented Grose as he slipped the iron bracelets over her wrists.

To Ellarie's surprise, they found Joyce sitting up, arms draped over bent knees that were drawn up to the chin and her gaze on the empty cell across from her. "Sweet little Bernadine, it's good to see you." Her voice was laboured as she spoke, burdened by the pain rippling through her, though she fought to not show it. "It's good to see anyone that's not in a uniform."

"Hello Joyce, it's good to see you too," Ellarie responded with a hard swallow. Indeed it was good to see Joyce, even in the pain-racked and tortured state she was in.

Once within the cell and unrestrained, Ellarie was at her side.

Grose went back to retrieve the supplies from where they lay near Jorgia, leaving Ellarie and Joyce a private moment.

"How are you?" Ellarie asked in a whisper.

A pained heave left Joyce before she answered. "I'm in agony, Ellarie. It kills me to be so near Merion and not be able to touch her or look upon her. I'm a few metres away from my love and yet loneliness is all I feel." Joyce's voice broke slightly and her brown eyes grew moist. "I hardly notice the throbbing in my back when there is so much longing in my heart."

Without hesitation, Ellarie wrapped an arm around Joyce's neck and drew her into a long hug, careful to not put pressure on her agonised back. Her body shuddered as Ellarie's touch drew the sobs from her. "The worst of it is that I know the next time I see her, we'll be standing at the gallows with ropes on our necks. I won't be able to save her. All I can do is watch when the trapdoor opens. I'll never hold her again or kiss her tender lips. I won't get another chance to tell her how much she means to me and how much I love her. I miss her spirit, as fiery as her hair. If she were in this cell with me, I'd still have hope. Now all I have are nightmares of watching her die before my very eyes and me helpless to stop it."

"It's not over, Joyce. We're not dead yet, we have to keep hope alive. Because it's all we have left in here," Ellarie answered softly. "Merion longs for you as much as you long for her and if her fiery spirit could break down walls, you two would be together again. You have to keep your spirits up too, for her and for the hope that you'll see her again."

The groaning of the rusting hinges on the cell door filled the room. Ellarie glanced up to see Private Grose silently going about the task of laying the buckets, basin and the last pitcher of water inside for them. With the door secured again, he stood there uncomfortably for a moment before declaring that he was going to retrieve more hot water and striding away.

Gingerly, Ellarie began to release her hold on Joyce, extending far enough to look her in the eyes. "I don't know how much time Grose is giving us, but you should sit up on the bucket and let me have a look at your back."

"I'd do it all again, you know," Joyce blurted out while Ellarie tried to coax her to take a seat. "They can flog me until flesh gives way to bone, but they'll never make me regret loving Merion Dollen. No amount of bars, chains or whips will make me love her any less.

"Aye, I'm a woman who loves other women and what of it?" she asked rhetorically. "If the gods take issue with that, then the gods themselves can take it up with me, they don't need mortal men to make me suffer. I should think that if they are gods of eternal reach and power that they can do it themselves."

"You shouldn't be saying things like that aloud, miss." The two women looked up to see Private Grose having returned, a pitcher of boiled water to hand.

"You're right, I wouldn't want them to charge me with apostasy and sentence me to death," Joyce answered with the biting sarcasm Ellarie had known her for. "They might take away all of this luxury that I do so enjoy."

"Lieutenant Crispin called a halt to floggings without *his permission*," Grose explained, overlooking the sarcastic retort. "He didn't put a halt to them entirely. If what you're saying right now reaches the wrong ears, then he may still yet consent to a lashing."

"Joyce, you should listen to him," warned Ellarie, gravely concerned that the woman may get another repeat of the trauma already inflicted upon her.

She would not be deterred from her rant and powered on, "If the gods declare that this love I have for Merion is wrong, then fuck them. They had the power to make me any way they chose and yet they made me as you see with the knowledge of where that would take me. Before I was ever born, the gods would have known that I would be damned to the eternal flames of Aren's Lair and they went ahead and made me anyway. In the face of that we're supposed to blindly believe that Ios and Iia are loving gods? No, that's not love, that's sadism."

"Say no more! I'm trying to give you a little bit of easement, stop throwing that back in my face and please stop talking before you get me hanged with you," Grose insisted, his voice filling with fear.

Ellarie shared his worry. "Sit on the bucket, Joyce and let me clean your wounds."

With a gentle push to Ellarie, Joyce gritted her teeth and rose under her own power until she was standing tall. She cut a fearsome looking figure in the ugly shift and with her dirty, blonde locks matted as they were. It was no secret that Joyce was above average strength and Ellarie and the other Thieves knew that when provoked she was downright intimidating. In that moment however, Ellarie saw something terrifying. This was a woman with nothing left to lose but a life that was to be spent incarcerated.

"You want to give me easement, is that it? Then help me and mine get out of here or give me the mercy of a quick death. Take that rapier on your hip right now and stick it right here," she said, pounding a fist beneath her left breast.

The Private was growing frustrated with Joyce. "You know I can't do that, but if the other guards hear you, they'll ensure that you're tortured."

"Tortured?" Joyce incredulously repeated the word. "I'm tortured with every single minute I have to spend in this cage. I'm tortured with the constant reminder that Lady Orangecloak, my friend and the woman I served, who stood for everything I believe in, is rotting in a cell in Atrebell. That's if she hasn't been executed already. Yet, what tortures me most of all is the knowledge that the love of my life is not two metres away and I can't see or speak or touch her and never will again. I have to spend the last of my life wondering every morning if today is the day that I'll have to watch my one love hang by the neck and *die*. That is torture and agony far worse than any lashing.

"You can give Bernadine all the ointment and bandages in Biddenhurst and she'll never be able to cure the wounds this place has inflicted on my mind. As long as my fellow Thieves are bound by these bricks and bars, then those wounds, Private Grose, shall remain open."

"I'm sorry that I can't close those wounds no more than Bernadine can," Grose uttered in a melancholic tone. "This is as much as I could give you, so please take it while I can still extend the offer."

Joyce wrapped her hands on the bars and leaned even closer to the Private. "Is that all you can do? Patch me up so that I can die another day, another way?"

"Aye, that's it." He shrugged in return.

The tall blonde pushed herself back from the bars. "Well, that's all that can be done then, isn't it?" With a grimace, she pulled her shift off and stood before Grose and Ellarie with all exposed. She sat down hard on the bucket and looked at Ellarie. "Best get to work, Bernie." Her gaze went back to Grose. "Would you care to watch, Private?"

Joyce offered, her sarcasm returning to the forefront.

Grose chose to ignore her and laid the jug of water in the wheelbarrow. "If you need this, Bernadine, just let me know." Turning sharply on his heel he spun away, walked nearly out of sight and remained there, with his back to them.

If anyone ever doubted the grit and toughness of Joyce Keena, then that doubt be would cast aside if they saw her back. Whoever had taken the whip to her was much less merciful toward her than they had been with Lazlo and Jorgia. Where those two were a mess, Joyce's flesh was a total ruin.

Ellarie wiped and scrubbed her friend, turning rags and water an ugly, dark colour. Through it all, save for a few grunts and moans, Joyce made no complaint.

The last of the salve was all used to coat the red, weeping gouges that stretched all the way to Joyce's ribs in some cases. She flinched at the first touch and then went still and silent until Ellarie completed the grim task.

Before Ellarie could finish, they were disturbed by the ruckus of the outside doors opening. "Lieutenant Crispin," said Private Grose dutifully, standing at attention. "How may I serve you, ser?"

"Lord Taves has requested that the most honoured of our guests be invited to a matinee performance at the outdoor theatre," he replied mockingly, still carrying that disgusting metaphor about.

"Understood, ser, how many of them has he requested?" the guard replied.

"We're going to take the Queen Bitch and the Red Bitch for certain, how fare the wounded?" The volume of the Lieutenant's voice dropped as he closed the gap between himself and Grose.

"They're not well, ser," Grose answered truthfully. "The one back here is still being tended on and the other two are weakened considerably by the infection that set in."

Joyce's hands went to cover her breasts as Crispin stepped past Grose to gaze in at her.

His eyes were cold and void of empathy as they looked over the pair behind the bars. "Fine, she may stay behind. We'll take the other two women and the pretty man. I'll tell Lord Taves that this one was being stubborn and took a swing at one of our men so we left her locked up for our own safety. Having three out of the four of them should suit him fine enough, anyhow. You will stay and make sure our little nurse there goes back to her own cell. She's not to be left alone, understood?"

Grose nodded, "Aye ser, you have my word."

"Good. That'll be all, Private." The Lieutenant spent no time waiting for a reply and was gone in a hurry. There were footfalls and voices to be heard in the distance and one above them all nearby. "On your feet, Red Bitch. Go to the back wall and put your hands upon it with your feet spread."

"Private Grose, what's going on?" Ellarie asked in as loud a whisper as she could.

"They're executing the Thieves members that were here before this lot and Lord Taves wants your lieutenants to bear witness to it," he answered quickly while maintaining his position ahead of the cell Ellarie and Joyce were occupying. "Just be quiet and finish wrapping."

"Oh, Merion, please be strong," Joyce muttered under breath.

Ellarie added to the quiet wish as she kept applying ointment. "And be silent. Don't give them cause to hurt you." She patted Joyce lightly on the shoulder. "That should do it. Lift your arms and I'll put on the bandages."

"Alright, faggot, it's your turn!" a deep voice boomed from just out of sight.

"What do you want?" Lazlo's pain stricken voice called back.

"Get up, you shit stain," the guard demanded. "We're taking you outside to watch your old friends dangle."

There were groans from Lazlo, likely produced from him trying to move in his beaten state. "You'll have to help me up."

"Oh, I'll help you alright," the jailer replied impatiently. "With a helping foot to the fucking face, now, get up!"

As Ellarie heard the key turning in the lock on Lazlo's cell, she began to fear the worst.

Grose moved out of sight suddenly, toward Lazlo's cell. "Wait, Mich, Crispin gave orders not to hurt them anymore. Here, let me help you get him up."

"The Lieutenant said not to whip the bloody freaks. He didn't say I couldn't kick 'em," the one Grose identified as Mich argued.

"It doesn't matter if you're using a whip or a boot, you can't beat them," Private Grose countered quickly. "If Lord Taves sees marks on the prisoners, we're all in deep shit. You go get the irons, I'll get him up and ready for you."

"Don't tell me you're going soft on this bunch, Grose. Next thing I know, you'll be running to Phaleayna to go join up with them," Mich said with a loud, hawking ball of spit that Ellarie hoped landed on the ground and not on Lazlo.

"I'm only following orders, Mich," Grose protested in defence of himself. "Now either you help me get him up or go get the leg irons."

"Don't you fucking order me around, Grose. I could rip your throat out with one hand if I felt like it," Mich threatened, in spite of the fact that Ellarie could hear him walking away.

"Here, give me your hand," she could hear Grose offering. "You've been beaten up enough as it is, you don't want more."

"I wasn't trying to, I assure you. I sincerely need help to get up," Lazlo responded with an audible grimace.

Once Mich returned, shackles and cuffs could be heard being secured into place and Lazlo was led out without further exchange between either of the three.

Private Grose looked in on the two women just as Ellarie was tying the last of Joyce's bandages in place. "Please, tell me you're done. I need a break."

"Aye, just about finished. And thank you for sparing Lazlo from that brute," Ellarie said with a respectful nod in Grose's direction.

"Don't thank me, I'm just following orders," Grose answered, folding his arms and looking away. Somehow Ellarie didn't think he was being truthful, though she decided against seeing how far the Private's empathy extended.

"There, that should do it," Ellarie commented when she finished with Joyce. She swooped up the shift from the ground and held the bottom open. "Put this back on."

Without protest, Joyce obeyed, her arms slumping at her side once she was dressed again. "Thank you, Bernadine and you too, Grose. I apologise for directing my anger at you earlier, you didn't deserve that."

Grose gave a sigh and returned to the front of the cell. "Just say your farewells. I need to bind Bernadine's wrists again and get this stuff out of here so I can go sit down."

As Ellarie stepped in close and put her back to the bars, she was grabbed quickly in a hug by Joyce, who held tight and put her lips almost directly to Ellarie's ear. "Stay strong, stay sharp. It's just like you said: we're not dead yet, you have to keep hope alive, for all of us, as you have always done, Ellarie."

"And you as well, Joyce," Ellarie whispered back. "If for no other reason than for Merion, for she loves you more than life itself. Don't do something to cast your life away so easily, fight for it and for her with every last breath you have."

Firm hands reached for Ellarie through the bars and drew back her arms to lock the shackles into place on her wrists. "Come along now, it's time to go," Grose muttered lowly. "You'll get to see her again in a few days when you can change the dressings."

Once returned to the cell she now had to call home, Ellarie found the day ticking by at a laboriously slow pace. She walked as much as the tight space allowed, lay in the hay pile and stared out her window until her knees and feet ached. There was nothing to see and nothing to do but wait for Merion, Lazlo and Bernadine to come back. For a time, she began to worry and her mind wandered to a dark place where no one returned.

Some day that will come to pass. These cells will be emptied before too long, while Lord Taves still finds value in hanging us, Ellarie reminded herself.

She had taken to her hay pile again, facing the outside wall and forcing her eyes shut and trying to imagine she was anywhere else. As Ellarie began to nod off, a commotion at the doors roused her from the state of near sleep she had reached. Quickly she was on her feet and pressed to the bars of the cell.

Rattling chains echoed off the walls and Ellarie held her breath until Merion was in sight and confirmed to be responsible for at least some of that noise. Not far behind was Lazlo, his head down and face hidden behind his mop of unruly curls.

Once Merion was free of her bonds, she went to the window in her cell and buried her head in the arms she folded upon on the sill.

It wasn't until the guards had left and silence had fallen over the cell block that Ellarie finally dared to whisper. "Merion, talk to me," she tried, hoping to coax her sister from her place before the tiny, barred window.

Merion raised her head and looked over her shoulder at Ellarie. Her face was mournful, but within there was an emotional void behind eyes that had once been bright and vibrant. "You want to know what happened."

"They are all dead, every last one of them. That much I am

certain of," Ellarie answered sombrely. "We are the last Thieves in Biddenhurst."

"That...That is the result, aye," Merion said with a hard swallow.

Ellarie knew there was more than Merion was saying and waited for her sister to reveal what she knew.

"When Larissa stepped onto the scaffolds, she could barely stand. The strain of being up in that device we saw her in and wherever they kept her afterwards had rid her of all her strength. Yet, when the guards held out the rope, she stood tall and embraced it. I saw the strangest thing just then and at the time I didn't understand what I was seeing, but now I do. Larissa's face was streaked with tears as she waited for the trap door to open. At first I thought she was crying in the face of death, but the more I looked at her, the more it became apparent that they were not sad tears, they were tears of joy."

While Merion talked, Ellarie slowly sunk down until she was seated on the floor, hands still clutching at the bars.

"I wondered why she cried so happily at the moment before her death and now I know," Merion pondered aloud until she was down at a level with Ellarie again. "It's been two years since she was taken from us. You remember, don't you? It was late summer when it happened. Think about that, she's been in here ever since. In that time, that young, vibrant woman was broken down so badly that she was joyous at her own end. This place and the people within it made sure that she believed death was the only way out. To her, that noose meant freedom."

24
TRYST

When Tryst had laid eyes on Tusker's Cove two nights prior, he had expected that his sad little party of three would be leaving it much the way they had entered. That notion was dispelled just a day later, when Harold Bickerington insisted that they join him aboard his ship, *The Myra*.

As it was, Harold and his fleet were going forth to the fishing grounds for a last haul before the winter. The trip required heading south as far as Portsward, to gather the other vessels located along the north coast in the tiny villages and have them congregate in the city. Once there, they were to gather supplies and make for the frigid northern waters between Illiastra and Drake.

At first, Orangecloak had politely declined the offer, not wanting to burden the captain and his crew with smuggling the three travelers into Portsward. It was Sheila Bickerington who had rightly pointed out that the party was now in civilisation. Getting to Portsward unnoticed on foot might be much more difficult than going by sea on a ship with a trusted captain and a good crew. The next morning, Tryst, Orangecloak and the wounded Fletchard went to the wharf alongside Captain Bickerington himself and boarded the ship he was so very proud of.

The passengers were given their own cabins and free reign of the areas below and above deck. Both Orangecloak and Fletchard admitted to Tryst individually that they were grateful for being aboard the ship compared to being on foot, and all three were noticeably less tense.

On the second morning of their sea voyage, Tryst slept fairly late. He had woken previously to relieve himself in the privy, when the light of day had just begun to illuminate the morning sky. The thought crossed Tryst's mind to greet the day and break his fast with the crew of *The Myra*. However, it occurred to him that a good sleep might well be hard to come upon once Portsward came into view. There was little doubt in his mind that the coming days with Lord Greggard would be pivotal for both he and Orangecloak. Rest would have to come now, if Tryst wanted any at all. On that thought he had relented, relinquishing himself to a few more hours of blissful sleep, lulled into it by the gentle rolling of the ship beneath his bunk.

When Tryst finally did rise, he found that the galley was spotlessly clean and empty at this hour with breakfast having long been served. Given that, it meant Tryst was left to his own means to procure his morning meal for himself. The quiet kitchen was soon filled with the noise of a loudly boiling kettle of hot water and the smell of fried fish and thick sliced potatoes.

Upon speaking to the select members of the crew that passed through the kitchen, Tryst discovered that both Orangecloak and Fletchard Miller had yet to wake. Knowing that, Tryst ensured that when he gathered ingredients for his meal that he cooked enough for the three of them.

Neither had woken by the time Tryst was finished preparing the meal, so he resigned himself to eating without company. The time spent alone picking over his meal led Tryst to thinking about Orangecloak once more, as he often did as of late.

Tryst was undeniably enamoured with the woman and was enticed by the idea of getting close to her. Where most might be turned away by her seemingly strange behaviour, Tryst felt only more attracted. This was a woman unbowed by the currents of society, a solid rock against a rapid river that was determined to be just who she was. She had confidence and strength within that Tryst admired deeply, traits that shone through those deep blue eyes that stared daggers at him. Despite the subjugation of her gender, she stood proud as a woman and refused to stand second to any man.

Yet, behind the bravery and bravado, there was fragility. The death of the men in her party and the capture of her friends in Argesse had wounded her harder than even the prospect of her own death.

For all the traits of a warrior she bears, her heart is soft, thought Tryst to himself. *Those fortunate enough to gain the bond of friendship with her are held tight and dear. She lives hard, she loves hard and she falls hard. For all I think I understand of her, there's much and more I may never. A beautiful enigma wrapped in a faded old cloak the colour of a peach, that's what she is.*

"Is there no breakfast left?" asked the deep, rasp-addled voice that could only be Fletchard's. The man looked dishevelled and unkempt, even for the standard he had been keeping since leaving the Hotel Dupoire. A rough but full beard had grown out and his hair had grown just long enough to beg for a combing. The clothes on his back bore mud and grime where once they had been splendid on that night in Atrebell. He had been the only one of the three that had declined an offer to have his garments washed in Tusker's Cove, for reasons Tryst didn't care to find out. Even the sling he still wore to support his wounded arm was looking dirty. If not for the thick patch around his left eye, Fletchard could pass for someone else and that someone was a broken, drunken waste of a thing.

Tryst gestured toward the kitchen beyond. "I made plenty enough for three. There's hot tea, fresh codfish and sliced potatoes, if you'd like."

Fletchard began lumbering in the direction Tryst pointed him before stopping abruptly and turning back towards him. "Any beans? I'd kill a man for a plate of baked beans."

Somehow I have little trouble believing that to be true, Tryst thought while answering him. "I'm afraid not, but I made generous helpings of the fish and taters. Help yourself, but be sure to leave enough for Orangecloak."

"Not to worry, I'll make sure your little lovey has her plateful," Tryst heard him patronisingly scowl back.

Tryst let the slight wash over him with a shake of his head. He was about to rise when the bounty hunter returned to the galley and plunked down across the table from Tryst with his plate and cutlery in his good hand.

There was only the sound of Fletchard chewing loudly on the fried potatoes for some time, though Tryst sensed that the bounty hunter had something on his mind.

It wasn't until Tryst had placed his empty teacup atop his plate and made a move to leave once more that Fletchard finally spoke up.

"I had a gander outside this morning," he started in. "We passed Crabber's Inlet in the night. If we keep our present pace, we'll be in Portsward this evening."

Tryst looked him over curiously before replying in a tone that matched his curiosity, "Aye, it seems that way."

The lone eye of Fletchard's went to Tryst. "After we reach Portsward, how long do you think it will take to get me out of this shit heap of a country?"

"A few days at most, I would imagine." Tryst shrugged at him. "Though I could be wrong, it all rests upon on how soon Greggard can requisition a ship bound for anything west of Drake that you could safely stow away on."

"I'm sure the good Lord Schemer will arrange me something then," Fletchard casually spoke between chews. "Even if I misbehaved a little along the way, I should still have enough goodwill with him to warrant hasty and safe passage out of this forsaken place."

The statement was confusing and Tryst made no qualms about it. "I don't follow you."

The last of breakfast was shoved into Fletchard's mouth while he looked over Tryst with a humming noise and a mischievous grin. "No, you definitely don't follow. I can tell truth from lie better than most and you're positively puzzled. Looks like Lord Schemer kept some of his schemes from even his sharpest sword." Fletchard stood from the table as he swallowed his meal, letting his fork and knife clatter onto the plate loudly.

He stepped out from the bench and left his dishes where they sat while still keeping his gaze on Tryst. "All this time I thought you knew and it turns out you didn't know shit." He chuckled lowly while wiping food from his face and beard with the back of his hand.

Before Tryst could ask Fletchard what he was talking about, the bounty hunter spun on his heels and left the galley, still laughing under his breath all the while.

Tryst mulled it over briefly while returning to the kitchen. *I know Greggard had a hand in Fletchard capturing Orangecloak. Fletchard indicated as much when we met in Atrebell and he told me that the Conductor had sent him. Beyond that, though, I have to wonder what connection those two might have.*

With no appearance by Orangecloak the entire time Tryst had

been eating, he decided to clean up the kitchen and wash the used dishes. He heaped a plate with the remaining food on the counter in the kitchen and went to work washing the dishes, cooking utensils and the dining table. Ensuring everything was dried and stowed away before deciding to bring breakfast to Orangecloak in her cabin.

Collecting the plate of fish and potato slices and making a fresh pot of tea with cups for the two of them, he departed for her room. Given that both of his hands were occupied and having no place to temporarily place anything, he had to knock upon the door with his boot. "Good morning, my lady. Are you awake by chance?" he called through the door to her.

From within there came hurried footsteps and the sound of the latch being undone. "Is something the matter, Tryst? Oh!" Her eyes went wide when she saw the burden in his hands and she stepped back without another word to allow him in. "I wasn't expecting breakfast at my door." She spoke with what could almost be called delight in her voice as Tryst stepped through and laid her meal on the small desk in the room.

"Aye, when you didn't turn up in the galley I thought I might bring your breakfast to you, to save you the trip," Tryst gave with a smile and a nod while looking her over. She was in a state of undress, clad in nothing more than her smallclothes and the white, lace trimmed tunic the Dupoire daughters had given her.

She inhaled deeply. "It smells just fabulous, did Kerrell make it?" Orangecloak asked, referring to the right hand man and chief deckhand of Captain Bickerington. "It smells of those Johnahn spices he likes to use."

While taking the liberty of pouring tea for the both of them, Tryst gave answer, "It was I that cooked our breakfast, actually. I hope you like it, I haven't had to cook for myself in quite some time and I fear my culinary skills might be spotted with rust."

"I'm sure it's as good as everything you cooked over the fire for us," Orangecloak said while taking a seat on her bunk with her plate to hand. With a gentle pat of the bunk, she invited Tryst to join her. "Come, sit, I'd enjoy the company."

"What I cooked over the fire was just plain fare stews and wild game," Tryst said with a shrug as he took up her invitation and seated himself near her on the bunk. "It was mostly just sticking stuff over a spit and trying not to burn it too badly. Working with a supply of ingredients and spices is something entirely different. In Atrebell I never had to worry about it as there were always cooks on duty, save for the twilight hours, and a meal was constantly at the ready. Prior to that though, I was cooking several times a week at the University."

That seemed to catch Orangecloak's curiosity. "I would have thought you had a cooking staff there as well."

"Well, in the Academics hall, aye, they're fully staffed," Tryst explained with his first sip of tea. "Much further up Fuwachita Mountain in the Combat Hall though, the students learn to cook as part of our survival studies and then we get assigned kitchen duty."

Orangecloak finished her first bite of the fish and let slip a glimmer of a smile. "Tell your instructors that the Lady Orangecloak herself says that they taught you well," she jested.

"I'm sure they would be glad to hear that from such a respected and popular figure in Illiastran politics," Tryst lightly kidded, toasting her with his teacup.

For a second, he thought he saw her call back a chuckle. "Is that what I am now, Tryst Reine, a 'popular figure in Illiastran politics'? My people will be glad to hear it, until now they thought I was just a rebel. Turns out I'm actually an unelected minister."

Tryst had to laugh at that. "One doesn't need a seat in the Parliamentary house to be an effective politician."

"Wise words, Tryst," Orangecloak replied, before gesturing toward the porthole on the outer wall of her room with her fork to change the subject. "Have you had a look outside today? We're near Portsward. That's the King's Quays right outside. You can even see the statue of King Tolleras I, the first King of Illiastra, perched on the south hills. There's a whole line behind him of all the other kings, but he stands like a giant above them. Have you been?"

He gave a reply with a shake of his head. "I'm afraid I've only had the pleasure of seeing it from afar, but I take it you have?"

Orangecloak laid down her now empty plate and turned her back to the wall behind her pillow to face Tryst. She kept her teacup to both hands and left a leg to freely dangle off the side of the bunk. "Indeed, it's quite a wondrous place to visit. I made a point of going there after a protest in Portsward. It seemed like a good place to hide for a few days while anyone looking for me would be running in every other direction to hunt me down."

"I certainly can't argue with your logic," Tryst agreed.

"Greggard has told me that most people generally avoid the King's Quays. Even Captain Bickerington has said he would rather face a storm head on then take shelter there. It's not somewhere anyone would think to look or would be willing to search."

She shook her head slowly. "I can't take the credit for going there, that was Lazlo Arbor's idea. He wasn't a regular part of my traveling party, but I had encountered him in Weicaster and he stayed with us for the trip north to Daol Bay and Portsward."

"Ah, Lazlo Arbor," Tryst mused. "It might not surprise you to learn that he was the second most sought after member of your group. If there's one thing the EMP hates as much as a woman in power, it's a gay man making a fool of them."

Orangecloak was quick to correct Tryst. "He goes either way, actually," she said, drawing Tryst's gaze just in time to catch her restraining a grin. "He seems to prefer men, though any woman lucky enough to have him for a night is in for quite a treat."

"First-hand experience I take it?" Tryst asked in a jovial tone.

The grin slipped its way loose at last. "Indeed, right there in King's Quay."

Tryst's hand ran over the growing beard on his face. "Something tells me that it was quite the experience."

"Aye, Lazlo Arbor was a proper lover." She turned morose at her recollection of her friend, the smile slipping away as fast as it had come. Having laid down her empty cup, she pushed from the bunk and stood up, as if to try and walk away from the memory.

"He *is* a proper lover," Tryst corrected her. "The man yet lives."

She looked away from Tryst before answering that. "He lives now in Biddenhurst, Tryst. Behind those walls, he's as good as dead in there, they all are. In all your time in the Lord Master's service have you ever heard of anyone who entered that place and lived to see the world outside its walls again?"

When Tryst couldn't think of any examples he shook his head. "I can't say I have."

Orangecloak turned away from him and strolled toward the porthole. "The answer is no, Tryst. If someone had found a way to escape, don't you think we would both know of it? I've lost enough of mine own Thieves to that place and not one has ever come back to me. I have no reason to hold out hope that Lazlo, Ellarie and the others will fare any better."

"Don't be so quick to forsake hope, my lady," Tryst said, following her to the porthole and leaning over her shoulder to take in the view with her.

For that Orangecloak seemed to have no response and they let the silence stand for a time, simply gazing out through the circular frame of thick glass together.

Outside the day was sunny, though the cold touch of the glass proved there was no warmth to be found. The number of ships trailing alongside and behind *The Myra* had grown once again and Tryst now counted a half dozen in sight and doubtlessly more aft and starboard of the ship. Beyond the fishing vessels that bobbed upon the rolling waters lay the sharp, ruggedly endearing cliffs of the north coast. Jutting sharply from the waves and glistening brilliantly in the sunlight where the waters touched them.

The fleet had kept close to the land, hailing into the harbours, coves and bays with lantern by night and horn by day as they went by. As *The Myra* would drift on by each town and village, more ships joined them. Most of these were smaller than *The Myra*, though some matched it in size. The only member of the fleet that truly towered over Captain Bickerington's prized ship was an imposing four mast schooner earnestly named *The Flying Whale*. The massive ship was reduced to spending the voyage perpetually lumbering at the rearmost of the caravan. It was, in the words of Kerrell Greenlee, "A floating icehouse" out of Morrisvale, one that practically required every working age male in the small town to sail.

"There, do you see King Tolleras?" Orangecloak said while nodding her head in the direction of the derelict port of King's Quays. "Lazlo told me that it reminded him of a mother duck leading its ducklings to water."

On the southern point of the shallow, narrow harbour it stood: a mighty pillar of sculpted stone rising tall amid the cliffs. It was a massive thing, with the sharp looking points of its crown cresting just above the hills on which it was based. The face was stern, set amongst a flowing beard with blank eyes staring westward at the roaring ocean before it. Stone robes flowed to sandaled feet, marvellously carved in what Tryst could only imagine was a decades-long effort. In his lowered right hand was the hilt and part of a broken blade in what Tryst had been told was once a complete sword that extended to the base. The left arm was bent at the elbow, ending in a jagged lump that had been a fist at one time, lying upon his breast above the heart.

Time had given its best effort at eroding the stone monarch away. His nose was but a stub, every part of the sculpture facing the ocean was pocked with holes and there were several bare chunks gone from the torso. Yet, still he stood, keeping silent vigil over the abandoned town that had served as a port and a vacation residence for Phaleayna's kings.

The rest of the visual representation of the line of Phaleaynan kings stretched behind King Tolleras' statue as far as the eye could see. Each one only reaching to the waist of the first, posed in various, noble, warrior stances.

"A great wonder of Illiastra." Tryst said in awe. "And their existence is nearly forgotten by almost every person that lives outside the northwest coast, as are the kings themselves in all but name. How many people have read the books and scrolls of history and know how King Tolleras founded the Kingdom of Phaleayna? How many know of King Theric the Terror or his grandson, King Malleon the Sixth, known as Malleon the Gentle-heart, who repaired his family's legacy? Behind those stone faces are generations of deeds both good and bad that the EMP's century of ignorance has erased from the memory of Illiastra."

"I know of many of them," Orangecloak declared. "There was a time in my youth when I read whatever books I could get my hands on." She leaned back and looked over her shoulder at him. "I've done more than that though, Tryst, I've been to the crypts in the foothills behind Phaleayna. It's something of a rite of passage for initiate Thieves, to venture through the halls of the dead to see the great men and women that came before us."

Once done with staring at the statues, Tryst stepped back from the porthole and returned to sitting upon the bunk. "It must be a humbling experience to walk amongst the last resting place of such renowned and exalted people," he commented.

Orangecloak remained at the window, her eyes unmoving from the nearby shores as she answered in a low voice that bordered on a whisper, "They're nothing but bones covered in dust and cobwebs. Most of the crowns and armour have nearly rusted away and their fine clothes were eaten by the rodents and insects that have served as their company. The last ones interred there are eight hundred years old, but most of the dead have been there for a thousand years or more. It is humbling, aye, for you learn just how fragile we, as beings, are. You see the short span of time we're given in this world and how easily we can be snuffed out of existence.

"Humans are not great, Tryst, we're merely average. We're vulnerable to more diseases and ailments than one can count and easily broken and killed by the most innocuous of things. We're just a flesh and bone vessel to carry about a brain that's advanced enough to know it's a brain. Kings, queens, lords, ministers, patriarchs, soldiers, peasants, thieves and raiders, we're all the same that way."

Tryst picked up on where she was taking the conversation. "Tell me then: what is it that makes individual people great in the eyes of the many?" he asked softly.

"That's the question that Yassira Na-Qoia, leader of the Island of Phaleayna sent us to the Royal Crypts to answer," Orangecloak replied, turning her head towards Tryst. "It is only when we answered that question, if for no one else but ourselves, could we become members of the Thieves."

He followed her statement with another query. "So what was *your* answer, might I ask?"

"It was *our* conclusion, if truth be told. A party of eight had gone together to answer what is known as The Thieves Riddle: Ellarie and Merion Dollen, Joyce Keena, the cousins Lazlo and Donnis Arbor, Coquarro, Myles and I. We toured the ruins and then split off into small groups to dwell on it, as we were told to do. I was paired with Ellarie, my closest friend at the time. It was she and I that worked out the riddle together.

"Our first thought was: is it intellect? Surely those with higher intelligence are great people, I reasoned. They have a greater capacity to understand and learn than the average person. A glance at that line of kings out there will tell you different, though. Men of low cunning can rule above the most brilliant minds with impunity simply by the sheer luck of being born from the right loins. As for a genius, they can still be killed and eternally silenced by just the bare hands of an idiot." She began to step back towards the bunk, stopping before Tryst.

"Then we thought that maybe it is gold that makes certain people great. The man who wields the wealth can pay for intellect and strength to serve him, after all. Every single one of those skeletons laid out on the plinths in the crypts was wealthy in life. The kings alone were born into riches they could never hope to spend in their living hours. Yet, all that gold and silver in life didn't make the skeleton of the king worth anything more than the skeleton of his servants.

"After all, neither servant nor king can take the gold with them from this world when they die."

She was before him then, standing with her arms folded as she picked up her story. "Ellarie argued, 'If not intellect or wealth, perhaps it is strength, then?' She had a point, for in ancient, tribal times it was the strongest warriors that led the largest tribes. It is common knowledge that rulers the known world over employ only the strongest knights and soldiers to guard them, their people and their realm. That's to say nothing of the reverence owed to the Combat University you come from. Yet a pox or a poison can destroy the greatest warrior without a blow. Even you, Tryst, if the Lord Master cornered you and turned a dozen riflemen on you, then the Master of Blades himself could fall at the command of a decrepit, old man."

"Indeed I could," Tryst agreed with a nod. "So what is it then? If it's not strength, money or intellect that makes a person rise to a level of greatness that warrants their immortalisation in a colossal stone avatar, then what does?"

The bunk creaked ever so slightly beneath Orangecloak's slender frame as she sat down beside Tryst to look him straight in the eyes. "The greatest trick we have ever pulled on ourselves, Tryst Reine: power."

Tryst was certainly intrigued by this point, though it was more than that. She was letting him in, giving him a glimpse of her world and her past and that prospect more than anything else excited him. "What brought you to that conclusion, might I ask?" he put to her, to keep their conversation going.

"Bones," she stated confidently. "The kings are laid out in the middle of these big rooms. Their undertakers would just leave them out on a plinth and let time go to work turning them to dust. The walls of the rooms are lined with alcoves for younger siblings and other royalty, all decaying at their own leisure.

"Outside those big, ornately decorated rooms are shelves full of little wooden boxes with brass plates on them all along the dark and unadorned hallways. Do you know what they keep in those?" She waited until Tryst shook his head before going on. "Yet more bones. Servants mostly, some are cousins of Kings, royalty of lesser familial branches, even cats and dogs. They would just boil the flesh off and lay out the bones all compactly in the little boxes. Here's the thing I noticed though, looking at all those bones: there's no difference between prince and pauper. I had no way of knowing if I was even looking at Kings on the plinths. Who's to say no one switched the bones on the pedestals with the bones in the boxes? What difference would it make? There's tombs for the knights too and the scholars and the great artists. The rich, the strong and the brilliant were all lying there together with friends, families and servants and no one is any better or worse than the other.

"That's when it dawned on us, Tryst. That's when we knew why some bones were laid out in a macabre display and others were stowed away on shelves like fine dinnerware: the ones in the little boxes had believed the ones in the tombs had power. It's the grandest illusion of them all, Tryst. Power is nothing but smoke and shadows.

"A strong man, even one like you, may be able to defeat every person in the world in single combat. Yet, for all of that, his rule is only good so long as the people collectively decide not to smother him. Just as the intellectual can be ignored or the rich man's coin can no longer be accepted as currency. It is us, as a society, who grants power where we see fit and we're only too quick to forget that we can take it away just as easily. We choose to see those in power as above us on stone thrones and the truth is that the throne is made not of stone, but of bone. We are those bones and if we all choose to oust the man we let sit upon us, then his seat is no more."

Tryst nodded thoughtfully as she finished. "I have heard a similar message before, albeit without the anecdote about the crypts behind Phaleayna."

"You're talking about our crossing in Aquas Bay," Orangecloak confirmed before Tryst could. Her eyes went to her hands on her lap before darting back to meet Tryst's gaze with a slim smile working its way along her lips. "I'm glad you remembered, though. To be honest I had hoped that you, above all, would truly listen to what I was saying."

He reflected on the memory warmly, grinning freely at the thought of it. "I had so many questions for you, so much more I wanted to hear, but that damn guardsman got close enough to make a grab at your boot. Before I knew it, you were bounding up over the side of a building in a red, orange and green blur."

She shrugged. "I'm here now, what would you ask?"

I would ask a million things and one, Tryst thought before replying. "I remember the last thing you were speaking about was that the many should not fear the few who claim power. If you say power is but a trick, what would you put in place of what we have now?"

There was confidence in her eyes as she spoke. It was a telling look that told Tryst that this was an arrow in her quiver she had at the ready and was a target she had feathered many times before. "When I was first in the field as one of the Thieves, with the stars as my ceiling and the grass as a pillow, I went to sleep dreaming of what a free Illiastra was. In those days I thought the best way to be free would be to let everyone live as they might. That would be absolute freedom, wouldn't it? Let everyone simply make the rules for themselves, no one taking claim over lands, no one kneeling to anyone else. No one could say, 'That's my land, you can't build there' or 'that's my apple tree, you can't eat them apples.' Everyone just shared what we in the world have between us all, as equals." Orangecloak shook her head with a snort at the thought. "I was naïve, I admit. I didn't know anything at the time and I still know nothing, in truth.

"It was much later that I learned that we need leadership and that not all people are fit to lead, for themselves or otherwise. We need laws and justice in place or we'll soon have people who kill and steal and rape simply because their own personal moral code doesn't prohibit it.

"There are gangs of men south of the Varras River that already believe that their ways of pillaging the homes of good, honest people is acceptable. It was when I saw the aftermath of these raiders with my own two eyes that I learned that anarchy can only breed chaos. Leaving every last person to make their own laws would only work if every last person had the wits and morals enough to not harm the person next to them unduly. The sad truth is that we as a species are not that far advanced. We are not elves, after all, and even they have some form of governance in place."

Tryst stroked the burgeoning beard on his face while posing his next question. "Anarchy can only breed chaos, that is certainly true, my lady. Have you understanding of the Elven nation? They have a form of leadership that, by our own standards, would be idyllic and utopic. How well do you think their system could be implemented in human Illiastra?"

"I don't, quite frankly. Not in our lifetimes, anyhow. It would require a level of change beyond what can be achieved with just empowerment of the masses. In fact, we would need a shift in the thinking of society as a whole, which is something that is not achieved overnight. From what I have seen, beliefs tend to have laboriously long deaths."

He considered his next question for a moment. "Then what do you propose in the interim between a generations-long, society-wide turnover in thought?"

Orangecloak didn't hesitate to answer. "A basic democracy, for a start. Everyone needs as much of a say in how their country and region is run as they do in their own household. We need to be involved in a decision making process that doesn't come to a screeching halt after we've finished electing delegates and leaders."

"A worthy goal if I may say so," Tryst began to say until a loud knock on the door interrupted their conversation.

After the knock came a clear, male voice of the person without. "Milady Orangecloak, Captain Bickerington has sent me to find you and your party."

"Is it urgent?" Orangecloak asked loudly of the person outside without rising from her bunk to answer the door.

"Not terribly urgent, no, but there's not much room for delay, milady," the as of yet unidentified crewman answered.

Orangecloak gave Tryst a brief glance of suspicion before replying. "You may let the captain know that I'll join him on deck in a moment when I have dressed."

The voice called back through the wooden door. "That would be unwise, milady. Might I speak with you in person? It's Kerrell Greenlee, milady."

"Just give me a moment, please." Orangecloak rose to her feet and scrambled into her worn leather trousers, lacing them up in haste before opening the door and allowing Kerrell inside. "What seems to be the problem, Kerrell?" she said as the tall, handsome fellow dressed in dark grey trousers and a blue, knitted sweater stepped into the room. He strode with a casual manner that belied the relative urgency to which he afforded his message.

"Forgive me for disturbing you, milady," Kerrell started before espying Tryst seated upon the bunk. "Oh, and Tryst is here as well. Good, that'll save me from having to find you."

"Good day, Kerrell. What brings you to us this morning?" Tryst asked, despite having a good inclination of what that answer might be.

The sailor smiled proudly as he explained. "It's about your

disembarking in Portsward. The Captain would like to meet with you in the cargo hold and tell you of the idea that the crew and I came up with. I shall fetch Fletchard, if you would like to head on down there yourselves."

"Very well then, we'll do that shortly, Kerrell, thank you," Orangecloak answered.

That earned a quick nod from Kerrell who began to show himself out, only to stop in his tracks and turn back to them. "Oh yes, the captain bid that you refrain from going above decks anymore. Our fleet is at full force and while you have our assurances that no one aboard *The Myra* would dare speak of you being here, we can't say the same for every man aboard every other ship. I hope you understand, milady, we're looking out for your own wellbeing."

"I understand only too well, Kerrell," Orangecloak answered him before clearing her throat. "Tell Captain Bickerington that we'll be with him shortly, I'm sure we'll find our way."

With a final nod, Kerrell excused himself and left Tryst and Orangecloak to themselves.

Once Orangecloak had finished getting dressed in her leather outfit, complete with the signature cloak, they departed for the cargo hold below.

It was just a short walk for the two of them down the corridor to the ladder that led into the bowels of the ship. As their feet touched the floor, their ears were bombarded with the sounds of sawing and hammering. What they found, once they followed the noise further into the hold, were a pair of sailors gathered around a small work area with boxes pressed into service as tables. Between them sat two oblong crates, their lids removed and their contents being neatly stacked in the corner by a deckhand Tryst knew to be named Cren.

Of the captain there was no immediate sign and the three working men seemed to take no notice of the other arrivals as they toiled away on the pine containers. Together, Tryst and Orangecloak waited on the edge of the cleared construction area, content to let the men work in peace.

The names of the men doing the modification work on the boxes were Ghoren and Alphonze, Tryst seemed to recall. The former was a man of his mid-fifties, tall, slender and clean shaven. His partner was about a decade younger, half a head shorter and bespectacled. Tryst had seen the same two men paired with one another regularly since boarding the ship.

"I see you found your way," said a voice from behind Tryst, one he knew to be Kerrell once again. With him was Fletchard, looking just the same as he was when Tryst had last seen him in the galley.

Tryst glanced over his shoulder at the sailors as he replied. "Aye, the lads are hard at work, it seems. Though it remains to be seen just what they are doing."

"Captain Bickerington decided to leave the explanation in my hands," Kerrell said apologetically, strolling into the work area to get the attention of the working trio. "*The Myra* is nothing if not a demanding mistress and he's unable to leave the wheelhouse.

The hammering, sawing and stacking stopped as the three realised they were no longer alone and everyone exchanged hellos and shook hands.

Orangecloak stepped up to the crates, a hand running along its edge while she inspected the interior. "What is it that we have here?"

"Crates, milady," Cren answered dryly.

Fletchard groaned, his lone eye rolling impatiently. "Of course they're crates. What are you doing to them to warrant our attention?"

Kerrell jumped in before Cren could speak up again. "These crates are being modified for your use. This is how we're going to get you to the Simillon Manor unseen."

"Go on," Orangecloak urged Kerrell, having taken no umbrage at either Cren's jape or Fletchard's condescending retort.

The first mate jumped in happily to explain. "As you can see we've unloaded the crates. As it was they were only carrying the caribou pelts we were planning to bring to market anyhow. Alphonze and Ghoren, meanwhile, have been busy constructing a false bottom and cutting air holes in the boxes. We're going to put two of you in one box and one in the other with all your equipment. Once that's done, we'll put the lid on the false bottom and refill it with hides to conceal you. Our hoist will sling you right out of the ship and into a wagon. That, in turn, will take you right to Greggard's manor and no one will be any the wiser."

Orangecloak's face gave away her concern. "No one will think it strange that two large crates are being shipped directly to Lord Greggard's home? Everything here would normally all be going to storehouses, would it not?"

"True," Kerrell said with a shrug. "The thing to remember

though is that at his core Greggard is a merchant and not just any merchant, but the Lord of Foreign Trade. Even if asked, all we have to claim is that this is his personal supply to be taken to furriers of his own choosing or to be used for sampling and bartering. Worry not, I'll ride to him beforehand and let him know of your arrival, and he'll have the paperwork drafted to correspond with the order. The purchase may come across as odd, but on the surface everything will look entirely legitimate and pass any initial inspections."

Orangecloak waited until he had finished before commenting again. "You've put a great deal of thought and effort into this Kerrell."

"Why, thank you, milady," he said gratefully. "I am merely doing my job to ensure that the needs of the ship, crew and passengers alike are seen to. The captain laid the task in my hands and I can only hope my solution is to his and your satisfaction."

Tryst glanced Orangecloak and Fletchard in turn before speaking up. "It sounds to me like a good plan and I see no other options available to us apart from attempting to sneak off on foot under cover of darkness. It has my satisfaction. Though, I can't say as much of my other two travelling companions."

The room was as silent as a crypt, save for the scrape of Orangecloak's hand caressing one of the pine boxes. All eyes were on her, waiting for her decision and watching her mull it over to herself. "I can't say I like the idea of being wedged into total darkness in a small box. I'm at the mercy of Greggard Simillon, who I was to believe was my enemy. Though, it seems that my options are limited."

Fletchard growled impatiently. "Yes, your fucking options are limited. You can get in the box or you walk on foot. Either way, make up your mind and shut your damned mouth."

The agitation dwelling within Orangecloak was practically palpable as she let Fletchard's curtness roll over her. "If I had wanted your counsel, I would have asked," she muttered back without giving him as much as a look, before turning towards the Captain's most trusted man with her decision. "Kerrell, thank you for all your work putting this together, my life is in your hands."

"I will do my utmost to ensure that your trust is not misplaced then," Kerrell said with half a bow before departing again.

After that came a brief exchange of pleasantries between Orangecloak and the three workers, during which Fletchard left without another word. The workers spoke amiably about their jobs and the weather, jesting lightly all the while until Orangecloak finally said her farewells and promised to see them all over dinner.

It was on Tryst to retire to his room and exercise, though Orangecloak asked of his intentions for the afternoon and inquired if he might spend it with her. It was a request Tryst was only glad to agree to and together the pair made for her cabin once again, inarguably the more spacious of the two.

Along their route, Tryst stopped off to the dining hall and grabbed an ornate wooden box from a shelf within. He tucked it under his arm and refused to tell Orangecloak what was in it until they were within her room.

"Can I know now what is in the box, Tryst?" Orangecloak asked almost impatiently.

Gingerly, he opened the varnished wooden container and began undoing small brass latches that held it together until the box was lying flat across the desk. On the inside, the base, lid and walls were painted to look like beautiful plains of grassed and forested land with a roaring river running through it. Seated in the middle of what was the base of the box was a velvet bag containing instruction cards, a pair of twelve sided dice and miniature, carved wooden figurines and props. "It's a game, Orangecloak. I thought it might be a pleasant way to pass time."

"This is *A Road to Adventure*," Orangecloak said at once in recognition. "I had owned it as a little girl. It's been some twenty years since last I had even seen it. Oh, Tryst, I would absolutely love to play."

"Then by all means, let's do just that," Tryst said gaily, gesturing open handed at the chair opposite to where he was about to sit. "Perhaps you would like tea and biscuits to go along with it?"

Orangecloak agreed with the sentiment but stayed standing. "That would be wonderful, Tryst. Why don't I get us the refreshments while you set up the board?"

Before Tryst could offer to do both, she was gone out the door happily, leaving Tryst no room to suggest otherwise.

By the time Orangecloak returned with their refreshments, Tryst had the game set up and they were ready to play.

The rules of the game were simple enough: the board had designated paths marked out in squares. Once a figurine of an adventurer was chosen, the dice were rolled and you moved the figurine about the board. Landing on squares with specific markings required drawing a card from a matching deck. Each card contained a scenario the adventurer was to contend with. The fate of the adventurer was decided by a second cast of the die. The goal of the game was to reach a mountain and slay the great, five headed chimera within. The luck of the die determined if the adventurer lived or died, and if they failed to survive, any other players could find their way to the mountain and challenge the beast themselves.

They played four rounds of the game together, with Orangecloak successfully slaying the chimera first in all but one game. While they played, Orangecloak and Tryst conversed on light and mostly impersonal matters. Orangecloak plied Tryst with questions about Drake, wanting to know more about the wintery lands and its people, and in turn Tryst asked about Illiastra's Southlands. Besides Aquas Bay, the world south of the Varras River was a world unknown to Tryst, apart from stories told by Freyard Archer, who was stationed at Fort Dornett.

To Orangecloak, however, it was those harsh lands that she called home. A vast wilderness bordered north and south by the Varras River and the Southern Mountain chain that separated the southlands from the Ocean of the Endless Storm. Within this boundary was a sea of grass and forest, not unlike the painted board on which they played their game. Spotted amongst the sea of green were ancient ruins, walled towns, the two cities known as Aquas Bay and The Warrens and the many encampments of the raiding gangs.

Of the raiders Tryst knew a great deal, on account of the deep-seated hatred his friend Freyard Archer bore them all. The decorated Master-at-Arms spent much of his time leading a large ranging of fellow soldiers to hunt the raiders in their stolen homes.

As Orangecloak was presently pointing out, there were numerous gangs comprising the legions of outlaws. Of those numbers, three stood with the largest: the Sons of Valdarrow, the Forsaken and the Moon Raiders. Beyond them were smaller bands, some named, others not, with most pledging some sort of fealty to one of the three largest and deadliest gangs.

"It's just the Sons and Forsaken now, is it not? The Moon Raiders were killed off by Freyard Archer and his men, or so he tells it," Tryst had interjected while Orangecloak was explaining the various gangs.

"You know Freyard Archer?" Orangecloak met his eyes at that.

"I'm not surprised. We call his men the Sun's Rangers. They're almost like a gang themselves, albeit one with a fort and moral fibre. I always felt Ser Archer was an honourable man, for what I knew of him."

Tryst grew curious. "Did you meet him personally?"

She answered with a disappointed wrinkling of her nose. "I never had the pleasure of meeting him personally, though some of my thieves did. The closest I ever came to him was from a distance. Myles and I were hiding within the tree tops while Coquarro treated with him below. I know Freyard saw me and knew I was there, sitting above him in a big redwood tree. He could have cut the tree down and captured me and yet he settled for a quick, wordless glance. Coquarro informed Freyard that the Forsaken had sent an armed band of attackers creeping toward Fort Dornett and where they could find them and Freyard left us be.

"How could I not respect the man after that? I knew he had no quarrel with me and mine, so I gave him no reason to start one."

After that, they spoke no more of her deceased friends or Freyard or raiding gangs and contented themselves with idle chatter over their game.

As the sun descended on the ever shortening winter days, there came a knock at the door from one of the deckhands to notify them of dinner. "We'll be right there, Walton, thank you," Orangecloak called out to the voice on the other side.

"You're getting to know the crew I see," Tryst commented warmly while disassembling the board game.

The shift in topic seemed to dampen Orangecloak's mood, yet she seemed to want to speak of it. "They're quite friendly and talkative. You can't help but like them. Well, most of them are anyhow, I've noticed there's a distinct divide between the majority of the crew and the captain's closest men. Even Kerrell, despite his pleasantry, is masking the emotional burden of their recent past."

It was indeed a grim topic that thought led to and though Tryst felt poorly for bringing it up, he spoke further of it. "Aye, when they dock in Portsward, the captain will be expected to report what happened with their Tower of Ios. If the Triarchy expects the blaze to have been as a result of foul play, then they may launch an investigation of their own."

"I would think that they would be glad to be rid of two child molesters they had been trying to hide," Orangecloak added.

Tryst tucked the game under his arm and stood up. "If there's one thing I have learned of the Triarchy since I've been in Illiastra, it's that they are more than capable of meting out their own brand of justice, however lopsided that might be. Captain Bickerington taking those matters into his own hands would vex them to no end."

Orangecloak grew frustrated with that. "Then the Triarchy should take care of the soiled members of their flock themselves. They know exactly who are committing these crimes yet only work to shield them from justice."

Tryst gave that a thoughtful nod. "They could, but doing so would mean that the same men who claim to be oracles of Ios would have to admit to allowing child molesters into their ranks. The Triarchy would sooner paint a portrait of infallibility, as do their allies in the EMP. You'll almost never hear one or the other admit they're wrong, as you well know."

They were in the hallway on route to the galley by then, with Orangecloak reaching Tryst's conclusion before him. "They instead act as though their clergymen have committed no crimes so that they don't have to police themselves, thereby removing the risk of having the populace realise they're capable of error."

"Precisely," Tryst agreed as he held open the door to the galley. "As you know yourself, the people aren't so easily fooled though. There are those who would cling to whatever lies the Triarchy or the EMP release, but many are not so wilfully blind." He finished the sentence while passing through the threshold and into the warm, aroma filled dining hall behind Orangecloak.

The benches scraped along the hardwood floor in unison as Harold Bickerington and his crew rose to their feet upon noticing Tryst and Orangecloak standing in the room. "Be at ease, gentlemen," Orangecloak offered. "I am no one that you need rise for."

It was the captain that replied for the crew. "Your humility is boundless, my lady, nonetheless, the respect of me and my crew is unwavering." He turned his attention towards the youngest of his deckhands. "Cren, fetch two plates of supper for the lady and the blade master, I'll have them seated beside me. The rest of you on the left side shall slide down to make room for them." His eyes fell back to where his guests stood. "Sit, I have the need to speak with you both."

To Tryst and Orangecloak's delight, they discovered that the evening meal was cooked by Kerrell, as it had been the evening before too. The man was well versed with his spices from Johnah and the Island Nations and used whatever he could get his hands on, Tryst had come to learn. Tonight was no different and Tryst and Orangecloak were given bowls of duck soup cooked with long thick noodles, chopped green bell peppers, sliced carrots and leeks.

The captain waited until Kerrell had taken his seat at his right side and Cren had plunked down a pair of wooden goblets filled with blueberry red wine before saying a word.

"Kerrell tells me that he's brought you into the cargo hold to show you our work." Harold Bickerington's voice was void of emotion, likely drained from the thought of his coming meeting in Portsward.

"Aye, he did." It was Orangecloak who spoke up, just as Tryst was about to do the same. "Everything is satisfactory, Captain. I think your method will suffice to see us off the ship."

"That is good to hear." The captain spoke in a tone as flat as the table his forearms rested upon, eyes gazing into his tumbler of rum. "In a few short hours, we should be rounding the turn into Twin Bay and by the midnight hour we'll be docked in Portsward, gods willing. The current plan is to offload you in the early morning hours, while the dawn is just starting to make its rise and darkness still favours you. We will put two of you to one crate and the third person shall ride with your things in the other. I will leave the decision of who goes where to you, my lady."

"That all sounds more than fair," Orangecloak agreed, the look on her face told Tryst that she already had a fair idea of how that arrangement would work out.

"It is going to be a trying day for the both of us tomorrow, my lady," Bickerington went on to say while idly circling his spoon about his soup. "I know what I must do and I do not relish the task. As a fellow leader, I would think that you above all would agree that leadership frequently requires doing the unpleasant, oftentimes alone and at great risk."

Tryst could see Orangecloak swallowing hard at that, staring hard into her own supper. "I agree wholeheartedly, Captain. Leadership is not just about ordering people around, it's about having responsibility for, and accountability to, those you lead. There are times, like the ones we face on the morrow, when we must speak and decide on behalf of those we lead. It shall be difficult for the both of us. However, I feel that we will both do what is right by our people.

The captain had leaned back in his chair while she spoke, listening intently while thumbing at the brown suspenders that held up matching trousers over a starched, cobalt blue shirt. "You speak wisely, my lady. However, while I acknowledge that we both face arduous times ahead, only one of us is trying to rally the whole country to their side. Tryst has told me that the other two members of the Musicians you have met are both willing to vouch for you. It took quite a few of us, but the Musicians have succeeded in giving you the gift of another chance. We do this not for you, but for the hope of what you might bring to Illiastra.

"I would not presume to tell you how you should use this gift for it is not my place. I simply ask that you take stock of everyone who has made it possible for you to be here and do what you think is right. Not just by the Thieves, but by those of the Musicians who have helped you, and most of all, by the people of the Illiastra."

"I understand, Captain. Thank you for your counsel," Orangecloak answered with a solemn nod. "And may good fortune be upon us both tomorrow."

25

ORANGECLOAK

In a group like the Thieves, stealth was tantamount to success. Orangecloak had made it her lifestyle to always look for the most obvious route and take it only as a last resort. She was accustomed to the unconventional and clandestine ways of getting about. Whether it was jumping onto moving trains, climbing trees and scaling rooftops or trekking through underground tunnels and sewers, she had thought she had done it all. From within the pitch black, stuffy, restrictive confines of the bottom of a slatted pine box, she realised how wrong that thought had been.

Inside this box, it was a blinding, restraining experience that forced her to rely on senses other than sight and left her at the complete mercy of strangers. Even the air holes that were cut in the short ends of the boxes had been made to look like hand holds. The clever disguising of the holes granted Orangecloak and Tryst a steady airflow, but prevented them from seeing anything.

At first she had tried to get herself excited about it. This was a whole new experience, after all. That excitement quickly abated, however, once the false bottom of the crate was nailed shut a few dozen centimetres from her face. The sailors had tried to make the predicament as comfortable as possible by lining the bottom of the crate with caribou pelts and cushions. It was a gesture Orangecloak appreciated and one among several she reminded herself of once she found that she could scarcely roll over in the tight space.

Even when she did move, she was practically atop Tryst, who was lying to the left of her. Though Orangecloak was loath to admit it, she was glad to have him with her. Being alone in the darkness while being hoisted and jostled about as cargo was an unpleasant experience to say the least. The decent company served to make it all that much more tolerable.

The last time I was locked in total darkness, I was alone and sure my death was at hand. It was Tryst who bore me from that certain death. Compared to that, this darkness I can handle with ease, Orangecloak had reminded herself while the block and tackle swayed the crate to and fro as it rose from the depths of *The Myra's* hold.

The crate bumped and nudged against things occasionally, but the lifting was far from the worst experience Orangecloak had ever experienced.

A sudden gust of cold, salty air blew through the air holes of the box, heralding their arrival above deck. They touched the deck briefly while the crew switched the crate from the block and tackle to what she was told would be a treadwheel crane mounted on the dock. In what seemed like only seconds, Orangecloak and Tryst were swinging through the air in their blindness again.

The sheer helplessness of the situation was what bothered Orangecloak most of all. She couldn't move, couldn't see and was at the mercy of the dockworkers handling the machine. There was nothing she could do but lie silently and hope she didn't plunge into the frigid waters of the bay or crash onto the dock below.

With a sudden thump and a bump, the crate came to a shaky rest in what Orangecloak could only fathom to be a wagon. In the absence of sight, Orangecloak turned to her other senses to help her have some sort of notion of what was going on about her. There were voices all around, muffled but distinguishable. At first they were the familiar voices of Captain Bickerington's crew, loud and clear as they called out orders to one another. After the flight from the ship to the dock, the voices grew strange, with the thick accent of the north coasters giving way to the more diluted dialect of the city folk. There were screeching seagulls, creaking ships and the gentle rolling of the waves to be heard behind voices both near and far – all the standard fare of a busy port town.

The smell of the salt sea had wafted heavily into her nostrils when the crate had rose above the deck. The air was less fresh than it had been in Tusker's Cove with an odour of rotting fish seeming to cling to the air.

Orangecloak had to imagine that the captain had opted to dock *The Myra* on the northwest side of Portsward, along the Fishermen's Wharves. A wise choice in her opinion, as docking near the naval ships in the belly of the harbour would put too many suspicious eyes on the ship and its cargo. Out here the poor folk minded their own business, which was catching enough fish to feed themselves for the winter to come. A few boxes of caribou pelts for the richest man in town were of no interest to fishermen who could scarcely afford to look upon them.

While they waited for the second crate containing Fletchard and their belongings to arrive, Orangecloak tried to pick up what the men on the docks were saying to one another. There were many voices and the crate made hearing them a challenge. From the snippets she could pick up though, there seemed to be something major occurring in the western half of Illiastra. To hear them tell it, all the concerned eyes of Illiastra were suddenly cast towards Portsward and Daol Bay, the two cities of Twin Bay.

An excited voice came so close that Orangecloak had to believe it was standing just outside the wagon. "What have you got on the back of this one, mate?" it called to whom Orangecloak could only guess was the carriage driver. "Rifles I bet, the fishermen in Daol Bay said we'll all be in need of them soon enough."

A second voice answered back, "Rifles from Tusker's Cove? No lad, they don't have the rifles to give. I've got two crates of caribou pelts here for Lord Greggard himself."

"Well, he'll be selling them for rifles then, I assure you that," the first voice replied, more distantly this time.

She felt Tryst lean in close to her. "They sent the Raven to pick us up," he whispered.

Orangecloak's mind immediately went to her lieutenant by the name of Edwin, also known as the Raven for his jet black hair and beard. It was him she had left as castellan of Rillis Vale when last she had departed. Though, whomever Tryst was referring to was someone else entirely. "Who's the Raven?" she asked with a whisper.

"A man in the employ of Lord Greggard, carriage driver mostly. Though he's also a messenger for the Musicians and one of Greggard's most trusted workers. A strange fellow by anyone's standards, but a good man nonetheless."

In the tight space, Orangecloak rolled as much as she could to face Tryst, despite the fact that she couldn't really see him. A movement made difficult by the pair of cloaks she wore as blankets, wrapped snugly about her to ward off the cold that crept in. "They were talking about rifles, I wonder what for."

"I have no idea, but whatever it is, I'm sure Lord Greggard is involved. No doubt we'll know soon enough," Tryst replied softly.

The second crate thumped and banged its way down beside them moments later and Orangecloak hoped the landing was as rough on Fletchard as it had sounded. There were other noises then, mostly men shouting commands to one another and the sound of ropes tumbling over the crates and being pulled tight to hold them in place. A crack of the reigns later and the wagon jolted to life beneath them.

The ride started smoothly enough, as the wagon wheels rolled over the smooth concrete of the wharf, though that soon gave way to the rougher gravel road. Orangecloak listened for noise, any noise above the sound of the wheels grinding the dirt, but the steady racket seemed to fill her ears every which way.

The cart made a left turn and Orangecloak tried to visualise the route the driver was taking. Portsward hadn't been too long ago visited by Orangecloak and she tried to remember the layout of the city to pass the time.

The Simillon Manor is on the north side of Portsward, but in the eastern corner of the city, she recalled to herself as she tried to picture it. The manor and its grounds happened to take up a large swath of the district, seated on a low, gentle hill and looking like it was nestled in its own little forest.

Another turn later and Orangecloak was sure she felt the cart rising slightly on the front. They were heading uphill and soon she was hearing the sound of dozens of voices all talking at once. *Paulder's Square,* she guessed. It was once the site of a demonstration she, Coquarro, Miles and Lazlo had led, the same one that had taken them to King's Quays afterwards.

It was not the main center of the city, but it was the site of the government house where the city council met. The surrounding neighbourhood was inhabited by the wealthiest denizens of Portsward and the square shared in that wealth and the image it provided. Orangecloak recalled the quaint, marble fountain in the center of the square with its statue of some dead lord seated lazily upon a palanquin. The featureless, sculpted heads and shoulders of his carriers being the only way to know it was in fact a palanquin the statue was on.

Orangecloak could hear the water spouting from what she knew was the statue's outstretched and upturned right palm as they passed close to it.

All around the marble fountain and its circular patterned brick façade stood whitewashed buildings of varying heights occupied by wealthy and lavish offices, banks, stores and upscale lounges. It was a place Orangecloak had detested in her visits, one that stood as testament to the wage gap between the working and business classes.

It was then that it dawned on her that the voices were not merely people chattering through a normal day of the week. There was a commotion, one they were getting steadily closer to.

"Tryst," she whispered through the black. She called his name again when no answer came and finally resorted to nudging his arm.

A grunt and a stifled yawn escaped Tryst. "Huh? What's going on?" he whispered back.

"You were asleep?" Orangecloak kept her own voice to a whisper but couldn't contain her bafflement. "How could you sleep at a time like this?"

She could feel Tryst rolling to his side to face her direction before he answered. "Because I'm lying down in a tight space in utter darkness, what else is there for me to do?"

"Do you hear what's going on out there?" Orangecloak asked. "Something's afoot."

Tryst fell quiet for a moment to hear the ruckus himself before responding. "A crowd has gathered, they sound worried and concerned, even a little panicked. I think we might be in Paulder's Square, unless Raven circled down into the Throat and is taking the long way around." He hummed aloud ponderously. "Are they shouting about you, I wonder? News of your capture would have long spread here. Perhaps the Lord Master is even claiming you've been executed."

Orangecloak shook her head as much as she could, before realising the pointlessness of doing so in total darkness and speaking up. "No, I can't see these types being too upset at the prospect of my death. Whatever happened has affected them personally."

"Aye, you might be right about that," Tryst began to answer.

A loud bang on the side of the wagon nearest to Orangecloak

gave her a start. She rolled over and put her back to Tryst, her hand darting for the curved, blacksteel dagger on her hip.

"You there!" a regal sounding man's voice from without shouted. "Aren't you Lord Greggard's carriage driver?! What's he got to say about this madness?!"

The man Tryst called Raven made a polite response. "My apologies, good ser. If you want to know Lord Greggard's opinion, you'll have to speak with his castellan, not his chauffer."

Tryst leaned in close to Orangecloak's ear to whisper as the wagon slowed to a near halt. "It's still early in the morning. This must be dire news to attract such an incited crowd on such a frigid dawn."

The Raven begged to be allowed through the throng to no avail for some time. All the while people were being pushed up against the wagon, making it rock and bounce from side to side with every passing person. "Why did he have to come through here?" Orangecloak was growing more agitated by the second. "He could have avoided the square entirely."

"Perhaps the mob formed after he went to retrieve us," she heard Tryst suggest from over her shoulder.

Orangecloak grumbled at that. "Someone should tell this man that the direct route is not necessarily the best route. We're going to be swarmed."

The cart began to move once more before Orangecloak's worry could grow any further and soon the voices began to fade.

When things grew relatively quiet, Tryst spoke up again. "It would seem the trouble has passed. I would say we just rode by the Government House. Those fellows are prone to much bluster but little physical action. That's what men-at-arms and sellswords are for."

Orangecloak huffed at that. "Yes, the luxury of being able to pay someone else to dirty their hands on your behalf," she said sarcastically. "You wouldn't be familiar with that at all."

That drew a laugh from Tryst. "You've got me there."

The remainder of the ride went smoothly and Orangecloak shifted herself onto her back once more and out of Tryst's lap. She sighed and tried to relax, though with every creaking of the wagon, she knew they were drawing closer to the Simillon Manor. Everything since escaping Atrebell was about this moment and it seemed as though everyone she met had a stake in the meeting that was to come.

A great many whom Orangecloak had spoken to along the way

were putting stock in her and the outcome of this meeting. The Dupoire family had business interests that benefitted themselves and their dwarven people. Then there was Jack Paylor, the voice for the gay members of society who could not reach out to Orangecloak. Lastly, there was the Bickerington family, who had opened their home and their hearts to her. It had taken a great deal of courage for them to deal with the crisis visited upon them by the Triarchy and even more courage to reveal as much to Orangecloak. They had no reason to trust her or even open their door to her, yet they put faith enough in her and Tryst and even Fletchard to keep their secret.

Of course, Orangecloak could not think of the Bickerington family without thinking of Louisia. The young woman's hope for a brighter future was the only beacon of light in the darkness that had consumed Tusker's Cove. The morning after arriving in the rustic, rural town, the deaf girl had asked Orangecloak, through her brother, if she could interview her. While Orangecloak had thought the request odd, she had agreed and was led to a small study located off the sitting room where Arthur had extracted the arrow from Fletchard.

Orangecloak had found Louisia seated there at a desk with inkpot, quill, parchment paper and a large, blank book spread out before her. The girl had claimed that there had been no one else in the known world she had wanted to speak to as much as Orangecloak. It was all Louisia could do to contain her excitement at the reality of that very thing happening in her own home. "I have interviewed Kevane Dupoire and his daughter Tinnia and of course Lord Greggard, among others. Though, all of them pale to having a chance to talk with you, my lady," Louisia had said through Arthur as Orangecloak had taken a seat before the small desk the diminutive girl sat behind. Orangecloak recalled Louisia's face beaming as brightly as the red, short sleeved, satin dress she wore. With her long, brown, curly hair and slender face accented by an adorable little nose, there was no doubt that Louisia was a pretty girl.

When Orangecloak asked why Louisia was sitting before a blank book, Arthur had let his sister answer in her own words through him. "I like to record the conversations I have with the interesting people I am fortunate enough to meet," he spoke as his sister signed with her hands in their invented language. "I write their answers in shorthand on the parchment and then write them out properly in the large book, later. My goal is to move to the Midlands of

Gildriad where a woman, even a deaf one like me, has every opportunity at both an education and a career. Hopefully, these interviews will be interesting enough that they will warrant publishing there. I am certain that your interview will be the cornerstone on which the whole book rests. Of course, this all depends on whether or not you approve the recording of your responses. I will respectfully refrain if you decline."

"I see no reason to decline your request, Louisia," Orangecloak had said on the embarkation of their discussion. "If you think my words will help your book sell, then I shall do my very best to ensure that they are worth reading."

After that, the first thing that Orangecloak had learned about Louisia was that as long as she had her brother about to translate, Louisia could talk the night away. There was no question that the brilliant siblings were both engaging and Orangecloak had found their conversation quite interesting, hanging on every word Arthur translated back to her. It was nothing short of exhilarating to watch the hyper intellectual teenagers turn spoken words into hand signals in rapid succession.

Once they had begun, the two women had talked until called for dinner, discussing all manner of things that Louisia could think of. All the while, Arthur sat patiently with them and translated every word of it back and forth, even chiming in from time to time to add to the conversation. Given the nature of Orangecloak's fame, most of the questions Louisia asked of her were political in nature. These, Orangecloak answered easily, given her staunch positions on governance and equality.

When they had first begun, Orangecloak had spoken in slow, concise sentences, wanting to give Arthur time to translate and Louisia time to write. What quickly became apparent though was that Orangecloak's method seemed almost insulting to the brilliant siblings and soon she was speaking as loquaciously as she pleased. Insofar as Orangecloak could tell, they never missed a word that she said.

As their interview progressed, Orangecloak began casually inserting questions of her own for Louisia, asking the teenaged girl of her aspirations and dreams in life. It turned out that Louisia's interest in travelling to the Midlands of Gildriad was primarily so that she could attend its highly respected university. Her brother shared the same goal, though they differed on their preferred fields of study.

Arthur had all the intention of seeing his medical career through to his doctorate and while Louisia found that field interesting, her chosen pursuit was history. "This world we live in is rich in history, much of it all but lost," Louisia had explained through her brother's translations. "I feel that though I cannot hear the people of today, I can certainly read the words of the people of yesterday. There are great mysteries written in our past and nothing would give me more joy than to uncover them."

Ever since the memorable interview, Louisia had been in Orangecloak's thoughts. *Louisia is a vibrant and brilliant young woman who could contribute a great deal to Illiastra. It is quite saddening that being both a woman and a person with impairment requires that she must leave to find her place. She deserves a chance to succeed in this country as much as anyone else.*

Something Louisia had told Orangecloak after the interview had ended stuck out to her from the moment it was said and Orangecloak thought long on it. "What I find most inspiring about you, my lady, is that you are a champion for not only women, but for honest people from all walks of life," she had signed to Orangecloak. "I dream of the same Illiastra you do, one where a deaf girl has as many opportunities as everyone else. Where women like us and people like me are free to learn, allowed to work and able to contribute. Please, don't give up. You have to fight not just for the Thieves, but for those who cannot fight for themselves."

As she had so many times before, Orangecloak came back to the same questions she asked herself: *if people bestow so much hope in me, is it my place to dash those hopes? Yet, must I bring this country to a war to keep those hopes alive? Is there truly no other way?* As usual, she still felt no closer to an answer.

The loud squeal of iron gates on hinges begging for oil assaulted her ears and shortly after, the wagon took a wide turn. They were on a quiet, secluded, winding path then. The iron shoed feet of the horses clopped on a stone road, birds chirped out their songs and the atmosphere took on a sense of calm.

Another left and two more right turns later, everything came to a soft stop and the Raven spoke up. "Home again, ladies," he said to what Orangecloak could only assume were the horses drawing the wagon. "Just a moment and I'll go grab the lads in the stable. You've earned a brushing and a bucket of oats today." Everything went deathly quiet for a time, a silence that reminded Orangecloak just where she was and the nervousness set in once more.

A hand gently squeezed hers as Tryst seemed to sense her concern. "This is it, my lady," he whispered softly and reassuringly. "Our journey is at an end for now. Meeting with Greggard will be the easy part, you'll see."

Orangecloak didn't share his nonchalance and tried to swallow her worry back down. "So you say," she said.

It wasn't long before they heard the bantering and footsteps of several men approaching. The wagon began to move again, forwards, then backwards on an angle until it lightly thumped against something solid. There were all sorts of noises to be heard then: the ropes that moored the boxes being undone, steel buckles on the horse's bridles being unclasped and what sounded like barn doors swinging open.

The Raven called out from what seemed to Orangecloak like a fair distance away, as if he were already in the process of leaving: "Just place them down in the vault lads. I shall return in a moment to check the contents once I fetch a prying bar."

Once the Raven had gone, the remaining voices began debating over the best way to lift the crates. Hands pulled at the hempen rope handles on Orangecloak's container sharply to judge the weight and more debating ensued. Soon there were even more voices, all male as far as Orangecloak could tell, and finally, they agreed on how to lift the hefty crates.

Orangecloak braced as best she could while the workers counted down from three to slide one of the boxes from the wagon. The sound of wood scraping wood echoed throughout their box but she and Tryst stayed put and for now, she could breathe with relief.

"Easy! Easy!" one voice called above all the others as the wagon bounced from the sudden release of weight.

"I'm losing it!" another shouted and then there was a loud crash and a bang.

Orangecloak held her breath and eyed Tryst as much as she could in the darkness, the two waiting to hear if Fletchard had been discovered. If Fletchard had audibly responded to being jostled and dropped, his moans didn't seem to have been heard over the shouts and curses of the workers at one another.

A voice with a higher pitch than the previous one yelled out jokingly, "You're lucky you didn't break that thing, Tommy!"

The second fellow responded with another string of curses and the lifting resumed without issue. Minutes ticked by slowly while Orangecloak and Tryst could only wait for their turn to be moved into the basement. "By Ios' name, I hope this second one is lighter," the man named Tommy who dropped the previous crate said upon return of the workers to the wagon. His hope was soon lost when the box containing Orangecloak and Tryst was, if anything, heavier. The men struggled with the crate, moving down a flight of steps one foot at a time. Within the box, the pair lay braced, trying to keep from their weight from being shifted about and unbalancing the load.

The carriers laid the crate down hard, all of them grunting under the strain of it. With a few shoves, the men seemed satisfied with its resting place and made their departure. Doors were slammed and latched into place and the chatter of the workers fell out of range.

"Now we wait," Orangecloak whispered after a deep breath.

"It shouldn't be long," Tryst replied with a yawn. "Might be a good time to catch a little nap, not much else we can do until Raven gets back with that prying bar. Even then, he has to remove all the pelts and lift the false bottom. That's even if he picks the right box first, we might be waiting longer if it's Fletchard who gets first pick."

Tryst was soon softly snoring beside Orangecloak, though for the life of her she couldn't fathom how he could sleep at a time like this. *He said the journey is at an end for now. He feels safe here, like he can relax for the first time in a long while,* Orangecloak reminded herself. *Even the Master of Blades is exhaustible.*

Despite trying, sleep would not visit her as it did Tryst. She pulled her black cloak to her chin and resigned herself to listening and waiting for the Raven to return.

For a time she lay there, hearing nothing and seeing less until her mind began to wander away until she was back aboard *The Myra* on the first night of its departure. After dinner with the entire crew of the ship, she and Tryst had retreated to her cabin to speak in private. They had spent some time talking of political matters in the Parliament of Illiastra and had worked up a thirst.

Tryst then took it upon himself to procure them some hot tea, returning several minutes later with a pot and two cups to hand. "Kerrell was making lemon tea when I went to the kitchen and graciously offered us half of his kettle," he had proclaimed happily.

"That was very generous of him. I don't know that I can recall the last time I had lemon tea," Orangecloak had said from where she sat on her bunk while Tryst poured her a cupful. "If memory serves me, it was after Mell the Huntress and a small band of her Thieves captured a three wagon caravan belonging to Minister Deltin of Densington," she pondered aloud while taking a few hot sips. "He was coming from Aquas Bay with a sizeable quantity he had bought directly off a Johnan merchant ship. Mell and her crew robbed him of everything but the clothes on his back and left him and his entourage hogtied in the middle of the road."

A low chuckle rumbled forth from Tryst before he sat in a chair at the tiny desk beside the bunk. "Now that you mention it, I recall a report being filed directly to Grenjin Howland regarding that. Minister Deltin formally requested that I and a group of Honourable Guards personally hunt down the Huntress."

"I recall the tea being delicious and his money putting clothes on a lot of poor backs and food in a lot of poor bellies," Orangecloak commented dryly.

Tryst had raised his cup in toast before taking a hearty drink of it "Money very well spent then, in my opinion."

The mention of the Lord Master and Minister Deltin had spurred Orangecloak to steer the conversation toward a more serious matter. "You know a great deal about this troubled realm, Tryst Reine. Serving a Lord and the Lord Master has made you privy to a great deal more information than most, am I right?"

"Aye, why do you ask?" a nonplussed Tryst replied.

She was quick to follow up with another question. "Then you would certainly know how the Thieves and the refuge of Phaleayna earn our coin?"

Tryst took a deep breath to think about his answer. "As your name implies, your primary income is generated through thievery, or so I had been told. An act you commit almost exclusively against the members and associates of the Elite Merchant Party and the Triarchy."

She nodded in answer and set her emptied cup onto the nightstand. "That's right. What you may not be aware of is that most of those earnings are liquidated into material goods: food, clothing, supplies, that sort of thing."

"I see..." A lone eyebrow on Tryst's face had crept upward and he pivoted his head ever so slightly as she spoke. "I'm confused,

Orangecloak, where are you going with this?"

It had saddened Orangecloak to say what came next. "You are a mercenary, Tryst Reine, albeit, one from a reputed and honourable branch of mercenaries. I recall you telling me that your current contract is with Lord Greggard and that when it is done you are free to do as you please. As much as you would like to work for me, I'm afraid that the Thieves don't have the available financial assets to be able to afford an expensive sellsword. If you think I can offer you a contract, then you are sorely mistaken."

"That is what this is about?" Tryst had asked rhetorically, moving from the desk chair to the bunk beside her. "I don't require a contract or financial compensation for my work. I can pledge my sword to your service just as well as any swordsperson in the known world. My offer of such still stands."

It was Orangecloak's turn to be confused. "I'm sorry, what offer are you referring to?"

That earned Orangecloak that sly smile of Tryst's before he tried to jog her memory. "You don't remember?"

"Remember what?" she answered question for question again.

His voice dropped low. "At the hotel, we were eating and drinking alone. You had consumed a little too much."

The memory was fuzzy, but Orangecloak seemed to recall some of what she and Tryst had talked about that night over excellent wine and better food. "I remember something about it," she had said, blushing at the memory.

He looked to her knowingly, trying to help her focus in on something specific. "I made an offer to you that we never spoken of afterwards."

Orangecloak tried to recall, but the only thing she remembered was the drunken kiss and anything she might have said was lost to her. "What offer would that be?"

"I told you that I would gladly follow you." He had begun to lean in closer, to the point where Orangecloak could smell his lemony breath upon her neck. "I tell you now that if you should want me, I will swear to you my allegiance upon my sword. That is the greatest honour a Swordsman of the Combat University can offer."

"Yes, I seem to recall that now," she had said while lowering her voice to a whisper. "That you offered to go with me should I so desire and...I never gave you an answer, did I?"

Tryst had answered her in a voice as soft as satin, "No...We never spoke of it again, but now I remind you that my offer still stands. You need not decide now, my lady. After Portsward, I will lay my sword at your feet and pledge myself to you. Should you pick it up, I am yours to serve as your protector, your council or whatever else you desire for as long as you wish."

That drew a hard swallow from Orangecloak and she could find no reason to deny his wish. "When I'm done exchanging words with Greggard Simillon, you may place your sword at my feet and I will give you an answer at long last. You deserve that much, Tryst Reine."

"And that is all I ask of you, Orangecloak," Tryst replied with a slender grin working across his face.

A door swung open abruptly on loud, whining hinges, startling Orangecloak and making her jump. She thumped her head roughly against the false bottom of the box and stifled a moan, settling instead for a few grunted expletives.

I feel asleep. I don't recall nodding off, but how would I know the difference in here? she thought to herself while Tryst stirred beside her and began to shift about.

Orangecloak rubbed her sore forehead and turned as best she could toward Tryst. "Someone's here, hopefully it's that Raven fellow to spring us from this."

"Fantastic," Tryst commented sleepily. "My bladder was beginning to complain quite loudly."

The voice of Raven could be heard outside. "Get the lights, my dear," it said to someone.

A foreign accent owned by a female voice called back, "Right, we should hurry, it must be unpleasant in there."

"It's no tea party, I'm sure. Help me get this lid off," Raven spoke sarcastically.

The sound of the nails reluctantly giving up their hold on the main lid ripped through the container and Orangecloak felt relieved that it was she and Tryst being released first. The two people went to work unloading pelts, armload after armload, each one being plopped down nearby with audible thumps. When the box was at last empty, they could hear hands scraping the false bottom from the other side.

Orangecloak swallowed hard, pulled back her cloaks and wrapped her hand about her dagger.

Sensing her apprehension, Tryst reached over and squeezed

her free hand gently. "It's alright, Orangecloak. No one here is going to hurt you," he said softly.

As much as she tried, Orangecloak's nervousness crept through in her voice. "I'm in the manor of a Lord of the Elite Merchant Party and lying absolutely prone in a box. We're at the mercy of whoever is on the other side of this sheet of wood, Tryst. These men have been my enemies for my entire adult life. Yes, I promised everyone I have met along the way here that I would meet and speak with Lord Greggard. That doesn't make this any easier of a thing to do or make me any less apprehensive."

Tryst seemed about to speak when the dim light of the cellar room rolled in atop them.

The left arm went instinctively to shield Orangecloak's eyes as she adjusted to the sudden brightness. She was lying there, blinded by the light and totally vulnerable to whoever stood above her, feeling as helpless as a babe.

"There now, give me your hand, girl, and I'll help you stand," spoke the Raven dryly. "Preferably the one on the dagger, I'd rather that thing not turn up in my throat later."

Once her eyes permitted her to stare into the lit room without irritation, she saw he was indeed not alone. Orangecloak tried to think of two more contrasting figures standing above her, but there was none she could think of. On her left was a man with a gaunt face and a bent nose that had clearly been broken before. He was leathery and haggard, looking like a man who had rode unprotected through the harshest known weather on a daily basis.

Meanwhile, his very antithesis stood looming over Tryst in female form with two slender arms crossed over one of the most lithely and shapely frames Orangecloak had ever seen.

"Why, if it isn't Yahmina Windleaf, as I live and breathe," Tryst proclaimed as he sat upright in the box. "I see Lord Greggard has been recruiting in Fuwachita again."

The woman replied warmly as she took his now outstretched hand and yanked him to his feet, "It is good to see you as well, Tryst Reine. If only the circumstances were better."

Orangecloak was helped up by both the Raven and Tryst and was finally able to give the other woman a proper visual inspection.

What stood before Orangecloak could easily be described as the very image of beauty. Hers was a face as fine as porcelain, lined as if it had been shaped by a god and coming to a perfect point on the chin. Her eyes were a magnetic blue and the tip of her elven ears poked ever so slightly through golden locks of silky blonde strands that tumbled elegantly beyond strong shoulders.

"I didn't think to find an elf here," Orangecloak commented as she reached to shake her hand.

"We tend to turn up in the strangest of places," the elven woman replied in a friendly voice that was as improbably close to perfection as the rest of her.

Tryst gestured toward the hard looking man that had helped Orangecloak stand. "My lady, might I introduce you first to Clinton Magpie, servant and chauffer to Lord Greggard, he's the man I called the Raven."

"You might call me the Raven as well, if it suits you, my lady," Clinton said with a polite bow before turning his attention to the box containing Fletchard. "If you'll excuse me, I was told there was a party of three. I'm going to venture to guess the third member is in this crate. Otherwise there's been a grave mix up."

By the time Orangecloak glanced back towards Tryst, he had already exited the box and Orangecloak quickly followed suit.

"My lady," Tryst said to get Orangecloak's attention once more. "Allow me to introduce the finest archer I have ever seen and a fellow student of the Combat Arts University of Drake: Yahmina Windleaf."

The elf smiled at that with the whitest, prettiest teeth Orangecloak could imagine. "I am also a dual blade wielder, though I am certainly not the finest in that field, am I, Tryst Reine?"

"It's not as though you didn't give me my fair share of bruises in the trying," a laughing Tryst answered before pressing with a question of his own. "Whatever are you doing here, Yahmina? It's a tremendous risk for both you and Greggard if you're found to be working for him."

Orangecloak glanced between the two of them. Their eyes were locked and they seemed to be studying one another. To what end Orangecloak couldn't tell, though there was clearly history between them that went beyond sharing study halls in Drake.

Yahmina offered a casual shrug in response. "Is it not as dangerous for you to be seen with Lord Greggard? Things in Illiastra are changing rapidly, practically overnight. A female bodyguard of elven origin isn't as strange a sight in the west as it once was."

The elf's vagueness befuddled Orangecloak. "What do you mean?" she queried.

Yahmina finally broke her gaze with Tryst and turned to Orangecloak. "The Illiastra you knew when you entered Atrebell is not the same Illiastra you have emerged to, my lady. Lord Greggard's castellan eagerly waits to explain it all to you and I have acquiesced to allow him such. Once your companion is freed from his box, you'll have the answers you seek."

"If you helped, he'd be freed sooner," the Raven suggested with a grunt as he popped the lid off with his wrecking bar.

Even to her own chagrin, Orangecloak helped with the unloading of the caribou pelts, stacking them up in the box she and Tryst had just exited. In no time at all, Fletchard was freed and Tryst and Orangecloak were reunited with their things. They slung their satchels and weapons over shoulders quickly while Raven and Yahmina cleaned up and sealed the crates.

At once the tension between Fletchard and Orangecloak became obvious to the new strangers in the room.

"How quickly can I be out of this place?" Fletchard barked at Raven, who met his question with a look of derision.

The rail thin, wisp haired, man politely answered, "You'll have to talk to Councillor Maurice about that. He's handling all of Lord Greggard's affairs in his absence.

Fletchard grunted. "Then let's find this Maurice. I'm sick and tired of riding about in crates and gallivanting through mountains and forests for this fire haired wench who stares pure death at me."

"You killed my friends and later attempted to kill me, I have no reason to treat you any other way," Orangecloak said while trying and failing to conceal her contempt.

The Raven was between them then, calm and rational amidst the storm. "That is quite enough. I will not permit fighting within milord's walls. Milady, if you would follow me, I will guide you to Councillor Maurice and we can begin the process of getting this one away from you."

The bounty hunter pointed a finger at the other man. "My name is Fletchard Miller."

Without so much as a glance, Raven turned his back to Fletchard while making for the stairs and waiting for no one to follow him. "With all due respect, I don't care what your name is."

The five of them climbed a narrow, winding staircase after that, with Raven leading the way and the others following behind. At the top of the stairs, Raven opened a plain looking door that opened out onto a magnificent, white-walled corridor. High, vaulted ceilings and long paned windows gave Orangecloak the impression that she was in a Tower of Ios rather than a manor. All about were fresh flowers in pots on pedestals and upon the windowsills, filling the view with all the colours of the rainbow and the sweetest scents one could desire. Red carpets ran along the main walkway of the floor, with white tiles of ceramic beneath. Matching drapery of velvet hung from every window, tied with ropes of shimmering golden thread.

Somewhere in the distance, Orangecloak could hear a number of stringed instruments being played, at least two violins and a cello for certain. Their music was of a slow tempo yet played roughly, as if by less experienced hands.

Footsteps reached her then, coming from her right. She turned her head sharply to see a man in violet robes traced with golden patterns strolling casually along the hallway. His skin was the darkened hue found mostly among the Johnans. Above the neck he was without a single hair as far as Orangecloak could see and his smooth, bald scalp reflected the light as he passed beneath the windows. The face of the man was highlighted by the glittering white teeth of the wide smile he wore upon noticing the new guests emerging from the cellar. With a quick step he plucked a rose from the nearest planter and strolled more quickly towards the party gathering in the hallway.

"Hello, my new friends," he started with a grand, sweeping bow that saw the long sleeves of his robe billowing in the air. "I bid you the warmest of welcomes to the manor of my dearest friend, Lord Greggard Simillon. In his absence, I have the pleasure of being the castellan of his household as well as the councillor for the Gunridge district of this beautiful city of Portsward. My name is Maurice Kett and I am humbly at your service."

Tryst spoke up with a smile to match their host's, "That's quite the introduction, Maurice. It's good to see you as well."

The suave gentleman spoke in the exotic accent found amongst the Johnans from the north central region of that southerly nation. "Ah, you'll forgive me, Master of Blades, for my gesture was not so much for you as it was for this picture of radiance that is the lovely

Lady Orangecloak," Maurice said in offering her the flower. "For you, my lady, I gift a rose as beautiful and fair as yourself."

The man was flattering, though Orangecloak expected as much from one of noble rank and all of it was taken with a grain of salt. Still, she remembered some courtesy must be shown towards her hosts. "I thank you, Councillor. You're too kind," she said with a polite nod as she took the rose to hand, taking care to not prick her fingers on the thorns along the stem.

When the chance arose to speak, Tryst took it. "Where is the Lord Greggard that he's unable to receive us?"

Councillor Maurice answered quickly, "He was summoned to Daol Bay on urgent matters I would rather discuss with yourself and the Lady Orangecloak in private, if you wouldn't mind. These are things that can wait to be discussed until later, after you've had a chance to settle in and change out of that bedraggled clothing and into something more suiting of your surroundings." Their gracious host gestured in the opposite direction from which he came, towards the longer side of the corridor. "Come, I will have baths drawn for you all, and food and drink prepared for when you are finished. We have luscious robes of fine silk you may wear, or something warmer perhaps if you are feeling chilled?" Maurice didn't wait for an answer. "No matter what you desire to wear I can have it brought to the guest rooms. Come, come, we must be off."

Orangecloak grew slightly wary at his urgency to get them moving, though a quick glance to Tryst seemed to alleviate her worries. Upon his gallant face there was not as much as a hint of concern. He knew this place, this manor and he felt safe within its walls. On his confidence Orangecloak rested her own doubts and followed Maurice down the long hallway.

At the first intersection they reached, the Raven took his leave of them and said his goodbyes, though Yahmina did not follow as Orangecloak expected and instead moved onward with them.

They entered the guest wing of the manor and it was here that Fletchard left them, being shown to his temporary quarters by Yahmina. He offered naught but a grunt in thanks and closed his door roughly before either she or Maurice could give any instructions.

Tryst's room was beside Fletchard's, though he had the manners to thank his hosts.

"Yahmina will call on you later, Tryst," Maurice told him. "I shall tell you all you wish to know over dinner."

"Then I shall see you all at that time," Tryst replied, giving a last wink to Orangecloak.

For Orangecloak there waited a larger room, away from the guest chambers and beside what she could only guess was Lord Greggard's own solar. "Yahmina will come around for you as well, my lady. After you've had time to clean and decompress. In the meantime I have duties of my own," Maurice spoke sweetly with another grand bow as he began to take his leave.

"Before you go, I have something I'd like to ask," Orangecloak said to catch Maurice's attention as he and Yahmina began to take their leave of her.

The two of them stopped and turned about to face her again. "Of course, my lady, you may speak freely," Maurice said.

"I just wanted to know who else might be attending this dinner meeting," she asked timidly.

"It will just be you, our Master of Blades, Yahmina and I," Maurice answered. "I apologise, my lady. I'm sure you can understand that being castellan of such a large building while maintaining my own manse and a district in this city leaves me incredibly busy. Is there anything else before I take my leave?"

Orangecloak eyed the pair, her heartbeat growing in her chest. *It's always a game to the nobles, no matter where they're from.* "No, that's it, just that and...Thank you, for helping me. I've received such generous hospitality along the way and I don't know if I deserve it."

That smile of Maurice's returned, followed by a deep laugh. "If the Musicians didn't think you deserved it, we would never have let you hear our song, my lady." He bowed for the third time. "I must go, but I shall see you soon."

She watched them walk away until they went out of sight, turning at the same corner Raven had taken moments ago. *If they insist I play their game, then play I shall.*

26
TRYST

The morning sky was grey and overcast, looking as though it may burst and spill the snowy contents of the foreboding clouds without notice. Within the meeting room of the Simillon Manor the light was dull, with the guests and hosts alike engaged in a grim game of quietude. Even the usually loquacious Councillor Maurice Kett was as silent as a corpse, sitting with his hands folded neatly upon his robed lap.

Waiting was a trying game that Tryst had never been fond of, yet one that nobles insisted they play. This morning, it was the Lord of Foreign Trade and Relations and Minister of Portsward making them participate, building anticipation for his eventual grand entrance.

It was more than the waiting that brought the quiet tension, Tryst knew. The presence of Fletchard Miller was still a sore point for Orangecloak and she veiled her displeasure behind an icy wall. At the very least Tryst was glad that Fletchard had opted to finally bathe, shave and take the time to ask for new clothes. He'd even shined his cuirass to the bright lustre it once bore when he had presented Orangecloak to Lord Master Grenjin Howland in Atrebell. Now Fletchard looked presentable in a new, slashed brown and yellow doublet, with his hair neatly combed and his beard trimmed back from its unruly state.

Tryst ran a hand over the beard he'd begun to cultivate himself from his time in the wilderness. It was noticeably darker than the long red mane that ran to the small of his back, yet he had been reluctant to shave it. His hope being that no one would notice the disparity between head and facial hair. If they had made note, no one had yet to say anything about it.

Of their gracious host, there was still no sign. According to Yahmina Windleaf, Lord Greggard had returned to Portsward that morning and was in fact somewhere within the large manor. As was common with nobles, however, he was fashionably late.

It was a show of rank to leave your subordinates waiting on your arrival, something Lord Master Grenjin had explained to Tryst in his early days as the old man's chief protector. "If they are not willing to wait for you, they will not be so willing to obey you," Grenjin had explained sternly. "It's the ones who fidget and squirm in their chairs, lacking for both respect and patience that you weed out, for they do not know their place. By contrast, any Lord or King that waits on his subordinates is King or Lord in title only and might as well wear a maid's apron."

The practice was one that had come to be followed by all Lords and Ministers of the EMP, even those like Greggard Simillon. Tryst glanced to Greggard's tall, empty chair at the head of the table. It was ornately carved from mahogany with a plush, blue velvet seat cushion. Its backrest was an elegant web of varnished filigree topped with a marvellous letter 'M' resting on two hands in the middle of shaking.

To the right of the valuable piece of furniture was Maurice Kett, indicating his right hand position. Bedecked in a fine, elven-made suit of dark red velvets, Yahmina had taken a place to the right of the councillor of the Gunridge district. Two seats down sat Fletchard, arms folded across his chest, lone eye staring idly out through the windows behind Tryst and Orangecloak. The lady had donned her gifted dwarven tunic and the faded and scuffed green leathers that she had been wearing before her capture, the orange cloak worn above all.

The table had a lovely spread of hot tea buns, scones and rolls with warm pats of butter to side for breaking the fast of those gathered. Aside from Orangecloak, none had decided to partake of the food. "It wouldn't be right to let this food go to waste," she had reasoned while buttering a pair of buns and pouring a cup of tea.

Orangecloak was biting into her third bun when the doorknob of the meeting room finally turned and the door opened.

The Lord Greggard Simillon showed himself in, looking

resplendent in a three piece, charcoal grey suit. He wore a black, velvet half-cape draped from his left shoulder, topped with a gold fringe epaulet and embroidered with a golden thread letter S. His short, wavy hair was showing signs of greying, though was full and robust for a man midway into in his fortieth decade. Greggard was as slender as Tryst remembered, with a confident stride to him as he made his way to the head of the table.

The room rose to stand for him, with Orangecloak rising as quickly as Maurice, much to the surprise of Tryst. Her face took on a harder expression, one that spoke of confidence and readiness. This was the moment she had been anticipating since she had been freed from the Atrebell dungeon all those weeks ago.

"Good morning to everyone," Greggard declared warmly to the attended, smiling with his mouth and his kind, deep, hazel eyes alike.

Maurice responded from where he stood, "My lord, it is good to see you are well. I trust your trip was fruitful?"

"It was indeed, my friend," replied the Lord of Portsward, extending a nod toward his councillor while slowly approaching Orangecloak from where she stood. "My dear Lady Orangecloak, words cannot express what an honour it is to finally make your acquaintance," Greggard spoke sweetly as he took her hand, bowing politely to lay a kiss upon the back of her fingers. "I deeply apologise for not being in Portsward when you arrived. I sincerely hope my friends have been hospitable to you in my absence."

Much to Tryst's awe, Orangecloak gave a polite nod and bow of her own to Greggard. "Indeed they have, as have the friends of yours I have met along the road that brought us here. They all send their fondest regards, my lord."

That remark made Lord Greggard smile quite broadly. "This is quite pleasing to hear, my lady. I am most glad they accommodated you on such minimal of notice." He made a sweeping gesture to everyone else. "Please, everyone, be seated and partake of this lovely spread we have before us. You shouldn't have let it grow this cold on account of waiting for me." The lord finished his rounds around the table, taking time to shake hands with Tryst and the remaining guests in turn before taking his place at the head of the table.

Once he was seated, Greggard saw to it that the food and tea was passed out and small talk made over the relatively simple meal.

When appetites seemed to be unanimously whetted, Maurice

led the way on conversation: "What news from Daol Bay?"

"I'm so glad you asked, Councillor," Greggard said as he replaced his teacup. "Much has happened, I'm afraid, but the biggest revelation is that it would seem that we are no longer living in the nation of Illiastra." Greggard's voice was one of restrained excitement as he delivered the news to his guests.

Confused looks were exchanged around the table until Orangecloak spoke up to ask the obvious question on everyone's mind. "I venture to guess that Lady Marigold Tullivan has officially seceded from Illiastra?"

The news was not surprising, least of all to Tryst. Maurice Kett had told of Marigold's lot in life to Orangecloak and Tryst on the eve of their arrival. Her father, Marscal Tullivan, Warden Lord of Western Illiastra, had succumbed to the consumption illness that had plagued him for quite some time. With her sister, Serephanie, still missing and unaccounted for, the death of Marscal meant that in title only, Marigold Tullivan was now the Warden of Western Illiastra and Minister of Daol Bay. A marriage contract arranged in Marigold's childhood denoted that in the event of Marscal's demise, the Tullivan girls were to be wed to Lord Eamon Palomb's twin sons. An arrangement, it became clear, that neither Marigold nor Serephanie had wanted any part of.

Instead of waiting on her betrothed, Marigold had called together all the ministers attending her father's funeral. Once gathered, she announced her intention to stay as sole ruler of the western portion of Illiastra. It was an act of open rebellion, one that saw her breaking national and theocratic law alike.

The ensuing rift between the ministers of the West that were to serve beneath her had put everyone west of Obalen and north of Aquas Bay on edge. She had supporters, namely Lord Greggard himself, though for every supporter she had, there seemed to be an equal amount of dissenters. That didn't even begin to address how the Elite Merchants to the east would respond.

Lord Greggard gave Orangecloak a wink and a smirk. "Quite so. It would seem we are now within the boundaries of the autonomous nation of West Illiastra."

There was no holding back the smile that crossed Tryst's face as he spoke on that. "Marigold is a brave woman. The other half of Illiastra will be forced to respond now and she will be branded a traitor to the realm. What success has she yielded from her trip south? Has she at least brought her own ministers to heel?"

Tryst was referring to the latest news Maurice had relayed to them. Lady Marigold had organised a long tour by train to visit with her allies and abstainers alike to the south of Daol Bay. The objective was to encourage the holdouts to rescind their objection and support her claim. If the offer was rebuffed, Lady Marigold would give the remaining objectors the option to resign, at which point they could remain in West Illiastra or leave peacefully by ship.

Those who joined with Marigold would be given the retired title of Interim Sealord of their district until such a time that an honest, democratic election could take place. The first to embrace their renamed title was Greggard Simillon, who now titled himself Sealord Greggard Simillon, Lord of Foreign Trade and Commerce. The ministers of smaller holds that had joined her initially were all welcomed into the new fold and retitled as well. As for the loyalists to the EMP, they retreated back to their holdings and clung to their old title of Minister.

It was in the wake of these events that Marigold had planned her campaign and the result of said planning that Greggard had been summoned to hear.

"Of that she has had marginal success," the newly made Sealord said casually. "There was an incident that resulted in violence with one Minister Nothram, however. Fortunately for Lady Marigold, she had half a dozen of her finest guardsmen protecting her. There was a loss of life, I'm sorry to report. A civilian woman was killed during a macabre display of intimidation by Minister Nothram and immediately after one of Lady Marigold's guards was grievously wounded during an assassination attempt on her life."

"That's awful," Orangecloak commented sadly. "Those poor people, I hope neither of them suffered long."

Greggard let his tone grow morose. "The woman perished quickly, which is as good a thing as can be said in the face of such a barbarous act."

"What of the soldier?" Orangecloak met his eyes as she asked the question.

Greggard's eyebrows rose in unison at the query and Tryst noticed a slight waver in his lip. "It is kind of you to ask. Alas, the poor fellow unfortunately lingered in agony for some days after taking his wound. I attended the funeral that Lady Marigold held for him upon her return to Daol Bay and it was a touching tribute to the man. Lady Marigold has a big heart. I think you would like her."

"It might be that I would," Orangecloak said, trailing off.

As Orangecloak let the conversation hang, Tryst took the opportunity to drive the conversation back to its roots. "Your manner of speaking implies that you were in Daol Bay for more than a funeral, Lord Greggard."

"That would be correct, Mister Reine," Greggard confirmed in a grave voice. "Lady Marigold has decided that Minister Nothram's actions shall not go unpunished. Five days, that is what she has given me to ready the warships in my port and assemble my standing army. The first battle in what will no doubt be a full blown civil war will be in Nothram's home of Pelican Harbour."

The air seemed to flee the room at that, with no one having any response as the repercussions of what Greggard was saying sunk in. Tryst met a curious glance from Orangecloak before she turned her attention back to the Sealord and his councillor.

Maurice asked worriedly, "Five days, is that enough time? How many of our ships and men is she requesting for this assault?"

After a deep breath, Greggard gave answer, "In terms of naval power, we'll sail seven of mine and eight of hers for a total of fifteen vessels. I've sent word to Tippard for Sealord Mattersly to send a pair of ships as well, for support. Though at fifteen, we already triple what's docked in Pelican Harbour."

"Samhais Morton won't impede him?" Tryst queried. "His sister is Eamon Palomb's wife. I would think if any minister in the west is bound to the Palombs, it would be him."

A mischievous smile marked Greggard's lips. "Lady Marigold assures me that Minister Morton is of no concern to us. In fact, he's already being tasked to keep other detractors of Lady Marigold distracted with a private summit meeting to be held at his manor in Weicaster Bay."

"This is new information," Maurice stated with a tone of mild surprise. "So she was able to bring him over to our cause?"

Greggard spoke while looking only at Maurice, as if the other four were merely spectators to their conversation. "A temporary truce, she was scarce on any other details."

Maurice continued on with his questioning, "What of Samhais' sister, Jorette? I have no reason to believe that Lord Eamon Palomb is above using his own wife as a hostage to keep her brother from aligning with Lady Marigold."

"He's not above that, or using his two youngest children for that matter," Greggard added. "It's common knowledge that Eamon Palomb is a man of few scruples. However, I can only take Lady Marigold at her word. No doubt she harboured those same concerns when she met Minister Morton."

Tryst interjected to direct Greggard and Maurice back to the topic at hand. "Lord Greggard, might it be presumptive to think you'll be traveling with Lady Marigold?"

He nodded toward Tryst in reply. "Indeed, I shall be in her accompaniment as part of her war council. She's leaving her uncle, Rory Tullivan, to manage the affairs of the city in her absence. I must admit that my trust of the man is limited for he does still bear a love for the ways of the EMP. I can't see him betraying the offspring of our dear late Marscal, though. His loyalty to his brother runs deeper than any political ideology."

From Tryst's side, Orangecloak found her voice once again. "If you're pinning your war hopes on Lady Marigold, does that mean you no longer have any use for me?"

"Nothing could be further from the truth, my lady," Greggard countered. "With Lady Marigold putting a civil war at our feet far sooner than we could have anticipated, the need for you is greater than ever it was."

"Only if you assume I am a willing participant in this game of violent politics," Orangecloak said coldly.

A look of contriteness crossed Greggard's face at that moment. "My apologies, my lady, I did indeed assume too much. However, I still feel as though I was correct in my assessment."

Tryst watched as Orangecloak's brows furrowed and her eyes narrowed in on Lord Greggard. "What would make you assume that I am a politician at all?"

Greggard seemed only too glad to answer that. "It goes without saying that politics is the same whether you are from high birth or low. For you to rise as high as you did in any political setting speaks of, at the very least, a remarkable cunning. To continually survive in your profession, with alacrity no less, while being a wanted woman by both Triarchy and EMP alike speaks volumes for your political savvy."

Orangecloak spoke boldly to that, "I suppose that is a fair enough conclusion to reach, aye. However, how is it that you know such things about me to say as much?"

The sealord smiled slyly. "As to that, I have had servants and guards alike hear your speeches and protests, with further reports coming from as far away as Aquas Bay. The general message you speak of is change. You seek for women of all walks of life to have the same rights as men and for queer folk to be able to live freely and proudly. You want the Triarchy out of the personal lives of Illiastra's residents and for scepticism and non-belief in the gods to not be treated as mental illness or a crime. You desire for elves, dwarves, Amaroshan and human immigrants alike to not be treated as second class citizens or barred entry to the country. Is there anything I happen to be missing?"

The look they shared was one of mutual respect, Tryst knew. They were both impressed with one another and seemed to be enjoying their exchange.

As Orangecloak answered Greggard, there was what might even pass for a smile on her lips. "I also have protested for certain actions deemed felonious to be decriminalised entirely, given that these laws were only put in place to shore up the prisoner population in Biddenhurst. You and I both know that Mackhol Taves treats his prison like a business and his prisoners like a commodity. He's turned what should be a method of correction and rehabilitation into a slave market," she put in confidently, waiting a moment before noting, "though, when you listed my demands, you left out the most important one of all: a fair and democratic government, chosen by and overseen by the people."

"I think they are all noble and honourable demands, my lady," Maurice commented. "The people are fortunate to have such a fervid champion in their corner."

The elbows of Lord Greggard perched on the armrests of his mahogany chair as he leaned forward and tented his fingers. "Yes, they are noble and honourable and I know how earnestly you seek them. The problem, though, is that neither the Elite Merchants nor the Triarchy will ever so much as entertain any of your demands. If you want these things to happen, you know the EMP has to go. I can tell you that those old men will sit there and cling to power no matter what the cost to the country or the people within it. If change cannot come from within, then it must come from without. You know that and you know how that change must come about."

"That is where we disagree, my lord," Orangecloak retorted. "In the people there are numbers and numbers cannot be ignored. There is more than one way to incite a revolution."

"Ah, a revolution, that's what you seek," Greggard spoke calmly and almost a little patronisingly. "I've always felt like the word revolution is just an elegant means to say 'civil war between people and their government'."

"With all due respect, Lord Greggard, I beg to differ," Orangecloak countered.

"How many revolutions in the history of our known world have come without a cost of human life, my lady?" Greggard asked rhetorically. "Centuries ago, the Knights of Northern Gildriad refused the orders of their king. Instead of slaughtering and enslaving the people of the defeated Kingdom of South Gildriad, they led a revolution against their own crown in the North. Tens of thousands died. Just as many as had died in the War of Crowns that the knights had marched to South Gildriad for in the first place."

Orangecloak looked eager to speak up, but waited politely as Greggard went on. "I wager that you met my dear friend Jack Paylor as well. Did he tell you that he's a veteran of several conflicts? He fought beneath my father in one of those, a revolution on Vellick Island by the oppressed Calaranians. Revolution is an idea as mired in blood and destruction and death as war. It merely has a prettier name, nothing more, nothing less."

She was ready with an example of her own. "You forget that Drake liberated itself from their monarchy in ancient times, even before the First Hero emerged from their snowy lands. That was a revolution and a bloodless one by their historical accounts."

"Indeed it was, one made possible by a soft king by the name of Yokotori, if I recall correctly," Greggard quickly replied. "His father was the despised ruler that necessitated the uprising, but the people couldn't oust him. Instead, they waited for his kindly successor. You will find no such kindness in Lord Master Grenjin Howland, my lady."

"If one of the Tullivan girls is missing and the other is in open rebellion, then wouldn't that mean that Grenjin Howland has no heirs?" Orangecloak asked in a tone that was ever so slightly smug. "Perhaps you should have set Tryst on killing him."

Greggard's glance fell on Tryst as Orangecloak asked the question. "As to that, perhaps Tryst here would be so kind as to answer you."

He cleared his throat and turned in his chair to face Orangecloak. "The Lord Master does indeed have heirs. The Tullivan girls, as women, are not entitled to inherit anything. However, they were given the title of heir in honour of being the oldest children of the marriage pact. The actual inheritance would be collected by their husbands upon marrying them."

"The husbands are the heirs now, then," Orangecloak correctly surmised. "If I recall correctly those heirs would be the twin sons of Lord Eamon Palomb, no less."

Greggard spoke up. "Even if you only judge them by their father's reputation, it should be clear to you why Tryst preserved the life of Grenjin Howland rather than extinguish it."

Tryst jumped back in. "It was yet another advantage to my hiring. Greggard was concerned that someone within the EMP might make an attempt on Lord Master Howland's life to hasten the rise of the Palomb twins. A move that would be disastrous, to say the very least. I've learned in my time beneath the Lord Master that he is far from the worst ruler we could have. He is undoubtedly rapacious and paranoid, a poor combination by any standard. Yet when it comes to his subjects, he's merely apathetic. The Palomb boys, on the other hand, are pure sadists.

"I will be the first to say that apathy is not a desirable trait in a ruler. However, if one must choose between a Lord Master who is either apathetic or sadistic, then the former is the clear choice."

Orangecloak eyeballed him warily. "You have witnessed their cruelty first hand, Tryst?"

"Aye, just once, it was the incident where Ren was captured," he answered reluctantly.

"You were there?" Her eyebrow shot up in disbelief. "When they beat those women, as Ren told me they did, you did nothing to prevent it?"

This wasn't something Tryst was eager to reveal, yet he would not deny it either. "I was disguised as a feeble old man, as I often do, so that I might walk amongst the people unnoticed. If I had revealed myself, then I risked revealing everything we had worked so hard for. I couldn't, there was just too much at stake and I knew the women wouldn't take more than a strike. Eldridge and Pyore are cruel, of that there is no doubt. However, they're guarded by their much older cousin, Captain Geddrick Palomb. He's not only charged with protecting them from physical harm, but from any reputational harm they could do to themselves as well. I had no doubt that if they raised a hand, it would take no time for Geddrick to step in, lest they cause too much of a scene. Ren rose to the rescue before Geddrick though and the result is what Ren told you. It was difficult for me to sit idly by-"

"-Not that difficult obviously or you would have done something." Orangecloak cut him off curtly while staring daggers at him with those fierce blue eyes.

"My apologies, Orangecloak, though, it goes without saying that if I had saved those women from a backhand blow, then you would be swinging from a gibbet by now. The risk of everything unravelling was too great and as much as it pained me to have to do nothing, I simply could not act." Tryst gently laid a hand upon Orangecloak's forearm as he continued, "The fact that you were brought before me that very night proved to me that I made the right choice."

With a sudden twitch, Orangecloak shrugged off Tryst's hand and averted her eyes from him. The red haired woman took a deep breath and moved on, seemingly trying to let Tryst's inaction go by and turning her attention back to Greggard and Maurice. "These twins, they're cruel and heinous, that much we know. So, your goal instead is to fight a war with Grenjin Howland and hope he lives long enough to see himself deposed. You still have yet to explain how I am of relevance to any of this. If you have Marigold as your figurehead, what more do you need? She is a woman, wealthy and independent and has support from a strong portion of her new nation. I fail to see why a poor woman, one who is believed to be the dead leader of protesters from the Southlands, is of any use to you now."

It was Greggard who took the lead answering that. "I assure you, my lady, that Marigold is no mere figurehead. That woman is every bit as independent as you would like to believe. I, her steward Oire and uncle Rory are merely advisors and her decisions are hers and hers alone."

Greggard paused for a sip of tea before going on. "As for your role, originally it was *you* who was our choice to lead the revolution. You have something neither Marigold nor I or anyone in a position of power in Illiastra has: the people. As much as you're long to admit it, you are a household name and an icon in Illiastra. Unlike me, Tryst or even Marigold, who all have history with the EMP to shake, you have a clean slate in the eyes of the populace. You are the hero they want. The one they wish to believe can free them from their oppressors. If you can mobilise them, we, the Musicians, will fund, arm, counsel and train you to lead them."

"How is it you intend to train me? You have no more experience in war than I do and even less experience in combat," Orangecloak proffered.

It was with a long look towards Yahmina that Greggard answered that question, a telling smile upon his face all the while.

Orangecloak turned her attention to the elven woman. "I thought you told me over supper yesterday that you were hired to protect Lord Greggard's children?"

Yahmina replied amusingly, "I was, though you may have noticed that Lord Greggard has no children here right now."

"That's not true, I've heard children playing at their games and making music," Orangecloak said, looking a little confused on the whole matter.

Greggard took it from there. "I am currently housing some nieces, nephews and cousins of a little more distance. Those would be the youth you've heard about the manor, no doubt. My own two daughters and my dear wife are wintering in our manse on Barkis Island among the more tropical climes of the Crescent Isles just north of Johnah. I sent them with a fine retinue of servants and guards to ensure their wellbeing and safety, and absolved Yahmina's contract so that she might serve you instead. My daughters, Isabelle and Almyra, were in tears at Yahmina's departure though, the poor things. She explained to them that she has greater need here and that she and I were going to make the world a better place for girls like them."

"That is a nice thought to leave them with," Orangecloak commented. "I know what it is to want to give hope, even if it is a fool's hope." She sighed and idly ran a hand through the red locks she had brushed and let fall across her shoulders in their natural wave.

"It is no fool's hope if you add your strength to that of the Musicians," spoke Maurice, his deep, clear voice carrying across the table and bouncing off the walls. "We do not come before you as merchants or politicians, though we understand if you see us that way. We are but men and women stretched across the known world that only want Illiastra to prosper at long last. Free from the oppression and tyranny of the ruling government and its religious ally. The same as you, my lady, the only difference is we are ready to take up arms for this cause."

"And I am not," Orangecloak stated bluntly.

"Yet you will sit there and judge Tryst Reine for not saving those tavern girls from the wrath of the Palombs." Greggard added, almost brazenly so.

Orangecloak scoffed. "My reluctance to lead a needless slaughter and Tryst's inaction are far from comparable."

"Are they?" Maurice chimed in. "It would seem to me that they are not such different things. Tryst decided not to get involved at the risk of blowing his cover when Eldridge and Pyore became violent with a pair of women. You refuse to get involved with your band of Thieves when the Elite Merchants and the Triarchy grow violent with your fellow citizens."

"We step in when we can," Orangecloak replied back hastily.

Greggard spoke next, "How exactly do you step in? If you abhor violence and refuse it, then how do you prevent it? Use your bodies as human shields and run away from the bullets and blades? No, I don't think so. There's not a mark on you to say you've ever taken a blow, no more than I."

"You're being facetious, Lord Greggard." There was fire in Orangecloak's eyes at that moment. "You clearly know that we Thieves are trained to defend ourselves and that we have a past addled with blood and violence."

"Not just a past, but your present," Greggard stated bluntly before continuing his line of questioning. "Are there not bands of people in the Southlands led by a former Illiastran soldier that fights under your name against the raiding gangs?"

Orangecloak winced at that. "You speak of Old Bansam," she answered quickly. "He is affiliated with the Thieves, aye. Though, I can see how the line between affiliation and membership can be blurred."

Greggard nodded, his tone returning to a near soothing level. "Considering he was a member at one point, aye, there would be a level of confusion there. The general populace certainly doesn't see much of a difference, I assure you."

"And I suppose that you do not see much distinction, either,"

Orangecloak said after a deep breath, conceding that point to Greggard. "If associates of mine are involved in the constant fighting south of the Varras River, then it looks as though I am involved as well, or at least condoning of it. Is that the way of it?"

Maurice tenderly handled the query, "It makes you seem like a hypocrite, my lady. You stand on the rooftops in Hercalest and Daol Bay and encourage peaceful protest while the Warrens and Aquas Bay see your kin spilling blood at their gates."

"The raiding gangs are merciless and savage," Orangecloak offered in her own defence. "More importantly, whether I condone it or not, Bansam will fight them. It is a grievous waste of my Thieves' lives, yet the man and his band do get results. The roads in the Southlands are far safer now than they were in my youth. The gangs lose territory constantly because of the efforts of people like Bansam, Mell the Huntress and the men out of Fort Dornett calling themselves the Sun's Rangers."

Though he masked it well, the mention of the name of the Sun's Rangers gave Tryst pause. *That would be Freyard Archer and his men,* he recalled to himself.

"Indeed they do," Greggard said thoughtfully before posing his next question. "So, tell me, if the Sun's Rangers and your friends Mell and Bansam sued for peace with these gangs, how well would that turn out for them?"

It was a trap and the look on Orangecloak's face told Tryst that she was well aware of that, yet she answered anyway. "They would die, as you mean to suggest I shall for trying the same with the Elite Merchants. You would compare the political party that has allowed you the financial means to build this manse with bloodthirsty marauders?"

"They are not as different as you think, my lady," Greggard said with a morose sigh. "They both greedily take whatever they can carry and keep coming back for more. Neither one has a value for life beyond an individualistic definition. They kill all who oppose them and either enslave or impoverish the ones that don't resist. The Elite Merchants are far more eloquent and subtle in their means, yet they are still just raiders dressed in livery."

Maurice followed Greggard's train of thought, "One could make the opposite comparison between the Thieves and the Musicians too, my lady. We both seek to change Illiastra for the better of everyone, whether they're women, queer, immigrants, dwarves, elves, half-elves or humans of colour. You see, my lady, while the EMP and the raiding gangs share the goal of control by instilling fear, the Musicians and Thieves share the goals of freedom and equality."

"I don't know..." Orangecloak said, trailing off in thought for a moment. "I don't know a great many things, but least of all I don't know if can be the warrior you desire me to be. I can use a sword and dagger, and as Tryst and Fletchard can attest, I'm no stranger to a bow and arrows, but to use them to kill another person? Worse yet to command others to do so, knowing that people will die fulfilling those commands and because of those commands? No, I don't know that I can do such a thing."

Greggard addressed her concerns. "You are the Field *Commander* of the Thieves," he said, adding emphasis to the word. "You were nominated and elected to do just that."

She nodded slowly. "To command, aye. I never agreed to lead them in warfare."

"Your predecessor had no qualms about it. What was his name again? Merry?" Greggard stated rather boldly.

Orangecloak's face wrinkled a tad at the mention of the former Field Commander. "His name was Marros Delauren. Aye, he fought and his fighting got him and forty of the best Thieves I have ever known killed. You need not remind me, gentlemen, I was in Yaelsville."

The revelation surprised Yahmina, Greggard, Maurice and Fletchard alike. "You have my apologies, my lady," Greggard said solemnly. "I had no intention of dredging up painful memories."

"You didn't know, apologies are not needed, my lord." Orangecloak cast her eyes to the ceiling a moment and took a deep breath. "You have laid much at my feet to think about. Certainly, it is true that war is coming whether I will it or not. That decision has been made by Lady Marigold, and now I must determine what is best for me and my Thieves. I will need time, as I'm sure you can appreciate that such things are not considered so lightly."

"Of course, my lady, my home is yours for as long as you need to consider everything," Greggard said with a cordial nod. "Soon, you will even have the whole manse all to yourself, save for my staff."

"What of your nieces, nephews and cousins?" Orangecloak asked sceptically.

"They and their attendants have only taken up temporary

residence from more easterly residences," Greggard explained. "I will be sending them all onward to Barkis Isle for their own safety and to provide much needed companionship for my daughters. Soon, you'll be free to wander my halls as you please, my lady."

"I see." Orangecloak's tone became heavy with concern, "Might I change the subject for a minute? I am wondering if you had any news of my friends that were captured in Argesse."

The high backed chair Lord Greggard occupied creaked as he sat back in it. "If only I did. The last I had heard was that they had reached Biddenhurst and that news is not recent. Beyond that I do not know. Do not despair, my lady, no news might not be a bad thing in this case. If they were dead, that is something Lord Mackhol Taves would waste no time in making known."

Orangecloak had a thought on that. "If they were executed, he would spread the word. However, if they had perished accidentally, then he might not say anything about it. Furthermore, that they're in Biddenhurst at all is an uncomforting thought."

Maurice leaned forward to have his say. "With all due respect, my lady, certainly you and they knew that was an accepted risk to begin with."

"Of course we did, we all knew our lives and freedom were forfeit if we were apprehended." The words echoed from Orangecloak in a defensive tone. "That doesn't mean my concern in their capture is misplaced."

Tryst was marvelled with her eloquence and poise. Here, she was indeed a leader and that same confident woman he had seen protesting in the market square in Aquas Bay. Her face was iron and her emotions tightly guarded.

All her worry was for naught, Tryst thought to himself as he gave the rigidly postured woman a quick look from the corner of his eye. *This game is not so strange to her after all.*

The glance from the weary looking eyes of Greggard spoke similarly to him before they fell back to the Lady of the Thieves. "At any rate, I am glad you asked of your friends for I was able to obtain one thing relating to them before I left Atrebell to return here."

Orangecloak's eyes lit up. "What is that, might I ask?"

Greggard reached into the inside pocket of his jacket and produced a folded pair of papers that he passed to Tryst who handed them on unopened to Orangecloak. "One of the guards at the southwest guard station in Atrebell is a friend and was able to do me the favour of sneaking me a copy of the inmate list."

She took the papers gently and let them fall open in her hands. "I appreciate this, Lord Greggard. If nothing else, I will now know for certain whom I have lost behind those sinister walls."

Tryst watched her eyes running over the words. They stopped on the first page, something written there having caught the eye, before flipping to the next page hurriedly. "Interesting..." she said in a low voice, trailing off on that lone word.

Maurice and Greggard shared a glance before the former resumed talking, "You're most welcome my lady, I'm only glad to give you even this small token. I assure you that if I hear anything more on their plight that I will pass it on to you."

"You mean that you will pass the information on to me if I agree to aid you?" Orangecloak asked as she folded the papers and tucked them into a pocket in her leather coat.

The Sealord of Portsward relaxed in his chair, propping an elbow on the armrest and supporting his chin in his hand. "Of course, if you decline the offer to align with me, then I very well have no way of finding you, do I? You saw the lengths I had to go to just to get you to my table at all."

Orangecloak answered in a tone that bordered on sounding bored, "You hired Tryst to feed you secrets from Grenjin Howland's table and told him to stay there unless I turned up."

"That's part of it, yes," the corner of Greggard's mouth curled ever so slightly as he answered her, seemingly amused by the red haired woman's knowledge on the matter. "Though, it is not everything."

"Might I inquire as to what I am missing?" Orangecloak asked, interested once again.

Greggard eyed Fletchard for but a second before looking back at Orangecloak. "It seems you do not know to what I am referring, that is surprising."

Frustration began to set in on Orangecloak's face. "I do not know what exactly?"

"Your capture was no mere act of happenstance, my lady," Greggard said with a sigh. "Lord Mackhol Taves knew of your whereabouts the entire time you were in Atrebell and intended on capturing you himself."

Orangecloak was unfazed. "This in itself is not news to me, Tryst told me that much."

"Perhaps not, but evidently there are things that neither of you know." Greggard swallowed hard before going on, "I learned of Mackhol's plot while I myself was in Atrebell and hastily set a plan of my own into motion. It didn't involve Tryst, but it did involve a bounty hunter I had noticed was on the same train as I bound for Atrebell."

A fiery look came over Orangecloak's eyes as she glanced between Fletchard and Greggard, considering the implications of what he was hinting at. "You..." She started, putting her palms against the table and pushing herself back in her seat as the shock almost tangibly washed over her. "You had some hand in what happened in Atrebell?"

The sealord glanced at his solemn councillor, cleared his throat and went on, "I hired Fletchard to bring you all to the dungeon in Grenjin's manor knowing Tryst would spring the three of you as per his contract. I am deeply sorry that your friends lost their lives. I assure you that it was never my intent."

"Nor mine, as I have already tried to explain," It was Fletchard who had said that, opening his mouth for the first time in the meeting.

"If you knew where I was, then why not send your messenger to warn me?" Orangecloak asked flatly. "I could have fled Atrebell and Myles and Coquarro would still be alive."

"By the time my messenger would have gotten to you, all the exits from town would be on heightened security." Greggard sighed despondently. "Anyone with the hood of the cloak drawn was stopped and scrutinised and red haired women of your age and dark skinned men were being detained in the streets and held in lockup for identification. You had no way out, my lady. The trap had been sprung. I knew that Fletchard was in town, though and I sent the Raven to him with an offer: I'd give him twenty five thousand gold for the three of you, that's half the bounty on your head. All he had to do was get you to the manor and aid Tryst in helping you escape later. I told him to expect no payment from Grenjin, but to not turn you over unless Howland falsely promised compensation. This way I knew Fletchard would be left for Tryst to 'handle' and he was. Everything fell into place to see you out of Atrebell safely."

Orangecloak directed her attention toward Fletchard. "And you, why didn't you tell me any of this before?"

"Would you have believed me?" Fletchard said, throwing his

hands up in the air in exasperation. "You spent all this time staring death at me and cursing on me, would you have listened to me if I tried to explain myself? You and I both know you wouldn't have given me a chance, especially with Ren standing before you like a shield for half of the journey.

"I also thought Tryst knew and would tell you, but I found out while we were still aboard *The Myra* that he didn't know shit. Greggard knew and I had hoped he would tell you, so I waited. I let people hurl their names and insults at me, like that fucking bald bear of a man in the woods. As for you, I tried to avoid you as much as I could. Now we're here and now you know."

Greggard gestured toward Fletchard calmly, trying to further defend their actions. "Fletchard here, at my request, gave up his business and his livelihood so that you might avoid a fate that ended in Biddenhurst."

"He still killed my friends and later tried to kill me," Orangecloak stated with a shake of her head. "This is not something so easily forgiven."

Fletchard leaned forward in his chair in Orangecloak's direction, forearms resting on the table. "I admit I was foolish to have hired those drunkards," he began with his voice as soft as Tryst had ever heard it, despite the deep, raspy edge to it. "I needed the numbers to force your bodyguards to surrender. If it had been you alone, I would have taken you myself. However on my own against three, your men would have challenged me and I knew then I'd be left no choice but to resort to violence or retreat empty handed. You don't get to be so well known as a bounty hunter if you're shooting all your bounties. It is common knowledge that you make more money if your target is alive and unharmed than you would for a corpse. I have always aimed to take my quarry as peacefully as possible and that was what I set out to do that night.

"My temporary employees, despite my efforts to teach them in such a short span of time, didn't retain any of that. They panicked when your friend Myles sprang to his feet and the shaggy haired drunk shot him dead. Then, that one Coquarro came at me with that hooked blade and fury in his eyes and I had to act. It was kill or be killed, so I killed. It was not a choice I had any time to deliberate over, or was even able to deliberate at all. It was instinct. Someone was going to die. If it had been me, those idiots I hired would have likely run off and Myles would still have died in your arms. You and Coquarro would have been left for Mackhol Taves' men to take to Biddenhurst, beyond where even Tryst Reine or Lord Greggard could have saved you."

Orangecloak folded her arms across her chest. "Putting aside that night for a moment, you still tried to kill me outside of Tusker's Cove. You wrapped your hands around my throat and tried to choke the life out of me."

The bounty hunter lowered his head for a moment before returning the gaze of his lone eye to Orangecloak and answering her, "My patience had reached its limit. The hermit had run it nearly dry to begin with and you took what was left. I wasn't going to kill you, even if I wanted to. We all know Tryst wouldn't allow it. But I would get to take some of my frustration out on him for making it look like I tried. I apologise for that as well, to the both of you. It wasn't becoming of me. It's not who I am, truly. I didn't build such a reputation as bounty hunter by being impatient and quick tempered."

"This is big of you, Fletchard," Orangecloak said after a clearing of her throat. "I have to admit there was much I did not know and that I too was caught up in my grief for Myles and Coquarro. I will miss them terribly until the day I draw my last breath, but the time for mourning them has long passed. You and I both have wide spread reputations and I did mine a disservice as well in how I treated you. I am the Field Commander of the Thieves and I should act as such in all things. I was taught by Yassira Na-Qoia that bearing a grudge on your shoulders for too long will only break your back."

She leaned across the table toward Fletchard, her voice dropping a little lower. "That night we spent with Jack Paylor, were you listening outside when he spoke with Tryst and I?"

"Aye, I was," Fletchard answered, mildly confused.

There was a brief hesitation before she went on, "Did you hear what I said when Jack Paylor asked what I would do to punish you for the events in Atrebell?"

Fletchard took a moment before responding, seemingly trying to recall the words. "You said something about ensuring that I never forget the names of your friends, if I'm not mistaken."

Orangecloak leaned forward. "I did and you not only remembered that but you remembered their names. Your cohorts' names escape you, but those of my friends were quick to your mind. I know that I will never forget that night in Atrebell and I don't think you will either and that is enough for me.

She sat up tall, her hands palms down and relaxed on the table before her and looked square at the bounty hunter. "I forgive you, Fletchard Miller."

A deep breath escaped Tryst as Orangecloak said the words and the tension seemed to seep out of the room.

Tryst scanned Fletchard's face and he seemed to feel relieved himself. "I thank you, my lady," he said in a voice that seemed genuinely surprised. "I forgive you as well, for your treatment of me."

"For that, I thank *you*," Orangecloak said with a courteous nod.

She turned her attention back to Greggard and Maurice who had been sitting quietly, exchanging glances the entire time she spoke. "With that being dealt with and out of the way, I think it can be said that I owe you a debt of gratitude, Lord Greggard. If not for your quick decision to aid me, I would be in a far worse predicament. I had walked into a trap that I feel was laid with help from someone in my own camp and sprung from it by men I thought were my enemies. I thank all of you for that. As well as those that helped us along the way. I would never have made it without the work of the Musicians."

"My lady, I am only glad I could help," Greggard replied with a radiant smile that shone as much from his eyes as it did his upturned lips. "I think that together, the Thieves and the Musicians can help each other achieve the peace and equality we both seek for Illiastra."

Orangecloak leaned back in her chair once more. "Then I think we should discuss what you would have me do."

"And so we shall," Greggard answered.

27

ORANGECLOAK

We are fine, Red, I assure you. Please, tell us more of your stories," said Coquarro, calling Orangecloak by the only name he ever had for her. She was dreaming, she knew, but she was with her friends and she was happy, if for but a minute. Beneath the moonlit trees of the Southlands, they were whole again. There was no blood, no horrific gunshot wounds, just her old friends as she had known them in the good times.

It felt like hours had passed with them atop the simple, wooden hunter's blind. It was peaceful up there, nestled amongst the branches of a particular, gnarled oak tree that stood all on its own in a clearing amongst a grove of towering redwoods.

In that time, Orangecloak had told them of everything that had happened to her since they passed away. She recounted how she met Ren and Tryst on that terrible night in Atrebell and her travels through the northern roads that led to the dwarves of the Dupoire Hotel. That, in turn, brought her to the forest beyond that and her encounter with the hermit Jack Paylor and even the scuffle with Fletchard. That part of the story had angered them both, as she knew it would. Not even speaking fondly of the brilliant and eccentric children of Captain Bickerington or her sea voyage to Portsward seemed to settle them afterwards. Up until then, they had listened quietly and eagerly as she spoke of her adventures.

When Orangecloak had finished telling them of the meeting, Myles had grown sullen. "You forgave the man who killed us? Are we not worth avenging?"

Orangecloak opened her mouth to answer only for Coquarro to speak first. "What would vengeance gain, Myles? Will we be given new bodies and sent back to the world of the living?" he asked the rhetorical questions in a sardonic tone. "She did what was right for the Thieves, the people and herself alike. I am proud of you, Red. I know that was not a simple thing for you to do."

"When you loosed that arrow at Fletchard, you should have aimed for his heart," Myles declared angrily whilst he paced.

"Myles, you were always so short sighted," Coquarro sighed with a slow shake of his head. "Obviously, Lord Greggard has a plan for Fletchard. There is purpose for him that could benefit everyone in Illiastra. Dead, he is but a carcass to the world and when the satisfaction of revenge ebbs away from Red, Fletchard will be of benefit to no one. This is not about us, not anymore. Our time is ended. Red has to think about those who still yet live, like Lazlo and Merion. If Fletchard can perhaps be of use to her in saving them and toppling the Merchants, then I say his toll for taking our lives will be paid in full."

Myles relented and slowed his treading. "Perhaps you are right, Coquarro."

Her tall, dark friend from Johnah had been sitting at her side the entire time, his long, dark blue woollen coat wrapped around his shoulders. "You should want her to forgive Fletchard for no other reason than to give herself closure, Myles. It is like my Aunt Yassira is fond of saying: 'Anger will only fester in the pit of your stomach and sicken you if you do not let it go.' You want the best for Red, you always have and this is what is best."

"I'd rather not fight with you, Myles," Orangecloak finally got a word in. "Not now. I know this is but a dream, but why can't we enjoy this, whatever it is?"

Myles resigned himself at that. "I suppose you're right. Let us enjoy the starry sky together one more time before you wake." With Coquarro to one shoulder and Myles to the other, they sat in silence, their backs to the old oak tree and their eyes on twinkling stars above.

The warmth of their bodies beside her felt as real as life. The rising and falling of their breathing, the touch of Myles' knee grazing hers, even Coquarro's muscled shoulder for her head to rest upon. For the moment she was content and she pushed away the sadness of knowing that it would end too soon.

As with all things, that time did come and at first she protested. "Just five more minutes like this, please. I'll never have it again, what's five more minutes in an eternity?"

"You are waking, it is time," Myles said in voice that was both sad and gentle.

The strong, wide hand of Coquarro squeezed her shoulder. "Go on, Red, Myles and I will be alright."

Reluctantly, she stood and shuffled to the edge of the small, square platform where they had been sitting and turned to face them. "I'll never forget you, no matter where I go or what I do, I promise."

"We know, Orangecloak," Myles smiled through his moistening brown eyes.

"Go with our love and live so that our deaths are not in vain," Coquarro added.

A tear began to streak her cheek as she lowered herself to the next branch and she looked back one last time. "I love you too. Goodbye, my friends." And with that she descended the oak tree.

The room she woke to was far away from that tree in the Southlands. It felt like she had travelled all those kilometres in a blink and was landing back in the guest suite of Lord Greggard Simillon's manor in Portsward. If not for the fact that she was dressed in a plush robe, linen trousers and a sleeveless tunic and not her green leathers, she might have believed it.

A soft featherbed waited nearby with thick blankets, but she had managed to nod off in a hard, mahogany desk chair. Spread out across the matching desk before her was a vast and detailed, albeit yellowing map of Illiastra. Lord Greggard had brought it to her on the night after their fateful meeting, joined by Yahmina and Tryst, and together the four convened until the midnight hour. Using strings, tacks and little carved, wooden figurines, Greggard had outlined the plan he suggested for Orangecloak and the Thieves to follow across the parchment. It was one he admitted to have been cobbling together since Orangecloak and Tryst had disappeared from Atrebell all those days ago.

As had been promised, Orangecloak was left with all their suggestions and the final decision was hers to make. Twice the sun had crossed the sky since then and she felt no closer to a resolution.

The whole thing had originally involved Orangecloak traveling through the winter and making a pre-emptive strike with all her marshalled might at Layn. The town was centrally located in the heart of the Southlands with the claim of being the home of Ser Farrell Holleran, the renowned Silver Knight of the last King. In truth, the town surrounded by wooden palisade walls only bore the same name as Ser Farrell's home. The statue of the man and the ruins of his birthplace were a few kilometres away and overgrown with dense forest. His ancestors still remained in the new incarnation of Layn, forced from their first town by repeated attacks by raiding gangs three decades ago. What constituted as Layn now was a fortified settlement that had grown from a small outpost to a bustling centre. As other villages and hamlets were abandoned and resettled within the relative safety of Layn, the timber logs had been extended and built anew to allow for more space. The added security of walls and an armed garrison had been its saving grace in the face of the increasing presence of the raiding gangs.

What Greggard proposed was to gain lawful entry to the town and coerce the mayor to willingly hand operation of his armed force over to Orangecloak and her Thieves. Since returning from his latest excursion to Daol Bay, Greggard had made an addendum to his plan: Orangecloak was to withhold any operations until the first quarter of spring. Greggard had reasoned that the eastern lords and ministers would be calling their armies for the impending conflict with Lady Marigold. With all attention focused in the west, Orangecloak would be free to strike where she may in the Southlands with naught but skeleton garrisons to oppose her.

"What made you decide on Layn?" Orangecloak had asked Greggard first and foremost after he had finished the presentation of his grand plan.

He had been only too happy to explain, "Why, for centrality, my dear. You have a direct route to your home in Phaleayna, which should give you a good route for supplies and soldiers. The Warrens are almost a direct run south, meaning Minister Clay Harlowe and any soldiers of his will be easy to contain. At the very least, they will have to resort to taking the long way around Layn rather than marching right through it. Everything west of Layn is where the raiding gangs dwell, we can thank the Sun's Rangers for driving them that far west."

Though she had great doubts about the plan, she withheld even the hint of such from her voice and stuck to probing questions. "My goal is to simply contain Minister Harlowe?"

"You're to keep him busy, harry his supply lines." Greggard had pointed out, "The Warrens supply the greater portion of Illiastra's coal. Without Clay Harlowe's stores, the west can survive and broker deals with Drake and Johnah and even the nations of Gildriad if we need to in the meantime. However, the east will have nothing fresh if you cut them off from the Warrens. Their supplies will dwindle within half a year and the small mines in north of the Varras will be unable to keep up with the demand."

"This wasn't your initial plan. You had more in mind than distracting Clay Harlowe and keeping his coal south of the Varras River. I would hear that plan too," Orangecloak had insisted while eying the map.

"Aye, that much I cannot deny," he sighed. "Lady Marigold made my original idea quite moot. I was going to make the Southlands the center of the war. It now seems that war will be at my doorstep. The focus of all the belligerents, including me, will need to be here." Greggard's eagerness seemed to dissipate with each sentence.

"Either way you looked at it, there was going to be innocent casualties," Orangecloak had surmised. "The Southlands is the most sparsely populated area in all of Illiastra with the Varras River as a natural boundary."

"If there was a war within Illiastra, it stands to reason that the Southlands would be the most suitable location." A hand of Greggard's had gently rubbed her shoulder. "I'm sorry that it happens to be your homeland."

It did bother Orangecloak to see the lands she knew as home offered as sacrificial collateral damage. Despite the raiders and the unforgiving wilderness, or perhaps because of it, the people of the Southlands were a resilient and vigorous folk. Many of these folk she knew as hard working individuals trying to survive amidst a world Illiastra had mostly tried to forget. They deserved to be protected, for she felt they were hers as much as anyone was. The Thieves had been allies to the mayors of the villages and holdfasts that dwelled in the stone and wooden walled keeps. These were men who had to answer as puppets to their ministers and lords, but were of births as low as their charges. They sided with Orangecloak and their true loyalty was with her. She was of no inclination to abandon them, or force her will over any of their towns. If she was to have a part in this coming war,

Orangecloak herself would define it.

This was a notion she had left unsaid to Greggard and even Yahmina. The elven woman had sworn herself to Orangecloak the evening after the first meeting with the Sealord of Portsward. Yet, her original contractor was Greggard, who paid good money to bring her to Illiastra from the university in the Fuwachita Mountain in Drake. Orangecloak couldn't be certain that the elf didn't have certain loyalties still tied to Lord Simillon. *Yahmina will have to earn her place, as Tryst did,* Orangecloak concluded.

For the first time since curling up in the chair hours ago, Orangecloak stood up and stretched her stiff limbs. A flagon of red wine had been left on a small round table near the door of the room and Orangecloak decided to fill a cup for herself.

She walked the large room, as she had been mostly doing for the past few days, opting to stay cooped up rather than risk being discovered by Greggard's extended family and their staff. A quick trip to the privy with a wash of the hands and face at the basin afterwards and Orangecloak found herself back before the desk and the map upon it. Her sight fell on the town of Layn once more, a red tack wrapped with a matching string protruding from the dot that indicated the town's location. No matter how many times she mulled over the proposed operation, the thought of commandeering the town brought butterflies to her stomach.

Despite its discolouration, the map was of fairly recent make and took into account the ever-changing boundaries the raiding gangs had loose dominion over. Even so, Greggard had drawn circles of his own to indicate even more current boundary changes amongst the gangs. Between Fort Layn and Aquas Bay, there was not an inhabited town to be found, though five forts dotting the Varras River banks stood heavily garrisoned. At the far southern reaches of the raiders' lands lay the abandoned ruins of Amarosha City, now just a stony haven for little else but ghosts. In the distant past, it had once been the centrepiece of a prospering nation of half-elves that had been Phaleayna's greatest ally.

The city had been destroyed during the war in the time of the First Master of Blades. The nation was amalgamated with Phaleayna and the Amaroshan people were granted citizenship. Then, the Triarchy slowly cut away at the rights of what they called the Halfbreeds. The faithful labelled them as abominations against Ios and encouraged violence and death towards decent folks whose sole crime was to have been born at all. What remained of their people, typically characterised by dusky human features and elven ears, had been given refuge by the Elven Forest. The same nation, that over a thousand years prior had driven the first Amaroshans out, had come to their rescue when the Triarchy pushed for outright genocide.

Orangecloak laid a finger upon the spot where the forgotten city sat nestled in the side of the mountain range that ran the entire southern edge of the continent. It still had tall, foreboding walls, albeit crumbling in places, but nothing she couldn't fix with a few investments from Lord Greggard and Kevane Dupoire.

No, too far south into the raiders' lands and too close to Aquas Bay for comfort, Orangecloak thought dismissively of the idea. Her eye caught something on the map and she looked further north from the old city, to an area on the eastern edges of the raiding gang's territory. A line had been drawn atop the script after the Forsaken had claimed the area around the valuable piece of ruinous real estate. Through the thick marking she could tell what had been written there in the tight handwriting of the original cartographer: Yaelsville.

She realised then why Layn had seemed like such a terrible idea to her. *The footsteps of Marros are not ones I wish to follow,* Orangecloak mused to herself grimly. *If I go through with Greggard's plan, then there are good odds that I will die in Layn much the same way my predecessor died in Yaelsville.*

Orangecloak found herself staring at the name of the town Marros had sacrificed himself and the Fearless Forty for. In her mind's eye she saw the dead in front of gates of Clay Harlowe's group of amalgamated mining towns collectively named the Warrens. Men, women and children they were, the runners from Yaelsville that the young group of Thieves had tried to lead to safety.

The town of Yaelsville itself had been left to fall into ruin, unburnt and untouched to send a message. Orangecloak and Lazlo had gone back after discovering Rillis Vale and leaving the surviving Thieves to hide there. The image she and Lazlo had discovered in what had been the town square of Yaelsville had never left Orangecloak: the heads of the Fearless Forty had been mounted on spikes in a morbid circle around the gibbeted corpse of Marros. The carrion birds and maggots had been gorging on human flesh and most of the remains were merely bone. Lazlo had vomited on the sight of it, but not Orangecloak. She had resolved herself to be steeled against it, to not let the last act of the EMP's thugs make her retch.

Idly, she traced her finger along the path she and Lazlo had walked to take them back to Rillis Vale, their hearts heavy and their memories scarred. She stopped at where she knew there was a clearing where the pair had come across the camp of Old Bansam and his men. The old warriors had finally arrived in Yaelsville from dealing with an attempted pillaging of Phaleayna by the Sons of Valdarrow.

She and Lazlo had stayed in the camp for the night and told Bansam everything that had happened. By morning, Bansam had broken camp and promised to clean up the mess the EMP had left and put Marros' remains to rest.

The entrances to Rillis Vale were not marked on any map, but Orangecloak knew where to find them.

Lazlo stumbled on the first entrance here, in a small cluster of boulders, she reminded herself with a tap of her finger in the place where they had found their underground home. The spot was nearly directly between Layn and a fort of the same name on the Varras River. Once the Thieves were inside the massive caverns, they had uncovered six more entrances that were either in working order or easily made operational again. A dozen more tunnels ran like snakes this way and that from the main area, though their exits to the surface were beyond repair.

For a moment, she thought Rillis Vale might make a formidable headquarters for a war effort. Though, if it was ever discovered or its location leaked, then it might lead to disaster. Her eye went back to the fortress just to the north again, remembering what Greggard had said about soldiers being redeployed to the warfront effort in the west come springtime. Fort Layn was a tightly walled, octagonal structure that sat on the river's edge and overlooked a wide, lifting bridge. It sat centrally to everything north and south of the Varras and had become the main link between the two halves of Illiastra.

It also happened to boast the engineering masterpiece that was the largest rotating cannon in the entire known world. The massive, imposing beast stood amid a spherical housing atop a tower that rose up in the centre of the fortress. From within its home, the cannon could turn three hundred and sixty degrees and be elevated a full forty five degrees from its horizontal base. The steel bore and neck of the cannon protruded from the structure, dauntingly huge and firing specially made shot that was twice as large as regular cannon balls. It also had the rare distinction of being able to fire six consecutive shots before needing to be reloaded. It was a feat Orangecloak would have thought impossible had she not witnessed the thing being fired for testing purposes. The heavy firepower and range of the beastly cannon meant that the fort required fewer men to defend it than its counterparts along the south banks of the river. From the best estimates her scouts had retrieved over the years, Orangecloak knew there were no more than fifty men manning Fort Layn at any one time. That number that would likely be halved to accommodate the needs of front line efforts should the EMP engage Lady Marigold and her rebellion in West Illiastra.

Orangecloak's heart began to beat faster as the idea came to her. *Perhaps if I, Tryst and a handful of my stealthiest Thieves go over the wall at night with grappling hooks, we could get in with little opposition,* she began to ponder. *I could send three or four to open the gates and that same number to subdue the engineers that operate the cannon. Even the numbers I should have in Rillis Vale could take and hold Fort Layn then. Who would dare oppose us? Head on would be reckless for EMP and raiders alike with that cannon turning to stare them in the face wherever they might strike. If mine are on the walls, with double the numbers Layn normally has at all hours of the day, no one can even hope to take the fort as I plan to.* Orangecloak ran it all through her head again, eyes fixed firmly on the fort's location on the map all the while.

This could work, she realised with nervous excitement. *We'll control the main gateway to the Southlands from here and for once the Thieves will actually have solid fortification to mount defences. We can even raise an army behind these walls.*

Orangecloak decided then and there that only Tryst would know of this plan for now. Greggard, Yahmina and Maurice would be led to believe her goal was the town of Layn. This was *Orangecloak's* plan. If war was coming one way or another, then she was going to stake her own claim in it.

She put a finger on Portsward again and began to trace her own path that would take her first to Rillis Vale. With great care taken, she had carefully left all of Greggard's strings and pushpins where he had placed them and instead committed her own revised route to memory. *There's a lumber camp here,* she said to herself, tapping the large, wooded area east of Daol Bay. *They've sheltered Myles, Coquarro and I before, they surely will again. Strike south and slightly east from there and I'll emerge from the Daol Woods on Longbarrow Plains. Two days south from there to the Varras River and I'll be between Fort's Plackett and Benton, go wide around Benton and use the north shore entrance to Rillis Vale. I can take Fort Layn from the Rillis Vale exit not a kilometre away.* Orangecloak followed the path backwards and forwards again looking for faults such as obstacles and paths that westward bound soldiers might take.

"This could work," she said in a voice that wanted to shout as she paced before the desk in the soft slippers Greggard had given her. The last of the wine in the silver goblet trickled down her throat and she went to the table again to fill it. Once there, she opted instead to return to the desk with the entire flagon, reasoning with a merry shrug that she was likely going to drink the whole thing anyhow. However, finding a place along the edge of the map for the wine jug proved a slight task and it ended up on the western seaboard.

A pair of papers that had been sitting nearby were tipped to the floor inadvertently and Orangecloak scooped to pick them up. *The prisoner manifest,* she noted sadly, holding the two pieces of brown parchment side by side under the light of the electric lamp on the table. Her attention went to two names and their descriptions below.

Prisoner name: Ellarie Dollen. Hometown: Atrebell City, Atrebell Region. Year of Life: Twenty-Forth. Date of Birth: 60th of spring, in the Year 1790, IR. Hair: Black. Eyes: Brown. Build: Slim. Markings of distinction: None. Prisoner issued number: 10562-1-8.

The entry had caught Orangecloak's attention straight away, but it wasn't until she saw another description at the end of the page that it made sense to her at all.

Prisoner name: Bernadine Voyer. Hometown: Wyford, Warrens Region. Year of Life: Twenty-First. Date of Birth: 7th of autumn, in the year 1794, IR. Hair: Black. Eyes: Green. Build: Slim. Markings of distinction: None. Prisoner issued number: 10569-1-8.

Ellarie's birthdate was off by seven days, which Orangecloak thought might be a misprinting until she noted that Ellarie's eye colour was wrong too. She couldn't make heads or tails of it until Bernadine's entry jumped out at her: their eye colours were switched. The girls bore a slight resemblance, near the same height and size, light complexions and dark hair. Anyone who knew the two would never confuse them, but to strangers one could pass for the other and no one would give it a second glance. The swapped eye colours said to Orangecloak that the two women had switched identities. It was a keen strategy, as Ellarie, being a known lieutenant of Orangecloak's, would likely be under higher security and greater restrictions than a presumed lackey like Bernadine. It wasn't much of an advantage, but it was better than none at all, Orangecloak knew, and more than anything it told her that Ellarie was refusing to give up.

Ellarie is still fighting. Even knowing that her life is condemned to end in the bowels of Biddenhurst, she keeps hope alive. If this war rolls over Illiastra and I avoid it, can I say that I am fighting? Orangecloak asked herself while laying the papers down atop the map, letting them rest between Biddenhurst and the Varras River.

Even without war, how can I go on as I once did knowing where Ellarie and her unit are? If for nothing or no one else, I have to bring them home. They were willing to risk everything for me and I should do no less for them. I don't yet know how, but a way must be found.

As she stared at the map in hopes an answer would come to her someone came knocking at the bedroom door. Orangecloak rose hurriedly and shuffled towards the entrance.

"Who calls?" she asked.

"It's Tryst, I was hoping we could speak privately," the instantly recognisable voice on the other side of the door answered.

The deft hands of Orangecloak worked the key into the lock to allow Tryst in. She nearly closed the door on his face when she caught sight of him, momentarily disbelieving it to be Tryst at all. "Your hair…" she gasped as he crossed the threshold with a mischievous smile on his face.

That drew a gentle laugh from him. "Aye, that's what I had come to talk to you about."

The long, red mane that reached his tailbone had been cut back to the shoulder blades and the fire extinguished for a dark brown to match his beard.

"Whatever possessed you to do such a thing?" Orangecloak asked, still in shock as she closed the door behind Tryst and took a better look at him.

He gazed around the room casually, his voice matching his behaviour. "We're not in the northern wilds anymore. If I'm to continue on with you in any capacity, I need to be able to blend in amongst the people. That exceptionally long hair, in any colour, was too defining of a trait and it needed to go. This is my natural shade and the length is more commonplace. No one will know me like this, or at least not as easily."

Orangecloak still had doubts of it. "If I'm not mistaken, I thought there were rules in the Combat University against the cutting of one's hair? You use hair as a measuring stick of sorts to determine tenure, if I remember right."

"You're not entirely wrong," Tryst began. "It's not against any rules, but it is a tradition amongst the combat students to shorn their hair off completely when they earn their right to study and then never cut it again. It is a way held on to for many reasons, one being that if an Expert in the field such as I needed to go into hiding he or she can easily cut their hair back to something similar as I have done. In this way, we can say that simply by our age and short hair that we mustn't be Experts of the Combat University of Drake or our hair would be longer. Those who go bald might cut off the remnants of their hair as well, or a warrior who disgraces themselves might choose to cut off their hair in penance. Among other reasons, the point is that the practice is far from forbidden. Mine is still long and I'll grow it out once more. For now though, letting it fall just beyond my shoulders and putting it back to my natural colour suits our purposes."

Orangecloak watched Tryst's face as he talked, noticing a sort of queer smile as he spoke that struck her oddly. "You didn't cut it just for my sake," she surmised when he finished his explanation.

"Well no, I didn't come here just to show you my hair, please, sit," Tryst said while motioning towards the desk.

On her way back to take a seat, Orangecloak grabbed a glass from the small serving table beside the door. Without asking if he wanted refreshment, Orangecloak filled the glass from the wine flagon and handed it to Tryst. "Tell me over wine. I fear your news is going to be unpleasant, so we might at least have something to drink with it."

"Very well," Tryst said as he accepted the cup, raising it in unison with Orangecloak before taking a taste. "Lord Greggard has recognised that our contract is now complete," he declared promptly upon swallowing. "I am officially an available mercenary again."

"Why, this is good news, Tryst," Orangecloak spoke light-heartedly knowing there were things yet to be said that would offset the good tidings. "You're free to pursue whatever you would like once more, unbound by contracts."

Tryst's eyes seemed to land everywhere but on Orangecloak as he spoke, "As to that, he acknowledged the completion of that contract of service so that he might table a new one."

Orangecloak kept her calmness. "What does this new contract entail, might I ask?"

He almost looked ashamed as he answered, "It would seem that Lord Greggard would like to acquire my services in the upcoming battle that's to take place in Pelican Harbour."

The idea sank in for Orangecloak and she gave herself a moment to respond with a slow sip of wine. "Does that man think of anything besides war?" she asked rhetorically with a despondent sigh. "Have you accepted this new contract?"

"I have not," Tryst confessed. "I wanted to let you know of it before I made a decision."

She shrugged nonchalantly. "What does it matter if I know? You're not sworn to me, go do as you wish."

His brows furrowed at that. "It does matter, I told you I would offer you my sword when my contract was complete and you had decided on your own fate."

"As you can see, I have yet to make any final decision." Orangecloak said, gesturing towards the open map on the desk. "I'm wintering here in Portsward and won't be going anywhere until spring. If you want to fight for Greggard between now and then I'm not standing in your way."

"The payment Lord Greggard has promised me for the job will go a long way towards your effort, whatever that might be," he reasoned nervously.

"Don't go into this battle to raise funds on my behalf," Orangecloak told him after another sip of wine. "I haven't decided if I'll even accept your sword. That's even if you manage to come back alive from this."

"Are you afraid that I'll die?" Tryst asked worriedly. "You need not fear such a thing, Orangecloak. I promise you I'll come back."

She shot him a sarcastic glance. "Do you think I haven't heard such before? The names on that manifest on the desk had made similar promises to me, as did Myles and Coquarro and many before them." Orangecloak crossed her legs and leaned back in her chair with wine goblet to hand while keeping her icy composure. "When the world around you is at war, there's little point in making such promises, they're largely out of your hands to keep."

Tryst pressed on from the comment. "It is a stealth mission Greggard has in mind. I'm with a small unit that is going to be stationed in the forest outside Pelican Harbour and I will be under the assumed identity of a man from the northern shore. The beard and the hair will lend itself to that."

"Yet your bright, green eyes will betray your origins," Orangecloak pointed out.

"That is a risk, aye. I could just say that my mother was a Gildraddi, though," Tryst countered.

That raised another question Orangecloak had: "I thought Greggard had said the attack was primarily taking place from sea? What use would he have for a unit hiding in the woods?"

To that Tryst had a ready answer: "Greggard has reason to believe that if Lady Marigold attacks the harbour from the sea, Minister Nothram will not surrender until his own life is in immediate danger. The goal with this backdoor infiltration is to force Minister Nothram to yield before the primary battle is at his doorstep. There's no denying my skills would aid in this."

"I have no doubt they would," Orangecloak said wearily. "Does the contract only cover this upcoming operation?"

"Aye, it does," Tryst answered.

Orangecloak was just about done with this topic and gave Tryst a tone to reflect that sentiment. "Then, by all means go right ahead, I'll be right here when you return."

"Very well, then," Tryst said while reaching underneath his cloak to produce the sheathed blacksteel sword that was his signature weapon. "As part of my disguise I'll be arming myself with standard issue weapons. Would you hold this and my other effects again?"

"I shall, if this is what you wish. I give you my word that I will protect your sword until you return for it," Orangecloak answered, taking the blade in both hands for a moment and letting it rest on her lap. "In the meantime, come, let me show you the plans I have been working on," she said to change the subject from the topic of him going into battle.

Leaving no detail omitted, Orangecloak spent the next several dozen minutes explaining all she had concocted to this point. The blacksteel sword was laid atop the map, across the icy wasteland known as the Impenetrable Tundra that stretched the entire northern reaches of the known world. She showed Tryst the lines of string and the tacks that had been Greggard Simillon's plan and then her own, unmarked path that only Tryst was to know of for now.

Tryst listened intently, leaning in over her shoulder and following her finger as she went from point to point on the map.

When she was finished, she turned to him. "Have you any suggestions?" she asked.

He waited a beat, running a hand over the brown beard covering his jawline. "You certainly know the Southlands a fair deal better than Greggard. There's only one concern I have," Tryst said while planting a finger squarely on Layn. "This is the middle ground between Fort Layn and The Warrens and the very town you sought to keep out of the line of fire. Do you think Clay Harlowe could make a base out of it on the road to attacking you?"

"Clay Harlowe won't attack a town in his own realm that I don't hold," Orangecloak said, confident in her answer. "Mayor Torell might have to tolerate having the minister within his home, that is true, but the mayor is a friend of mine. If Minister Harlowe is plotting in Torell's keep I might as well be a fly on the wall. I'll know his plans before he can make any sort of move against me."

"Are you going to tell Greggard any of this?" Tryst asked casually, taking a seat on the corner of the desk to face her.

With a shrug, Orangecloak sank bank into her chair and took a sip of wine. "I have no intention of it and if you're any friend of mine, then neither will you."

"You have my word, Orangecloak, I assure you," Tryst stated before asking another question of his own. "Do you have any idea what sort of state the remaining Thieves are in?"

"No and that's something that has been worrying me," she answered with a sigh. "They surely believe that I am dead or at the very least captured by now. Before I plan another move, I should at least find out who has taken the mantle of Field Commander and what direction they're leading everyone in."

He let out a low, ponderous hum. "Perhaps you should make contact with them soon. Even if just to let them know you are alive and to have someone that knows you confirm that you are not an imposter. Do you have any agents in Portsward you could speak with, by any chance?"

Orangecloak nodded in answer. "Aye, my recruiter for the west coast is stationed in town. In his prime he fought under Old Bansam, both in the military and in the Thieves. Even then he served to assess and place Bansam's recruits and he had a great knack for it. The man's name is Charl and he took a bad wound to the leg fighting the Moon Raiders gang, forcing him to retire from active duty. As a recruiter he is still able to put his skills to use in a setting much more suited to his current capabilities."

As Orangecloak spoke, Tryst swirled the wine in his cup and looked to be considering everything she said, waiting until she finished before adding in his own commentary. "Good, if he is here in Portsward it shouldn't be difficult for you to make contact with him. You should make arrangements to do that sooner rather than later, if for no other reason than to let the others know you live."

"Agreed and with that said, I would like you to come with me." she proffered to him. "We should make the arrangements to go looking into town before you leave for battle."

Tryst sucked his teeth glumly. "Fletchard and I are to be at the docks by the midnight hour, I'm afraid."

"That's this evening, why so soon?" Orangecloak asked nonplussed.

"It seems Lord Greggard was able to find a ship for Fletchard. It leaves under black sails in the dead of night," he answered.

"He's leaving on a smuggler ship." The tone in Orangecloak's voice gave away her amusement. "I'm guessing it arrives under such clandestine conditions as well, anchoring far out into the harbour with landfall made only by rowboat."

"Yes, as a matter of fact," Tryst chuckled. "You don't become Lord of Foreign Trade and keep that spot without getting to know the underside of that world. Not to mention, a man as conspicuous as Fletchard Miller is not an easy one to sneak out of Illiastra without someone noticing. Under black sails is the best bet."

Orangecloak finished her wine and laid the goblet aside decisively. "It's settled, then. I'll go tonight with you and Fletchard." She pushed herself to her feet quickly and went for her cleaned suit of leather hanging in the wardrobe beside the featherbed.

"You would do well to take Yahmina with you too," Tryst advised her concernedly. "I'll not be returning to the manor until the battle is over."

"*If* you survive that battle, that is," Orangecloak corrected him dourly while pulling on the tight fitting, green trousers from beneath her robe. "Even you can be killed, Tryst. Don't ever be too sure of yourself. What business do you have on the docks to keep you there so long that it leads directly to the battlefield?"

"I have to board a ship as well," Tryst explained, having stayed where he was when Orangecloak went to change. "You remember that big, bloated, floating icehouse Captain Bickerington had at the tail of his fleet called *The Flying Whale*?" She turned to meet his stare and gave him a curious nod before he went on. "I have forged documents that its captain shall be signing for me. He's to give me receipts for payment of travel and I'm to pay him for a trip I did not make.

"After that, I have draft documents for a Stefos Buchlan from Nettles Cove to report for service. There's a real fellow there by that name, but he doesn't know he was to be drafted. Greggard and I just picked him from a census because he was near my age, size and general description. I'm to change into the clothes of a commoner from the north coast and go from there to a recruiting office. The rest of the ruse will hinge on how well I can fool the men in the uniforms."

Orangecloak was satisfied with Tryst's explanation and moved to dismiss him. "Very well then. Do me a favour and go inform Yahmina that I'll have need of her tonight. We'll be going to the *Sea Star Inn*. I've been there before, if she's not familiar with it. Return when you are prepared to leave, I'll be ready by then and we shall all travel together."

"Certainly, I'll return for you in a short while. I have to pack the few things I can take with me and sign my contract with Greggard," Tryst stated while crossing the floor of the room. He stopped at the door and turned back to her. "I suggest taking your blacksteel dagger, the streets are very dangerous at night and you can be killed just as well as I can."

It was well after nightfall by the time Tryst returned for

Orangecloak, carrying all his worldly possessions. Included amongst it being his steel mask and a small bag of coin that he told her she might borrow from.

As soon as she had eyed the bag, Orangecloak had remembered something important. "If I might, I will need just three coppers."

"They are yours, then," he said while pressing an uncounted handful into her palm while looking over her attire.

Orangecloak had decided on wearing both cloaks over her leather suit and the tunic gifted to her by the Dupoire family. The heavier black cloak was placed atop the signature, frayed orange, to conceal it against eyes that need not see it and provide more warmth. Her hair she had tied back into a simple tail to better conceal beneath her hoods. On her hip rested the dagger in its sheath, as Tryst had suggested. When he came, it was the first thing he reminded her of and Orangecloak had brushed aside her cloaks to show him that she was not without it.

"Should you wear the orange cloak?" he asked worriedly when he noticed it beneath the black bear fur of the outer layer. "If it is seen, you'll be known right away."

She gave a single nod. "It is a risk, but one I must take. The orange cloak inspires people as much as the rest of me ever could. Where I am going, it will open more doors than any sword or uniform."

"If you insist, there is little else I can do," Tryst said with a shrug, disinterested in pushing the matter any further. "Come then, our company awaits us."

The hallway outside her quarters was unusually dark, as the way was normally illuminated with electric lamps set in the wall opposite the window side. They had all been extinguished and the moons were both in hiding this night, leaving only the pitch black for Tryst and Orangecloak to navigate through. Soon enough, the path they were taking felt familiar and it became apparent they were leaving through the same cellar that she, Tryst and Fletchard had entered from days before. Down here they had allowed for a single bulb dangling from the ceiling to be lit and standing beneath its glow was Fletchard Miller.

He had acquired thick leather gloves and a long, black, hooded woollen coat that reminded Orangecloak of the dark blue one Coquarro used to wear. The coat was a size too big for the bounty hunter and it made him look broader than he actually was. His things were slung across his shoulder in his satchel and on his side hung a new, unadorned, falchion sword.

Of Yahmina there was at first no sign. Orangecloak's gaze went around the room several times without seeing anything, until the faint rustle of a cloak caught her attention beside the outside exit.

The elven woman was as silent as a cat from where she stood outside the light of the bulb, peering through a small hole in the doors. Her cobalt blue, thick cloak was colour matched with a suit of leather armour beneath.

"Good evening," Orangecloak said, greeting them both.

"It is snowing," Yahmina replied. "I don't think it will get much worse though, so travel should be safe. I suppose that would constitute a good evening." The woman had a frank way of speaking that Orangecloak wasn't quite accustomed to. Nonetheless, she found herself liking the elven woman. She exuded the confidence of a battle-hardened warrior and even unlike Tryst, seemed to always be at the ready for danger.

By contrast, Tryst was downright carefree, even though it was he who was the Master of Blades and Yahmina who was the lesser rank of Expert of Blade and Bow.

The elf turned to look at Tryst and Orangecloak, inspecting their attire briefly until she seemed satisfied. "Are you armed, my lady?" she asked Orangecloak in a flat tone.

Though it seemed to Orangecloak that Yahmina knew the answer already, she offered an answer nonetheless. "Aye, I have a blacksteel dagger with me."

"Good. Where Tryst tells me you want to go is not a safe place after dusk," Yahmina answered sternly. "There are ruffians about and the guards themselves won't offer you any help. Not that you need me to tell you that, I'm sure. At any rate, let's be off." With that, the elf shoved open one of the two double doors and walked into the night.

Fletchard offered them an exasperated roll of his one eye that for once wasn't directed at them and followed Yahmina, with Orangecloak and Tryst behind him.

It was crisp and cold, with the winter settling in quite comfortably over the city. Snow fell in large, heavy flakes with a foreboding thickness and it was quite apparent that Portsward and Daol Bay were soon to be under a considerable white blanket.

The party all had their hoods drawn, and within minutes Orangecloak could see flakes gathering on the head and shoulders of her companions. The streets were well lit by the time they first set out, illuminated by electric lamps on tall poles that cast a ruddy glow to the ground below. Yahmina led the group well away from where the light fell and kept them to the darkness as much as the snow allowed. It had accumulated quite a bit since Orangecloak had arrived in Portsward, making the walking more of a chore than they would have liked.

The town gave way before them as they came to the top of a steep hill. Below, Orangecloak could see a smattering of lights through the snowfall and little else. A Tower of Ios stuck its peak high into the sky and a few warehouses and factories with their tall chimneys along the waterfront seemed built to compete with its height, but nothing could stand above the Tower. It was law that it should always be the tallest manmade point in any settlement and that happened to be one law Greggard hadn't circumvented.

Orangecloak found herself staring at its burning beacon in the tower's peak. The way it glowed in different shades of blue and white as it burned brighter than anything in the town below was nearly mesmerising.

The hill sloped gently here and at the bottom forked to the south and the west. It was the south road that Orangecloak knew she and Yahmina must take. For the other two, they would have to report to the same wharf that they and Orangecloak had disembarked *The Myra* from a few days past.

When the fork rose to meet them, they gathered away from the streetlamp that shone upon it. "This is it, then," Fletchard said while turning to Orangecloak. "Odds are that our paths will not be crossed again, Orangecloak. I hope some good can come out of the brief time that they did."

"I hope for that as well. Farewell, Fletchard. May the winds be ever in your favour," Orangecloak responded a little sadly. She extended a hand to him and there was a brief pause before he took it and shook it firmly.

"Farewell to you, Orangecloak," he added rather softly. With a last nod, he turned, the darkness engulfed him and he was gone, leaving Tryst to catch up with him.

Orangecloak nodded in the direction he had gone and spoke to

Tryst. "You should go before he gets too far away."

"He won't walk too far on me, I'm sure," Tryst's voice was full of melancholy. "But I suppose you're right. I'll see you when I return."

"That's *if* you return, Tryst Reine. War is not a trifling thing," she reminded him again.

"But of course," he answered. "Let's hope the battle unfolds in my favour then."

Orangecloak offered Tryst the same handshake. "I shall hope for no less. Farewell, Tryst."

Though Tryst took her hand in response, he did not shake it. Rather, he held it between his own and looked her in the eyes. "Farewell, Orangecloak," he said softly. With that, Tryst let her go and walked away.

Don't die on me. Orangecloak said to no one when Tryst's footfalls fell out of hearing.

With Yahmina now at her side, the pair continued on alone into the ever-beating heart that was Portsward's downtown. Orangecloak remembered from previous visits that the pubs and taverns only closed when the light of dawn peeked above the eastern hills. Between the midnight hour and the waking, the streets between the various drinking holes were a hive of scum and drunkards. Down here and between those hours, a woman was but an object.

As it was, women were forbidden from being out beyond the midnight hour thanks to the chauvinistic law upheld by the Triarchy. Being caught meant the night was spent in a jail cell. For the most fortunate, they were merely returned to their male guardians the next morning. Some had enough frivolous charges added to their original transgression that they soon found themselves on the next train to Biddenhurst.

The lawmakers had long decided that women in any form made for far better slaves than the savage drunks or other delinquents that might accost them. Even if one of the brutes was caught in the act of raping a woman by the guards, it was the victim who almost always faced the harshest punishments.

The Triarchy's own scriptures blamed the women, as men were, according to its own words, filled with urges and were not under any obligation to control them. That sort of jilted logic was among the first things Orangecloak sought to change. Every man that had come under her leadership in the Thieves knew as much. They understood that their urges were their own to control and should they not, there was no one but themselves to blame for it.

Perhaps it was the cold air or the heavy snow, but tonight Orangecloak felt a strange calm in Portsward. As the homes and businesses of the working class encompassed the pair of them, it came to Orangecloak why that calmness prevailed: the streets were near empty. Even so, Yahmina veered them off the main road and into an alleyway as soon as the opportunity presented itself.

The alleys and rooftops were Orangecloak's main access ways as it was, yet even she had a particular aversion to alleys after dark. It was no secret that the Thieves were not the only ones who sought the paths unseen.

"The weather must be keeping everyone in," Orangecloak commented in a low voice to Yahmina. "I've never seen Portsward this quiet at any hour before."

"If you asked Lord Greggard, he would tell you that this was all the doing of him and Marigold Tullivan," Yahmina said in return without stopping. "Now that Western Illiastra has declared itself a nation in its own right, Lord Greggard is no longer concerned that his outward actions might invoke the ire of the Triarchy or the EMP. No matter what way everything unfolds from here on out, he cannot go back to the way things were. He either thrives under Lady Marigold, or dies under Lady Marigold. There is no middle ground any longer. In the eyes of the east, he is as much of an outlaw as you are, my lady."

"I still don't know what this has to do with the streets being bare," Orangecloak put back to her as they exited an alley and hurried across the wide pathway of Seaside Road, Portsward's main thoroughfare.

Yahmina dropped to a knee and peeked out around the side of the alley to ensure there was no one about. "Yes well, as for that," she finally answered. "Lord Greggard and Lady Marigold alike have passed some new legislation that aims at making things a bit easier on the streets at night for our gender."

That piqued Orangecloak's interest. "What sort of legislation?"

The elf rose from her crouched position and turned to face Orangecloak. "For one, curfew for women is lifted and we can be out at any hour now. For another, the right of guardianship over women is no longer enforced. Women are free to work and earn their own wages, and are free to vote and even be elected to office. Basically, we're free to damn well do whatever men are free to do. We can even enlist to be soldiers now."

Orangecloak was pleasantly surprised. "All that in such a short time, it's no wonder she's been such a polarising figure."

Yahmina glanced out onto the street once more but stayed put as she responded to Orangecloak. "Indeed. However, the Triarchy has stated that Lady Marigold's laws are in defiance of Ios and therefore she and all who follow her are blasphemers and apostates. Only the bravest women dare venture out after dark for fear that the big brethren in the burgundy robes will arrest them. It's not only women that have become afraid though. The Triarchy has also taken to charging the drunken scoundrels as apostates for public debauchery. They too hide in fear of being drafted into the burgundy order."

"This was the very sort of thing I was afraid would happen," Orangecloak said with a grunt. "What are we stalling for?"

Yahmina glanced over her shoulder to the street once more before answering, "There are two men loitering over there, close to the Sea Star's front door. I'm waiting for them to move on."

Orangecloak strained to see through falling snow but could see little more than shadows beyond the lights of the homes and establishments. "I see nothing."

"That's because your eyes, pretty as they might be, are not elven," Yahmina answered rather brusquely. "You told me at one point that you travelled with an elven man for a time after leaving Atrebell, was he blind?"

That annoyed Orangecloak and she made no qualms about it. "You're being facetious. Tyrendil's eyes were as good as yours."

"That is good to know," Yahmina commented before gesturing toward the street. "The men have staggered on down the road, now we can move. " The elven woman left the cover of the alley, making no effort to wait.

Orangecloak went forward cautiously, looking left and right down the street for herself before darting across the near vacant road to the inn on the other side.

Yahmina cracked the door open and held it just wide enough to allow Orangecloak and herself entry into the reception hall of the three-storied inn.

The lights were dimly lit and sparse, and it made the place look dank and uninviting to the uninitiated. Across a long floor covered in an equally long, worn red rug sat the front desk and a man of about sixty. There was nothing extraordinary about him with his trimmed, grey beard and a hairline that had retreated halfway to the back of his head. He was nose deep in a ledger book, feather quill to hand, when the hooded pair entered the building and he gave them only the slightest of disinterested glances.

"I'm sorry, ladies, we're full up tonight," the man spoke without even bothering to look at them. "You might try *The Good Wind* or *Hetchman's Inn*, although the latter has had a recent rat infestation."

Orangecloak stepped forward and strolled confidently to the desk where the man sat.

"Look, I told you-" he started to say again, finally mustering the energy to look up.

"We're not here for a room." The words were out of her mouth by the time she closed the gap. "I'm here to deliver a gift."

That caught the innkeeper's attention and a greying eyebrow shot up along with his head. "What gift might that be?" he asked Orangecloak curiously.

She leaned in and dropped her voice to a whisper, "I bring you the colours of freedom."

"And just what are the colours of freedom?" the old fellow inquired, his eyelids narrowing.

The words were ones Orangecloak herself had come up with as a password of sorts and she recited them back for him: "It is gold upon a shield of green amidst a field of orange."

He was looking over the two women curiously, tongue rolling over his bottom lip in judgement before speaking again. "Might be that it is, might be that I prefer copper to gold."

"Then I shall give you two for your trouble and one for a tip," Orangecloak said while reaching into her pocket to produce a handful of copper coins. Two she placed face up and side by side, the face of Grenjin Howland's father in profile facing to the left on both of them. A third was placed with the dove of the EMP facing up.

The deskman scraped the coins off the worn, wooden surface and let them drop somewhere unseen. "Your price is fair. I have a message for you as well," he stated while glancing around to ensure no one was listening in. His fist rapped on the desk sharply once, then again and followed with a rap-a-tap, rap-a-tap, tap, tap, tap. Three fingers he flashed quickly and two he laid against his right cheek. He rubbed his face thrice with the digits and went back to his ledger as if no one were there at all.

Without another word needed, Orangecloak beckoned to Yahmina quickly and went for the staircase beside the front desk.

The elf followed dutifully and wordlessly at Orangecloak's heels as she ascended the steps.

The third and last floor was Orangecloak's destination and neither one utter a sound until they were off the landing and into the narrow corridor beside it.

"You didn't think the Musicians were the only ones with secret codes did you?" she grinned slyly over her shoulder at Yahmina.

"Of course not, I must say though that I'm quite impressed all the same," Yahmina answered back, nearly bumping into Orangecloak as she stopped before the second door to her left. "How do you know this is the door?"

"He showed three fingers and laid two on his right cheek, nails down. That means the door we seek is the third floor, second door on the left from the landing." Orangecloak answered in a whisper. She paused and took a deep breath, balled her hand into a fist at her side and began knocking upon the door. Two hard knocks, a rap-a-tap, rap-a-tap and three more tuneless knocks to follow. Twice more she repeated the pattern and took two steps back when she was done.

Yahmina looked from the door to Orangecloak and back again several times, waiting for one or the other to move. After what felt like a few minutes, Yahmina seemed about to speak when the door opened but a crack before them.

"Yes?" an old, deep voice from within a blackened room asked.

"I seek you," Orangecloak answered quickly.

"And who sent you?" it asked once more.

Orangecloak drew back her hoods to reveal her face and hair beneath. "No one, though I hope you will make an exception in this particular instance."

"Yes, I suppose I shall," the old voice put back to her in an aloof tone, giving away no surprise at who he was looking upon. The door creaked open wide enough to allow Orangecloak and Yahmina into the darkness inside and was closed shut with haste behind them. A light flickered from a table in the far left corner and then another from the right and the room took on a dim glow.

"Either death is a lie or the lie was your death," the owner of the voice commented while looking upon Orangecloak with sombre, wizened eyes. He was a man of his late sixties, skinny as a twig, greyed and leaning on a cane. Wrinkles had worked their way into his face from long days under the sun and he had a pronounced limp.

"That would be the latter, Charl," Orangecloak returned with a slender smile for him as she took in the room. It was then that Orangecloak realised that what she thought was three people in the room was actually five.

A young woman near Orangecloak's age and a man who looked slightly older stood quietly in the corners beside the lamps. Awe and wonderment upon their faces as they realised who stood before them.

Orangecloak bowed her head politely. "Hello there."

From behind her, Charl stepped as quickly as his limp would allow until he was before the two strangers. "My lady, this is Amyla Spade and Athelbert Fauster, two new recruits who arrived from Obalen some time ago." Charl gestured an open hand towards the two young people and then to Orangecloak. "Amyla, Athelbert, allow me the honour of introducing you to the Lady Orangecloak, Field Commander of the Thieves."

The girl dropped to her knees before Orangecloak, tears welling in her eyes as she tried to stammer out some words. "It's you," she managed. "How can this be? We were told that you were long dead in Atrebell and that the woman wearing your cloak was a fake."

"That was merely a lie spread by the Merchants after I slipped through their grasp," Orangecloak answered her. "Now stand, my dear, I require no such displays of fealty."

The man named Athelbert helped the woman back to her feet. "I told you that, Amyla. She's not a high born, nor a lady proper, she is one of us. We need not grovel."

"Indeed so, it's a pleasure to meet you, Athelbert," Orangecloak began to say while extending a hand for him to shake.

He returned the offer with a smooth hand. "My friends call me Athel and I do hope that you might do so as well."

"If Athel is what you prefer, then that is what I shall call you," Orangecloak spoke in a friendly tone to the man before turning back to the woman with the head of long, dark curls. "Amyla, it's an honour to make your acquaintance as well."

Before a handshake could be offered, Amyla drew Orangecloak into a tight hug. Yahmina tensed up and put a hand to one of the elf blades strapped to her legs, only relaxing when Orangecloak gave her a look of reassurance.

Amyla let Orangecloak go as suddenly as she grabbed her. "Oh my, I shouldn't have done that," she said, becoming embarrassed. "I'm so sorry, milady. I just got caught up in the moment. I'm just so very glad that you're alive."

"There is no need to be sorry, my dear. If anyone has to apologise it is me, for I have forgotten my manners." She turned to Yahmina beside her, as silent as a stone. "Charl, Athel and Amyla, allow me to introduce Yahmina Windleaf, an Elf of the Forest and an Expert of Blade and Bow from the Combat University of Drake."

Charl looked Yahmina over suspiciously as she lowered her hood. "This is the same elf that's been seen around Portsward guarding the children of Lord Greggard Simillon."

The elf turned sharply on the old man. "That I am, but you need not worry about I or Lord Greggard, we are not your enemy."

"No, not now, I suppose." He added as their eyes met, "We both have bigger issues." He broke Yahmina's gaze to look over Orangecloak. "And you and I have some stories to exchange by the look of things. Come, sit." The elder gestured to a small, simple table and four chairs in the middle of the room. "Amyla, be a dear and fetch some wood to stoke the fireplace with, there's a chill seeping into the room," he said while turning to the recruits. "Athel, we'll take some tea and maybe scones if you'd be so kind as to go to the kitchen and retrieve some for us."

"Aye, ser," they both answered him quickly and left the room before Charl could take a seat at the table.

The old man waited until the recruits had closed the door and both Orangecloak and Yahmina were seated before speaking up again. "I could sense you wanted to talk without them here. It's been a while since they've come to me, though it might be some time before I can send them on to Phaleayna for seasoning, what with the coming war. They've surpassed all my suspicions, though. They'll be loyal to you, of that I have no doubt."

Orangecloak nodded at that. "I trust your judgement on the matter, Charl. I thank you all the same for giving us the privacy to let me know as much."

Charl changed the subject demandingly. "I'll hear your story now. I must know how you went into the depths of Atrebell's dungeon and emerged again not only alive, but free and in the company of Greggard's housecarl."

Starting with the painful memory of the deaths of Myles and Coquarro, Orangecloak recounted the events of her escape. Her more intimate moments with Tryst and any mention of the Musicians, she carefully omitted. The Dupoire and Bickerington family were merely mentioned as sympathisers to Orangecloak's cause. Even Tryst Reine was spoken of as a contracted mercenary in the employ of Greggard alone, with no further allegiances.

She had gotten into talking of the meeting with Greggard and Maurice when the two recruits returned from their tasks. The girl was carrying an armload of firewood that looked larger than she was and Orangecloak moved to help her. "No, my lady, I wouldn't think of it," Amyla said with a measure of strain in her voice. "I carried it this far, I think I can manage to lay it beside the fireplace."

Behind Amyla came Athel with a wooden platter filled with tea and scones for all.

Charl motioned to the two Obalenites. "Sit, young ones. Eat up. Orangecloak, you may continue your story at your leisure."

While Orangecloak concluded her account of recent events, Amyla went into the hallway to find a spare chair for the table, offering the remaining one to Athel.

The old man waited until Orangecloak was finished before offering commentary on it all. "A vaunted mercenary, a lord, a man who is a sea captain and government minister both, a hermit and a dwarven businessman," Charl mused aloud. "All working to help you move about the northern reaches of Illiastra. Offering food, shelter and counsel along the way out of the goodness of their hearts. If I didn't know any better, I'd swear that the Thieves weren't the only underground threat to the Elite Merchants."

Yahmina gave Orangecloak a hard look, convincing her to refrain from telling Charl that he was correct in his assumption. Instead, Orangecloak decided to press on with the reason she had sought him in the first place. "Charl, speaking of the Thieves, what news do you have of them? I've been out of contact for some time and I haven't been able to get any fresh information. Surely news of my capture has reached Phaleayna and Rillis Vale alike?"

He bit into a scone and chewed it for what seemed an eternity before answering. "Everyone thought you were dead or locked in the

Atrebell dungeon. Either way, no one south of the Varras River thought you were coming back. Personally, I had thought that if something were to happen to you that Ellarie Dollen would be the natural choice for a successor. Yet, when you went down, so did she, along with Lazlo and their units. So now, with only the meek Edwin the Raven and the apathetic Garlan Vahn to stop her, Mell the Huntress has assumed power."

Orangecloak grew despondent at that. "I had feared as much."

"Don't fret too much, she has opposition," Charl added with an encouraging wink.

A twinge of excitement fluttered in Orangecloak's stomach. "Who might that be?"

Charl hesitated a moment, wearing a strained face that looked to be having trouble recalling. "The dancer from Collura, his name escapes me."

Orangecloak answered for him, "That would be Reed Eldeen." This was a glimmer of hope. Among Orangecloak's supporters, Reed was among her most ardent and assertive. "Of course, if there is anyone I have left that would have the fortitude to stand up to the overbearing attitude of Mell the Huntress, it would be Reed. There's little that man fears and she wouldn't make that list on her best day."

"That would be him," Charl said. "The vale is divided in support between the two. It hasn't yet come to violence, at least as far as I know, but you know what Mell is capable of as well as I do."

Orangecloak nodded thoughtfully. "Indeed, it is trying. Hopefully, when I return I can bring peace between them and unite the Thieves once more. What of Bansam?"

After pouring himself a cup of tea and buttering a fresh scone, the old man replied, "His latest letter indicated he was embroiled in conflict with the raiding gangs, as usual. Apparently they're getting bolder as of late. Something to do with the Sun's Rangers staying holed up in Fort Dornett, likely on account of the coming war and redeployment of the soldiers in the river forts."

"Those aren't good tidings," Orangecloak decided.

Charl agreed, "Coming from Bansam, they so rarely are."

Orangecloak glanced between the two fresh faces. "I'm sorry that the Thieves you have come looking for are in such a state of disarray. We're usually a more organised and functional group." The sad smile Orangecloak wore did little to assuage the unspoken concerns of the two. "While we're on the topic, what brings you both to Portsward seeking recruitment?"

The pair looked at one another, seeing who of them would speak up. It was Athel, with his short, brown, wavy hair and neatly kempt beard that responded for them. "Well, as Mister Charl said, we're from Obalen. We were forced to run, or well I was and Amyla came with me rather than stay, after what they did."

"Who are they? What did they do?" Orangecloak inquired concernedly.

Amyla fielded those questions, her voice on the cusp of breaking and her eyes filling. "They were Triarchists. My brother Lennick, Lenn for short, he had invited me over for dinner. Athel was working at the time. The Triarchists came and broke the door down. A big brute in a dark red robe led a mob and he had some of Lenn and Athel's neighbours with them. The big one said that my brother and Athel stood accused of being reprobates in the eyes of Ios for lying with men. He told us that the neighbours had even confessed to witnessing it. Lenn didn't even get to say anything in his defence. A group of men just grabbed him and started dragging him out of the house." Amyla began to sob then and Athel rose from his seat and went to her side to comfort her as she went on, "I tried to stop them, I fought them as best I could, but there were so many of them. The one in the robe held me down until they'd taken Lenn and then he had the gall to say that he was going to give me lenience by not charging me with 'Aiding an Apostate'."

She wiped the tears from her face and continued, "When they left, I went to Athel, I knew there was no one else I could go to. The city guard wouldn't dare intervene, but I had to do something, I couldn't let them kill my brother."

Athel picked up the story to give Amyla a break. "She came to the clinic where I worked as a nurse and told me what was happening. We went to the Tower of Ios in the town square, but we were too late. They lit the kindling beneath Lenn and burned him alive at the stake."

Orangecloak cast her eyes down to the table and shook her head sombrely. "That's reprehensible. I'm so sorry that you had to witness that."

"Amyla almost charged headlong into the throng," Athel added. "I stopped her and we went to my parent's home to hide for the night. I suggested that the only safe place in Illiastra for me now was with the Thieves and Amyla wanted to fight for those like me. Our search led us here, where, after much searching, we found Charl."

"I want to avenge my brother," Amyla declared through the tears streaking down her face. "I want to fight so that men and women like Athel don't have to hide in fear of death for the crime of loving one another. Have I come to the right place for that, my lady?"

In Amyla, Orangecloak could see Ellarie Dollen staring back at her. Like Ellarie, Amyla was a protector, but her protection had failed. This young woman sought vengeance and a chance to right her perceived wrong for being unable to stop her brother's death. She was emotionally wounded, like so many other Thieves before her.

"You have indeed come to the right place," Orangecloak said with a single, solemn nod. "The both of you have. I cannot promise safety, not as long as you serve beside me. Your lives will be fraught with danger, as I fear I will have need of fighters and healers alike in the coming seasons. However, you will be fighting as part of the Thieves and we fight for equal rights for the oppressed." Her chair scraped on the floor as she slid it back and stood up straight. "Your battle is my battle, friends. I stand with you."

"Thank you, my lady," Amyla managed to get out between sobs.

"There you both have it," Charl said, evidently satisfied with the outcome. "The Lady Orangecloak herself has brought you into the fold. I'm afraid you'll have to stay here until I can manage to arrange transportation south of the Varras River though, no telling when that will be now that the trains don't run to Obalen anymore."

To that problem Orangecloak found an immediate solution. "Yahmina, would Lord Greggard be opposed to making room for two more at the manor?" she asked.

The golden haired woman shrugged. "I hardly see why he would be. His relatives should all be gone by morning and him two days later for battle with Marigold."

Orangecloak nodded at that and turned back to the new recruits. "Then it is settled. Amyla, Athel, gather your things, you will be staying with me at the manor."

28

ELLARIE

The snow grew deeper by the hour, covering the buildings and gravel beyond the window beneath a blanket of pure white. *You were right again, old man,* Ellarie reflected as the kindly face of the elder of Tabelan flashed before her mind's eye. The tiny farming village north of the Varras was a rare haven for the Thieves. Every spring since Orangecloak had become Field Commander, it had fallen to Ellarie to visit the town and get the yearly weather forecast from the Elder. This year, he had called for snow and lots of it from late autumn to early spring. She had to wonder what he would think when the woman he fondly called 'the Little Squirrel' would not visit him this spring or ever again.

"Are you sick of staring at snowflakes yet? I know I am," Merion whispered in a bored tone from amid her hay pile.

"We had best get used to staring at snowflakes." Ellarie answered her sister from where she stood at the window. "The Elder of Tabelan said we would be seeing more than usual."

She shrugged at that and ran a hand through her red tangle of hair. "Perhaps, but he's been wrong before. I remember hearing an old tale that said the dwarves once believed that their god Aren controlled the weather. If that were true, then he is a fickle deity, prone to changing things seemingly at a whim. I take no faith in the predictions of the weather, no matter if it's an aged farmer or a learned scholar making them."

It was a welcome change in their mundane existence just to talk about something other than despair and death. Even if Merion was dour and gloomy about it, which given their circumstances, Ellarie could hardly blame her for.

"Have you been talking down the line yet this morning?" Merion asked, referring to the act of whispering to the inmates visible to the left and right of the cell opposite of the speaker. It had become their only method of communicating with the others.

"Lazlo is still sleeping and Billie has taken to trying to stare me to death," Ellarie replied with a roll of her eyes. The naivety of the substitute for the late Nia was beginning to grate on both sisters. It was clear that Corporal Cornwall was just happy to be rid of the former washerwoman and bedslave, but Billie was having none of it. Her mind was consumed with delusions of love that she believed Cornwall had for her and nothing said to the contrary had made a bit of difference.

Etcher, situated across from Billie, had risked having the guards swoop down on them in his effort to try and snap some sense into her just two days prior. The woman had taken to fits of rocking back and forth and mumbling about the corporal and how he was going to save her. "He's not coming back, girl," Etcher had told her firmly in his deep, soothing voice when he had grown tired of the redundant display.

"Yes he is, he loves me, he told me he does and he's going to come get me. You shut your filthy thieving mouth and don't talk to me. You'll get me in trouble when he comes back."

Wholly unmoved, Etcher kept talking, "If he loves you, why are you in Biddenhurst at all? Wouldn't he do everything he could in his power to ensure that the one he loves most does not rot away in a place like this?"

"Because I ran away from my father's care when I was thirteen and I stole things and sold myself to stay fed," she had confessed quite readily. "I broke the laws made by Ios himself and this is where people who break the laws of gods deserve to be. Corporal Cornwall helped me realise that and you know what? Even though I'm a filthy, worthless criminal, he loves me anyway."

"What do *you* think you deserve?" Etcher asked her calmly.

"I'm a criminal, this is where I belong." Billie's answer came with a measure of disbelief. "I am just glad that Lance showed me mercy, took me into his care and convinced them not to execute me."

"That's not what I asked, Billie. What do you think you deserve for the crime of survival?" Etcher had persisted, his voice growing just slightly louder.

"Corporal Cornwall told me-" she had begun to answer before Etcher cut her off.

"I know what Cornwall told you, but I want to know what *you* believe you deserve."

The look she had returned him was one of utter bafflement. "I am only a stupid woman, it doesn't matter what I think."

That was all Merion could take of the conversation and she had jumped in at that point, quite loudly and angrily. "Who told you that?"

Billie had turned to face the wall separating her and Merion and talked directly to it. "It is written in the *God's Gift* that women are stupid creatures made only to serve men. We are not smart like them."

"Have you ever read the *God's Gift*?" Etcher asked quickly, before Merion could get in another angry retort.

"No, because women aren't supposed to read, that's for men to do," she had dutifully answered just as quickly.

Then it was Ellarie's turn. "Every woman sharing this room with you can read, child."

"Well, you're not supposed to," an exasperated Billie exclaimed far louder than she should have. "We're not supposed to worry about things like that. We don't have the minds for it." The poor thing had begun to grow more irate by the minute. "We're meant to be good wives to our husbands and do as we are told. I ruined myself, but Lance helped me find my way back to Ios and now I can be a good wife to Lance and make him happy. So, even though I have to stay in Biddenhurst for the rest of my life, I have a chance to repent for my crimes and make things right with Ios. I love Corporal Lance Cornwall. He saved me from eternal damnation, and with his help, I'll be with Ios above when I die and Lance and I will be together forever."

"She is indeed ruined," Merion added frustratingly. "That fucking Cornwall has completely destroyed her mind."

"I heard that," Billie spoke up again. "I'm going to tell Lance what you said when he comes to get me out of here."

"Be my guest," the redhead shot back.

"Stop talking to me, all of you. I'm not supposed to talk to Thieves, you're the worst people of all and I'm a good person now. I'm not like you anymore and I can't be seen by Ios to be talking to you." Billie said, bordering on shouting.

"Etcher, no more, we don't need attention," Ellarie ordered loud enough for him to hear from the cell beside her.

They had left her alone from then onward. Ellarie felt a pang of pity for the poor thing, watching her grow more despondent and unhinged by the day. The concern now was that Billie would try to explain who she was and ask for Cornwall. The guards would never believe her and if they did, they protected their own. Billie would be severely punished for such an accusation and it was very likely that the rest would not be spared either.

All while Ellarie had been thinking back to the encounter, her sister had been engaging with Etcher, who in turn was talking up the line to the others.

"Jorgia's back is aggravating her again," Merion reported back finally. "Do you think Grose will let you change her bandages?"

"That decision is not Grose's to make. We've been denied by Lieutenant Crispin himself," Ellarie let her tone fall flat at that. The thought of getting to see Jorgia, Lazlo and Joyce every day had been a small joy and even that miniscule thing had been taken from her.

"You believe him too easily," Merion scoffed.

"What does it matter if I believe him, Merion?" Ellarie groaned. "Even if he's lying through his teeth, I'm locked in this cage and there's not one thing I can do no matter who made that decision."

Merion wasn't backing down. "How did you convince Grose to help at all in the first place?"

"That was different. They were visibly suffering and near death. As far as Grose or anyone else is concerned they're going to live now," Ellarie answered dejectedly.

There was a sigh from Merion at that and she turned away from her sister and went back to her conversation with Etcher.

With little else to do, Ellarie decided to return to her little window, losing herself in her thoughts while watching the falling flakes. *Joyce, Merion and Lazlo are all lieutenants themselves, yet it's me they turn to as a leader. How can I be responsible for them when I'm locked up in here? In the field I could issue commands and I had people to answer them. I had control. In here I can do nothing for anyone and there's no one that can follow my instructions.*

"Bernadine, it's feeding time," Merion called, to draw her back.

"Who is serving?" Ellarie asked while sauntering back to the bars of the cell.

"Icicle for certain and two more with him, one of which seems to be Straw Beard, but the last voice is unfamiliar to me." There were no doubting Merion's abilities and once again she was proven correct when the guards came into sight.

Straw Beard came first, pushing that noisy little wagon that was used to carry the food. As he had been known to do, he went to the back of the room first to start dispensing the bit of bread and water the guards laughably called food.

After him came a broad shouldered fellow in a long, thick coat and leather gloves, sauntering in between the cells with Icicle at his side. His face was weather beaten, with high cheeks and a nose permanently shaded a deep pink. Coal black hair and shoulders were shimmering with the recently melted snow upon them. His gaze was to Ellarie for but a second before he became struck with Merion. "I was told that you didn't have Orangecloak," he stated in a voice tinged with an accent that marked him from Farmourd.

"We don't, you're looking at the Red Bitch, Royen," Icicle replied frigidly.

Royen ran a gloved hand across his jaw as he looked over Ellarie's sister. "Why don't you just stick a cloak on this one and say she is Orangecloak? It would have fooled me," he chided.

Icicle didn't share the jest and his tone remained at its apathetic natural state. "That would become a problem when Atrebell produces the real Orangecloak that they're keeping in their dungeons." He thrust a finger in Ellarie's direction and changed the subject. "This one here is just a footpad. You'll never get that redheaded one, but this one is eligible."

That statement and the judging eyes upon Ellarie made her suddenly feel very nervous.

"I like this one. She could pass for the Queen Bitch up at the front," the strange guard intoned with a quick lick of his lips.

"When will the Matron be gracing our presence, ser?" Straw Beard jumped in as he returned from delivering bread and water to Joyce, Donnis and Lazlo.

"She'll be here in the afternoon. That fat lump Taves calls a nephew is escorting her," stated Royen before looking in the direction Straw Beard came from. "Who is down that way?"

"Oh, down there? No one you need worry about, ser, just a male foot soldier, the Pretty Man and the Big Bitch," Straw Beard said with an almost cheerful shrug.

"I'll see these rebel lieutenants for myself," Royen declared, strolling away and leaving the others behind. "Walk with me, Corporal Berrit, you can handle the introductions."

The presence of Royen and Icicle was briefly removed and Straw Beard moved in to issue Ellarie and Merion's meagre rations of food. "Eat up, ladies," the ale-bellied sot with the thin wisps of facial hair suggested. "You've got a big day ahead."

As curious as Ellarie was to decipher what Straw Beard was referring to, her attention was focused down the corridor to Lazlo's cell and the two guards peering in at him.

"So, you're the one they call the 'Pretty Man'," Royen mocked. "I had heard stories that you were a fierce swordsman, but all I see is a scrawny little fruit."

From where he sat, Lazlo gazed upward lazily. "Let me out of here, put a sword in my hand and we'll see if you still have the courage to say that, guardsman."

I told you to shut your damn mouth, Lazlo, Ellarie angrily thought to herself.

"Perhaps I will for some entertainment," Royen answered, amused by Lazlo's spirit. "When spring returns and the fighting square has opened, I might like to match steel with such a notorious figure. Nothing would give me such great pleasure as to disembowel a faerie like you. Tell me, boy, how many men of Captain Hoyt's did you kill before you were captured?"

"Not enough," Lazlo answered sharply.

The room went deathly silent, the air sucked from it all at once. A lump began to form in Ellarie's throat and she dared not look in Lazlo's direction.

It started with a snort and soon Royen roared in a deep laugh from the pit of his stomach. "I like that answer. You've got a brass set of balls for a faggot, I'll give you that." His tone went grave again. "I'll almost feel bad for you when the rope tightens on your neck."

"I'd rather die in that fighting square, if it's all the same to you," Lazlo put back to him. "I would get a good death and you would get the honour of saying you slew a lieutenant of Lady Orangecloak. Imagine the fame and recognition they'd bestow on you for that. I think the heralds would sing your name every time you entered a room: Royen, slayer of Lazlo Arbor. I think that has a good ring to it."

"It does, but the lists in the fighting square are not my jurisdiction. However, since you can't go petition on your own behalf, I shall take up your cause. Consider it a token of respect from one swordsman to another. I hope for both our sakes I can get you that honourable death." Royen turned his attention from Lazlo to Icicle. "Who else is back here?"

Icicle curled his nose in disgust as he answered, "Just the Big Bitch and one of the Pretty Man's flunkies there."

Royen ignored Donnis entirely and looked in on Joyce. "Well I'll be fucked!" he boomed. "I guess a name is not everything is it? She's not so big at all, comely too, if I do say so."

"Joyce is more than comely," Ellarie heard Merion whisper to herself, clinging tightly to the bars. "She's beautiful. She's *my* beauty and I want her back."

It was Icicle who explained the name. "She's the tallest of the Three Bitches and unassumingly strong. She's not that big next to a man, true, though it was reported that this one killed four in the skirmish in Argesse."

"Four is it? That's impressive, especially so for a woman," there was a rise in Royen's voice as he said as much, before sucking his teeth regretfully. "If you were a man, it might have been more. Perhaps you'd all not be here. It's a shame, but you womenfolk have to learn that you're not meant to be fighters and soldiers. Even when you try, you might get a few kills, but you'll always lose. You lost in Argesse, your fearless leader lost in Atrebell and Mell the Huntress will lose if she shoves her ugly face north of the Varras River."

Ellarie couldn't discern what was being said specifically when Joyce replied, though her tone was deathly serious. Yet, despite her serious nature, Royen found what Joyce was saying to be quite amusing. "So says I, yes and so says all of history going back to when the three gods made the world and then fought over it," he told her. "Who won that war? Not the dwarf god Aren and not the goddess Iia, but Ios himself. He rules above the world and men rule in his name below. That is a lesson you will learn at the cost of your life."

"If that is all, ser," began Icicle, cutting in before Joyce could say anything in response. "We have much work to do before the Matron arrives and we really should be getting to it."

"You have a *great* deal of work to do," Royen guffawed as he began walking back towards the exit, giving Ellarie a last glance as he did. "This place and the people in it smell abominable. Everything will have to be cleaned for the Matron's tender, womanly sensitivities if you don't want her giving a poor report to Lord Taves."

Icicle readily agreed, albeit with a pronounced apprehension in his voice. "Of course, ser. Leave it to us, we will not disappoint."

The sound of the outside door of the cellblock slamming shut was still bouncing off the walls when Merion pressed her face to the bars and whispered to Ellarie, "Execution day is upon us."

Ellarie was unsure. "Were the others clean when ushered onto the scaffolds?"

Her sister took a moment to remember. "I suppose not, but we're considered to be of more value than they were. I would think that Lord Taves would want us to look our best when we die. Think about it this way: no one looks twice when someone stomps a sewer rat to death – we saw it all the time in the cities. Now, recall how badly the townsfolk in Layn reacted that one time when a guard shot a friendly hound dog for stealing a sandwich from his lunch pail."

There was still too much doubt for Ellarie. "You raise a point, but Icicle said that whatever the Matron is coming here for that you, Joyce, Ellarie and the men are not eligible. We're missing something here, Merion."

"Perhaps they're starting from the bottom," Merion suggested despondently. "Hang a few pretty ones first, to make the rest of the Thieves take notice."

Something dawned on Ellarie then. "The rest of the Thieves..." she repeated. "Merion...When the guard was talking to Joyce, he said that the EMP would defeat Mell the Huntress should she come north of the Varras."

"He did and it's very likely she might," admitted Merion, missing what Ellarie was thinking. "You know as well as I that Mell is very reactionary. Once she hears what befell us, there's little doubt that she will marshal what's left of our ranks and march. What of it?"

"When we left, Edwin the Raven was castellan. He's always the castellan when we and Orangecloak leave Rillis Vale all at once," Ellarie pointed out.

Merion's answers were almost lazy in their delivery. "Edwin's a pushover and Mell does as she pleases, it's not exactly a great secret."

"The way he said it though, it was as if he knew that Mell was Field Commander now," Ellarie pointed out. "There was not even a mention of Edwin."

Her sister shrugged, unconcernedly. "Have the EMP ever considered Edwin? I would be surprised if they even knew he existed. Mell is loud and boisterous and she carries her banner proudly into battle with the raiding gangs. I would say as far as the government is concerned, if Orangecloak, Lazlo and the Three Sisters are all gone, then the only visible member of the Thieves that's left is Mell."

"And Old Bansam," Ellarie added.

"Bansam is an *associate* of the Thieves, there's a difference," Merion corrected her. "That's not even taking his age into account. They're not going to pay much consideration to him. To what difference this all makes to us now."

"Probably none, I suppose," Ellarie agreed, before raising a further point. "The Thieves were founded by the EMP, Merion. It's not impossible to think that despite Marros' rebellion and Orangecloak's continued animosity towards the EMP that someone else in the fold could be swayed towards corruption."

"Not impossible, highly unlikely though. Orangecloak never demanded loyalty, but she had a way about her of earning it quite easily." There was a sombreness seeping into Merion's voice just then. "We loved her. We all did."

Ellarie was quick with an answer for that: "Except Mell."

"They fought quite a bit," Merion admitted. "But Mell respected Orangecloak."

"Respect and loyalty are not the same," Ellarie argued. "That guard Royen just said he respected Lazlo right after he called him a fruit and a faggot. Royen's respect for Lazlo is not going to save him from the gallows and it won't stay Royen's blade if they meet in the fighting square.

"Mell can have all the respect in the world for Orangecloak and I'm sure she does. However, loyalty is what Orangecloak needed from her and Mell would never give her any measure of that."

Merion stopped to consider that for a moment before responding, "Orangecloak never stood in the way of Mell's desire though. She never advocated for it, but she recognised that Mell's efforts aided in keeping the raiding gangs from getting too close to Phaleayna."

"And yet Mell wanted more," Ellarie returned with fervour. "She sought for the Thieves to focus all of their efforts on battling the raiding gangs. It was Orangecloak who refused to issue any such command and only allowed Mell to seek out willing volunteers to fight for her own gang."

The doors leading to the guard room swung open loudly and a number of men could be heard shuffling into the room. Ellarie and Merion stopped talking immediately and stepped back into the middle of their cells. A single voice that Ellarie knew to belong to that of Lieutenant Crispin was issuing the guards commands at the front of the room. His attention, though, soon turned to the prisoners.

"Alright, maggots, I want to see every one of you on your feet!" he bellowed down the corridor. "You're each going to get a cube of soap, a rag and a bucket of water that will be left outside your cell. When you are given these items, you will remove your shift and the wraps on your feet and pass them through the bars."

The sound of the other Thieves scrabbling to their feet filled the air and behind it came the first wooden bucket thudding and sloshing down. Lieutenant Crispin's voice drew closer as he continued on over the racket his men were making, "You will have ten minutes to clean yourselves. During this time, we will be flooding the chutes beneath your cells to flush out the latrines. When we are done, you will be given material to dry yourselves with and new, clean shifts. Anyone who refuses to wash will be forcibly held down and scrubbed clean against their will. We will not tolerate filth on the day that the Matron is scheduled to come through here."

Ellarie noticed a snide smirk on Crispin's face as he marched on by in a fresh uniform, hands clasped behind his back. The other guards continued laying out buckets, rags and tiny chunks of soap that looked as though they had been hacked with a particularly blunt butter knife. When at last they finished, Crispin had come back and was standing between Etcher and Billie's cells, eying the washerwoman mischievously.

"Inmates, disrobe!" he commanded.

On cue, Ellarie had pulled the rutty thing that had passed for clothing over her head and hastily unravelled the browned strips of cloth that had bound her feet. The thought of bathing, for whatever reason and even with a ratty cloth and a jagged piece of soap was too tempting for her to care.

Let them gawk if they want, Ellarie thought as she dipped the rag and soap in the bucket of lukewarm water. *If my options are to expose my naked form to them or have them enter this cage and expose it themselves, I'll take the former every time.*

It was then she noticed Merion, still clothed and unmoving. Daring not to speak with Lieutenant Crispin so near, Ellarie shot her sister a firm stare and motioned for her to remove her shift. Merion stood her ground and steadfastly refused, much to Ellarie's frustration.

Crispin began to lose interest in Billie and turned in the direction of the sisters and Ellarie felt a lump form in her throat. She stood up quickly and locked her gaze on Crispin, running the soapy rag about her breasts and torso in a way that might distract him. When she saw a grin cross his face at the sight of her, Ellarie knew she had bought some time. The diversion was not certain to grant much of that and Ellarie shot Merion the briefest of glances to try and convey that immediate concern.

Merion held out for another moment or two, before finally realising that Ellarie's sultry display was for her benefit. With a disgruntled face, Merion disrobed reluctantly, stuffing her shift and footwraps between the bars and taking her toiletries to hand.

Ellarie was relieved that her sister had finally given in, yet the fact that Crispin had yet to move on was giving her concern for herself. Against better judgement she decided to engage him. "Do you like what you see, ser?" she asked lowly.

"Why yes, I certainly do," he answered playfully. "It grieves me to no end that I'm going to have to send such a pretty thing to the gallows." As if he suddenly realised how much attention was being paid to Ellarie alone and how odd it may seem, he turned and left her, glancing back over his shoulder briefly. "Life is unfair like that," he told her. "We never get what we want."

A wave of relief came over Ellarie when he had moved on and she looked scornfully at Merion, who was hunched over with her back to the bars. Crispin had paid her little mind for now, but Ellarie didn't think Lazlo, Donnis and Joyce would keep him for long.

By the time Crispin began his return walk to the front of the cellblock, Ellarie was knelt over trying to wash her feet. The floor was cold to the touch and she was hoping she could hold her balance on one foot to keep from having her bottom touch the cool stone.

"On your feet, inmate," she heard Lieutenant Crispin order and obediently she stood, almost slipping clumsily in the process.

To her surprise, Ellarie saw that the command was directed at Merion, who was still hunched over, washing herself timidly.

"I'll not say this a third time: on your feet, inmate!" he declared quite loudly.

Stand up, you fool, Ellarie thought as she anxiously watched. Ever so slowly, Merion uncurled herself and stood straight, albeit still facing away from everyone.

"Turn around, inmate," he demanded in a deep, sly voice.

Merion held again and Ellarie could see her breathing quite anxiously.

Crispin raised his voice louder once more. "Inmate, I have ordered you to turn around! Obey or there will be consequences."

Again Merion responded, albeit slowly and using her arms and the rag to cover her breasts and womanhood.

"Lower your hands, inmate," Crispin's patience was at an end as he said as much. "I will only say that once."

Trembles rippled across Merion's skinny frame. With a deep breath and a look of pure malice, she summoned the willpower to remove her hands from her private parts and stood motionless before the Lieutenant.

"Was that so hard, inmate?" Lieutenant Crispin asked rhetorically in a voice that he might have thought to be soothing. "You have a lovely body, my dear."

Ellarie watched her sister's eyes look anywhere but upon the lieutenant as he kept staring at her naked form.

With a click of his teeth, Crispin moved on. "Some days I really hate my job, but every now and then Lord Taves throws me a bone like this and it's not so bad for a time," he added almost cheerfully before departing from sight.

Their time with the water and soap came to an end and soon the buckets and rags were taken away. In their place, they were left with threadbare lengths of old cloth rags to dry off with and shortly after new shifts were doled out. The lieutenant women and the men were given the crimson, just as they had in Atrebell, with the same numbers painted upon the sleeves. As for Ellarie and the other women of no rank, they were garbed in white with their numbers painted in a bright red upon a single shoulder.

Prisoners from elsewhere in the city with fettered feet were led in and given mops and brooms to clean the corridor floor. They were all middle aged and had likely been behind the walls of Biddenhurst for some time. None dared to raise their head or even glance at the Thieves in their cells and were soon gone once their task was complete.

Lastly there arrived a grey haired man in a white smock with a bag beneath his arm. To either side of him were an escort comprised of the guard Merion called Greenboy and Private Grose and the three walked immediately to Lazlo's cell, ignoring everyone else entirely.

Ellarie could hear the old man explain in an authoritative voice to Lazlo that he was a doctor and was there to inspect his wounds and dress them if need be. Although Ellarie couldn't hear Lazlo's words, she suspected that by the tone he was taking that he was resisting.

The doctor turned to Private Grose on his left. "The patient is refusing treatment and is hostile and dangerous. For reasons of safety, both my own and his, I have to refrain from treating him. I can determine that he seems healthy and he is not showing any signs of lingering illness from infection. I will counsel that whoever was tending to the wounds previously to continue to do so regularly. However, I will not be setting foot in that cell, Private."

"Very well, Doctor," Grose affirmed. "The inmate named Bernadine Voyer has been doing an admirable job of taking care of the wounded. If you could put your counsel and an order for supplies in writing for Lieutenant Crispin, I'd be most appreciative."

"That I can do and if that will be all, I shall be returning to my clinic," the doctor agreed as he began walking back up the corridor without as much as a glance toward anyone else. "I'll have my assistant run that note over to you before sundown."

Grose gave Ellarie a passing glimpse as he followed the doctor out and soon the room was quiet once more.

"It looks like your job is safe, Bernadine," Merion commented sarcastically.

Ellarie shook her head. "No, Lazlo, Jorgia and Joyce are safe."

Her sister gave a puzzled look. "What do you mean?"

"You heard every word of what was said when I talked Grose into letting me help them," Ellarie said to jog her memory. "Don't you remember what he said of the doctor?"

"He mentioned it would be in our interest to not have him

about." Merion seemed not to be paying much mind to it as she leaned on the bars. "He never said why."

"I don't know that I want to know why." Ellarie shuddered. "That doctor seemed disinterested with Lazlo and didn't even check on the others. Still, the look Grose gave me made me think that we dodged an arrow."

There was a groan from Merion at that. "And hopefully that will be the end of it. He's gone, let's worry about what's to come."

"I suppose that might be best," Ellarie said as a measure of reassurance. "If Orangecloak were here, she would probably be telling me to stop worrying so much anyhow."

Merion seemed to find that amusing. "That's because she already worried enough for everyone as it was."

In spite of herself, Ellarie had to crack a tiny smile at that and let their conversation end.

She retreated to the little window yet again. The snow was still falling, though it was now reduced to a mere tumbling of large flakes here and there.

A guard that Merion had named Slink came and went twice afterwards and Ellarie surmised an hour had gone by. Outside there was scarcely any movement and within the walls there seemed to be even less.

Merion had taken to her hay pile and was staring blankly at the ceiling, her hands propped behind her head and hair tucked into the hood of her shift.

Now and again Ellarie would take a break from the window and stretch her limbs, but with little else to occupy her, she always returned to leaning on the sill.

The wind had dissipated to a gentle breeze and the falling flakes danced upon it with a casual grace. Ellarie put her focus on a single one and watched it roll and rise on the gusts, staving off its descent to the ground with every fluttering of an updraft.

To her left two shapes suddenly came into view and Ellarie craned her face as much as she could to see them. They were a plump man in a guard's uniform and a tall, slender woman wearing a fine fuchsia cloak with a trim of white fur around the hood and shoulders. They strode past quickly, the woman hiding her face beneath a hood she held in place with a gloved hand.

That must be the Matron, it dawned on Ellarie. *It was said that she would be arriving with a fat nephew of Lord Taves. That must be them now.*

She broke away from the window, went to the bars of the cell and pressed her face between them. "Merion, the Matron is coming. I just saw her pass before my window," her heart began to race in her chest as she whispered frantically.

Her sister answered without moving from where she lay, "What would you have me do? Stand up and run around in circles?"

The lackadaisical answer frustrated Ellarie, yet she didn't know what else she expected from Merion. "You should at least get up."

"You heard the guards, whatever is going on today, I'm not eligible for," she replied lazily. "It really doesn't matter what I do."

Ellarie moaned aloud at that. "Yes, well *I am* eligible if you haven't forgotten. For my sake could you at least act concerned?"

"Calm down," Merion sighed unconcernedly. "You know as well as I do that any minute now the guards are going to burst in here and order all of us to stand up anyhow."

No more than five minutes later the doors swung open and what sounded like a herd of guards came stomping in.

"Inmates, on your feet!" Lieutenant Crispin ordered in the most commanding voice he could evidently muster. "Come on now, all of you! Rise for the Matron at once or I will be quick to authorise floggings again!"

With all the energy of a lethargic snail, Merion clambered to her feet and brushed the hay from her shift, rolling her eyes all the while. "This should be interesting," she commented dryly to Ellarie.

"How many have you flogged as it is?" Ellarie heard a woman's voice that could only be the Matron's ask at the front of the room. She sounded confident and strong, yet Ellarie discerned a gentle lilt to her tones as well.

There was a moment's hesitation before Crispin replied, "Just three, madam and the deeds were done without my consent. I quickly corrected the issue, though and saw to it that the wounds of the recipients were well tended to."

"You say *just three* like it's a trivial thing to lash at someone's back repeatedly with a leather whip," the Matron said disapprovingly. "That will be the last of the flogging, Lieutenant and I'll keep what you have already done between you and I. Lest Lord Taves catch wind that his prized prisoners have been harmed."

"Yes, Madam, as you say," he relented almost immediately. "Inmates, the Matron will be speaking to you all individually. You will answer her truthfully and be on your absolute best behaviour. She is here to take one of you into her service and if you are selected, you will do so without resistance or there will be consequences. Am I understood?" He took the silence as affirmation and after a beat spoke up again. "Excellent. Madam, you may begin at your leisure."

"Thank you, Lieutenant," the Matron said, taking over from there. "Do remain near in the event I have further questions for you."

From there she began with Bernadine, asking the woman posing as Ellarie her name, age and what her role within the Thieves had been. Although Ellarie couldn't hear any responses, they seemed to be to the Matron's satisfaction and she moved on without further inquiry. After going through Allia, Coramae and Jorgia in the same fashion, the Matron was just forward of the space between Ellarie and Merion's cells. From what Ellarie could see of Billie, she seemed to be acting quite skittish in the presence of the Matron, who in turn skipped Etcher entirely for the odd woman. "What is your name, miss?" she asked in a suspicious tone.

"My name? It's uh, Nia." Billie hesitated for a second while she tried to recall the correct surname. "It's Nia Hedgeworth."

The Matron was not so easily swayed and she stepped in closer. "You don't seem so sure of that. Where are you from, Nia? How old are you? What was your position with the Thieves? Who did you serve under?"

The scraggly looking woman cleared her throat and tried once more to pass off her ruse. "I ah, um, that's...I'm Nia Hedgeworth, I'm twenty four years old, I'm from Phaleayna and I was a robber."

Not even close, Ellarie noted, pinching the bridge of her nose in disgust. *And not even the least bit convincing.*

However, the Matron seemed to have no further questions and abruptly put her back to Billie and moved on.

Ellarie got her first good look at the women at that. At best guess Ellarie placed the woman at about fifty years of age, with a lithe body that was almost elven in dimension. Her hair was light brown, but as the light from the windows fell upon her, it took on a reddish hue as it fell beyond her shoulders in elegant waves. With only a quick look, one might have mistaken her for a woman of high birth. Though, the more Ellarie looked at her, the more she sensed something off about the Matron. Beneath her cloak she wore a velvet dress of pure blue that was made for a wider woman and fell just slightly baggy across her small bust and hips. The skirt was frayed at the bottom and bore distinctive stitching around the area of the right knee from having been torn and repaired.

As the woman neared, Ellarie readied herself for questioning, running through potential answers in her mind one last time. Before the woman could say a word she caught sight of Merion across the corridor and did a double take, leaving Ellarie behind for the moment.

"You there, what's your name?" the Matron asked with a gasp.

Merion glanced past the Matron at Ellarie warily, before answering in a befuddled tone, "I'm Merion Dollen, one of Orangecloak's lieutenants."

"My apologies, for a moment there I thought you were someone else," the Matron realised, her voice dropping back to where it had been. "No, now that I get a good look at your face, I know I was mistaken. My apologies once more, I never meant to startle you."

The eyes of Merion looked all about the strange woman with an eyebrow raised querulously. "Apology accepted, ma'am," she mumbled.

Wordlessly, the Matron left her and turned to Ellarie. "It seems you're the last one for me to talk to. I'm told there are two more men and a lady lieutenant further down and I'm looking for an unranked woman, so, this ends with you. Now tell me, lass, what is your name?"

"My name is Bernadine Voyer," Ellarie answered, trying her best to look timid.

"That is a lovely name. Where are you from and when were you born, Bernadine?" she asked next, giving her a thorough visual assessment all the while.

"I'm originally from a little place called Wyford down in the Southlands." She grew more confident in her answers now, having recited them for so long for just such an occasion. "It's gone now, having been overrun by the Sons of Valdarrow. My family and I relocated to Layn when I was young. I was born on the seventh of autumn in the year fifteen thousand and seventy nine by elven reckoning."

The Matron gave her a squint at that. "Are you telling me that you're only twenty one years old?"

"Yes, that's right," Ellarie replied courteously.

"I would have taken you for a little older, perhaps closer to twenty five or so. Has anyone ever told you that you bear resemblance to Ellarie Dollen?"

She nodded. "Yes, we've been mistaken for one another before. We've been told we look more like sisters than she and Merion do."

"There is no doubt about that..." the Matron said ponderously. "Tell me, Bernadine, when you were in the Thieves, what was your primary duty?"

This Ellarie knew without question. "I was a scout mostly, though I had other assignments as well. None within the Thieves were usually assigned to just one task, ma'am. We could be given any number of jobs."

"So you've got a little bit of experience at everything then?" the Matron replied, evidently pleased with that answer.

"Yes, ma'am."

"Well and good." The Matron bowed. "Thank you for your time, Miss Voyer."

Ellarie fell silent as she watched her stride back to the front of the room. Merion was eying her sister cautiously but Ellarie dared not to speak with so many guards present.

From somewhere by the main entrance, she could hear Crispin and the Matron talking, though their voices were so low it was hard to make anything out. After a time, she broke off from him and the sound of her boots tapping the floor in slow steps filled the air. There were other boots making a ruckus too, and someone left the cellblock, slamming the door behind them hard.

Things settled again to a point where Ellarie could hear the Matron talking to some of the other girls near the real Bernadine, asking more questions of them. Yet again she skipped on by Etcher and Billie and paid Merion another curious glance, finding herself before Ellarie once more. "I've made my choice," she declared loud enough for all to hear.

"And who would that be madam?" asked Icicle, walking into Ellarie's view from where he had been at the front of the cells. His arm was bent at the elbow with shackles and chains draped across a forearm, ending in a fist clenching a ring of keys.

Her smiling face fell on Ellarie. "I'll take Bernadine Voyer."

At once Ellarie felt her stomach flutter as the guard wheeled about and went to the door of her cell.

"Go to the back of your cell, place your hands behind your head, spread your feet and press your face to the wall," Icicle commanded sharply while sticking a key in the lock.

"Take me where?" Ellarie panicked, freezing in place. "Are you going to execute me?"

"Why of course not, Miss Voyer," replied the Matron softly. "I'm taking you into my service at the request of Lord Taves himself. I am going to be moving you to a much nicer place than this and you will be answering directly to me from now on."

"You can't take me, ma'am. I have a job to do here," Ellarie put back quickly as Icicle beckoned to another guard out of sight for assistance.

The Matron was beside Icicle then, with a hand on his shoulder. "Guard, hold on a moment," she insisted as she turned to Ellarie. "What job do you have here?"

"It is my job to tend to the wounds of Lazlo, Joyce and Jorgia who were badly whipped," Ellarie explained as her heart raced in her chest. "The dressings on their backs will need regular changing. I was trained in that when I was with the Thieves. Please, let me stay, ma'am, they need me."

There was a pause while the Matron considered what Ellarie had told her. "I see...Who trained you to do this? Was this a doctor with proper medical certification from the University of Weicaster or perhaps from the University of the Gildriad Midlands?"

"I don't know, ma'am. The lieutenants were all trained by Doctor Ganzing who lives in Phaleayna. I have no idea where he was educated." She caught the slip she had made and ran with it before anyone could detect as much in her voice, "And I was in turn trained by Lieutenant Merion over there, ma'am."

"This Lieutenant Merion taught you how to treat wounds?" the Matron queried, her gaze going to the red haired woman she spoke of.

Ellarie realised that the Matron was picking up on her meaning and suddenly, she felt calmness come over her. "Yes, that's right, ma'am. Merion Dollen taught me everything I know."

She watched Merion's eyes grow wide from behind the bars as her sister grasped what Ellarie was attempting to do.

"Very well then, if Miss Dollen here taught you all you know, then she should have no trouble handling the task herself when you go to work for me," the Matron decided with a folding of her arms.

"Madam, I don't think that's possible," Icicle interrupted. "We've been ordered by Lieutenant Crispin to not take the Thieves officers from their cells for any reason."

"I am here under the authority of Lord Mackhol Taves, guardsman," the Matron declared boldly. "Furthermore, he would not be pleased if he found out about what you did to these prisoners and unless you would have me tell him, you will obey my order."

That seemed to be the extent with which Icicle was concerned. He shrugged at her and opened the door of Ellarie's cell. "You heard the woman, inmate. She's taking you with her. Go to the back wall."

This is the right thing to do, Ellarie reminded herself as she was bound hand and foot in similar heavy chains to what she had been wearing upon arrival to death row. *This is for Merion.* When Icicle was done with the task, Ellarie found they had been joined in the cell by Private Grose and the two led her out into the corridor. *This is for Joyce, Jorgia and Lazlo. In fact, this is for all of you.*

"Alright, Miss Voyer, we have to get some shoes on those feet and a warm cloak to wrap you in for the walk to your new lodgings. Let's move along," the Matron said while sticking her hand into the crook of Ellarie's elbow. "I've kept my guard waiting long enough."

"Wait," Merion spoke up as Ellarie was led away. The Matron stopped and looked over her shoulder to where Merion's cell lay. "Might I have a word?" Merion asked, reaching an arm through the bars towards Ellarie.

The Matron gently turned Ellarie about and nudged her towards the red haired woman.

"What in los' name are you doing, you sweet fool?" Merion whispered as she reached an arm through the bars, wrapped it about Ellarie's neck and drew her close.

"It's alright, Merion. I'm no good to anyone locked up in that cell," she whispered back. "I don't know where I'm going, but we have to take what comes our way, right? In the meantime, when I'm gone, you'll get to see Joyce."

There was a deep breath from Merion as she held her tight. "I love you. Wherever they take you, whatever happens, don't you ever forget that, do you hear me?"

"I won't." The two parted enough for Ellarie to look her sister in the eyes. "Not ever."

29

TRYST

Corporal Stefos Buchlan, ser, I was ordered to report to you," Tryst Reine said with a proper salute as he stood before Captain Wynne Nathers of the Illiastran Army's Flying Hawks Company.

"Is that so?" the surprisingly young captain answered apathetically, his attention on anything other than Tryst. "You have papers to prove that?"

"Aye, ser, I certainly do," Tryst replied, reaching into the inside pocket of the teal jacket of his standard issue, West Illiastra military uniform. Tryst had never worn a uniform like this before. The closest he had come was the silken vest and trousers that all students of the Combat University wore in training, but even that outfit wasn't required attire. The whole thing was stiff and binding and he would have traded it all for the soft, supple leathers that were left in Orangecloak's guest room at the manor of Greggard Simillon.

A gloved hand all but yanked the papers from Tryst's and looked over them with total disinterest. "From Nettles Cove I see. What did you do there?"

"I'm a farm hand, ser," Tryst answered quickly and dutifully.

Nathers chortled. "A farm hand? What the fuck is there to grow in Nettles Cove?"

Tryst deigned to return the laugh. "We can get a fine yield from potatoes in the warm months, but mostly we raise sheep, ser." He was, after all, supposed to be playing the part of a proud resident of the North Coast, he must bear the comment, not remark upon it.

"Yes, I suppose so," Nathers said over the sound of the ruffling papers. "Well then, that raises more questions, boy. Is there an explanation as to why a shepherd got drafted and sent straight to the Flying Hawks?"

Somehow, Tryst managed to feign nervousness as he answered the question. "There is, ser. You see, the truth is that I haven't been living in Nettles Cove all my life."

The Captain looked up at Tryst suddenly at that and studied his face. "No, I suppose you haven't." He paused for a second and in that second Tryst thought his ruse had been seen through. "My, that's a bright green set of eyes. The only way to get eyes like that is to have the blood of old Gildriad in you. Is that where you come from?"

"Aye, ser," Tryst said, his racing heart nearly betraying the still face he wore.

The soldier shrugged nonchalantly. "Still, I don't see why you're here with me. You got a story to tell me? Here, sit. I'll pour us a drink of rum. If you're going to serve under me, I'll want to know your story. Plus, it's something of an old tradition in the Hawks to have a drink and a chat with the captain upon joining. The reason for that was so the captain could better get to know the men and women he was to be working with."

Captain Nathers popped a cork from a flask that had been sitting just out of hand's reach on the table in the pavilion tent. "That captain now happens to be me. So sit, boy, tell me how a Gildraddi of some supposed fighting skill came to end up herding sheep in the bleak hole they call Nettles Cove."

It was a lie, one spun by Greggard that Tryst had to memorise, but it was flavoured with bits of truth. Greggard had insisted that the best lies were fabricated on such a premise.

The mother of the real Stefos Buchlan had the words 'Foreign Birth' listed for her birthplace in the census, meaning she was almost certainly an immigrant from outside Illiastra. From this minor detail Greggard concocted a story about a former female soldier from the Knightdom of Gildriad. The lie went that she was amongst the Knightdom's naval fleet when they rescued a fishing vessel under attack by a corsair ship. Stefos' father happened to be one of the rescued fishermen. They met, fell in love and Stefos was the product of that. They returned to Nettles Cove to raise him in his youth and in his teenage years his mother had taught him how to fight like the Knights of Gildriad. These skills learned in adolescence he had honed into his adult years.

With cup to hand and a boot propped on the table, the Captain listened attentively to the story, without comment, complaint or waning interest.

Tryst slammed down his empty glass. "Next thing I know, I have draft papers in my hands and no real reason to refuse them. My country has called on me and I have answered."

Nathers slid his own empty cup onto the table. "You're an honourable lad, Corporal Buchlan. I wish I had the time to see how seasoned your abilities are. Alas, you've been sent to me on too short of notice. You must have really impressed your recruiters though, no one has ever been sent to me straight from the rookie barracks."

That gave Tryst a brief pause and it took him a moment to think of something to say. "I shall try to do you proud, ser."

The chair beneath Nathers creaked as he set himself back to the floor and he clapped Tryst on the shoulder. "You showed up, that makes me proud enough."

Captain Nathers proceeded to prate on endlessly about all manner of things with Tryst feigning interest all the while. Every now and again, Tryst would spot other members of the Flying Hawks passing in front of the campfire outside the open tent flap. Two even took the time to look within and snigger. Evidently, it was a rite of passage to merely tolerate the loquacious captain.

"We have two women in the Flying Hawks now," he explained after a time. "They came with us from the east. Over there they were only associates, but once we threw in our lot with the west, they were legally allowed to join. You know, I've always been a supporter of women's rights, and those two out there can fight as well as any of the men here. Then there's that Lady Orangecloak." The mere mention of her name piqued Tryst's interest in what Nathers was saying. "I only wish I had the chance to have met her. From what I heard, she was a fine Field Commander for the Thieves and her women fought every bit as hard as her men. It's a damn shame that old bastard ended her life."

Tryst fed the Captain a lie, to see what he knew. "I heard she was shot dead on the street in Atrebell."

The captain looked at Tryst in surprise. "Not so, boy, she was captured alive in the streets by a bounty hunter, that one-eyed prick that used to be set up in Daol Bay. Wretched Miller or whatever his name is. No matter, he's gone too. Word is that the very thought of paying out all that gold for Lady Orangecloak sent that old Lord Howland into fits. Most likely he had that master swordsman of his slice the bounty hunter up like a ham. An earned fate for helping to take such a beautiful woman out of this world, I say. I'd have run him through myself." Nathers suddenly fell sombre and quiet. "She was too good for Illiastra. We didn't deserve her, we didn't support her." He looked away from Tryst briefly. "*I* should have supported her. Illiastra collectively failed that woman, her and her kin that they took in Argesse. That was the real reason I brought the Flying Hawks over to Lady Marigold. I made the mistake of not supporting the one woman in this country with balls. I'll make up for that by helping the next woman to have grown a set."

"If I might ask, ser, what did you hear happened to Lady Orangecloak?" Tryst asked with feigned worry, knowing exactly where she was. "The news takes so long to work its way to the north coast that I hadn't even heard of her capture until I got off the boat in Portsward."

Nathers was silent for a moment, save for a long deep breath. "What I heard, from close sources, was that they hung her in the dungeon underneath the Atrebell Manor. The ceilings are low so they couldn't drop her down and break her neck, so the pricks did it the slow way and drew out her suffering. Parliament was in session then too, so my money says that the sadistic piece of shit that runs Biddenhurst probably suggested they hang her that way."

A gloved hand rubbed the bearded jaw of Tryst in a worrisome fashion. "That is truly awful. Not even the mercy of a quick, clean death," he said, waiting a beat before pressing for more. "What do the people make of it? Surely the voices on the streets are talking."

"Man and woman alike mourn her, boy." The Captain was terribly melancholy as he spoke, "We encountered a mural someone painted on the side of a train as a tribute, on the east side of Forrenton. Apparently, similar sentiments are popping up all over the place now. On buildings and walls mostly, but wherever someone can draw her face or scribble her name she's turning up, sometimes the tribute is even as simple as a big splash of orange paint. It's not coming without a price, though. East of Obalen, it's punishable by death to do any of that now, as the poor, dead bastard we cut down from the lamppost beside the train had sadly learned."

A sudden push to his feet seemed to indicate that Captain Nathers was done with their conversation. "I've talked your ear off long enough for one night, boy. We've got a lot of work to do ourselves in the next few days and thinking about Lady Orangecloak won't make that any easier." His head went out through the flap of the tent. "Chesley, come here, boy."

From outside a wiry, blond haired lad in his teenage years appeared. "Yes, ser, did you call on me just now?"

"This is Corporal Stefos Buchlan, the newest member of the Flying Hawks. He'll need a tent set up." He turned to Tryst with a twist of his head. "You're the odd man out, I'm afraid. It does mean that you get your own tent, though, so that's an added bonus."

"That's fine, ser, thank you." Tryst bowed respectfully.

Captain Nathers turned back to the lad. "When you've got him situated, be sure to bring him around the camp and introduce him to everyone. You can tell him how we operate around here and answer any questions he might have. Until he dismisses you, you're under his charge tonight. Understood, Cadet Chesley?"

"Yes, ser, understood," the young man said with a courteous nod before turning to Tryst. "If you would follow me, Corporal."

The two set out after exchanging salutes from the Captain. The lad held the tent flap open for Tryst and as it fell, he could see Wynne Nathers pouring himself a second drink of rum.

Outside there was order and relative tranquillity. Those talking did so at respectable levels. There were patrols moving about on the perimeter and cadets shining boots, sharpening swords and greasing pistols in the light of the fire. It wasn't until they reached the caravan wagons that Chesley came to a stop. With a keen memory of where everything was, the cadet hauled out all the tools needed to set a tent and laid them in Tryst's arms. Atop the pile, he placed a dagger in a black leather sheath. "Everyone gets a company dagger, ser, and might I say, welcome aboard. Your best place to set is to the left of the others. If you set on the right side, you're likely to get smoke from the campfires. The wind isn't blowing the other way."

"Aye, I'll do that, thank you," Tryst said with a polite nod.

Before Tryst could say another word, the lad was gone without so much as a farewell. Tryst took the tent to the covered grove where the small encampment lay and went about finding a place to pitch. It had been quite some time since he had to make a tent, or the means to make one. In recent memory, Tryst could think on a few nights spent between Atrebell and the Hotel Dupoire when one might have been quite useful.

The tent was eventually set up in fairly short order and Tryst sorted through the items issued to him upon his acceptance into the West Illiastra Military. First and foremost was the cumbersome rifle, fitted with a bayonet on end of the barrel. Tryst plucked the slender blade from its holding and put it beside the plain, unadorned rapier and the considerably more ornate dagger he had just been gifted. There was no weapon Tryst loathed as much as the firearm, and if this one didn't have the bayonet, he would have no use for it at all.

A flimsy sword and what amounts to a cumbersome spear, that's what I'm armed with, Tryst thought to himself as he dug out oilcloth and whetstone to sharpen the three blades, such as they were. *No sight was as welcome tonight as this dagger.*

His crunching footsteps in stiff, leather boots brought Tryst back to the crackling fire and the small group seated around it. He espied an opening between a husky lad and a dusky woman and that was where he seated himself. "Good evening," Tryst said by way of greeting to all of them.

The lot went broke off their conversation and looked Tryst over judgingly while he got comfortable and started sharpening the rapier sword.

A balding fellow who looked like he had a dozen years on Tryst spoke up from the opposite end of the fire. "What's your name, boy?"

"I thought it was only the captain that called everyone boy?" Tryst answered jokingly.

The man didn't seem to be the jovial type and folded his arms before answering, "You're boy until we say otherwise. Now, what's your name?"

Tryst cleared his throat. "It's Corporal Stefos Buchlan."

"Piss on that," said the husky fellow beside Tryst with a gob of spit on the blaze, making Tryst suddenly that much more nervous. "Your outside rank isn't worth shit here. Again, what's your name?"

Tryst answered again, a little more forcefully, "My name is Stefos Buchlan, from Nettles Cove on the north coast."

The man with the receding hairline chortled at that. "Remind me to thank Wyvern tomorrow morning, Mink. It seems he has given the naming over to us."

"I'll put it on the agenda, Vole," answered a pale, skinny fellow with beady eyes all dressed in warm furs.

The one named Vole looked to the group. "So, lads, what do we name our new mate?"

It was the thick, muscled fellow with the shaggy beard occupying the space beside Tryst that spoke up first, "He's got bright, green eyes that have been hopping between each one of us since he sat down, so I say Hops ought to be his name. You know, short for grasshopper."

"No good, Yak. We had a Hops in living memory," Vole answered quickly while scratching his stubbly chin in contemplation. "Still alive, actually. Though, he's feeble now."

Another unidentified lad, near Tryst's age and seated between he and Yak jumped in. "I say Moth. First thing he did when he got left on his own was to get drawn to the fire."

Vole clicked his teeth at that. "Look at this fellow, he's not so plain as to have the name of a bug you'd squish under thumb, he needs something better than that. You've been awfully quiet, Vix, you have any ideas?"

The woman turned to Tryst to look him over in contemplation. She had the alluring eyes and skin tone to mark her to be most likely from the Crescent Isles, or her bloodline at the very least. A long, dark head of hair fell straight down her back and blended in with the black cloak she wore about her shoulders. "This one is a foreigner. Gildraddi, if I'm not mistaken, of the old blood. There's a mysterious aura about him and I can tell that this one is a born warrior." She turned her gaze to Vole. "He should have the name of a fierce, predatory animal."

"I've been in this company for nearly ten years and I've only ever been given the glorified word for a field mouse for my name," Vole complained. "This arsehole shows up one night and gets a good predator title? Bloody lovely, that is."

"You told me that you came to this crew as a scout, Vole," Yak countered lazily after a sip from a tall horn of ale. "And field mice are sneaky little things, like a good scout ought to be. So, I think it fits you. Besides, when has Vix ever been wrong when it comes to figuring others out? If she says that he gets a fierce name, then that's good enough for me."

Vole threw his arms up in surrender. "Alright then, I throw it out to the rest of ye, what do we call him?"

"How 'bout Cougar?" said the fellow that had suggested Moth moments before.

The man named Mink scoffed at that suggestion. "I don't think that'll work, Gull. It needs to roll off the tongue more and it's got too many noises in the word. Well, that's not right, what's the term I'm looking for, Vix?"

Vix looked at Mink. "You're referring to syllables. Aye, it does have too many, it's not a bad start though," she corrected him.

"I got it!" Yak exclaimed excitedly. "His name ought to be Lynx."

All eyes fell towards Vole, Tryst's included. The balding man took a deep breath as he looked into the flames and for a time said nothing. "I'll have to check the register book, but I don't think there's a Lynx in living memory." He slowly pushed himself to his feet and looked directly at Tryst and Tryst alone, staring hard into his eyes. "Barring some mistake in my memory, forcing me to declare otherwise, I hereby declare you to be named by my authority as a First Lieutenant. Furthermore, I decree you to be a member of the Flying Hawks Company. Welcome to the fold, Lynx."

A polite applause followed Lieutenant Vole's declaration and Tryst rose to bow, resting his right hand, clenched in a fist across his chest as he did so in response. "You honour me, ser and I thank you all for your generous welcome." Tryst spoke the words as he had seen done before by new guardsmen at the Atrebell Manor. When no one raised opposition to his manner, Tryst returned to his log seat.

As quickly as Tryst could take a seat, Yak turned the conversation to the wild game to be found in the area and he was practically forgotten. Despite that, Tryst was overcome with the strong sensation of being watched and followed the feeling to Captain Nather's tent. The flap was lifted back ever so slightly and Tryst could see the man they called Wyvern staring back sternly and suspiciously. He looked away when their eyes met and Tryst tried to think no more of it, watching the flap fall and come to a rest.

"I suppose you have questions," Vix said from Tryst's side. "I would, were I you. That must have been confusing to watch."

He shrugged casually. "You all named me Lynx. From listening to you all, I assumed you all take codenames in place of real names. I guess you do away with ranks as well."

"Very observant of you, Lynx. Shy do you think we do that?" she asked, likely to see how much more he could deduce on his own.

Tryst turned to the fire and thought about it for a second. "I gather the names are not chosen from a random pool, but contain an indication of rank in name alone. The others were trying to give me insect names first, which would to them mean I was perhaps low in skill, experience or something of that nature. Instead you vouched for something stronger, because you didn't base your judgement on your own position, like Vole did."

"This is true." She smiled, pleased with his answer. "You are a strong and fierce man, Lynx. There is a warrior within you and even if the others can't always see past their own place, I can."

"Of course you can," Tryst said jovially "Vix is short for Vixen. The Fox is a cunning predator that seems to persevere through everything thrown at it. You have a fitting name."

That got a soft laugh out of her. "Well yes, Vix is a good name to have, but I didn't always have it and it was not long ago that I was given it. Before the Flying Hawks picked their side in this conflict, women were not allowed to serve in the Illiastran Armed Forces. I and another woman now named Cloud were associates of the Hawks, but even that had to be kept in secret."

"And now you're fully fledged and pledged," Tryst kept the light-hearted tone going. "If you don't mind my asking, since the Flying Hawks couldn't take you, what stopped you from instead joining up with the Thieves?"

She raised her eyebrows at that. "That's a good question and the easy answer is that I wanted to make a difference. As noble as Lady Orangecloak's goals were, I never felt she was fully committed to fighting for them. She stayed the blade where her foes were only happy to use it. If I, as a young woman, wanted to fight for the Thieves, my only option was to join up with Half-Mad Mell's band and fight the raiding gangs. That seems to be a losing and unyielding struggle and serves no purpose beyond wanton bloodshed."

"I thought you said the Flying Hawks were a company under the Illiastran Military?" Tryst feigned, already knowing much of the group from his own time working for Grenjin Howland. "How do they serve the needs of a young woman?"

Vix looked at him from the corner of her eye while he

sharpened his sword in the light of the fire. "Had you heard of the Flying Hawks before you were dispatched to us?"

"I had not," Tryst lied.

"Then we have done our job well, I suppose." She nodded while watching the flickering flames. "I should tell you of what we do."

The Flying Hawks, she explained, were an order dating back three centuries. They had been instituted by the government and its army of the day to serve the interests of the nation, untethered by the whims or policies of a governing body. Although founded to be an armed overseer of government and army alike, their role evolved over the years to encompass other work suited to the skillset of its members. Soon, the Flying Hawks were involved in spying on other nations and secretly intervening in foreign conflicts by aiding the side who best supported the interests of Illiastra. They gained power and influence in the underbelly of governance and the Flying Hawks proved that even they were no exception to the corruption of absolute power. Before long, they were wading into the waters of national conflict as well. Assassination, fraud, graft, or embezzlement – there seemed to be no limit to what the Flying Hawks would do to maintain their position. With seemingly untouchable laws on their side that prevented outside measures from touching them, it took a hierarchical collapse from within to end that chapter of the Flying Hawks' history.

In the past century, the Hawks had attempted to return to the roots of the organisation and at times seemed to be on the road to that goal. However, for every step forward, it had seemed like the EMP were forcing them to take one or two backwards. With the support of the majority, Captain Nathers made the bold move to slowly and quietly sever the Flying Hawks' ties to the EMP for the last time. Afterwards, with all of the EMP's attempts at contact ignored, the Flying Hawks lost their government funding and had to begin accepting private security contracts. The pay was meagre compared to what they had been getting, but it was enough to maintain their small base in the equally small town of Karsil.

Vix didn't know if it was Lord Greggard or Captain Nathers that had made first contact with one another after Marigold's secession. What she did know was that both sides had immediate use for one another and the Flying Hawks migrated west at the first opportunity.

During the story, the others aside from Yak had departed one after the other, until just the three of them remained to tend the fire. The only new addition to the circle was a sinewy lad with reddish hair, who had taken a seat to the other side of Vix while she had spoken. He stayed silent the whole time and patiently waited for introduction.

With the brief history of her company explained, Vix finally turned to the young fellow. "Wedge, this is the newest member of the company, we just named him Lynx."

Tryst laid the oiled and sharpened sword aside and reached behind Vix to shake the hand of Wedge. "Pleased to meet you, Wedge."

"Lynx is a hefty name," The man offered in reply. "I hope you can live up to it."

Vix interjected, "It was I who steered the group towards a strong name."

Wedge shrugged and turned his gaze towards the flames. "Then who am I to argue?"

She ignored him and turned to Tryst. "Lynx, allow me to introduce Wedge, he or Yak usually partner with me."

"That reminds me, whose turn is it tonight?" Wedge chided.

Vix's jaw dropped and she made a playful slap at Wedge. "You're terrible."

"Oh, I am terrible alright, and yet, still your first choice for a partner on a silent job." Wedge glanced sideways at Vix. "So what does that say about you?"

"That I like you better when you're quiet," she codded back.

A big, bellowing laugh came forth from Yak. "No comeback for that one, Wedge."

The three of them continued to jape and carry on, and after a time. Tryst was laughing right along with them. On his own, Wedge would seem abrasive and insensitive with his mocking, depreciative style of humour. That was where Yak provided counterbalance by throwing the sting of Wedge's remarks back on him. The slender lad was able to show in those moments that he was a willing recipient of his own brand of humour. Amidst all that was Vix, who seemed to have a comical anecdote for every joke and delivered them with a fantastic sense of timing. They gave Tryst a sense of welcome and inclusion that he hadn't felt since his days among the halls of the Combat University.

When the three showed signs of sleepiness, Vix turned her

attention back to Tryst. "Lynx, where did you pitch your tent?" she asked him.

Tryst glanced towards the grove. "Oh, under the trees with the others. Cadet Chesley pointed it out to me. Why do you ask?"

"Chesley?" pondered Yak for a moment while he tried to recall the cadet. "Ah yes, that would be Squirm. We found him shivering in the snow in a little town on the outskirts of Hercalest region a few winters ago. His parents were shipped off to Biddenhurst for something, he didn't know what and I don't know that anyone ever looked into it far enough to find out. Anyway, whatever it was, it left him orphaned, so Wyvern took him on as a squire. He's a cadet by rank and that's as high as he'll rise. He's harmless, and that's not a quality one wants in a Flying Hawk. However, he's a good little squire and camp attendant, so we take care of him. We're all he has."

"I need not wonder how he earned the name Squirm," Tryst commented.

To his surprise, the others didn't seem to understand, and Vix fielded the question they all seemed to share. "What do you mean?"

It was left to Tryst to explain, "Captain Nathers, or rather, Wyvern, ordered Squirm to show me about the camp after he fetched me a tent. He ran off as soon as he put tarp and pegs in my arms and I haven't seen him since."

The three exchanged looks of suspicion until Vix said what they all seemed to be thinking, "That's not like the boy. He's been nothing but entirely obedient to Wyvern."

"Did you spook him somehow?" Wedge queried, for once in seriousness.

Tryst gave a nonplussed shrug. "Not that I could tell, I barely spoke to him."

"That is most bizarre," Yak said with a voice of wary and a hand stroking his thick bush of a beard. "I'll have a word with the boy, to see why he abandoned his duty. No need to bring this up to Wyvern."

Vix dusted herself off and stood up. "That's not why I brought it up, Lynx. It is beyond odd that the boy would behave like such, but Yak will deal with that. I asked because the members of the Flying Hawks divide into groups of four and we need a fourth in our crew. Any man to be named to the Flying Hawks in such short order must be of considerable skill. We are but three who either get divided to two or given a temporary replacement. Will you be our permanent fourth member, Lynx?"

"It's to become a bidding war for my favour, is it?" Tryst prodded to lighten the mood.

"Anyone with even half their wits can see that you're a dangerous fellow, the kind that a person would be far better off to have with them than against them," Wedge put in.

Vix was standing before Tryst then, her hands on the hips of her dun brown, loose fitting trousers. "The others are either intimidated by you or they have enough numbers for their parties. We lack on both accounts. We've been searching for a fourth for some time and we're not letting the first new face in months slip away to one of the other groups. So what say you? You can break that tiny tent and sleep in our pavilion. It's got a brazier for warmth and hammocks for your comfort."

"Who am I to refuse such an offer?" Tryst stood up and outstretched a hand to Vix to shake. "Consider me your fourth."

From that night onward, Tryst was constantly in the company of Vix, Wedge and Yak. Their spacious tent was attended by a cadet named Cob, a sobriquet which Tryst thought unfitting, yet the young woman of sixteen years wore it with pride anyhow. She was but a skinny thing, with hair the colour of straw, light complexion and two of the darkest eyes Tryst had ever seen.

The Flying Hawks were at the forefront of the army on the march towards Pelican Harbour. Their days started when the two moons were not yet ready to step aside for the sun and lasted until the former pair returned. They were the scouts, the outriders and the first line of offense all rolled into one complete, deadly package.

A valuable asset to any army, Tryst thought to himself after their first march. *Small wonder why Greggard thought it so prudent to whisk them away from the reach of the EMP.*

On his first morning Tryst was woken by Cob. The others had already risen and left the tent and only their squire remained. "Where are the others?" Tryst had asked after greeting girl and morning alike.

"They left to gather fresh news and supplies," Cob answered cheerfully while setting the little table in the middle of the pavilion tent for breakfast. "I was told to let you sleep a little longer to give you a good rest and ensure you were equipped and ready for the day. You should rise and eat while you have time, though."

While Tryst sat before his meal of ham, a half cob of corn and buttered toast, he was presented with a bundle of clothing by Cob. Once he had a look through the pile, he found it consisted of a hooded parka, suspendered trousers and fingered mittens, all in mottled white and grey. "I didn't know the Flying Hawks adhered to a uniform," Tryst had stated while finishing his meal.

"We don't, this is to blend in to the environment," the girl replied before turning back to her regular duties of packing up their encampment. By the time Tryst had donned his new attire and armed himself with his sword, knife and rifle, Cob had summoned him to the armoury wagon. "I hope you have no problem with not using a rifle for the time being."

"I don't, but why would that be?" he answered curiously.

Her own answer was right to the point: "Too noisy, we prefer crossbows. They are more suited to our tasks. Maybe when we get to the harbour the Captain will order rifles, but for now, you'll be using these," she said while holding out a crossbow and a quiver of bolts.

After exchanging his standard issue rifle for the crossbow, Cob showed Tryst to where his three cohorts had gathered. All the Flying Hawks assigned to morning duty were gathered in a circle around a box, waiting on the captain to mount it and deliver orders for the day. "Good morning, Lynx," Vix said with a smile. "I see Cob looked after you this morning and got you well equipped. I trust you're comfortable with the gear you've been given?"

"I bid a good morning to you three as well," said Tryst with a smile of his own. "Everything should be fine. I don't see any issues arising from using a crossbow. Truth be told, I prefer it over a rifle."

"That's good to hear, we have little use for such noisemakers. Our motto of sorts when it comes to combat is 'Be Quick. Be Precise. Be Traceless.' Firearms are quick, they can be precise, but such a loud bang makes being traceless quite difficult," she said with a wink.

"In that we are entirely agreed. I've always preferred a bow for my ranged targets. It was the armed forces that put a gun in my hands," answered Tryst with a confident smirk.

Just as Vix opened her mouth to say something to Tryst, the Captain emerged from his tent. "Fall in, Hawks," he commanded in a gruff tone. "Today is the first day of our operation to take Pelican Harbour. Should we succeed, we'll become an invaluable asset and indebted ally of the Western forces. Anything less than absolute success is complete failure from here on out. We have to be in top form every time we gear up. That starts now and does not end until I declare the mission to be complete. Am I understood?"

"Aye, Captain," the group answered in unison.

Wyvern looked over his company with a prideful nod. "That's good to hear, ladies and gentlemen. I have devised the pairings list for today. Remember not only your own name, but those of your comrades as well and know who is supposed to be with whom." Captain Nathers delivered the speech in a commanding, inspiring tone and stopped only to clear his throat before diving into the list of names. "Flint and Kegs, Blue and Elk, Dog and Owl, Snow and Hare, you lot will be outriding the left flank. Vole and Mink, Wedge and Yak, Mist and Pike, Ox and Cane, the right flank is yours. Finally, our forward scouts for the day: Jay and Cloud, Birch and Frost, Colt and Lock, Vix and Lynx. The others will be at the ready and move with myself and the camp. Our main priority is to keep the movement of ourselves and the armed forces as secret as possible. You are to consider every civilian and soldier you see as a loose set of lips. Any people we come across are to be taken into custody and held as guests until this operation is complete or until their identity and allegiance can be verified. Do I make myself clear?"

"Aye, Captain," the group answered again, this time with Tryst himself adding his voice, now that he knew the proper response.

With that, the Captain pumped a fist high into the air. "Hawks, take flight!"

"Take flight!" all answered and broke to go about their tasks for the day.

The three that were his new companions fell in about Tryst as they headed back towards their pavilion. "Scouting on the first day, Lynx, you can thank me for that," Yak claimed with a slap on the back.

"What did you say to Wyvern to encourage him so?" Tryst queried curiously.

Vix chimed in with the answer. "I took the liberty of letting him know that we had claimed you for our band. He asked for Yak and Wedge to vouch for you as well. Before you know it, they had done such a fine job that Wyvern said he wanted to see your skills for himself. Here we are. Yak and Wedge are mounting up to outride the right flank and you're with me, scouting ahead on foot. It's an exhaustive job, but it will let us test your mettle."

"Then I hope I can live up to your expectations," Tryst

commented in earnest.

Yak gave Tryst a hefty slap on the back. "We shall soon find out. Let's go, Wedge."

After the other two men had gone on their way, Vix led Tryst back to their encampment for a final equipment check before heading out. Atop the gear Tryst had already been given, he was also burdened with a satchel of tiny red flags on needlepoint sticks. "Every hundred meters or so, stick one of these in a tree. It will let the rest of the caravan know that we've inspected the terrain and deemed it clear," Vix explained.

Once Vix had gathered her own satchel of food for the day, the two of them were quick to catch up to the other scouts. Vix ensured that Tryst was given a round of introductions upon arrival at the muster point. The first hand Tryst shook was that of Cloud's, the other female in the ranks of the Hawks.

"Before you ask: no, I'm not from Drake, I'm albino," she said with a jovial smile.

"I might have made that mistake myself," Tryst returned in matching tone. In truth he knew the difference, having spent so much time among the light skinned, white haired Drakians of whom the complexion and hair colour came naturally to. Though, there certainly was no mistaking how Cloud came into her name, with her head of long, ivory locks.

The others were all Illiastran in origin as well and though their heights varied, their slender builds did not. The scouts were as nimble as squirrels and as quick as the spotted cats of Johnah. As fast as Tryst could keep up on the ground and on foot, the others were scaling and leaping through trees, eyes darting every which way.

Vix was right, this was an exhaustive job and if Tryst himself weren't in peak physical form, then he would have been left behind a dozen times before midday.

"What's wrong, Lynx? Can't keep up?" Vix joked, noticing much the same herself when they stopped to take a brief break.

"I'm not a climber, I'm a fighter," he chided back. "Put a sword in my hand, then you'll see what I can do."

Vix gave a sly wink. "I'll hold you to that."

The remainder of the day went much the same. Tryst was surprised in himself for being able to keep pace from the ground, jabbing the little flags into the tree trunks as he went.

By nightfall they had stopped again, waiting on the patrol guards to relieve their position. Back at camp, they found their pavilion tent erect and waiting for them. A campfire lay before it with Cob tending a roasting spit above. They reunited with Wedge and Yak and the five of them recounted their day. Things were largely uneventful outside the camp, as there would be very few people in the forests at this time of year.

Within, there was what Tryst could only label as organised chaos. The Hawks were at the forefront and Captain Nathers held meetings with the other officers daily and seemed to grow more stressed by the minute. Yet the camp moved ever on, crawling slowly forward towards Pelican Harbour.

Tryst was moved about from scouting forward to guarding the outskirts of the moving army, from day to day. The only one of the group that switched out position with Tryst was Wedge. Yak stayed on horseback and Vix was ever out in front.

On his first outing with the bearded man, it was explained to Tryst why. "Each group tries to stay at four, two stealth agents, one strong-arm and a flex. You're the flex now, Lynx, and I'm the big, lumbering muscle. Vix has no need of me yet, so I sit out here on a destrier and wait on her call."

Compared to the urgency with which Vix and the others conducted their scouting work, riding with Yak was greatly relaxing. "The camp caravan moves like cold molasses and there's not a damn thing out here but deer and the furry little creatures," he explained almost lazily from his saddle that same day. "We need not push ourselves too hard, Lynx. There will be time for that when we're outside Pelican Harbour."

When Yak had brought Tryst to where the horses were hobbled, Tryst was almost immediately handed the reins of a brown mare. The beast was smaller than Wildstar, his own horse from his days in Atrebell, yet Tryst couldn't help but be reminded of his friend.

Did you make it to Obalen? Tryst wondered of the courser to himself. *I'm sure the stablemen there would have given you good care and a good home, even if Obalen is a less than ideal place to be now.*

It was doubtless that as the crossroads between the east and west that Obalen would be a centrepiece to Marigold's war. Oddly enough, Tryst had heard little to nothing from Greggard that resembled concern for the city. It gave Tryst the impression that

Greggard didn't seem to find its inevitable occupation by the enemy to be too concerning.

Things stayed quiet until the sixth day, when Tryst and Yak returned to camp in the evening to find Wedge and Cob without Vix. "Cloud and Jay trapped a trapper," Wedge answered apathetically while nibbling on a leg of fire-roasted chicken. "They're busy escorting him to the rear of the convoy. He claims he knows people in regular service who can verify his identity and that he's no threat to us. He also said he had a family living in his cottage nearby, so the others went to find this cottage and let them know the trapper is safe and will be returned unharmed to them soon. So Vix and I were left to inform Wyvern of all of that. Well, that's what she set off to do. It doesn't take two to relay information."

By the time Vix returned she looked equal parts dismayed and exhausted, something Yak lacked the subtleties to not mention. "Vix, I take it things went poorly with the trapper?"

"Everything's fine, the man claims he's from Galdourn." Vix turned to Tryst and her tone became explanatory in nature. "The minister there is Ike Slake, a holdout to Lady Marigold, but he lacks any sort of military capacity to offer any resistance."

"I hadn't known that, there is little news in the north that can be called fresh," he stated in what he hoped was a convincing manner. "What of the trapper, could you confirm his story?"

Vix was handed a plate of food by Cob and took a few bites of the fried onions before continuing her update. "He claims that he knows an officer in the Western army. Jay and Cloud are escorting him through the caravan to try and confirm as much," Vix stated before completing the same story Wedge had already told them.

"Is there something else?" Tryst added concernedly.

She smiled tiredly. "Worry not. It has just been a long run today. I'm already longing for my cot and a good sleep."

Both Tryst and Yak thought it best to leave things there and said no more of the matter. The rest of the evening was spent with Tryst and Yak recounting the uneventful day they had and Cob relaying news from within the caravan.

The next morning, Tryst rose and broke his fast with the others. Immediately Tryst took notice of Vix and thought she seemed back to the normal of what he had come to know of her. The four set off to the morning meeting, leaving the cleaning and disassembling to

Cob.

As usual, Tryst alternated with Wedge from the previous day's placement and set off for another day of scouting after the morning meeting with Vix.

The days went on as they had been once more, with little aberration until the eighth sunset. The camp was abuzz by the time Tryst and Yak could turn over the reins of their horses to the stable hands. Wedge and Vix seemed to be caught in the excitement as well, with the former pacing anxiously before Cob's fire and the latter wearing an untameable grin. "Lads, I have good news," Vix gave as a warm welcome. "We are now directly east of Pelican Harbour. The real operation begins tonight."

"At last, I've been waiting eagerly for this day," Yak proclaimed with a thump of a fist on his thick chest. "I was afraid my muscles were going to waste away waiting for a fight."

"What is our new course of action?" Tryst asked eagerly.

"Before dark, the Flying Hawks will leave the rest of the armed forces behind and travel south by a kilometre," their fair squad leader began to explain. "Then we strike directly west. By morning we should be at the southwest corner of Pelican Harbour and quite literally in Minister Nothram's back yard. While Marigold's naval forces attack the mouth of the harbour and draw Nothram's eye that way, the armed forces on foot shall besiege his eastern gates. All the while, we slip over his walls and penetrate the manor with little resistance. If all goes as planned, Nothram will order a surrender before little or any blood can be shed."

"I guess we had better get a quick meal and prepare," Tryst stated when she finished.

"You're absolutely right, Lynx," Wedge beamed after a deep breath to compose himself. "Tonight the Flying Hawks prove their worth to Lady Marigold's cause. She will see that we are indispensable and remove any further doubt of such from her conspirators' minds. This is what we were bred to do and causes like Marigold's are why we were bred to do this: for the people of Illiastra. Not for any political party, not to further the control of the Triarchy, but for *all* of the men and women of this country."

By the twilight hour, the Flying Hawks were well away from the pack. The Wyvern had delivered a similar, albeit more rousing, speech when he called his soldiers. Afterwards he laid out their plan and announced the members that would be involved in the assault on the manor. The small bands within the Flying Hawks were being deployed together and to Tryst's surprise, Vix's crew had been one of the four selected for the frontline offense.

The first to congratulate them on the achievement was Vole, whose own crew would be among the frontline. "It looks like we shall get to see if you've earned that name, Lynx," Vole had stated with a hearty slap on the back.

Now though, save for the collective footsteps in the freshly fallen snow, all were silent. Seventeen they were, in their mottled white suits and guided by the light of the two moons, shining bright for once. The four groups were led by Vix, Vole, Snow and Jay, with Wyvern himself leading them all. Each of them bore a dagger and sword on their hips, save for Yak, who preferred an axe to a sword. Snow and Jay's teams had crossbows slung across their backs, one among every group carried medical supplies and Vole's crew bore grappling hooks and lengths of rope. Together, they trudged through fresh fallen snow, varied in their equipment, but unified in their cause.

"Halt," Wyvern commanded to the group as he came to stand by a tall tree. "Mink, shimmy up and see if you can see the lights of the town. We should be near."

"Aye, Captain," the man called back before disappearing quickly up the long limbed sentinel. The others waited patiently, all their senses on high alert. Minutes ticked by before they heard Mink scrambling back to the ground to report his findings. "I can see the town lights. We're roughly five hundred metres away, give or take."

"Close enough," Wyvern replied with a measure of gravity to his voice. "We split up from here on out. The most important thing to stress in this mission is that you're to avoid killing if at all possible. The men and women of this town are Westerners, just as Lady Marigold is. She gave us this task to spare lives on the front lines from both sides. It will not suffice if this devolves into a massacre. Subdue and restrain should be the first actions, use lethal force only if your life or the lives of your teammates are in immediate peril. Am I clear?"

All sixteen answered as one: "Aye, Ser."

The captain moved on hastily, "Vole, your team will breach the town wall. Subdue any sentries you find and leave your grappling hooks for the others. You'll attack the north wall of the manor's rear yard. Remember, silence is the key. If you make any errors, they will fall to the rest of us as well."

"Understood, Captain," Vole answered before disappearing with his three into the night.

Nathers turned his attention to Snow and Jay's teams. "You lot have the east wall. You're in their back yard and it's the longest trek across the manor yard, so you'll end up drawing the most attention. Keep the guards distracted and pinned down with crossbow bolts from a safe distance until the north and south wall teams can close the pincers on the manor. Once you see us breach the doors and windows, you charge."

The two lieutenants responded in unison with an, "Aye, Ser," before they darted off, leaving Wyvern with Vix's team alone.

"It looks as though I will be going with you, Vix," the Captain said while letting his gaze fall to the four left standing with him. "We breach the south wall with the same objective as Vole's team: enter the manor through the first floor windows, subdue and restrain any who resist and take Minister Nothram alive."

"I understand, ser," Vix replied. "Shall we set out?" The foreboding, ominous way with which she said the words made Tryst suddenly tense.

"We shall, but first there something which much be addressed and dealt with, lest our mission become potentially compromised," Wyvern said before turning his focus solely to Tryst. "Hawks," he commanded. "Show your talons."

The sound of steel sliding from sheath echoed in Tryst's ears all about him and before he could draw his own steel, his three companions had him outflanked. They were silent and as still as stone, all manner of friendliness vanishing into the night air with their steaming breaths.

The captain himself left his sword at his hip as he stood before Tryst. "Before I allow you to take part in our operation there are some things you should tell me, Tryst Reine."

They know, they all know and they have for some time, Tryst thought to himself regretfully. He stayed calm and quiet, waiting for Wyvern to speak.

"From the moment you stepped into my tent, I knew precisely who you were," Wyvern started after Tryst deigned to say anything. "I don't know if Lord Greggard thought he would fool me. I would like to think a man in such a position of power would not be so careless as to make such a mistake. I would like to think that Greggard knew that I, the captain of the Flying Hawks, a group devoted to the gathering of information, would figure out his flimsy ruse. Or does he so arrogantly think I am such a rube as to be so easily flummoxed?"

Tryst weighed his answer carefully. "I don't know what Lord Greggard's intentions were. I am merely following the instructions of my contract with him."

Wyvern cocked his head to the side. "What instructions might those be? I'll have them all. You may be the Master of Blades, but how do you like your odds against four of the Flying Hawks? Consider that before you choose to deceive."

"I never assume my victory is certain," Tryst said as he raised his hands in surrender. "And I assure you that my orders were not harmful to the people or the cause of the Flying Hawks in any way. I was told to assist your operation as Lord Greggard believed my skills would be an asset to your group. That is the absolute truth."

"Then why didn't he tell me the truth of who you are?" Wyvern inquired while reaching inside his coat. He drew a sheaf of papers and thrust them at Tryst's feet in the snow. "Why would he play me with this false identity? Aye, I won't deny the skills of the Master of Blades would be 'useful'. They'd be more useful if I was aware that they were at my disposal."

The wind carried away several pieces of the parchment and neither Tryst nor the Flying Hawks made a move to collect them.

"I do not know, I promise you," Tryst responded gingerly.

"I think you do." It was Yak who spoke up, grinding his leather gloved fists along the hilt of his heavy war axe. "I like you, Lynx and if I offer you any council before I'm forced to kill you, it's to be completely honest with us."

"The man speaks wise counsel," commented Wyvern dryly. "There would have to be a reason why Lord Greggard would not want it known that the Master of Blades, Illiastra's most wanted man, is in his service, even amongst his allies."

Tryst shook his head dismissively. "There may well be and yet I do not know what those reasons might be."

The captain kept his stern gaze firmly on Tryst. "I think I know the most important reason and her name is Orangecloak. The lie told to the masses is that she is dead. The story I happened to hear is that she's in the dungeon of Atrebell and you're guarding her, waiting to drop the axe. Lastly, there's this little tale circulating that you are the most wanted man east of Obalen. There were orders sent to all the holds still under EMP rule that you are to be killed on sight as a traitor to the realm. Strangely, they also say that you pinched the orange cloak and might have hung it on the shoulders of a red haired woman you hope to claim is Orangecloak. Yet, here you are, working for Lord Greggard, who defected from the Elite Merchants and joined Lady Marigold's cause. You can see why none of this seems to add up to me. So tell me, Tryst Reine, Master of Blades: where is Lady Orangecloak?"

The question hung on the light wind that blew at Tryst's hair. He waited, glancing at Wedge and Vix to either side of him, weighing the options before him. "I propose a trading of information. You answer a question for me, I answer one for you."

Wyvern seemed to find that amusing. "Do you think you're in any sort of position to be negotiating that sort of deal, boy?"

"I believe I'm in the perfect position to level that offer," Tryst countered. "I'm under no obligation to speak and if you kill me, any information I hold is gone into the wind. That wouldn't do for the Flying Hawks, would it? Information is your currency and letting that turn to dust in your hands would be a terrible bit of business."

Tryst thought he heard a chuckle escaping from Wyvern as he considered what Tryst said. "What would you like to know, boy?"

"How did you know who I was, if you knew from the very moment you laid eyes on me?" Tryst tabled to him.

Wyvern scoffed. "Such triviality, but if that's all you seek an answer to, then I'm happy to bequeath that information. You and I were both in the hand-to-hand tournament held in honour of the Lord Master's birthday in Hercalest four years ago. The birthday celebration part was purely farcical. We both know it was merely a show for Howland to display his new personal bodyguard. He wanted the world to see what awaited them if they tried to make even so much as a threat on his life. There was a long list of men that signed up for that and among the names on the list was Wynne Nathers of the Flying Hawks, then still a lieutenant."

The memory came back to Tryst then. "I recall loathing that tournament. It was the Lord Master's idea, not mine. I also recall all of my opponents and you were not one of them, Captain Nathers."

"No, much to my own chagrin I was pinned by Bronoghan the Bull, a mere man-at-arms stationed at Fort Dornett on the Varras

River," Wyvern regretfully admitted.

"That man-at-arms weighed in at an excess of one hundred and twenty five kilograms, as I recall," Tryst added. "Now *him* I do remember fighting."

The Captain smiled at the memory. "And I remember your knee shooting into his face as fast as a lighting strike. That big, tall prick hit the mat like a fat sack of bricks.

"Every man among the lists wanted to fight you, boy," Nathers continued. "They all sought the glory that would come with being able to say they were the one to defeat the Master of Blades in hand-to-hand combat, myself included. I can assure you that every last one of them committed your face to memory as I and even my squire did. It's your eyes that betray you, Reine. I've seen the Gildraddi Green before. So has Squirm, but your eyes are different again from even that. He remembered you straight away when he saw you. The two of us knew you were among our camp and your teammates knew when Vix came to make her statement about the trapper that was apprehended."

Nathers held his hands out, palms up in a show of good faith. "Now, we've told you everything you wanted to know, so, I'll start you with an easy question of ours: why, given that we've known of your presence, do you think that we've not killed you in your sleep yet?"

Tryst took a moment to consider his answer. "You want information from me."

"We do," Wyvern said with a nod. "We want to know where Lady Orangecloak is. There is much misinformation coming out of the Atrebell Manor since the last night of the Autumn Parliamentary Sessions, yet in every report your name crops up. So, I'm certain that you have had a great hand in everything to do with Orangecloak from that point onward. Whether she is alive or dead, we would know, for there is great value in knowing such a thing."

"I cannot give out information if I fear it might be sold to my enemies," Tryst countered. "How can I be certain that anything I might divulge will stay between us five?"

Wyvern shrugged nonchalantly. "If you were sent by Lord Greggard and his allegiance to Lady Marigold is true, then your enemies are also the enemies of the Flying Hawks. I understand your concern though, so I shall sweeten the deal by showing you something." Reaching into a pocket in his trousers, the captain produced a folded envelope with a broken seal. "We received this just prior to our defection becoming known to the Lord Master. Wedge, give the Master of Blades some light so that he might read."

Doing as he was asked, Wedge produced a damp rag, unrolling it to reveal flint stones contained within. A limb was snapped from a nearby tree and pressed into service as a torch with the rag wrapped about it and the flint put to work lighting the oily cloth. Wedge held the torch for Tryst, leaving him little recourse but to inspect the letter in the envelope.

It was written by the familiar hand of the Lord Master's steward Hossle. What he had written on behalf of Grenjin Howland was of no surprise to Tryst, having expected no less from his former employer and his rampant paranoia. When Tryst had finished, he nodded to Wedge to indicate as such, folded the letter back into place and returned it to Wyvern. The torch was snuffed in the snow and Wedge unsheathed his sword once more.

"The Lord Master sent you a personal request to find and apprehend me with a promise to restore your funding, no questions asked, should you succeed," Tryst said in a tone that sounded nearly bored. "This would certainly contradict those things you told me in your tent the night I arrived."

Nathers hummed and tapped a finger to the side of his nose tellingly. "Aye, if Orangecloak was your prisoner in Atrebell, then I think it rather odd that the Lord Master would ask us to hunt you down. That told me that all but the last story were most definitely false. The strangest thing is that it makes no mention of her though, just you. I ask you to end this mystery for us once and for all, boy: where is Lady Orangecloak?"

Tryst wrestled with the knowledge, wondering what would be his best course of action. He did not know if they could be trusted with the truth, yet a lie would mean the deaths of most of the people present. Even considering his skills, Tryst could not exclude himself from that count. He decided to take a gamble, anything he said now would be, yet he knew where the odds lay most in his favour. There was little trust to be placed in the Flying Hawks. Just as Orangecloak was sceptical of trusting Tryst, the Hawks had a reputation to be considered. They were merchants as much as the shopkeeps, peddling in information with a currency of violence and a history of bloodshed. To them, the whereabouts of Orangecloak, no matter what their opinion of her, was simply a lucratively high priced piece of inventory.

They will get selective honesty, Tryst decided. *I shall try to satiate their appetite with scraps of truth and hope they grow satisfied without the full meal.*

"Lady Orangecloak is safe," Tryst offered carefully.

The words fell on the group with an almost tangible weight. All eyes fell to Captain Nathers standing before Tryst, his face expressionless save for a raised eyebrow. "Safe can mean different things to different people, boy," he began. "A jailor would consider his prisoner safe if they were locked in an iron cage, just as a parent would say their child is safe if they were tucked into a warm bed. You know I need more than that."

Clearing his throat, Tryst divulged a little more, "She is within Lady Marigold's newly defined Western Illiastra and under the protection of a fellow alumnus of the Combat University of Drake. That's about as safe as one can get on any part of this continent."

Wyvern audibly sighed at that remark. "We are to believe that your allegiance was so easily swayed? You've been the guardian of the Lord Master Grenjin Howland for over four years and suddenly you've thrown in your lot with the Thieves? You'll forgive me for being cynical, surely."

"I haven't changed my position on anything," Tryst responded sternly. "I was born and raised in the Midlands of Gildriad and made a man in Drake. My life has been spent amongst people who enjoy the freedoms and rights that Lady Orangecloak seeks. Do you really think that four years of tending to the security needs of a greedy despot would skewer decades of knowledge and logic so drastically?"

Wyvern began letting the questions fly quickly. "Why aren't you with her now? Why join us at all? What part has Lord Greggard played in all this?"

Tryst laughed under his breath. "You grow greedy yourself."

The impatience of Wyvern was becoming apparent. "Answer the questions, boy."

"Very well," Tryst shrugged. "Lord Greggard is an old acquaintance of mine. As far as he knows, I have parted ways with Lady Orangecloak and she has been reunited with her Thieves and is on route to the Southlands. I showed up on his doorstep looking for a short contract to raise the funds needed to sail back to Drake, as I'm practically copperless right now. I had to leave my money in the Imperial Bank of Atrebell and the recent secession of Western Illiastra has made retrieving it impossible. The contract Greggard offered was to lend my skills to this mission, as you already know, to improve the odds of its success. In reality, I wanted the job to help cover the cost of travel for Orangecloak, myself and my acquaintance from the Combat University on our journey to the Southlands."

Nathers seemed to be weighing the information in his mind before responding in a contemplative voice, "This is expensive information. The EMP would pay well to know where you and Lady Orangecloak have gotten to. It is fortunate for you and her that what I have told you of my respect for her is true. Knowing she is alive and under the protection of one of the world's foremost swordsmen fills me with great joy. Now, I am in quite a predicament, Tryst Reine. I cannot let her protector rush into a life-endangering mission. Please, go back to Orangecloak, keep her safe and get her back to the Southlands so that she can raise the banner of the Thieves."

"With all due respect, Captain, I cannot do that until the mission is complete," answered Tryst sternly, brokering no argument.

"And I cannot risk having you die come the morning," the Captain gave back.

Their eyes locked as Tryst returned the verbal volley: "I have no intention of dying on Minister Nothram's doorstep."

"No one ever intends on dying, yet all of us do," Wyvern stated. "If you are intent on going into this battle, then I won't deny you, as I do admit you have a useful set of skills. It is not just I who you must get permission from." The captain turned to the lone female among them. "Vix, this is your foursome, will you accept Tryst Reine?"

"Ser, are you truly reserving final judgement to me?" Vix asked cautiously, to which she received a single nod from the Captain and took the cue to continue on. "We have little time to waste, yet I will say this: I am disappointed to have been so deceived, Tryst Reine. If what you say is true about Lady Orangecloak, then I am of the same mind as Captain Wyvern. You should go protect her, for she is more important than any one of us and with or without you, Minister Nothram will fall today. Yet, we do have a need for you to complete our four."

She stopped long enough to sheathe her sword, an action the others followed in suit. "You may fight beside us today and leave, should you survive. However, in return for overlooking your deceit, there is now a debt owed to myself, Wedge, Yak and Cob. Should we ask a favour of you within reason and capability, you must oblige. Am

I understood?"

Tryst breathed a sigh of relief. "I humbly accept being in the debt of your fine group. Call on me when you would and if what you seek is in my power, it is yours."

"Then, until Pelican Harbour is ours or you fall, you shall continue to bear the name Lynx," Captain Nathers confirmed in a tone that mirrored Tryst's own relief. "Vix raised a valid point, we have spent considerable time dealing with this, let us be off."

The five set off at a jog to make up for the time lost, reaching the town to find it still blanketed in darkness.

The south corner of the east wall was where they found the grappling hooks left behind by the others. Wedge was the first to scale the wall, with Vix close at hand. By the time Tryst, Yak and Wyvern were able to join them atop the bailey, the other two had found the first man to fall in the battle. "He saw one of our groups coming," Vix declared in a whisper to the group. "There's blood on his blade, he fought back and wounded one of ours."

"He didn't fight back for long," the Captain surmised as he looked over the body of the young man. "Come, the manor awaits and we're already late."

The eastern wall of the manor property was lined with the eight Flying Hawks designated to the spot. They stood out from the grey, brick wall like sore thumbs in their mottled white suits, huddled low and awaiting a signal. Vix's unit neared slowly, with a hand signal issued by Wyvern to let the huddled mass know that the approaching group were friendly. "I saw the fallen soldier atop the town wall, which of ours took a wound?" the Captain asked when they were close enough to whisper, wasting no time on greetings.

A member named Thorn spoke up. "Hare took a deep, nasty slash to the thigh. We got him off one wall, but I don't think we can get him over another and he definitely can't fight."

"So be it," Wyvern said and turned to Vix. "I'll take Hare's place on the east wall of the manor. Get into position and wait for the signal from the harbour."

Vix nodded and the four left for their place in the shadow of the high walls bordering the home of Minister Nothram.

Crouched low, with their backs pressed to the south wall, they waited. From their position they could only see the sky above the harbour and hoped that from there they would see the signal.

"Daylight will soon be on us," noted Yak in a low voice. "I thought the signal was to come before dawn?"

"That's what we've been told," Vix answered in a whisper. "Stay vigilant, it will come."

A scattered few flakes of snow began to tumble down and Tryst focused solely on them as the time ticked by. It was deathly quiet in Pelican Harbour, windless and calm, almost unnerving, given the chaos that was set to erupt at any moment. In the distance, a lone pair of footfalls ploddingly crunched through the freshly fallen snow of the night. Just as the walker sounded close enough to see, his steps were drowned out by a pair of concussive blasts from mortar cannons that filled the air. The four turned their heads together in the direction of the sea, watching as two explosions rocked the hillsides on either side of the mouth of the harbour.

"That would be our signal," Vix said, leaping to her feet. "Let's get a move on. Lynx, Wedge, boost Yak to the top of the wall first. He can lend a hand to the rest of us."

Wedge flattened his back to the wall beside Tryst and cupped his hands to support Yak. "They blew the guard towers protecting the entrance of the harbour," Wedge exclaimed excitedly. "That will draw the town's forces toward the Daol Bay fleet."

"Aye, it's time to nick the head off the beast while its back is turned," Yak added, having waited eagerly for this moment for some time. Tryst and Wedge shot him upward and onto the top of the narrow, three meter tall wall. He swung a leg over and perched there, extending a hand to Vix as she was vaulted up to his level and descended to the other side with nary a sound. After her came Tryst with assistance by Wedge, who then practically ran up the vertical brick structure to reach Yak and Tryst's waiting hands.

As the men joined Vix, she nodded towards the east wall where white shapes were already traipsing across the snowy back yard, crossbows at the ready. "We should all hit the building at the same time, we'll split up from here on out. Yak and I will take the window nearest to the front of the house, Wedge and Lynx can enter from three windows down. That should space us out evenly."

The last sentence had barely left Vix's lips when gunfire erupted from the manor into the back yard. "They know we're here. Move!" she declared, breaking into a sprint.

The four split into two and made for the manor as fast as the snow would allow them to run. The aim of the riflemen within the manor was on the eight attackers in the rear yard of the manor and Vix's unit arrived at the building's walls unscathed.

Wedge yanked his dagger from its sheath and used the pommel to smash in the glass and unlatch the window. "We're in the kitchens," he noted before slipping through the window ahead of Tryst. Two cooks were within and one was already running for cover as Tryst joined Wedge in the stuffily hot room. The remaining fellow came at them with a cast-iron frying pan, cursing loudly at Wedge. A frantic parry later and Wedge had him disarmed of the kitchen tool, letting it bounce across a table noisily. With a furious elbow to the face, Wedge dropped the cook to the floor to clutch at his shattered nose.

Tryst grabbed the terrified fellow who had hid within a cupboard and drew him out by the jacket. "Where is Minister Nothram? If he surrenders, no one else need be harmed or killed. Just tell us where he-" A loud series of gunshots ripped through the home, cutting off Tryst's words. He shoved the screaming chef back into the cupboard and barred it shut to keep him there.

"They're firing within the manor!" Wedge yelled. "The others must have breached the windows as well, we have to hurry."

"VIX! NOOO!" the thunderous roar of Yak echoed from somewhere unseen. "No quarter for the lot of you!"

"I think they got Vix!" Wedge shouted frantically, making for the doorway with haste.

"Wait! We don't know what's out there!" Tryst grabbed to stop the man, but not quickly enough and his hand closed on empty air.

Wedge yanked the door open and bolted into a hallway beyond. As he began to give pursuit, another pair of shots bounced off the walls and rang painfully loud in Tryst's ears. He peeked into the hall and saw a pair of uniformed guards hurriedly trying to reload their weapons before a downed and bleeding Wedge.

Tryst took his chance and charged them before they could finish the task, unsheathing his dagger as he ran for the duo. One tried to raise the bayonetted rifle and for his trouble was left with the short blade protruding from his shoulder. As he wailed over his wound, his accomplice was taken to the floor with the weight of Tryst's body. They tussled briefly until Tryst was able to get atop him, take his rifle away and repeatedly drive a fist into the soldier's mouth and nose, painfully breaking a fair smile to bits. *Better off toothless than lifeless,*

Tryst reasoned as he left the fellow writhing on the ground.

The dagger was yanked loose from the shoulder of the screamer, now slouched against the wall. He bawled out and swung with his uninjured arm, quickly finding it ensnared in Tryst's grasp. A quick snap broke the soldier's wrist, ensuring he wouldn't raise his rifle again.

Tryst went to Wedge and found him already dead, with one of the shots having hit the left side of the chest. "I'm so sorry, my friend," he uttered quickly, having no time to offer anything else for the body.

It was in a study that Tryst found Yak. Three guards of the manor lay dead or dying on the floor and there seemed to be no surface without blood upon it. Near the remnants of the broken window they had entered through sat Yak on his knees, cradling Vix in his arms, his blood soaked axe lying beside him.

"Is she alive?" asked Tryst as he sheathed his dagger and crossed the room.

"Barely," Yak said between heaves. "Where's Wedge?"

"Dead. He rushed into the hallway when you started shouting and he was shot for it," Tryst answered while checking the soldiers for signs of life and finding none. "I need you, Yak. Come with me."

"*She* needs me," he said while keeping his eyes squarely on Vix. "*You* can bugger off."

Tryst knelt beside Yak and looked upon the woman. Vix had taken the blast from near range to the right side of the chest. Her left hand clutched the mortal wound and her eyes had become glazy, staring into a nothingness that was miles from the carnage. "It's no good, she won't make it."

"I'm staying with Vix all the same. I won't let her die alone," the large man stated firmly. "Stay or leave, but do so quietly and quickly, Lynx."

"Yak..." Tryst began to say, before thinking better of asking for assistance again. "Don't get yourself killed, stay low."

A quick squeeze of the shoulder and Tryst left the last of the unit behind.

There was fighting in the hallways and rooms between the Flying Hawks and the guards of the manor, but nowhere among them did Tryst see the Minister. Tryst headed for the staircase, encountering a single guard on the way. The man tried to use the bayonet on the barrel of his gun to thrust at Tryst. It was a slow attempt in a narrow hallway and the soldier had little room to manoeuvre. Tryst evaded the jab, grabbed the gun by the barrel and yanked it from the fellow's hands, smashing the butt into the face of the soldier in quick succession.

Another Flying Hawk lay face down and dead at the foot of the stairway, his white suit soaked in red. Tryst stopped short and peeked upwards from around the corner. At the landing of the second floor was a lone man in the midnight blue uniform of the armed forces of the EMP. Like Tryst, he had taken a position of cover against a wall. The soldier leaned out just long enough so that Tryst could see an upraised pistol and a sleeve decorated with the gold bars that identified him as an officer.

That's most likely the captain of the town guards, Tryst surmised. *It wouldn't be unlike Nothram to save the best to protect his own damnable hide.*

Tryst turned the corner and made a loud stomp on the bottom step and leapt back to his cover position. The officer fired and made a hole in the wall opposite the stairs.

While the man was trying to reload, Tryst was on him. Having taken the steps two at a time to reach the top, he had collided with enough force to take the guardsman off his feet and into the wall behind him. The plaster of the wall crumbled under their combined weight and they landed on the floor of a bedroom. A girl in a nightgown began screaming and fled beneath her bed as the two men rolled on the rug beside her. The guard lost his pistol in the collision and was going for the sword on his hip. Before it could be produced, Tryst grabbed the wrist with his right hand and drove his left fist into the soldier's diaphragm. A loud groan escaped the soldier as the air was forced from his lungs, leaving him gasping and useless. Tryst seized on the moment of opportunity and drew the man's own sword, pressing it against his throat.

"Where is Nothram?!" he yelled at the captain.

The girl shouted from beneath her bed where she wept uncontrollably, "Please, don't kill Captain Hardnall!"

The eyes of Tryst went to her when Hardnall failed to answer between gasps of air. "Tell me where your father is and I promise you I will end the fighting," Tryst offered her.

At first, the girl wailed and turned her face away from Tryst, so he asked her again, louder and more demandingly.

She finally relinquished, "He's in his room. It's the last door down the hallway! The last door! Please don't hurt Captain Hardnall or Father, just make it stop!"

"I'll do my best, miss," Tryst answered her before turning his attention back to the captain. "On your feet, get in front of me."

Hardnall was yanked roughly to a standing position and his sword pressed against the small of his back. Tryst's free hand grabbed the collar of the captain's coat to hold him in place. "Don't make any sudden movements." Tryst ordered. "The girl seems to value your life and I don't want to break my promise. Let's go see Nothram."

Tryst marched his captive down the hall slowly, expecting other armed men to emerge from the other doors they passed. When they reached the last door, Tryst leaned in as close as he could to the Captain's ear. "How many men are with the minister?" he asked.

"Just two and they'll shoot if you open that door," Captain Hardnall replied, uttering his first words to Tryst.

Tryst flattened his back to the wall on their left, adjusting the sword tip to lay against Hardnall's hip while keeping his right gripped on the man's coat. "Then you open it. Don't give them any reason to do anything to you, if not for your own sake, then for the girl's. She doesn't need to cry any more this day."

The captain waited a beat while he considered his options, finally relenting reluctantly before knocking on the door in a particular pattern. "Minister Nothram!" he called out loudly. "The men accosting the manor have been contained to the first floor, but we can't hold out much longer. Might I come in to discuss our strategy?"

"No!" an old voice replied from within the room. "We hold it to our last! Marigold Tullivan will never have my surrender!"

Hardnall's eyes went wide and met Tryst's, sharing in his shock. "That fool will let you all die rather than yield to a woman," Tryst commented in disbelief.

Numerous footsteps began thudding up the stairs and soon the Hawks were upon them, kicking in the door to the room nearest them and eliciting more screams from the girl as they did.

"Hawks, stand down," Tryst commanded authoritatively. "Nothram is here, send for Wyvern!"

He was joined by Jay's crew, all four unharmed and whole. "You're certain he's in there?" asked the blood spattered squad leader.

Tryst answered quickly, "Aye, their Captain here says there are two guards with him."

Jay nodded and turned to his unit. "Oak, Crane, breach that door. Cloud, when that door is open, the four of us will go in and subdue the guards and we'll leave the securing of Nothram to you. Lynx, restrain your prisoner."

The man in Tryst's custody was mentally defeated the moment he heard his employer command that every fighting man in his command were to die.

Tryst wheeled him about and walked him back to the room with the girl. "This fight is done, we both know it. I'm going to let you go to that child and comfort her. Protect her, for she is not guilty of the crimes of her father. Don't do anything to make me regret this."

"I'm done," Captain Hardnall said with a despondent sigh. "You'll get no issue from me."

"Good, go to her before they break down that door," Tryst said as he released his grip on the disheartened soldier. "It's about to get very chaotic in here."

Tryst kept the sword and left the captain at the threshold of the girl's room, returning to lend support to Jay. His men named Crane and Oak had been searching for a makeshift battering ram and had settled on a nearby bench. While they went to work making splinters of both the door and bench alike, Tryst flattened against the wall beside Cloud.

"Are you with us, Lynx?" she asked over the ruckus of the crashing wood beside them, a coil of hempen rope in her hands already tied in loops and knots.

A nod served for his answer.

The door made a loud crack and fell inward. Both Oak and Crane dropped the bench dove away from the entrance as the last of Nothram's guardsmen fired their pistols simultaneously.

Jay gave a roar and the four, including Tryst, fell in behind him, descending on Nothram and the pair of guards.

The Flying Hawks, even without Tryst, were far more skilled than the common foot soldiers and with two to one odds against them, the soldiers both were disarmed and subdued with haste.

Tryst took a measure of satisfaction in seeing the albino woman tussling with Minister Nothram. He had swung a candelabrum, of all things, at Cloud, though she quickly deflected it and tossed him over her pivoted hip to the floor. For a brief second

Nothram struggled, but Cloud handled him on her own without issue.

If only both Marigold and Orangecloak could see this, Tryst thought to himself. *Minister Nothram hogtied and forced to surrender by a woman. Hard to say which one of them would enjoy it more.*

Seconds later, the Wyvern stepped into the now cramped room. "Well, isn't this a delicious piece of irony?" he asked as he cast his eyes to the sight of Cloud straddling Nothram's back. There was a look of satisfaction on her face as she put the finishing touches on the knots binding the minister.

"That's fantastic work, Cloud," Wyvern complimented her with a pat on the shoulder. "Lady Marigold will be sure to hear of who arrested Minister Nothram. I know she will take great pleasure in it."

Nothram spat and cursed from where he lay on the rug, still beneath his arrester. "I'll never surrender to a woman!"

Wyvern replied in a calm, measured voice. "It looks as though you don't have a choice, Minister Nothram. Or I suppose I should say 'Former' Minister Nothram. Your Captain of the Guards has already been dispatched to raise the white flag and spare the lives of the men you would so wantonly waste on foolish pride." He turned his attention to the men of the Flying Hawks, still holding the yielded guards. "Take these two and corral them with their comrades, we're still trying to find a place to hold them all temporarily. Lynx, when you're done, I'll have a word with you. You will find me with Yak, who is right where you left him."

The lower level of the manor was in a state of disarray. Tryst descended the stairs to find the furnishings broken, walls and windows alike pocked with holes and the wounded and dead of both sides lying on the floor where they fell.

Of the four teams to attack the manor, only Jay's came away without losses or injuries. The first familiar face Tryst had seen among the dead was Mink. He had been the Flying Hawk that Tryst had earlier discovered at the foot of the stairs, shot clean through the throat by Captain Hardnall.

His team leader, Vole, had lost three fingers on his right hand and to hear the medics talk, he would be lucky to regain the use of it.

As for Snow's team, all but he had been lacerated or shot in the melee, though he recorded no losses. That included Hare, whom Tryst would learn was later found by the foot soldiers of Marigold's army against the manor wall after the fighting had stopped.

Sometime after Tryst had left Yak, Vix had succumbed to her wound. The burly man was still on his knees, clutching her lifeless body and sobbing softly when Tryst stepped into the room.

Wyvern was already there, waiting and looking over the body of Wedge, who had been carried within the study to clear up space in the hallway outside. The weary and drained captain closed the eyes of his fallen soldier and slowly stood to face Tryst. "I hope you plan to honour that debt you owe us, Lynx," Wyvern whispered softly, his eyes on the distraught Yak, cradling Vix nearby. "For I believe we will need to ask for repayment far sooner than I had wanted."

30

ORANGECLOAK

It had been a simple enough question she had asked of Yahmina and the answer was simple in itself: "She's eager."

"I suppose she is, but what else can you say of Amyla?" Orangecloak asked, probing for a more thorough answer.

Yahmina was quick with a question of her own: "Do you have suspicions of her loyalty?"

"I have suspicions of everyone, Yahmina," Orangecloak answered drolly from the chair at her desk, cradling a large mug of hot, green tea to hand. "It comes with the territory of being Field Commander of the Thieves. You have to learn to see behind the eyes of every face you meet and hear the words their tongue doesn't say. Though my judgement is not fool proof and I sometimes seek out a second opinion. So, with that said: what do you say of Amyla?"

The elf took the time to think about her reply before putting it to words. "Amyla is a fierce little fighter and I think I can upgrade her to live steel before the spring. She learns quickly and, as I said, quite eagerly. As for her loyalty, she seems to be most loyal to vengeance. Both she and Athel are still in the throes of grief for her brother. The difference is that Athel is in mourning while Amyla has let her emotions manifest into anger and rage. It can make her dangerous, even unpredictable. That underlying danger is also a detriment to her fighting ability. If she fights in anger, she will leave herself open to careless mistakes on the battlefield, mistakes that could prove fatal for you and her alike."

"Your answer suggests that you still assume I am going to war," Orangecloak said, glancing up from the map on her desk.

Yahmina replied without hesitation, "And you keep trying to convince yourself that you won't."

Orangecloak let her have that one without further retort. She had come to value the elf's brutal honesty over the last few days. With Tryst and Greggard gone off to the battle in Pelican Harbour, Orangecloak had found her company reduced to Yahmina and the recruits from Obalen for the most part.

Councillor Maurice made a point to visit, but not daily, and the servants had proven themselves to be poor companions. Though friendly, they were entirely too formal and seemed totally unable to speak to her as they might with each other. Holding a conversation with them had been a battle unto itself and one Orangecloak had surrendered before long.

They've been servants their whole lives and likely their families as well for generations under the Simillons. All they know of conversation with those they tend upon is courtesies, even when I insist that I am no different than they, she had long surmised to herself. *They will never see me that way, no more than Amyla does. I am different in their eyes and perception is in the eye of the beholder.*

The young woman still looked upon Orangecloak with awe and admiration, treating her as if she was a Queen of old Phaleayna. To Amyla's credit, she was far more pliable than the servants and Athel was more amicable again. There hadn't been any formalities out of him since meeting Orangecloak at the *Sea Star Inn*.

"I'm a surgeon's nurse," he had stated proudly to Orangecloak. "When you spend your days with your hands covered in blood, trying to stop diseases from eating away at man, woman and child alike, you don't see classes. High birth, low birth, disease doesn't discriminate. It will feast upon you no matter how much coin is in your purse. When my enemy is so indiscriminate, it leaves me no room to be either. If you come into my clinic, I will stand by Doctor Zetheran and aid you, no matter whom you are. I bestow the same level of courtesy to all, much to the chagrin of any highborn that has been under my care."

Yahmina perched herself on the end of the desk, drawing Orangecloak out of the memory. "She makes a good sparring partner for you, though," the elf added to her review of Amyla. "Once we got beyond the point where she could dare to take a swing at you, that is."

"Then I thought she wouldn't *stop* swinging," Orangecloak replied, reflecting on the memory.

"It was good practice for you and a much needed release for her," Yahmina said nonchalantly. "From the first night I saw her, it was easy to see how consumed she was by her brother's death. I understand where her fury comes from. To your credit, you dodged most of her blows admirably. If only you had dodged *all* of them."

Orangecloak shifted uncomfortably in her chair, taking the weight from her aching left hip to her throbbing right. "Indeed, I've taken my share of welts and bruises today."

"I say they were earned," Yahmina stated frankly. "Luckily for you, her daggers were only wooden. Amyla fights like she's half mad, she gave you ample openings time after time to disarm her and knock her down and you tried only to defend."

"It's as you just said, she fights like she is maddened," Orangecloak responded defensively. "I couldn't seem to get a blow in with her hacking at me like an overcooked steak."

"I would have," the warrior woman of the Elven Forest put back to Orangecloak.

She raised her cup of green tea to Yahmina. "Then tomorrow you may fight Amyla and demonstrate how to get around her offence."

"Consider it done."

The new day came and Orangecloak found herself sitting on a thick branch overlooking a snow and mud covered clearing in the woods near the manor. Her attention was on the sparring contest below, watching as Amyla grew more and more frustrated with Yahmina. The elven woman was dodging and parrying with just one of Orangecloak's wooden swords with ease, having left the other one beneath Orangecloak's tree with their water canteens and provisions.

Every time Amyla pressed, Yahmina found a place to stick the point of her sword in Amyla's borrowed leather armour or drag it along a vital spot and say a single word: "Dead."

Within a dozen quick, splintery deaths, Amyla was livid and breathing hard while Yahmina stood poised and ready. "Calm yourself, human and take a rest. Your anger blinds you to the point where this is no challenge at all," she said before turning to Orangecloak. "It's time you came down from up there and sparred. You've watched me long enough. Let us see if anything has stuck with you."

With a backward roll, Orangecloak slipped silently from the tree and landed tidily on her feet in fine form.

"I'm impressed," she heard over her shoulder, turning to see Athel strolling through the woods in search of them. "That was quite the landing."

"Have you come to learn at the feet of Instructor Windleaf?" Orangecloak asked the approaching man in a jovial tone.

Athel spoke leisurely, clad in a dark blue cloak that was clasped at the shoulder and further held tight by a hand. "Nay, the only blade I wield is a scalpel, or a knife being pressed into service as such. I treat wounds, I don't cause them."

Orangecloak gave him a nod. "I can respect that, Athel. Then surely there must be something to bring you all the way out here to the courtwood?"

His eyes scanned around at the clearing, looking unimpressed with it. "I had wanted to see this training facility Amyla had spoken so fondly of. From what I can see it seems to be little more than a muddied field, though."

"Not so," Yahmina said, having overheard Athel. "Through the forest on the other side of the clearing is an archery range I devised for myself. Go and have a look."

The wooden blade Yahmina had been using flew through the air deftly from her hands towards Orangecloak. She caught it carefully by the hilt, despite it being little more than a weighted practice sword.

"My lady, Amyla awaits the pleasure of your wooden blades," Yahmina declared as she reached the tree.

Orangecloak grabbed her second sword from where Yahmina left it and went into the clearing where the muddy and sweaty Amyla was still on a knee taking a rest. Seeing Athel still standing beside Yahmina to watch the sparring seemed to spur the curly haired brunette's spirit and she rose to meet her challenger.

While she stretched her arms and legs, Orangecloak gave her simple instructions. "Same as yesterday, Amyla, you will show me no easement."

"As milady so wishes," Amyla answered while lunging at her. Orangecloak swatted the blow aside and began to retaliate, stabbing and slashing at the woman. Orangecloak had the height and reach on Amyla, though the difference was not so great as to make the contest unsporting. The frustration in Amyla grew and Orangecloak pressed her own attack further, driving Amyla backward. Finally, Amyla's rage came forth in an angry fury and she parried and swung at Orangecloak's face with her left blade. It was a high arc, easily ducked, that left her open for a jab in the ribs with the wooden blade in Orangecloak's right hand.

"Dead," Orangecloak declared in victory.

"By Aren's balls," Amyla cursed through gritted teeth as she turned back to face Orangecloak and take a deep breath.

Yahmina called out from where she spectated beside Athel. "That's better, my lady. Amyla, you need to focus. Balance your emotions and keep them in check. Both of you, back to where you were and go another round. We will go for best eight out of fifteen."

Amyla shot a glance at Orangecloak. "The elf is going to drive us to madness," she muttered under her breath.

"She's an instructor," Orangecloak reminded her in a low voice, herself only having found that out the day after the fateful visit to the *Sea Star Inn*. "It's her job to drive us to our edge, to see if we can look into the abyss at its end and come back unscathed."

Amyla politely bowed at that and lowered herself into a ready position. "Wise words, milady. Let's find that edge and dance on it."

Their timber blades continued to clack loudly through the morning air. Orangecloak and Amyla were evenly matched in many ways, but Amyla's frustrations dictated the direction of each match. Four more contests went unanimously in Orangecloak's favour, ending on her decree of "Dead!" each time her blade found its way to the padded leather coat Amyla wore.

"Three more and the lady Orangecloak will win quite decisively, Miss Spade," Yahmina astutely observed. She was alone by then, perched on the same branch Orangecloak had been seated upon before the exercise began.

It wasn't until Yahmina had gotten their attention that the sparring woman had noticed the absence of Athel. The exhaustion was setting in on Amyla, the evidence of which being clearly heard on her voice. "I know, Instructor, I will try harder. Where has Athel gone?"

"Where indeed, I wonder?" Yahmina facetiously queried, her voice dripping with sarcasm. "Did you see him leave, my lady?"

"I did not," Orangecloak admitted, getting a sense of where Yahmina was taking this particular lesson and playing into it.

The elf shrugged ever so smugly. "Then I should declare you

both dead and forsake this sparring entirely. On the battlefield you need to keep your senses alert of everything going on about you. Concentrating too closely on one person or thing will blind you to everyone else and leave you wide open. We are taught to look for such weaknesses in the Combat University. A warrior paying attention to one's surroundings can dispatch a great number when his foes are so singularly focused."

When both participants nodded in understanding and caught their breath, the Elf relented, "You may continue on though, I would like to practice my archery before the sun is set. The score is five for my lady, none for Miss Spade. Match six, let it commence."

The sixth match was quick, as Amyla found a second breath and wasted it on anger again. The practice sword in Orangecloak's left managed to find its way directly to the heart after another wild swing from Amyla.

It was the seventh match that surprised both Yahmina and Orangecloak, who found herself flat on her back, with both her red hair and green leathers caked in brown mud. Orangecloak's swords were out of hands reach and atop her chest sat the skinny frame of Amyla Spade. The tip of one of her own wooden blades pressed beneath the chin of the woman she was now pledged to. "You are dead, milady," Amyla said in heavy breaths through gritted teeth.

You are more like Ellarie Dollen than you might ever know, Orangecloak thought in that moment. Behind the dark eyes of Amyla sat a hatred for a world that had robbed her of normalcy and wronged her family. That same malice had lived within Ellarie when they met and over time Orangecloak was able to soften her dear friend's loathing into discontent. Back then, though, she had years to do that and during that time had never led Ellarie into battle. There was no such allowance for Amyla. Orangecloak and Yahmina had only so much time to help her emotionally and during that they were training to shed blood.

The sudden and brutal death of her brother had shattered Amyla's world, as Ellarie's had been shattered by the intolerance of her father. The difference between the two was that Orangecloak had helped Ellarie to put the fragments back together while Amyla was merely learning to avenge the broken shards.

"Are you hurt, milady?" Amyla withdrew the blade and became suddenly concerned. "I am so sorry if I have hurt you." She fell back on her bottom and off Orangecloak's chest. "I'm so sorry, milady. I don't know what came over me."

Orangecloak answered calmly, trying to mask her fear, "I'm not hurt, Amyla, please, help me up." The woman leapt to her feet and held out a hand for Orangecloak to grab. "Pick up your blades," she instructed Amyla. "The score is six to one. We have at least two more matches to settle this ahead of us."

Timidity took over Amyla in the next match and she practically let Orangecloak disarm her of both blades. Orangecloak won with ease and Yahmina was the first to say as much. "You're not fighting back, Amyla. I'm not counting that match, the score remains as it was before. Commence match eight when you are ready."

"I'm sorry, Instructor Windleaf," Amyla stammered.

Yahmina hopped down to the ground and walked into the fighting ring to face her dark haired pupil and her downcast eyes. "Look up at me," she instructed, guiding Amyla's head with a finger beneath the chin. "If this was a real battle, your foe would have done the same as Lady Orangecloak. Do you understand?"

Amyla shrugged off the elf's finger. "It's not a real battle. We're practicing in a muddy, snowy field with wooden toys, for Iia's sake."

"But if it were, you would have failed in your duty to protect the one you have sworn your life to. Another blade would have gotten beyond you and potentially to her," Yahmina explained sharply, gesturing her head in Orangecloak's direction. "If you want to learn to fight, you must exorcise such weakness. Your knees practically buckled when you merely thought you had hurt Orangecloak. What will they do if something should actually happen to her?"

"I won't let that happen," a defiant Amyla declared.

Yahmina folded her arms and stared down the former maid from Obalen as she continued to lecture her. "If your resolve is broken so easily, then the choice will not be yours. To be a warrior you must first be a smith and such faults must be hammered from the sword until all that remains is hardened, unflinching steel. You cannot let emotions cloud your judgement on the battlefield or you will most certainly pay for that mistake with your life."

"Did you not say to me when I agreed to this training that Combat University candidates are rejected for being unfeeling?" Amyla countered.

There was no doubt that Yahmina was ready for just that very question. "To be void of emotion and to control one's emotions are two different things entirely, Miss Spade. It is said that Mackhol Taves is void of emotion. The cruelty he not only condones, but demands of his guards in Biddenhurst, is inhuman. He is a terrible person and would be a terror on the battlefield if he could swing a sword, but he could never join the Combat University. What we look for in our students is heart, courage and the fortitude to do what is needed to prevent such heinousness from lording over the known world."

Amyla's jaw dropped and she looked upon Yahmina incredulously. "Then why was your so called 'Master of Blades' working for Lord Master Grenjin Howland? Is Grenjin not the very definition of heinous?" she shouted back.

Before Yahmina could answer, Orangecloak did. "The character of Tryst Reine is not in question, Amyla. I can vouch for him."

"Then why did he work for Howland?" Amyla asked again crossly. "Why did he stand aside while men and women like my brother were put to death?"

Orangecloak replied once more, trying to assuage Amyla's doubts. "There are a great many reasons for that and I can assure you it was not easy for Tryst to sit idly by. The short answer is that you or I or the men and women of the Combat University or the Thieves cannot help everyone. It is the greater good that is weighed before an individual need."

"That is correct, my lady," Yahmina nodded approvingly. "It is taught to us early in our training that we should always strive to do better by ourselves, by our neighbours and by the people we share this world with. Though often, what is best for one might be detrimental to the neighbour and helping the neighbour might harm the many. It is learning to balance such that the University aims to teach. If a student lacks emotion entirely, they cannot understand what it is to make such decisions. On the contrary to that, if the student is unable to take absolute control over their emotions, then they cannot hope to make those decisions with a clear, unbiased mind. Do you understand, Amyla?"

The young woman shrugged in response, her hands and the blades clutched in them falling limply to her sides. "Then why fight at all? Wouldn't violence make us just as bad as those who would use it against us?"

"That is a very important question," Yahmina responded

reassuringly. "There are people in the world like Mackhol Taves and the raiding gangs of the Southlands who are void of empathy and consumed by greed and malevolence. These men, and even women, will not hesitate to resort to the most violent and unthinkable measures to achieve their goals. They would kill, maim and torture those who resist and rape and pillage as they go. When there exist those who will go to the greatest extreme to hurt their fellow citizens, what resort is left for those who would stop them? It takes those with constitution, fortitude and strength to counter such tyranny, savagery and brutality."

Yahmina's voice rang of pride as she spoke and she kept her gaze locked on Amyla. Though, it occurred to Orangecloak that the words seemed to be as much for her as they were for her sparring partner. "That is what the men and women of the Combat University fight for. We have to know the value of life. Only those who understand that value can shoulder the burden of being able to take it. When a potential student puts themselves before us, it is the job of instructors like me to determine if they know this. Those that have this understanding and possess the potential to physically and mentally handle the toll may join our ranks. They train in arms in our halls and bathe in the collective knowledge of centuries of valiant and honourable warriors before them. When we know the burden is something they can bear and their skills have been properly honed to defend the vulnerable and oppose those who would bring suffering, then 'they' become 'we'."

Amyla's brown eyes glanced to Orangecloak, a look of hope suddenly appearing in them as Yahmina's words sank in. "Does the fact that you're training me mean that you think I have the understanding and the skills to join the school in Drake?" she asked.

"I am not an Initiation Instructor, so some might say I lack their insight to be able to judge properly," Yahmina answered with a clever smile. "For what it's worth though, I think you do. Consider that if I didn't, I wouldn't be sharing my knowledge with you at all," the elf said while looking to the sky.

Orangecloak followed her line of sight to where both the white and red moons were now visible in the darkening field of blue. "The day wanders ever closer to dusk. Tomorrow we will come back here and the day after that and so forth until this snow has receded and your skillset has grown."

"Yes, Instructor Windleaf," Amyla answered with a newfound sense of pride. "Are you dismissing us for the day?"

"Indeed, you have both done enough for today. I shall meet you both for dinner later," Yahmina replied, spinning on her heel and strolling away.

Orangecloak had already gone for the water canteens hanging on a tree nearby, leaving her new friend to follow.

"Does it make you nervous, my lady?" Amyla inquired as she joined her. "To be training to fight like this, I mean. All I've ever known of you and your Thieves are the protests. You're not fighters, at least not this sort of fighting."

A loose trickle of water ran down Orangecloak's face as she swallowed hard. "I'd be lying if I said it didn't make me nervous."

"I'm nervous too," Amyla said. The palpability of that nervousness was evident in every word she spoke. "I just want to slow everything down."

The statement struck Orangecloak as odd. "Why is that?"

"Just a few weeks ago, I was a maid for Minister Felton of Obalen. Making beds, emptying chamber pots, that sort of thing. All I could think about was getting home to my husband in the evening and visiting my brother and Athel in my spare time."

That revelation surprised Orangecloak. "You were married?"

"Aye, I suppose he's filed for spousal abandonment by now though," Amyla said sadly with a little shrug. "He will know what happened to Lenn and from there will figure out what became of Athel and me. Don't be mistaken, he won't care that I left. In fact, I would say he's already proposed to that ample, blonde haired nanny that works for Minister Felton that he always so desired."

Amyla gazed out at the sparring area longingly. "All of that feels as though it was a lifetime ago, like it was some other woman who was a maid with a disloyal husband. Now, I'm swinging wooden swords at the Lady Orangecloak and an elven instructor from the Combat University is teaching me how to protect you. Everything is moving and changing so fast, I feel like I haven't even had time to mourn my brother. I just...I just wish it would all slow down, just so that I might have the chance to catch up."

"I'm sorry, Amyla," Orangecloak said softly, her hands going to Amyla's arms when it seemed she seemed on the verge of weeping. "I have taken you in to my fold and your concerns are now my concerns.

I'll help you and Athel get through this as best I can. We have the winter. I know it's not much, but you'll come through this. You're stronger than you know."

"My lady, I'm not worthy of such kindness," Amyla told Orangecloak with a shake of her head that sent brown curls tumbling about her shoulders.

"I happen to think you are." Orangecloak smiled before turning toward the direction Yahmina had gone. "Come, the day grows late and I'm exhausted."

By the time Yahmina had relented, she had worn both her students to the breaking point of exhaustion. Soaking in the hot waters of the bathtub in her quarters brought Orangecloak the first bit of relief of the day. It was difficult to think of a body part below the chin that wasn't throbbing from the exercise. Yet it was a good pain, one she welcomed in a strange way. There was a time when she trained daily and was constantly beleaguered by aching muscles and treated the pain as a sign of growth. Even those days felt like a flickering memory now. For a moment, she even began to doze in the wet heat and her eyelids grew heavy with fatigue.

Though her eyes had fluttered only briefly, Orangecloak had no way of knowing how long she had nodded off for when she heard a tiny knock on her door. She jolted awake with a splash as she heard a timid, little voice call her name from without.

"Miss Orangecloak, are you quite well?" It was Daisy, she realised, the brunette handmaiden that tried to tend on Orangecloak hand and foot whenever she was inside the manor.

"Yes, Daisy, I am, is anything the matter?" Orangecloak answered, careful to not give invitation to enter.

"Oh, okay." The young maiden seemed to pause a moment on the other side of the heavy, ornate door to the bathing room in Orangecloak's guest chambers. "It's just that Councillor Maurice is without and would like to see you. Shall I send him away, milady?"

That surprised Orangecloak and her mind raced with questions. "Councillor Maurice has come to the manor at this hour? Is it urgent?" she asked the maid.

Orangecloak could almost hear Daisy fidgeting nervously outside the bathing room. "I...I didn't ask. It's not my place to ask the noblefolk of their business, milady."

There was nothing to be done about it. The councillor was not a man to be deterred and he was her acting host after all, it would be rude to refuse him. "Very well, Daisy. I will see him, but do be sure to keep him outside until I am dressed."

"Yes, milady, of course," Daisy replied to the door.

It was only when her footsteps fell distant that Orangecloak actually stepped out of the bath. A warm, fluffy towel awaited her and shortly after an equally warm, green robe that was so long it gathered about her feet. Her hair hung in damp ringlets about her, even after she had tried to dry them with the towel. She had no time to even attempt to dry it further and opted to tie it up in a quick bun.

When she had drained the tub and emerged from the bathroom, Orangecloak found her handmaiden waiting beside the hallway door. "You may see him in now, Daisy," she said while seating herself at the fine chair behind the spacious desk. Atop it sat the large map of Illiastra that Orangecloak had been using. Despite the fact that it still bore no marks to indicate her own plans, she folded it quickly and laid it aside out of sight.

The Councillor of the Gunridge district was clad, as usual, in the fancy, embroidered robes that were the common dress of the nobles of Johnah. Today he decided on a bold yellow with cloth of gold trim and heavy looking sleeves that concealed his hands. "Good evening, my lady, I hope I am not disturbing you," he said by way of greeting, moving past Daisy without so much as a hello.

Orangecloak responded in the noblest sounding voice she could muster, "Not at all, Councillor, do come in and be seated. I sense you have some news to share?"

Maurice wore a polite smile that Orangecloak could see beyond as he moved gracefully toward the desk. What this man could tell her could probably fill an ocean. "I do bear some tidings that I wish to share, aye." Though that answer told Orangecloak she would be likely to only get a puddle's worth. "Dear maiden," he said, addressing Daisy. "A snifter of brandy would suffice right about now, if you would. Perhaps some wine for Lady Orangecloak?"

"No wine for me, but I will take a pot of black tea, Daisy, thank you," Orangecloak said kindly, making a point of making eye contact with Daisy.

"Yes, milord and lady, as you wish," the maid answered quickly before departing, leaving Orangecloak alone with Maurice.

Orangecloak jumped to what she expected was the heart of the matter. "Have you gotten word from Pelican Harbour?"

"Alas, I do not. I wait patiently every day for such," Maurice answered despondently while lowering himself into the armchair on the other side of the desk.

Orangecloak opened her hands wide in puzzlement. "Then what is it that brings you, Councillor? Usually your visits to the manor come much earlier within the day, so it strikes me as odd that you're here at this hour to specifically seek myself."

"This is true, though today I was ensconced in a meeting with the other councillors of the city on a matter of some urgency, hence my late arrival. Tell me, my lady, when you went into town the other night, did you not notice that the streets were strangely barren?"

She nodded gravely. "I did, I was given to understand that the reason for that was due to an increased presence by the Triarchy's hooded enforcers."

Maurice flicked his index finger towards her affirmatively. "Indeed it is and that is precisely the problem. The Triarchy fights the rule of Marigold as vociferously as they once opposed you, my lady. It seems a woman of any background in Illiastra being anything more than subservient is too much for the most devout to stomach."

Orangecloak exhaled at that. "I know her struggle all too well."

"You would also know that the Triarchy fight with fear and manipulation," Maurice said. "It's hard to combat an enemy that claims it has a supernatural, all powerful deity in its corner and can convince the populace into believing such. Whether or not they can produce evidence becomes irrelevant if no one calls the bluff of the threat. It seems my fellow councillors are among those feeling threatened by the fear mongering of the most pious and the citizens seem to be faring only a little better. Meanwhile, the enforcers are doing as they will, arresting anyone breaking Triarchist law, punishing them as they see fit and defying the orders of the city watch. Despite my pleas for unified action against the Triarchy, the councillors are wont to get between them. It seems they fear that they will incur the wrath of Ios for disturbing the work of his so called 'Blessed servants.' It is a troubling situation to say the least."

"That is troubling," Orangecloak agreed. "I assume you have some sort of contingency plan in place to deal with the Triarchy?"

"We do. It's been largely ineffective thus far, though," Maurice admitted reluctantly with a sigh. "Greggard and I met with the city's

Patriarch and his Triarchists after Greggard returned from the funeral of the late Lord Marscal. At first, Greggard asked them for understanding and proffered that perhaps the *God's Gift* was wrongly interpreted when it came to women being leaders or even having basic rights. When that request was met with flat refusal, he then sought to pay for their blind eye on the matter, an offer they thought insulting to their gods. Lastly, Lord Greggard gave them an ultimatum: they could prove the existence of their gods and in the absence of evidence the Lord Greggard would refuse to adhere to their laws any longer. They balked at this too and insisted the *God's Gift* was all the evidence that would ever be required. It only escalated from there and soon the holy men were all shouting over one another at Greggard, hurling insults at he and I and calling us blasphemers and heretics and heathens. I had to call the city watch to have them all ejected them from the town hall for fear of violence.

"Things since then have gotten drastically worse. Lord Greggard made a motion to remove the untaxed status of the Triarchy and charge the Portsward Tower of Ios a decade's worth of back taxes. He gave them a third of a season to pay down no less than the bare interest on the taxes or face eviction from their leased property.

"As you can tell from your visit to the town, the fires are still burning brightly in the Tower of Ios and we've not seen a copper of tax payment. They've barricaded themselves within and decided they will no longer recognise the laws of heretics and instead will be enforcing Triarchy law. To do this, they send out their burgundy brothers by night to harry those they find in the streets. There's been bloodshed, between the bastards with the bastard swords and the city watch, mostly, but civilians have been caught in the chaos as well. That's why the streets are so barren: there are two sets of contradictory rules for the townsfolk to live by after sundown and no one wants to be caught in the middle when they clash."

She waited until Maurice had finished before giving a reply of her own. "The Triarchy made my own life agonising at every turn and all this time I had thought that they and the ruling class were hand in hand. It's altogether foreign to hear that the two longstanding allies are now at odds."

The door creaked open as Maurice opened his mouth and he closed it in a hurry, abstaining from speaking at all when Daisy moved into the room. She came bearing a silver platter and atop which sat a steaming pot of tea with cups, sugar and milk. Beside the tea and its accessories was a basket lined and covered in cloth napkins and a decanter of brandy with an empty snifter. "Milord and milady, I do hope you don't think it presumptuous of me, but I took the liberty of bringing you some warm buns that were just being pulled from the oven. I thought you might be hungry."

"Thank you, though I will just have the brandy," Maurice replied stiffly to the maid without so much as much as a glance.

Orangecloak smiled politely for the girl. "Thank you, Daisy. I could certainly go for something to eat. That was thoughtful of you."

"Tis nothing, milady," Daisy blushed, as Orangecloak found she did often when praised even the slightest. "I'm happy to serve."

"You are dismissed for now, girl." The command came abruptly from the councillor, and to Orangecloak it even seemed curt. "I'll come find you when the lady and I are done talking."

Orangecloak was not about to let the friendly little maid leave on that note. "Daisy, Councillor Maurice sees a need to speak with me in private. When we're done, please come back and have some of this fresh bread and tea with me. I'd hate to see it go to waste."

That brought back the wide grin of the maid. "Certainly, milady, as you wish," she said with a bow before departing the room.

"That sets a bad precedent, my lady. By being overly kind to the servants, it casts your hosts in a poor light," Maurice commented dryly while pouring his brandy.

"You were a servant once yourself, Councillor," Orangecloak replied while stirring sugar and milk into her tea. "How is it that you can speak so lowly of those doing a job you once did?"

"Careful, girl, your words have the potential to wound me," Maurice spoke in a playful tone with a raised eyebrow. "It's rather quite the contrary: being of low birth gives me an appreciation for Daisy and the other servants that those like Greggard lack. It's that when folks like you and I are so outwardly gracious to the serving staff that we remind both worlds that we are but outsiders in the upper echelon. There is always a game at play, regardless if I am speaking to handmaiden Daisy Scullard or Lord Master Grenjin Howland. We all have a shell we wear to show the world what we want to see. It shields who we are beneath and reflects what we want others to believe. I want the world to see a wealthy, successful man of the noble class from Johnah. I dress in the robes worn by those of noble origin in my homeland, though I had never worn them until I came here. It is what one would expect a man of my station and ethnicity to wear, so I wear it and play my part. There is no one that would think I was actually born in a filthy shanty in the slums of the city of Azarai. However, I dropped the first half of my surname and altered my forename and was given leave to call myself a bastard of my former employer, the nobleman Vernon Dawe.

"The mask I wear is the face that everything of the upper crust of society is supposed to be. It is a heavy burden and one I must carry from dawn to dusk, every day, with everyone."

"Except me, it seems," Orangecloak noted in a flat voice.

The councillor rose to his feet and walked about the room as he spoke. "You are like me, my lady: a great pretender. As much as I like Daisy, and believe me, I am rather fond of the girl, she is not. Her heart is embroidered on her sleeve for all to see and as such, she must be played to see only the shell, lest she unwittingly gives up the ruse."

He stopped before the muddy, green leather coat she had hung over a chair near the fireplace. Ever so gracefully, he held up a sleeve for inspection with his left hand while his right still held the brandy snifter. "You and I are much alike, my lady. I could sense a kindred bond between us from the moment I laid eyes on you. We climbed from the pit that we were born into with blood and sacrifice. You may dress in torn clothing and play the part of a pauper, but like it or not, you are now part of the ruling class."

She swallowed hard at that, her eyes going to the crackling fireplace for a moment. "You did not come to compare life stories, Councillor. Have you any other news I should hear?"

"No, I suppose I didn't. The truth is I came to tell you a few things and because I had just come from Yahmina's chambers with the promise that I would escort you to her. Your instructor has requested to speak with you."

"Very well, give me a moment to clothe myself and I'll join you in the hallway," Orangecloak said as she slid her chair back, glad for any reason to end the conversation.

For her outfit she had only her leather leggings, doeskin boots, dwarven tunic and green bodice. Despite offers for new clothing from servants and hosts alike, Orangecloak had turned them all down in favour of her meagre selection. Skirts, corsets, dresses and frilly blouses were not Orangecloak's idea of comfortable attire and that had been the entirety of their offerings.

For a moment she considered the orange cloak as well and her gaze fell to where it lay folded and hidden beneath her pillow. She hadn't worn it since her fateful meeting with Greggard Simillon and with good reason. There were too many eyes in the manor and none of them did Orangecloak trust, regardless of Greggard's vouchsafing. The cloak was her most identifiable mark and without it she could pass for merely being a visitor with red hair, a somewhat uncommon, but otherwise completely unremarkable trait.

Once dressed and in the hallway, she found Maurice staring through one of the tall windows overlooking the moonlit courtyard.

"You look resplendent as always, my lady," he complimented her generously when he turned toward her. "Have you been to the upper floors of the manor yet?"

"I'm afraid I have not," she answered. "I've kept myself hidden away as requested. I have only been to my room, the meeting chamber and the outer yards with Yahmina and Amyla for our daily training."

Maurice made a wide gesture with one of his long sleeves down the hall and began walking with her. "Then allow me to show you the way."

"You said there was other news I should know. Is it from Biddenhurst by chance? Has there been word of my lieutenants?" Orangecloak asked as they got underway.

"I fear that our days of obtaining news freely from the east are at an end, my lady," Maurice admitted regretfully.

She turned to face him. "What could have happened to make you say that?"

"Obalen is lost to us," he sighed. "As a result, our railway has been severed from rest of the country, effectively hindering our communications and influence."

Orangecloak was baffled to hear it. "This is a great loss to the cause, how is it that Lord Greggard and Lady Marigold did not try to seize it first?"

Councillor Maurice had no issue with explaining further. "Lord Greggard tried to appeal to Minister Felton through conventional methods and evidently the Elite Merchants or the Triarchy had gotten to Obalen first. My wager would be on the latter. Felton's a pious sheep of a man. It is common knowledge amongst the ruling class that the Triarchy controls Obalen, not Felton. He capitulates to whatever they say without question. I counselled Lord Greggard to send steel instead of paper, but he didn't seem too concerned with taking Obalen at all and saw the letter as merely a formality."

"I would think it inevitable that the EMP would cut off West Illiastra from the railways and Obalen would be the most natural juncture at which to do that," Orangecloak pondered aloud as Maurice led her up a marvellous, dark varnished staircase. "Furthermore, Obalen is only a strategic location when you consider it from a locomotive perspective. I've been there, Councillor, many times. They have no defensive perimeter at all and only a single guard tower. Neither side will be able to hold it very long from the other."

"These points are all well and good," Maurice said in agreement. "The problem is that Obalen gives our enemies a base with which to attack us from. It will turn this newly crowned nation into a theatre of war, and even if we win, we will have nothing but ruins for our home. The railway severance also creates a major problem for you, my lady."

"And what would that be?" she queried. "I'm well accustomed to trekking across Illiastra on foot, I assure you. Even stowing away in the cargo cars of trains is a luxury."

He shook his head. "That is not what I was referring to. If soldiers cannot access our ports to reach Aquas Bay and man their ships, then they will have to go over land."

Orangecloak filled in the rest for him. "They will need to cross the Southlands, lest Aquas Bay become isolated from the rest of Illiastra. That is an issue, though if a great portion of the Illiastran army treks into the Southlands, there is little my Thieves could hope to do about that."

Maurice seemed ready for her to say as much. "They can, if you can unite the people of the Southlands and marshal an army of your own. I admit that I know little and less of the Southlands compared to you, my lady. What I do know is that there are but three ministers residing south of the Varras River. Only Aquas Bay and Minister Petor Polliane are completely untouchable by you at this point. Our reports seem to indicate that Clay Harlowe's hold on the Warrens is tenuous at best. That still puts him in a better position than Minister Josch Bight, whose grasp of power only extends as far as the outer walls of the westerly Fort Plackett."

A shiver went through Orangecloak as they walked slowly

down the spotlessly clean hallway. The more she listened, the more it became apparent that the goals of Lord Greggard and Councillor Maurice were not completely aligned. "This had me thinking, my lady," he continued. "The sooner you can strike south, the better."

And there it is.

"Lord Greggard had intended that I stay until spring," Orangecloak softly reminded him. "He insisted that my contributions were not needed until then."

For a moment Councillor Maurice was mum, save for a queer look he gave to the empty hallway ahead of them. He glanced over both shoulders, and seeing no one, turned back to Orangecloak. "Follow me, for there is something I would show you."

His casual pace quickened to a stride and Orangecloak adjusted to keep up. They stopped at the hallway's end and turned to climb yet another set of stairs, these ones narrow and all but hidden in the outer walls. *These are servant's passages,* Orangecloak realised.

They emerged at the top of the stairs on what seemed to be the floor containing the Simillon family's sleeping chambers. It was quiet up here, scarcely lit save for a few electric lamps mounted in wall sconces. "Where are you leading me?" Orangecloak said while lowering her voice to a whisper. "I get the feeling we would not be permitted to be up here."

Maurice put a finger to his lips to silence her as he cautiously looked about once more. "You're right, we're not welcome to explore this far, so be sure to keep your voice down. There's not like to be anyone up here at this hour, but we must not risk it."

He led her to an old, oaken door, beautifully moulded and varnished to a dark lustre. The two of them slipped inside, with the councillor letting the door open just enough for them to squeeze in. A great feeling of nervousness tinged with excitement had overcome Orangecloak as she wondered what this great mystery could be.

The room they entered was already illuminated by two lights situated on a distant wall. Without much else, Orangecloak could tell this was the master chamber of the manor. A large, high posted bed sat in the middle of the floor and draped with blue silk so fine it was practically transparent. The accompanying furnishings were lavish and likely expensive beyond reason, topped here and there with the personal effects of Lord Greggard and his wife.

As she let her eyes adjust to the dimness, she noticed Maurice moving towards the lights out of the corner of her left.

"Here, have a look," he called to her.

Orangecloak went and stood beside him, her eyes befalling a large painting situated on the wall between the two light fixtures. At first glance it looked like the three most prominent figures of the Triarchy: the ruling god Ios, standing tall and proud and garbed in white robes to the left of a globe of the known world. His right arm stretched from Gildriad across the sea to clutch tightly at the land of the Atrebell region of Illiastra. On the opposite side of the blue, green and brown sphere stood Iia, the subjugated goddess. She wore a shimmering white gown and a striped cape coloured with a mixture of green, gold and red that was lifted by the wind. An arm of the goddess was outstretched, reaching to touch the world so greedily guarded by Ios. Beneath gods and globe alike was the fallen god of the dwarves, Aren. Lying on his side, naked but for a loincloth with his wrists bound in black, iron shackles and clutching the ankles of Iia. The whole thing was painted with oil on canvas, intricately detailed and full of life. There were so many little touches and flourishes that Orangecloak could have spent years scouring it and not found everything the artist had crafted.

"It is simply astounding, Councillor," Orangecloak said with a voice full of awe. "Though, I'm still not sure why you brought me all the way up here to see it."

"Look at the faces of the gods and tell me who you see, my lady," he suggested.

She first studied the face of Ios and saw the lines of age in his cheeks and the wrinkled brow that led to a sharp nose below it. Most of all she saw the dark, piercing eyes that stared harshly and enviously at Iia. "Ios seems to bear a striking resemblance to Lord Grenjin Howland," she observed before moving on to Aren, his eyes cast upward at the goddess standing above. A dark, course beard lined his face and his body was clearly dwarven, resembling the people that were once his most devout worshippers. The eyes were green and the face red and ruddy in the cheeks and nose from a mixture of hard weather and strong mead. "The face of Aren I do not know, though neither do I know Chief Robarte of the dwarves and yet I reckon they are one in the same here."

Lastly she came to Iia, her gaze locked on Ios with eyes of the brightest blue and a look of determination. The face was pale and smooth, with the faintest whisper of a smile on slender lips. Encapsulating the visage were flowing ringlets of red tumbling over lithe shoulders onto the tricoloured cape of green, gold and red.

No, not red...Orange.

"Iia...She is..." Orangecloak gasped, taking an idle step forward as she became fixated on the face of the goddess.

"She is you, Lady Orangecloak," Maurice answered for her.

Orangecloak shook her head in disbelief as she continued to stare at the painting. "I have never seen this before. Who painted it? How did Lord Greggard come to have it? I thought it was forbidden for artists to paint my likeness. Why would he risk being caught with it?"

The councillor stepped ahead so as to be directly at her side again. "Your image is forbidden and satirical imagery of the gods and the EMP is equally so. This came from the Shadowed Gallery, my lady."

Orangecloak was only passingly familiar with the Shadowed Gallery, which was a gallery in name only. In truth, it was a network of artists who sold their work to wealthy men with coin enough to buy expensive and forbidden art. From Orangecloak's general understanding, there were pieces depicting her image sold in these backroom dealings. Only two of these had she ever seen and neither were as exquisite or immense as the one before her.

Maurice lifted a long sleeve in the direction of the painting as he talked. "As we couldn't have a member of the EMP ever be found to be buying from the Shadowed Gallery, it was my benefactor, Vernon Dawe, who we sent to procure it for Lord Greggard. Even Bradico, the artist behind this masterpiece, was personally on hand to sell what I believe to be his finest work."

"Why did Greggard want it at all?" Orangecloak asked, still awestruck by the canvas.

"Why indeed?" Maurice responded tellingly. "Why would he put Tryst Reine in Atrebell as a safeguard for your benefit? Why would he explicitly state in the contract that Tryst was to bring you to him? Why has he been so insistent on aiding you?"

Orangecloak refused to believe what he was suggesting. "That's madness, Councillor. The man is a happily married father."

"And where are his wife and children? Sent away to keep them safe from the war, aye, that's a clever excuse, I will give him that."

"I'm to believe you're outing the lust of one of your closest friends for my benefit?"

"There are times when the best way to help my friends is to protect them from themselves," Maurice admitted despondently. "Also, I made a promise to his wife Lorna that I would strive to prevent Lord Greggard from ever finding himself in such a compromising situation. Not that I think you would consent or that he would do anything more dishonourable. Rather, I would like to keep Lord Greggard from putting himself in a position to besmirch his honour at all."

"I understand, I'll consider what you've suggested, Councillor. Thank you for showing me this," Orangecloak said as she took a last look at the painting and at the usage of her likeness to represent the goddess of the Triarchy.

"We should leave. Yahmina is surely growing impatient waiting on you by now," Maurice said with a gentle hand on her shoulder. He led her out of the room and back the way they came, looking out for servants all the while and finding none. Not another word was spoken until they were before the door to Yahmina's room on the second floor. "You will keep what you saw and what we spoke of between us, won't you, my lady?"

She nodded in response. "Of course I shall, I realise what a risk it was for you to show it to me at all. I will not misplace your trust, of that you can be sure."

"Most excellent, my lady," the councillor replied with a slow bow. He turned his attention to the door and gave a soft knock, "Yahmina Windleaf, your guest has arrived."

"Come in, please," Orangecloak heard from within.

They found the elven woman lounging across a chesterfield amidst a room that looked more like a library than a bedroom. She was clad in naught but a white, sleeveless, satin and lace nightgown, her golden locks falling haphazardly where they may. "What kept you both? I was beginning to wonder if the good councillor had gotten lost after he left here the first time," Yahmina said with a friendly smile on her face while she laid aside the book she had been reading.

Maurice politely laughed at the jest. "I apologise, the lady and I began talking and time quickly slipped away on us."

"No harm done, I was quite enjoying spending time with Athel, the man knows his literature," the elf replied while turning her attention to a bookshelf in the back of the room. Orangecloak hadn't noticed the other fellow back there thumbing through a thick text.

"Good evening, folks," he called from the back of the room.

"Hello, Athel. I would love to stay and converse with you all, but I am afraid that I must be going," Maurice said with a much quicker bow than he had given Orangecloak in the hall moments before. "I have a home of my own I must return to and duties that require my attention and so I bid you all a good evening."

Following a collective farewell, four became three. It was only when Councillor Maurice had shown himself out and closed the door behind him that Orangecloak finally spoke up. "I understand you requested to see me, Instructor Windleaf," she stated while stepping further into the room and looking about.

It was smaller than the guest quarters given to her, but still seemed long and cavernous. To the right of the entrance lay a wall of bookshelves nearly reaching to the ceiling. Opposite of that it looked like a normal bedroom, as if a library had encroached upon the domicile and claimed half of it for itself. A chesterfield with dark wooden legs and frame and a beige floral pattern sat nearest to Orangecloak. Further down were a dresser, clothing cabinet, full length mirror and a door presumably leading to a lavatory and finally a large bed in the far left corner.

"I did indeed, my lady," she said with a soft, noiseless roll to her feet. From beneath the bed she drew what sounded like a bundle of sticks that were tied in a roll of burlap. "A carpenter's apprentice dropped these off to me earlier, take a look and see if they suit you."

The elf laid the pile at Orangecloak's feet, undoing the twine bindings in a flash to unveil that the sticks to be a varied stack of wooden weapons.

There were spears with weighted heads, longswords made for two hands, axes of various lengths in double and single headed options and daggers for thrusting and slashing. All were made of what looked to be maple or other similar softwood. "I had sent for these the same day of the meeting with Greggard," Yahmina explained while standing up with a wooden longsword to hand. "I had envisioned it would be you and I sparring with them. Fortunately, you have a partner of similar skill level now. Starting tomorrow, I will be switching up your arms at random. You will learn to fight with, and against, a mixture of different weapons, you and Amyla both. Together, we will learn where your strengths and weaknesses lie. What say you, my lady?"

While Yahmina spoke, Orangecloak had knelt and inspected the weapons for herself. By the time the elf had finished, Orangecloak was holding a pair of two-tined, wooden hand claws. "Fascinating, I had heard there were people who fought with claws fastened to their hands, though I had never seen such before."

"The Drakians used them quite extensively until the last century," Yahmina explained casually. "Now, they've fallen into disuse. I maintain that they are far from obsolete and rather think that they are simply forgotten outside of the Combat University."

"Amazing, I think I'd like to give them a try some day myself," she said before gently laying them back among the pile. "If truth be told, I'm not sure if we will have the time to gain any level of skill with all these weapons. It may be better if we try them all and leave the decision so that you might narrow it down to a few that you think Amyla and I have the most potential with."

"We have all winter. I think I can sort that out long before then," Yahmina answered incredulously. "Or is there something else?"

Orangecloak paused a second before delivering the inevitable news. "We may have to leave sooner than anticipated."

Athel snapped his book shut with a loud thump and turned to face Orangecloak. "And why would that be?"

"Please, have a seat and I'll tell you, for there are some things you both should know." Orangecloak gestured to the chesterfield, waiting for them both to be upon it before going on. When she was finished, both knew of the matters in Obalen, its occupancy by the EMP and the need for the Southlands to have firm opposition to the forces of Illiastra's ruling body.

"Amyla will be most upset to hear this," Athel replied when she finished, understandably morose over the news. "She and I have many family and friends in Obalen. I do hope that they are all safe."

Yahmina had different concerns. "A winter's march, is that the way of it? It wouldn't be easy, my lady, but it could be done."

"When has anything worthwhile ever been the easy thing to do?" Orangecloak countered with a confident smirk.

"I'm with you, Orangecloak." Athel stood up tall and proud, a full head above Orangecloak. "I am no fully fledged doctor, but a nurse is still a valuable asset in the wilds."

"You would be very valuable to our cause," Orangecloak reassured him. "Trained and knowledgeable healers are few and far between in the Southlands. I have no doubt that your skills would be put to great use, my friend."

Yahmina was on her feet now as well. "My lady, does this mean you are going to war?"

Orangecloak took a deep breath to consider her answer. "It means that I recognise that this is larger than both I and the Thieves combined. I acknowledge that even if I run and hide that this war is going to happen. I realize that it's not about me, that the world has all but forgotten me now and that I need not get involved. But the Southlands, my home, will soon be under siege by an army trying to parade their way to Aquas Bay so that they might take ships and assault West Illiastra. If the EMP wishes to roll an army through my home, then who else should be standing at the door to deny them?"

"There is no one else, milady," Orangecloak heard from behind her. She turned to find that Amyla had joined them, having entered unheard. Before a word could be said, she was on bended knee. "Milady, I swear myself to you as Athel did before me. I'm with you until the end."

Orangecloak gently took her hand and drew her back to her feet. "Rise Amyla, if you wish to show your loyalty to me, then do not kneel at my feet, but instead stand with me."

"I will stand for you whenever you would call upon me, milady," Amyla said diligently.

"I know you will," Orangecloak stated warmly. "And on the morrow you will be called upon to train with me. The pace will be faster and more gruelling than it has been, though I would not ask this of you if I did not think you would rise to the occasion."

The girl nodded without hesitation at that. "I promise that I will not fail you, milady."

As promised, Yahmina did amplify the training. She began waking both women at the crack of dawn and keeping them afield until nightfall from the next morning onward. The weather was cold and wet, yet neither of the three complained of it. Every time Orangecloak and Amyla sparred they did so with a different weapon combination, searching for strengths and weaknesses in using each under the attentive eye of Yahmina.

Within a few days it was discovered that Amyla had a knack for using the two tined hand claws and they became a regular part of her training. Orangecloak excelled with dual blades, particularly with a dagger in her left hand and either a sword or a hatchet in her right. Yahmina had also invested time in showing Orangecloak how to use Tryst's bow as a melee weapon, should her foes get in close while she was wielding it.

Beyond a dual blade combination, Orangecloak also found herself taking to the spear. It seemed like she was able to score victory over Amyla half a hundred times while spinning about with it. As it was, the grace and agility that was required of the Thieves complimented the spear nicely, and some, like Merion Dollen, even preferred it as their primary weapon. As a result of Orangecloak's own success with it, both she and Yahmina agreed the spear should be her second weapon of choice after the dual blades.

Eventually, once Yahmina had determined that Orangecloak and Amyla were ready, she inserted herself into their sparring matches again. It was well into the third week of the intensified training before either Amyla or Orangecloak were able to even so much as land a blow on the elf though. Despite their sharpened skills, neither of them could still truly beat Yahmina, yet the fact that they both had been able to get through her defences was victory enough.

On a near daily basis the manor was visited by Councillor Maurice. Occasionally he would brave the cold and oversee the training for himself, though more often than not he waited until mealtime to speak with Orangecloak and her company.

As for Athel, he spent his time in the large library of the manor. Lord Greggard was an avid reader and had amassed quite a varied collection of books and Athel was poring over as many as he could. When he grew tired of reading he went into the town with the Councillor and returned on foot alone after dark.

After some time of clandestine travels, he revealed to Orangecloak what his trips into Daol Bay had been for. "I promised that I would serve you and I am no fighter, at least not in the physical sense, anyhow. What I am is a nurse and my skills require a particular set of tools to be of use to you. I had to leave nearly everything behind in Obalen after the Triarchists killed Lenn, so I had to rebuild my medical kit from scratch," he explained while bringing forth a wide knapsack that opened from a hatch on the front to reveal rows of shelving within. "As it were, Maurice agreed with me. What you see here was not only paid for by him, but he also helped me to find some of the more rare items. With this, I should be able to take care of most injuries and maladies that we could potentially encounter."

"This is an invaluable service, Athel," Orangecloak had said, ever grateful. "We are fortunate to have you with the Thieves. I'm sure you can understand that it is very difficult for us to find people with legitimate medical training."

The days continued on in this manner with little aberration for the most part. A notable exception to the schedule was when Yahmina decided on the dawn of the third week that Amyla was ready for live steel. For once, Orangecloak and Amyla were given a much appreciated day of rest while the elf went into town on her own to place an order with a smith.

It was Mezzoday, or hump day, of the fourth week that Athel came looking for them during training. "Ladies, I hate to interrupt, but I've been sent to summon you all to a meeting," he declared loudly, causing the three of them to halt their current exercise.

"Who is calling this meeting?" Orangecloak asked through quickened breaths.

"A visitor and that is all I am permitted to say on that front," Athel shrugged without a hint of worry. "It is urgent, but our guest does not seem troubled, if that helps."

"Perhaps it's the smith," Amyla suggested.

Yahmina agreed as she laid aside the wooden sword she had been using. "It may well be. Either way, we should take a break and see what they want."

The three were led by Athel to the same room Lord Greggard had used to conduct his fateful meeting with Orangecloak. His place at the head of the table was now occupied by Councillor Maurice, who was happily looking over a small scroll that he held unfurled in both hands. "Come in and take a seat, my friends. Please, do not look so worried for I assure you the tidings I come bearing are fortuitous."

Orangecloak tried vainly to mask her excitement. "Is it from Pelican Harbour?"

The councillor shoved the roll of paper in Orangecloak's direction with a finger as he answered, "Indeed, a dove arrived by way of Daol Bay. Have a look for yourself."

She took it to hand and read it aloud for the others to hear. "Nothram surrendered and Pelican Harbour is now Lady Marigold's. No heavy losses for either side. Will be staying here until further notice." Orangecloak turned the slip of paper over and laid it back on the table when she found nothing else written on it. "There is no mention of Tryst."

Maurice seemed perplexed by that. "I would not expect that there would be. A dove is a fast means of transportation, but there is no guarantee it won't fall into wrong hands before arriving where it should, if it does at all. Lord Greggard would not make mention of Tryst for that very reason, my lady."

"I suppose not," Orangecloak agreed. "Still, it would be good to know what came of him." She sighed quickly and changed the subject. "This is fantastic news for Lady Marigold. As I had been given to understand, Nothram was the most vocal and volatile of the resisting westerners. It will certainly send a message to the other holdouts."

Yahmina was quick to add to Orangecloak's thought, having taken the paper to hand herself to read. "It is a huge victory for women if one thinks about it. An army governed by a woman has defeated a man who thought he could not be bested by one. Once the word spreads through Illiastra, others will realise that the fairer sex are not so weak and powerless. We can be called upon to lead just as well as men can. It is an inspiring moment to be a woman in Illiastra, if I do say so."

"This also creates a blind spot for you, my lady," spoke Maurice enticingly. "The Lord Master will have no choice but to put the better part of his forces towards quelling this rebellion. A poor girl that many believe dead and who may or may not be lingering in Illiastra is now of least concern to Grenjin Howland. He has to deal with the powerful opposition rearing its head in the west. If you head for the Southlands as soon as possible and strike while the beast has its back turned you could deal a critical blow."

"That is all well and good," Orangecloak concurred with the Councillor. "Though Tryst wished to join us. I gave him my word that I would wait."

"That may take weeks," Maurice countered as he stood up and prepared to leave. "I would advise you to move sooner. You have Yahmina and Amyla to fight at your side and you are not the defenceless kitten you were when you arrived here. Tryst can join you later. I am sure he can find his way to the Southlands. I'll even arrange a detail of guards from my own household to go with him and join the Thieves, should you like."

Orangecloak shook her head in refusal. "I made my promise,

Councillor. I'm sorry, but I will delay my departure until he returns."

"Then let us hope he makes haste in returning to you if he is not dead. I shall bring you word as soon as I know anything, my lady and that is my promise to you." He bowed before the three women and Athel. "I bid you all a good day."

Yahmina made a move to stand. "We should return to training, our day is wasting."

"Please, sit, I have some questions," insisted Orangecloak, gesturing to the chair nearest to where she already sat.

"Certainly, my lady, what would you ask?" Yahmina inquired curiously while slowly lowering herself back down to her chair.

"You knew Tryst Reine from the University in the Mountain and you've walked among the common guards of Illiastra," Orangecloak said, looking her straight in the eyes. "Tell me, how difficult would it be for a standard soldier to kill him in combat?"

"I don't know that there is a single man, or woman for that matter, that could beat him in single combat outside of Myolas Himmato. He is Tryst's one rival. Everyone else might as well lay down their arms and beg for mercy.

"In the chaos and disorder of battle though, even a man like Tryst Reine can be cut down. I would put his chances of survival above that of a normal man-at-arms, though I would by a liar if I said with absolute certainty that he would live." The elf stood once more. "And you know I am not one to lie, no matter how sweet I might think those lies would taste to you. Anyway, it is near enough to the lunch hour that I think we could break for it early. Then it's back to the field for further practice. We should not dawdle, for we have lost too much daylight as it is. Was there something else you wanted to ask me?"

Orangecloak nodded slowly. "There is, Yahmina. I may be a leader of a group seen as militaristic, but I admit that I know nothing of the ways and means of proper military speech. Could you teach me the words to say when someone pledges their sword to me?"

She watched as Yahmina's lips curled upward ever so slightly. "I can, my lady. I have a book you might read that has the words you seek. After practice, I shall bring it to your room."

That night she lay awake into the late hours, though no matter how she tossed and turned in the large bed, sleep would not come for Orangecloak. She was glad the battle was won for Lady Marigold's side and though it was the outcome she had been hoping for, it had created a new wave of uncertainty. She knew she should be sleeping, given how tired her body felt from the rigorous training she endured with Amyla and Yahmina. Yet, she lay awake, staring at the crackling fireplace, waiting.

A movement on the end of the bed caught her attention and she looked to find that she was not alone in the room as she had thought. "Hello, Miss Skittles, nice of you to join me," Orangecloak said to her unexpected guest.

The fourteen-year-old cat was the Simillon Manor's mouser, or she had been in younger years. Now the old, black on white feline spent her days lounging where she pleased. As of late her preferred place had been in the bend of Orangecloak's knees when she was lying on her side. Her black-capped head and a single white paw draped relaxingly atop Orangecloak's legs, practically begging to be petted and purring softly when she got her wish.

"It's nice to have some company, if only I had known you were at the manor sooner," Orangecloak found herself whispering to the content kitty. "It seems like every time I find new company, they go away in the end. I suppose that's life, especially a life like mine. If you spend your days on the edge, eventually someone is going to fall off. Twice now it should have been me and twice I was pulled back from the brink. So many others that have stood on that precipice with me have not been so fortunate. Now, I have to wait to know if Tryst will join the list of the fallen."

She sighed and scratched behind the cat's ears. "I worry about him, I suppose that's foolish of me, yet I do. By the gods, what is wrong with me? I am the Field Commander of the Thieves, I can't be longing for someone like I am some sort of lovesick, adolescent girl. Yet, here I am, staring at a sword on the desk and hoping that the owner of it will soon be running back. This is madness and I should be ashamed of myself. What is there for me to even like about him? Sure, he's fairly handsome, though not the most handsome I have ever seen. Lazlo Arbour, for instance, is far more comely that Tryst Reine. The lead ranger out of Fort Dornett is another."

The cat woke long enough to shake its head and lick its chops before settling back to her place atop Orangecloak's legs, content to listen to her. "Perhaps it's more than that though. Once Ren left and only Tryst and Fletchard remained to our party, I came to rely much more on Tryst. He proved that my reliance was not ill placed and that he sincerely wanted to help my cause. That means a great deal coming from someone like him, you know."

She chuckled aloud. "Listen to me prattling on with this utter foolishness. I will give him two weeks and if he is not back by then, I simply must move on." Her eyes went back to the sword in the red scabbard on the desk, before it resting a small, black book Yahmina had delivered earlier. "He so badly wanted to lay that sword at my feet and swear fealty to me. It would be a shame if he could not come back to wield it."

Miss Skittles gave a yawn and Orangecloak found herself following suit, her eyes getting heavier by the second until at long last she dozed off.

By the end of the week there came visitors in the form of a smith, his apprentice and a leather armourer. The lot arriving to complete the weapons order Yahmina had made. Before the elf saw them in, she explained to Orangecloak that these three were in fact members of the Musicians. According to Yahmina, the master smith was among the best to be found in all of Illiastra and his residence in Portsward was no mere happenstance. Lord Greggard had scouted and contracted the smith to serve him and the Musicians above all others and once his trust was assured, he was sworn into the organisation.

The men were waiting in the sitting room off the main entrance of the manor when Orangecloak, Yahmina and Amyla joined them. Various products of their labours were laid out on the low table nestled between a pair of matching chesterfields, their rough shapes visible beneath a white cloth. However, what caught Orangecloak's eye first were not the oblong shapes on the table, but two tall stands covered in long, white sheets.

A bald, middle-aged fellow whose thick, hairy arms gave him away as the master smith stood and spoke first. "Lady Orangecloak, I am honoured to make your acquaintance," he said as the other two followed suit and rose to their feet. "My name is Clayton, a humble smith out of Farmourd. Allow me to introduce my apprentice, Fenton from right here in Portsward and my chief leatherworker, Mikhayle of the Cabathos nation in the Crescent Isles."

Of the apprentice most would say he was a plain man to look upon, especially standing beside a Cabathosi for contrast. There was little Orangecloak knew of their people. They resided upon a quiet collection of isles that had somehow avoided the seemingly endless series of wars that plagued the Crescent isles. She did know, though, that the brightly painted leather clothing and long hair tied in thick, unruly knots were the traditional dress of the Cabathosi, and in that, Mikhayle represented his people well. She had to wonder if beneath his floor length coat was a body full of equally bright tattoos, which was also a cultural signature of his homeland.

"The pleasure is all mine, I assure you," Orangecloak said with a polite handshake to each of the men in the noblest voice she could muster. "If I might ask, to what do I owe this pleasure?"

"We have come to show you the fruits of the labour Lord Greggard and Ser Yahmina requisitioned of us these many weeks ago," Clayton answered in a proud and formal tone.

"Then by all means, I would like to see your work," the Lady Orangecloak offered.

"If I might be so bold, it is I who would start," the Cabathosi man declared in a heavy accent while he whipped the sheet from one of the stands in a loud whoosh. Beneath was a leather suit mounted on a mannequin and dyed a deep blue that was nearly black. "This is for the woman with the head of dark curls." Mikhayle explained while opening the jacket to reveal a thick woollen doublet beneath.

Amyla stepped forward timidly, her jaw dropping. "For...For me? I don't know what to say."

The foreigner chuckled. "Aye, if one is to be a protector of Lady Orangecloak, then one needs the proper armour to protect oneself as well. Come forward and take it to try on."

"I can't believe that this is for me, it's just splendid," Amyla complimented while she ran a hand over a sleeve of the jacket. "I'll try it on right away."

Before Amyla could take the clothing from the stand, Clayton stepped forward. "Perhaps just the jacket and doublet for the moment, we have some other gear we would have you try on with it."

On cue, Fenton the apprentice reached to the table and produce a special pair of gloves that resembled the gauntlets worn by the knights of old. "Slide your hands in here when you are ready," he instructed Amyla as she slid into the doublet first and then the jacket.

Smith and apprentice alike helped buckle the gloves in place. Lobstered plates rippled up the wrists and knuckles, and atop the back of the hand was a single, fierce looking ridge of steel. As Amyla looked over her fearsome gauntlets, the apprentice produced a full set of hardened, leather pauldrons. They fit snugly over the jacket and buckled across the breasts in an X. Long leather straps hung to her hips and supported oddly shaped, matching sheaths. The smith himself took one of Amyla's hands and guided the steel ridge on the back of the hand into the opposite sheath until there was an audible clicking noise. When Amyla drew the hand back, the gauntlet was armed with a two tined claw twice the length of her fingers. She went through the same motion with only guidance this time, to snap the second set of claws into the glove.

Once Amyla was armed in her new weaponry, Orangecloak had to admit that it lent the woman a fearsome appearance. Even without the claws, the gloves added a hard surface to her fists. All seemed to agree that the whole ensemble was a good fit for the scrappy fighter.

Once she was shown how to sheathe and disengage the hand claws, Amyla and Mikhayle removed the leather trousers from the mannequin and she left the room to change.

Attention turned back to Orangecloak, and for her they produced a hollow headed hatchet made of bright, shining steel. Its hilt was wrapped in green leather that was close to the colour of the suit she was known for wearing.

"I chose the hatchet as your gifted weapon after careful consideration of your skills," Yahmina elucidated as she watched Orangecloak lift the weapon and test its weight. "I also thought it would be a fitting choice to accompany your blacksteel dagger. They are both light and do not hinder movement like a longer blade might. The hatchet also makes for a practical tool on the road and would not encumber you like a spear sitting diagonally across your back. Given that you will already be carrying a satchel and most likely Tryst's bow, it seemed like an easy decision."

"It will do wonderfully," Orangecloak responded gratefully. "Thank you all so much."

"My lady, does a good weapon not need a good belt and scabbard with which to carry it on?" Fenton the apprentice asked, extending his arms towards Orangecloak to bequeath her with a long, brown belt. It bore a holster for the hatchet to one hip, with a covering for the head and a horizontal sheath in the small of her back for the blacksteel dagger.

"I don't know how I can thank you all for these gifts,"

Orangecloak began.

Before she could begin thanking them further, Clayton spoke up. "That is not all, my lady. Mikhayle still has another gift for you."

The second stand was unveiled and upon it stood a forest green suit of leathers like none Orangecloak had ever seen before. The jacket alone was stitched and tooled with fine, intricate, symmetrical patterns all about it. Upon the back, it bore the same knotted symbol of her orange cloak painted in gold. The shoulders, wrists and elbows were noticeably given additional padding and the left arm had a bracer pattern sewn into the leather. "Here, lift it and see how light it is," Mikhayle said in offering her the jacket.

Inside the jacket was lined with soft satin and indeed felt much lighter than she had expected as she took it to hand and felt it for herself. She ran her hand down the smooth interior and paused when her fingers grazed over something. "What am I feeling here, between satin and leather?" Orangecloak asked curiously.

"I had hoped you would notice," the leatherworker replied excitedly. "What you are touching there is mithril mail."

Yahmina's pointed ears perked at the mention of the word and she stepped in closer to touch for herself. "How is it that a human came to possess a sizeable quantity of mithril? Are you aware of how obscenely expensive it is?"

"I am and this piece has been with my family for several centuries," Mikhayle answered with a single, firm nod. "My ancestors recovered it from a shipwreck on the beaches of Cabathos and kept it as an heirloom. It was passed on to me and I brought it with me to Illiastra, in hopes I might find a fighter worthy of wearing it."

There was no holding back the scoff from Yahmina. "Your family found a piece of Elven armour and instead of selling it for the thousands of gold it is worth, you are just going to give it away? How very altruistic of you."

The Cabathosi found that quite humorous, evidently, and chuckled hard. "In truth I wanted to see if there was a smith in Illiastra who could work it. When none, even Clayton here, could do so, I decided that I would incorporate it as it was into a work of my own. Unfortunately, the men who could afford such finery don't deserve it, so I decided to hold on to it until someone worthy of it came along. That such person is the Lady Orangecloak and I am only too glad to be able to make such an outfit for her."

"I am incredibly grateful," Orangecloak said, bowing before them. "I shall wear it with honour."

The man with the strong foreign accent continued, "The people of Cabathos have a tradition of wearing something to shield our backs. It is an old superstition that many believe will keep others from betraying us. I don't know how true that is, but the gesture is sound."

Yahmina spoke up again. "At any rate, mithril is impenetrable. You won't find a better material in armour." She turned to Mikhayle. "If you were looking for someone in Illiastra to work it, you did not look far enough. In the known world there is only the Armourer's Guild of the Vale within the Elven Forest who knows the secrets of crafting mithril and they keep those secrets very closely guarded."

"So I found out when I arrived here," Mikhayle said jovially. "I even travelled to the border of your lands, Ser Yahmina, and was rebuffed at the treeline, despite my intentions."

He took a breath and turned back to Orangecloak. "This type of leather, while not of elven quality, is near it. You will find it tough and durable and yet flexible. Even the bodice is comprised of it. The one thing I omitted from my normal armour is heavy plating sewn throughout. I had thought it would make the outfit too heavy for someone who relies on agility."

"You made the right choice, Mikhayle," Orangecloak said, having slid the jacket on while Mikhayle and Yahmina were talking. "Even with the mithril it is very light on the body. I cannot thank you all enough for everything."

"You are quite welcome, my lady," Clayton said. "You should also be sure to thank Lord Greggard and Councillor Maurice, for it was they who shared in the expense."

"I shall do that, Clayton," she said appreciatively. "You have my deepest gratitude."

"Oh, my lady, your jacket is just splendid!" Amyla proclaimed as she re-entered the room, now dressed head to heel in the deep blue leather suit she had been given. "It suits you perfectly. Now we really look like fighters."

"You do much more than simply look the part, Amyla," Yahmina spoke up. "You and Orangecloak *are* fighters, both in body and spirit."

With that the elf turned to the others. "I think we shall postpone training for the day and see to it that our guests are properly hosted. I'll have the staff prepare us a nice dinner. On the morrow, you will both wear your new leathers to training, as you will have to get accustomed to fighting in them."

Without fail they appeared the next morning in full gear, sparring with wooden replicas of their chosen weapons until their suits were sweaty and muddy. When done sparring, they fought straw dummies with the real steel, getting accustomed with the weight and feel of their new arms. By night they cleaned their leathers and oiled and sharpened their blades until all shone brightly again, ready for another day of hard training.

A week and a day later, the two were sparring once more. Amyla was pressing hard with an attack, fiercely flashing the wooden claws perilously close to Orangecloak's face. Not one blow had landed thus yet and Amyla was growing tired. Orangecloak waited and let the desperation set in.

Parry a jab from the left claw and evade the right, look for the opening. There. Amyla was ready and slashed away the wooden axe that was making for her stomach at the last second. The quick reaction put Amyla off her rhythm and brought with it a stumble that Orangecloak quickly seized upon. Amyla's right handed slash went wild and high and Orangecloak ducked below it and around Amyla to her back. In a smooth, fluid motion, Orangecloak's arm and practice dagger were soon wrapped around Amyla's throat.

Orangecloak's eyes scanned the grove of trees where Yahmina normally sat and judged their sparring contests and found the elf was gone out of sight. "Tulip," Orangecloak whispered in Amyla's ear, uttering the safety word they had designated to signify an immediate stop in their battling.

"What is it?" Amyla said, herself lowering her voice to a cautious whisper.

"Yahmina's gone, that's not like her," Orangecloak answered as she released the woman from her grasp. The two slowly approached the wooded area and found their food and water canteens undisturbed. Voices reached Orangecloak's ears and she pointed out the direction to Amyla, finding that she had heard them as well.

The pair crept through the woods as noiselessly as the dead leaves and fresh snow would allow until the voices became discernible.

Amyla's breath turned to steam before her in the chilly winter air as she listened keenly. "I see two people there," she observed. "A man and a woman for sure, do you recognise them?"

Orangecloak shook her head in response, continuing to study the strangers. The man looked to be a husky fellow with a bushy brown beard tipped with frost. His companion was a girl Orangecloak figured to be about a decade her junior with long blonde hair in a neat braid. The two were dressed alike, in thick winter suits in mottled white from head to toe.

Neither one seemed to be talking, yet there were two voices exchanging with one another, obscured from view by a thick spruce.

A twig snapped beneath Amyla's boot when she tried to step forward and the man and girl turned their heads sharply in the direction of the two women. The four stared at one another and the jaw of the girl dropped as the strange pair both realised just who was standing to Amyla's left.

An amused Yahmina shuffled backward a step, revealing where she had been standing behind the tree. "It looks as though your plans just evaporated."

"I suppose they have," a second, familiar voice replied as its owner emerged beside Yahmina, clad in the same clothing as the other two and wearing a joyous grin on his face. "Hello, Orangecloak. It's good to see you again."

"Tryst Reine, I am glad to see you again as well," Orangecloak answered with a swallow, trying to show restraint.

Tryst inclined his head towards the two that looked to be with him. "My lady, might I introduce my new friends? This is Cob and Yak, formerly of the Flying Hawks Company, whom I was fighting beside at Pelican Harbour."

"It is a pleasure to make your acquaintance," Orangecloak replied with a nod, laying a hand on the shoulder of her friend. "This is Amyla Spade, a new recruit to the Thieves."

"Lady Orangecloak," said the bearded fellow she had to guess was the one named Yak. "If it would please you, myself and Cob have come to pledge our service to you as well."

As much as Orangecloak wanted to trust Tryst's judgement and as desperate as the Thieves were for new blood, she still did not know these people and could not accept them so easily. "With Instructor Windleaf's permission, I think we should adjourn for the day to the manor and we shall discuss things over lunch," Orangecloak offered, putting things off for the moment. "You must all be starving."

"I think that would be wise, my lady," the elf answered, gathering Orangecloak's gesture for what it was. "Let us be off."

While Yahmina showed everyone to the private meeting room, Orangecloak took the chance to retrieve her signature cloak and a certain sword from her quarters. She fastened the cloak across her shoulders and the sword onto the open space on the left hip of her new belt.

When at last she returned to them, she found that Athel had been summoned as well and had placed himself beside Amyla.

The six rose in unison for Orangecloak, casting their gaze to her while she crossed the floor.

"Please, be seated, I require no such displays of fealty," Orangecloak said to them as she took the lone empty chair in the room at the head of the table.

No food had yet been served and the five seemed as though they had been waiting on her to arrive to even begin conversing, so Orangecloak took the lead. "Tryst, I believe you have yet to meet my newest recruits. We were acquainted the same night you departed. Amyla's name you know and beside her is Athelbert Fauster. They both hail from Obalen, where the Triarchy took Amyla's brother, who was Athel's companion."

"They burned Lenn alive at the stake," Amyla spoke up, her eyes downcast to her hands folded neatly on the table. "I am sorry, my lady, there is no need to soften the blow for mine and Athel's sake. What the Triarchy did should be known."

"I am so sorry for you loss," Tryst answered solemnly. "It is a pleasure to meet you, despite the dire circumstances that brought you both here."

Athel glanced up and met Tryst's eyes. "I don't know that we would have met under any other circumstances, Ser Tryst."

"You may be right, Mister Fauster," added Tryst with a nod.

Athel extended a hand and they shook. "Please, Athel is fine," he told Tryst.

"Then you may call me Tryst, without the 'ser'," Tryst warmly intoned, letting a smile flicker on his face for a second.

Orangecloak chimed in, "Athel is a nurse and Amyla was a maid, though she has since had a change of careers and has decided to take up arms."

"Both of which would be very useful to the Thieves," complimented Tryst before he turned to the potential recruits he had brought. "I think Yak and Cob here would be most useful as well. Yak is a fighter, accustomed to a covert style similar to the Thieves. Despite his size, he moves with an uncanny gracefulness. As for Cob here, she was in training to be a Flying Hawk and was a camp attendant and squire for the group I was assigned to."

"There sounds like there is a story here as to how they came to be with you here in Portsward, Tryst," Orangecloak said with intrigue in her voice. "I should hear it, I think."

"Very well, then." Tryst cleared his throat and began. He explained how he had been assigned to fight with the Flying Hawks. A group, as Tryst explained, who was formerly an independent, clandestine branch of the Illiastran military who defected to West Illiastra when Lady Marigold seceded.

It was further explained that all members of the Flying Hawks were identified by pseudonyms, even Tryst who had been known as Lynx. Tryst told how the leader of the Flying Hawks, Captain Nathers had easily surmised Tryst's identity and had spent their first meeting talking about Lady Orangecloak. This Captain Nathers claimed he was a sympathiser and had otherwise hinted at the shady events surrounding Orangecloak's capture and incarceration, all of which Tryst seemed to be tied to. Apparently the Captain kept his awareness of Tryst's identity from him and let him find his way into one of the subgroups within the Flying Hawks.

It was under the leadership of a woman named Vix that Tryst had found himself and it was there he been acquainted with Cob and Yak. Prior to battle, his ruse was called out and he was forced to confess that he had not in fact done Orangecloak any harm and was in fact in collusion with her. The others were even willing to let Tryst return to Orangecloak at the conclusion of the battle with only one condition: they wanted a favour to be called on at any time. Tryst agreed to the conditions and they went into combat together to take the manor of Minister Nothram. During the course of the battle, both Vix and a third man in their group named Wedge were slain. With Tryst due to depart after the battle, it would mean that Yak's group was no more.

Without a group, a Flying Hawk could appeal to the others, and there had been other losses and there would be other openings, but

Captain Nathers had another idea: he wanted to lend Orangecloak his own support in the form of giving her two of the Flying Hawks.

Yak spoke up, his voice full of sorrow at the recollection of his slain friends. "Captain Nathers claimed that had he known you were alive before he agreed to serve Lady Marigold that he would have sought you out instead. Many within the Flying Hawks support you, milady, and the Wyvern chief among them. Had he come into his position sooner, we would have given you our full strength."

"I have heard of the Flying Hawks," Orangecloak said. "Though, last I heard they were led by Hank Harding, a puppet of the EMP. For a long time I feared I would find them on my doorstep at a moment's notice. But luckily, Harding was as lazy as he was corrupt."

"Milady, I should say something that Tryst doesn't yet know," Yak went on. "Captain Nathers did not want to call in the favour so soon. Rather, he had wanted to wait until it was a better time for both him and you. However, after Vix heard Tryst say that Wedge was dead, she made it her last wish that Cob and I go with Tryst and join you." The burly, bearded man trailed off for a moment and stared at the ceiling. "Just before she died in my arms."

Orangecloak took a deep breath when Yak finished. "Captain Nathers and I both seem to be of the same mind when it comes to honouring the last request of the dying."

"I failed Vix, milady," Yak said suddenly, his brown eyes locking tight with Orangecloak's. "It should have been me that went through that window first and taken the pistol fire. That should have been my duty to my leader and in that I failed. I swear on Vix's memory that if you allow me the chance, I will redeem myself for having failed her. I don't know that I am worthy of serving you, milady, not after failing Vix. Yet, I would humbly ask for the chance all the same."

"I understand your pain, ser. It was only recently that two of my closest friends died before my own eyes. I still see them when I go to sleep and they will never leave my memories. I also lost many more behind the walls of Biddenhurst and may never see them again. Conflict is woe and misery for everyone involved and there is no guarantee that any of us will live to see the end of it. I trust Tryst Reine and his judgement and if he vouches for you, I will give you the chance you seek. I will honour Vix's last wish and her memory," Orangecloak offered sombrely as she shared her painful memories. Her attention turned to the light haired girl. "And what of you, Cob, what would you seek of me?"

The girl was nervous and hesitated with her answer for a second. "I...I...I would seek...I'm sorry, milady, it's just that you're *The* Lady Orangecloak. You're wearing the cloak and everything, I can't believe I'm sitting here and you're there and we're talking. I'm sorry. I shouldn't be acting this way, it's not proper."

"It's alright, Cob. Why don't you start with your real name, I'm not sure I like calling you after an ear of corn," Orangecloak said lightly, trying to ease the tension.

The teenaged girl composed herself and began again. "It's Merith, milady, Merith Tailor. I'm from a little town called Hulting in Galren region. I was a squire for Vix when she was an illegal freelancer for the Flying Hawks. We joined up officially with them when they switched sides for Lady Marigold. When Vix was given her own group, I was squire and camp attendant for the three of them and for Tryst for the short time he was with us. I would do so again, for you, if you would have me. I can do a great many things: I can clean, cook, sew, start a fire, sharpen weapons and set a tent, whatever you need."

"It would seem you have a great list of talents alright and I welcome you to the Thieves, Merith Tailor of Hulting," Orangecloak said kindly to the shy girl, watching as she blushed. "Yak, might I ask what your real name is?"

"It's Paderon Pendergast of Trout Brook, also in Galren region, if it pleases milady," he answered diligently. "I would prefer to keep the name Yak, as I find it far more intimidating than Paderon or Paddy, but the choice is yours."

"I rather like Paderon," Orangecloak said thoughtfully, running the name through her head. "But if Yak is what you prefer, then I shall call you by that."

The head butler and the servants entered the room shortly after, bringing with them a lunch of lentil soup and thinly sliced, roasted beef sandwiches on freshly baked rye bread. The seven dined together and Tryst, Paderon and Merith informed the others of the fallout of the battle. Orangecloak and her trio learned that Tryst's group had left Pelican Harbour before the ship bearing the Lady Marigold could safely dock, so neither of them had seen her. However, they could confirm that it was mortar fire from her fleet that heralded the start of the battle.

"Did Nothram surrender peacefully?" Orangecloak had asked of

Tryst and Yak.

A sly grin crossed Tryst's face as he answered, "Nay, kicking and screaming as a woman named Cloud roped him hand and foot. I couldn't think of a more deserving end to his reign: to be brought down by a member of the gender he so vehemently loathed."

"That is fitting for him," Yahmina concurred. "I had the misfortune of meeting the man once. It was hard to say if he despised me more for being an elf or a woman-at-arms."

When a gap in conversation presented itself, Amyla timidly asked, "What do you think Lady Marigold will do with him?"

Tryst fielded that one. "The Wyvern told me that Lady Marigold issued an arrest warrant for Nothram on the charges of murder, attempted murder, unlawful detention and assault before the battle began. She will most likely extradite him to Daol Bay and put him on trial for all of that. If he's guilty, I cannot fathom Marigold sparing him from execution."

The conversation tapered back to less macabre topics like the weather until the dinner was done.

Yahmina suggested they all retire to the nearest sitting room for tea while the servants cleaned off the table and they all agreed upon it. Leading the way was the elf, leaving Orangecloak and Tryst to delay for but a moment.

Tryst stopped before her, a smile playing at his lips. "I came back, Orangecloak, as I promised you I would."

"I'm glad you did," Orangecloak replied, her voice going soft as his bright green eyes of the old Gildraddi bloodline pierced her with their gaze.

"Will Tryst and my lady be joining us today?" Yahmina called while leaning on the doorframe of the sitting room.

Orangecloak turned away from Tryst to the elf. "Yes, Yahmina, we'll be right there."

The pair found the others standing in wait for them when they entered the sitting room. Orangecloak's hand brushed her left hip and she remembered what lay there. "Tryst Reine, I have held your sword for you. I mean to return it." She pulled back her cloak to reveal the sword hanging from her belt.

"Why thank you, my lady," he answered with sudden formality as the sword was laid in his hands. In one smooth motion, he unsheathed the blade and swung to a knee before her, holding the deadly weapon out in both hands. "As I promised before I left: I offer my sword to you, Lady Orangecloak, to wield as you so wish."

"I accept your gift," Orangecloak started in a strong voice, pausing for a second while she recalled what she had read in the book Yahmina had given her. "I declare that a weapon this fine should have a worthy hand to hold it. Tryst Reine, Master of Blades, you would do me a great honour to wield this sword on my behalf."

"If that is your wish, then I shall grant it, my lady." He accepted the sword back in his hands, laid it at her feet and bowed his head. "I promise that for as long as I so live that I shall do you no dishonour. Your will is mine and my life is yours to command."

The others in the room had all remained standing during the pledging and starting with Yak, they began to kneel, until all five had joined Tryst on bended knee.

As Orangecloak stood there, smiling so proudly, she sought for words to say to them and at last they came to her: "Rise, my friends, you are all now members of the Thieves. Rise, for we do not kneel to one, rather, we stand for all."

Starting with Yahmina, they all rose before Orangecloak. She extended a fist in their direction. "In the Thieves, we have words of our own. We stand fist to fist, knuckle to knuckle in greeting and parting to say these words, and from me you shall learn them. Please, join me."

One by one they came to stand in a circle around Orangecloak, their own fists touching hers.

I had never thought that I might say these words again.

"We are the Thieves," she began, her pride radiating with every word. "Stealing back freedom."

The *Gold & Steel* saga has only begun.

Stay up to date at www.thegoldandsteelsaga.com and be the first to know when the second volume, *The Worth of Gold*, will be available.

About the Author

Christopher Walsh is an author from the Southern Shore on the Avalon Peninsula of Newfoundland, Canada. After spending several years travelling and living across the country, he returned home, and in 2011 began crafting the world of *Gold & Steel*. *As Fierce as Steel,* the inaugural entry in the series, is also his first foray into the published literary world.

CPSIA information can be obtained
at www.ICGtesting.com
Printed in the USA
LVOW11s0032091116
512194LV00001B/6/P